All That Glitters

THOMAS TRYON

ALFRED A. KNOPF
New York

For Annie

THIS IS A BORZOI BOOK
PUBLISHED BY ALFRED A. KNOPF, INC.

Manufactured in the United States of America

CONTENTS

Babe   5

Belinda   103

April   155

Maude   255

Claire   359

In 1888, the year that the French showman Georges Méliès presented his first magic-lantern show in the Théâtre Robert-Houdin and projected magic-lantern pictures onto a screen, Los Angeles was an inland metropolis of some twenty-five thousand people, with little to distinguish it from a hundred other cities eagerly sprouting up around the country. A scant eight miles northwest of the "downtown" intersection a married couple with the commonplace name of Wilcox purchased generous tracts of subdividable property on the cheap, where they planted barley fields and citrus trees—lemon and orange and grapefruit. They put up a house, "Queen Anne" in style, replete with turrets and gables, with a few outbuildings, and a windmill that pumped water, and, not unnaturally, the dusty road that ran through the center of the ranch they named after themselves: Wilcox.

At a later time, Mrs. Wilcox chose to do a bit of traveling. She journeyed by train to the east and by ship across the Atlantic, and on board the ship she met a woman who was returning to her home in England.

"And where do you live?" inquired Mrs. Wilcox of her new friend.

"Oh, we live out in the country," the Englishwoman said, and told Mrs. Wilcox the name of the place.

"How pretty!" exclaimed Mrs. Wilcox, and when she got back to Los Angeles she gave her citrus ranch the same name. She called it

HOLLYWOOD

And the magic began. . . .

$Babe$

In those far-off days, those olden golden Hollywood days back in the thirties or the forties, a cumbersome touring car of the Reo manufacture was frequently to be seen traversing the streets of Los Angeles. This capacious and ponderous vehicle, the kind that would stand out anywhere in any time, was most likely driven by a burly figure wearing a dark suit whose seat and elbows were shiny, and a visored chauffeur's cap, emblem of his trade. His name was Sluggo McGurk and he was an ex–middleweight contender out of Elk Fork, North Dakota, with the flattened, pulpy ears known as "cauliflower," and a nose broken numerous times, and he sported a fifteen-hundred-dollar wristwatch, diamonds and platinum. His passenger, his constant and near-sole passenger, was a woman. She displayed expensive furs of fox, mink, or ermine, and long antelope gloves and diamond bracelets, and she showed a creamy décolletage. She had bright blonde hair, the same "platinum" shade that Jean Harlow had popularized and that manicurists and five-and-ten-cent-store salesgirls imitated to the best of their pocketbooks' abilities. Her eyelashes were long and curled and thickly mascaraed and she outlined her eyes like an Egyptian queen, and when she talked it was in a kind of coaxing drawl, not southern but slangy and raffish, and she wore an amused expression on her face. By 1938 this was not only the highest-paid female star in the movies, but also one of the most famous women in the world, after Eleanor Roosevelt, after Madame Chiang Kai-shek, after Wallis Simpson, and after Greta Garbo. Soon she would be as famous as any one of them. . . .

But that was back in the thirties and forties. Today, in the seventies, see where we are: Hollywood Memorial, where the movie stars get put away. Jesus, it's hot! Personally I don't care much for funerals—funerals are for the dead, not the living. When you're dead, that's what they give you, a funeral.

Anyway, here we are, baking in that inglorious South Hollywood sun while it beats down in one relentless glare, its rays murkily piercing through a thick, grimy scrim of haze and smog, and not a hint of breeze. My swollen eyes sting and water. With the exception of the officiating priest and the body in the casket, everyone present, so far as I can tell, is wearing dark glasses, as though to prove beyond a doubt that we are indeed in good old Tinseltown.

I played a little scene in my first movie within these cemetery walls. I must say, the place hasn't changed much, though at the time Cecil B. De Mille was still alive and kicking, cranking out the remake of *The Ten Commandments*. Now C.B. lies in yon splendiferous crypt, granite as the old man's jaw, the schist in the stone as glittery as Jayne Mansfield's bathroom. Scattered around and about, earning a well-marbled rest, is a galaxy of glittering names: Douglas Fairbanks (Sr., not Jr.); Peter Lorre; as well as two renowned *Our Gang*-ers, Darla Hood and Alfalfa Switzer (separately interred).

Tyrone Power is buried somewhere nearby, and farther off the crypt of Valentino rears up in dubious Spanish taste, though that old-time Hollywood cliché "The Woman in Black," mourner of mourners, no longer makes her yearly epiphany at the gravesite; she, too, has cooled, and is probably buried somewhere in the neighborhood so she can be as near to Rudy in death as she was in life.

Right now the clock hand is on the prick of noon and the carillon is sounding. I recognize "You Light Up My Life." Mindlessly I wonder if the original Debbie Boone version is equal to Hollywood Memorial's. Close by, among the mourners, someone is throwing up his breakfast, or perhaps is merely emotionally overcome. People can get like that at funerals.

When I played my deathless scene in these precincts thirty years ago and more, all was rest and quiet. A suitably reverential ambience. Now they've built a string of grungy shopping malls just beyond the wall—there's a goldfish shop, a video palace, a Mexican chili parlor—while in the lily-scented air the pervasive thrum of congested traffic is recognizable along Santa Monica Boulevard. That way lies Paramount Studios and Marathon Street, this way lies Columbia and old Desilu, yonder lies Hollywood and madness.

If you haven't already, check out the coffin. It's see-through. Quite a novelty, huh? Look at it, resting on its pink-scalloped catafalque, the bead-fringed, swagged baldaquin above, the solid banks of roses, gardenias, other hothouse flora (the gardenia blanket cost six hundred, easy, and is rumored to have been sent by Frank Adano, but since Frankie himself is very dead this seems unlikely; in truth, I sent it in Frank's name).

Inside the glass coffin lies Our Heroine, royally embalmed and made up, wearing a gown of ivory satin (or "ekkroo," very Babe), her blonde tresses lushly curled, a tiara of rhinestones—"strictly for effect"—sling pumps on her feet. Will her ten toes curl up, I wonder, like those of the Wicked Witch of the East when Dorothy's house landed on her? Will the coffin crack when they drop it in the hole? But of course there's no hole; Hollywood Memorial Park not give holes—not for the likes of Babe Austrian, anyhow. The coffin will find eternal rest in the mausoleum, stuck away in a large marble drawer among many drawers, a veritable filing cabinet of celebrated corpses. I am being irreverent, I know, but let's not take this whole number too seriously.

And why, you may well ask, a glass coffin? Is she Sleeping Beauty, Snow White, Evita Perón? I hide my smile, thinking of Sleeping Beauty imprisoned under glass, waiting for the kiss of love to restore her to life. But nobody's kiss is ever going to restore this beauty; there's not a breath left in the old fraud. This whole thing has been a fairy tale, a charade in the good old Hollywood style. "The Life of Babe Austrian." And who will play it onscreen? Not Judy, for sure. And where is Betty Hutton when we need her?

I'm standing here choking on the smog, Angie is next to me on one side, Pepe Alvarez on the other. We practically have to hold each other up. "Conspirators" is the word for us. No, that's not really true. Actually we're upholding legend. Hollywood depends on its legends—"legend" connoting a certain paucity of truth; we won't find much truth around here today.

I note how few others among Babe's older friends seem to be present at these cryptside obsequies. But, then, I quickly remind myself, why should there be, when Babe outlived almost all of her contemporaries? Though I myself am here as a bereaved friend of the deceased, still I am an alien, or at least feel like one. I knew Babe over a period of more than thirty years, but it isn't she, the late, great Babe Austrian, who has drawn me hither, but another, to whom I humbly pay my silent tribute. Rest, perturbèd spirit—I am silent as the everlasting tomb, granite-mouthed. My lips are sealed just as the crypt will soon be.

Look, what I know, I know. And what I set down now in these pages is not the heresy it may appear to be; rather, it is the plain and relatively unvarnished truth. If Frank were still alive, he would certainly support me in my intention to tell it as it happened. I believe that Frank, who was responsible not only for Babe's career but for so many others, would want the truth revealed; he always loved a good laugh. Certainly Babe wanted it, requested it of me—dying wish and all that. Besides, the real story is too good to be buried here with Babe.

As for me, the name's Caine. Charlie Caine. Not Charles Foster Kane —there's the obvious difference in spelling, and also I seldom use my middle name. Moreover, *Citizen Kane* was released in 1941; I considerably before that.

I hail from that same small American whiz-through town that half the nation comes from. I am possibly its most famous citizen, not that that counts for much. I'm hardly its "favorite son." I've yet to move or shake the world much, but I've found my niche and that alone has taken some doing. I cling to this, my niche; I nestle there, quite comfortably. I live part-time in New York City, part-time in Los Angeles, *near* but not *in* Hollywood, on a street without sidewalks where it takes forty minutes to bring the police if you're being ripped off. I used to act in the movies, but haven't seen the inside of a studio in many years, nor care to ever again —I really hated getting up at that ungodly hour. My friends are trained; they let me alone from eight to four to get my writing chores done, and I turn out something reasonably publishable every few years. I know where the bodies are buried. And, given the chance, I tell.

When I got here, April first, some thirty years ago, they were tearing out the goldfish pond in the Paramount gardens. That fishpond used to be famous. Dottie Lamour once posed beside it in a sarong, Veronica Lake in her peekaboo bang; Bing Crosby tapped his pipe out against its rim. But sacrilege was committed: the pool was ripped out, the hole macadamized so studio heads could park there. That same day, April Fool's, as I walked around the lot I saw the writing all over the wall. What did it say? "Many are called but few are chosen"? Maybe. I don't think so, though. For sure it didn't say that someday somebody was going to try to make a movie star out of someone named Pia Zadora.

Babe Austrian was clearly one of the chosen ones. And after she was chosen, she proved indestructible, a Hollywood institution, like Hedda or Louella and Oscar and C. B. De Mille, like the Farmers Market, freeway smog, Barney's Beanery, Knott's Berry Farm, and the forecourt at Grauman's Chinese. Babe Austrian was a *star*. A big shining *star*. She was a star through five decades and longer—a show-biz phenomenon, one of the Greats. She was a major stage and vaudeville attraction before I saw the light of day, and the first time we met I was barely twelve years old. "Met cute," as screenwriters like to say, so cute that if I'd been five years older I'd probably have gone to jail for the number I pulled with her. Though

I was only a Cub Scout at the time, my actions were hardly of Cub Scout ilk, and as it was, I got kicked the hell out of the Beaver Patrol. I'll get to that unfortunate encounter presently. Babe and I met a second time aboard the Super Chief; this was on V-J Day, August 15, 1945, halfway across the state of Iowa, with fairly deducible results; she was a famous movie star, I a mere nineteen-year-old sailor heading for the ComPac fleet. And we met yet a third time in a Seventh Avenue hotel suite during a New York heat wave in the early fifties.

Speaking of heat, today it would soften an interstate highway. Not a healthy, bright heat, like a hot Fourth of July in Missouri, not even the humid heat of the Eastern Seaboard in August, but a thick, greasy heat, rancid, like oleomargarine on a slab of moldy bread. Cut it with a knife. Look at the way those gardenias are already wilting around the bier. I notice how the priest is managing a little savvy. He's donned smoked glasses, along with the rest of us. They look good on him, too, real Movieland stuff. The smog gets to us all, even Holy Mother Church. And even the limo drivers in their badly wrinkled suits of sweaty broadcloth leaning against the black cars lined up along the curve are wearing them. Surely this isn't merely Babe Austrian's funeral; they must be sodding down some Mafia chieftain, a *capo da capo*. I'm reminded of the demise of Frank's famous mobster pal, Bugsy Siegel, lo these thirty years ago; funny, wasn't it, how Frankie left Bugsy at the rented residence of Miss V. Hill a scant six minutes before the guns began blasting away. I mean, he was *out* of there—had a hot date, otherwise he'd have been perforated, too.

As I understand it, Bob Hope's been asked to say a few words today *in memoriam.* This is good, I think. Babe should not be laid to rest without a touch of Hopian gallows humor—Babe always loved a good gag. Did she ever! Glancing around among the somber and attentive faces, I see Phyllis Diller's; she appears to have the church giggles, as befits. Oh, Phyllis, if you only knew. Dean Martin is as tanned as a cigar-store Indian, but looks strangely sober and a bit sheepish. Dino loved the Babe. Does he want a drink? I wonder. I know I do. And I'm A.A.

My wandering mind tends to wonder what those two news hens—gosspists, Hedda Hopper and Louella Parsons, would have made of this scene. Hedda, née Elda Fury of Altoona, Pennsylvania, was a terror, a badly biased "reporter" of Hollywood Didos, but I think she'd have gotten a bang out of this ersatz pageantry. (Hedda was sharp as the proverbial tack; Lolly, usually sauced, never knew her spigots from her sprockets; but both had long been amused by Babe Austrian, as indeed who among us gathered here was not?)

Bob has finished his bit and now they're wheeling the coffin away. It's on a cart something like a hospital gurney; its wheels squeak. Into the crypt goes Babe, just like your stock certificates and the family jewels. Everybody's splitting now, can't wait to get home to the pool. A vodka-tonic awaits. I bet even the priest could go for a tall, frosty Tom Collins about now. Spike heels are sinking into the turf all over the place. Notice how everybody's talking at once? Nobody's wiping any eyes or blowing any noses or going prostrate from grief. George Burns dies, you cry a little, maybe. "Poor George, we'll sure miss him," sniff, sniff. But not with Babe Austrian. With Babe you say, "What a great old broad," and you drag out one of the old jokes—"Babe Austrian's car breaks down, see, and there's this hick farmer driving a load of hay, see, and so Babe says, 'Hay, fellow—' "

Like that.

When I was six or seven I heard my first Babe Austrian joke. My brother told it to me; we were sliding down the cellar hatchway doors and I got a sliver in my behind. And I saw my first actual picture of her on the back of a Dixie Cup cover. I peeled off the paper disk with its tab and there she was, an ice-cream icon, radiantly platinum, flashing those pearly-whites, with this prominent pair of tits, curvy in a way that gave seven-year-olds big ideas, not that we could do anything about it . . .

I saw my first feature movie in the year 1931. Babe Austrian was not in it. Jackie Cooper was. I was led by the gentle, callused hand of our hired girl, Jessie, following my older brother with his hand in my mother's, across the marble lobby of the Loew's Poli Theatre, the premier movie palace of our city, whose wondrously tall mirrors reflected glittering sights I had never thought to see in this lifetime. I have vivid impressions of crystal chandeliers, dripping prisms, a bubbling fountain, also marble, a grand staircase, broad, with many narrow steps and brass railings polished to a gleaming finish, and standing easels advertising scenes of garish or allur-ing form from the Coming Attractions. In the eye of memory, that movie lobby seems large as the municipal railroad station waiting room, and as glamorous as the Hall of Mirrors at Versailles.

Our arrival at the Poli Theatre had been timed to coincide with the commencement of the early-evening show. My father was to meet us there after business hours, but when we got to the theatre he was nowhere to be seen and Mother said we would just go ahead on in. Walking past the discreetly located candy counter (no popcorn at Poli's—yet), we encoun-tered a broad bank of closed brass-framed doors, at one of which an usher appeared, dressed in a nifty bellboy's red uniform with frogging and gold buttons, a navy-blue stripe down each trouser leg, and a trim pillbox on the side of his head anchored by a strap under his chin, and reeking of aplomb. When the door closed behind us, I found myself drowning in the most palpable darkness I had ever experienced. The newsreel was on. I instantly panicked; my ears were assaulted by the deafening sounds of rapid gun and cannon fire, while a soundtrack voice accompanied by imposing blasts of music intoned a majestic narration (I think the Japanese had invaded Manchuria that spring), and I clung the tighter to Jessie's hand.

Another usher, picking out the way by the discreet pencil beam of flashlight, conducted us past the top of the first aisle, across the rear of the theatre to the farther aisle, where I glimpsed my first sound-film image: a heap of civilian corpses in a blasted railroad station. Still clutching Jessie's hand, I followed obediently down the sloping, carpeted aisle to perhaps midway, where the pencil light directed us to four seats at the side. The others went in first, I the last, with the aisle seat saved for my father. As my eyes adjusted to this velvet void, I became aware of rows of human heads protruding in front of me, and wildly leaping images on the screen that seemed to my young mind scrambled, almost abstract, and it was all I could do to look, so overwhelmingly huge did they seem, so filled with light and shadow, so far beyond my powers to conjure or imagine.

At length the newsreel ended and I felt a sense of relief and a return to some sort of reality as the curtain closed across the screen and the footlights came up to warm the spangled pleats in shades of pink. Patrons filed out; others entered and were seated. As I gazed about, I saw theatre boxes above, to right, and to left, and a lofty rococo ceiling whose gorgeousness in retrospect defies description. I recall giant frescoes sprawled across that blue plaster expanse with gods and goddesses contending *à la* Tiepolo in Venetian grandeur. The plasterwork was a riot of rococo and there was a giant chandelier hanging down from the center of the medallion.

As I was staring up at this astonishing sight, the lights went slowly down again and I was once more plunged into that overwhelming, womb-like darkness. Always sensitive to my moods, Jessie patted my hand reassuringly and slipped a comforting arm around me, drawing me close as though firming me up for greater shocks to come. Then, while the curtains were still closed, a pattern or design was flashed on the folds of material, which, as they began to travel apart to a fanfare of music, revealed more and more clearly on the white screen the image of a bearded lion that moved its head and gave off ferocious roars. Was this lion real?

I believed it not to be, yet it seemed very real to me at that instant. The lion's head was framed by a circlet of scroll-like tapes with lots of little print that I couldn't read. Poli's played only MGM and Fox pictures, and already the *Ars Gratia Artis* of Metro-Goldwyn-Mayer was impressed on my fevered brain.

On this particular occasion we were on hand to be entertained by the MGM studio's latest hit release, *Fanny and Kiddo*. The film starred the famous acting team of Crispin and Maude Antrim as well as Jackie Cooper, and it was solely because of Master Cooper that we were present at all; in 1931 young boys could be taken to see Jackie Cooper more or less with impunity. He had a grin like a yard of picket fence, and he could cry buckets; I never saw a kid-actor cry the way Jackie Cooper could. Our second movie was *Oliver Twist*, our third *Skippy*, to be succeeded by a seemingly endless string of "literary" offerings—*Great Expectations, David Copperfield*, and the like, with maybe a *Tom Sawyer* or a *Huckleberry Finn* tossed in for good measure. Though he never held any great brief for the movies, Dad nonetheless believed in "the classics," and he believed that Jackie Cooper was a Good Influence.

But where *was* Dad? The credits were unrolling and still he was nowhere to be seen. Even my mother, usually the soul of calm, evinced signs of anxiety and was peering over my shoulder. I saw her relieved smile; and I looked up as a tall figure, picked out in the reflected light falling from the screen, materialized out of the darkness and slid into the empty seat beside me. How had Dad found us in that enormous cave of night? Wasn't that clever of him? He gave my thigh a friendly squeeze, set his straw hat with its jaunty band of maroon-and-navy-blue grosgrain on my lap, and with a wink turned his Arrow Collar Man profile up to the screen, and at that same moment, returning my attention to the picture, I experienced the miracle of movies as I saw and heard my first talking actor. Jackie Cooper, aged ten, was talking to a confederate as they went about setting a pail of whitewash on the doortop—the idea being to drench the enemy—but the plan went awry when "the colored maid" entered instead. She let out a scream as she was doused with the stuff, and Jackie and his chum ran off. As I said, a miracle.

Anyway, *Fanny and Kiddo*, adapted from the children's classic of the same name by Ginna Josepha Johnson, was a step up in Jackie's budding career, while Maude Antrim was essaying one of her first "older" parts. Maude played the part of Fanny Mallotte, owner-manager of a traveling show, and her equally famous husband, Crispin, played the part of a carnival barker. As I recall it, I was able to follow the simple story with little trouble. Fanny comes across Kiddo (Jackie) crooking money from the box-office till and, rather than snitching on him, she endeavors to make a good boy of him. After many misadventures, Kiddo turns over a new leaf and at the fade-out, wearing an Eton collar and a cap with a tassel, he marches off to school to learn how to be a man while Fanny bids him a tearful farewell at the picket gate.

We had no time to be disappointed at the end of the movie, for there immediately followed the Coming Attractions, wherein I was first exposed to the actress the world has come to know as Claire Regrett. She wasn't a star then, just a featured player in a Warner Baxter movie, and I could read the bannerline printing that leaped out at me: "Hollywood's up-and-coming star—Claire Regrett at her temptingest!" (I heard my father groan at this solecism.) "This woman is bad but dying to be good," said the announcer; then there was a brief shot of Claire in the gutter, being helped to her feet by Warner Baxter, followed by: "Sinner or saint? Only God knew the truth." Then she's in church talking about becoming a nun and I hear Dad groan again and he puts a hand over his eyes.

Finally he leaped up and jerked his head at us, and we dutifully followed him up the aisle and out into the spring darkness. We didn't even get a soda at the ice-cream parlor next door, but were summarily paraded to the car, parked nearby. If it hadn't been for Claire and the preview, we'd have had ice cream, and I held this grudge against her for a long time to come. Instead, we were hustled home, where Jessie had a shepherd's pie on *Lo* in the oven, then packed off to bed. And for the next thirty-five years I don't recall ever watching another movie in the company of my father, until it was me up there, and even then he was hardly what you'd call "keen."

Quite simply, he didn't like the movies. A rabid individualist, he wasn't susceptible to their charms, and his shrewd Yankee intellect pierced the best of their obvious artifice and sham. Movies *were* sappy. Even as children we knew that the stories were mostly lousy, the actors lousier. But what we *did* know—and my father may have also vaguely realized, but didn't care to admit—was that the movies were here to stay.

In particular, his opinion of movie actresses was low, you could even say narrow-minded. Those he condemned ranged from Theda Bara to Joan Crawford to Jean Harlow, for her braless interpretations of tin-plate blondes, and, of course, Claire Regrett, for her boilerplate sluts and easy-virtue ladies. "A glorified lingerie model," he called her. He didn't even like Fedora, something I *never* understood. I don't think he actually even saw her in anything, certainly not her sound films, but he considered her screen image scandalous. Fedora was a femme fatale like Pola Negri and the rest of that spiderwebby sisterhood. Two screen females he could stomach: Sonja Henie and Minnie Mouse.

Nevertheless, within four or five years after that first dip into the movies I knew the inside of every first-run house in the central city area, the Poli (MGM and AyanBee, later 20th Century–Fox), the Poli Palace (in the next block north on Main, where the holdovers played), the Strand (Warners and RKO), the Allyn (Paramount, exclusively), E. M. Loew's (Columbia and Universal), and the Regal (holdover Warners and RKO). Then there were the second-run, outlying houses—the Princess, the Rialto, the Crown, the semi-distant Colonial, as well as the cheap grind houses on North Main, all beyond the moral pale, and that local nadir of moviedom, the Proven Pictures Theatre, where drunks spat in the aisles and the older guys felt up girls in the back rows. And last, the State, at the far North End, where the touring swing bands played, along with a Republic or Monogram feature—if you could call any Monogram a feature!

Before long we had our weekend moviegoing down to a near-science. As soon as Saturday chores were done, we lit out for whichever show had been picked. Properly managed, you could watch two shows straight through (two ninety-minute features, two co-features, the Coming Attractions, the newsreel, a cartoon, and sometimes even a "featurette" in Cinecolor). All this sandwiched in between eleven and five, with a hotdog and a malt at Kresge's five-and-dime, while you listened to the latest hits being played by a skinny lady sporting hennaed hair seated at the baby-grand piano with an ebony finish that had seen a better day.

Weekdays, the movies were definitely out, but that firmly stated parental ukase never deterred me. At "Rise and shine," I'd sometimes report in sick, claiming to have a sore throat and a headache, I couldn't possibly make it to school. No sooner was my mother out of the house, however, leaving me in Jessie's care, than I was up and dressed and out on the yellow trolley car, heading uptown to catch the latest "Gold Diggers" when the movie house opened at ten o'clock. Twenty minutes to town, ninety for the picture, twenty minutes back, I'd be safely tucked in bed by the time Jessie appeared with lunch on a tray, and nobody the wiser. That's how smartass kids got to the movies in 1935. If this kind of illicit traffic had ever been discovered by my father, the consequences are unthinkable.

Actually, there were moments when he did own up to having enjoyed the performances of, say, an Irene Dunne, maybe a Claudette Colbert—not as in *Cleopatra* with her snaky hips and cast-iron bra, not as in *Sign of the Cross*, either, with her asses'-milk baths, but as in *It Happened One Night*. Irene might act a little jazzy, as in *Theodora Goes Wild*, but everyone could see she was a lady, he said, and she did a neat little trick with her teeth that he liked. Once he even admitted to liking Roz Russell, who hailed from nearby Waterbury, and he certainly enjoyed Maude Antrim a lot. Maude was his latter-day Bernhardt, and if *she'd* ever come to town he might even have asked for her autograph. (She did but he didn't.) Maude Antrim, he claimed, always reminded him of Mother—ours, not his—and he admired Cary Grant extravagantly, especially Cary's swank wardrobe—the two-tone spectators, pleated slacks, swing-back jackets, Prince of Wales plaids, pencil stripes in his shirtings. Babe Austrian movies, of course, were anathema.

But the time was fast approaching when not only Babe's movies but the lady herself were to take an important part, not merely in my education, but in my life. Later, Dad was heard to bemoan the fact that it was Babe Austrian who'd come to town and not Maude Antrim. (They said, untruthfully, that I'd assaulted her and shouldn't be let loose on the community without a collar and leash. Not true.)

It had recently become the weekly parental practice to dispatch my older brother and me to art classes at the Hartford Atheneum, where each Saturday morning, in company with twenty-five or thirty other students, we would perch on stools with charcoal stubs, sketching from the "undraped" form. Undraped *plaster* form. The Atheneum was a good (bad?) example of the dolorous Gothic style that was in flower when the building had been erected over a century earlier, with ivy-covered stone and mullioned windows, but it was nevertheless just *there* that I had my first live sight of the Babe. And it was at this point that I discovered to my amazement that even the Babe Austrians of the world had their woes. It was along about this time, the spring of 1938, that Babe's name made that notorious list put out by the motion-picture theatre owners of the country and published in *Variety*, the so-called Box Office Poison list, which should have written *finis* to her movie career. Truth to tell, it did her no end of harm, even though she had plenty of elite company—Dietrich was on that same list, so were Katharine Hepburn and Fred Astaire, as well as Claire Regrett. Garbo would probably have been eligible, except she had *Camille* in second runs around the country and *Camille* was doing well. (*Camellia*, Babe's famous parody, would do even better, but that came much later on.)

But if you ever knew Babe, you knew she wasn't about to be flattened by a bunch of cigar-chomping, pot-bellied Kiwanis chiefs from Terre Haute and points west. When her latest picture, *The Girl from Windy City*, went into release, to sorry reviews and sorrier box-office receipts, she simply faced the music—and in the most literal sense. Against his better judgment, she persuaded Frankie Adano to book her into whatever vaudeville houses survived in that mid-Depression era of radio's Jack Benny and

Amos 'n' Andy. And, of all things, she took up playing the trap drums. No kidding, you can check the newspaper files in any large city around the country and you'll see that in the year 1938 Babe Austrian was indeed playing a new live act, seated up on a platform with that peroxided hair, beating out double paradiddles, and chewing hell out of her trademark bubble gum while she flashed her teeth, beat the dumbo with her foot, and rolled the sticks between her fingers. Oh *yeah!*

And she sang her famous "Windy City Blues":

> *"Oh I got those Windy City blues,*
> *They send a chill right down my spine,*
> *Oh I got those Windy City blues,*
> *'Cause I lost that man of mine. . . ."*

As it happened, a bunch of us went to see *Windy City* on the afternoon of the day it opened, and you could have shot moose in the theatre and never hit an antler. The place was plenty empty, and we saw the theatre manager gnashing his teeth when we came out into the lobby after the Coming Attractions. He did his gnashing with good reason, too; the picture really stank, one of the worst Babe ever made. But there she was, big and brassy as ever, in the "My Idea of Heaven" number, sashaying about a celluloid paradise, switching those hips and tossing one-liners at the colored actors, who wore big white wings and played golden harps while a celestial choir kept going "*Yeah* Babe, *oh* Babe."

By now everyone in the Greater Metropolitan Area was more or less aware not only that this turkey was limping along at the local theatre but that Babe herself was also set to appear "In Person" at the State Theatre up on North Main. To promote both the movie and her live stage appearance, she was scheduled to arrive on Saturday morning at the municipal train station, where she would be met by the Mayor, who'd present her with the official key to the city, and afterward there would be a motor cavalcade from the depot up to Main Street and right through the center of town.

Ah, for the feverish thoughts that swam through the air of my room that night, like so many fishes in the sea, and, oh, for the fetid dreams my perverted fancy concocted as I slept. That doll-like face my eyes knew so well, those platinum ringlets, those bejeweled fingers, those twitching lips and rolling hips, that inviting honkytonk voice—did I really sleep that night? I wonder. And, oh God, the tits . . . I wasn't fourteen for nothing!

Next noontime, at the Atheneum, when the bell rang releasing us from our two hours' enslavement to the Muses, we stampeded from the place into the bright sunlight and exciting holiday pandemonium of Main Street. Few scenes in my life have ever made such a dent on my impressionable mind as my first taste of what the Hollywood brand of hoopla and ballyhoo was and still is capable of. Bands played, flags waved, crowds cheered, there were photographers, reporters, policemen, remote units from the local radio stations. Both sides of Main Street were lined with a horde of screaming, bawling, shouting, gesticulating, popeyed gawkers standing tiptoe to see—what? Little, so far as I could tell, since I saw nothing but a beef trust of backs in front of me. A rusted drainpipe ran up one wall at the Atheneum entrance, and by some adroit maneuvering I managed to elevate myself above the heads of those in front, where I beheld a sight I shall never forget.

Out in the street, proceeding at a measured rate of speed along the thoroughfare, was an automobile—the automobile of our mayor, George Allen. I recognized him from his pictures in the paper, as well as the fact that he occasionally played golf with my father. The windows of the long, dark green automobile were rolled down, and behind his trademark pince-nez on a black silk ribbon he sat beaming and nodding, and at his side sat —BABE!!! Oh *yeah!*

If the Virgin Mary herself had been sitting beside Mayor Allen in his hammer-claw morning coat, his top hat, pearl spats, and spectacles, I for one could not have been more impressed. Less, actually, because I never really imagined the Virgin to possess breasts, while Babe—oh, there they were, those twin headlights, that gorgeous set of clydes sticking out to *there.* She was wearing a big cartwheel hat of black Milan straw (once or twice she turned her head and you could see it was a cut-out; her hair showed in the back). Her dress was shiny, cut low, with diamond clips in the corners, and she had ice on her arm up to the elbow. That was the arm she waved with; the other hand lay anchored in her muff—a silver fox muff that matched the fur chubby that was tossed over those shoulders —and it was hot that day. Hot, I'll say.

She smiled. Those pearly-whites flashed as if there were diamonds set between them, and you could see her eyes as they rolled about in her head like bb-shot. I felt myself stricken, then I went berserk on the spot. Heedless of my brother or our schoolmates, I leaped down from my perch and in seconds was shoving my way through the crowd, feeling hot and cold, as if I might burst or faint dead away. The slow-to-move were ruthlessly pushed from my path, the immobile became suddenly active as I weaseled my way through the press of bodies until I emerged at curbside just as the official vehicle, preceded by a marching brass band, drew abreast.

Looking neither left nor right, I plunged from curb to street, launching myself in a beeline for the main attraction. I saw nothing else, I had eyes only for her and the cartwheel hat, the flashy dress, the agreeably demonstrated pulchritude, that darling pink-and-white face, those flaxen curls. Nearer I came and nearer to the goddess; perhaps I was reaching out with my hands as though to *grab*—something!—I don't remember, but *forward* I went, closer, until I was *beside* the car, onto whose *running board* I, without so much as a by-your-leave, *sprang!* I wrapped one arm around the doorpost and stuck my head *inside* the *car!* I could *smell* her! Jesus, what a whiff! What a *scent!* Was it "Midnight in Paris," the dime-store perfume in the dark blue bottle, or the one with the man bending the lady backward in her ball gown over the piano? I stared for what seemed minutes. I was aware of eyelashes about a foot long and curled like the tines on a hayraker. I saw a coat of heavy orange stage makeup, and a startling nakedness, an alarming vulnerability in the person of the goddess, as if mere mortals such as I were not supposed to be seeing her in such close proximity.

She was a lot smaller than I'd imagined (Babe was only five-two without her platforms); Mayor Allen, not so tall himself, dwarfed her. But I was hardly aware of him as I stared at my quarry. She had a jeweled bag in her lap, and gloves, and the rocks on her free arm gleamed and coruscated like crazy. Her eyes were large and china blue and reminded me of the eyes in a doll. But though the eyes may have been large, the hands and feet were small. Teeny-tiny. I saw this right away. And—gad!—her little shoes were toeless, with tiny bows and spike heels.

She showed no alarm at my incursion, only a measure of mild surprise mixed with amusement. What was this dumb squirt-gun going to do to *her?* She smiled at me, that gleaming, porcelain smile that was hers, all hers. This was heady stuff and I had the feeling I was going to pass out. I didn't faint, however, but leaned farther inside, saw those snaky hips in that shiny black stuff, caught the sheen of sheer silken hosiery; I was suffocating from my passion and, reaching into the car with my fingers begrimed with charcoal from school, I—

pinched her!

God's truth. I pinched her on the thigh. Today people tell it that I pinched her on her ass; I didn't. She was sitting on her ass. But I do remember putting my index finger and thumb together and squeezing that holy flesh. It seared my pads and burned away my fingerprints forever; I leave none wherever I touch, that index finger and thumb are blistered but absolutely without whorls, only smudges. Believe that as you believe in a heaven yet to come.

I heard an exclamation of horror from Mayor Allen, and was aware of his indignant stare behind his pince-nez, and his mouth, open like a fish out of water, gulping air. Then, as I took my hand away, I *saw* Babe pat her cartwheel hat or maybe just her hair, and roll her eyes, and I *heard* her say:

"S'aw right, sonny, help yourself."

It's true, every word. I heard it with my own ears and Mayor Allen later verified it, though Babe herself later claimed not to remember having said it, which may be regarded as odd, considering how she could always recognize a good line when she heard it.

There was no time for more. I'd had all I was going to get of Babe Austrian for this and many a year to come. A burly arm seized me about my middle and I was torn bodily from the running board, and while the car rolled forward in the procession, I was left in the toils of John Q. Law, three feet off the ground, swimming in the air. I saw faces—staring, laughing, ridiculing faces. As I was plunked down on my two feet with no ceremony whatever, I saw, protruding from the window of the mayoral vehicle, one little baby hand, languidly, eloquently waving—itty-bitty waves. Then it was gone.

The effects of this minor escapade were manifold. I made the evening edition, my picture was plastered on page three, my name was set down in the annals for posterity (wrongly spelled, my age falsely reported), my father was obliged to draft a letter of apology to the Mayor, while I was sternly forbidden the inside of any movie house for a period of two whole months. And I commenced a lifelong association with Babe Austrian. Oh *yeah!*

Babe's story is one of the Plain Tales from the Hollywood Hills, the legends that star the great ones of Hollywood's Golden Age, those blinding, glitzy, rhinestone days of platinum hair, of lamé gowns, white fox furs, belted polo coats and pale fedoras, bearskin rugs, glass brick and chrome by the acre, of oversized upholstered furniture, tinted mirrors, and white rococo plaster, of wide shoulder pads, top hat, white tie, and tails, of silver cocktail shakers and satin mules and swimming pools shaped like Acapulco Bay, of running boards and white sidewall tires, of klieg-light premieres and Medici mansions, of Deco and dating and Coconut Groves and eating inside the crowns of Brown Derbys, of the pogrom-sent moguls of Panatella and Casting Couchdom, of toe-tapping, finger-snapping, Busby-crapping Bakelite and Mickey Mouse (before Disneyland), of rat-a-tat gangsters and Gary Cooper tall as stilts and Carole

Lombard acting screwy, in a time when the inmates did not run the asylum but were kept where they belonged, in padded cells, when if youth ever had its fling it was only at the whim of its elders, when the very worst product the majors could crank out was somehow more satisfying than most of what's squeezed today from the Melrose Avenue sausage factories.

"We had *faces,*" says Gloria Swanson, and is photographed amid the baroque plaster ruins of the old Roxy, crushed beneath the wrecker's ball; gone but not forgotten. They also had glamour then, and a veil of mystery, and attraction and elegance and a sinful purity, the innocence of nursery babes, and the overpowering loftiness that elevated them to that heady Olympian realm where they dwelled, and not their most sullied or foolish acts could degrade the diadems they wore like the haloes of ten thousand virgins. Gloria was right: they *did* have faces then. And class. Didn't they? Lotsa class. When weren't the guys in white tails—Gary, Cary, Melvyn, Randy, Fred? Swank, pure swank.

In the matter of screen "type," as they like to call it, Babe always fell between stools. Neither the rare exotic of her middle movie period (Dietrich, Garbo, Fedora), nor the all-American girl (Janet Gaynor, June Allyson), nor the Perfect Wife (Myrna Loy), nor the generously endowed Florodora blonde on the *Police Gazette* (West, Grable), nor the floozy-*cum*-nun (Claire Regrett), a Babe Austrian could have flowered only in the U.S. during the second quarter of the twentieth century, and by her own admission could never have done it without Frankie Adano. Generous to the last, Babe was still proclaiming the same thing on her deathbed, for the same—yet far, far different—reasons.

In addition to being Babe's manager in the early days, Frank was also generally and elliptically referred to as her "boyfriend." This meant to grownups that they shared a bed, while to us young fry it meant something like cherry Cokes on Saturday nights after a roller-skating party. But everybody knew about Frankie Adano, and you'd hear talk about his underworld connections (he'd grown up with Benjamin Siegel, better known as Bugsy; later he had truck with Al "Vegas" da Prima, "Ears" Satriano, and "Moonskin" Spaccifaccioli), though the manicurists used to say Frank was better-lookin' than Clark Gable or Bob Taylor. And just at this time—Babe's visit to our town—everybody knew Frankie had dumped her for Claire Regrett, whom Louella Parsons said he was "squiring" and the guys joked he was "screwing." Doubtless some of each.

People like to ask what Frank was "really" like, as though I or anyone would really know. Frankie was Frankie, a little like Caesar, all things to all men—but seldom like Caesar's wife, above suspicion. Frankie was always suspect, even when he was innocent—like that rap he did a year and a half for. Frankie was what he was. He was lucky, that's one sure thing. In his time he'd ducked more than one bullet and lived to tell the tale. And he always came up smelling like a rose, no matter what—at least until the end.

For me his name still conjures up the Golden Age of Moving Pictures. Anyone who knows anything about Hollywood knows how truly he was always at the dead center of things, from way back in the early thirties clear through the sixties, even the seventies. Hook or crook, Frank was certainly one of the most dramatic, colorful, powerful, and imposing figures in the whole industry, a crackerjack agent who was wooed and courted and deferred to, who was ass-kissed and ass-kicked, loved and hated, who made or remade movie stars by the fistful. Think of them— Babe herself; Maude Antrim; her husband, Crispin; April Rains; Kit Carson; Belinda Carroll; Julie Figueroa; Claire Regrett; and all the others. His was a stylish career that managed to survive unsavory Vegas alliances, his friendship with Bugsy, scandals of sex and murder, even the Senate crime hearings.

To me Frankie was a saint. He was my agent, and I respected and appreciated him. He was always four-square with me—a little nutty maybe; still, you had to admire him—love him, even. Generous to a fault. Thoughtful, considerate—a really classy gent—he used to remember to wire my mother flowers on her birthday, or he'd send her theatre tickets when she was in New York. Once, when a picture of mine was playing at Radio City Music Hall, he had her whole bridge club limo'd down from Hartford to see the opening, with lunch in the Rainbow Room afterward. Mother declared that outside of her husband, Frankie Adano was the best-looking guy who ever lived, and that *he* was the one who should have been in the movies. Mother was not alone in her opinion. People always used to say he could have had a Hollywood acting career himself if he'd wanted to—look at George Raft. But Frankie was too smart for that bull. He knew which end of the trombone the music comes out of.

Frankie had a genius for recognizing the potential in actors before the studios ever laid an eye on them, sometimes before the personalities themselves even knew what they had. Take Babe, for example, his first big success; or April Rains, who was a total unknown; then there's Kit Carson, the ex–beach bum; or look what he did with Claire Regrett, who was only Cora Sue Brodsky when he first knew her, behind the hosiery counter at Gimbel's; or Belinda Carroll, found singing for nickels on a street corner across from Echo Park.

There are those who still claim he was nothing but a two-bit opportunist, but he had the manners of a duke. Why else would spectacular dames like Barbara Stanwyck and Roz Russell have had him for a friend? For a while, after Thalberg died, he dated Norma Shearer before she remarried. A guy doesn't pull the wool over the eyes of ladies like that; they've been around the hall, they know the score. They could always spot a three-dollar bill.

And Babe Austrian? Well, there are a few—more than a few—interesting sidelights to *that* fifty-year career, most of which Frankie was a party to. Babe adored him—in her younger days, that is—worshipped the ground he walked on, even after he dumped her for Claire Regrett, and after Claire, Frances Deering, the beautiful lumber heiress, who of all the beauties was finally the one to snare him. Think of the long list of women he had—who else could have juggled them all, and with his finesse? What Frankie knew, you don't learn. Putting it Babe's way, "Honey, you either got it or you don't. And if you don't, don't come around." Oh *yeah!*

Certainly it's not giving away any secret to state that Babe Austrian and Frankie Adonis were two parties in an open-ended romantic relationship existing without benefit of clergy, a relationship of such duration and depth that it seemed like a fact of life. Nor did it seem to be any secret that they were getting it on. We knew it, even back then. In a day when the overworked tag of "sex symbol" hadn't been thought of, those two were just "sexy," and that was a given. Winchell was always writing them up; the local newspaper carried Walter, and I chewed up the lines looking for BABE (in caps; all celebrities were in caps in our paper) or FRANK ADONIS, as he was later known, "the Italian Clark Gable."

Frankie was dark and slick, all patent-leather, Italian flash; Babe was blonde and diamond-flashier. She could have seen her face in his hair, so brilliantined was it, while he could probably catch his mustache in her lavallière. It was Frank who got Babe her first Hollywood contract. Sure, *you'll* say she was signed when she was in New York, playing in *Lola Magee*, but you'll be wrong. When Babe was grabbed for pictures it wasn't in New York or anywhere near it, and nobody but Frankie could have pulled off that clever job of work.

There are many versions still making the rounds concerning how they met, including both published autobiographies. In his, *Just Call Me Lucky*, Frank states, with surprising discretion, that they were "introduced" by a "mutual acquaintance," whose name he assures us he has forgotten, but claims this introduction took place at Risenweber's. Babe, on the other hand, states in *Oh Babe!* that they met at the Belmont race track, which heaven knows they both frequented often enough. Either story might be true; neither is. I'm putting this down for the record: this is the version Frankie himself confided to me not long before he died, and swore was gospel.

The facts were these. Frank's ma, Maxine Fargo (Maxine had remarried after old Tony Adano's death), was living on West Fifty-fourth Street, and I mean *West,* right in the heart of Hell's Kitchen, as they called it then. Frankie Adano, a second-generation Italian with both Neapolitan and Sicilian connections, was a small-time grifter and chiseler, out to make a buck and do himself whatever good he could manage. He was a street kid, a regular Dead Ender, good-looking and smart. One of his best friends was a guy named Benny Siegel, nicknamed Bugsy, who at a later time all by himself invented a place in the Nevada desert called Las Vegas. The pair of them used to snitch ladies' alligator bags and Kolinsky scarves or swipe counter merchandise from Manhattan department stores. Once they picked on some dame in the subway, beating her up and yanking her pocketbook off its strap. The woman was an off-duty cop; she nailed Frankie, Benny ran away, Frankie did his eighteen months.

But that didn't stop him. In time he and Bugsy gave up petty crime and worked their way up to bootlegging and became bag-runners for a numbers racket. They rubbed shoulders with the mob and won reputations for being sharp, dependable, and ruthless. Frank's then-girlfriend was a hot little Jewish number named Cora Sue Brodsky, a girl with the makings of a broad. As I said, she sold lingerie at Gimbel's, and she lived with her family in Bensonhurst and yearned like crazy to be a movie star. Frankie promised Cora Sue he could do the trick. He snapped his fingers to show how easy, got her moved into a flat on East Twenty-third Street, and Saturday nights often found him in the basement of her building, stirring up in set-tubs the gin that his customers claimed to like but which more often than not tasted of soap, bluing, and bleach. Cora Sue would hang around, waiting for the next batch to be bottled, even helping him do it, and when the janitor was off-premises Frankie would take her to the janitor's bed and give her a good weekend *shtup,* which helped her complexion and kept down her level of complaints. Cora Sue was willing, nay, eager, to stick her legs in the air, because Frankie was going to make her into this big movie star—that's what he told her anyway. But this was B.B. —Before Babe. After Babe, Cora Sue never stood a chance. But she loved him anyway.

Babe was a baby vaudevillian. She came out of Chicago, having grown up in Cicero, where the infamous Saint Valentine's Day Massacre took place. She was known variously as "Baby Polly," "Pretty Polly," sometimes "Chicago Polly," and she recited cute verses, did comic and dramatic monologues, danced with her own shadow in a Pierrot outfit, and worked in living tableaux, until she was too old to be "Baby" anything anymore and she became Babe, which, fortunately, she had the curves to merit. But she didn't get rid of "Baby Polly" altogether; she made her into a character, a parody of a cute, lisping child who asked risqué questions and supplied her own humorous answers. Babe or Baby, the act was big-time all the way.

When she and Frankie met in 1930, she was appearing on Forty-second Street at the Julian Eltinge Theatre in her play *Lola Magee*, and her star was waning. She'd been in several editions of the Follies, Ziegfeld having become intrigued with her Polly character as well as her ability to belt out a song and hit the last row in the balcony. She'd been in editions with Fields, with Will Rogers, even old Trixie Friganza. Fanny Brice had been her nemesis.

But her current vehicle, *Lola Magee*, was strictly for the beer-and-pretzel trade. It had boffo laughs, but its main attractions were Babe's husky voice, her baby-blues, and that rollicking set of curves. In a three-month period Frankie saw the show seventeen times. At that time he was working at a tango parlor on West Forty-sixth Street where you could go and get your exercise in the new imported dance craze. Of all the studs who were available as partners, Frankie was *primo*, and the girls used to fall over themselves getting his arm around their waist. He was a snaky dancer, smooth and elegant and completely serious about it, as though in exhibiting the subtle but sexual innuendos of the tango he were undergoing some profound metaphysical experience. It was no joke. He was crazy about dancing, he loved displaying his agility and grace—the grace of a black panther, according to some who saw him. He had a wasp waist and wore spray-on pants, so tight he couldn't sit down, and those yellow pearl-button shoes; spats, too. The girls went cuckoo when he got his thigh in their crotch and rubbed them up until the honey dripped. Between his dancing and his gambling instinct he was pretty well set up for the life work he was already carving out for himself, and in this year of 1930 he had privately decided that a cute little trick named Mabel Osterreich from Cicero, Illinois, was just the meal ticket he was looking for. The way Frankie reasoned things, he had what she wanted, he was perfectly willing to give it to her, and he would make her what is today called a superstar. So he dumped Cora Sue Brodsky on her Brooklyn keester and went all-out for Babe.

Always a ladies' man, Frankie had in fact what the girls were looking for, what Cora Sue had panted after. That is to say, though relatively slight of stature, he was hung like a horse. He sometimes referred to that particular portion of his anatomy as his "pride and passion," and was boastful of his endowment. In fact, he enjoyed showing it off, and in typical Neapolitan style he sincerely believed he was put on this earth to make the opposite sex happy. He didn't have any name whatever at the time, except as this hot tangoist, but in his tight striped pants, his yellow shoes, his chamois vest, his Borsalino, he cut a dashing figure around Broadway, where the lights were bright.

One day he made up his mind that he was going to treat Babe to some of his "pride and passion," and he hiked over to the Eltinge before the matinee and flashed his personal engraved card at the stage door. The obliging doorman carried the card inside, then came back and gave him the gate. This made Frankie angry. But he was always the type of guy to make his own luck when things didn't fall his way, so he took the bull by the horns, and in the most literal sense. One Wednesday afternoon he waited at the end of the stage-door alley until he saw Babe's private car arrive for the matinee. She was then the "great and good friend" of a certain Waldo Niemier, a burly sub-contractor from Ho-Ho-Kus, New Jersey, and after every performance Waldo's driver would take Babe to Ruby Foo's, or to Sardi's, or the old Delmonico's. On this particular afternoon, just as the car started up, Frankie stepped out of the shadows, opened the door, and jumped in, announcing to the startled passenger that he had a present for her; it was right there in his fist. So declaring, he flung himself back against the pearl-gray upholstery and exhibited for her delectation his rampant "pride and passion."

"Take a look, Babe," he breathed hotly, "it's all yours." And it did live up to its rep; every raging inch. Then, while he rolled his eyes and snorted in imitation of a bull, Babe slipped out the stickpin from her hat and gave his throbbing pride and passion a healthy jab. They said you could hear the howl of pain clear over to Broadway. As the car ground to a screeching halt, with his wounded pride fast wilting in his hand, Frankie threw open the door and staggered onto the curb, blind with rage and agony. As it happened, in addition to curious passersby, a Times Square mounted policeman was also on hand to witness the spectacle, and when he questioned the occupant of the limousine as to what the trouble was, Babe replied:

"He was tryin' to stick me up, Officer. Take him away and book him."

A citation for disturbing the peace and impairing public morals was written, and Frankie spent the balance of the day in jail before he found a mouthpiece willing to bail him out.

Furious, he plotted his revenge, and at the next Saturday matinee a phalanx of ferocious harpies was seen marching from Broadway toward

the Eltinge Theatre, where they stormed the box office. Calling themselves "Mothers for a Moral America," they carried signs reading "Babe
Osterreich sinister influence on young America," things like that, and
ringed the lobby so no one could buy a ticket. There was also a gang of
news photographers and reporters on hand, and as a fracas ensued between the irate "Mothers" and the would-be audience, mostly male, one
of the photographers managed to sneak into Babe's dressing room, where
he snapped her in the embrace of a fifteen-year-old boy whose nether
quarters beneath his shirttails appeared to be bare. The resultant picture
is the comical one everybody knows today. "Broadway star *in flagrante
delicto* with under-age son of boiler superintendent," read the florid caption. Babe's show never played that matinee, the Black Maria arrived, and
she was hauled off to the pokey, to that identical jail where Frankie had
been incarcerated earlier that same week.

Lola Magee had been what might be called a so-so hit. After this,
however, all was changed, and Babe was never the same again. The box
office was mobbed, this time by sensation-seeking audiences, the play
became famous, all New York was fighting for seats, and the theatre was
sold out weeks in advance. Babe remained in her cell two nights instead
of the single one that was required, and, knowing a bad thing when she
smelled it, she later held a press conference outside the jail. The "Mothers
for a Moral America" were exposed by a traitor in their midst, who
declared that each of the bogus "Mothers" had been paid five bucks a head
to storm the theatre, while the "under-age son of the boiler superintendent" was disclosed as being a forty-three-year-old dwarf from a Forty-
second Street flea parlor. And the whole farrago was exposed as a hoax
perpetrated by none other than Frankie Adano!

Tit for tat. For years afterward, Frankie wore Babe's pearl stickpin
in his cravat and loved to tell the story to friends, though it never got into
print. While nursing his injured "pride," he also nursed a grudge against
Babe, now his declared quarry. He went up and down Broadway betting
that he would give her the business before the week was out, and what
was more he'd take her to Havana for the weekend and screw the hell out
of her at the Nacional. He bided his time, waiting for his chance, which
he seized on another matinee day when the doorman was still at lunch,
slipping the relief man a box of Corona Coronas to look the other way,
and sneaking into Babe's dressing room.

Hiding himself behind a painted screen, he waited until Babe entered
with her maid. When the maid stepped out to fill the water pitcher and
Babe was in the can, Frankie locked the door and was waiting for her.
From all reports it was quite an encounter, a noisy brouhaha in which

Babe lobbed the entire contents of her dressing table at him, Frank fielding the rouge pots and cold-cream jars until he managed to get close enough to tackle her and by sheer force bear her to the floor—except it wasn't the floor but a pillowed chaise longue where he fell on top of her, and pretty soon there were no more protests from the lady. Frank, a smart business-man, was finally giving her the business.

They held the curtain nearly an hour that day "due to technical difficulties," and when Babe finally went on it was said she gave the best performance of her career as Lola. That night there was a champagne supper at Lüchow's at which Frankie reputedly downed three and a half dozen oysters—"for purposes of fortification only"—and the next day Babe returned Mr. Ho-Ho-Kus's car and uniformed driver. The morning papers reported that she would be taking a short hiatus—in Miami Beach, as it happened—and that her understudy would *not* go on in her place.

After that Frankie collected the bets he'd chalked up and it became quickly known that Babe Austrian was strictly his territory and that he was running the whole show, his intention from the beginning. He went into his Pygmalion act, revamping her from top to bottom; he changed her name, redesigned her figure, and sent her to Pelletti, who saw to such streamlinings in those days. He got her top salary for the show, got her dressing room redecorated, got her a new wardrobe, onstage and off, got her a bigger, brighter sign on the marquee, and ran the show to sold-out audiences for eleven more months.

The rest is, as they say, history. Babe Osterreich was no more; Babe Austrian was born, and within a year had become a major star on Broad-way, one of the prevailing sex images of the time. The next step, inevita-bly, was Hollywood and the movies. Frankie saw to that, too, and at the train station the "Mothers for a Moral America"—the same contingent of belligerent females he had corralled to storm the Eltinge Theatre—were on hand to send Babe off on the 20th Century Limited with a floral wreath, this time naming her "Star Performer of the Year." To say the least, Frankie's ex-girlfriend Cora Sue was miffed—Frankie was supposed to have made a star out of *her*. Before leaving town, however, he did pay for some rhinoplasty and dance lessons, then gave her a kiss and said toodle-oo; he and Babe were off to Lotusland.

It was an interesting coincidence that the Broadway house Babe had packed in *Lola Magee* was the Julian Eltinge, named in memory of the most celebrated female impersonator of the period, whose genteelly ren-dered portrayals of fashionable "ladies" carried him to vaudeville stardom and eventually to Broadway, where he was regarded, not as any sort of show-biz freak, but as a genuine "artiste" plying his legitimate and hard-learned craft.

Eltinge bowed offstage in 1941, after a long and successful career that spanned some forty years, from vaudeville and the Palace to his name in lights on the Great White Way. Having retired from the scene, he staged a comeback during the war at Billy Rose's Diamond Horseshoe, where he succumbed to a heart attack, just coming offstage, still in high drag. Julie died for his art.

I mention this merely as a sidelight, since Babe Austrian was indubitably the most imitated performer of the century. Her clothes were copied, her millinery; her punchlines were famous. "Got something for me, boy?" was as famous as Greta's "I vant to be alone," while "Get off my porch" was the catchphrase of the day. She popularized the tam-o'-shanter so it sold by the millions, and when she took up golf, women from Maine to California hit the fairways with their five irons and caddies. Her collection of French Impressionists rivaled that of Edward G. Robinson's, while her absence from the track on race day was judged a bad omen. But this is getting ahead of the story; the Monets and handicappers came later.

In the year preceding their arrival in Hollywood, Frankie Adano had discovered his center of gravity, and when he and Babe rolled into Tinseltown he was determined to be taken seriously. They put up at the Beverly Hills Hotel in "adjoining rooms" and made sure they were seen everywhere together. It was at Santa Anita that they made their initial splash, where they posed for pictures and Frankie made his oft-quoted comment, "We came to shake the grapefruit from the trees and the stars out of the skies." And shake they did. Together or separately they created the kind of flurry that the town adored. Frank's first purchase of note was an expensive car, a landau with enclosed cab, open driver's. He hired a chauffeur, stuck him in maroon livery with black froggings, and told him to drive Babe around town, from Hollywood to Beverly Hills and clear out to Santa Monica. And just as he planned it, her advent amid the coconut palms of Hollywood caused its share of comment and speculation among the natives, who like most natives were of a fairly restless nature.

One thing seemed most apparent: Babe Austrian was made for the movies, just as the movies seemed to have been invented for her. So that no one was more surprised than she and Frankie to find the studios behaving standoffishly. Rather than the hot ticket she'd been in New York, Babe was perceiving herself to be a little frog in a big Hollywood pond. It didn't seem to matter, the length of her car, the number of her furs, even the square inches of diamonds she sported; she was treading water, getting nowhere fast, and neither she nor Frankie seemed able to break the logjam.

In addition, there was a curious social situation prevailing in the environs of Beverly Hills: the stardom conferred on Babe in the East did her little good in a town that was as caste-conscious as Calcutta. Because of her naughty image, there was an unfortunate stigma attached to Babe's person, and it was preventing her entree into the front parlors of the rich and famous where deals were made, parts cast, careers made.

Frankie was quick to note the openly offered snubs, though it was being made clear that he himself was welcome almost anywhere (they should only have known about *his* checkered past), and he was frequently invited to gatherings without Babe, which made for some difficulty. But since it was a basic tenet of the industry that a lot of movie deals were cut at Saturday-night social gatherings, and since everything depended on his getting Babe a picture as quickly as possible, they discussed the matter between themselves and were in accord: when Babe might attend a gathering, she would; when not, Frankie would go alone and try to harrow the arid fields of Beverly Hills.

Besides, her day would come. If the smart matrons of Beverly Hills, Bel Air, and Brentwood chose to snoot her, she didn't care; she wasn't there to be social anyway; she was there to get famous and make pots of money. "I don't take things lying down unless I happen to be," was to become one of Babe's famous lines, and she went on making herself as conspicuous as she could. Not only was she seen regularly at the race track, she lunched at the hotel pool and let the tourists snap pictures of her, she tooled around town in her car, she went regularly to the theatre, and took in a bunch of movie matinees. All in all, a far cry from the oddball recluse she would become in later years, when people went mad to catch even the tiniest glimpse of her.

There are several famous personalities, among them we can include the Babe, who owe their film careers, at least the start of them, to one person unique in Hollywood annals. You probably don't hear much too much about her these days, but Viola Ueberroth, intimate of the greats and the famous (one-time mistress of Clark Gable; she paid to have his ears pasted back), "discoverer" of the great Fedora, doyenne of the Bel Air circuit, operator of the infamous Friday Night Carmel Drive Poker Battalion, renowned Beverly Hills hostess, and intimate of the movers and the shakers of the town, was and remains a filmdom institution. Still going strong in her late seventies, she's part of the old Hollywood, the one that's dead and gone and isn't likely to return.

Having got her early start as a lowly steno at the old AyanBee Studios on lower Sunset Boulevard (where her brother, Sam, was first a publicist, then a producer), by the time Babe and Frank arrived in town Viola had established herself as a shrewd and canny agent as well as an intimate of the powers-that-be. Already her regular Friday-night poker game was an institution, and the fact that Sam was one of the more prestigious producers at AyanBee Studios hurt her not at all. Some years before, it had been Viola's unfailing eye that had fallen upon the forlorn, unknown figure of Fedora on a streetcar en route to the beach and had been instrumental in getting her her first Hollywood part, setting her on the road to international stardom. What Vi had done before, Vi could do again.

As luck would have it, Viola was already well known to Frankie, and he to her. He'd met her in New York at a Lamb's Frolic and they'd managed to get on so well that he'd asked her for a date, one that had ended up, as he'd planned, in her bed. It was a fact that Vi, not one of God's prettiest creatures, had been made love to by some of the biggest studs in Hollywood, and if he'd wanted to, at the time Frankie could have carved his name right there on her thigh. So no wonder that it was Vi who now came to Frank's rescue.

The fact that Constance Bennett as well as certain other screen royalty wouldn't offer Babe the time of day held no water with Vi, nor did it keep her from jumping wholesale on Frank's bandwagon. Besides, she was shrewd enough to realize that Babe Austrian was a walking gold mine, a Fort Knox with tits, as her brother Sam would one day put it.

So, standing up to the beldames of the film colony, Viola proceeded to invite both Frankie and Babe to her Friday-night poker sessions. And if there was one thing Babe knew, it was cards. She'd been a hard-nosed player since her teens, when she'd get into a game with the stagehands, and this had been one of the things that had helped cement her relationship with Frankie. And now it helped provide her with her first movie role, at AyanBee Studios, and under the aegis of Sam Ueberroth.

AyanBee, that crumbling silent-picture studio, which was said to be held together with a little spit and lots of adhesive tape, was definitely in need of a hit, and a prodigious hit at that. Vi happened to recall a script that her brother had bought years ago and that had ended up on a shelf collecting its share of dust. The property was called *Pattycake, Pattycake,* the saga of a naive girl straight off the farm who falls in love with a medicine barker in a traveling show and ends up a star on Broadway. Certainly not an original story, but there was a character there that Babe could play, a wisecracking know-it-all who was always on top of everything.

Yet when it came to casting, Sam proved a hard nut to crack, especially since his wife, Pauline, was one of those Hollywood spouses who eyed Babe with disapproval. But Vi soon took care of that, and upon

Pauline's discovering for herself that Babe wasn't at all like her projected image, but a sweet-natured girl with a good sense of humor, she began adding her own blandishments to Viola's. Together they persuaded Sam to drag out the script of *Pattycake*, with Babe in mind; Vi slipped a copy to Babe to look over, and in a weekend she'd completely rewritten the thing, calling it *Broadway Blue Eyes*, giving it a stronger plot line and surrounding herself with four or five leading men to cast her spell upon. Harry Shine, one of Mack Sennett's old comedy directors, was dragged out of mothballs to perform director chores, and in no time AyanBee Studios had the moneymaking hit it had been looking for. In fact, it could be said that Babe Austrian saved the lot (Fort Knox with tits, indeed), and with this resounding success her star was catapulted high into the Hollywood firmament. In hardly any time at all Babe's name was a household word, and Babe Austrian jokes quickly replaced the farmer's daughter and Little Audrey variety, and shopgirls across the country began peroxiding their locks and wearing ankle socks and a hair ribbon to match their outfit.

Then came *Pretty Polly*. It had been Frank's original idea of teaming the two unlikeliest show-business personalities anyone could hope to find, and he came up with a winning combination that led to three of the biggest laugh riots of the thirties and did much to foster the illusion of the so-called screwball comedy. One evening he'd taken Babe down to the Biltmore Theatre to see Crispin Antrim and his wife, Maude, in a play, and sometime during the second act the idea struck him. With Crispin's droll wit and impeccable manners, his high style and crisp, gentlemanly airs, the great Shakespearean actor seemed the perfect foil for a Babe Austrian. Frankie envisioned a story in which the two could rub up against each other (after a fashion) and produce laughs. Never especially noted for his comedy performances, Crispin Antrim nonetheless proved an adept farceur in the old tradition, while Babe's broad delivery of a socko gag was already well demonstrated. After the curtain fell, Frankie conducted her backstage to meet the famous actor, and was pleased to see how well they got on.

Next day Frank huddled at Metro with Irving Thalberg, who quickly got the message. The fact that Crispin was years older than Babe only added spice to the idea, and Frank went away to think some more. Sometime later he came up with the idea for a backstage story, called *Footlights*, which eventually became *Pretty Polly*, the story of a newcomer to the Follies who meets a broken-down actor whom she turns into a slapstick comedian and who ends up the star of the show. The critics dismissed it as cheapjack Hollywood stuff, but nonetheless it made customers everywhere weep buckets.

Frank's idea of teaming Babe and Crispin paid big dividends. *Pretty*

Polly was followed by the even more successful *Delicious*, about a board-inghouse keeper and his daughter running off counterfeit bills on an abandoned printing press, and the third, *Manhattan Madness*, contained some of the funniest screwball scenes ever filmed—the story of a rich playboy producer of Broadway musicals who bets his theatre that he can make a star of the girl who works in the hashhouse around the corner. His efforts to create a singing comedienne out of little Mitzi bear fruit and—guess what?—he ends up marrying her.

Crispin Antrim, who lived at Sunnyside, the palatial house he had built for his wife, Maude, and that rivaled Pickfair as a royal palace and Hospitality Hall for visiting firemen, made a small fortune from his comedies with Babe, but for unspecified reasons the lady never set foot inside those lofty precincts. People said Maude herself was the cause of this rejection, though I never found reason to give the report credence.

By now Babe's career was in high gear. In less than three years she'd got a beach house in Santa Monica and had become one of the biggest and most dependable attractions in movies. Thalberg, then turning out the elite glamour product of MGM, thought he saw in the comedienne further possibilities as yet untapped, and when Crispin Antrim suffered an accident, it was Irving who had the idea that resulted in Babe's being cast with the four Marx Brothers in what was to become their biggest hit after *A Night at the Opera*. Far more than merely the love interest, Babe played the wily Flaxie de Mer, alias Gladys Smith, who managed to steal from Groucho every scene she played in *All at Sea*.

It was also during this period that Babe, needing a place in town, moved to the Sunset Towers, a notably glamorous landmark on the Holly-wood scene. As you drove west along Sunset Boulevard toward the section known as the Strip, you passed, among other remarkable sights, Schwab's Drugstore (where Lana Turner was not discovered), Frascatti's of happy memory, the Garden of Allah and the Villa Lorraine, and farther west, on the south side of the street, the Sunset Towers. Financed by a prominent industrialist and motorcar magnate, its *moderne* style and ex-travagant exterior embellishment were pure Art Deco, and its eleven stories were surmounted by a spacious penthouse where for a number of years the industrialist had housed his inamorata, a celebrated beauty and ex-chorine. The apartment had a marvelous view of the hills to the north and the flats to the south, and to the east and west the Sunset Strip snaked like a well-trafficked ribbon between Hollywood and the old Beverly Hills bridle path.

In a later epoch, movie fans driving past would point aloft to where Babe Austrian was at home, as though the late-burning lamp in her bedroom were a beacon—a beacon that declared to the world that Babe Austrian was alive and well, living in sin with no one knew which, or how many, oversexed studs.

By the mid-thirties, with her easy, freewheeling style, her unblinking candor, her high humor, her oft-quoted wit, she was the hottest thing to hit Hollywood since Lupe Velez. In addition, she had stuffed her head with all sorts of information and if she played dumb, believe me, it was only playing. Along with Connie Bennett and Claudette Colbert, she was one of the top female moneymakers in the years 1934–37. Only Maude Antrim beat her out in '37. And by then she'd become a fashion plate as well; Adrian was dressing her, in a much more subdued style than her former gaudy image, and when he got her out of those long skirts, she was discovered to possess two of the most shapely legs God ever gave a woman, legs that a Grable might envy.

During the war years she easily maintained her position as a mainstay of the studio, and by the time June Allyson came on the lot in 1942, Babe had been there for eight years, and the Marxes were long gone to Eagle-Lion and film oblivion. In the famous *Life* shot of the celebrations of twenty-five years of MGM, it is a startling omission that Babe Austrian is not among the luminaries. "More stars than there are in heaven" was the slogan, and she was assuredly one of those. The fact was, Babe *is* in many of the shots from that *Life* sitting—she is positioned on the left, next to Arlene Dahl, wearing a navy-blue tunic and skirt and surrounded by ostrich feathers—but the shot that was used in the magazine and became famous doesn't show her. Promptness was never Babe's long suit; people had been waiting for her all her life, and she figured they'd wait for her that day to begin. They didn't, the editors chose one of the early shots, and here is the result.

Meanwhile, the redoubtable Vi Ueberroth was greatly responsible for the new Frank Adonis who was emerging, chick from embryo. To look at her today, it's not easy to imagine Vi as ever having been physically attractive or having had a high-tech sex life, but the chances are strong that for a period she and Frankie enjoyed intimacies, though neither of them was the type to kiss and tell. Whatever the real relationship, theirs was a friendship of long standing, and as the secretary from AyanBee on lower Sunset rose in the eyes of the industry and became the doyenne of North Carmel Drive, she continued to enjoy a special friendship with the Black Wolf, as Frank was sometimes called.

In 1932, when he first arrived in Hollywood, Frankie Adano had one client, Babe. In just a few years he had changed his name to Frank Adonis, had formed the Adonis Actors Agency, and had a client list the length of your arm. He hadn't, however, done it entirely on his own. And he'd had strong support from others besides Vi. One of these, an unlikely benefactor and sometime mentor, was none other than the kingpin of MGM, Mr. Louis Burt Mayer himself. No one knew how this strangely matched combo had got its start; some say it was because of their frequent meetings at the track, some claim it was because Frankie knew the prettiest ladies in town. But however it began, from Mayer Frankie went on to enjoy the acquaintanceship of much of Hollywood's royalty, and to see him making an entrance at one of their parties in a well-cut suit of tails was a sight to behold. In the early thirties every movie actor worth his salt wore white tie and tails in his parlor, bedroom, and even bath pictures. Cary Grant, Gary Cooper, Georgie Raft, Warren William, Edmund Lowe, Astaire, Gable, all sported their best soup-and-fish, but few of these idols of the silver screen were ever so dashing as Frankie Adonis in his evening rig. He was in fact buried in his, and why not, since he'd lived so much in it?

But the major change in Frank's life at this time was in relation to Babe. There was a series of public quarrels, soon he was looking for surcease elsewhere, and he found it in the arms (and bed) of Claire Regrett, née Cora Sue Brodsky, who had in just a few years become one of MGM's leading female stars.

Cora Sue's miraculous transformation from lingerie salesgirl to chorus cutie to ranking star was the start of what was to become one of the great screen legends. After Frankie split for Hollywood with Babe, Cora Sue grew more determined than ever to make it big "out there," so she quit the chorus line and hopped a train. And on that train, the story goes, she met a Hollywood producer, our friend Vi's brother, Sam, who said he could make Cora Sue a star as well as Frankie Adonis could. She let him. How much she let him or how often remained a matter of conjecture for some years, but the fact remained that in not too long a time Cora Sue Brodsky's dreams came true. Claire Regrett was born, and before long she left Sam's AyanBee Studios for Metro, eventually won the Oscar, and stayed a reigning Hollywood star for almost forty years until she retired and died, alone and all but forgotten, in a New York penthouse.

Certainly there's no denying that Claire formed an important, even integral, part of Frank's life, and it's a matter of record that their liaison continued off and on for more than thirty years. The embarrassing scene she made at his funeral has become part of Hollywood lore, and the rivalry between her and Babe has passed into the pages of the town's history.

As far as Babe was concerned, Claire Regrett had stolen her lover, if not exactly out from under her then possibly from on top of her. Babe was a faithful soul: if she liked you, she liked you for good, no matter what others might say. By the same token, if she didn't like you, nothing was going to change her mind. And that's how she felt about Claire. She'd disliked Cora Sue Brodsky when they were both back in New York, and she hated Claire Regrett even more. Though she was then enjoying a huge personal success of her own, it rankled in her breast that Cora Sue had managed to become this larger-than-life Hollywood figure already on her way to having her own cult and her own legend. When Frank came into a room now he went first to Claire, then to Babe, and then, most important, back to Claire again—during a highly public dinner they were observed by Louella to be holding hands and twice he leaned to kiss the back of her neck. Babe, seated with a pair of studio flacks and a hairdresser, pretended not to notice, but it was plain that she was furious and could easily have taken an axe to Miss Regrett's scalp.

Claire took much pride in the fact that she had got her old lover back, and at Babe's expense. When Frank visited her set, Claire would wait for a break, then haul him off to her portable dressing room, where she'd tell her maid to get lost and lock the door; then she and Frank would go at it while people on the set joked at the way the trailer rocked as Frankie gave her the same business he used to give Babe. One day someone walked past and, through a window whose curtains Claire had neglected to close, glimpsed her feet shod in spike heels sticking straight up in the air while she moaned, "Oh, Daddy, give baby that big lollipop."

But the day came when Babe had the last laugh, for Frank's interest in Claire again dwindled down to the last of the wine. He refused all invitations to join her in her trailer, having started dallying with a little Latin tootsie he'd brought to Mayer, who'd given her a part in a low-budget picture; her sensational bust was already attracting attention. Her name was Julie Figueroa, a girl he'd found checking hats at the Florentine Gardens on Hollywood Boulevard. Now Babe and Claire had something in common; they were both yesterday's news and might have enjoyed commiserating, but they still would have nothing to do with each other, while *la señorita* Figueroa was lapping up the cream.

Frankie's reputation as a swain, lover, and general, all-round Hollywood cocksman increased in direct ratio to the large number of females he was servicing at this point. Some twenty years hence, he would engage in a rivalry with Sam Ueberroth over the affections of a pretty UCLA coed, and Frank would get one of his testicles shot off for his trouble, but until then he was letting no grass grow under his feet; at least not until he met Frances, who would be the one to get him to the altar.

Yet even though in this period he no longer shared Babe's bed, Frank still played an important part in her life. There were no recriminations; she kept the jewelry he'd bought her—a not inconsiderable treasure—as well as the famous Reo motorcar. And soon she began her search for a new man, a search that took her through a motley series of lowbrow types, consisting in the main of prizefighters, pool sharks, muscle-enhancers, and the like. There was even a bullfighter or two. Occasionally these athletic figures gave way to even lesser-lifes, to known frequenters of Mafia hang-outs, dese, dem, and dosers with scars and police records. Babe never had pretensions about herself (unlike Claire Regrett, who had many and hoarded them all), and, being the queen of Cicero, she'd had plenty of exposure to gangland types. Now it seemed as if, having had Frank Adonis, there was no other man for her, no one of any class. Give her a jug-eared welterweight any day, or a blackjack dealer with a diamond on his pinkie finger. She always claimed "Moonskin" Spaccifaccioli was, despite his bad complexion, a great lay, and maybe he was.

These were the wide-open, lusty days of moviedom, and when Babe wasn't at the studio, her greatest passion was playing the ponies. Each morning she perused her *Daily Racing Form*, even before she checked out her stocks and securities in *The Wall Street Journal*. She toured the racing circuit every season, from Hollywood Park to Santa Anita, and ended by making the sporting trip to Agua Caliente. (Caliente was outside scruffy, crummy Tijuana, and it was generally conceded that a prominent movie figure could go there and play fast and loose in private, or not so private, and not be pilloried for scandalous behavior.)

When the familiar Reo appeared, people would note that Babe was on hand to watch the track. Her driver and general factotum these days was the middleweight ex-prizefighter Sluggo McGurk, who'd been punched so hard so many times that his head sloshed, but when Sluggo was on tap no one messed with Babe, not if he was smart. Unless, of course, he happened to be one of Bugsy Siegel's lieutenants, that duke by the name of Al "Vegas" da Prima, of whom Babe was rumored to be currently enamored. She and Al were known to have shacked up at the Hotel Del Coronado near San Diego on several occasions, and when his yacht, the *Black Star*, was anchored in Catalina harbor, a pair of binoculars could discern at the rail a figure that certainly resembled Babe Austrian; though no one could actually prove it was she, it was reported that way in the press.

Penned Louella:

What in the world are things coming to around here, anyway? What famous film blonde has lately been seen aboard the yacht

of what friend of what well known gangland figure and real
estate investor? Naughty, double naughty, little miss, you ought
to have your bottom spanked!

Ironically, there wasn't much truth in these rumors, since at that time
Babe hadn't ever been aboard a gangster's yacht. The truth was, the
woman on the *Black Star* was another person altogether.

Back in her old New York days Babe had a close friend with whom
she'd appeared in a couple of shows. The friend's name was Patsy Doyle,
and the two girls were not dissimilar in looks. Men occasionally mistook
Patsy for Babe, or vice versa, and once Babe even dispatched Patsy on a
date in her place. When her movie career took off, Babe sent for Patsy to
be her stand-in. Patsy jumped at the chance, and soon there were two
Hollywood blondes riding side by side in the back of the Reo, one the star,
the other not.

Patsy Doyle was a good-time girl all the way. She was made for
Hollywood; maybe not stardom Hollywood, but girls like Patsy always
helped fill out the fringes of the place. She was without ambition, caring
nothing for the art of the cinema, though she was apparently well versed
in other, less esoteric arts.

Eventually she married a high-roller type they called Snake-Hips,
who wore a white fedora and took all her money for gambling. Given
Patsy's deliberate aping of Babe's peroxided hair and flamboyant dress, it
was understandable how the two women might be confused in the public
eye, and Babe didn't care enough about what people thought to clear the
matter up. To hell with Louella and all her tribe!

This is how I reencountered Babe Austrian: in the spring of 1952, she
returned to Broadway, an event that proved to be a triumph. The revival
of *Lola Magee* was her own idea, though her career was still being master-
minded by Frank. I was brand new in New York at the time, having
graduated from college and playing a small part in my first Broadway
show. My days of pinching movie sex symbols were long behind me,
though the intervening years had done little or nothing to dull the memory of those pretty feet, those baby-blues, that shapely shape, as exhibited
in the car of the Mayor of Hartford, Connecticut. (Actually, I'd encoun-
tered her one other time, on a moving train. But more of that anon.)

Over the years I'd followed her glittering career with interest, she
then being the only star of magnitude with whom I had ever scraped
acquaintance. I'd seen her *Lola* at a Sunday-night Actors' Fund Benefit,

a raucous evening if ever there was one, and a performance that served
only to rub up a keener appreciation on my part for her comedic talents.
With due respect to both Fanny Brice and Barbra Streisand, I thought she
was one funny lady.

Months later I was working with Tallulah Bankhead in a revival, and
when I came offstage one night early in the run there were some people
waiting in my dressing room. One of them was Max Hollywood (his real
name), an up-and-coming Broadway hotshot agent who said he had
"plans" for me. These plans involved the person of Miss Babe Austrian.
Lola having closed, she was going to tour a new play around the summer-
stock barns, and she was looking for someone to fill out her cast. Max
turned me over to the tall, lantern-jawed young woman, Beata Saggiter,
who had just begun as his assistant.

Though it was only May, that week the temperature soared freak-
ishly, day after day hovering in the high eighties. My appointment with
the star was postponed twice, but finally Beata confirmed the date as
locked in for Friday at 2:00 p.m. and said I should meet her at Sardi's. I
arrived in loafers, khaki slacks, and a navy polo shirt. "Jesus, Charlie,"
Beata greeted me, "what's this?"

"What is what?" I countered.

"You can't go see Babe Austrian looking like Joe College. Don't you
own a dark suit?"

Sure I had a suit. One. Blue serge. Hot.

"Go put it on. I'll wait," Beata decreed. I hopped the subway down
to the Village, pulled the suit out of the cold-storage bag, and was back
at Sardi's in forty-five minutes.

"Jesus, *Char*lie," Beata wailed, "what is that smell?"

Mothballs.

We cabbed up to Babe's hotel. First we waited downstairs in the
lobby, then in about an hour were allowed to head on up to the suite. It
was big Sluggo McGurk who greeted us, and we sat around on the
horsehair sofa for about ten hours, with only a drugstore fan and a pitcher
of lukewarm "ice" water for cooling purposes. I was sweating bullets
while we waited; I felt nervous, my mouth was dry, I drank the water,
I sweated more. Finally Sluggo reappeared and told me to get up and
follow him. "Not you," he said to Beata, and preceded me into an adjoining room.

In a large, tall-backed armchair sat Babe Austrian, looking me up and
down as I trod in, wiping my brow. "Pleased ta meetcha," she said as I
approached the throne. She seemed a little nervous, even shy, as I gave
my name.

"Charlie, huh? I used to know a Charlie." She rolled her eyes and ventured a tiny smile. "Charlie Peekoe. Smoked Cubano-Cubanas. Ran a numbers bag. Good guy, had a club foot, but he was a dancin' fool. Sit down, honey, take a load off. How you been?"

I said I'd been fine, exerting whatever charm I could muster, all of it damp.

"Max says you're gonna be a big star. Whaddya think? You want to be a star?"

I guessed I'd like to, "if I could find the right parts."

"You look like you already got good parts," she replied without missing a beat. Sluggo was standing by the window, staring out at the view. The room was hot and he was sweating the same way I was, but Babe sat there cool as a cucumber. The blue eyes again raked me tip to toe and she asked me how tall I was.

I told her.

"Umm. I like six-footers. And you probably have a couple extra inches to boot, hm?" She asked me to stand up and turn around; as I obliged her she made suggestive noises. "I suppose I could get you the right part if you could come up with the right parts for me. Whadda ya think?"

Jesus.

All the time she was sitting on that throne, *vibrating*—like an Oldsmobile warming up a bad battery. I thought the whole thing was some big put-on, but no, she was dead serious. She was still a sexy dame, I was a young stud to her, and it was play and pay all the way. This was no act, this was Babe.

"You seem nervous," she said. "Are you?"

I blamed the heat and mopped my face with my soggy handkerchief. The suit weighed ninety pounds if an ounce.

She was looking hard at me, I could tell. The long eyelashes went bat bat bat. "Haven't we met someplace?"

No, I lied, we hadn't met. "I'd remember," I said blithely. She studied me some more and I could tell I was bothering her. I was sure I wouldn't get the job.

"Say, Slug, how's about catchin' yourself a beer," she told the gorilla by the window. Sluggo took the hint and sauntered into the other room. I wondered what Beata would do to him, or vice versa. Babe sat studying me some more.

"Care for a cigarette?" I asked, taking out my pack.

"I don't smoke. It hurts muh voice. I'd prefer if you didn't, either."

I pocketed the cigarettes. I was sure I'd shot myself down.

"We got this show," she said. "You ever heard of it? Sort of a little comedy. Some jokes. This guy wants to bring it in next fall. Nice little part for a young man. 'Bout your height. I like tall men, makes me look small, vulnerable, you know?"

"Windy City?" I said, trying to sound savoir-fairish.

"Huh?" she said.

" 'The Windy City Blues'? 'I love that Windy City where the men are tall and brown in that oh-so-toddlin' town'?"

"Oh. Oh yeah. Heh heh." That was her song, but my knowing a line didn't win me any Brownie points so far as I could see. Finally I blurted out that actually she was right, we had met before. Oh? And where was that? On a train, I said. Which train? Super Chief. "Oh? Wonderful train. I take it all the time. I don't like to fly," she said. "This fortuneteller said I'd be killed in a plane crash. I always listen to my fortunetellers—you do that, too, you'll live longer. How'd you say we met?" She drilled me with a look.

Oh, I said weakly, it was just sort of in passing.

She touched her hair. "Oh, *en passant,* so to speak."

"I told you then I wanted to be an actor."

"No kidding. Small world, isn't it?" She was staring harder and I felt myself getting hotter. Goddamn air conditioning. Did she remember or didn't she? I still couldn't tell. "Yeah," she said, looking me over again, "you're tall all right. Dark, too."

She sort of rocked around in the chair before posing her next question. "Just how experienced are you?"

I said I was in a show, that I'd done stock.

"Stock, huh? Who'd you work with?"

I mentioned two or three fading names—Ruth Chatterton, Kay Francis, Flossie Reed.

"She must be ninety, Flossie. This dame who's your agent. You and she an item?"

I explained that Beata's and my relationship was strictly professional.

"Good. Keep it that way. She says you're with Tallulah. But Tallulah's closing. Could you get out of Tallulah and come with me?"

Not *too* eager, but: "Sure. I think so. Yes. Very much. I'd like to work with you."

She vibrated a little more. "Umm. The feelin's myutchul, I assure ya." She touched the platinum scallops in several places.

When she asked if I'd ever met a movie star before, I said I hadn't, except Ozzie Nelson, whom I'd met with my Boy Scout patrol when we were taken to the theatre stage door—"in Hartford?" I ventured carefully. "The State Theatre?"

"Oh yeah. I played the State. You're too young to've seen me."

"I saw you."

"No kiddin'." She seemed to come alive slightly. "You really saw me? Betcha don't remember what I was wearin'."

I described her outfit as accurately as I could remember. She inspected her nails and rearranged several bracelets on her arm. "Hartfid, huh? Good town, Hartfid. They had a parade fuh me."

I agreed Hartford was okay.

"Good place to be from, huh?" She laughed at her little joke.

"Did you enjoy the parade?" I dared ask.

"Yeah, why not? I rode with the Mayor. He was a screw. Kept puttin' his hand on muh knee."

"I know." She shot me a look. "I was there."

"You were where?"

"On the running board."

"What were you doin' on the runnin' board?"

"I wanted to see you. Close up."

"Didja? How'd I look?"

"Great. You looked swell." There was a beat while she looked at me and I looked at her. I wanted to look away, but could not do it. "I pinched you," I confessed.

"Get off my porch! How old?"

"Twelve."

"Jeeze, you kids start early."

"Don't you remember?"

"Lotsa bozos pinch me. It's muh type. How'm I s'posed to remember some kid with merit badges? Get serious. Time's up, so long. Tell her we'll call you."

"But don't call us," I said, the old show-biz kiss-off.

She summoned Sluggo, who quickly showed himself. "This number's leavin'. Show him the door." I waited for her to put out her hand, which she did not do.

"Well? What happened?" Beata was steaming because she'd been excluded; an agent should be allowed to stay with the client.

I shrugged. I didn't want to tell her I'd blown it with the Hartford Pinch. "She'll call us," was all I said.

Beata owned some street verbiage and used it. "What'd she do? Unzip you in there? Give you some head?"

"Jesus, Beata, can it."

I found out later that Sluggo had overheard her crude remark and it went straight back to Babe. Babe didn't like it, not at all. And they never called about the show. I read in *Variety* that another guy—tall, dark—had the part. I thought, Screw it. It was two more months of Tallulah showing her crotch.

But as things turned out, I did get a summer in the country—of sorts. The guy Babe hired came down with mononucleosis and took to his bed, and I got this hurry-up call from Max saying I was to go right over to the producers' office and sign a contract, then I was to go down to a Second Avenue rehearsal hall.

"Should I put on my blue suit?" I cracked; Beata used her vocabulary again.

As I mentioned, the interview in her hotel suite wasn't the second time I'd met Babe Austrian but the third. By now I'd begun to count. If she hadn't remembered the first time, I wondered if she'd remember the second, the time on the Super Chief, heading west at the end of the war. I was a navy signalman and had been granted liberty. While I was visiting home the A-bomb was dropped on Hiroshima and Nagasaki and it seemed the war in the Pacific would quickly end. But before this could happen I found myself stuck in a coach seat all the way from Chicago to the Coast. It promised to be a tedious and uncomfortable trip until I chose to visit the club car.

So there I am all duded up in my best pressed whites downing my rye-and-ginger-ale. I'm feeling hot and sharp and all man, and who do I see sitting across the aisle from me reading *Look*, with these itty-bitty shoes and a silver fox chubby over the shoulders, but this movie blonde. I counted back the years; only seven had passed, but though I was now grown up, she hadn't changed at all. As I sat debating whether it was appropriate to refresh her memory, she kept flipping the *Look* pages and absently tugging the hem of her skirt over her kneecaps. Every time she bent forward she showed her cleavage and I knew she knew I was looking at her and I think she knew I knew she knew I was looking at her.

She got up, dropped the magazine in her chair, and ankled on out of there without a look left or right, up or down. That evening, after dinner, I went back to the club car. It was around ten-thirty and there were few drinkers on tap. But there she was, this time reading *Photoplay*. The car was swaying and I sort of let it throw me into a seat, not right next to her but one chair away.

"Yeah," she says to me, "take a load off." Then she asked me my name and I told her. Then I said, "I guess I don't have to ask yours."

Heh heh. Oh, really? Who did I think she was? Her name, she said, was Gladys Lillie, "but just call me 'Glad.' " She came from Battle "Crick" and was the Popped Rice heiress—"you know, exploded out of cannons?" Where was I going? What was my ship? What did I do? Like that. She could have been Axis Sally, but she wasn't. Neither was she "Gladys Lillie." But I called her "Glad" anyway. I told her my life story, she told me hers, part, anyway, but longer than mine. She kept crossing and uncrossing her legs. She had real nylons on, or maybe it was her underwear that made slicky sounds, and she was wearing the same perfume as seven years before. Tigress, she said, and made a noise like one. Grrrrr . . . Every time she moved her legs she moved her purse, this giant-sized pocketbook, and every time it moved it clinked. I was wondering what was in it that made it look so weighty and made such a noise. By now we were somewhere west of North Platte and she and I were about the only passengers in the car. Finally the porter came with his little round tray and said it was last call. We had a nightcap. Pretty soon they began shutting off the lights and giving us looks. The next time she moved her purse she unclasped the flap and I took a gander inside. It was filled with bottles, those miniatures they sell on planes and trains—Smirnoff and Vat 69 and Johnnie Walker Red Label. She said it was always well when traveling to be prepared.

"Like a Boy Scout?" I ventured.

"Don't mind if I do," she replied pokerfaced.

Ha ha. She was a card. Then she suggested that since they were turning out the lights on us, I might care to come back to her stateroom and have another nightcap. Maybe I'd like to change from rye to brandy, it made a nice nightcap. Would I? I did.

The next day found me at breakfast with a minister from Indianapolis. Talk about the Reverend Davidson in *Rain*. I got a heavy morals lecture with lots of hellfire and brimstone thrown in; penises were designed by the Almighty for purposes of procreating and urinating only, *nothing* else! I asked him if he was acquainted with "Old Lady Five-Fingers," but this geezer was a real coconut.

Shortly after I returned to my seat the conductor arrived with a note. "From Miss Lillie," he said almost in a whisper.

I read,

Dear Charlie, it was nice meeting you as we did. Didn't we laugh a lot? You're very smart, very. You'll go places some day. I won't be able to see you again this trip since I'm having a migraine, they usually last a couple of days. I wish you well and don't forget, the club car's air-conditioned. Yours truly, Gladys Lillie.

And I didn't even get an autograph; she hadn't signed her real name. But I wasn't despondent for long, because when we went through the next tank town, there were people lined up on the station platform and along the tracks with placards reading "War Ended!!!" "Japs Surrender!!!" "It's All Over!!!"

Boy, I thought, *was* it all over.

And now, seven years later, I was about to go into rehearsal with her. No one could blame me for my trepidation, because even though the play was a so-called pre-Broadway tryout, everyone concerned knew going in that the thing was a stinker.

Babe was a tartar to work with. Being the acknowledged star, she loftily appropriated anything good out of anybody else's lines, if she thought she could get a laugh with it. At one point I devised what I believed to be a catchy piece of business with a bunch of flowers, and when the director chuckled at it, she whirled on him and said, "Don't you think it might be funnier if *I* smelled the bouquet?" Our director, a notorious alkie, didn't care if she or Garbo smelled the roses, so Babe kept my bit. By the end of the day a distinct *froideur* had arisen between us.

We rehearsed to little avail, but there was no help for it, open we must, and did. This was up in Connecticut, and everyone from the city came up to see this "pre-Broadway tryout." It was Turkey City all the way; they were gobbling "disaster" everywhere. Babe got out her trusty pencil and began cutting, rearranging, and rewriting. Her jokes were corny, but she got more laughs than before. In the second act she came on in this monster fur coat—it was monkey fur, looked more like a gorilla suit, she'd bought it out of a Paris fashion show—and when she appeared in it, she brought down the house. Strictly a sight gag. She entered stage right, stopped, got her laugh, then crossed to left and lit a cigarette, then shed the coat, handed it to me, and said to put King Kong in the hall closet "and don't forget to feed him." That kind of stuff. They lapped it up.

The young actress who played the other half of the love interest was cute and pert and we began sleeping together right off. Her name was Jenny Burton and she simply moved into my room at the inn where we were staying. But when Babe got word of this arrangement she didn't like it and made no bones about it. I stood my ground. She could steal my flower-smelling onstage, but offstage my life was my own. "Besides," I told her prophetically, "we plan to get married."

"What're you talkin'? You just met her."

"Haven't you ever heard of love at first sight?"

Her fuse began to sputter. "Never mind the hell about love at first sight or anything else, just you don't let anything get in the papers you're shacked up with this piece-goods."

Thereafter our relationship grew more and more icily polite. By now

I wasn't so sure but that she remembered the Super Chief and didn't want to let on, which was okay with me, since I didn't want Jenny to get wind of my brief relationship with the star.

It was during that initial week's run that I met Frank Adonis for the first time. He'd come up to Westport to catch Babe's show and he stuck his head in my dressing room while I was making up. He gave me this maybe/maybe-not look of appraisal, then told me I was going places. "Maybe I'll catch you in Hollywood, kiddo." I didn't want him to catch me in Hollywood, I wanted him to catch me now—and sign me and make me a goddamn star! But he shot me with his finger and was gone, whistling a tune. I caught him passing my window and hollered that he'd been whistling in my dressing room and we were in for nothing but bad luck.

I wasn't wrong, either. Our concerted efforts would never see the bright lights of Broadway. Yet as we continued our tour, every management insisted we fulfill our obligations, and because of Babe's name we played to packed houses at every performance. Even the blue-haired matinee ladies tittered at the risqué lines she had interpolated into the script, and some of her ad libs brought down the house. We never, any of us, lost track of the fact that we were on a stage with the famous Babe Austrian.

When we traveled, the rest of the cast, myself included, went by bus or train, while Babe rode alone in her car, always with the trusty Sluggo at the wheel and with her little Chihuahua, Tiny, in her lap. Everywhere we played, it was a scandal among the theatre apprentices that the star was doing it with her chauffeur, which managed to add a certain *frisson* to what was otherwise a boring, in fact embarrassing, tour. Only once or twice did she allow her reserve to break down. It was just hello, good morning, good night, have a nice day off, and that was about it. Everyone called her "Miss Austrian," including myself, who'd known her more intimately. She never mingled, either with the cast or the backstage crews, never gave a party, never bought anyone a token good-luck present. Never let her hair down—except once.

Passing her dressing-room door one night, I glanced in and saw her at her makeup table, staring into the mirror at herself. Her robe was partly open and those major boobs were hanging out. Without looking at me she extended a hand to halt me; then, covering herself, she asked me to come in. "Sit down," she said, "take a load off. You know, you're pretty funny out there. I ought to squash you like a bug, but I let you have your head. You know why? There's only one star in a show, but the star's got to have support. The better the support, the better the star; the better you are, the better I am, get it?"

I said I got it, and soon we were getting along better. She wasn't so bad, when you got to know her. Problems—she had problems, like all those ladies, wanting love and acting neurotic as hell. She needed someone around to talk to, to make her laugh, tell her she was terrific. I did all three. It wasn't so hard; she *was* terrific, after her fashion. She started writing this play about an older star and a young man—said we'd take it to Broadway, her and me. I suggested she write in a part for Jenny. That was the end of that.

One night, in the middle of a scene, a very Lubitschy one—Babe and I were supposed to be dancing and drinking champagne—she dropped her glass and swooned outright in my arms. I stood there staring blankly at the audience with this dead weight hanging on me, while the stupefied stage manager merely goggled. I hauled Babe to the couch, where she lay softly moaning and clutching her abdomen, then I hustled offstage and rang down the curtain.

She was suffering an appendicitis attack and was in need of immediate attention. She couldn't walk, but lay there sweating on the sofa until a hastily summoned ambulance carted her off to the local hospital. The rest of the cast went back onstage; the wardrobe girl read Babe's role, tendering one of the more interesting performances of a femme fatale known to the American theatre.

We were scheduled to end the tour over in the Poconos, but due to Babe's unexpected surgery, we found ourselves back in New York before the end of August. I started pounding the pavements, occasionally with Jenny Burton at my side. This was in the days of "making rounds," going to each casting office and putting in your bid for a part, making sure they had your résumé and pictures. By the time September was out, Babe Austrian and summer stock were things of the dim past; Jenny had moved in with me on West Thirteenth Street; we were going to be the new Lunt and Fontanne. Before long things began to break for me. Max Hollywood landed me a part, I was seen by an important casting person, was sent to be interviewed by an even more important Hollywood figure, and pretty soon I was on my way west. Jenny went, too, not just for the ride: we were Mr. and Mrs. Lunt by then.

If my troubles seemed to be ending, Babe's seemed to be just beginning—medically, anyway. We read that she was going into Harkness Pavilion for tests. The papers hinted that she was having the whole thing tucked, but I got it straight from our director that she was having female problems and that her ovaries were being offed. It was hysterectomy time for Babe Austrian.

When I was still a toddler, I learned to tell my right hand from my left by my mother's dressing-table drawers. "Get me my red dotted scarf out of my lefthand drawer," she'd say, or "Bring me my pocketbook from my righthand drawer." In similar fashion I identify past years from the women in Frank's life: he had a date with Cora Sue Brodsky on the night the stock market crashed, he was seeing Babe Austrian in 1930, he brought her out to California in the winter of 1932 and was her more or less constant companion until around 1938 (excluding several amorous interludes with Claire Regrett), when Babe took to the road with her drums (and I pinched her in the parade). Then, just before Pearl Harbor, he met Frances Deering of the Seattle lumber Deerings, and married her in 1942 after a whirlwind courtship. But life with Frances was no bed of roses. For another husband she probably would have made a perfectly good wife— for a magnate, a captain of industry—but not for Frankie Adonis. Frances was smooth as Parian marble, and just as chill, awf'lly Upper Bryn Mawr, and she ran a taut ship. Her mock-Tudor house on Rockingham in Brentwood was neat in the way a museum is neat, everything kept under glass, including her spouse.

Not surprisingly, it wasn't long before Frank started straying, taking up first with Belinda Carroll, who held the inside track until the early fifties, when he began a sketchy affair with Belinda's best friend, Angie Brown, whom he most likely would have married if he'd ever been able to get free of Frances. Except that in the early sixties along came Miss UCLA, April Rains—four years, no more, for that one, though it almost sent him around the bend—and then nothing serious until the last years, when he and Belinda finally got back together. And Belinda, having been really crazy about Frankie since she was a kid, now couldn't make up her mind; then when she did, he got himself shot. But that's another story.

Babe, Claire, Frances, Belinda, Angie, April, I count six; that's almost one and a half per decade of Frank's entire adult life. It sort of makes me wonder how he fitted them all in.

When Jenny and I arrived in Hollywood we booked in at the Villa Lorraine, a hotel on the Sunset Strip where many New York actors stayed while doing a picture. We came in the spring and it was really Southern California weather, clear skies, warm sun, people in shorts and sandals. You expected to see Alice Faye and Tony Martin out for a stroll, or maybe Robert Taylor and Barbara Stanwyck horseback riding along the old Beverly Hills bridle path. We went to a sneak preview in Studio City— it was Jimmy Dean in *Rebel Without a Cause*—and we were standing in the lobby after the screening when a woman came flying out crying, "A star is born! A star is born!" She was Ann Warner, wife of Jack, and she was right. We guessed that's how it always happened in Hollywood. We stopped to chat with a group, one of whom was Jimmy Dean's agent, Dick Clayton (Jimmy wasn't there), and when the group broke up I got a friendly wave from a familiar figure: it was Frankie Adonis.

When I'd met him in Westport when I was with Babe's show, he'd predicted I was going places. So? Here I was, ready to see my name in lights, but if he meant to do anything to ensure that, I hadn't heard a word about it. Still, to be a client of the Adonis Agency was a cherished hope, and I was theirs for the asking. Anyway, after a brief exchange (Babe was right, Frances was like the Polar Cap), as a parting shot Frank said, "You'll be hearing from me, kiddo." Jenny was thrilled, but I told her that was all Hollywood talk, it didn't mean a thing.

I'd hate to hang for as long as it took me to hear from Frank. It happened, though. I pulled up at the stoplight at Doheny and Santa Monica one day (the same intersection where one day many years later I would see Elizabeth Taylor in her Rolls-Royce heading west, and Richard Burton in his Rolls-Royce heading north, both talking on the telephone in their respective cars—one assumed, to each other—as they waited for the light to change), and I heard my name bawled out (we didn't have car phones in those days). It was, of course, Frank, and in his passenger seat sat none other than Sir Laurence Olivier, to whom, in Frank's cool fashion, he introduced me.

"Listen, kiddo," he shouted across Sir Laurence, "why don't you follow us to my office and I'll sign you up, whaddya say?"

Nonplussed, I blinked and nodded. Within the hour I was a client of the Adonis Actors Agency, and Frank was my agent for the next sixteen years.

At the time Jenny and I were still parked at the Villa Lorraine, and it was Frank who dug us up our first Hollywood apartment. Someone owed him a "favor," and since a tenant was moving out, and Frank's girl at the time, Angie Brown, was still living on the premises, we found ourselves on North Cadman Terrace, lessees of a one-bedroom domicile with one garage. My car got dirty, a lot.

Our building, though spacious, had only six units, very chic, done in California Regency—putty beige, black and white, understated elegance with lots of dentil moldings, bull's-eye windows, and a couple of good French lead statues. The front, or more spacious, quarters were known by the tenants as the Grand Trianon, while the back studio apartments over the garages were known as the Petit Trianon, separated by an unpaved alley where the trash cans were kept. These alleys were the kind that crisscross behind all the apartment dwellings in that section of Beverly Hills—except that where we were, on North Cadman, wasn't B.H.; we were B.B.H., Barely Beverly Hills. You could *say* you were Beverly Hills but technically you weren't.

Floyd Judson and Marie, his wife, a team of psychologists, lived downstairs in the front; upstairs was a hard-of-hearing duffer whose bathroom was directly behind our bedroom, and when we were in bed we could hear him splashing around in his tub—"the bather," we called him. Elsewhere in the small complex was an assortment of types, including a Mocambo "hat-chick" girl named Fern, and a talented young actress under contract to Warners, and her untalented newlywed husband. In the back, over the alley, were two studio apartments, each occupied by a colorful tenant. The north apartment was inhabited by a terrific-looking tootsie; sure, Angie probably looked to most people like one more Hollywood bottled blonde, but you can believe me, she was special. Movie fans may recall her as Angelina Brown, one more pretty Columbia starlet who didn't make it. But, then, in Hollywood there are ways and ways. She'd had a whirl at the movies ten years earlier, had given it all up to marry Eddie LaStarza, the Most Famous Baseball Player in the World, had a deep sexy voice and figure to match, wore Don Loper clothes, and did some modeling on the side, while her son by the MFBPITW went to a military academy. Like Frankie, she came of Italian stock and she maintained a gorgeous figure—she had the greatest pair of legs since Betty Grable, was in fact a good friend of Betty's; they occasionally played poker together. She always had a tan; her hair was the color of cornsilk, but out of a bottle: the roots were often darkly telltale. And she had cheekbones to rival Colbert's.

By this time Frank had been married to Iceberg Frances for a dozen years; things hadn't worked out well, but she wasn't about to divorce him —nor did he seem particularly to want a divorce. That dilemma would come later, with April. But just then, in the mid-fifties, he was happy seeing Angie; he kept her tucked away, and if people knew about the relationship, they weren't saying much. There seemed to be some kind of gentlemen's agreement where Angie was concerned, not to involve her publicly or link her in print with Frank's name.

It's logical and fitting that Angie should have been on that extensive list of Hollywood beauties being "squired" about town by Frankie Adonis, but she wasn't called "The Mother of Us All" for nothing. Angie was great of heart, profoundly wise in a way some women do well to be wise, sympathetic and understanding. She took a very wry view of life, not jaundiced, just ironic. She had pushed her talent as far as it would go and she knew it; smart lady, after co-starring opposite Ross Hunter in a Columbia B flick, she "retired."

These days Angie was moonlighting. She'd got a job singing in a West Hollywood nightspot called the Trey Deuces. She didn't know it then, but it was Frankie who'd stopped by and held parley with the proprietor, who, after some "persuasion" and having his palm well crossed with silver, auditioned Angie and hired her. She sang two shows a night and kept her Loper job, too. But she didn't move out of the Petit Trianon —said she couldn't bear to be away from Dore.

This guy Dore lived in the other studio apartment, and if Belinda Carroll was Angie's best girlfriend, her best "boy"friend was her next-door neighbor. Dore Skirball was the house character, and his relationship with Angie was a warm and abiding one; indeed, they were friends to the bitter end. Dore loved Angie like—well, a sister, I suppose. He'd had a sister once; she'd died in a car crash, and he looked on his gorgeous neighbor as a kind of substitute. Dore loved to chatter, so did Angie, but Angie was a good listener, too; I think this is one reason they got on so well. His campy, bawdy jokes and outrageous behavior kept her in tears, and they seemed to send and receive on the same wavelength. Many's the night when we were trying to get to sleep after an evening, and me with an early call, Jenny and I would hear those two laughs ringing out from across the alley into the wee hours.

Something more should probably be said about this character, Dore Skirball, a.k.a. Dore Oddball and Dore Screwball, both of which epithets were, to say the least, fitting. Dore was "family." You couldn't help liking him, though not everything about him was likable. Despite his outrageous behavior, his desire to shock, his need to attract attention, his giddy frivolity and love of luxury, underneath all the glitz he was solid and sober, sharp as a tack, sometimes even wise as an owl.

In his time he'd been a jack-of-all-trades, a crack fighter pilot with three Jap planes to his credit and medals which he almost never acknowledged, a piano player (once the accompanist of a famous singer), and he had a sketchy dance background, having once studied with Martha Graham. He'd finally settled on an antique business because he'd known period furniture all his life, had picked it up in museums and galleries during his travels, and he knew a cabriole from a gateleg, a *pompadour* from a *duchesse brisée*.

Dore hadn't spoken to either of his parents for years (they didn't approve of his lifestyle), and he had no living brothers or sisters, but he was beloved of an aunt who lived in the town of Torreon, just across the state line near Yuma. Aunt Bobbie kept a chicken ranch there and ran a roadside stand specializing in "Aunt Bob's Ribs and Chicken," and according to Dore, she was the only relative he really gave a damn about.

He wrote her faithfully and remembered her birthday and Christmas with lavish if inappropriate gifts—one year an expensive negligee with maribou trim, another year a Georgian silver wine cooler that set him back hundreds. The woman neither drank nor entertained, but she used it to cool her Dr. Pepper. Dore was "different"—a lot different, especially back in the uptight fifties. Gay as pink ink, and you either liked him or you didn't, take your pick.

He was often misunderstood, people were frequently offended by his flamboyance, but he didn't care. "Take me as I am, ducks, because that's the only way you'll get me," he seemed to say. He wasn't arrogant, he wasn't above it all, he simply made no bones about life, and if he caused pain and trouble for himself, he was prepared to face the consequences.

Having lost his shirt in his antique business due to an unethical partner, he was currently working for an upholsterer employed by all the top decorators in town. He was also a chef of note. He loved to bake, called himself "Betty Crocked," and he *was* that a lot of the time, for when he baked there was always a shot of vodka in a tumbler at his elbow. He was generous with his time, his abilities, and his talent, and he possessed that rare gift that Noel Coward employed to denigrate his own considerable powers, "a talent to amuse." Dore's was no small talent. He was outrageous, he was charming, he was witty, and, first, last, and always, he was funny. He had framed the famous *Life* shot of Gloria Swanson in evening gown with cigarette holder posing amid the ruins of the Roxy theatre. Below it he had written the caption: "They should have left the theatre and torn Gloria down." Even when in the dumps and wanting to cut his throat, he could find something to joke about (often himself), even if it was gallows humor. It was what got him through, he said. Once he stuck his head in the oven, gas on, thinking to kiss the world goodbye, but when Angie found him and called the fire department, who brought him back from the brink of the abyss, as he came to and saw a uniformed fireman in the doorway, all he could say was "Get the name and phone number, ducks, and find me something pretty to put on."

In addition, his taste was impeccable, if a trifle *exquise*. His apartment —a one-room studio with bath and pullman kitchen—sparkled with mirrored screens, white-painted fake brick, whitewashed ceiling beams, bleached and pickled shutters, deep slipper chairs done in a natural linen stripe, the floor covered in coco matting. In 1956 Dore Skirball was far ahead of his time in matters of décor. A small mirrored bar was crammed with glittering crystal and silver, and a surrounding mural executed by a friend, ersatz Venetian scenes with white monkeys cavorting across painted panels, hung on the linen white walls.

He also had a pair of goldfish in a bowl on the piano, whose names were pronounced "Sy-*philis*" and "Gon-*oria*" and who had been given to him by no less a personage than Claire Regrett, for whom he'd done a quantity of decorating on the side and whom he referred to as "Miss Clutch" when she wasn't present. It was of Claire that Dore had conceived the remark "To really know her you have to read between the lines in her face." He used to be in and out of her house all the time. He loved telling wicked stories about her and her studs, the real dish, and you knew he couldn't be making it up, not a word. Like the time she met a marine gunnery sergeant at a USO party, took him home, sneaked him into the house, and kept him locked in her bedroom until the Shore Patrol came and hauled him away and gave him a general court-martial and six months at hard labor. (Brown Derby wags said they'd rather take the six months in the stockade than a week locked in Claire's bedroom.) Or the time she laid out a grand buffet whose centerpiece was two huge blue tins of Persian caviar, and when one famous guest allowed as how she might have some, the serving attendant said, "Oh no, Miss Hellman, those cans are both empty. She just puts them out for show." Or how her sense of etiquette dictated the use of place cards in little silver holders when there were only four guests for dinner; the way she called a napkin a "serviette," curtains "drapes," and a house a "home"—"*Thank* you *so* much for visiting us at our lovely 'home,' bless you, darling"—attempted her shaky French on Italian waiters, "studied" *Romeo and Juliet* every morning until she could more or less recite the balcony scene, then cadged the great Olivier into playing opposite her in her living room; how she picked out a dress at Don Loper's, then bought everything to match, creating symphonies of chartreuse, cerise; how she sent illuminated copies of the "Desiderata" to everyone at Christmas, then collected them again and sent them the next year as well —"These words have so much meaning to me, I hope you may find something among them as well, bless you darling and a Merry-Merry Happy-Happy." How she spent half her life at a desk replying to mail in her own hand, on her famous amethyst stationery, scribbling scribbling away, with no sign of writer's claw; how she ran a mail depot out of her garage and entertained her fan club at a yearly gala when she gave a conducted tour of the premises wearing suit, high heels, hat, bag, and gloves. One day when she encountered Dore before going to a lunch, dolled up to the nines with furs, gloves, jewels, hankie, and asked him "How do I look?," Dore replied, "Go back upstairs and take off any three things."

They were always having little spats, "lovers' quarrels," Dore called them; Claire would get mad and begin throwing whatever came to hand, and sometimes Dore would come back with cuts or bruises. But on the occasions when they *were* speaking he'd go out to her house and try on her latest headgear, her Walter Florells, her Lily Daché's, her John Frederickses. She must have had a hat collection in the hundreds, and it was from Claire that Dore got a lot of his drag: beaded dresses, fur pieces, gloves, wigs, and those anklestrap shoes she loved and made famous. Claire indulged him because he was a great convenience to her; he'd do anything she asked and she kept him busy waiting hand and foot on her. He was enslaved to her stardom but he didn't care. Who else was as close to such a luminary, and if he had hitched his wagon to a star, that was his business, wasn't it? He could get mad at her, too: "Look up 'bitch' in the dictionary," he said to Jenny one day, "you'll find her picture." And "She's the only witch who rides around on a whisk broom."

Once, when I was working opposite her on a TV show, I asked Dore for a message to give her and he said, "Tell the bitch that Wendy says grow up!" It was all too much, of course, but, then, everything about Dore was too much. Then came the great falling out and they were no longer speaking. He never said what had happened, but he was sorely hurt and disappointed and he never mentioned her much anymore, and after that he moved away and it was a long time before anybody found out exactly what had happened to cause the rift. All we knew was that just when Dore had his act going hot, she sent her car and driver around to collect all the dresses, shoes, and other drag he'd acquired from her over the years. Dore just dumped them into the alley and let the driver scurry around in the dust retrieving them.

Dore was not only a man of parts but a talented performer as well, and occasionally he appeared at the Trey Deuces, the *boîte* along Santa Monica Boulevard where Angie sang. There he rendered his impressions, not only of stars he was acquainted with such as Claire, but of other famous screen legends as well, Davis, Hepburn, Marilyn, Luise Rainer. Generally recognized as far more than just another female impersonator, he went in for a full characterization, looked for the mannerisms to punch up, and he was brilliant at voices. There was something almost uncanny about his vocal mimicry of Marilyn, a little trick he did with his voice that made his impersonation both telling and ridiculous, both a parody and a personal comment on Marilyn's childlike vulnerability. And though he'd never met her, he had Babe Austrian whittled down to a fine point in terms of voice, gesture, and mannerisms. Babe was his real heroine; he loved hearing Jenny and me tell stories about our summer's tour with her, and he incorporated many of her lines into his everyday conversation as well as his act. "Get off my porch" and "Take a load off" became almost as much his as hers.

His dream, of course, was one day to meet Babe face to face, to have her come and watch his act. He even pleaded with Angie to persuade Frankie Adonis to bring her to the club, but it was no soap—at first. Babe didn't favor men who took her off. Then, since no one seemed able to oblige Dore with a meeting, it occurred to me that I might be instrumental in arranging one. One day, after a business lunch with Frank and an Italian producer who might "have something" for me, as we were saying goodbye in the parking lot Frank handed over to me a manila envelope with a script he'd forgotten to deliver. The envelope had Babe Austrian's name on it and he asked if I'd drop it by the Sunset Towers—"just leave it with the doorman."

I hightailed it home and shouted across the alley to Dore; in two minutes we two were heading across town to keep a fated rendezvous, carting along a couple of corrugated cartons from the trash cans, which Dore was busy emblazoning with stickers reading

FOR MISS BABE AUSTRIAN—FRAGILE—DELIVER BY HAND ONLY

Often as I'd passed that famous Hollywood landmark, the Sunset Towers, I'd never put a foot inside, and was fascinated at the prospect of seeing it. When we pulled up in front we jumped out as if we were on a life-or-death mission, leaving the car for the doorman to deal with, only to be halted at the reception desk. I introduced myself as Mr. Adonis's "personal assistant," while Dore was *my* "personal assistant," carrying a shipment of expensive Austrian glassware for—who else?—Miss Austrian. I said we were expected.

When the guy sat down at the switchboard, we sprinted for the elevator, and the door closed on his angry orders to come back.

Upstairs, the door was opened by a black woman in full alpaca uniform, cap, and apron, looking like one of Babe's colored maids from her early movies. This, I knew, was the famous Sugar May, a kind of benign Louise Beavers who talked darky talk and held the door wide while we trooped in with our deliveries.

Dore stood in the middle of the room gawking at the decor, and I inquired as to the whereabouts of Sugar May's mistress.

"Miss Babe, she at the track," Sugar May informed me. I asked if I might be permitted to use the telephone. The instrument was pointed out to me, a small room off the hallway, mirrored all to hell, with its own baby chandelier, some framed prints along French lines—lots of lace, garters, fluffy beds, pink tits, and cunning crotches. Pretending to place a call, I afterward made believe I had "Mr. Adonis" on the line.

"I'm sorry, sir, Miss Austrian is at Hollywood Park but is expected. Shall we wait, sir? Very good, sir, we'll do that. Miss Austrian's maid-of-all-work is with us."

Sugar May chortled at this, saying, "I is mo' like the maid of *no* work round here. Yawl wants coffee while you's waitin'?"

Before long Dore and I were sitting in the kitchen, klatsching away with the hired help. Dore was in hog heaven and we were laughing so hard that no one heard the foyer door open.

"Sugar May? What the hell are these damn boxes doin' on my rug?"

Sugar May grimaced at us. "Missus be home early. Yawl best come along."

She lumbered out of the kitchen, we following at her heels to face an indignant Missus.

"These mens done bought you's stuff," said Sugar May cheerfully.

"Stuff? What stuff? And what the hell are they doin' sittin' in the kitchen?" Babe demanded.

"They was havin' theys coffee while they wuz waitin'," was Sugar's truthful reply.

Before Babe could say anything, I stepped forward. "Hello there," I began, "remember me?"

She eyed me closely. "What the hell are you doin' up here? I thought you were in pictures. You a delivery boy?"

I explained that I had brought a script from Frankie. "Dore, come say hello to Miss Austrian." Dore moved slowly and dreamily toward her, mumbling that he was happy to make her acquaintance. Babe shot me a look as if to ask what kind of contraption this was. "Dore's an impressionist," I volunteered. "He was anxious to meet you."

"Dying," Dore croaked.

"Pleased ta meetcha, dear," she said politely. "Now, get off my porch, will ya, I gotta lie down, my skull's killin' me. I lost a bundle."

As she started across the room I hurried after her.

"Dore has a terrific act. He does you. Frank's seen him. They'd be pleased if you'd come see the show."

"Freebies," Dore added.

She glared at him, then at me. "Look, sonny, Frank and I don't agree on a lot of things. And I don't go out in public, Frank knows that. Leave the script on the desk there. And thanks."

She disappeared into the recesses of her bedroom, where I glimpsed a large bed on a dais, upholstered in white satin, with a plumed baldaquin and lots of swagged gauze. When I returned to the living room Dore was still gazing around at the conglomeration of furniture and bibelots. Babe's taste in furniture and decor was not for everyone; in fact it was for damn few, we had to agree. I settled for placing the envelope in a prominent position in the center of the French *bureau plat.*

"What is this stuff?" I asked Dore, never sure of my periods. "Louis the Fifteenth or Louis the Sixteenth?"

"Louis the Hotel, dear," came Dore's reply. He showed his teeth to Sugar May as we exited. "You may keep the cartons, ducks," he told her.

No one got a bigger kick out of Dore's antics and imitations than Frank Adonis. Recently things were beginning to get to him; not just Hollywood, not just his unhappy marriage, not just the effort he put forth daily, masterminding the intricacies of over a dozen high-priced careers, dealing with the delicate temperaments of the likes of Claire Regrett and Belinda Carroll, as well as Babe herself. He was having other troubles. These, however, he kept well hidden behind the suave, man-about-town façade he'd been showing the world for years—hidden even from me, with whom he'd shared a lot in a relatively short time.

Anyway, Frank kept coming around, taking Angie out to one nightspot or another. And frequently, when the door opened, he'd find not only Angie but Dore as well, all got up for his amusement as Babe, wearing something black and sheer, or Marilyn, in her white pleated *Seven-Year Itch* dress, or whoever he'd decided to be that night. In fact, more than once Frankie saw one or another of the many delivery boys who arrived with liquor, cigarettes, or groceries floored after being greeted by the ersatz "Babe" or "Marilyn" or "Bette," convinced they were actually in the presence of the real thing.

Having met Babe in person, Dore wanted more than ever to have her see his club act, and I approached Frank on the subject. Surprisingly enough, he seemed perfectly willing and said that somehow he'd manage to haul Babe over to the Trey Deuces one night to take in the act. "Leave it to me, kid." He figured she'd get a laugh out of it—not like Miss Clutch.

I wasn't in town when this encounter took place, but I heard about it later. By now Dore was really packing the joint, especially on weekends, and Frank reserved a table for himself and Babe. Apparently Dore gave his all that night, and when he came on there was an extra buzz of excitement in the room, since Babe had been spotted in a corner, hiding behind her shades. She, however, sat like a bump on a log, never applauding, never cracking a smile, never a peep. After a while Dore attempted to acknowledge her presence.

"How'ma doin', hon?" asked the stage Babe of the real one.

"Lousy," came the reply from across the room. "Somebody get the hook."

"Dear me," said Dore without missing a beat, "I'm glad you came, Miss A, but I wish you'd left your hostilities in the toilet."

"Get off my porch, sister," Babe called back, then tried to get up, only to fall back in her seat. She was plotzed, and Frank, fearing worse was to come, got her up again and hustled her out through a side entrance.

Dore was crushed, and I heard all about it the day I came back from location, when he thanked me for trying and mentioned how touched he was by Frank's note of apology. After that you didn't hear him mention Babe anymore, and somehow the fun went out of the thing. Even then, he didn't take Babe out of his repertoire; he was too cagey for that.

Shortly after this, Dore celebrated his birthday and we were all invited to a special performance at the Trey Deuces, which, as it turned out, was also to be his closing show. Recently he'd received some glowing notices in one of the trade newspapers and had been offered a booking at a Key West club called Coconuts, so he was packing up his trunks and hitting the road with all his "ladies" in tow.

From time to time Jenny and I would get a postcard from him. "Wish you were here and I were there," "This is the land of milk and honey and I'm milking them, honey"; like that. We did miss him.

Then the old world took a couple of wacky spins, and when it stopped I found myself a man of several changes. Alas for the Trianons, Grand or Petit, the place seemed to empty itself, and in the space of a year most of the old faces were no more. Angie had a quarrel with the landlord and was first to leave; next was our aged friend behind our bed, "the bather." Also went Fern, who decided to marry one of her many beaux, and, most unexpected, Dore likewise threw in the towel. After six months he'd come home again, saying that the road was not for him, but before he could get himself relaunched in Hollywood, he got a call from his Aunt Bob, the one with the chicken farm outside Yuma; apparently she was ill and needed him to help her run the place for a while, and, being Dore, off he went to the desert to ride herd on a flock of chickens.

Jenny and I were the last of the old bunch to abandon North Cadman Place, but this was no time to be sad about leaving. I was experiencing a distinct pick-up of career, with a relative rise in salary per picture, so Jenny began combing the hills above the Strip for a house. She found one halfway up a charming, winding, palm-lined street—two bedrooms, with a glamorous night view of the city grid. There was neither pool nor room for one, but that was all right—we managed with a small fishpond under a ginkgo tree, two dogs, and a cat.

Every major career has its ups and downs, it's part of show business, and when you're the kind of superstar that Babe was, it wasn't easy to maintain either momentum or equilibrium. Shirley Temple's movie span was a brief eight years, if that, whereas Babe was still going strong in the 1970s. But there were those times when she had to take up the trap drums or find some other clever gimmick to keep herself in the public eye. For a while she'd become the "Prune Juice lady"—everyone remembers those ads, a svelte Babe in a clinging gown holding up a glass of juice, with a balloon coming out of her mouth saying, "I have a happy morning because I drink Purefroot Prune Juice," the implication being that prunes were a laxative and kept her plumbing in perfect working order.

By the time the forties rolled around she'd done her last Metro films (*Broadway Melody of 1942* and *Millie from Piccadilly* in 1943) and had gone back to the scene of her earlier triumphs, AyanBee, to make the first of her Technicolor pictures, *Peaches and Cream, Mademoiselle de Paree,* and her last for a while, *USO Girl.* One of those Hollywood all-star spectaculars, it was the bomb of all bombs and it effectively finished her off, at least for a time. She announced herself as "retired"; then the next thing we knew the U.S. government was announcing that Babe Austrian would undertake a tour of the European theatre of operation as a real-life USO girl.

When she came back home, one of the last entertainers to return from the front, the war was over and she had recovered some of her former popularity. She recorded an album of her hits—"Windy City Blues" and "Get Off My Porch" were two favorites—and she began doing clubs. She opened in Miami at the Eden Roc and was one of the first world-beaters to appear in Vegas at the Frontier Hotel. But as the years went by, Babe was yet again becoming a shopworn angel, and by 1958 she was pretty much tarnished goods. Even Winchell was referring to her as a "Gone-bye Girl," while others were proclaiming that she really *was* box-office poison. Luckily Frank was still her agent, and negative thinking like Winchell's only acted as a goad to Frankie.

In the old days there used to be a joke around the business: Frankie Adonis never took things lying down but Babe Austrian always did (big laff). Both were scrappers, both could take it as well as dish it out, and neither was a quitter. What followed, therefore, in the colorful career of Babe Austrian came not as a matter of course, but as the result of hard work on Frank's part, as well as some shrewd maneuvering. There was all this talk that Babe was slipping; talk she'd slipped; talk that she was washed up. One month, in her fan-magazine column, Parsons took Babe to task in a typical Open Letter to a star in need of chastisement. ("What Can You Be Thinking Of, Ann Dvorak?" was one of Lolly's choicer items, a spanking in print because Ann had been turning down parts and quarreling with her studio.) This letter of Lolly's was entitled "Quo Vadis, Babe Austrian?" and it went:

"Dear Babe, Whatever is happening to you these days? That's the question your many fans want to have answered. Whither goes thou, Babe? After saving our famous relic, AyanBee Studios, and making them more money than they'd seen in years, after adding to the everlasting glory of Leo the Lion in that too too funny Marx fellows picture, and now suddenly we have this parade of stinkeroos. What can you have been thinking of by doing *Son of a Gun?* And what can Frankie Adonis be thinking of, letting you appear in such a dud? If that's a comedy I'm a monkey's aunt!"

The letter went on in this vein, exhorting Babe to find a suitable script and get her act together: millions of people were just sitting and waiting for her to make them laugh again. What Lolly had not known at the time, nor had her colleague and rival, Hedda, was that even as the Fat One was typing out her letter, Frank Adonis had been doing just that: finding a good script for Babe. Sticking his neck way out, he was about to launch his own personal production, to star Babe in what was to become the classic *Camellia*.

Louella might well have wondered where Frank was going to get the money to finance such a move, but Frank wasn't telling. It wasn't too long, however, before the news leaked out that he intended financing his picture in a co-production deal between some Mexican gamblers and some of his Vegas friends, including Al "Vegas" da Prima and da Prima's pal "Ears" Satriano. There was a hitch in the proceedings, though—an "unfortunate" death aboard da Prima's yacht, anchored off Ensenada, where he and some of the boys had been whooping it up with a covey of girls from Gina's in Tijuana.

Da Prima's current light-o'-love was none other than Babe's stand-in, Patsy Doyle, who'd been running for Congress with the boys for some time. There was a fracas aboard the yacht, and the unlucky Patsy caught a bullet. Her body got washed up on Rosarita Beach, while the yacht hightailed it beyond the twelve-mile limit. Nobody paid much attention until the dizzy Louella came up with the garbled rumor that it wasn't really Patsy who'd been shot, but Babe herself. When Frank heard this he merely laughed, reminding everyone that Babe was at that moment more than three thousand miles away, in South America. Louella was obliged to eat her column for breakfast. But then she turned around and stung Frank's behind, charging that he was the one who'd deliberately started the rumor in the first place and that he'd done it as a cheap bid for some badly needed publicity to boost Babe's sagging career.

Ever one to take potshots at Lolly, Hedda declared the whole thing a tempest in a teapot; she had the real scam: not only was Babe a continent away from the scene of the crime, but she was romantically involved with the Peruvian Tin King, Conçon "Rollo" de Hualada, with whom she was currently whooping it up down in Buenos Aires.

The movie business rejoiced that Babe hadn't been the victim but, rather, her lowly stand-in, just another Hollywood trollop who'd got it through the heart with an Italian Biretta. Peroxide tootsies like Patsy were a dime a dozen, but to lose Babe Austrian and have her body washed up among the sand crabs, even though her career had been heading for Endsville—well, nobody wanted to see her go down the tubes. The unfortunate Patsy was buried near Caliente, where she loved to play the ponies, and is remembered mainly for her appearance among thirty other blonde chorines in a little opus called *Moonlight and Pretzels,* which hit the screens back in '34.

Maybe Frank *had* actually begun the rumor; I wouldn't have put it past him. By fair means or foul, a healthy boost was what he intended to give Babe's career, though few knew then, as few know now, exactly how far he was willing to go to make it all pay off for Babe. You might say it had become a mania with him—that her star that had shone so brightly for so long should continue shining undimmed. And there was no doubt that she was badly in need of some rethinking. The aging process is generally accepted as being far more cruel on the female of the species than on the male, and this certainly was true for Babe, as for any other Hollywood sex symbol. Her career had been floundering, and it was a measure of Frank's entrepreneurial shrewdness that he erased her from the scene at precisely the moment when such a removal was most appropriate, then returned her to the scene at an equally opportune moment.

However Frankie managed it, there was a media "leak," noting that Babe Austrian had been seen several times in Buenos Aires being squired about by this Sr. Conçon de Hualada, and later visiting some of the hill villages whose narrow thoroughfares she negotiated in a white Rolls-Royce, a vehicle hardly likely to obscure her presence south of the border.

Speculation and wonderment again became rife as the old image of Babe Austrian suddenly took on a whole new aura. She was no longer the shopworn article the press had been making her out to be—passé, full-blown, even tarnished—but, rather, some striking, elusive creature whose voice and intonations were the more precious for having been lost to us for a period; a national treasure, the more highly to be cherished because she had lately been treated so indifferently, cast off like an old shoe.

Babe certainly was having a time of it with her Tin King, and the press had a field day. Her swain lapped up the headlines gladly, seemingly bent on keeping their names and pictures in the papers. They called him "Rollo" of the Argentine, and the "Calf of the Pampas," suitable epithets, both. No beauty, Rollo was short and plump, he had a little twist of a mustache, and he enjoyed bowing and kissing ladies' hands, Alphonse and Gaston rolled up in one. (Maude Antrim was heard to say that he looked like a cross between a May Company floorwalker and Thomas E. Dewey.) It was reported that in one month he'd sent Babe over seven thousand dollars' worth of flowers. Harking back to earlier days when Babe was seen up and down Broadway in the limousine belonging to the butter-and-egg man from Ho-Ho-Kus, she was now to be viewed everywhere riding in Rollo's Rolls-Royce, an amusing euphony which got plenty of play in the world press—which was exactly what Frankie wanted. For, despite all the doomsayers of Hollywood, he was determined to star Babe in his production of *Camellia*, a send-up version of the Dumas classic.

The matter of the feud between Babe and Garbo, reports of which filled the columns of *Photoplay* and *Screenland*—this, too, was the promotion of studio flacks. It all started with this hilarious take-off on Garbo's famous *Camille*. If she had never played another role, her interpretation of the worldly, doomed courtesan would assure her a ranking place in cinema history, and the decision to spoof the film had obvious merits so far as the box office went. The by-now-hoary work of Alexandre Dumas *fils* had provided cinema fodder for the great Bernhardt when she was in her seventies; her death scene in the flickering celluloid is a moment of high camp in the way she spins her body like a top into the arms of her lover and then expires, *clunk!* Others had played the fated lady, too, but Greta Garbo had made it her own, and fifty years later there still is nothing dated or stagy in her performance—her every moment rings true and sure, imbued with a tragic irony. It was never Babe's intention to hold her fellow artist up to ridicule, but merely to satirize the kind of archaic, hothouse flavor of the original work. With her familiar bag of tricks—the batting eyelashes, the rolling hips, the barroom tones—with the exaggerated curves of the period costumes, the whole overblown concept that made *Camellia* what it was, she produced a prodigious hit that remains the high point of her art.

It was also one of Hollywood's first runaway productions; not a foot of film was rolled in town but, rather, all was shot at the Charabusco

Studios in Mexico City, where Frank had set the star up in the villa of an ex-president of the country who'd taken it on the lam when a four-million-dollar deficit was suddenly discovered.

The country was delighted to play host to America's famous blonde and gave her a warm welcome. *Sí Babe! Sí-sí-sí! Qué muchacha allegra! Olé Babe!*

"O-lay yourself," came the goof-retort.

This "south of the border" period of Babe's life marked the beginning of her whole later epoch, in which the canon was fully laid down that was to produce the legend. First came *Camellia*, then a new nightclub act, carefully planned and overseen by Frankie, and it was no shock to him at least when *Variety*'s report under "New Acts" hailed the appearance of Miss Babe Austrian at Las Floridianas in Acapulco as a noteworthy event.

The review appeared on the usual Wednesday, in typical *Variety* ese:

> That blonde bombshell and glittering symbol of old-time show business, the intrepid and still-sexy Babe Austrian, hit the stage of Las Floridianas like a bolt of lightning. Spanked out in a blue spangled dress, coiffed and gemmed like the queen she is, she took stage center and belted number after number for a fast-paced fifty minutes that had the audience falling over itself to give her kudos. The array of flowers at the last were enough to see the Ali Khan married again. Among old faves were the Babe's trademark, "Windy City Blues," as well as "She Had to Go and Lose It at the Astor," "I'se a-Muggins" (a borrow from old Thomas "Fats" Waller himself), and "When It's Bedtime Down in Boom-Boom Town," and certainly not for the kiddies' ears.
>
> Wearing a collection of dazzling gowns that would turn the eye of Josephine Baker, our Babe paraded herself before a hosanna-laden audience of international figures who were spellbound by the songs, dances, and yaks being handed them by this trouper, looking younger than springtime and twice as fresh. Her curtain speech is a masterpiece of witty rhetoric, it warms the heart and brings the act to a smash finale. Talk is she'll next take it to London then Europe. On hand was Old Faithful himself, Frank Adonis, pulling the strings and bringing us a Babe we've hungered for. Old-timers wept sentimental tears while tyro viewers applauded themselves silly. New Yorkers, cry your hearts out, 'cause the word is Babe ain't a-comin' home.

The review was signed "O'Brien," *Variety*'s Mexico City stringer and an astute critic. People began sitting up to take notice. If Babe Austrian *had* retired, or in all seriousness intended to, that retirement had now ended and she was back doing business—that's show business, folks! And it was that same act that was to form the cornerstone of the remainder of Babe's life and career, which to my mind were one.

By the time Babe had fully reemerged, it was the spring of 1963. That winter I'd gone to North Africa to do a picture, and when I was finished shooting Jenny joined me in Morocco while I polished off my loops in a dingy sound studio in Madrid. Then we ventured across the Mediterranean, eventually heading for Rome, which at that time seemed to be the heart of the whole movie industry, and where Frank's other clients, Kit Carson and April Rains, were already working on a major spectacle. It was no secret to anyone that Frank and April were seriously involved, and clearly there was trouble waiting in the wings. But as Jenny and I followed the spring north into Sicily, all was yellow daffodils and happy prospects. We put up at the Risorgimento in Taormina, waiting for Frank to arrive in Rome, where we were to join him. But first he had to stop in London to see to matters concerning Babe Austrian, the final, carefully planned step in her magical restoration.

Those were the four months which later became known to us as The Summer of the Purple Grape, token to the amounts of red Italian Valpolicella, Barolo, and Chianti Reserva that were consumed. Taken all in all, it was an unforgettable time, as bad as it was good, and we all came in for our share of headlines. When September came round, it found me on the Dalmatian Coast making another picture. Jenny was still with me, and when we finished we headed for London, where we sublet a cold-water flat behind Harrod's while I waited out yet another film, to begin in Paris late that winter. In the meantime Frank had arrived in England with Babe in tow, prior to her opening at the Café de Paris. All London was geared up for Babe's appearance, Frankie having managed his promotional work well; the advance notices from Mexico and Lisbon were sufficient to stand the town on its ear. This was the time of the Beatles' invasion from Merseyside, the time of "I Wanna Hold Your Hand" and "Puff (The Magic Dragon)," of miniskirts and Carnaby Street.

And now into the very heart of swinging London stepped that artifact of another, earlier age, Miss Babe Austrian. What had Frankie done? Why had he decided to bring her into that city at just that time? The international headliners of the period were the same ones we'd been seeing for years—Noel Coward, Marlene Dietrich, Danny Kaye, Judy at the Palladium—those surefire headliners who were like money in the bank to their managers, the scent of whom was like a sizzling T-bone steak to the public at large. Oh yes, Master Frank knew well what he was up to that winter when he came across with the Babe.

These are some of the things he did to promote his star—the same old star, but a whole new ballgame. First, he four-walled the old Maiden Lane Cinema for a month's period prior to Babe's club opening. He rented the space and put on his own sensational show, bringing to London ten of Babe's best-known films, all the way from *Broadway Blue Eyes*, her first hit, to *Fiji Fifi* and the ill-fated *Windy City Blues*, along with the justly famous *Sheik of Araby*, not forgetting the three well-beloveds with Crispin Antrim, *Pretty Polly*, *Delicious*, and *Manhattan Madness*. Also to be viewed were *Peaches and Cream*, *USO Girl*, and *Mademoiselle de Paree*, those latter-day efforts that showed Babe in glorious Technicolor, films that hadn't played London since the war. (Noticeably absent was *Dixie Belle*, her biggest flop.) All these to play simultaneously with the opening of *Camellia* in the West End. And to several evening screenings at the Maiden Lane Frankie invited a symposium of cinema buffs and critics who were admirers of Babe's film work and voluble on the subject of her special brand of comedy.

With Babe were her pianist, Waldo Dacey, who was to remain with her for the rest of her career, along with Pepe Ventura, her new manager–*cum*–hair-stylist, part Mexican, part Arapaho Indian, who would also be at her side as long as she appeared in public—and after. These days she was rehearsing long hours for her club opening, but Frankie let it be known that on one or two occasions she would be on hand to reply to questions from the audience. Since the Maiden Lane was now on its last legs, having suffered considerable damage during the war from a buzz bomb, Frankie brought together a group of preservationists who formally declared the building a historic landmark. He plastered its front with the most garish display of Babe hoopla, including a ten-foot replica of the star in her costume from *The Sheik of Araby*, whose form both undulated and spoke in those inimitable accents. Londoners went wild.

Next Frank got her on the BBC. Staid old British Broadcasting played host for *Everybody's Babe*, she was interviewed for all to see, and the Queen Mum was quoted as saying, "She seems quite a sweet old dear to me." Babe herself cut the piece out of the paper and stuck it to her dressing-room mirror.

Jenny and I went to the opening as Frank's guests. We even sat at his table with Frances, who'd flown over for the event. Among other ringsiders we spotted the Snowdons, Charlie and Oona Chaplin, Josephine Baker, in from Paris, Grace Kelly there with the Prince, Liz and

Burton, the Duke de Vedura, the Marquis de Cuevas—name them, they all came. Babe Austrian was hot stuff.

She even got away with that corniest of show-biz tricks, the sing-along. "Come on, louder, you guys, I can't hear you!" She had them in a frenzy. Later, in the Green Room, the line waiting to pay their respects to her was as star-studded as the ringside had been. Everyone wanted to have a word with her, and the social invitations came fast and furious. Frankie was on hand, making sure the right photographs were taken of Babe with all the right people, celebrities and royals alike. It was a night of nights.

It was the same thing all over again when she got to Paris months later. Wisely, Frankie had booked the Trocadéro well in advance, the best room Paris had to offer; and, equally wisely, Babe had been boning up on her French, and the place was flabbergasted when she waltzed out and began with her Mademoiselle de Paree brand of *parlez-vous*.

Everything fit together now—it was all gravy, there for the lapping up. But, as so often happens in the best of times, it was just here that fate chose to play the lousy trick she'd been saving up for so long, the blow that was designed to knock Babe Austrian back on her uppers. Everyone remembers that terrible accident.

Taking his cue from the reception at the Command Performance, when Babe had created such a sensation on the ramp, Frankie had worked out more or less the same staging for Paris. There was a pozzarella, or horseshoe ramp, built out into the audience, where she could really get close to the paying customers. She always loved working the pozzarella with its twin rows of bulb lights, and it was here that she met disaster. Her habit was to move out and around the ramp, accepting the flowers and tributes that enthusiastic fans and patrons thrust at her, leaning down to touch their outstretched hands, returning the flow of love and affection she received from them. Nightly it was her great moment and she always made the most of it.

One night, a Saturday, there was a man in the audience, a beefy cheese salesman from Düsseldorf who'd had a bit too much schnapps, and when he put his big mitt out to her she accepted it as she usually did. He took her hand in his and held on tight, until she felt herself being pulled off balance; he went on pulling, and a cry of surprise and alarm filled the room as she feel forward and landed with a crash in the pit.

Screams rang against the ceiling; the audience jumped to its feet and began to mill, and for a moment it looked as if there might be a panic and stampede. Frankie savagely pushed his way to the spot where she lay with her injured back, knocking aside one helpful man who was trying to lift her, shouting, "Don't move her! Don't move her!" She lay there on the floor until the house was emptied, when she could be safely moved out on a stretcher. She couldn't talk, the pain was so great, and the doctor gave her shots to knock her out. Next morning the disheartening word flashed round the world—Babe Austrian had suffered a broken back. Her performing days were now over, she was finished. That's what they said: show biz had seen the last of Babe Austrian, and she of it.

Everyone believed it; everyone except Babe, that is, and the astonishing fact is that exactly nine weeks later to the day, Babe Austrian again appeared before another select audience at the same Trocadéro. She played the show in a plaster cast, starting at her neck and going clear to the base of her spine, and when she came onstage in the wheeled contraption Frankie had had constructed, she delivered the wisecrack that was to follow her the rest of her life. Slapping her hands on her hips and giving the audience a wink, she said, "Well, ya can't say I didn't fall for ya." The place went wild. Josephine, *La Bakair*, was again in the audience and she stood up from her seat to pay Babe the tribute that by now is an old story. Paris took her to its Gallic heart, and she ran at the Troc for a total of one hundred and forty-five consecutive performances.

It took another seven months for her injury to mend, yet she never missed a performance that whole summer. And when it came time to tape the show, as had been arranged by Frank for Euro-Television, she performed without a hitch. When it was over, she collapsed in her dressing room and Frankie sent her down to Lausanne to have the rest she deserved. And when she finally returned to the U.S.A. a year later, and put her little size sixes down on American soil, she grinned at the battery of TV cameras and said, "Find me a place to lay my head, boys," show business was changed, too.

"I've come back to separate the men from the boys and the sheep from the wolves," she kidded. It was not merely the catchphrase of twenty years ago, but a political referendum. Cleopatra's triumphal entry into Rome was no more rousing an event than Babe's reappearance in New York City on that warm spring day in 1965. And as Julius Caesar himself had engineered the one, Frank Adonis had brought off the other; it's no secret that he was the moving force behind the wild and frantic tribute New York paid to Babe after all her years away. If people thought that Frank had lost his knack, that he didn't have the know-how anymore, they needed only to observe the frenzy that was whipped up in the streets of Manhattan for the granddaughter of an Alsatian immigrant and a Norwegian milkmaid.

Babe arrived in New York on May 10, 1965, when the *France* steamed up the Hudson and docked at the old *Normandie* berth, and Babe was swung from "A" Deck in a floral-decorated breeches buoy, to be deposited on the pier, where Mayor Lindsay presented her with the traditional welcoming Key to the City. "Look out, boys, Babe's back in town," she said, brandishing the giant beribboned key for the newsreels. "With this thing I guess I can open any door in Manhattan."

And she was, for a certainty, back in town. Now the lady had come home to reclaim what was rightfully hers, the hurrahs of her fans of almost forty years. The reporters were fascinated and full of their typically "of interest to our readers" questions.

"Hey, Babe, how long have you been abroad, anyway?"

"All my life, sonny, all my life."

"Just how old are you, Babe?"

"Old enough to know better and young enough to enjoy it."

"Are you home for good?"

"Good or bad, whichever turns up first."

Babe had arrived in New York to find *Camellia* playing all over town. The enormous success of the revival of this film could only have delighted her, and the movie box-office lines worked in concert with her new Broadway show, one of Frank's devising, that incredibly successful one-woman evening called *My Head on a Silver Platter*, that opened at the Booth Theatre, the same house that had presented Bea Lillie in her famous solo run.

Meanwhile, it got in the columns that she'd had her face done; I decided the rumors must be correct, because the next time I saw her she certainly had a new look. This was a year or so later, when she went on *The Ed Sullivan Show* for the first time, plugging her show. She looked great, had lost weight, which Frank was always trying to get her to do, her cheeks had taken on a sculptured look, her hair was better dressed, and she belted out her numbers with obvious relish. Ed himself seemed awed by her—the Babe legend was hard at work even on the Great Stone Face—and he stumbled around more than usual as he ad-libbed with her. "A ver' great performer, ver' ver' great. Thank you, Babe Osterreich," forgetting she hadn't been that for decades. That was Ed all over.

In this, her first nationally televised appearance, she sang two numbers, "The ABC's of Love" and "The Windy City Blues," and engaged in the notorious Scheherazade sketch, a naughty parody that started all the trouble with Cardinal Spellman and nearly got Ed, a staunch Catholic, taken off the air.

That she should be censured for so mild a form of humor both irked and amused Babe, and she willingly entered into a joust with the eminent prelate, whom she and others affectionately called "Sally." When asked by reporters why she thought the Cardinal was mad at her, she replied, "Aw heck, fellas, if the Cardinal was holdin' anything against me, I guess I'd feel it, wouldn't I?" And "The reason His Eminence is studyin' my act so careful is, he wants to do me on TV. I don't mind, honest, I been doin' him for years." "Sally" Spellman didn't dignify such quips with a public reply, though it was known that in private he fumed and wanted to have the woman excommunicated until it was discovered that she'd been baptized a Lutheran.

There was a personal encounter of sorts, cleverly staged by Babe herself. Upon learning that a prominent public figure was having his son and heir baptized at Saint Patrick's Cathedral, Babe called in a favor and wangled an invitation. She arrived early, in a big hat with plumes—you couldn't have missed her in a crowd of ten million—and when His Eminence got a load of her, he reddened with anger.

"How'm a doin', guy?" came her question as she slipped him a wink. Her question elicited no reply from His Eminence, but Babe had made her point, and the incident made the afternoon editions. Later she reported that she thought the Cardinal looked great and that he had "a real swell place there. And we were all crazy about his hat."

Head on a Silver Platter copped a Tony that year, so did Babe, which seemed to surprise nobody but herself. Everybody else took it as a foregone conclusion that she would win. She donned a man's black tuxedo for her appearance—nothing new in that, Dietrich had been doing it for years—but when she came out from the wings, cleverly disguising the slight limp she still had after her Paris fall, her reception was tremendous. It was as if the New Yorkers, those hard-nosed, jaded denizens of Broadway, had been too long denied the opportunity of applauding her. Her thank-you speech got an undeniable quota of laughs, to wit:

"Gee, I don't know what to say. In fact I'm nonplussed. Honest, I've been plussed by a lot of guys but tonight I'm really nonplussed."

Further words followed in which she offered heartfelt tribute to Frankie:

"All I am I owe to Frank. Frank Adonis made me—and don't one of you crack a smile."

The public gratitude she paid Frankie was generous and well deserved, so filled with good humor and honest affection that it stole the show, and people spoke of it feelingly for long afterward. All she was she owed to herself and the God-given talent that had kept her a star for forty years, but without Frank, where would she have been? Frank knew better than anyone what he had wrought, the jewel he had polished, and just what it had taken to keep her name up there in lights.

With the huge success of *Head on a Silver Platter*, plus a newly recorded album, and the bounty of free publicity given her by the Cardinal, Frankie now sent the Babe off on what became the first of three highly successful tours, reminiscent of her vaudeville beginnings and was as carefully plotted and executed as the road tours of such self-managing attractions as Katharine Cornell and the Lunts—and every bit as triumphant.

When her show reached Los Angeles, Jenny and I were again in attendance. You never got tired of seeing it; it was that kind of evening. In New York she'd had Reggie Gardiner to bring her on and compère the show, but Reggie hadn't wanted to tour, and Cyril Ritchard had gone in before she opened in Atlantic City. Opening night at the Los Angeles Biltmore was one more triumph in a parade of triumphs, this an especially piquant one in the wake of being labeled a has-been, and Louella's Open Letter. If Lolly ever wanted to know what *bad* happened to Babe Austrian, here was her answer: packed houses, sensational reviews, and as warm a welcome as she'd had in New York. And she deserved every bit of it. Babe was still big-time all the way.

Since her fall in Paris she'd never again used a pozzarella, but remained safely behind the proscenium arch. By the same token, she'd kept aloof from her fans, terrified that a similar mishap might occur. Still, I thought it would be okay to stop back and say hello to her, but when we arrived, her manager, Pepe Ventura, refused us entry to the dressing room. "Miss A is not receiving visitors this evening," he informed us grandly; "she's going directly to her apartment. She's very tired." If I found this behavior odd, Jen shrugged it off as mere temperament. "After all, she *is* getting on, isn't she?" So much for old friendships, I thought.

She played a full eight weeks in L.A., then went up to San Francisco for another six, and closed in Seattle at Christmas. After that Frank got her to lay off. But not for long . . .

At some point during these various comings and goings, Jenny and I had begun experiencing domestic troubles. Nothing really earth-shattering, but not just spats, either. Having decided she wasn't in love with the idea of acting but was interested in other aspects of the movies, she'd got a job assisting an important costume designer and she was working on a western shooting up in Kanab. After I'd put her on the plane to the location,

I came back to our house on Sunset Plaza (which we lovingly called "Sunset Placid" because our life had been so tranquil there) and our German shepherd, Bones, who whimpered for days after his mistress flew away.

Nor was I the only one around town to be feeling the yoke of domestic dissatisfaction. Frank was showing signs of severe home wear. His affair with April had gone sour, following a series of breakdowns—she had been in and out of sanitariums—but he still would have married her except for the fact that Frances had refused to divorce him.

And then there was Angie Brown. She'd been wearing her heart on her sleeve for years, but she, too, had finally given up on Frank, realizing hers was a one-way street called Back and there was no chance of her ever getting together with him again. Five years ago she'd moved, first to Palm Springs, eventually to Cathedral Wells where she and her second husband, a rodeo clown named Cloud Howdy, owned a roadhouse on the outskirts of town that served the best barbecue and chili west of the Pecos.

People used to gas a lot about Angie, saying she was going to pot down there in the desert, putting on weight and forgetting to dye her roots, and to this sad end had she come, a sleazy saloon and chili joint in Cat Wells, but I knew differently. Angie loved that hokey old place; it held lots of happy memories for her, and she somehow suited it, I thought, not the movie Angie of *Too Many Girls* and *Three Men on a Horse*, but the real Angelina Brunetti; just as Cloud Howdy, this rodeo character she'd been sleeping with for some years, suited her, too. And she'd more than proved the deep affection in which she was held by the natives: she ran for public office and found herself elected mayor of the community. It's true, Angie was now Her Honor.

Sure, she'd spread a bit; sure, she had a big butt—so what? What woman hasn't by the time she hits sixty? (That figure is approximate; nobody ever really knew how old she was. The records state that she'd married Eddie La Starza at age twenty; make of that what you will.) In any case, her age doesn't matter, for what I really want to mention here has to do not with Angie so much as certain others.

By this time I'd begun writing, and I'd gone over to a location in Tucson, where a picture I'd had a hand in scripting was before the cameras. Angie called me there to say she was close by in Scottsdale, playing in a golf tournament, that Cloud was back in Cat Wells minding the bar, and why didn't I come see her when I was finished?

I said I had a better idea. As long as we were in the neighborhood, why didn't she meet me in Yuma and we could do a surprise drop-in on our old chum Dore Skirball at his chicken ranch in Torreon, which I knew was somewhere south of Yuma. I hadn't seen him in years, but from Angie I'd heard that he'd taken up his ranching chores with uncharacteristic seriousness, that his aunt hadn't succumbed to her attack, and that he'd apparently found his niche in life and was making the most of it. It seemed that, rather than clamoring to get back to the bright lights of West Hollywood, he was more than happy to stay put down on the farm.

Angie and I met on the outskirts of Yuma and stayed overnight at a Ramada Inn, from which she telephoned Dore in Torreon. Next morning I was awakened by a pounding on the door, which came bursting open. When I groggily came to a sitting position, I was greeted by what seemed an apparition. Standing on the threshold was Dore Skirball.

"Howdee, pardner! Could anyone please give me the time o' day?"

It wasn't really him but a sort-of-Dore, certainly not the Dore we'd known at the Trianon. He'd lost most of his hair, what remained was white, and he looked like one of his old comedy characters, Cowboy Bill, in his pipestem jeans, his high-heeled cowboy boots, bandana, and ten-gallon hat of white straw, bowing his legs and talking in a thick Texas drawl.

The three of us had breakfast at a coffee shop on the highway, and while we dunked our bear-claws, Dore brought us up to date on his doings, and his Aunt Bob, who was now in her seventies. Afterward, he stopped at a drugstore to buy Bobbie some hair color; then I followed him in his van while Angie rode with him out to "Cactus Gulch," which is what Bobbie called Torreon, some twenty miles away.

From afar I saw the sign we'd heard so much about in the old days: "Aunt Bob's Texas Fried Chicken & BBQ Ribs." We left the highway a hundred or so yards before, driving over a newly rolled road to a ramshackle house set back among some tamarisk trees, by a bend of the Torreon River, which wasn't much more than a muddy creek—but, according to Dore, was loaded with the biggest, most succulent catfish to be had anywhere. And there on the porch was this good ole pioneer lady jest a-settin' and a-rockin': Aunt Bobbie herself. She jumped up and sort of loped out to meet us with long butch strides, and in her good-natured, down-home way she reminded me of Charlotte Greenwood, a real Aunt Eller type.

She gabbed with us for a good hour, repeating all the latest cowboy jokes; then she and Angie trooped inside to oversee lunch, while Dore showed me around the "ranch." I found it difficult to act impressed by the layout, but he was so proud of the place I mustered up a show of enthusiasm. And, in truth, the roadside stand, "Aunt Bob's Chicken Inn," was doing a land-office business. I could see how Dore must be raking in the dough, because during the whole time we were there, no fewer than half a dozen vehicles were parked in front.

Later, while Angie took Aunt Bobbie upstairs to give her hair a touch-up and set, Dore led out some horses and we went for a desert ride. I could see why he liked the place so much. Torreon was a lovely spot, the roads arrowed straight to the horizon "thisaway and thataway," the only thing showing aboveground being the ragged lines of tamarisks, with their feathery branches like the lacy trees in Chinese T'ang paintings. The West seemed to suit Dore somehow. The sight of him on horseback seemed an odd one, yet he sat his horse well. In his jeans and wide-brimmed Stetson, the squash blossom silver-and-turquoise belt, the printed orange bandana at the throat, he looked a real hand. He took me down to a bend of the river which he called the Snake's Back, where we sat in the shade and did a bit of fishing with poles he'd thought to bring along. While I never got a bite, he hooked three big ones in a row—"For your lunch," he told me. I wasn't much on catfish, but I kept my mouth shut. Angie could have my share.

Back at the chicken spread, I stood amazed as Dore cleaned and cooked the fish himself, breaded them in cornmeal and some tasty seasoning. And if he'd cooked up a beef Wellington for us, he couldn't have served it with more pride and panache. We ate lunch on a picnic table under the trees; in addition to the catfish there were crispy, golden sections of chicken, along with hot buttermilk biscuits, the best cole slaw I ever ate, as well as beefsteak tomatoes drenched with a zesty dressing, and baked Texas barbecued beans, raring hot and of a far different sort from the calmer Boston brown beans I was used to. For dessert there was homegrown Casaba melon and home-churned ice cream.

I'd already fallen in love with Aunt Bob—but that was no news: everyone did. Bobbie was one of those old-fashioned, down-to-earth women who, having worked hard all their lives and having blessed little to show for it, were bent on squeezing every last bit of enjoyment out of what time was left to them. We got along from the start, and after lunch, while Angie and Dore sat talking in the porch shade, Aunt Bob invited me to look around. As she led me upstairs she confided to me how much it meant to Dore to see me again and that I'd taken the time to pay him a visit.

"But I came to see you, too, ma'am," I said, and she gave me a playful slap.

"Don't you 'ma'am' me, you big Hollywood galoot. Call me Aunt Bob like everyone else."

Dore's room was surprisingly spare and plain, but crammed with his usual welter of books and magazines, and on the bed a primitive patchwork quilt that must have been worth a piece of change. I thought what a far cry this was from his old digs over the trash cans of B.B.H., and from all those endless drinks and dinners, those nutty evenings at the Petit Trianon.

" 'Twas a long time ago, I guess," Aunt Bobbie agreed soberly as we went along the hall. "I do urge him to go over to Hollywood and visit his friends, but he don't seem to want to leave."

"Doesn't he ever miss the city?" I asked.

"Not so's you notice," she said philosophically. "I must say, I do favor having him around. You get my age, you like a bit of comp'ny. And he does make you laugh, don't he? And if he gets cabin fever he can fly himself straight to Yuma, or if he gets bigger ideas, Houston-Dallas is only a skip away."

I had to confess, it was good seeing Dore again, and I was amazed to see how he'd come to terms with life; it isn't always easy for a person to give up "the show business," as Aunt Bob called it. When I asked Dore if he missed the old days at the Trey Deuces, if he didn't yearn to come back and start in again, he shook his head. He said that the Sunday evening when Frank had brought Babe around and she'd proved such an embarrassment had pretty well scotched him. The only thing he did of that nature now was to call the square dances at the monthly hoedown in town. When Angie joined us we spent an hour or so talking about the old days on North Cadman—happy reminiscences, but for Dore no regrets.

Next morning both Angie and I felt a real letdown at leaving Cactus Gulch and the muddy Snake's Back, and especially sad to say goodbye to Aunt Bobbie. Later I wrote her, thanking her for a good time; she wrote back, and as it turned out we corresponded for years. With time, Aunt Bobbie became a kind of presence in my life.

When Jenny came home from location and learned about this little jaunt to Arizona, she was even jealous that I'd found this new friend, and she took it in bad part that Angie had "lured" me over to Torreon. It went so far, actually, as to become one of the wedges that time and circumstances were driving between Jenny and me. Our difficulties, far from being over, seemed to be only beginning.

. . .

These days Frankie was in many ways changed from the old Frankie of the thirties and forties. Things had been gnawing at him around the edges. Life was earnest, life was real—and getting realer every minute. In sum, Frankie's vaunted luck had changed. The scandals and personal tragedies that had beset him, starting with the loss of April, then Frances's death, then that of his beloved mother, Maxine, and the changing tenor of the entire movie industry, all had worked their miseries on him. He was fatigued; life, once so varied and colorful, had lost a lot of its savor. The old rules no longer applied, and he didn't like having to play by the new ones.

Yet always there was Babe, the great Babe Austrian, who was greater than ever. She had been his first great creation, and maybe she would be his last, too, for at the business of the Comeback, Frankie Adonis was a past master. He seemed to know exactly when to unveil the "new" Claire Regrett, the "new" Belinda, the "new" Babe. His unerring instinct in such matters all but guaranteed success.

Having closed in *Platter,* Babe had filmed the movie Frank had been working on for her for four years, and again the fact that *Gracious Me* became a hit had as much to do with Frank's involvement as Babe's own. Babe Austrian and Walter Matthau made as good a comedy team as Babe and Crispin Antrim or Babe and Groucho, and audiences were convulsed. That year there was an inordinate amount of excitement in the six weeks preceding the Academy Awards, and already the odds were being chalked up in Vegas, where a substantial claque of Babe fans was betting on her. Comedic performances seldom if ever beat out the heavyweight dramatic roles—there were only a few like Judy Holliday in *Born Yesterday,* and she probably won because the opposition was split between Swanson in *Sunset Boulevard* and Davis in *All About Eve*—but this time a lot of the odds-givers were looking for a major upset in the Oscar derby. Unlikely as it seems that any adult would not have seen *Gracious Me,* for the sake of the few I herewith include bits of the *New York Times* notice by Bosley Crowther, who made it clear that here was no average Hollywood bio epic, another *Jolson Story* or *Night and Day,* etc. "Not necessary to adhere to facts for facts' sake. A loose jumble of fun-filled events with musical cues abounding. Aldo Ray never better. Produced by Frank Adonis, etc., etc."

By the time *Gracious Me* reached the nation's screens, thanks to Frank, Babe was so solidly launched along the comeback trail that she'd become a household name. It was astonishing, the way she was knocking them dead in Vegas, on the road, and, as importantly, on television, which meant that she was finding her way into the middle-American living rooms of Kalamazoo and Cedar Rapids. Babe never minded hitting the common denominator—so long as it wasn't the lowest one—and she thought a box with dials and a screen in every parlor was jim-dandy; she'd grace the invention any chance she got.

She didn't win the Oscar, of course; Maggie Smith got it that year, but the loss never fazed Babe; she was always a good loser. She continued making TV guest appearances, she played the Vegas clubs on a more or less regular schedule, she wrote her second book of memoirs—*Life Is Just a Bowl of Cherry*—and her version of the Jerry Herman song "The Man in the Moon Is a Lady" made all the charts for a whole summer.

Everything was spinning like a top, but like a spinning top, in time things lost their momentum, Babe's career as well, for on a certain night —a famous night, as it later turned out—of Christmas week in 1973, Frank Adonis was shot to death in his Palm Springs garage, and with his end came a lot of other ends. With Frank gone, the spark seemed to go out of Babe's career and she entered into a period of virtual retirement. She withdrew to her penthouse, where she sat in isolated splendor, sometimes going out for a drive to the beach house at Santa Monica. Friends of mine would sometimes see her touring in the back of the old black car, her features swathed in net, hidden from the world, while Sluggo with his shiny suit and fifteen-hundred-dollar watch drove her where she willed or they would stop by the pier and she would sit staring out at the water for hours at a time. Once or twice they saw her get out of the car to use the public toilet.

She must have become bored with watching the water, because before too much time went by she'd gotten her act together and taken it on the road. She was touring in *Platter* again, playing to a whole new generation of fans who'd seen her old movies on television.

We met again, Babe and I, and under circumstances of a somewhat offbeat nature. This was in the winter of 1974, in Chicago, where I found myself in the middle of a cross-country publicity tour set up by my publisher, beating the drums on behalf of my latest book. Since I had a heavy schedule of interviews that carried over from Friday to Monday, I was trapped in Chicago through the weekend. Glancing at the local TV guide, I found a five-day run of Babe Austrian films playing on a local station including *Everything From A to Z*, its sequel, *Everything from Soup to Nuts*, and most notably, *Frankie and Johnny*. Paging through the "Guide to Nightlife" or whatever it's called, to my surprise I found that Babe herself was in town, playing *Head on a Silver Platter* in yet another farewell tour.

I had arrived late the night before, and by the time Friday rolled around I was having morning coffee with entertainment and book editors, some of whom came from as far away as Cleveland to ask their thrilling questions. My final stint that evening was the taping of a show called *Here's Sandy*. Now, Easterners and Westerners probably wouldn't have heard of this show, but Midwesterners were devoted to it, and at that period no celebrity passed through the city of Chicago without putting in an appearance on it. Also scheduled was the Babe.

As my good luck had it, Belinda Carroll was also in town, likewise book-plugging; her autobiography, *My Way, Always*, was just hitting the best-seller lists. Our paths had converged twice already when we'd appeared as guests on local talk shows. And when our latest TV hostess, Sandy Becker, saw what she had on her plate, namely three individuals, each of whose lives had been touched by Frankie Adano, she tossed the script out the window half an hour before taping and decided to offer up to the viewers a round-robin of questions and answers regarding the Real Frankie Adonis.

This concept made all three of us guests uncomfortable—there were too many things about Frankie none of us wanted to see turned into talk show gossip—and we proceeded with more than the usual caution. We were on the air when I glanced round and saw the producer talking into the ear of the cue-card writer. In seconds a card flashed: "Ask Carroll about Adonis murder." Obviously, Belinda wasn't meant to have seen the card, but she did, and she blazed out, saying she knew what was up and she wasn't talking. This resulted in cutting tape, TV's number-one no-no, after which, having deleted Belinda's outburst, Sandy resumed with interesting questions regarding MGM in the great days. The show was not what you'd call a triumph.

After the taping Babe invited me to ride back to the hotel in her limousine, a thoughtful gesture I readily accepted. She never mentioned Belinda at all, though she had plenty to say about Sandy Becker's producer. En route she suggested I come see her show, which I was happy to do, having no other plans. She had a house seat put up for me at the box office and I went and laughed my head off; she really was funny. "Rolling in the aisles" is a show-biz phrase invented for performers like Babe Austrian. Though I knew her act so well by now, I marveled at it all over again. She reached out and touched something deep in the audience, old and young alike. She was nostalgia personified; the oldsters enjoyed the kind of poignancy she commanded, while the younger ones felt they were viewing the living legend—which they were. Oh *yeah!*

When I went to bed that night snow was falling outside. I've never thought of Chicago as being an especially pretty city, not in the way that, say, Washington can be, or Paris, or even New York. But there was a pretty magic about the way the softly falling snow began to cover up the streets and buildings. I sat there at the window, reflecting on the strangeness of life and its little quirky coincidences that afforded one such weekends as this, such chance encounters with the likes of Belinda Carroll and Babe Austrian.

Tomorrow we would doubtless go our separate ways, having come together for this moment of time, during which our old friend Frankie had been the common denominator. There was Belinda flogging her Hollywood tragedy, I my novel, and Babe the single product she ever had to sell, herself. It had been an odd rendezvous, and, as things turned out, it lasted longer than anyone thought it would, for when I awoke in the morning it was clear that we were "having a bit of weather." The light snow that had been so pretty to look at the night before had in the wee hours become a good old-fashioned Great Plains blizzard, ferociously blanketing the whole Midwest, and, not incidentally, making travel impossible. Chicago's streets were all but empty; there were only the plows out, doggedly trying to clear paths, while the snow was coming down so thickly that there wasn't a chance of a plane's getting out.

We found ourselves holed up there in the Ambassador East and I had to scramble to reorganize my schedule. There were some domestic problems as well. Belinda had been occupying one of the larger suites, which she was to have given up this morning, for some foreign notables were scheduled to arrive by train and her rooms were reserved. Obviously the management didn't know the lady well. Belinda Carroll had been brought up in the great days of Lana Turner and Ava Gardner—in those days Lana and Ava weren't put out of their hotel suites for anybody, foreign notables or not—and twenty years later Belinda wasn't about to relinquish *her* rooms to anybody, either.

Making a stab at easing things, I suggested that she take over my suite, a corner one, up high, and perfectly acceptable. A grateful management said it could oblige me with a single room, and that's how things were arranged. Belinda's forty-seven thousand suitcases were sent up, while my two went out the door. I ordered my breakfast in the hotel dining room, reading the papers while I ate. Then, when I went to the desk to ask for my new key, the clerk told me I wasn't staying in that room as planned.

"Your things have been moved to Miss Austrian's suite," he informed me. He popped the bell, and a bellhop was instructed to escort me up in the elevator. I was completely mystified.

"Good evening, Mr. Ventura," I said as Pepe, Babe's formally titled

"Associate Producer," met me at the door and ushered me in. He explained that Babe was still abed, but since she had the extra space, she was offering me a bedroom until the weather improved. Since to my knowledge Babe had never been noted for her beaux gestes, I had trouble assimilating this sudden switch; still, I decided to accept it in the generous spirit in which it had apparently been offered. But if I imagined that sharing her suite was to improve personal relations between us, I was wrong.

Because the city was experiencing difficulty clearing the streets, all Chicago was effectively immobilized. From my window I could see that everything was nailed down hard and fast. Meanwhile, Babe was out of sorts because her evening appearance had been canceled, proving that the show does not always have to go on (she claimed in an interview that it was the only time she'd ever missed a performance anywhere under any circumstances), and she remained incommunicado to all comers, myself included, and except for one time, which I'll get to, I never laid eyes on her during the two and a half days I was obliged to accept her hospitality.

On Sunday I called Belinda and we met for dinner in the Pump Room to catch up on news. She looked sensational, the way movie stars always ought to look. Wearing simple navy blue and modest jewelry, she sat beside me in the booth, her classic features illuminated by the flickering candles while strings played softly in the background. We spoke of Frank and of Angie Brown, and of Maude Antrim, of whom I entertained the happiest memories. I congratulated Belinda on her book, which seemed headed for a large success. I knew how hard she'd labored over a typewriter: it wasn't one of those "as told to" numbers; she took pride in the four hundred pages that had been written with a pen dipped in her life's blood.

It hadn't been easy for her, baring her soul in such a public way, especially the sections of the book dealing with her daughter, Faun. I suppose it was inevitable that it should have been a best-seller, containing as it did an inside view of one of the most scandal-ridden lives in the history of Hollywood. The thing was, she'd been able to let her own sweetness of nature come through, no easy matter under the circumstances. Belinda couldn't know then that she was headed for the biggest success of her career, that she was to receive the accolade of the entire industry, to win a sensational Broadway triumph, and that everything she'd always hoped for was at last to come to her. With, of course, the obvious exception: Frankie Adonis, who was lost to her forever, as he was lost to all of us who loved him. So near they had come, she and he, so close but no further, and now it was ended for all time.

Belinda was now some fifty-two years old, Frankie had been dead for two or three years, and she still mourned him because she had loved him. To all intents and purposes, she was alone these days—I knew she had no love interest. And she was studying acting again; she still wanted to be a great actress. You had to applaud such tenacity, such doggedness of purpose. Who in the history of movies had ever ridden such a bumpy road as hers, who had risen to where she had and somehow, no matter how perilously, been able to maintain herself on those dizzy heights?

Quite a girl, Belinda.

When we'd finished our coffee she suggested we put our noses out the door and see what the weather was like. We bundled up well, me in the only coat I had, she in the fur coat Frank had given her on their last Christmas together. As we slipped out through the revolving door and a blast of cold air hit our faces, I felt her slip her warm hand in mine and we headed into the wind. The city had an eerie feeling, as if it had been deserted by everyone but us and the very few other brave souls who had ventured forth.

Unbelievably, by the time we got to the water clock at the Loop the snow had begun falling again, as if we hadn't had enough by now, and we were forced to cut short our venturing-forth. She would have gone on, but I convinced her it was foolish: we were tired and needed our health if we were going to keep going with our tours. But as we retraced our steps I became aware that things were somehow different. As a result of that little walk of ours, when we came back into the warm, brightly lighted hotel, with the wind shut out, I felt a growing sense of intimacy between us. Nothing to put your finger on, but our relationship had shifted, even if only slightly. We stood close together in the elevator, our bodies touching as we went up. I decided to take no liberties when I walked her to her door, but when I put the key in the lock she surprised me with a kiss. One that probably meant nothing to her but meant lots to me; a kiss that with time was to take on even greater significance.

In consequence of which I was in no mood to be trifled with, and I wanted only to get to my bed as fast as possible; but no such luck. As I let myself into the Royal Suite I found Pepe Ventura in the living room; he rose abruptly and snapped off the TV. I had the idea he'd been waiting up for me.

"Well, hel-*lo*, " he greeted me in that snide tone of his, "back so early? Did you have a nice dinner?"

I said I had, yes. Nice.

"Not much fun eating alone, I guess." His eyebrows were dark and thick and perfectly arched; not without the aid of tweezers, I suspected.

Ignoring his supercilious manner, I took off my coat, and as I hung it in the closet I asked how Babe was.

"Miss A is fine," he returned pointedly. "As a matter of fact, she's been waiting. She'd like to talk to you before you retire. Though it does seem to me—"

"Yes?" I was getting lots of attitude here and, frankly, I didn't like it. "*What* does it seem to you?"

"Never mind."

"But I do mind. I gather you think I haven't done my job or that I've been lax in some way as regards—*Miss* Austrian. But just let me lay it on you, pal: I don't know how long you've known the lady, but I've known her for damn near forty years, giving me the edge, don't you agree? I'm always available if she wants me, but I got the impression she preferred being left alone. Which sort of frees me up to have dinner with anyone I care to, right, pal?"

"Please don't call me 'pal'; my name is Pepe."

"Right, pal." I went to the bar, poured some mineral water over ice, and walked to Babe's door. Pepe flew to block my way.

"Wait—don't go in there!" he hissed. "Miss A may not be dressed to receive."

"I was taught to knock," I retorted, veering away toward my own door. "Let me know when Madame's got her shit together. I'm going to have myself a footbath and a pedicure."

While Pepe knocked discreetly, then slipped through Babe's door, I went into my room and lay down on my bed, staring moodily at the window, which had over a foot of snow on the sill. I'd picked up the phone to place a call when Pepe appeared in my doorway.

"Finished your bath already?" he asked with that mixture of pretension and queeniness I disliked so. I waited and he said, "Anyway, Miss A will see you now."

I put down the phone, got up, took my glass of mineral water, and walked past him, heading for Babe's room. But he slipped by me to sidle up to the door, where he applied the same discreet knock as before, waited a moment, then turned the knob and gave me an elaborate "Please to enter" gesture.

"Hullo there," Babe greeted me from her bed. She was propped up against a mess of pillows. The covers were scattered with various publications—I glimpsed *The Wall Street Journal*, weekly *Variety*, *TV Guide*, *Business Week*, even the *Kiplinger Report*—and though she wore glasses, as if she'd been reading any or all of these, the lights were turned down. Obviously she made herself at home wherever she happened to be. It was quite a picture; she looked dwarfed in the oversize bed, her hair was wrapped in a black net, but she had her war paint on and even her long eyelashes. I wondered if I should flatter myself that I was the reason; wondered, too, if she'd get out of bed to scrape it all off before retiring.

She motioned for me to draw up the chair, and as I did she thrust out the flat of her palm at me and, as though to warn me away, said, "That's far enough. Sit down, take a load off."

I sat and she proceeded to interrogate me as to my evening's activities. I made no secret of the fact that I'd dined with Belinda.

"She tryin' to put the make on you? She hot for your fair white body?"

I grinned cockily. "If she were, she wouldn't have much trouble." I thought I'd get something back, but as she frowned, considering something, I noticed a sudden rustling movement under the covers and in moments the famous Chihuahua, Tiny, had wriggled into sight, poking its pointy face from underneath the covers. Babe caught the creature up and hugged it against her breast. "Nice Tiny, sweet Tiny," she crooned, and the dog settled down against her, its tail wagging. Babe stroked the pale belly with her long-nailed hand, while she gave me the full once-over.

I was amused when she actually said "Humph!" It sounded old-fashioned and somehow endearing and I was prepared to be conciliatory, but she seemed bent on provoking some sort of quarrel.

"I heard you and her were living together in sin. Up there at old Maude's place. With the daughter right there in the house and everything. Sounds pretty tacky to me."

"Does it?" I countered briskly. "I guess some people are better equipped to judge what's tacky than others." I didn't pause, but plowed straight on. "As for our living together, if you'd ever been to Sunnyside you'd realize that the guesthouse, where I stayed, is a long way from the main house, where Belinda lived, and you should also realize that she would never have been interested in me, since at the time she and Frank were planning to get married."

She pursed her lips and gave the dog a wettish smack. "Maybe it wasn't Belinda after all; maybe you were boffing old Maude. At her age, too. What some dames will do for a lay. Talk about cradle-robbing."

"Maybe so, maybe not. One thing we know—it wasn't on the Super Chief. Was it?" I sat back with a smug look. Babe and the dog both eyed me with some puzzlement.

"I don't get it. What's that supposed to mean, 'Super Chief'?"

"Golly, and all this time I thought you were busy treasuring the memory of our little cross-country rendezvous. As we hurtled through the night, wrapped in each other's arms—all across Wyoming—or was it Oklahoma?"

She frowned. "What're you talking about—Wyoming? Super Chief? What's the gag?"

"No gag. For your enlightenment, Miss A, I have reference to the end of the Second World War, in which I was privileged to play a minor role—V-J Day, August 15, year of our Lord 1945. Miss Gladys Lillie of Battle Crick. I mean, *you* remember Gladys Lillie, don't you?"

She slid her glasses down her nose and regarded me suspiciously over their rims. "Listen, buster, just what're you inferring?"

"No no no, lady," I corrected. "I'm *implying; you* can *infer* whatever you like. I merely meant that one of my most treasured memories is of that night. Can you really have forgotten? I'm really surprised—I thought I'd made a better—um—impression on you."

She gave me a sour look and stuck her glasses back firmly in place. "I can't be expected to remember every guy I come across. Nineteen forty-five? You must've been a baby."

"*You* didn't think so. I seem to remember you—ah—said you liked doing your bit for the boys. 'The brave boys who are facing death all over the globe,' I believe that's how you chose to put it. Rather delicately, I thought, considering how robustly you did your bit for *this* boy."

She grew more indignant. "You got me mixed up with ten other dames, sonny," she said, refusing my look. "I never went around screwing sailors on trains."

"Maybe, but the Super Chief wasn't just *any* train," I said wickedly. "Don't you remember, you said it was 'a silver bullet speeding to the heart of love'? Of course, that was during the night. Next day you didn't know me from Adam."

By this time she was really giving me the fisheye. "Look, Strongheart, if this is some sort of joke—"

I leaned back in my chair and watched her for a moment. Then: "Yeah, yeah, sure," I said, "that's it, just a joke. Forget it. I was just pulling your leg."

There was another pause; then, adjusting herself against the pillows, she said, "That's okay, *I* was the one who was pulling *your* leg. Sure, I remember you. You were this cute-lookin' guy in sailor blues and you had all these battle ribbons across your chest. You kinda caught my eye. Nice. It was very nice. We really celebrated—didn't we?"

"You had that pocketbook. That big pocketbook, full of—"

"Yes? Full of what?"

"I was just wondering if you'd remember. You had a lot of those miniature bottles of booze."

"I remember. You drank Johnnie Walker Red."

I was impressed. She really did remember. But she still hadn't come out with why she'd sent for me, and I wasn't up to prompting her or trying to figure the thing out. Even in the light from the bedside lamp, which she kept dim by hanging a pink silk scarf over it, she showed the age she hid so well onstage. Her voice sounded tired, and I remember wondering if she wasn't coming down with something.

She pushed her head back into the pillows and gave me another look. "Why did you bring up those things?" she asked. "Why didn't you mention them before?"

I smiled and shrugged. Who knew? Again she scrutinized me, and I got the impression there was something troubling her—something she wanted to get off her chest. I couldn't be sure, but I was studying her just as hard as she was studying me. Finally she made a negligent gesture, as if none of this really mattered, and I took that as my cue to leave. She didn't press me to linger.

When I'd climbed into bed, after checking the latest snowfall, I thought over our little interview. Obviously she hadn't remembered me at all. If she had, she would have recalled that, VJ Day having fallen in August, I would have been in summer whites, not winter blues, and that I'd worn no ribbons, since I'd never been decorated. No doubt it was some other sailor she was remembering, on some other train.

I must have dozed off in the middle of these musings for the next thing I knew—this was late, probably after two, though I never looked at my watch to verify the time—I was wakened by the instantly recognizable smell of smoke. And where there's smoke, there's fire. I sprang out of bed and dashed into the sitting room, switched on the lights to see an ominous pall curling from under Babe's closed door and slowly rising to the ceiling. I shouted the alarm and grabbed the phone. I saw Sluggo come charging out of his room—I remember the pajamas, striped in black and yellow, his hairy chest—he banged on Babe's door, then crashed inside. The smoke blossomed out like the mushroom cloud of an atom bomb. While I was warning the desk of our situation, Sluggo staggered out, cradling an inert Babe in his arms. Meanwhile, Pepe had appeared and was taking hold of Babe's lower extremities and following along.

I hung up and went to help him—the smoke was thick, we were all coughing as the haze grew worse around us—and my next thought was that Babe was dead, asphyxiated before Sluggo had reached her. I used the next moment to throw the windows open; then Sluggo passed her to Pepe, who'd climbed out onto the fire escape.

It was freezing out there. I ran and dragged her fur coat from the closet and stuck my head out the window to wrap it around her. Sluggo snatched it out of my hands and threw it over her. Babe gave a low groan; my God, I thought, looking at the top of her wigless head as she stirred in his arms, she's nearly bald—hardly a normal reaction to the danger we all had been in. Then the door burst open and half a dozen firemen in rubber boots and helmets came clomping into the room with axes and the working end of a hose.

The captain said Babe had obviously fallen asleep with a cigarette, but I corrected him—she didn't smoke. It was the silk scarf over the light bulb. I moved aside as two firefighters dragged a smoldering queen-size mattress into the sitting room, followed by another man holding a limp Tiny.

"Dead?" I asked, taking it. He shrugged. I carried the dog into the hallway, where a clutch of curious hotel guests huddled in nightdress. Something told me the dog wasn't dead, and I opened its mouth and began blowing air down its throat.

"He's crazy," I heard someone say. "You can't give artificial respiration to a dog."

But I wasn't the crazy one, he was, for, to my relief, the dog revived. When its eyes were open and I saw that it was breathing regularly, I went to tell Pepe, only to discover that he and Sluggo had taken Babe down in a service elevator to a waiting ambulance.

When things had quieted down and we were assured that she was out of danger but would be spending the night at the hospital, the management found another room for me, small and smelling of fresh paint. I stayed up most of the time with the dog, and in the morning they brought my clothes and gear in on a trolley. By mid-morning the word came that planes were flying out of O'Hare and by afternoon I was winging my way to Cleveland, the next leg on my journey. I had left Tiny with Belinda, asking her to get the dog into Pepe's hands before they all left for California.

The night's events made the news; all anyone could talk about was the nocturnal rescue of Babe Austrian from the "deadly conflagration"— there'd been little fire—by "a trusted retainer." No mention of yours truly.

After Cleveland, I hit Detroit, and in the coldest of weathers I spent another week and a half making up for lost time and leap-frogging all over the Midwest, eventually arriving back in New York around mid-March. Perhaps a month had gone by when one morning I got a phone call from a secretary at my publisher's office. A Mr. Ventura had telephoned from Los Angeles and could I return the call as soon as possible? I wasn't eager to be back in touch with my friend Pepsi, but I was curious, so did as requested.

"Thank you for returning my call," Pepe said in those quincelike tones of his. And then he got to the point. "Do you think you'll be returning here any time soon? Miss A would like to see you as soon as you get back."

I said I had no plans for returning until the Fourth of July weekend. "Is she sick?"

"Not really. A few complaints, nothing major. But she'd like a word or two with you if you have the time."

I said to put her on, but was kept waiting until I was about to hang up.

"How ya doin'?" came the familiar question. I replied in the positive; how was she?

"Okay, don't worry about the Babe. Only I was wonderin', when are you comin' out? I got somethin' I want to talk to you about."

I told her my plans and there was another pause. "Why don't you tell me now?" I suggested, with neither an idea of what the problem was nor how I might help. It didn't matter anyway: she wouldn't discuss matters by phone, and by the time I arrived in July it would be too late. We said goodbye, but when I thought things over, I began to wonder. Her voice had sounded weak, not up to snuff at all, and I had a feeling something was amiss. It being convenient for me to leave in time for the Oscars, I altered my plans, closed up the apartment, and headed for the Coast.

The night of my arrival I called the penthouse to let Babe know I was here. Pepe, gracious as ever, thanked me, said he would find time for an appointment, and took my number.

I didn't hear a damn thing for three days!

I'd forgotten about her when I got the call, saying Miss A would be pleased to see me the next afternoon at one. It was a command performance, no doubt about it, and, wondering what the big secret was, I planned accordingly.

It's sometimes said that if walls could talk, there would be no need for books—talking walls would have it all. I hadn't been inside the walls of Babe's Sunset Towers penthouse since the time Dore and I had dropped off the script for Frankie. But before my last trip east, several times as I'd driven along the curves of the Strip I'd noticed moving vans parked in the vicinity of the Towers—tenants moving out, however, not in. There was a noticeable shabbiness cloaking the building.

This place is dying, I thought as I crossed to the elevator and pushed the button. The elevator had been automated now, there was no attendant, and I rode up in silence, wondering what I was to find at the top.

Arriving, I pushed the bell and heard the chimes. I waited, glancing out the small window to my right, to where the streams of cars tooled up and down the Strip, and I glimpsed the slanting roofs of the Villa Lorraine farther east. I turned back as the apartment door opened and I was greeted, not by Sugar May, as of old, but by Pepe Ventura himself.

He looked the same, though his hair was longer and his mustache darker. He was wearing a patterned shirt, tight pants, and huaraches, and the same diamond glinted in his lobe.

"Hello, come in, I'm glad you're here," he said all in one breath, and, closing the door, he ushered me into the living room. I passed through the draped archway and entered what surely was by now a museum. The long, low-ceilinged room was hushed and still, reeking of stale air and containing little light. Each of the venetian blinds was drawn; several lamps burned dimly. It was all very Miss Havisham, as if the clocks had been stopped at the marriage hour forty years before, and with the rats still eating at the seven-tiered wedding cake. The whole place was like a cocoon, a time capsule, everything perfectly, intimately maintained just as it had been, everything stuffed or preserved under glass. Babe had made this space her monument.

Everywhere my eye fell there were movie-star glossy stills of Babe Austrian, culled from different periods of her long career; the thirties, forties, fifties, sixties—the decades seemed to roll themselves out before my eyes, Babe in all her incarnations. Interspersed with these were photographs of other celebrities: Cole Porter was there, Claire Boothe Luce, Al Jolson, Bob Hope and Martha Raye, Anita Loos, and so on, the superfamous of this century. There were also a number of Frank's pictures set about on the tops of chests, and on the wall the twin portrait of Babe and Frankie; the two faces looked out at me with their quizzical expressions, and I wondered if they'd found whatever it was they were looking for. There were other, single oil portraits of Babe, one in the altogether, as well as the famous nude statue by Italo Foscari in its lighted niche.

"Please sit down," said Pepe, entering behind me with brisk steps. He waited until I sat, then disappeared through the archway, and I heard voices in muffled conference. I got up again and went to one of the windows to tip a bit more light in through the blinds. I sat again. Waited. All was quiet, except for the Strip traffic far below and the ticking of a mantel clock. I looked around. There was no dust on anything; the pillows were plumped; there were current magazines carefully aligned on the mirrored coffee table; the gold-veined mirrored walls had been cleaned up to a certain height (but no higher: a man's reach; beyond that the cleaner could or would not go, and the surface was smoky). I noticed a cobweb in a corner. I had never seen a deader room; it reminded me of one of those anterooms in a mortuary where you go to view the remains of the dear departed. I also noted the indentations in the carpeting, carpeting that had somehow stood the wear and tear of time, and now had the heavy imprint of somebody's sturdy ground-gripper shoes. Their corrugations seemed to go in all directions. Footprints in the rugs of time.

I turned as Pepe reentered. He motioned me to a small sofa in a curved window niche looking out onto the terrace, where I could see a profusion of plants and flowers. There was a hose, a watering can, some gloves on a table, and I wondered who did the gardening. I sat where he wanted me to and he took a place beside me.

"I really should apologize," he began. "I can understand how mystifying this probably is to you."

I replied that yes, it did seem strange; I was trying to get my bearings with him; he, too, seemed odd. I couldn't put my finger on it, but there was something different in his attitude.

He flashed his white teeth under his Pancho Villa mustache. "I'm not surprised. But I'm sure you'll understand when I tell you that these have been our instructions. It's not that we're trying to be dramatic or anything or withhold information, it's just that—it's how she wants it."

"Miss A, you mean?"

"Yes, Miss A. You've been asked here in order that she may speak with you about a matter of considerable importance."

Fine with me. "What matter? And what importance?"

"I'm afraid that's part of what I'm not allowed to tell you. She wishes to do it herself."

"All right, I have no objection. When may I see her?"

"I'm sure it won't be very long now. Outside of yourself in Chicago, she hasn't had any visitors 'at home,' so to speak, in a long time. She's very nervous over seeing you again. There are some—some things she wishes to tell you. She's felt the need for some time, but it's only lately that she's found the courage to do so. She's been waiting for your return."

I glimpsed the burly figure of Sluggo lurking in the background, as though looking for something to happen.

"Am I to gather from all this that she's ill?" I asked.

"Well . . . some problems. One or two, but things are relatively under control. And thanks for coming so quickly. I hope you'll be easy on her."

Now, what the hell did that mean? The whole scene struck me as hoaxy, silly as a frat-house initiation. Was this Babe's passion for elaborate staging? Maybe the reason for all the delay was that she was inside trying to paste herself together so she'd look her usual glamorous self—the long lashes, the red fingernails, the works. Well, I thought, she put me up in the blizzard, I owe her this.

As I went on waiting, I was reminded of that other afternoon, more than twenty years ago, when I'd sweltered waiting for this very same individual but under far different circumstances. Promptness might be the politeness of kings, but it was not of movie queens, current or ex. I could hear a faint tinkling sound, chimelike and slightly Oriental, as if at any moment Gale Sondergaard might step through a beaded curtain and stick a dangerous letter in my hand. Pepe was making small talk, the worst kind: had I seen the latest movie, what did I think of the lovely weather, wasn't there a lot more traffic on the Strip, how long would I be staying in town, had I spoken with Angie Brown? I mean *bor*-ing.

Then apparently it was time. He got up and asked me to come with him. "It's all right," he whispered as we got to the end of the hall, where there was a closed door, "you may go in. And please, I beg you—be kind to her."

Thank you, Deborah Kerr. Babe undoing the buttons on her blouse. I'll be kind. Yes, sure, although I wasn't sure just how kind I was prepared to be. My motor was running fast as I opened the door and walked in. I shut the door behind me and paused to take in the scene—Babe's scene. More Babe-stuff: crystal chandelier with a velvet sleeve over the chain, Austrian shades ruched all to hell and gone, satin-tufted chaise stuffed with pillows, soft piled rug, lots of satin, lots of swags, windows with the lambrequin treatment, the bed raised on a dais, hung with gauzy panels that fell from the high ceiling to the floor, and there in the bed a figure, our Babe, well bolstered against pillows, staring straight at me.

"Oh you son-of-a-bitch," I swore softly.

"Hello, luv," said Dore Screwball.

I mean it.
Him.
There.
In the bed.
Her bed. The bed of Babe Austrian, the dead Babe Austrian.
What the hell!
My first reaction was, what's that fool doing in her bed? He doesn't belong there. Then in another moment I realized that, whatever else he

was, this was no fool, that he was not in *her* bed but in *his*, and that he did, indeed, belong there. The balding head, fringed by sparse, short white hair. The features naked, without their makeup, no face paint anywhere in evidence. Just as I'd seen him at the chicken ranch. Wearing a bathrobe of maroon flannel, a perfectly ordinary-looking, by no means new, a many-wearings, comfortable garment, the hands with noticeably short fingernails, no polish, those tired blue eyes looking up at me, doubtful, rueful, entreating understanding, yet somehow filled with the old Dore-wickedness. I was torn between anger and the desire to laugh, so I laughed. Nothing else seemed right. I laughed.

"Hello, Dore, what's new?"

"Same old shit, ducks. What's new with you?"

It was surreal. Weird, man, weird. "Good to see you, Dore. Tell me, how long has this been going on?"

"Years, luv."

"Yuma? Torreon? Snake Bend?"

"That was in-between. Babe was 'on vacation.' Come sit. Take a load off."

Though he spoke in Dore's voice, it was still her line; it rang falsely —for the first time. I took the chair and sat by the corner of the bed. How ridiculous. How grotesque. How inconceivable. Was this Grand Guignol or Keystone Kops?

I damned my stupidity, telling myself I ought to have realized it sooner, should have known how I and the rest of the world were being duped. And for just how long? A magnificent job it was, this masquerade, this beauty of a hoax that had been pulled on me, on us all. But how? *How?*

We stared hard at each other, back and forth, he and I, wondering what to say. He reclined there in that ridiculous bed, against the piled pillows, like something out of a movie. Something quaint, bizarre, totally unlikely—and yet he lay back with such an indolent air of—of "Dore-ness." The master of every situation, particularly one so *outré* and thoroughly outrageous as this one. Gloria Swanson wasn't even close.

"I must say, you don't seem terribly surprised," he said, looking miffed. "I thought I'd nail you in your tracks when you walked in."

"Damned clever, these Chinese."

He grinned that lopsided, jack-o'-lantern grin of his. "I suppose you must be wondering why I've asked you here tonight." He delivered the line and laughed.

I had to admit, it was funny. I'm not sure if I mean funny ha-ha or funny finger-down-the-throat, but it *was* funny. Maybe you had to be there. *I* was there, trying to take it all in my stride.

"Well. Is this a bitch or isn't it?" Dore asked, a bit sheepishly, I thought.

I agreed that yes, it *was* a bitch. I'd been set up, and what a set-up. I seemed to regard him as though through the long end of the telescope, a far distance down a long tunnel of years—nearly a quarter of a century of offbeat, crazy recollections. I knew I'd been had at Torreon, and God knew elsewhere, him and his Aunt Bob—I knew Aunt Bob had to be in on this—him with his fried catfish and his cowboy horsebacking. My mind seethed with questions, the most burning of which was When. When had it begun? For how long was Dore Skirball Babe Austrian, or, more to the point, how long was Babe Austrian Dore Skirball? What was behind it all? The questions were endless; I wanted the answers, but somehow this didn't seem just the right moment.

One look had told me he was sick, sicker than he wanted me to know, or perhaps knew himself. If he wasn't precisely at death's door he was certainly in the neighborhood.

"How are you, really?" I asked.

"Not top of the heap, as any fool can plainly see. I've got the heartbreak of psoriasis, ducks, I think I'm going to pop off." He saw my look. "No, not today, Chazz. I'm likely to be around a bit longer. But I had something on my mind, something I wanted to consult with you about. Anyway, I thought it was time to straighten out one or two small details before I do pop."

There was a sudden wriggling under the covers, and a small head appeared: Tiny, the Chihuahua of recent fame; then she sprang altogether into sight, flew across the bed, tail wagging, and plopped in my lap, where she began jumping up, trying to lick my face, as though to thank me for reviving her in the Chicago fire.

Dore patted his thigh. "Tiny, do stop." The sound of his own, real voice recalled many scenes from earlier times, and I was happy to be hearing it. But I wasn't letting him off the hook so easily.

"I know one thing," I said. "I know how Miss Italy's going to die."

"Angie? How, love?"

"By my hand. I'm going to murder her for this."

Dore wagged his head. "I really don't think so, ducks," he said.

"Are you going to tell me she isn't in on this whole thing?"

"No, I'm not, but it's not her doing really. She's only involved because someone had to be, after Frankie went. I couldn't do it all alone, you know."

I was at my most sarcastic. "I suppose not. After Frankie got shot. And while we're on the subject, just what *does* Frank Adonis have to do with this?"

"As it happens, it was all his idea."

"Come on, Eve, this is Addison, remember?" No one was going to convince me of that. A hoax on this grand a scale? It wasn't Frank's style.

Dore was bristling. "If you don't want to believe me, okay, you can get the whole story from Madame La Zonga." He shouted through cupped hands. "Miss Italy, get your ass in here."

I was totally confused as the door opened and Angie Brown appeared on the threshold.

"What the hell's going on around here?" I demanded. "You were supposed to be playing tennis in the desert."

I heard that delicious laugh as she hurried to kiss me. "You darling," she said, her arms still around me in a bear hug. "Fancy seeing you like this."

I held her away from me and looked at her. "What's going on here anyway?"

She played the innocent. "I don't know what you mean, Chazz. Nothing's going on, that I know of. Oh—you must mean our little masquerade; is *that* what he means, Dore dear?"

"You'd better tell him. About Frank. He doesn't believe me."

"I don't know *what* to believe. I wish somebody would explain."

I sat down and Angie perched on the other corner of the bed. "Dore wasn't kidding, Chazz; it *was* Frank's idea. His and no one else's. He had to do it; otherwise he would have ended up with his head in a bucket of cement."

"But why?"

"Because of Babe. The *real* Babe."

"And the *real* Babe? Suppose we agree on where she's at these days."

"Dead," they said in unison.

I could see how eager he was to tell me the whole story, but I could also see that he was exhausted and that my being there was a strain on him. I decided to let explanations wait and get to the reason for my being summoned in the first place. Suddenly he seemed to shrink in the bed, and I could see he was deeply distressed by something, something more than the state of his health.

"What is it? Something to do with Babe?" I asked.

He nodded, but warily. "Maybe—maybe we better save it for later. Better yet, let Angie tell you."

I could see he was tired, so I sat back and listened to Angie explaining how the back tenant at North Cadman Terrace had turned himself into one of the greatest female performers of all time.

She really *had* died in Mexico, Babe: at Rosarita Beach, aboard the *Black Star*. There'd been a drunken argument between Ears Satriano and

Al "Vegas" da Prima. Trying to intervene, Babe had got herself caught by a bullet. "They dumped the body overboard and lit out for calmer waters. Frank flew down to identify the corpse. The minute he saw that it was Babe, he knew he was in hot water. The idea came to him all at once. Luckily there was Patsy. Patsy Doyle was the answer, and he saw how to pull the whole thing off."

"But why did he identify her as Patsy?"

"Because," Angie replied, "if he'd said it really *was* Babe, he was in trouble with some very nasty characters. Between them they'd put over a million bucks into a movie, *Camellia*. If Babe didn't do the picture, Frank was a dead duck. It was up to him to pull the chestnuts out of the fire. So he did."

"Good old Frank. But who's 'they'?"

"The boys, darling. The Vegas gang, friends of Bugsy's. They'd rubbed him out, they could do the same with Frank. *Dore* was the way out. So Frank got Patsy to lie low, then he dug up Patsy's husband—Snake-Hips—paid him to say the body was Patsy's and do a big number about avenging her death."

"Yeah, but what about Patsy? What became of her?"

"She took the money and ran. Quite a chunk, as a matter of fact; she and Snake really put the screws to Frankie. He was in hock to the banks for that one. But he made it up on Dore. Anyway, Snake got a job at a dog track in Miami, Patsy bought herself a beauty parlor, and they settled down."

I blinked. This was all so neatly carpentered, I couldn't believe it. Yet I had to. This was no time for lies; I knew I was getting the real feed. Angie went on: "And when everything was tied up neatly in Mexico, he flew straight over to Yuma and Torreon, where he met with Dore and persuaded him to try the stunt on."

"Some stunt," I said.

"It worked, didn't it?" Angie said. "He brought it off—they both did."

"But how?"

"Well, the first thing to do was to let everybody see Babe—Frankie's Babe. Right away, pictures had to be in the paper. So he called me to help Dore put a wardrobe together. He needed the wigs, the shoes, padding, the works."

"You did all that?"

Angie grinned. "Why not? For Frank *I'd* have played Babe."

"Dore's better," I said.

"Isn't he! He was fabulous, right from the start!"

Clever Frank, he hadn't let Dore show his face anywhere close to home, where discrepancies might have been noted by the ultra-keen. Frank got the idea of sending him as far away as they could manage. As soon as Dore showed up in Buenos Aires, he checked in at the Plaza—checked in as himself, but checked out as Babe Austrian. "And in the meantime," Dore said, sitting up in bed, "there was Rollo."

"Yeah, what about that number? Rollo of Argentina? The Tin King?"

"He wasn't any kind of king," Dore went on. Clearly, he was enjoying himself. "There wasn't any real Rollo. Rollo was just one more impostor in the game, some joker who owed Frank a favor and worked it off by playing Rollo. Paid to chase Babe and create those screwball scenes to keep my picture in the papers. Then, when he wasn't needed anymore, Rollo got sent home to show off his mustache and spats."

"Then what?"

"Frank got the biggest theatrical bookers in South America to book me on a tour," Dore said. "Babe's 'comeback,' as they called it. I played my way up to Rio, then to Mexico City, but no closer to home. Frank wouldn't let me come back to L.A."

"And *Camellia?*"

"That was a pretty sticky wicket. I wasn't ready to put my face on the silver screen. But *Camellia* went before the cameras, right on schedule."

"But wasn't that just what you feared? Closeups?"

"There *weren't* any closeups. If you look hard, you'll notice that the closeups on Babe come only when she's playing Madame La Zonga, the fortuneteller."

How many times had I seen *Camellia* over the years since it was made? Babe Austrian's "perfect" farce? But not Babe—Babe hadn't been within a country mile of that film. It was Dore's, all Dore's. Dore Skirball gave good Babe.

"He worked so hard," Angie said. "No one knows how hard he sweated."

I could imagine. Such a metamorphosis couldn't come about with a mere snap of the fingers. But what daring, what foolhardiness—and what an accomplishment.

"It's true," Dore said. "Every word."

"Just where did your Aunt Bob come in?"

"She refitted all of Babe's wardrobe for Dore," Angie said.

"So what about that deal in Torreon?"

Angie looked at Dore, then at me. "You can blame me for that. When you mentioned you wanted to go catch Dore's down-on-the-farm act I panicked. I thought sure we'd blow it. We had to make it look like he'd been living there for years."

"What about all that business of the bedroom? All the books and stuff."

"That wasn't my room," Dore said. "It was Bobbie's sewing room, I hadn't been there for ages. When Angie said you were coming, we got together a lot of stuff to make it look as if Dore *might* live there. Not very convincing, I'm afraid."

"You had me fooled. What I don't understand is—why did you go to all the trouble? Frank knew, Angie knew, why not me, too?"

Angie shook her head. "No. Sorry, Chazz, but Frank wanted it kept secret. He made us promise. Nobody was to know, not even you. Don't take it personally—the more who were in on the gag, the more chance of its getting out. And if it did, Frank would pay the price."

"You really loved him, didn't you?"

She smiled, and let it pass. "Now we're going to leave you, Dore." She got up and held out her hand to me. "Come on. We'll let Hot Stuff here get his rest like the doctor ordered. You'll see Chazz again," she told him and took me out. When she closed the door she sighed and leaned wearily against the wall. "Well, that wasn't as tough sledding as I'd feared. He's been awfully upset—having to tell you. None of this is easy on him."

"What is it? How sick is he?" I asked as we went along the hall.

"He puts on a good show, but"—she shrugged helplessly—"he's chuckablock with cancer."

"Isn't there anything to be done?"

"Nope."

Poor Dore. When I looked at my watch and mentioned that I was now three-quarters of an hour late for my lunch date, Angie grabbed my arm. "No, wait, you can't go yet. You still don't know why he wanted to talk to you."

She looked through some papers on a table and handed me a fancily engraved envelope.

"What's this?" I asked.

"It's a letter from the Board of Governors of the Comedy Hall of Fame, stating that it's been their unanimous decision to present Babe Austrian with its annual award. They want to induct her into the Hall of Fame."

"But that's wonderful!" I exclaimed.

"Yes, it's a real coup for him. But there's a hitch. They expect him to appear. In person. On television."

"Can't someone accept for him?"

"Of course. But he really *wants* to appear, only he's afraid to. He thinks it wouldn't be morally right. It's a question of ethics. He thinks if he just stalls it, he'll—"

"Have it awarded it posthumously?"

"Something like that." She held the kitchen door for me and I passed through, only to get clobbered by another shock. Sitting at the table were Pepe, Sluggo McGurk, a man I recognized as Waldo Dacey, Babe's long-time accompanist, and a fourth individual, a woman. She turned round in her chair and I was looking at Dore's Aunt Bob. She jumped up and gave me a big hug and kiss.

"Many's the time I've hoped to see you again, Chazz, but not like this. Well, you've had the whole story by now. What do you think?"

I hardly knew what to say. Aunt Bob had been in the city since the arrival of the award announcement, and along with the rest of Dore's cronies had been trying to persuade him to accept it.

"Don't you think he should?" she asked.

"Damn right he should. God knows he deserves it." It seemed we were all agreed on that.

"And God knows he was much funnier than she ever was," Waldo said staunchly. "He's been laying them in the aisles for twenty years. And his audience was a lot bigger than hers."

"I can vouch for that," I said, remembering his Chicago appearance when they all but tore the place apart.

"Then you should darn well go tell him," Aunt Bob said. "Persuade him to do it."

"Is this what he wanted to talk to me about?" I asked. Angie nodded.

"Only not today," she said. "He's exhausted. Come back tomorrow. Talk to him. He'll listen to you."

So I left, wishing I was as sure of my powers of persuasion as Angie was. I'd never known Dore Skirball to listen to anybody.

And there you have it. Or, rather, there *I* had it. In spades. Was ever anything trickier pulled on us, all of us who believed—however little— in the truth of things, in the world's being round, in water's being two parts of hydrogen, one of oxygen, in the Trinity, the Seven Seas, Nine Muses, Twelve Apostles, and fifty-four American presidents? And one, count him, one Dore Skirball? Oddball. Screwball, too, don't forget, a real nut-burger. This clever fellow we'd been cozened and duped by, for how many years? By "we" I mean me and all the millions of others who were taken in by this incredible piece of trickery.

He really made me feel like a jackass. I kept going over all the clues that had lain there but I hadn't been smart enough to pick up on, all the times he'd deliberately fooled me—like the trip to Torreon and the Cowboy Bill scene.

Yes, we'd been duped, but I decided we'd better make the best of it, because there was nothing that was going to change the facts; and let me state it emphatically, *these are the facts*. No mistake, not the least possibility of error. And what conclusion is to be drawn from them? What theories to be posited, what to be deduced? This grotesque transfiguration, this Dr Jekyll into Miss Hyde (she never married, Babe; of course "she" never married). Marvin Breckenridge (Myra to *you*) had recourse to the scalpel, you'll remember, but the transformation of Dore Skirball into the fabled Babe Austrian, while less surgical, was far more effective in the long run, a psychological alteration that owed more to art than a snip-snip and some adroit needlework in a high-priced Scandinavian clinic. Physical scars had he none; yet as to the mental variety, I'm not so sure—or rather, I am *most* sure; he had them aplenty. Dore Skirball was to all intents and purposes a nonentity, born in the dun countryside of the Texas Panhandle, the dude who emerged not a butterfly, but a moth. Yet talented, so talented. Never had a lesson, never a coach, yet he had created out of that reservoir of talent an extraordinary being; for all that, he was that show-biz oddity, a drag queen. Worse, he had been pleased—almost until the end—to let his incredible masquerade pass unnoted by all but a handful of his fellow beings, and those few pledged to secrecy.

Yes, Dore Skirball had done something no other man had done in the entire history of show business. He had successfully taken the place of a female performer, had impersonated her onstage and off for years, and no one the wiser. I thought how difficult it was for most people to lead just one life with any degree of satisfaction, and then I thought how really difficult it must have been for him to lead two. While he may have enjoyed playing Babe at given times, especially the onstage ones, certainly he couldn't have wanted to be her *all* the time. Yet what choice had he? If ever a bed had been made that would have to be slept in, this was it. How taxing, to live day after day, month after month, year after year, under such circumstances. Very wearing, being a full-time Babe.

Plainly, it had been what Dore had wanted going in, but coming out, I'm not so sure. Nobody ought to get the idea that he'd ever *become* Babe —this wasn't the old movie gag where the dummy takes over the ventriloquist. Playing Babe had brought him two things, the glory he'd always craved and the opportunity to display his talent, plus enough money to keep himself in the manner to which he'd always wanted to become accustomed.

But in playing Babe, Dore had become a walking, talking self-denial. In acting out that role he had abandoned himself while creating his own myth, and in so doing had become the prisoner of that myth. The Frankenstein doctor's brainchild had grown into a monster, awesome and grim in its towering force, much more than some Karloffian movie creature with a steel bolt through the neck and a stitched-on forehead.

Now a party to this outrageous secret, I undertook to get to know him better, this masquerader, Dore Skirball. Yet, looking back, I find I never really got to know him at all, and I wonder if he wasn't unknowable to everyone, friends and strangers alike. I realize he was of a far more serious makeup than I recalled his being back in the zany days of the Petit Trianon, but, then, as we grow older we all find out how much more serious life is, or we should. If he'd once been a gay spirit, in the true sense of that word, he'd become a sober citizen in the years that had intervened. Funny, yes, witty, outrageous, yes, all those, but he'd seen enough of life to know just how earnest a proposition it really was.

Now, having lived the life of Babe Austrian, he was faced with dying his own death, the death of Dore Skirball. And though he appeared to be facing it with equanimity, I had doubts. Equanimity and mortality seldom go hand in hand; rather, they're mutually exclusive. However serene one may appear to be on the surface, there must be inner turmoil, regret, remorse, the deadening realization of things left unfinished or never begun, all skillfully hidden.

Still, Dore presented an admirable façade—if that's what it was. He seldom spoke of his wasting disease; he tried as best he could to behave as if it weren't wearing him down, even though his deterioration was perfectly obvious to all of us.

His secret remained a well-kept one. Of the living, only Aunt Bob, Angie, Sluggo, Pepe, Waldo, and myself were aware that the entity who inhabited the penthouse premises in the Sunset Towers was not that legendary show-business personality and star, Miss Babe Austrian, but, rather, the former chair upholsterer, female impersonator, and all-round Krazy Kat. That's how it was, and nothing was going to change that, not while Dore Skirball lived.

In the weeks that followed, I never heard him complain. He maintained a steadfast air of muted resignation, as if he'd had his fun and regretted none of it. Now time was running out and he would go gently into that good night. But afterward? What was to happen then? Was his outrageous secret to be carried with him to the grave? Would the world never learn that someone else, a male, had inhabited the person of the great star whom the public had known for fifty years as Babe Austrian?

I went back to the Towers and joined Angie in trying to convince him that there was nothing wrong in his accepting the award. I knew how important it was to him, but he had developed a bad case of nerves, as if he thought that to appear again as Babe in front of an audience might somehow expose the masquerade and hold him up to public ridicule. Because of his illness, to get up and be Babe again was going to drain him, and he was terrified of failing. His anguished expression was terrible to see. "But how?" he moaned. "How?"

"How what?" I returned with a studied show of nonchalance.

"How can I? Go? To the thing? How?"

"That's what Cinderella asked," Angie said.

"I know, fairy godmother, very funny."

"I'll tell you how," I said, deciding to talk turkey. "You get your ass out of that gauze cocoon you're lying in and you put on your drag—no, not just any old drag, I mean your highest drag, the very tip-top beaded drag, you put on your Tina Louise shoes and your Marie Windsor fall and your Grace Kelly gloves and all your diamantés, and you get yourself all cranked up—you take a deep breath and you simply go, that's how."

"God damn it, I can't."

"Why not?"

He began to blather and blabber and we sat there listening while it all came out. He couldn't possibly appear because the award was meant for Babe, not for him; the real Babe, not the fake. Babe was dead and he, Dore, was a fraud and how could he go and accept it when it wasn't his, it was hers, and he wasn't her, he was him, and she was Babe, and when he had to face Lucille Ball, Queen of Comics, in front of a TV camera and accept the award as if it were hers he meant his—it was too much.

"Bullshit," pronounced Angie and let him have it. "Look, pismire, you've been fooling everyone for years, and a good job, too—nobody ever tumbled, not even in Chicago, when Sluggo was dragging you out of the presidential suite and you didn't have a face on or a wig or anything but your own jockey shorts. Then was the time you should have been scared, but you weren't. Not for yourself, and not for being discovered. Fraud? Sure, if you want. But Dore gives good fraud, remember? Nobody better. Chazz is right; you haul your ass out of bed and get your act together."

Still he protested. "But I didn't earn it—it's not mine, I tell you."

"And we say it is! Maybe yours more than hers. Think about that.

Anyway, she's not here to get it. But you are. And while it seems not to have occurred to you at all, there's one person you ought to be thinking about right now."

"Oh God, don't tell me, let me guess. The Virgin Mary. Pope John the Twenty-third. Alaric the Hun. Peaches Browning. Mickey Mouse. Madonna."

"Don't be an idiot. You know who I'm talking about. And if Frank is the one who snared you into this life of deception to begin with, think how he'd feel, knowing you were being offered a place in the Hall of Fame for it all. It's a first, a real first. Frankie would love it. He's up there looking down and saying, That shithead gets the plum and hasn't even got the guts to pick it."

Dore shot his brows. "Somehow I tend to doubt that Frankie is 'up' anywhere looking down. Still . . ." He frowned and bit his cuticle while he thought. "I suppose you're right; Frankie would be mad. And I'd be an asshole. How often does a broad—or should I say fraud—ever get this laid on him?"

"Her."

"If you like. It's still confusing."

"Will you do it?"

"I have to sleep on it."

"You've already slept on it. Yes or no?"

His expression brightened. "All right, ducks, let's do it. There remains, however, the question of wardrobe. In the words of Marie Antoinette, I haven't a thing to wear."

I scoffed. "You've got a closet full of rags in there. Whatever happened to that gold lamé?"

"The Claire Regrett? You must be crazy—my Claire would never fit me now."

He was referring to his weight loss. It was his illness that kept getting in the way. I tended to forget this was a dying case, that the Dore—or Babe, rather—the one I'd seen in Chicago, was not the same person. This was a sixty-year-old man who'd bought his ticket for the Big Drag Show in the Sky and was soon to be on his way. Yet for now, just now, the last now he'd ever know, it all had to come off smooth as silk. Angel cake frosted with Dream Whip.

In the annals of filmdom the rites of passage from this world to the next are often accompanied by extravagant, even bizarre, obsequies. On film, a plump, crazed movie fan tears off the veil of Mrs. Norman Maine and

Janet Gaynor shrieks and faints in the arms of Adolphe Menjou. Norma Desmond in tapestried lamé has Eric Von Stroheim inter her pet chimpanzee in the rose garden. Trench-coated and dry-eyed, Humphrey Bogart watches Ava Gardner buried, bare feet and all, amid a sea of black umbrellas in the Tuscan countryside. Offscreen it's much the same: Hollywoodites like to bid adieu to their dear departed with richest pomp and no little circumstance; a really top drawer funeral will pull a score of limousines, easy; maybe forty or even fifty. A horde of devotees falls upon Campbell's Funeral Parlor on New York's upper Madison Avenue, where Judy Garland is coffined and blanketed under gardenias, though there's no dough to lay her away. At other funerals the called-upon stand up at the mike and say kind things about people they hated. As a wag once said when the services were packed for an unloved movie mogul, "Give 'em what they want and they'll all turn out for it." The histrionics of the grief-stricken Pola Negri at Rudy Valentino's funeral were nothing compared to those of Claire Regrett at Frank Adonis's, and while today we don't seem to have anyone prostrating himself over the Lucite coffin of the departed Miss Austrian (I have to tell you, the glass coffin bit was all Dore Skirball's own idea; he claimed it was the Snow White coming out in him), but I've been noticing the Instamatics clicking all over the place.

Yes, we're back at *that* funeral again: several Babe-mourners have had their photos snapped at the head of the corpse, braving the glare of those shining locks. You can't blame her fans for wanting to memorialize the moment—how often does a Babe Austrian die? Well, in this instance twice, if you get what I mean—but this is a special case. I'll say this for Babe, repose becomes her.

There's this woman, a real looneytune, her name is Sarah Walsomething, her whole damn life is funerals, nothing but funerals. She spends her every waking hour either going to funerals or scaring them up. The obituary page in the *Los Angeles Times* is her Bible. She doesn't subscribe to the paper, nor does she ever buy it; she grubs it out of trash cans and is reputed to spend endless hours jotting down the names of the deceased, the time of burial, and the location. She particularly enjoys reading the obits in *Variety* and *The Reporter*, for here the names of the Hollywood famous are more likely to be found.

To read ". . . Burial plans pending" annoys Sarah no end. She wants to know where they're being buried and when. The more famous, the harder she tries. She's even been heard to say that when Garbo dies, she plans on flying all the way to New York to be on hand for the burial. I have a hunch about that: I don't think Garbo will want a public display. But right now I'm wondering if she's here—not Garbo, Sarah whosis—

here at Babe's funeral. I mean, this thing is something to tell your children about. You want to write home about this one. They'd never believe it in Keokuk.

And what wouldn't Sarah give to know the truth? If she reads this she'll shit little green bugs. Is it really to be believed, that over there in that glass—plastic?—box lies the earthly remains of Babe Austrian a.k.a. Dore Skirball? I mean, how Monogram can you get?

I know that when what I've written here gets around, the cat will be out of the bag for sure. I told Dore I wasn't much interested in cats and bags, but he made me promise. It was part of the deal: if he got up there and accepted the award from Lucy Ball, I'd write the whole thing down, start to finish. And I have. There's no guarantee they'll print this, of course, but there's always the chance.

To the last he did a bang-up job. Really sensational. He was a super riot at the Comedy Hall of Fame thing, he had them rolling in the aisles. Gave them "Windy City Blues," a little "I'se A-muggins boomp-dah-de-ah-dah." The voice cracked once, but only once, and it never fazed him for a second. He just plowed right on through to the end. Ethel Merman nerves, that's Dore.

Th-th-that's all, folks! Time to get back to the old drawing board. Let's hear it for Hollywood Memorial. Bye, Bob; bye, Phyllis; bye, Dean. The media are interviewing Hope. "One of the really true show-business greats," I hear him proclaiming. I squeeze Angie's elbow as we pass; she stifles a snigger. "Truer words were never spoke," says Aunt Bob.

As we wend our way along to the parking lot we hear the carillon ringing, its clear, silvery notes that float out across the green grass, their sound reminding me of something Dore once said about Claire Regrett: being married to her must be like being married to Saint Patrick's Cathedral, because she clanged so loudly—"usually on the hour."

Ding-dong ding-dong. *Pax vobiscum,* Babe.

Belinda

I think I had always been a little in love with Belinda Carroll, or something akin to love. What name do you put to the passionately inchoate feelings of a thirteen-year-old for a young screen goddess recently discovered by him? So it was for me, back in the late thirties when her newly fledged career was just sort of bumbling along and I first saw her in *Honey Brewster*. In the next few years I and thousands of others like me watched her shed the last of her baby fat, grow breasts, find her waistline, lighten her locks, drive a sports roadster with wire wheels and balloon tires, wear an angora sweater, put flowers in her hair, and dance the rhumba. I applied myself zealously to Belinda-watching, and since I loved her desperately, I looked for a way to advertise my feelings.

One winter the cellar of our modest Dutch-colonial house flooded. This was weird, its flooding, when we lived on a hill, but there it was, water up to the knees of the Kelvinator washer, and when those waters receded, plumbers had to be brought in to do some work. When they left, there was a small patch of wet cement, some twelve by twelve inches, on the floor. On a whim I took a large spike and with loving care inscribed the initials B.C. over my own, with a plus sign in between, and enclosed the whole with a crudely drawn heart.

In those days there were three prime beauties in Tinseltown, three MGM beauties. Garbo was going or gone, likewise Claire Regrett, but there were Hedy Lamarr, incredible creature, Lana Turner, ditto, and Belinda Carroll. All three were favorite pin-up girls during the war, along with Columbia's Hayworth and Fox's Grable, but though the war was to bring me into contact with several stars, there was nothing doing with Belinda. I never laid eyes on her for another ten years.

I remember the first time I ever saw her in the flesh. It was at North Cadman Place, soon after I first went out to Hollywood to try my luck. I was waxing my surfboard in the alley, and when I heard a car behind me I turned to see this big white Caddy barreling along, kicking up a cloud of dust. The car screeched to a halt, and she stood up in it and grinned at me, this blonde creature in an angora sweater and a scarf tied cowboy style around her neck. "Hi, Charlie," she calls like we're old friends, "can I leave my jalopy here a sec?" She jumps out and hustles upstairs to Angie's. Then I hear them giggling up there and after a moment Angie hangs her head over the windowsill and says, "She wants to know if you're married."

I say to ask Jenny.

But I hurried my wax job along and when I went in again Angie's apartment was quiet; they'd gone off somewhere in her car, which was always parked out front on the street, while the white Caddy stood blocking the alley. The keys were in the ignition, so I moved it—one more movie star was nothing to the Beverly Hills cops—and I held on to the keys so she'd have to come and get them. When she came, it was Jenny who handed them over; I was in the shower. But she got the picture that I was married.

She's had a sad life, a rotten life in a lot of respects. Not many girls would have survived all the crap she went through in the forty-odd years since Frankie discovered her—the men, the binges, the nightclub fracases, the jails, the headlines—the murder—the comebacks, one two three comebacks, each one historical, each one again proving that you can't keep a good girl down.

The Belinda of today is hardly the Belinda I first fell for; of course she's not, none of us is the same as we were so many years ago. But though so greatly altered, she still has that same spark, that wonderful glow, that magical, impalpable Thing that made her a star. After everything else was burned away in the crucible, what remained was pure gold, and that's Blindy today, pure gold.

Claire Regrett was a self-made creation. She invented herself, and when one model went to the junkheap, a new model quickly appeared in its place, auto-incarnated, more modern, more streamlined, more in tune with the times. Claire was the phoenix, arising to new life from the hot ashes of its own immolation, feathers intact, her song renewed.

Belinda was another story. Belinda was nearly always the same; the basic model saw a few changes, a bit of updating, maybe a few of the latest attachments, but it was always the same—Belinda, through and through. Claire went on for nearly forty years, like Old Man Moses, and when she was done she was done and that was it. After her last vampire movie she pulled the plug on her career and curled up in her Manhattan penthouse and died. Belinda's still going strong, though, and she's not about to curl up anywhere unless it's on a Chesterfield sofa. If you could see her you'd know she's happy; she's put the past where it belongs, in the past, and bygones are all bygones. She may not always have been the most sensible girl, but she's fairly practical now; I might even say she's sage.

It was Frankie, of course, Frankie who made her. Belinda Carroll was really his creation, though many people still don't realize how much his creation she was. He loved her in a way that was so special, he had such high regard for her; even at her very worst he seldom got mad at her, the way he did with Babe or Claire or Frances or any of the rest—except April, of course; April was always that special case, wasn't she? But Frank discovered Belinda, got her established, had her trained; he even thought up her name—Belinda after Belinda Cox, a girl he'd known in high school, Carroll from Madeleine Carroll, the stately blonde English actress; he put up with her stage mother of all stage mothers, Eunice, who never received anything but good from Frank and who never paid him back in kind; he took Belinda to Metro, saw her set there, then because of her mother's machinations saw her booted out, only to make them take her back again. He found the Honey Brewster series for her, convinced the studio brass that she was a lot more than just another pretty face, a nice pair of boobs, then later saw her through so many of her troubles, her broken romances, her downslides, her vicious bout with alcoholism in the sixties, all the troubles that came from her fatal desire to do herself in any way she could manage it.

Frank was Belinda's storm anchor through so many years, the person who understood her best and who never stopped trying to make something wonderful of her. He did it, too. The shame is, he never lived to see her at the pinnacle she at last attained. Today she's retired, she's a hausfrau; all her homemaking instincts finally emerged—she makes scrap quilts, she sews baby clothes (for other women's babies), she does charity work ("The Frank O. Adonis Foundation for the Underprivileged of New York"), she leads the life of a solid citizen. No, no, she has no plans to return to the screen.

The lady who lives in Manhattan now and lunches and leads a useful, prosperous, happy life is a far cry from the twelve-year-old kid who was discovered singing pentecostal hymns outside the Four-Square Gospel Temple across from Echo Park in downtown Los Angeles. Leave it to Eunice Apper to be a devotee of Aimee Semple McPherson—Aimee, who couldn't keep her hands off the buttons on a man's fly if she tried. There was some kind of service going on inside; this was on Good Friday of the year 1935—historic date—and Frank had been downtown for a court proceeding. He happened by in his new car and saw this kid on the corner; she even had a tambourine in her hand; there was a small crowd around her and she was belting out "Nearer My God to Thee" as if she were going down on the *Titanic*. He tore around the block to check her out again, then parked and went over to speak to her, found out her name and that she'd been singing nearly all her life. She had that golden hair and those cornflower-blue eyes and he liked her manner. She was pretty, she was merry, she was ingratiating—she had STAR written across her forehead. He asked her the sixty-four-dollar question, would she like to be in the movies? Sure, why not? came the reply. He had a camera and was grabbing off a couple of shots when here came this broad-hipped Valkyrie flying down the steps, flailing at him with her pocketbook. That was Eunice, her mother, off to a bad start.

Eunice was a holy terror, and much has been written about the way she pushed her talented daughter, pushed hard at all the people who had her best interests at heart, how she finally got herself barred from the MGM lot, attempted to influence the child's career through a highly unsatisfactory home life, and in the end produced the neurasthenic teenager who thought life on a dance floor was much more important than life lived on the square. At sweet eighteen Belinda was already a frequenter of the Sunset Strip nightclubs, of which there were many in those days, and since she was past the age of consent nobody could do a thing about it. Unless it was Louis Mayer himself, who talked until he was blue in the face, though in the end even his fatherly pats did no good.

While it was Frank who'd brought Belinda to MGM, it was Sam Ueberroth who'd kept her there, even after her option was nearly allowed to lapse (at a drop of the hanky by Miss Claire Regrett; at that time they were still listening to Claire). Upon learning that Belinda was on her way out, Sam rushed from his offices on the other side of the lot straight to the Thalberg Building, where, the story goes, he shed real tears before the mighty L.B., pleading with him not to drop the girl, and threatening that if she was let go, he, too, would leave: he would take her to Universal or some such place and make her a bigger star than Deanna Durbin. L.B. never liked hearing about Deanna Durbin, who had slipped through his fingers but whom he always regarded as rightfully an MGM property, and while he had his Mickey and his Judy and his Lana, he thought again and had his secretary, the all-powerful Ida Koverman, call down to Casting and rescind the fatal pink slip.

The moviegoing public had already been treated to Judy Garland's sentimental singing of "You Made Me Love You" to an 8×10 glossy of Clark Gable in a *Broadway Melody* picture, but when Belinda Carroll danced with a dummy of Fred Astaire, audiences applauded the screen. This was in the justly noted Technicolor dream sequence from *The Prince and the Chambermaid*, when Sissie the chambermaid falls asleep in the royal suite and dreams that she's Ginger Rogers and that a mannequin in white tie and tails is Fred. Where did she learn to dance, this little girl of so many talents? A dance director taught her on her lunch hours, in the alley; she was learning camel walks and buck-and-wings between her Studies of the Ancient World and her English grammar.

Frank later confessed to me that he'd been awarded a secret bonus by Mayer himself for bringing Belinda into her own, with an extra five grand tossed in just for thinking up her name. Frank guided her career for nearly forty years and was responsible for most of her hits; but there was more than that to the picture, as we all know. The morning after Frank had been killed, when the papers were full of the thing, people liked to remember how Belinda Carroll had had that girlhood crush on him, her discoverer.

"I'll never marry anyone else," she was quoted as saying back then. "I don't care how much older he is, I want him to wait for me to finish growing up."

Schoolgirl crush, yes; but a bad one, very serious for her. It lasted for quite a few years, and if Frank had been in any way inclined to wait for her to mature, who knows what might have happened? When she was sixteen, he gave her a silver heart studded with baby diamonds, and she wore it for years. She saved every card, note, telegram he ever sent her, and had as many pictures of him as fans had of her in their collections. To her, the goddess, Frank was a god—Zeus, highest on Olympus, whose dark head was always surrounded by golden clouds.

Later on, when she was grown and Eunice was causing her all that unnecessary misery, Frank would be her sometime escort at one affair or another—this was before he married Frances, and it didn't hurt for him to be seen with his own discovery on his arm—but Eunice hated it. She detested the man, mainly because he'd wrested away from her any control over Belinda; but of course by that time it was too late, the damage was done.

Those were Belinda's plum years, the apple-pie years in which she made her fullest mark as that juicy, fruity blonde, that luscious creature from whose cherry lips "the honey fairly dripped." In those mad forties Sunset Strip evenings when the beat was Latin and the hips and asses swung in jungle prints on white crepe and the girls all wanted to look just like her, she was It. I mean *It;* Clara Bow couldn't hold a candle, and forget Ann Sheridan and her "oomph," whatever that was. There was Blindy-baby fanning her pretty tail around the floor at the Trocadero while the gardenia in her hair wilted and she danced with Ty and Hank and Butch and Bob and the rest of the wolfpack, little dreaming that, like the Trocadero itself, her life would become just another parking lot. Of course, it was the famous "Honey" pictures that did it—that Louis B. blend of vanilla milkshake, all-American-girl sex and flunked algebra —that really launched Belinda into the big leagues. This is interesting because the author of the first "Honey" script was none other than Frankie Adonis himself. The movie Honey was his creation, he drew the pattern of the character to fit Belinda's shapely shape, the role was surefire. (True, *Honey*'s were programmers, along with the Hardy pictures and the *Dr. Kildare*'s and the *Maisie*'s before them, but like those series, these were immensely popular. They were also Louie Mayer's pets. He adored the character of Honey, who was the world's great innocent, with that baby voice and those big blue eyes, the way she batted her lashes and showed off that glorious fanny. She was every guy's dreamgirl, and even before she'd become a full-fledged star, G.I.s were making her their favorite pin-up.)

People used to say she was just another dumb Hollywood tootsie cast in the dimwitted mold, but people would learn to eat their words. Maybe she wasn't a brain like Myrna Loy; what education she had she'd got at the studio school, but when it came to the abc's, she had something the customers were buying, and she put it all in a stack of angora sweaters two feet high.

When her life, personal and professional, began coming apart at the seams, no one was sadder than I, though what happened took on a quick, knifelike inevitability. No one that joyful and bursting with the juice of youth could have avoided being one more movieland statistic; she was in love with life, Romance was her courtier, illusion the pillow where she laid her pretty head. She was the girl of any man's dreams; she attracted men the way molasses gets flies. She was also the natural prey of unscrupulous males, and this was her lifelong problem. No—her *real* problem was in making up her mind among all her husbands and boyfriends and lovers, the ones she wanted and then didn't want and then wanted again, then didn't after all. It probably sounds crazy to say she was a one-man woman, but I really believe that way down deep she was, right from the beginning. The man, naturally, was Frank Adonis, only the two of them didn't know it; or maybe she did and he didn't. He was older, but not that much. She told me once that the other men in her life were only interludes, Frank was the main event, he was what she'd always really wanted. And I can believe it, even in the face of all the rest that happened.

What she most wanted was to be loved, really and truly loved. She craved love. She reached out for it everywhere she went, and when she was without it she went looking for it, often in all the wrong places.

She found it, of course, in Frank. I always thought she did. After that wild and restless careering around the movie curves, that long and fruitless search, all those scary romantic collisions she kept having over twenty-five, no, thirty years, to find everything she'd been looking for in Frankie Adonis, man of her dreams—there were palpable ironies involved there, and worse ones later, when he lay dead on a slab in the morgue and she'd lost him for all time.

He'd been first and he'd been last, first among the many, last above all. And,.in between, the others: no. 1 Dick Pritchard, no. 2 Perry Antrim, no. 3 Grant Potter, no. 4—well, no. 4 would have been Frankie if Frankie'd ever made it.

Everybody says Dick was a real sweetheart of a guy, would have made her a terrific mate—if she hadn't been an up-and-coming movie star and he hadn't been killed. Dick, alas, was short and sweet. She met him on a Government Bond Tour; they got married in Chicago when Eunice wasn't around; she followed him back to the training base and lived with him in the married men's barracks. Then she followed him to another base and lived in a Quonset hut; then she followed him to San Francisco and waved her hanky while he shipped out through the Golden Gate. Afterward she went back home, cried her eyes out, made peace with Louis B. and the studio. They stuck her in *Honey Goes to Mexico,* last in that series. She announced she was pregnant and Hedda said she was knitting booties, hoping for a boy. Dick Junior. Louis B. himself flew south with the bad news: Dick's PBY had been downed in the Lingayen Gulf.

She had to be sedated, she swore she didn't want to live, then she miscarried. Production on the movie location shut down, Honey finished going to Mexico on the Culver backlot, but there was no fiesta. Louella called her "Movieland's most tragic widow." Louis B. got one of his hot ideas and they came up with a script called *Wartime Widow,* the poignant story of a poignant small-town girl who poignantly faces widowhood, mostly in poignant black, until Young Doctor Malone moves onto the block and things lighten up. Van Johnson was the doc, and he carried the real-life widow to even greater heights of stardom. Black-and-white, made for 250 thou, big grosses, opened at the Capitol on Broadway, she did PA's nationwide, sold lots of bonds, got voted "Girl We Most Want to See Victory In With," forget the syntax.

In 1945, after the German collapse in France, they sent Perry Antrim home as one of the nation's most decorated heroes. Frank and Frances Adonis gave a party in his honor and the whole town turned out in best bib and tucker. Belinda was on hand. "I took a look at all that fruit salad and I just flipped," she was quoted by Ruthie Waterbury in *Photoplay.*

Having allowed her to admire his ribbons, Perry drove her home. She invited him in; they sat in the sunporch and necked until Eunice came down and threw him the hell out. "My little girl is still widowed," she informed Perry, pushing him toward the front door, "and she doesn't put out for servicemen, I don't care how many goddamn ribbons you got."

On the weekend Belinda kissed Eunice goodbye and went off—she said—to Catalina on a fun cruise with some friends. Actually she headed for Union Station, boarded the Lark for San Francisco, and en route was joined to Perry Antrim in the legal bonds of holy matrimony, standing up in the club car with Frankie Adonis and Angelina Brown for witnesses. Whom God hath joined together let no man put asunder. They honeymooned at the St. Francis and made every paper in North America. Eunice wept like Lot.

Now, forty years later, Perry Antrim remains that same glamorous figure whose name and face ring in the memory, reminding us of our lost youths and of the other great adventurers of that same generation, Lindbergh, Wiley Post, Richard Halliburton. As Hollywood's Crown Prince, heir to that great family of actors, whose likeness appeared regularly in the magazines from the day of his birth, he acquired that permanent ermine-tipped mantle of fame and glory that few may wrap themselves in. When Lucky Lindy set his *Spirit of St. Louis* down in Paris, Perry was only a boy, hiking at Yosemite (American rotogravures of the period show him perched on the top of Half Dome after scaling its granite face), a boy who enjoyed sports, especially sailing—when he was fourteen his father had bought him the *Guinevere*, that trim sloop which at twenty he traded in for the *Maude*, which he took round the world, visiting celebrated figures and heads of state.

When Belinda married Perry, he was the all-American warrior, the most talked-about and decorated hero of the war. At this time nobody had even heard of Audie Murphy, while the whole world knew who Perry Antrim was; they knew almost everything there was to be known about him—twenty years of Perry-watching had informed anyone who cared to know what he ate for breakfast (hot oatmeal, a banana, raisin-cinnamon toast), what he wore to bed (flannel pajamas), what his favorite color was (blue, like his mother's eyes), his favorite song ("Red Sails in the Sunset").

He kept on making headlines—right up to the end of his life, and after. From the grave he came back in black-and-white 5.0-pica print. That time he'd disappeared for good, and it was one of the saddest tales ever told, how the famous playboy-explorer went up the headwaters of the Oroyocco and never came down again until they brought his head out of the jungle, shrunk to the size of a croquet ball. I know you remember the grisly story that swept the nation in '54, but no one knows to this day if it was true that the head was indeed Perry's, even though the man who brought it out guaranteed its provenance when he tried to sell it to Perry's widow.

If Perry Antrim were alive today, as his mother was until only a few years ago, how many tales would he have to tell about his exploits, his adventures, his travels, his many meetings with the famous of the world? I always thought *The Seven Pillars of Wisdom* read like Little Orphan Annie compared to *Olympus Crowned* and *Letters from My Raft*, Perry's two most popular books.

No wonder the ladies were dazzled by him—what didn't he have? Background, fame, prestige, money, brains, looks, and an intrepidness not to be seen short of the exploits of Paul Bunyan. For a girl, to have grown up in the thirties was to have been charmed and fascinated from afar by this young god, and for a lad who'd never stepped in front of the camera —movie acting wasn't for him, he said—Perry Antrim was every bit as famous as Jackie Cooper or Mickey Rooney. For a decade and more, pictures of him had appeared regularly, Perry on the back of his famous horse, Ready-Go, aboard the *Guinevere*, performing prodigious feats with his archery set or his rifles, boxing with one of the professional pugilists his father had picked out for him to spar against, or showing some famous visitor or other through his equally famous "Playhouse."

As anyone over fifty knows, this Playhouse, so-called, was every bit as celebrated as the individual for whom it had been created. It was an amusing conceit of Crispin Antrim's that his son should be provided with a magical kingdom of his own on the grounds of Sunnyside, a boy's playhouse as might be imagined by some great artist. Consequently the building called "the Lodge," which had been built by the original owner as a guesthouse, was revamped into a boy's idea of heaven. The walls had been frescoed by Howard Chandler Christy in fanciful visions of castles with golden turrets flying scarlet pennants, broad green moors where silver-mailed knights jousted with lances before their ladies fair, a forest where Robin Hood robbed the rich to give to the poor, and where a rainbow arched across a vault of sky painted cerulean blue. From the carved beams were hung bison heads and the horns of moose and stags, there was an indoor slide from the second story to the first, there was a billiard table (gents shot pool, gentlemen played billiards), and in the lower room, surrounded by mullioned windows set with panes of colored glass, was a wide, deep window seat where a boy could loll over picture books containing tales of pirates and buried treasure or of balloon flights to the face of the moon. The Playhouse sat perhaps three hundred yards from the main house, and it was here that Perry always claimed he had spent his happiest boyhood hours. And it was here, to the Playhouse, that he brought his first bride, Claire Regrett, following their elopement. The house was enlarged, a kitchen was installed, as well as a nursery, and it was there that Claire, unaware of what lay in store, was obliged to live cheek by jowl with her in-laws. An impractical arrangement, for the couple did little more than sleep there; their real, practical life was lived at a three-hundred-yard remove, over at the big house, where the currents of the outer world stirred the curtains and Aldous Huxley and Stella Campbell came to lunch on squab under glass.

There were times to come when Claire would be heard publicly to damn the Playhouse and all its Bavarian gimcrackery, and while she herself had sewed the curtains for the rooms, it was Maude who'd picked out the chintz. The big conflict was over the Christy murals: a sacrilege to paint them out, declared Crispin, and so they remained, and Claire studied her Fanny Farmer cookbook amid medieval damsels and men of derring-do.

Finally the murals were taken down, their canvases carefully rolled and packed away, the plaster was painted Perry's favorite shade of blue, and all vestiges of a boy's playhouse were done away with, though it retained its designation for the rest of its natural life. The whole thing was a cunning idea, but of course fatal to budding matrimony. Better they should have begun housekeeping in a West Hollywood bungalow than to reside in that charming domicile under the benign wing of Maude and Crispin.

I can still recall a layout from an early *Photoplay*, showing the younger Antrims hanging out the windows of their bide-a-wee. And there was Perry in a Tyrolean hat, and Claire in a rickracked apron, whipping up popovers. And there were the two of them smiling skittishly in their bedroom, which featured a giant-size porcelain stove brought from Stockholm and converted from coal to gas to keep them warm.

It was all Crispin's doing, of course; he would have it so. He wanted his son close by, so they could talk things over every day and go riding together. It was an idea he had of family unity. Poor Claire was a novice when it came to such matters, and there was no way she could have successfully vetoed Crispin Antrim's plan. In fact she adored living there —at first. To be a member of the Antrim clan was a great step upward, socially speaking; to be living at Sunnyside, where kings and queens regularly swung in and out the doors, was an even greater coup. No woman in her right mind would have declined the opportunity—think of the publicity! And she suffered accordingly.

Not so Perry's next wife. When it came Belinda's turn she was able to profit from her predecessor's error. Also, by that time, after the war, Perry was older and more mature and realized that his father's romantic fancies could no longer rule the son's life, and so the younger Antrims purchased the Mandeville Canyon ranch where the senior Antrims could come and be entertained—and then leave.

It was judged a wise move, and with Perry as her husband it seemed that Belinda was finding happiness at last. That it was a love match there was no disputing. Theirs was one of the great love stories, on a par with that of the Windsors, though it may have lacked the same historical implications. But the Windsors were by now aging and middle-drawer, while the Antrims were set squarely in the top one.

They went to Chichén Itzá for their honeymoon, where Perry partook in a dig for ancient shards, since he was interested in Mayan history and culture. They took ship for Nome, where Perry studied the composition of the Alaskan tundra. His wife was photographed by *National Geographic,* wearing a parka of mink. Then they sailed for Genoa, and in Rome Perry was honored by the government for his bravery during the Italian Campaign. Field Marshal Montgomery himself arrived to be on hand when the young warrior was decorated, and a shot of the old warrior bussing the young warrior's wife hit the cover of *Life.*

During the seven-year period of this, her second and most blessed union, Belinda Carroll appeared in only two films, *I Only Loved You Twice,* opposite Jimmy Stewart, and *Tarnished Angel,* with Van Heflin. She did, however, star in a production of her own when she gave birth by Caesarean section to a female child, the adorable Faun, whom she had named after the cunning fawn sent her by a fan as a christening present. And if it was in any way prophetic that the spelling of the child's name differed from the beast's, referring instead to the mischievous goat-footed, horned creature who plays a flute and dances in the moonlight, no one realized it at the time. But of course no one was even thinking of such things as they all smiled down at the little swaddled darling in the antique cradle, the same cradle that had once held her own father. Maude had had the cradle put safely away in the attic, saved against the day when it would be needed again; it was brought down, refurbished, and the new infant placed inside, and Nana herself rocked it to sleep.

Half a decade of wedded bliss was all they had, one of the most famous couples in the world. The Lindbergh kidnapping having blighted his own youth, Perry had decreed that no photographs were to be taken of his daughter, that she was never to be present at interviews, and that she was to be kept out of the public eye. Belinda agreed; she didn't want her baby stolen by some madman. So the child was sheltered and kept apart, and no pictures of her were ever printed until Faun became interesting to the press for all the wrong reasons.

In 1950 Perry heard about Dr. Keynes, an English missionary who had gone into the Borneo jungle in order to bring the gospel to the native tribes, known to be hostile, and had not been heard from again. The desperate pleas of his wife for some brave man to go in and find her husband, dead or alive, moved Perry, and he announced to the press that he would undertake the dangerous mission; so good a man as Dr. Keynes should not be left to perish if it was possible to save him. It was fully two years before Perry was able to mount his expedition, and in June he kissed Belinda and his daughter goodbye, flew to Honolulu, thence to Sarawak, and on the first of July he and a team of seven men boarded small craft at the mouth of the Oroyocco and began motoring upstream. It was the last time any of the party was ever seen alive, and finally word came down via a local trader, one Lazarre, that the search party had fallen victim to a party of Dayak headhunters.

Belinda was devastated, and from her secluded widowhood she announced her retirement from the screen. Louis B. himself stated in the press that he would never hold her to her contract; she didn't have to come back to work unless she wanted to. She retired behind the gates of the Mandeville house, seeing no one but her closest friends and the family.

People began calling her the "bad-luck girl." That's a lousy sobriquet to hang on any woman, but especially on someone like Belinda. After she had lost two husbands, each of whom she'd loved, and given the unwelcome misfortunes that were to follow, you could say she'd had bum luck, but why underscore it with such a label? It started in the press, and it dogged her heels for years as she reeled from pillar to post, attempting to pick up the pieces of her life and only shattering it into smaller pieces.

For more than two years she withdrew into the protective shell of her sorrow, maintaining a stolid silence. For a while eager reporters had camped on her doorstep, hoping for a word, something, but it was time wasted. She never came out and few went in. One who did go in, and often, was her mother-in-law, Maude, who'd become widowed herself. A year following Perry's final expedition, Crispin died of an aneurism at age seventy-one. In keeping with his character, a modest funeral was conducted, the grand old man was interred at Forest Lawn, and Maude settled down to observe the rites of her newly acquired widowhood. Now she had lost so much, an only son plus her beloved husband of forty years. In their mutual sorrow the two women came closer and closer together, forging bonds that were to stand Belinda in good stead throughout the remainder of Maude's lifetime.

Then came the unfortunate business of the man Lazarre, who appeared on the scene to make his grotesque bid for fame. A letter from him had arrived at Mandeville addressed to Belinda Carroll Antrim, declaring that he was in possession of his remains and requesting an interview. Excited and unwary, Belinda agreed to see the man, and he came to the house. She received him in the living room, where she offered him tea and they talked. At some point he produced a small box, saying it contained the proof of her husband's fate, and when she removed the box lid she found a shrunken head inside. They took her away in hysterics and the man was thrown out.

That bizarre episode has been seen as the breaking point for Belinda Carroll. She went into an emotional tailspin from which she was not to emerge for a long time, a descending spiral, faster and faster. She began her heavy drinking at this point; there followed a series of minor scandals and run-ins with the police, pictures in the papers, even a story in *Confidential*, that notorious scandal rag of the period. There was even a suicide attempt, in reality more of a cry for help than an attempt to do away with herself.

Unable to deal with being a mother, she sent Faun away to a fashionable boarding school where she had many classmates who also came from movie-star households. Summers she was provided with a governess, and when her grandmother gave her her first horse, Faun seriously took up riding around the ranch and the hill paths of Mandeville Canyon.

Then came the unhappy night when Belinda went to a party at Malibu, got smashed, quarreled with her escort, left with his car, and on the way home ran the light at Pacific Coast Highway and Sunset. She struck another car, crashed through her own windshield, and became a statistic.

After that Maude persuaded her to go into a sanitarium, and she was away for nearly a year. She concluded this unhappy chapter in her life by renting out the Mandeville house to friends of Frank's, sending Faun to stay with Maude at Sunnyside, and leaving for New York. Why New York? She didn't know, really, but New York was big; maybe she could get lost there. Lost? She was lost before she ever quit L.A., but in New York she got more lost. Lost on a barstool at Goldie's, drowning in one big long Manhattan cocktail, with the cherry missing.

Belinda Carroll had a middle name, but you never saw it in print or on a theatre marquee. Her middle name was Trouble with a capital "T" and you'd hear people muttering, "God, Belinda Carroll's in trouble again." And you could usually believe it. New York was not generally prone to the Hollywood gossip—New York had its own gossip, and the recent escapades of Belinda Carroll didn't matter much in the face of local scandals. Frank flew in and talked with his old pal Ed Sullivan, and in no time Belinda was announced for a Sunday-night video spot. The nation watched in fascination as an obviously distracted Ed appeared in front of the curtains to say that, while he had looked forward to saying hello to that "wonnaful Hollywood storr, Miss Blinda Car'l," he must unfortunately forgo such pleasure, since "Miss Car'l" had been stricken by a backstage attack of unspecified illness and could not appear. An act of trained dogs was substituted. Next day everyone read in Dorothy Kilgallen that Belinda had been stricken by an attack of Vat 69. Blotto. After that she became a sort of joke. Miss Bad Luck again.

By then she'd racked up a collection of movies rivaling those of any other major star of the period. Seven Honey pictures, interspersed with other examples of the MGM product, playing opposite the top male stars on the lot, Gable, Stewart, Taylor, Tracy, Johnson, and Fred Astaire. She made her first Technicolor production, *Dancing on the Ceiling,* in 1945, and from then on she never made a film in black-and-white. She hoofed it with Fred in *Good Girls Go to Heaven,* with Gene in *After the Ball.* But bad luck dogged her. She was to have played Milady de Winter in the *Three Musketeers* remake until she slipped and fell downstairs, and Lana went in for her. A film opposite Orson Welles started up, then fizzled; she wasn't even paid. She was replaced on two other films, once when she contracted pneumonia after jumping into an ice-cold river in Saskatchewan (*King of the Royal Mounties,* opposite Jimmy Stewart), another after a near-fatal motor accident. She was secretly assigned the role of Annie, to replace Garland in *Annie Get Your Gun,* but her lymph glands swelled and she went into St. John's, while Betty Hutton got to sing "They Say That Falling in Love Is Wonderful."

But you couldn't keep Belinda down; it became a constant source of amazement to all Hollywood how she managed to get laid out flat, then rise and stand again, and face the cameras, and have another hit. Good story, bad story, the audiences loved her. *I Don't Care,* the film biography of Eva Tanguay, seemed to put the whole thing in a nutshell. Belinda didn't care.

Or didn't seem to. The fact was, she cared too much. But sometimes a person can slip, or fall, and not get up again, just lie there flat out, out for good. That's how it seemed in the late fifties, when she and her studio of so many years agreed to disagree, and she drove through the MGM gates for the last time, leaving her "Belinda Blue" dressing room to *n'im-porte qui*. And, just as when Claire Regrett had gone before her, it was the end of an era.

The next time I saw Belinda I was back in New York, having got one of the leads in a new play. Also, through Frank, Jenny had been hired to do the clothes for a costume epic at Fox, and so she'd stayed on the Coast—relieved, I suspected, to be seeing the last of me for a while; we'd been having a bad case of the seven-year jitters. Anyway, I'd lucked out and the play, having garnered some good reviews, was in for a run. I had this sublet over on East Thirty-second Street, and one night after the theatre I'm walking south on the west side of Lexington Avenue when the skies open up with no warning and it begins raining fish. I duck into this little bar, the Nag's Head—it's an unpretentious, cozy kind of place, the usual well-Manhattaned characters slouched at the bar, and a friendly bartender, providing you're not out to burn the joint down or pinch asses or anything; Freddie was his name. I grab a stool till the rain blows over, Freddie makes me a dry martini, and he and I have a chat. He hasn't seen my show, so I promise him a pair of house seats; he pays. Some guy is noodling the piano in the back and I see this blonde tootsie hanging over his shoulder, picking out notes on his keyboard. Then she slings herself up onto the piano, Helen Morgan style, and starts to sing "It's a Big Wide Wonderful World," but real slow and lowdown, sort of the way Streisand does "Happy Days Are Here Again." This dame's got a nice smoky tone and good diction, nice mike work, and I say to Freddie, Who's that? His answer floors me. It's Belinda.

"But don't tangle with her," Freddie says. "She's a creature of mood; she may take your head off."

I pick up my drink and move in closer; it's not easy accepting the fact that here's this big movie star, twenty-five years of MGMing under her belt, and she's singing "Big Wide Wonderful World" in the Nag's Head saloon. And I don't even recognize the voice. Her hair keeps falling across her eyes and she either kicks it back with a chin jerk or she does this really sensational gesture, slipping her fingers through it and casually drawing it back, only to have it fall again.

After "Wonderful World" she segues into "Gone with the Wind," not the "Tara's Theme" of Max Steiner but the Allie Rubel pop number Martha Raye recorded back in the forties,

"Gone with the wind,
Just like a leaf, you have blown away
Gone with the wind,
Our romance has flown away.

Yesterday's kisses are still on my lips,
I found a lifetime of heaven at your fingertips,"

a real torchy little number, and Belinda sang it really well, in a voice that by now had acquired this husky, whisky crackle in it.

Later, when she got tired of singing, she sat alone at the far end of the bar, well out of the light, and Freddie angled down and talked a little with her, and I saw her looking my way. Freddie came back and jerked his ear at her.

"She wants ta talk with ya."

Outside it had stopped raining. I had a radio gig in the morning and I was full of suppressed yawns, but I told Freddie to bring me another martini and I went down the bar and took the empty stool next to Belinda.

"Hi," she said, putting her hand in mine. It was soft and warm and very small as hands go. She didn't make a big deal out of anything; I complimented her on her singing, she accepted my praise gracefully, we spoke of Frankie, she cadged a drink from me, then another. I didn't mind; I enjoyed the idea that I was buying Belinda Carroll drinks.

She banged on in this Old Crow voice, calling out to Freddie for cigarettes, getting up to go to the john, stopping to shmooze with some people on the way back, and all I could think was, This is Belinda Carroll? I wanted to get away, but I was fascinated and I couldn't leave. She hiked herself back on her stool again and punched my arm.

"Charlie, Charlie—I know all about you. You used to live at the Trianon, din' you? With my friend Angie?"

"Well, we didn't exactly live together," I told her.

"I bet you'd of liked to."

I agreed.

"Angie's a good-looking woman. You got a wife still?"

Yes, I said, I had a wife, though I was in need of a pumpkin shell. "There I'll keep her very well."

She guffawed at that one. She said she thought a well-kept wife was an attainment. "All wives should be kept well." She giggled.

Yes, I said, and I guessed she was one who had been. I also knew she'd been a well-kept widow, since it was general knowledge that Perry had left her a trust fund that would see her well off for the rest of her life.

"Where *is* your wife, anyway?" she demanded. When I explained about the movie Jenny was working on, she grew scornful. "Huh—that smells of turkey already, don'tcha think? And I guess I know a turkey when I smell one. God knows I've done enough of them." She slurred her words and kept repeating her gesture of tossing back her hair, but it wasn't half so engaging as when she'd been singing.

It was getting late. The clock said two-twenty and I was wiped out, but she wouldn't let me go. She had things to get off her chest; she was like the Ancient Mariner, I the wedding guest, and I was obliged to hear her tale. I didn't really mind; at her very worst Belinda Carroll was always someone I enjoyed spending time with. I had a private word with Freddie, he got the kitchen to throw a couple of sandwich steaks on, I coaxed Belinda to a booth and tried to get some food into her. She poked at the steak and pretended to eat the sliced tomatoes, and when the waiter brought coffee she turned her cup over and demanded another drink; so it was steak and Scotch.

When I realized she'd eaten all she intended to—it wasn't much, and the Belinda of that era usually insisted on getting her own way—I suggested cutting things short. Then the real trouble began; she wanted to go on talking, first in the booth, then back at the bar, where Freddie was yawning and rolling his eyes at me to get her the hell out of there.

"Can't we go somewhere else?" she asked, when we stumbled out into the wet street. I gave her a flat no, I definitely had to be in bed. I asked her where she lived: the Elysée, she said; the Elysée was one of those small but smart East Side hotels; it boasted the famous Monkey Bar, where Nancy Noland used to sing. The Elysée was twenty blocks up Lex, and I wondered what she was doing down in Murray Hill.

Because of the late hour we had no trouble finding a cab, and on the ride uptown she was both humorous and talkative, keeping at me like a bulldog pulling on a rope. "I guess you think I'm a real mess, hm?" she said, powdering her nose in the overhead light. "I guess you'll be on the horn to Frank, telling him his Blindy's all screwed up, hm?"

I said I had no plans in that direction and she snapped her compact shut and gave me a sidelong look. Her hip was next to my thigh and I could feel the heat in it through the beat-up trench coat she had on.

"Listen, I was wondering," she went on. "Could you meet me sometime? I mean, could I see you? I'd like to talk with you. Unless you're too busy or something."

I said I had time. "Anything in particular you wanted to talk about?"

"No. Just, you know—talk. When?"

"Whenever you say. Would you like to come see the play some night?"

"I don't go to the theatre much," she said. Then added, "But in your case I could make an exception."

We made a date. I got her a house seat. I paid, she came. I could see that coif of shining blonde hair out there in the dark and I thought, "I'm acting for Belinda Carroll." The cast knew she was out there, too, and they were all agog, more agog when she came backstage and shook hands and was charming; some change from the Nag's Head. Afterward I suggested a bite at Sardi's but she asked for something less grand, so we went to Downey's and sat in a corner with people looking over at us and talked. She held down her drink intake and was very funny. She kidded about herself and the mess she'd made of things, but she didn't harp on her woes. Life was a joke, not to be taken seriously, and I thought, "Well, that's the only way she's ever going to get through it, so that's okay." She told me about her mother, that hectoring harpy Eunice, who'd caused her so much misery when she was young and who'd hated Frank so much; she talked about her kid, Faun, who since the age of ten had been becoming something of a problem even for the formidable Maude Antrim. Of course nothing was suggested as to why Belinda herself wasn't on the home front, taking care of matters herself, instead of toughing it out in New York. Or, better yet, why wasn't the kid here with her mommy?

It was odd, or maybe I only imagined it that way, how the conversation kept coming back to Frank. What Frank was doing, what Frank thought about this or that, things she and Frank had done, things Frank and I'd done that she'd heard about—she even made me tell tales about the tour with Babe Austrian the summer Jenny and I met. She obviously needed to talk about Frank, which was fine with me.

Reading between the lines of her conversation, I decided that this was somebody who didn't like herself very much, who'd lost her self-respect somewhere along the line. She'd cloaked herself in outrageous behavior, but it was a hair shirt she'd put on and I suspected it was giving her a bad rash. She desperately wanted Frank's good opinion, and I knew she'd been on her best behavior tonight so I'd turn in a good report. I tried to get across the idea that I wasn't a spy, and she needn't worry about my squealing to Frank—or anyone else, for that matter.

She asked about Jenny, and that took up time, and pretty soon I was hiding my yawns again.

"Come on," she said, pulling my sleeve, "I've bored you long enough. You've got to get your beauty sleep, you have a matinee tomorrow."

So we went along. In the taxi she was wonderfully sweet as she thanked me for the show and dinner, saying complimentary things that far exceeded either the merits of the play or my performance in it, but it was nice hearing them anyway. We exchanged a friendly kiss at the door of her hotel.

"Good night, brother dear," she laughed. She went in and I went on. And that, I decided, was to be the extent of our relationship. Oh brother!

I talked with Jenny every day, to find out how things were going out there in Tinseltown, and since there didn't seem to be anything wrong in saying so, I mentioned that I'd seen Belinda a couple of times, eliciting only the most casual of responses. I'd had the idea that maybe Jenny wasn't missing me as much as I cared to be missed by my spouse, but I chalked it up to lots of hard work and an overwhelming interest in the production, which despite Belinda's misgivings was the biggest break Jenny'd had and could possibly make her reputation as a costume designer. But I heard distinct overtones of pique in her response to my mention of Belinda, and the next time it happened she said something like, "You two are quite the pair, aren't you? You'd better be careful before you hit the papers."

How could she possibly have known? But there it was, the next Monday, in my friend La Hopper's column:

> What up and coming Frank Adonis client, now treading the boards of Broadway, is seeing what ex-Metro lovely, also an Adonis client? Rumor has it that the lady is auditing classes at the Actors' Studio, by way of a stage career. Certainly she's all washed up in flickers. As for the lad in question, his dressy wife is burning at both ends, seen in the Warner Brothers' Green Room with the studio's newest Sweater Boy and that same evening at Jack's-at-the-Beach with same. My spies tell me they were engrossed in deepest conversation.

The publicist for our show was ecstatic about the item and wanted to put it to further use until I told him to lay off. When Jen and I next talked, we joked about it all; the Sweater Boy turned out to be someone we both knew, an actor who was working in the picture, and they'd had a hamburger together, that was all. I likewise soft-pedaled the relationship with Belinda.

Was it a relationship? No. I didn't think so, certainly nothing to make the papers over. Just as she said, I was her brother, her birthday fell three days before mine, we were fellow Capricorns and had the weight of the world around our necks; albatross time.

We saw each other a couple of more times, but were careful about being noticed. Then I heard on the grapevine that we were deliberately lying low and people were talking, so we said the hell with it and went to Lindy's for pastrami sandwiches. That episode made Winchell.

We saw more of each other. I'd been gone from New York for some time, many of my old friends were by then working on the Coast, and the place seemed empty to me. Likewise, Belinda had few friends there, and she was lonely, so—we saw each other. It was good, I enjoyed it. We'd meet for a cup of coffee, or we'd walk over to the river. I still like recalling bits and pieces from those days in New York when I was first really getting to know her, the real Belinda, as they say. She really was on the ragged edge, and I liked to think I was giving her something, if only a helping hand. She even stopped drinking so much when she was with me; she'd have a Seven-Up with a shot of angostura bitters—what she called a "Carrie Nation"—and we'd meet at the Monkey Bar or at Goldie's and share the New York cocktail hour, which in those days was a lot of fun. She liked to dress up for these occasions, put on the dog, and I thought it was remarkable the number of people who'd stop by the table to say hello: Faye Emerson, Maggie McNellis, Yul Brynner, whoever wandered in.

In those days Marilyn Monroe and Shelley Winters were attending classes at the Actors' Studio, and one afternoon we ran into Shelley on the street. I had played a walk-on in stock when Shelley was the star, and since then we'd co-starred on television, and when she saw Belinda she started screaming how Belinda simply had to come up to the Studio and audition for Lee Strasberg. I had a picture of that and I gave Shelley the high-sign to can it about auditions, but *maybe* Belinda might like to go with Shelley and just *audit* the class. Well, that was fine, so off they went together, laughing and giggling like two schoolgirls.

But the seed was planted and the time came when Belinda did get up and do a job of acting. She really did—a scene from *The Country Girl*, wearing that damn trench coat and the babushka she put on so people wouldn't recognize her. She wouldn't take either of them off until Strasberg stopped the scene and asked why she was dressed for outdoors when the action was supposed to be in a theatre dressing room. He made her peel the coat off and reveal herself, and this did something to her; it made her prickly and angry, because she was overweight and trying to hide it. The babushka went, too, and her hair was full of tin curlers, so he made her remove those and comb out her hair during the scene, giving her an activity, and the scene—Odets, but not at his best—really took off. They talked about it for years, Belinda Carroll and her *Country Girl*, comparing it not unfavorably with Uta Hagen's original. Then she did a really dumb thing. Maybe she just couldn't help herself, maybe it was her overwhelming need to be loved, maybe it was just elemental wop-sex, but in any case she got involved with this actor she'd met at the Studio, some guy called Tony Dichi, an arrogant little Italian from the Bronx who thought he was Marlon Brando and did an unholy imitation of him. When he and I met, it was hands off; we both backed away. I knew he was using Belinda, just climbing right up her back, and I despised him for it. He was also screwing her, and I admit it; by then I was jealous; no right to be, but that's how it was. She and I even had fights about the little squirt, and then for a while we were out of touch, but I heard all the stories. People were talking, and not to Belinda's advantage. Again I had this impression that she was deliberately trying to do herself in; else why would she have picked of all people this little hard-on with his greaser curls, his blue beard, his Elvis Presley Roman-Greco lips, his muscles, and his leather motorcycle jacket? Later this "individualist" did a movie and a half and then went straight to Zipville.

But the depth of Belinda's fascination for this little gonzo was all too apparent. Things got worse; finally the column items started to break, and not blind ones, either. She was quoted as saying Tony Dichi reminded her of Frank—because Frank had come from Hell's Kitchen, too, west of Eighth on Fifty-second; were such things possible in that Eisenhower world? Shelley tried to patch things up but I said screw it, Shell, leave it lay. Lie.

One day I read in the *Times* that Jean Dalrymple had offered Belinda a part in a revival of *The Women* at the City Center, four weeks of rehearsal. She went off to Boston and never came back, not in *The Women* anyway. She'd pulled out of the show after some deep trouble in Beantown and that was it for her name up in lights on Broadway.

When she got back from Boston (in semi-disgrace, though the whole mess was sort of hushed up and made only the Broadway rounds), she was at frayed ends and trouble was still her middle name. Tony Dichi was no longer in evidence, but not long after her return she got involved with some stud who worked in a wire parlor handicapping the ponies, a real bastard. One night when he took her to his hotel she went to bed with him, then tried to roll him; he beat the living hell out of her, she was damn near dead when the cops got there. They hauled her off to Bellevue, of all terrible places, and when they got her stitched back together she was up for grabs. The guy even pressed charges; you remember the headlines on that one. They were going to send her to the Tombs, and I got this lawyer friend of mine to square things and I paid the scumbag to lay off. He dropped the charges; I went and fetched her and took her home. To my place, I mean. This would really make good copy, but what else could I have done? She could hardly walk or talk. I might have called Shelley, but she wasn't in town.

Ten minutes after I got her inside my apartment Belinda was asleep on my bed. I went around hiding anything that had the least alcoholic content, then hung up her things. When she woke up, I fed her soup from the corner deli and she was like some poor wounded bird, both wings broken, couldn't hope to fly. She had the TV in there, she was watching Howdy Doody and Gary Moore. Meantime I was on the horn to L.A., keeping Frank up-to-date on things. He asked me if I could put her up for a little while. I did, for four nights, and she damn near drove me crazy. She was becoming this God-awful chatterbox and you couldn't shut her up, racka-racka-racka all day long. All she wanted to do was sit around and drink and gab, while I got bleary-eyed and wondered what the hell I was doing, trying to help this looneytune. I didn't even like her much anymore; she'd taxed me far beyond my strength and I felt helpless. That's how it is sometimes when the weak ones take over the strong ones and wear them down. I felt sorry for her but she was getting under my skin, and four days at close quarters about did me in.

When I told her she had to move out, she went with no fuss, not back to the Elysée, but to a hotel a few blocks away, not bad but certainly not good. I saw her around the neighborhood from time to time. Drunk she was a mess, but sober she was still an all-right lady, though she suffered from bad hangovers and consequently was often in brittle shape. When she was sober I'd try talking some sense to her, about quitting the booze. I'd try to encourage her, but she'd grow abusive and then she'd get me pissed off. Around this time she wasn't just Belinda, or I guess what I mean is there were more than one of her—it was Joanne Woodward time and her *Three Faces of Eve*. There was this one I've been talking about, the would-be tootsie with too much gas in her tank; then there'd be the one in the torn trench coat and striped babushka taking her wash to the laundromat or shopping in the A & P, no makeup, hair a mess, scuffed penny loafers on her feet, seams not straight, a real blowze, but something friendly and ingratiating about her—nothing of the movie-queen stuff.

Then a lucky thing happened. A woman called Ronnie Alsop lived in the building, a fan of mine, as it happened, a pleasant, middle-aged spinster well on her way to being an old maid; Ronnie was going down to Tennessee to do research for a paper she was preparing on the TVA, and since her apartment was going to be vacant and a pet was involved, she offered the place to Belinda, asking that the cat be fed and the place not get burned down. We jumped at the chance.

Having her own digs seemed to help Belinda, for a while, anyway. The little apartment, conventionally furnished, with a fire escape over-looking a back alley, seemed to suit her. It had forest-green walls, white-enameled trim (badly chipped from wear), and lots of cabbage-rose chintz. There were books and magazines, records, a shelf full of cookbooks, and not a lot of space to worry about taking care of.

We observed certain proprieties: she never showed up at my door to borrow a cup of sugar or a ten-cent stamp; if she wanted me she tele-phoned first, and she didn't just crash in on my parties—not that I had many, but some nights after the theatre we'd have small get-togethers, occasionally at my place. It got to the point where I didn't like to include Belinda, because a drunk is a drunk no matter how famous, and the sight of her plastered all over the davenport wasn't very pretty. I didn't see why my guests should be bored by her, even if she'd once been in the Movie Top Ten four years in a row.

Belinda Carroll was a fallen star, no doubt of that, and at that period there was no reason ever to imagine she would rise again. To all intents and purposes she was a has-been, washed up in the business. After the Boston debacle no producer would take a chance on her. When spring was in the air I suggested bringing her to a guy I knew to see if he'd take her on for a summer stock tour; it took me weeks to get her to agree even to see him, and when I finally put the two of them together she waltzed in pissed to the gills, stood there wobbling on her spike heels, only to collapse in a chair. Then she tried to put the make on him, and when he didn't take to her charms she became insulting and the thing ended in another fiasco. I took him to an expensive dinner by way of thanks, but the damage was done, and Cape Cod did not see Miss Carroll in *Angel Street* that summer.

It wasn't anyone's business, but we'd begun sleeping together. Not on a regular basis, but it was probably inevitable that we should, propin-quity lending its usual hand. I felt guilty, a little anyway, as if I were taking advantage of a situation, and maybe I was, but not advantage of her. It seemed a natural result that we should make love sometimes after my show, and with Jenny three thousand miles away I fell willing victim to that old dodge, Well, what's a guy to do?

And it was nice. We'd be in bed, smoking and having a post-coital slug of hooch, the radio would be playing George Shearing, and I'd be thinking, This is wild, I've got Belinda Carroll in my arms, I'm making love to her. In one of these intimate moments I told her about the flood in the cellar and the patch of wet cement, the initials in the heart; she started to cry and said it was the sweetest thing she'd ever heard of.

She was getting hung up on me, I could tell, and I told myself I shouldn't get involved; my friends said it, too. She was in no shape to indulge herself this way, and of course they were right. What she really needed was some solid therapeutic help, but at that time she wasn't ready for it the way she was later on, when she really got down to brass tacks and joined Alcoholics Anonymous. But I found her a couple of books; crazy to have thought they'd help her, but I was really grasping at straws. I brought her Kahlil Gibran's *The Prophet* and Erich Fromm's *The Art of Loving*—this is a laugh, but I even got her to take a whack at old Dale Carnegie—anything that might have given her a toehold, but it never worked; she'd read a few pages and then the book would end up under a pile of lingerie in the corner.

She was an awful slob, too, and while I wasn't Norman Neatly, I did like things picked up. I had a girl who came in and cleaned once a week and I ended up having her go down to Belinda's and look after her, while I scrubbed my own toilet and scoured the bathtub. Not a convenient arrangement, to say the least.

One thing: I did get to know her. I did get to look behind the façade of a typical movie star and see the deadly doubts and fears that prey on that kind of personality, spoonfed by the studio so they can't make up their minds about anything, so they know nothing about the everyday business of living. This was a woman who'd had the adoration of the world, who'd dined with kings and emperors, who had only to crook her little finger at any man and he'd come running. She'd dated Jimmy Stewart and Cary Grant and Howard Hughes, but she couldn't wash out her undies or boil water. I even had to go down and put a fresh roll of toilet paper in the holder for her. It was pathetic, she was so helpless, and it was the studio system that had crippled her. And yet—and yet—she was Belinda Carroll, and I just felt this throbbing, burning need in her, she was so damn sweet and really kind; she knew about giving and not just her body—though she could give plenty of that. But she was never selfish (the only thing she took lots of was my time, but I could be generous, too), and when she wasn't smashed she was an amiable companion and I enjoyed being around her.

It was at this time that I was given a clearer picture of Belinda's mother, the terrible Eunice, who, having done everything in her power to push her daughter into the limelight, had turned around and done everything she could to destroy her success. On the one hand she'd mothered Belinda to death and on the other she'd ignored her whenever Belinda needed a mother she could go to.

I never knew the woman—she died of Bright's disease shortly before I arrived in California back in the fifties, and by then she and Belinda were estranged. She didn't even say that she was dying, but wrote a letter to be mailed upon her demise. Belinda had kept it and she let me read it. Its impassioned and accusatory lines were as destructive as Eunice could make them—and she was a master. All of her pent-up jealousy over Belinda's success was there to read (Eunice had once worked with a knife-thrower in a cheap carnival act and she was crazy about show business), filled with acrimony, criticism, and scorn, the sort of letter designed to lay a guilt trip on any sensitive person. It completely repudiated their relationship, blaming Belinda for all of Eunice's ills and misfortunes, and at the end she said she was glad to be dead because she didn't care to go on living in a world where there were such terrible people as Belinda Carroll (she hated the name, she said, just as she hated the man who'd thought it up: Frank Adonis was her *bête noire*).

But it seemed to me that, despite everything, Belinda must have retained some filial devotion, since she had with her several keepsakes of her mother: a vanity set with cheap silver backings, and some snapshots, pictures I looked at carefully, studying that rawboned, rubbery face that reeked of the kind of hopeless belligerency you sometimes find in photographs of the lower-class women of Depression America, the Okies out of Steinbeck. The wonder was, I thought, how did the woman ever give birth to such a beautiful child?

Belinda talked about her sister, whom she'd loved and who had died of meningitis at an early age, and her brother, who'd been killed in a strike riot at the Ford plant after being clubbed down by company goons. The loss of these two obviously had affected her own early upbringing and I was inclined to think it also affected her later behavior, both bad and good. Certainly it added to her fear of being alone in the world and her constant need of a man. Even if it was a one-night stand, that would do; she had a horror of sleeping alone.

I think maybe if she'd had a relatively decent and affectionate mother, things might have been different for her, certainly in relation to her own daughter. Maybe the cavalier treatment she'd given Faun had its origins in the way Eunice had treated Belinda. And maybe if Eunice hadn't tried to cram all that pentecostal Bible-thumping down Belinda's throat, she might have found her own path much earlier than she did. Fifty years is a long time to wait to discover that there's a Higher Power looking out for you.

I'd always heard a lot about Belinda through Angie Brown, who was her closest friend, going all the way back to the forties. Angie wasn't only man's best friend, she could be a girl's best friend, too. Maybe I haven't given Angie her proper due; some people say I ought to be writing about her instead of Belinda. It must have seemed to me back then that Angelina Brown was indestructible, though in the end, of course, she wasn't. In those early days she'd modeled dresses at Don Loper's establishment. An ex–chorus boy and Copa dancer, Loper had appeared in several wartime movie musicals performing "specialty numbers." Now he was "couturier to the stars," and many women, including Jenny, bought their clothes evening wear especially, at his South Rodeo Drive emporium, several doors away from Romanoff's Restaurant. Angie was his top model and brought in lots of customers. And she and Belinda were best friends.

Belinda seemed to be a bird with a broken wing, in need of Angie's help. Angie was madly in love with Frank, but so was Belinda—it was a kind of bond. By now she'd been around the block a time or two. She was a "friend of Howard's." There were lots of "friends of Howard's" in those days, the girls Howard Hughes had stashed away in houses and apartments around town, for he was justly reputed an indefatigable girl-chaser. People whispered that someday he'd marry Belinda, but Howard evidently had other ideas; no ring was forthcoming, though he did buy her a car, a blue convertible—"Belinda Blue," as it would become known, her favorite shade, which he'd had custom-mixed at the factory.

She called the car "Baby."

There was little doubt that the studio had big things in mind for its new blonde star. Now people were pointing her out as she tripped around the lot, angora sweater, sharkskin shorts, and plastic heels. She was everybody's darling, everybody's dream, and over in the Thalberg Building executives were rubbing their palms and counting their shekels.

One who blanched when Belinda came on the lot, however, was Claire Regrett. Claire was still one of MGM's top leading ladies, but about to become that worst of all things, an ex. When Belinda arrived, Claire was already poised to depart, her Metro days were numbered—but not Claire herself. Far from it. There was plenty of good mileage left on that chassis, and, being Claire, she was out to beat the world. But that didn' mean she had to be nice to this little stock girl Howard Hughes was banging.

It was true that Mayer gave Claire Regrett the shaft, that he told Frank he'd renew the option, then dropped it with one of the loudest crashes in all show business. One moment Claire was making five thousand a week, the next week zip. The next time she drove on the lot she found her dressing room being repainted and decorated—in baby blue to match the convertible parked in front. Claire fled in tears and later sent her maid to retrieve her effects. A comment of hers started making the rounds, and though it didn't get into the columns, it nonetheless did her a lot of harm. She was reported to have said that she was glad to have left MGM since it had become nothing more than a pastry shop selling cream puffs and tarts. The idea of Claire's calling anybody a tart was pretty funny, and she took a lot of flak about it, even denying—via Louella— that she'd ever said anything of the kind. Whether she had or hadn't was no longer the point. The point was that people *said* she had.

Still later Claire managed to have words with Angie over Belinda. This was at Loper's salon, where Claire also bought some of her things, and while Angie was modeling a number, Claire came out with something like, "I don't think so, dear—it makes you look cheap—like Belinda Carroll."

Angie saw red. She marched up to Claire, letting her have it with both barrels. "Look, little Miss Has-Been, where the hell do you get off calling anybody a slut when they invented the word for you? You, whose first movie was as blue as the blue Pacific, who got started tossing her legs for every producer on the lot, and who's got a mouth like a truck driver! Don't try to kid me; everybody knows you park up on the Ridge Route and do the late-night traffic as it comes over the hill."

Claire, who was not one to take such talk lying down, let Angie have it right in the chops. Loper came dashing in to stop the carnage, but not before nails got entangled in hair and a real kick, bite, and bitch fight took place between the two contenders. People talked about it for years.

As for Angie and Belinda, the paths of their lives took vastly divergent turnings, but the two women went on for years, best of friends, supporting each other, providing a shoulder to cry on. It was one of the most satisfying friendships in Hollywood, a rare thing among the kind of women who were used to being best friends at one moment, then not on speaking terms the next. Not Belinda and Angie; and both of them in love with the same man. These days I was wishing Angie weren't three thousand miles away in Cat Wells but right here in New York, helping take care of her friend. If ever anyone needed help but wouldn't ask for it, it was Belinda. And it wasn't Trouble in only the grand-scale things, major tragedies and the like; it was in everything, even the smallest.

I remember going down to her apartment one spring noontime; she was out on the fire escape sunning herself. We'd had a robust winter and she was reveling in the warm sunshine. She'd dragged out cushions, she had a magazine, the cat was there with a saucer of milk, and it was a scene of sweet contentment. Then I saw what she'd done to herself—she'd given her hair one of those home perm jobs and she looked God-awful. I always liked her with the simple shoulder-length hair she'd worn in the late forties, but short hair was in, and she was obeying the edicts of Paris. Now the home perm had really messed her up. The hair had been cut short, and that was okay, but she'd dyed it and it was all kinky and uncontrollable and she looked like an albino. I didn't say anything because I knew she'd get upset, but she pried it out of me anyway and we had a row. Finally I called a girl I knew who was doing the hair for a couple of big Broadway stars, and she took Belinda in hand; Belinda ended up wigging it for weeks until the kink grew out and she could be herself again.

She was fun, though, especially when she wasn't totally plotzed. We were good for each other; she made me laugh and gave me good advice (I thought) about Jenny, and I got her to put on the brakes with the booze. She said I was a party-pooper; and referred to me as "Mr. Toad of Toad Hall"; in return I called her "Mother Russia," because drunk or sober she was indefatigable.

It wasn't so long after this that the winds of change began blowing. First Jenny showed up unexpectedly in New York, wanting to know what the hell was going on. There'd been those items in Winchell and elsewhere, and she had blood in her eye. I didn't have to confess to any sins; she already knew all there was to know and was quick to say so. Needless to say, she and Belinda did not get on and consequently I wasn't seeing anything of my downstairs friend. Then Ronnie came back from Tennessee, forcing Belinda to move out. Then my show closed, and since there wasn't any sense in staying east when we had a house in California, we abandoned Manhattan Dreams and the theay-tuh and headed for home.

Though Jenny's nose was out of joint, Belinda did the noble thing. She sent us flowers and champagne and showed lots of class in the way she eased out of an awkward and potentially dangerous situation. I breathed easier, and the first week back in Hollywood I was cast in a *Playhouse 90*. Since doing live TV always made me a wreck, I had my hands full. I'll say this for Jen: angry as she was at my philandering, when it came to the work she was Jenny-on-the-spot all the way, cuing me and keeping dinner hot when rehearsals ran late. She always was a great hand-holder.

Meanwhile, back in New York: no sooner did I pick up sticks than Belinda went all to pot. I don't mean it had anything to do with my leaving, it wasn't that, but she entered a most difficult and shameful period. Everyone remembers the stories, the headlines, that made the news for weeks, one more juicy scandal attached to that famous name and face. She'd gone on with her classes, attending the Studio sessions regularly and even performing a couple more exercises in front of the group. They used to laugh at her, pooh-poohing the idea of some Hollywood blonde becoming any kind of actress, but I really believed she could do it and I always encouraged her. Well, she met that creep Benny Vidor, that phony no-talent would-be actor-director and all-purpose bullshit artist. Benny tied knots in her brain, and what others hadn't already done to her, he managed to do now.

First he got her to move in with him—she always liked to wake up with a man next to her, even a hairy ape like Vidor—but he treated her like dirt. Did she crave it? I don't know, but she sure stood up and took it. "Mother Russia" again. He used to bounce her off the walls and she'd have bruises, and when Strasberg heard about it he kicked Vidor out of class. Oddly enough, Belinda took his side and stuck up for him, even in the newspapers. Then there was The Scene. You remember.

A Friday night, they'd been to Downey's, had a few, gone home, started the usual argument, which evolved into a physical contest. He beat her up good, left her on the couch, and went to bed. Was awakened by neighbors below, complaining of water leaking into their bedroom. Investigation found the bathtub overflowing, Belinda floating in it, passed out, her life's blood running over the top and onto the pink chenille bathmat. They only just managed to save her.

Of course, in those troubled times there was always a sturdy bulwark for her: Maude, her ex-mother-in-law, who loved Belinda because she'd been so devoted to Perry; Maude would have done whatever was needed to help her, but Belinda was having none of that. She was standing on her own two feet even if she was falling down every four, and she wasn't about to cry uncle and go running home to any mother-in-law.

And where was Faun Antrim during all this? Mercifully, Faun was well out of things. By now she'd become Maude's responsibility, but the girl was awesomely precocious, and nobody was pulling any wool over her eyes, not even Nana. After I went back to L.A., I had a minor encounter with Faun, one I long remembered with feelings of distaste and regret. She must have been twelve or thirteen at the time. In those days there used to be a toy-town pony ride at the corner of Beverly Boulevard and La Cienega Boulevard, where the Beverly Center rears up now. Two of my married friends, Al and Bea Smith, used to take their kids to ride the ponies there, and one Saturday when I was helping Frank with some chores, we were downing hotdogs across the street at the little stand that's built to look like a real hotdog in a bun. After our lunch on the run I took Frank over to say hello to my friends, Al and Bea. They had two girls, around eleven or twelve, and with them was a playmate their age, and she was introduced to us as "Faun."

"Not Faun Antrim?" Frank asked. The girl stared up at him with the oddest look, really weird.

"What's wrong with that?" she demanded, her eyes snapping.

"I know your mummy," Frank said. "I saw her not so long ago."

"I have no mummy," she said. "My mother is a drunk and they've locked her up where she belongs." To this astonishing statement she added an even more shocking one. I felt my ears burn red and I moved away from the group with Al.

"Holy Christ, what's going on around here?" I asked. "Who's been filling her head with that kind of stuff?"

"She gets it at school," Al said. "Bad stuff, really terrible."

"Does she really think those things about her mother?" Frank asked, joining us.

"I'm afraid so. And worse."

"What's worse than a twelve-year-old calling her mother a whore?"

Then the fit really hit the shan. I'd seen how precocious Faun seemed to be, but how precocious she actually was soon came to light. She ran away from school, not once but two or three times, she cracked up a car, then she was caught in a theatre balcony in Westwood making out with a UCLA collegiate seven years her senior. After this, something far more shocking. First she damn near burned down the whole of Sunnyside: she'd left a burning cigarette on a two-by-four in the stable, some hay caught fire, the place went up, the whole hillside was burned black; this was during the dry season and the grass was like tinder. Though the fire department managed to extinguish the flames before they spread too far, two valuable horses died of smoke inhalation, and the stables themselves were destroyed, those handsome buildings that Crispin himself had designed, with the name of each horse above its stall glazed on an enameled oval.

Worse followed. Since Faun had made a major hobby of riding horses, Maude had engaged a riding instructor, a young Britisher named Buckminster Eaton, who came with the best credentials. One night when Maude arrived home after a dinner with friends, she found the hysterical girl, her face bruised and bloody, screaming that Bucky had tried to rape her and to protect herself she'd stabbed him.

Bucky later turned up after having driven himself to the clinic in Beverly Hills for emergency treatment; he'd lost a lot of blood and eleven stitches had been taken. Quite a gash. It was a dirty business, all right, one that served to send Faun's mother flying west on the next plane. Belinda was out of the sanitarium by this time, and in fair shape, and when she arrived she took charge. It was she who elicited the information that there was no rape involved, at least not on the part of Faun's riding instructor.

It came to light that for months Bucky Eaton had been fighting off the sexual advances of his young pupil, and when he finally rebuffed her by announcing his engagement to a Pasadena Rose Bowl beauty, the infuriated Faun had taken her revenge. The case was settled out of court, but everyone knew that a large sum of money had changed hands between Maude and Eaton. It didn't really matter—the money, I mean; there was plenty to cover such incidentals—but the thing took its toll. Bucky left town under a cloud, and Belinda, who'd arrived so calm and collected, began spinning like a dervish.

In 1963 she went to Rome to make a picture, *Zenobia, Queen of Palmyra*. As everybody knew, she really needed a job; she wasn't getting a nibble in Hollywood. In fact it looked as if no one anywhere would touch her, but Frank pulled another of his magic acts and got her signed on the dotted line. It was an Italian-French co-production, it paid only so-so, but she'd get the billing and they were going to find a top male star to play opposite her. (This turned out to be Jack Palance, but what the hell.) The Biblical epic was then in its heyday; they were grinding them out as fast as someone could come up with an idea. The old Fedora *Zenobia* had made money, so why not give it another whirl with the works: color, stereophonic sound, wide screen? They shot it in something called Cinema-Aspect 75, which was a lot of bunk; the prints were grainy, the color was washed out, but Belinda's face was up there on the screen again, which was what counted. There she was, back in the beads and feathers, cast-iron tits and a double lipline, with eight yards of braided falls, sexing it up at Cinecittà. Frank had told her that if they liked her, there might be a two- or three-picture deal, and to keep her nose clean, no booze. He subsequently found out that clean noses had nothing to do with no booze.

This was in the early part of '63, a year Jenny and I both remember with mixed emotions. Frank got me signed for a spy film to shoot in North Africa; mine was a dual role and looked interesting, and I'd get to ride a camel, not so interesting. Jenny would go, too. We'd been having more and more problems, the fights were coming thick and fast, we almost split up, but now we decided to try to save our marriage, and rather than costume another film, she'd take a break and go over with me. I was glad; I just couldn't see us hitting the divorce courts and doing the mental-cruelty bit. If we'd had trouble, it was my fault as much as hers; our careers had a habit of getting in the way of things, and when she made this generous offer I was pleased.

I finished the picture in seven weeks—we were slowed down by high desert winds—but when I'd polished off my loops in Madrid, Frank said why not come over to Rome, he'd get me another picture.

At that point Kit Carson and April Rains were halfway through *The Trojan Horse*. It happened that Claire Regrett was also in town, shooting one of her last, *Vampire of the Catacombs;* they had her working underneath the Colosseum with thousands of sets of bones and prune-dried cadavers. And with Belinda making *Zenobia*, things promised to be interesting. With her had come her daughter, Faun, more precocious than ever. In the wake of the Bucky Eaton scandal, and thinking it prudent to remove the girl from home, Maude had made a present of this holiday. Belinda had decided that it might be just as well for Faun to be close at hand while her mother was filming. And no doubt Faun's absence from Sunnyside was viewed as a well-deserved breather for Maude.

It was not a good time for Belinda. I found her greatly changed. The boozing had taken a heavy toll, and I didn't see how she could possibly photograph well, but Frank's report was that the producer was so enamored of her, it hardly mattered. Even so, things weren't made easy for her. True to her fashion, Claire seemed to break into print every other day, in the *Rome Daily American* or in *Roma di Notte*, and at one point she went to considerable pains to take Belinda to task publicly. Belinda was seeing a flamenco dancer she'd picked up at the Pippastrella who, she claimed, was bedding her in a most satisfactory way. Claire was not long in leaping into print, upbraiding Belinda as one of those Hollywood actresses who did nothing to uphold the standards of the industry and went around giving the business a bad name and what would the people in Duluth think? She added that Faun was nothing but a spoiled little brat and should be spanked for her behavior. (Faun *was* running wild with the younger movie crowd.)

Later there were harsh words when the two actresses came across each other in the lobby of the Grand, and, having had one too many, Belinda was heard to refer to Claire as "that has-been," which Claire countered by calling Belinda a "never-was."

Jen and I agreed that Belinda was once more deliberately setting out to do herself in, as if she were determined to spurn every opportunity that came her way, to defeat all attempts to help her, to toss back the lifesaver ring, as if she had somehow decided that good fortune was never to be hers and she had no way to go but down, down, all the way down.

At that point Belinda established in a peculiar category; she was like a queen without a kingdom, though she did hold court frequently, usually along Via Veneto, at Donay's or another street café. Her courtiers and servitors were mostly Roman riffraff, true, but to the Italians she was still a hot ticket. (They called her "La Bionda.") And often at her side was the almost grown-up sex kitten, Lolita herself, little Faun, her hair somewhat blonder than nature had decreed. And frequently between the mother and daughter sat the sleek and slick El Gatto, "the Cat." Not a painter but a flamenco dancer, Belinda's current flame masqueraded as a Spaniard from Toledo, son of a hidalgo, no less, but in reality he was a mongrel gypsy with a little Spanish blood and the longest sideburns this side of José Greco. His more intimate name was—what else?—José—"*il mio Joselito,* " Belinda called him—and he had earlier come to the world's attention by doing a gypsy dance under the windows of *la signorina* Ava, who at that time occupied a flat at the end of the Piazza d'Espagna and who had her own Latin, a courageous *torero,* and didn't need this ersatz "flamingo" dancer (as he had been called by Claire Regrett). Ava having ignored the would-be swain, Señor Joselito had proceeded to serenade yet another *signorina,* La Bionda, under *her* balcony at L'Albergo Grande.

All things considered, I deemed it wiser to avoid Belinda as much as I could. I saw her around, of course—Rome is a village and everyone sees everyone there, or did at that time. But we ran across each other one day at, of all places, the Trevi Fountain. Jenny had taken some American friends to see the gardens at the Villa d'Este and wouldn't be back until dinnertime. I was out snapping pictures of the sights, and as I came into the piazza who should I see posing for tourist cameras but Belinda Carroll. She was lolling in the sun by the fountain, having the time of her life, laughing and rapping with whoever happened along. I would have passed her by, but she noticed me and came rushing over. I took her to a café where we sat under an awning and had a Negrone apiece. Negrones are a deadly drink and I never cared for them much (Frances Adano had introduced me to them), but that was what we ordered. Belinda and I chatted away ten to the dozen about this and that, the unbelievable problems on *The Trojan Horse,* about Jenny—Belinda seemed especially interested in hearing about her; she even thought to ask about Ronnie Alsop, and we ended up dashing off a postcard to her. Naturally, we talked about the hottest gossip item going: Frank's affair with April Rains.

We had a couple more Negrones, then we abandoned the Trevi, and before I knew it we'd walked clear over to her hotel. By then we both knew what we had in mind, and we went up to her room. There were sessions of the Ecumenical Council still proceeding at the Vatican and our elevator car was full of priests. Belinda's eyes crinkled with merriment at the idea of what that collection of celibates would think if they guessed our purpose in ascending together to the *sesto piano.*

As soon as we entered the salon, I was confronted by the elaborately set bar Belinda maintained on a large refectory table. She didn't bother with room service, but dispensed the liquor in job lots; she could have run a good-sized party on what she had in stock. I poured Zubrovka vodka over ice and we drank healths, and then we began tearing off our clothes. I drew the outside shutters, allowing that wonderful Roman afternoon-siesta light to filter through. Meanwhile, the traffic had thinned, and its brazen cacophony dimmed away while we lay in the bed making love. To tell the truth, I never had the least thought of Jenny out at the Villa d'Este, not one; until afterward, and then I thought a lot about a lot of things. I even thought about what if someone besides those priests had seen us come in, what if they were downstairs, waiting for us to come out again?

After we made love, I found some of that slushy Italian pop music on the radio, and we lay on top of the sheets as we had so often in the New York days, smoking Gauloises, sipping our vodka, and talking quietly. We weren't kids, but we sure acted like it, even felt like it; Belinda was sweet beyond belief, filled with a warm gentleness and subdued humor. As she talked we kept stroking each other's hair; mine was long after my African stint and I'd left it uncut; who knew what kind of movie Frank might come up with?

Later, when the traffic had begun getting noisy again, telling me it was time to get going, I went into the bathroom and turned on the taps to fill the tub, then went back to bed to discover that Belinda and I weren't quite finished yet. After that we talked a while longer. As I recall the conversation, we were talking about love and happiness, marriage and fidelity, things like that. Perry Antrim had been dead for about ten years now, and though Belinda never said as much, I inferred that with his death all of her happiness had been swept away, and to her sorrow she never expected it to return. This of course was why she drank, to blot it all out. She said she certainly didn't intend to marry again—which only went to show how wrong people can be about themselves. She said she now had a full-time job with Faun; there was so much to make up for; she'd let the girl down terribly and wanted to do better. She had given El Gatto the El Gate-o; and as to the future, she didn't have a clue as to what she might do when her picture ended.

It wasn't difficult deducing from what she said that she held little brief for April, and it was clear to me that the green-eyed monster was involved here. I figured that since April had nearly twenty years on her, Belinda probably had a right to envy her that beautiful skin, those clear eyes, that healthy outdoors look, but I was taken aback by the vehemence of her feelings about Frank. "After Perry, he's the only one I really wanted. But he's crazy if he thinks Frances is ever going to give him a divorce. She'd die first."

At one point I shifted my position and as I glanced across the room I saw that the light through the shutters was being reflected in the floor in gleaming ripples. It took me a moment to figure out what was causing the liquid reflection; then I leaped up with a shout and rushed to turn off the tub. The floor was covered with my bathwater, and the Oriental rugs were sopping.

"What'll we do?" I wondered, while Belinda just giggled.

"Get dressed and scram out of here quick," she said. "Then I'll ring for the *portière* or someone."

I threw on my clothes, kissed her *arrivederci*, and left. Two of the same priests were in the elevator going down. When they saw me without Belinda, they looked a little disappointed. I couldn't blame them.

Each time I saw her she shook me up somehow. I didn't really understand my feelings then, but later I came to realize that I was probably in love with her but didn't know it. What struck me most about Belinda at that time was that her ore was being annealed in a furnace of her own heating. Something inside her was moving to put herself to the supreme test; she was searching, groping. One day she took some things out of her bag and I saw a book by Krishnamurti, and when I mentioned the fact, she denied ownership; claimed it belonged to a friend. I judged that she was doing some groping, she was on a search, and of course I was right; she wanted, needed, something—something that that damnable mother of hers had always denied her.

The thing was, I *liked* Belinda. Her problems of temperament and ego-boosting went beyond those of most stars-in-difficulty, yet she was kindhearted, she was sensitive to other people's problems, and she cared. Here's an example of what I'm talking about. It happened at a time when April and Frank and Jenny and I had been down at Capri during a break in April's shooting schedule. Somehow Belinda had got wise to the fact that Frank and April were now holed up at the villa of the Contessa Ingrisi, a rich American divorcée we all knew—everyone knew Dodi in those days—and Belinda decided to play spoilsport. She got herself invited aboard the *Calliope*, which was carrying on its illustrious passenger list no less a celebrity than Madame Callas herself. When Belinda dropped the news that Dodi Ingrisi was playing hostess to America's sweethearts, the yacht chugged off for Civitavecchia, where, as if on cue, the lovers appeared in full view, April giving Frank a hair trim on the Contessa's terrace. Photographs were snapped through a telephoto lens, they were sold to *Oggi*, and when they appeared, the jig was up for Frank and April. In the meantime Hedda Hopper had blown into town and hell was to pay, the biggest mess possible—with Belinda at the bottom of it all. When I found out about her involvement, I let her have it with both barrels. Filled with remorse over the mischief she'd caused, she went to April and apologized for her part in the affair, and as a result of that meeting the two women became friendly. Funny how things like that happen. Later, after Frank was killed, Belinda again went to April, to the place where she was institutionalized, to explain what had happened, but by that time April wasn't running on Standard Time and it was merely wasted effort on Belinda's part. But I think it's important to acknowledge these and other examples of her goodheartedness.

One day, when I got back to the hotel, Jenny reported that Belinda had called. When I got her on the phone, she sounded depressed and asked if we could meet. She began to cry and I promised to come, then had to invent an excuse for Jen, who wasn't fooled for an instant.

Belinda's woes were on the upswing. It was Faun, of course. She'd come home the night before and bragged that she'd lost her virginity. With whom? With her mother's discarded lover, the flamingo dancer.

I got in touch with Frank—he'd left Rome for England to make arrangements regarding Babe's London opening—and explained the problem. Did he have any suggestions? He'd already had a notion of what was going on; rumors flew around Rome like confetti and it never took long for the latest scandal to be reported. Frank said he'd see what he could arrange.

Next morning Faun received a curt note from her amigo, Joselito, saying he was unavoidably called out of town and regretfully would not be able to see her again. The day after, Faun was on a plane, booked via London over the Pole to Los Angeles, where Maude awaited her. No one mourned El Gatto, least of all Belinda. I had to laugh, though. What sprang our flamingo dancer out of Rome was a surprise invitation from Dodi Ingrisi to a large party she was giving for a movie producer who was looking for a Spanish dancer who could "flamingo" good. Joselito didn't get the job.

There was this about Belinda: she possessed the knack or ability to surmount whatever the winds of chance happened to blow her way. The mind of the public is notoriously short in such matters, they are a forgiving lot, and it wasn't long before most people had forgotten that the star of *Zenobia, Queen of Palmyra* had more or less disgraced herself in Rome.

This was just as well, and by the time she returned to the States no one was more surprised than she to discover that she was in love again. She'd met Grant Potter thirty-five thousand feet over Cleveland, New York to L.A. By the time the plane was over Albuquerque and the captain was announcing the Grand Canyon coming up, she was head over heels in love. Potter was a rich, aggressive contractor-builder with a variety of business interests, some of which took him to Mexico on frequent trips. He'd built a house in Acapulco and it was there, on a terrace overlooking the bay, with a vermilion sun setting into the gray-blue sea, amid a bower of flowers that smelled like heaven itself, that Belinda Laurel Seacombe Apper Pritchard Antrim became Mrs. Grant Potter. It turned out to be a mistake of no ordinary ilk.

For a while all went fine—of course it did. She adored Mexico, she became an aficionado of the bullfights, she learned sufficient Spanish to run the house smoothly, and she made a charming hostess. She even did a film, the unfortunate *El Gatto nel Sol;* the picture came and went like the mayfly it was. She kept her mahogany tan, wore beautiful clothes and expensive jewels, and was a worthy chatelaine to Las Flores Rosas, which was the name of the house. The President of Mexico was a frequent visitor, and several of His Excelencia's mistresses—not simultaneously, however. Grant and Belinda made a handsome couple and were frequently photographed together with their teen-age children, Faun and Dane. One shot even appeared in *Town & Country,* which had a lot to say about where Mrs. Potter stood at the moment on the social ladder. Who remembered Benny Vidor or the flamingo dancer now?

When Grant's business required his presence in Los Angeles, they usually occupied the Mandeville house that had been Belinda's and Perry's and which she'd had completely redecorated in all of Grant's favorite colors. There they lived the life of country squires, enjoying the rural atmosphere of the western Sunset area, yet being seen at all the best Brentwood and Beverly Hills parties. Hollywood proved that it can overlook both misfortune and bad taste when it elected to readmit Belinda to her former elevated status in its society; "forgive and forget" was its motto —"but don't do it again."

In return, the doors of the Mandeville house were flung wide, and celebrated guests came and went—producers, directors, actors and actresses, as well as many of Grant's extensive list of business associates, because it was all business, anyway, wasn't it? The marriage was a noble undertaking and we all gave Belinda full marks. Her efforts at creating a solid family unit were warmly chronicled in the papers, and the credit line

"Mr. and Mrs. Grant Houghley Potter" was often seen on the lists of charitable committees, and while Grant was occasionally mistakenly referred to as "Mr. Carroll," he took it with grace. That was what happened when you married a movie star, he said.

Jenny and I were invited to several affairs at Mandeville, and I found it easy to believe that Belinda had at last found the happiness she'd sought for so long. Then life took another little spin. By now Faun had graduated from Westlake School and there was a big party to celebrate. She went on taking her equitation classes and rode in the Westbury horse show and the one at Nod's Ridge, and Dane Potter often participated, for he enjoyed riding, too. A year after her high-school graduation, Faun made her debut at a party given by Grant and Belinda at the Bel Air Country Club; the tables were decorated in tuberoses and asters, with ginger leis flown in from Honolulu for the guests, and in the center of the buffet table there was a fountain of champagne from which guests might imbibe. The party was a big success and in another month Faun Antrim and Dane Potter were secretly married in Arizona. Seven months later the bride was delivered of an eight-pound, fourteen-ounce boy, christened Gary. Rumor had it that Faun lacked the maternal instinct. She turned her baby over to a nurse while she scooted around, and this lack of responsibility no doubt led in the long run to the child's mysterious disappearance. But that wasn't until some years later, when Faun had disconnected from the world and entered into the life of a Flower Child in the then-dawning Age of Aquarius, withdrawing to a commune to preach free love and raise bean curd and alfalfa sprouts, and then setting out to discover the wisdom of the East. Good luck!

For a time Belinda disappeared from my life—not that she'd been that much in it, but one way or another we'd managed to keep in touch. Jenny and I had even flown down to Acapulco for her wedding, and I'd seen the look of adoration on her face as she'd raised it to kiss her new husband. Grant seemed an uncomplicated kind of guy, four-square, the real McCoy, shrewd and hardheaded in business matters but a loving, tender mate and putty in Belinda's hands. They traveled a lot at that time, and she had everything any woman could possibly want—except a child, which they both wanted, the proof of their love; but it was getting late for her to have a baby. It helped some that their children had between them concocted a baby, but the fact that Faun and Dane were stepbrother and -sister added something slightly louche to the whole thing, something the least bit off, like Tuesday's fish. There were even mentions of that dread word "incest," as if by having fallen in love they'd committed some terrible crime, when of course there were no blood ties whatever.

The senior Potters were obliged to swallow their embarrassment when the baby was born with such obvious prematureness, though as grandparents they put a good face on the whole thing. But the future dimmed when it was learned that Dane, an exercise enthusiast, took a profound satisfaction in beating up his new wife, a habit he couldn't seem to break. Faun was fast becoming the battered bride, and the marriage was over before it began.

At the same time Belinda was discovering that her own union was all but on the rocks. The writing was not on the wall, however, but in a poison-pen letter addressed to her and signed "a friend," divulging the information that her husband, whom she loved and trusted, was secretly seeing a woman in San Francisco, a city to which he made frequent business trips.

I became privy to this little item because I'd accidentally stumbled across Belinda in the most unexpected way. Vi Ueberroth was practically one of the charter members of the Sand and Sea Club, that exclusive enclave on Pacific Coast Highway, an establishment catering to only the most exclusive social element in the city. Occasionally Vi would invite me out for lunch and an afternoon of sun poolside or, if I chose, a lie-out on the beach, listening to Vi chatter away; you could always count on Vi to bring you up-to-date on the latest dirt.

This particular afternoon, when she'd got into one of her beloved poker games, I went for a stroll along the beach. I suddenly discovered I had acquired a pal in the dog that ran up and barked for the stick I was carrying. I winged the stick, the dog bounded after it, pulled it out of the surf, and trotted back to me with the stick in his jaws. The next time I threw it, the dog dashed right across a blanket where two women were sitting with a baby under an umbrella, and then by golly if the dog didn't get the stick and plow right back across the same blanket, splattering water all over the place.

When I stepped over to apologize to the women, I had my surprise: one of them turned out to be Belinda Carroll.

"Well, look who's here," she said musingly, shading her eyes at me. "I was just thinking of you not two hours ago."

"What were you thinking?"

"I was thinking that it's been ages since I've seen you. You never call me."

"I don't know where to get you. I tried Mandeville. Aren't you there anymore?"

She shook her head so her hair swung and she drew me down and introduced her companion, a young Finn who was her current *au pair* girl, a buxom milkmaid type with the look of the young Bergman about her, hired to look after the three-year-old baby, whom its father had left with Belinda! Faun, fortunately, had no interest in hauling the baby around with her on her "spiritual pilgrimage."

When I pretended to suppose it was her own, she gave me a playful sock. "This is our beautiful Master Gary Potter," she explained. "Kirstig and I are baby-sitting while Dane is in Salt Lake City on business. Say hello to the nice man," she said, and the baby cooed. "Feel how heavy he is, this little dumpling," and she handed him over to me. I sat him aboard my thigh and dandled him a bit, until he began to squall and Kirstig relieved me of him.

"Oh goodness, I thought so," she said in her English-accented Scandinavian voice, "the little mischief has gone toy-toy in his nappy. Let me just go change him, I shan't be a minute."

With an apologetic smile she got up and bore the pooped-up baby away, leaving me to talk with Belinda, an interval both pleasant and enlightening.

The surprise of stumbling across her had taken my breath away, but now the mere sound of her voice worked like a tonic on me. There were little crooks and lines around her eyes that, while they made her appear older, were nonetheless intriguing. She was weathering, all right, but wonderfully. Her vivid beauty was paring down to a fine handsomeness rare in women, and I found her quite as extraordinary-looking as ever.

She seemed pleased to see me, too, and asked me many questions—about my health, my work, how things were going with Jenny and me. She'd rented a place here on the beach for the whole summer and urged us to come out any time we liked. The sun and salt air were good for the child and she was so delighted to have him. "Me, a grandmother? Come *on.*"

"And Faun? What's become of her?" I waited for her answer.

"I had a letter, surprise, surprise. Wrong—not a letter, a card. From Delhi. She's been at the Taj Mahal. There was some difficulty, evidently —they had to drag her out of the pool. It's against the law to swim there."

"What's she doing in India? Killing all the sacred cows?"

"She's meditating and learning yoga and has something called a mandala. She also has a mantra. Rings on her fingers and bells on her toes —I guess she jingles as she walks. She sent me a snapshot of herself with a diamond in her nose—how on earth do they get them to stay in? Now she's living at an ashram somewhere and eating goat cheese. She can even make her stomach touch her spine or something. But I don't think goat cheese is the answer."

Though she made light of the whole thing, I could tell that Faun was rattling Belinda's cage again. Because she seemed embarrassed to talk about it, I looked for another topic of conversation. "Where's Grant these days?" I asked finally.

She didn't look at me. "To tell you the truth, I don't know. Singapore, maybe. Or Botswana, or Honduras. Or . . . San Francisco . . ." The funny way she said it made me pay closer attention.

"What's in San Francisco?"

"Oh, you know, the usual—Nob Hill, Golden Gate Bridge—and somebody named Curtwright."

Who, I wondered, was Curtwright.

Candace Curtwright, it came out, was a San Francisco socialite type, glittering hostess, patron of the arts, chairman of the Opera Ball, thirty, blonde, and a dilly.

"Blondes are fatal for Grant," she said. "But what a way for me to find out." She fetched her striped beach bag, delved inside, and produced a letter, which she handed over to me. "Read it and weep, darling."

The letter, handwritten on drugstore stationery, said:

Must you spend your whole life being dumb? Did it ever occur to you why your darling husband insists on spending so much time these days in the lovely City by the Bay? As Tony Bennett says in the song, "I left my heart in San Francisco." You know, dear—where the little cable cars climb halfway to the stars? Take a tip, the name is Candy Curtwright, she's pretty and she's loded [sic]. But don't cry, it happens to us all. Just ditch the bum.

The lines were unsigned. I stared at them, trying to analyze the handwriting. There was something so blatantly vulgar, so cheap and obvious, even obscene about the note that I inwardly cursed its author. What kind of woman—of course it was a woman—could be so deliberately cruel?

I folded the pages to return them to their envelope, and as I did so, I caught the faint fragrance that clung to them, and noted Belinda's tentative glance from under her lashes.

"Mm." She wet her lips as she took the envelope back and stashed it in the bag. I wondered why she carried it with her. Presently Kirstig returned with the baby and we ventured into other realms of conversation.

An hour later, when I got back to the club and found Viola, who was sunny as Spain because she'd won three pots and filled an inside straight, I told her about the letter. Wise in the ways of her sex, Vi was neither as surprised nor as shocked as I. "Bitches, dear, we're all bitches," she said matter-of-factly. But I could see she was upset, for she liked Belinda and was one of the few women permitted to address her as "Blindy," the nickname Maude Antrim had given her back when she was married to Perry.

"Certainly it was a woman. I got her scent. And guess what it was."

"I know—Eau de la Skunk!"

"Try Jeunesse Dorée." This was the scent that Claire Regrett had invested her name—and money—in.

She laughed outright. "Oh, my dear, you don't mean it. Are you saying you detect the fine Italian hand of Madame Regrett in this?"

I pointed out that Claire was a notoriously bad speller. "Loded" was how she'd written it.

Vi mused about this and I could tell she didn't like it, didn't like it at all. "Claire was in San Francisco for the opera two weeks ago. *Pagliacci*, I believe she said."

"So there we are."

"Oh dear, oh dear," Vi said, shaking her head. "I really wish this hadn't happened. What a woman doesn't know—another woman will tell her. I'm afraid Blindy may take this too much to heart. I just pray it doesn't set her off again. You know—"

She tossed back an imaginary glass of Scotch and went to collect her winnings.

Though she had no occult powers that I knew of, it was exactly as Viola predicted: the news of Grant's infidelities snapped Belinda's lines again and she became a ship all at sea. This time her sails were badly torn, her rigging all tangled, her anchor torn away and sunk. She endured the shame of the divorce bravely enough, making another collection of head-lines and keeping tongues wagging.

To the loss of a husband (after the divorce, Grant married his thirty-year-old San Francisco socialite) must be added the shocking and mysteri-ous loss of her grandchild, Gary, whom she had adored and whom she mourned, while Faun's blithe attitude about the missing child only served to estrange mother and daughter further. The story of the tragic case sold papers for months; one lead after the other was turned up, only to prove another red herring or to end in some calculating person's believing it was chance to make money out of someone else's misfortune, in this case one of the most famous women in the country. As might have been expected, the mother was at the bottom of it all. Having flown in from India with members of the Hare Krishna cult she had made herself a part of, she arrived at Sunnyside, demanded that Belinda hand over the child. She drove him away in a van with flower decals pasted all over its exterior, the speakers blaring "Strawberry fields forever . . ." Neither Belinda nor Maude Antrim ever saw the boy again.

Faun was crucified in the papers, and Belinda was again pilloried, as if the thing had somehow been her fault. It mushroomed into a scandal of remarkable proportions when she, leaving her psychiatrist's office on North Bedford, was attacked by a hysterical woman who dumped a bag of garbage on her. Since a photographer had been conveniently on hand to record the incident, it seemed likely it had been a set-up, but it didn't help Belinda at all to see her picture plastered on page one. (Some time later I was hurrying to catch my flight out of Chicago, and as I ran for the gate I was accosted by one of those smiling Hare Krishnas who annoy travelers by handing them a flower and then cadging a donation; as I brushed angrily past the creature in her curry-colored rags, I was astonished to realize it was Faun Potter, or someone who looked a lot like her.)

The kidnapping was all Belinda needed to push her off the deep end. She began drinking again, more heavily than ever, and there were many repetitions of the kind of scenes she'd played before, the kind from the New York and Rome days.

Again, regrettably, I lost track of her. Jen and I were still having problems, I was being faced by important career decisions, and frankly my mind was in other places. But then there occurred the unfortunate business about Mel Beets, and that, of course, was the end. It was really the nadir for Belinda Carroll; after it she had no place to go but up; she'd been down about as far as anyone could go.

She'd always liked jazz, and back in the forties when she came to New York she'd sometimes go up to Harlem to hear the black musicians, Dizzy Gillespie and others, who she claimed "sent her." Now she'd latched on to a sax player who could be heard at The Joint, a place along the Coast Highway between Santa Monica and Malibu.

One day eight of us had driven in two cars up to Trancas, the only really good beach around in those days when the notorious Red Tide was running. It was a great day and we lingered for a long sunset cocktail hour; then, since everyone was starved, on the way home we stopped for chili and beer. By then it was after ten, but some of the gang were up for

a party, and since The Joint was just next door, they said they wanted to
go catch a couple of sets. Jenny poured cold water and party-pooped, but
it wasn't our car so she got overruled.

As we entered, there was a sandwich board at the coat-check closet
that proclaimed "Featuring Mel Beets," and there was an 8×10 glossy of
a black dude with a saxophone hung around his neck. Since it was still
early, there were plenty of tables, and we sat up front while a trio played
really cool stuff, the kind of fifties music that frosted a hot room and
reminded you of *Castles in Spain,* that terrific icy album that Miles Davis
put out.

While we sat listening, I noticed this woman at a table to one side;
she had a drink and there was an untouched club sandwich on the
Formica-top table. The way she sat, with one foot turned at the ankle, the
other foot resting on top of it, made me look closer. Sure enough: Belinda.
She'd put on weight—the reason I hadn't recognized her right away—and
she was looking her absolute worst, in slacks and a messy blouse and
don't-care hair. Afraid she might catch me staring, I looked away, and I
didn't say anything to Jenny or the others.

Then the set ended, the trio came off the stand, and a quintet came
on. Now I had my first look at this Mel Beets; he was the one people came
to hear, and pretty soon he began to wail on his sax. No doubt, he was
good, really cool. Not bad-looking, but nothing to write home about,
either—a trimmed mustache, neat hair, good hands with a careful mani-
cure; you could see the pale rose ovals gleaming under the lights. I was
always amazed at how some musicians could go clear out of things while
they were playing; this fellow was as far out as you can get.

But I didn't like him, only because of Belinda's interest in him, and
I found myself rejecting both him and his music. His eyes would occasionally flick over to where she was sitting. She looked zombielike as she
sipped from her drink and took extended drags on her cigarette, blowing
out streams of smoke that rose and dissolved in the blue lights, as if she
were trying to call attention to herself.

After a couple of sets the group took a breather. When they moved
off into the dark, I watched Belinda get up and head for the john. Our
group started talking, and the women said they were going to powder
their noses. I thought, God, if Jenny recognizes Belinda—

But when they came back there were no signs of anything amiss. I
got up casually and stretched, glanced around, then said I thought I'd
check the service for messages. I ankled over to where it said "Rest
Rooms" and ducked behind a ratty curtain that was half off its rod. At the
end of the passageway hung a lighted sign, "Telephone," and I went along

to it. The booth was hidden away under the stairs and it was in use. The light at the top glowed dimly and I could see a man behind the glass. Then I realized there were two people in there, but I didn't think they were using the phone. The man was wearing a white shirt; the back of his neck was dark; the woman's arm was white as she embraced him. As I looked away, to the walls that were covered with graffiti, I noticed two pairs of initials enclosed in a heart, making me think of a similar design in cement in the cellar of a Connecticut house. And now here we were, Belinda and I, in a California roadhouse, and she was getting banged by a black saxophonist, and my wife would be angry if she knew what I was thinking. I turned and went out.

"Anything?" Jenny asked. I shook my head.

After a while the musicians shuffled onto the stand again; they played a few riffs, feeling their way into something, but the quintet was now a quartet, because the sax player was missing. They started without him, "On the First Warm Day," a Bart Howard tune Mabel Mercer used to sing, and it jarred me, reminding me of New York, but my mind was still picturing the scene in the telephone booth—what if I'd just knocked on the glass and waved?

The guitar was taking the lead chords, and I noticed that Belinda's table remained conspicuously empty; the top was cleared of both glass and uneaten sandwich. Pretty soon Mel Beets reappeared, clipped on his sax, and slid into the measure; after a discreet interval Belinda stepped out from behind the curtain, ducking low in the light as she resumed her place. She carried a fresh drink, which she set in front of her while she lit another cigarette and blew more smoke into the blue lights. I couldn't resist looking at her, my eyes flicking back and forth from her pale face to the sweating brown one on the stand. She looked both nervous and bored. She studied her wrist in the light, then fumbled in her purse; she turned aside, bent her head, and jerked it once, twice, and I knew she was taking a snort. As she turned back she wiped her finger under her nose, a dead giveaway.

At that moment, her profile had fallen into full light, and I heard Jenny's low gasp and she poked me. "Look—it's Belinda Carroll!" she said in a louder voice than I could have wished for. The music level dropped at that moment and her voice carried, carried so well that Belinda glanced our way. She peered harder; then she jumped up, knocking over the table along with her drink. She stumbled and landed in the corner with a crash. I rushed to help her, pulling her to her feet but trying to keep her hidden with my body as I propelled her through a slit in the curtain.

We were standing in the passageway to the kitchen and I could hear pots being rattled, and voices. I tried to prop her against the wall and keep her upright while I caught my breath. She stared at me and kept repeating "Jesus Christ" over and over in a dazed, disbelieving voice. Wagging her head, she tried to shove me away.

"Don't look at me, Jesus, don't look at me!" she kept saying, still shoving at my chest while I stood there holding her up, trying to figure out what to do with her. Then a figure ducked through the curtain behind us and I felt rather than saw someone move in—this turned out to be the club manager—and relieve me of her weight. He didn't say a word, but as he took her away, I heard Belinda say my name. "He's a friend," I heard her tell the man, "Charlie—friend—" Then she was gone and I could smell fried onions from the kitchen.

I was ashamed to face my friends; most of them knew of my friendship with Belinda, and Jenny kept saying, "I don't understand, I simply don't understand." I didn't try to enlighten her, because I didn't understand, either, but there were domestic repercussions. At home, she had lots to say about the situation, words I didn't care to hear. I felt she was hitting below the belt and taking it out on Belinda for whatever had happened years earlier in New York. Then something got into the papers about a "famous forties star" hanging out at a beach dive because she was hung up on a musician who happened to be a gentleman of color.

One evening a few weeks after this, after we'd had yet another quarrel, I lied to Jenny by saying I was going to visit a couple of friends. I took one of the cars and on the merest hunch drove out to the beach. It was a Friday, and I may have been ill-advised to make the trip, but I'd been drinking since five and I had a good buzz on. I parked and went into The Joint and sat down at the bar. The place was already crowded and I had to crane and stretch to see over the heads of the crowd. The quintet was on the stand and I didn't even have to look to know that Mel Beets was in his place: there was the wailing of his sax to tell me. A further glance told me that Belinda was over there, too, at her regular stand, drink on table, her hair shining in the light. With her was a kind of duplicate job, also blonde, and though I couldn't see her face, I had a feeling I knew who it was. Maybe it was the spaghetti straps, the cinched-in waist, the tilt of the head, but I was pretty sure it was Angie Brown.

Sure enough, as I took my drink and headed in that direction, I heard her gleeful laugh, that big Italian guffaw. Sliding closer, I put my cold hand against her bare back. She let out a yelp, turning with an indignant look until she realized who it was; then she jumped up, threw her arms around me, and screamed with delight.

"Quiet!" "Shut up!" "Sit down!" came the calls, and "For God's sake, sit down!" I heard Belinda growl. She wouldn't look at me, but was trying to cover her face with the hand that held a cigarette. I sat. Angie clutched my hand, and while the number played on we exchanged a whole dialogue in total silence: she didn't really understand what she was doing there, Belinda had wanted her to come and keep her company; she didn't like the sax player; things were grim; she was glad I was there— why *was* I there?—she was *so* glad to see me; what could we do together to help our friend? When I lit Angie's cigarette for her, I could see by the match flame that like the rest of us she hadn't gotten any younger; but, God, it was good to see her. And then the music ended. As Mel set his instrument on its rack he glanced our way, then went off with his cronies.

Belinda gave me a hard glare. "What are you doing out this way again?"

"I happened to be in the neighborhood; do you mind? Do you mind?"

"I mind the hell out of you if you're trying to check up on me," came the sullen reply.

"He isn't checking up on you," Angie interposed tactfully. "He knew I was here and he came to have a drink, that's all."

Belinda used an expletive; I never liked to hear her swear and this one was a beaut. She eyed me with a kind of venom I'd never witnessed in her before, and I could believe many of the stories I'd refused to countenance before. I did my best to turn the corner, to brush past whatever it was that had loomed so suddenly. I said I'd wanted to see how she was doing and that I didn't have a telephone number for her. This much was true, though it didn't go down too well. Angie kept the conversation going until the musicians came back. When Mel Beets appeared in the doorway, Belinda beckoned to him and he came over. I got up and we shook hands while Angie performed the introductions. I was friendly, but not too; I said I'd enjoyed his music the first night and had come to hear some more.

"He's full of shit," Belinda snarled. "He wants to play daddy and see how his baby-bunting is. He doesn't approve of interracial fucking—do you, Chazz?" She drawled out my name and the word hung in the air.

Mel was scowling, not at me, but at her. "What d'you want to talk like that for?" he said in a low, smooth voice. "Why d'you rag him that way if he's your friend?"

"That's right," Angie put in. "We're all friends here. Mel, got time for a drink?"

"Yes, I'll have one, if it's all the same." He spoke politely, in a slightly southern-accented voice. His hands were on the table and I kept noticing their slender lines. A cigarette burned between two fingers and the smoke

curled between us. The waiter brought another round. "Let me," I said
to Angie, who'd moved for the check.

"Oh, let him, damn it," Belinda said. "That's what men are meant for,
picking up checks."

"Put a lid on it, babe," Mel said softly.

"Oh, go lid yourself," she returned.

"I mean it, babe. Can it."

"Well, fuck this, for Christ's sake, can't I even talk anymore?"

"Not like that. Not when you got friends come out to see you. Put
a good face on it, babe. Eat your sandwich there."

"Who's hungry?" She swore contemptuously; then the ashes from
her cigarette fell into her drink, and this triggered the most bizarre chain
reaction. With one vicious swipe she sent the whole drink flying, and it
splashed onto the nearest table, where two couples sat eavesdropping on
our table. Without pausing, Belinda snatched up Mel's drink and dashed
it in his face, cubes and all. When she jumped up, he tried to pull her down
again and she bit him. Then she snatched up the fork from her plate and
attacked him with it. It was sickening. Angie and I both went at her,
trying to pull her away, but something bad really cracked in her. She
kicked and scratched and fought like a wildcat; she was absolutely uncontrollable, and when first our chairs, then our table had been overturned
and Mel was bleeding, I took off my jacket and threw it over her head,
trying to subdue her, and we went to the floor. Her shrieks were hoarse
and intermittent and I could see her fingers clawing the air. Figures had
appeared from the kitchen and were staring down as we writhed in the
wetness, until I clambered astride her, holding her arms down while she
went on thrashing and kicking. No one approached us until, after what
seemed hours, I heard a siren's wail and then two cops rushed in. I didn't
want to let them near her, but they literally dragged me off her, and when
she was free of my jacket she scrabbled away from us. Then, as the cops
closed in on her, she went crazy again, cursing and kicking like a mad-
woman.

I'd never seen anything close to this; I couldn't even have imagined
such a thing. They used force to quell her, they handcuffed her and shoved
her toward the door. The overhead lights had come on, people crowded
around, and I heard the famous name being buzzed about while the whole
place ogled the scene.

"Hey, wait," I called, hurrying after the police, but I slipped in the
water and went down on my ass again. It was Mel who helped me up.

"It's okay," he said in my ear, "let them have her. I can get her out."

Angie, who'd run out with them, came back in shaking her head.

"Mel, are you hurt?" His arm was perforated from the hand up, the dark skin bathed in red, and she peered at him anxiously.

"It's all right, don't worry," he said, "I'll play again." His little joke. The pianist, a guy named Teddy, hit the keys, the waiters were cleaning up the mess, the lights went down, and Angie and I followed Mel into the cubicle where the musicians hung out between sets.

"Didn't I tell you the bitch'd pull something like this one night?" said Johnny, the guitar player. Someone had come up with a first-aid kit, and Angie was swabbing Mel's wounds with alcohol.

"I think we should take you to get this looked at," she said. "There's no telling where that fork may have been."

"Most likely in her mouth," said Johnny Guitar. Someone brought me my sport jacket. It was a mess. I felt for my wallet, but the pocket was empty. I looked in all the other pockets, then tossed the coat in the basket. Nobody knew nothin' 'bout nothin'. I told myself it was my own damn fault for meddling.

Mel said he'd meet Angie and me at the police station. She left her car and drove with me, but at the station there was a real foul-up. Belinda was giving the boys in blue more of the same—we could hear her strident voice coming from somewhere in back. Mel was at the desk talking quietly to the sergeant. "You know who that is?" he asked in his low voice.

"Damn right. Big stuff, she is. She's really buzzed. What's she on, anyway?"

"She's been ailing, she don't feel so good. Pills, maybe."

"You her friend?" the sergeant asked.

Angie pushed forward. "We're all her friends. She's sick, she needs help. Must you keep her in there? Can't we take her to the hospital, get her to a doctor?"

"Don't see her going anywhere in her present condition," the sergeant said laconically.

"What's the charge?" I asked, stepping up.

"Let's start with a d. and d. and then take it from there. When she quiets down maybe we can see about some bail. Why don't you folks go along home and get some sleep. She's not going to do anyone any good tonight."

"Officer, will this get in the papers?" Angie asked in a low voice. The sergeant shrugged.

"Not from these lips." He glanced around the room; there were a dozen people in it, each of whom knew that Belinda Carroll, world-famous star, was shut up behind those green bars. And God knew what was going to happen when they let her out again.

I waited with Mel while Angie went to telephone Maude for help, and when she hung up she reported that Felix Pass was on the way. Felix Pass was a brilliant attorney, one of Beverly Hills' best, but he couldn't get anyone to fix bail. Next morning Belinda appeared before Judge Eugene Hahn of the second circuit court of California and was sentenced by him to ninety days in the county jail. He was known as "Rockpile" Hahn.

Much was made of these events in the press, and the photographers had been accorded the privilege of photographing the prisoner at her arraignment. She had a black eye and a swollen lip, and her clothes were torn. Formalities over, they rode her down to Lincoln Heights, where she began serving her sentence. At first she was in a cell with a woman being held for possession of narcotics and child negligence. She got into a fight with Belinda and both women had to be placed in the infirmary. After that Belinda was given a cell of her own. At the end of twenty-one days Felix Pass got her released in the custody of her former mother-in-law and she was let out the back way. The press made capital of the fact that a Rolls-Royce with an Oriental driver arrived to pick up the freed jailbird and drove through the crowd that had gathered amid a flurry of flashing bulbs. Other vehicles trailed the Silver Cloud onto the Hollywood Freeway, coming off at the Bowl exit onto Highland, then traveling at a measured pace along Sunset into Beverly Hills. Just past the hotel, the procession turned into Benedict Canyon, then wound its way up and up among the green foliage until the passengers were looking down on the rooftops that dotted the landscape—most of them red-tiled in the old California mission style.

Close to the top, on Caligula Way, the Rolls proceeded through the twin gates of the famous estate known as Sunnyside, the residence that had been built by Crispin Antrim fifty years before. None of the pursuing vehicles was allowed to enter. The gates closed behind the Rolls as it drew up to the entrance, where Maude Antrim was waiting to help Belinda inside. The door closed, the car drove away, all was quiet. Belinda Carroll was not seen again for a long time.

That was it. They scratched her off, one more alkie, gone the same road as Frances Farmer and a host of other Hollywood beauties, talented ladies who'd skidded and forgot to jam on the brakes or braked too hard on the curves. In Hollywood gone is forgotten, and she was forgotten; mercifully, it seemed, because she didn't need cameras poking in at her or reporters with pencils in the bands of their fedoras, not that reporters wore fedoras anymore.

She was "under treatment," as it was generally stated in whatever notice was taken of her. She'd gone the way of all flesh, she'd been walking the Boulevard of Broken Dreams too long; had she been another kind of woman she might have taken the dive off the Hollywood sign. For two years she never appeared in public. A steady progress of medicos came in and went out through the gates, sometimes she was driven in the Rolls to a clinic for an X-ray or an EKG; that was about it. I was in Europe again and not privy to what was going on, but I wrote her, wrote often, though she didn't write me back. I wasn't any help anyway; I was drinking myself in those days—it's where I got my calories; I sure wasn't eating much.

One day an unobtrusive-looking car drove through the gates of Sunnyside. No one would have recognized the driver, but it was Belinda, driving herself for the first time in a long while. She drove over to Pico Boulevard, where she parked and entered a church. She walked down a flight of stairs and went into the community room. It was not smoke-filled, not did it have fluorescent lighting. She was surprised at the number of familiar faces she saw there; a couple of them were old friends, people she wasn't even aware had a Problem. Six times she went and never said a word coming or going. She hid her hair under a scarf, her eyes behind dark glasses. Her hands still shook and she was always thirsty. She drank lots of orange juice for the vitamin C, she chewed gum or her nails, and her voice developed an unattractive hoarseness. On her seventh visit, Angie accompanied her. Angie was the one who made her do it. She raised her hand and when she was called upon she stood up and said, "Hello— my name's Belinda Carroll and I'm an alcoholic."

Those were hard-wrung words for her, words that embarked her on a journey; not the kind you take for sightseeing, but the long, bitter journey that a soul in chains makes when it fights its way back from the darkest corners or up from the deepest crevasses.

I wasn't present to witness this crucial moment in the life of one of the world's most famous women—I was in New York experiencing a similar, crucial beginning myself—nor was I present on that famous night over a decade later, to feel the thrill of hearing her name announced to a worldwide audience of millions.

Holding the gold statuette they'd just handed her, she smiled to her many well-wishers in the audience and gave this speech:

"I always wanted to be standing here, like Bette Davis and Katharine Hepburn, my heroines, and be holding this little fellow in my hands. That I am standing here at all is as much a wonder to me as my having won tonight. I truly think I must be home in bed asleep and this is just a dream. But it's a beautiful dream, a lovely dream. I—I have a lot of people to thank, more than you can imagine and more than I can ever hope to think of." She went on to thank those people connected with the film that had won her the award, saving her deepest thanks for the man who'd made her. Upon mention of Frank Adonis's name the audience forced her to wait while they applauded; then she listed in turn each of the major stars whose careers Frank had either kicked off or helped to boost, with one notable omission.

Her closing remark was particularly heartfelt. "And I especially want to thank all of my friends who are all the friends of Bill and who have done so much to help me. You know who you are. God bless you, everyone."

Later on the wags were saying that she'd sounded like Pollyana, but what did that matter? She had her goddamned Oscar in her mitt. I've seen it. I've touched it. I've kissed the darn thing. But what most people wanted to know was, who were the "friends of Bill's" she was talking about? There wasn't really any reason for most people to know, but the ones who did had the best reasons in the world, because they were all saved. Back from the brink, out of the pit. They'd all come in out of the rain along with Belinda Carroll. Those people were in A.A., that most anonymous of organizations, but Belinda Carroll had gone public on a worldwide hook-up and that was the big hurrah. Pretty soon just about everybody knew who "Bill" was.

April

Back in the early thirties a young woman of no particular distinction arrived at the Hollywood bus station on Vine Street, a few blocks east of Wilcox Avenue, where Mrs. Wilcox's house had once stood. Like thousands of others, this screen hopeful had blown in from the American Midwest seeking fame and fortune. Her name was Peg Entwhistle, and like Dorothy she came from Kansas to the Land of Oz; but unlike Dorothy she never clicked her red shoes three times and got back home to an anxiously waiting Auntie Em. This was Peg's bad luck. At that time there was a local real-estate company owned by Mack Sennett and some lesser lights, and as a suitable advertisement for their company they erected a tall block-letter sign in the hills, spelling out in characters three stories high the name "HOLLYWOODLAND." A real smart deal. Today the sign still stands—part of it anyway—and with the passing of time it has become the unofficial trademark of Hollywood, suitably tawdry and commonplace, just the right degree of rundown tackiness. New York has its Empire State Building, Chicago has the Wrigley Building, St. Louis the Gateway Arch, San Francisco the Golden Gate Bridge, and Hollywood a battered realty sign.

As for Peg, she proved ordinary enough, hardly movie fodder, conventionally pretty, like ten thousand other movie-struck girls, with passable legs and firm breasts but little else to recommend her, including talent. She peroxided her hair and beat on the doors to fame and fortune for about two years, doors that stubbornly remained closed to her until, despairing of ever tasting success, our Peg climbed to the very top of the last letter of HOLLYWOODLAND—the thirteenth letter—and dashed herself onto the ground among the sharp yucca plants. The coroner's report stated that she died of a self-inflicted broken neck, but this was not strictly true: what Peg really died of was a broken heart.

They sort of told it all in *A Star Is Born*—only there the girl, Esther

Blodgett, really makes it. But the chances are something like a million to one. The smart ones hustle on back to the dime store or the farm, settle down with some guy in overalls, and raise kids that get mumps and measles. The dumb ones stick it out and end up like Peg, splat in the yucca patch.

Who can count those broken hearts of Hollywood? I've heard of a famous star of the forties who, suffering a severely altered lifestyle, actually lives out of her car, a vintage Plymouth; not quite a bag lady, but "car lady" is close. I know of another star who ended up waiting tables at a fancy Beverly Hills soda fountain, once serving coffee to the director who'd made her a star. And there's a third party I know personally, who's been hidden away in a rubber room for years; bent her mind over a guy she couldn't have—a married man; bad business. Sure, you know who I mean. Everybody knows about this one; she was a well-publicized commodity about twenty years ago. Hedda and Louella did their work well. That sad tale made good copy, start to finish. But probably you don't know the whole story. I knew her back in those days, happier, more innocent days; she was a happy girl, for a while, but the world's taken a turn or two since, and she's not so happy anymore. Maybe she'd be better off if she'd taken the plunge, like our Peg; who can say?

The thing was, my friend didn't really want to be a movie star at all, and you just can't do it that way. You really have to want it. You have to taste, smell, feel, eat, and sleep it. You have to screw your mind onto the idea of stardom, you have to have a built-in set of gauges and meters, little clock faces ticking away in your head, whole sets of gears that mesh and stay meshed. Maybe you go up, you go down, you go up again, like Belinda Carroll; maybe you start your climb at the horizon, you slide up to the zenith of the noon-sky, then you slide down the other side, like Claire Regrett. But you possess that necessary thing that makes a star— you *want* it. You'd kill for it. You'd murder your own mother. You thrive in the limelight, the camera likes you, the front office likes you, the fans like you, everybody likes you, you say yes yes yes, and there you are, one more shining star in the Hollywood firmament. Nobody ever made stardom who didn't want it. Except maybe April. She *didn't* want it, didn't want any part of it. But it happened anyway.

> *Dusty's good vibrations*
> *And our imaginations*
> *Can't go on indefinitely,*
> *And California dreamin' is becomin' a reality. . . .*

The perfect music for a perfect L.A. day is playing on my car radio. You couldn't ask for much better—just take a look at that sky. Pristine. Not a lot of smog, either. She had a great voice, Mama Cass, really mellow. I miss her.

And California dreamin' is becomin' a reality. . . .

Those were crucial years for me, the mid-sixties; the time of the Beatles, Sonny and Cher, the Mamas and the Papas, the Supremes. Frank had put my career in high gear. I was free-lancing the studios, Jenny and I were living in style on Sunset Plaza Drive and dining at La Rue or Scandia weekly. La Rue was at the foot of the street and was one of Frank's favorite eating spots as well—he used to take Frances there a lot. And, by the weirdest of coincidences, it was at La Rue that Kit Carson first came to light. No kidding, if you can believe it, the famous Kit Carson used to park cars there; that's where we first spotted him, when he was just plain Floyd Ayres, better known to his friends as Bud. I guess you're thinking with the way things turned out that he was probably better off parking cars, and I suppose you'd be right. Parking cars might have made him King of the Mountain compared with the way he ended up, but that's another story. No, it's not, not really. But at least he's not at the funny farm, like you-know-who.

The Asylum for the Insane at Libertad, California, may not be the worst place in the world—there are lots of others with far more degrading conditions—but it will do. This is where Anna Thorwald lives and eats and sleeps. Anna has her good days and her bad ones, doubtless more of the latter (how do you have a really good day at Libertad?). In the annals of psychiatry she's not a classic schizoid case, but she's an interesting one. Certifiably insane, true, but not a textbook specimen. Little word of her ever leaks out, though for years the various nurses and staffers at the hospital have been offered money to tell all. But they know they'd lose their jobs if they did.

I still go to see her, Anna. Not many people do—she hasn't any family left, she's pretty well forgotten by now—but I try to keep my oar in. April meant a lot to me in those days before she came to stardom, and I seem to be all that's left to her of the Hollywood she was so briefly a part of. It's not terribly far, the drive is pleasant. You go west along Sunset Boulevard past both Bel Air gates and the UCLA campus, where Anna used to be a student, and then turn right onto the San Diego Freeway going north and head west along the Ventura Freeway. Near Simi Valley you get off and drive some ten miles into the yellow foothills until you get to this place that at one time or another has sheltered several famous personages whose minds have faltered, like Anna's. She's been at Libertad for a long time now, she'll probably stay there to the end of her days—and I have to admit I hope that won't be too much longer.

To be truthful, I'm not really nuts about this Easter pilgrimage I'm making, but I guess by now it's become a habit. Easter, Christmastime, her birthday, other occasions, I try to go visit her, never knowing, of course, what I'm likely to encounter. Lately she's been getting steadily worse, and I find it tough sledding; I guess anyone would. Mrs. Kraft, who's in charge of administering the place, is a decent soul, and she does the best she can under the circumstances; always optimistic, Mrs. Kraft, but who can be optimistic about this case when it seems so evident that Anna will never get well, never get out of there?

Now I'm coming into Libertad; along about now I usually get this creepy feeling, picturing that grim layout of brick buildings. A necessary evil, I suppose, asylums for the insane; we have to have places like this, every state in the Union must have a couple, but I have such a deep-down wariness of this one. Booby hatches aren't my thing.

And there it is. Lovely, isn't it? Looks like a set for *Ramona* or a Cisco Kid movie, all that fake Spanish architecture, arches, red roof tiles, you expect to see people in serapes and sombreros. Just what the doctor ordered for a nice rest away from home: good fresh country air, you get a good night's sleep here. The chow's great, too. Shit-on-a-shingle is their stock-in-trade—and if you're lucky you may get "Jell-O jewels" for dessert. And the whole place, inside anyway, is painted that awful institution green. I think they think it rests the eye or soothes the nerves or something.

I'm taking along some flowers and candy, an Easter lily and chocolate-covered filberts. Sweets to the sweet, nuts to the nuts; Anna is both. I've prepared for my visit by accumulating a good hour and a half's worth of anecdotes and general news, gambits to keep the conversational ball bouncing. It's not an easy thing, this kind of visit, but I accept it as a kind of obligation. Frank would want it. If I were the one who was dead, he'd do the same for me, I'm sure he would. And I guess it's just as well that he can't come to see her anymore.

Mrs. Kraft sees me crossing the parking lot, greets me with a smile. You have to give the old gal credit, she's not a bad soul; she does her best for the patients, has their interests at heart. She chats at me a few minutes, tells me that Anna has been "in and out" of things all week but is a bit better today, looking forward to my arrival.

I guess I don't need to describe the "Community Room." Seen one

community room, seen 'em all. The door closes automatically behind me.
There's a regular echo in the room. It's large and the ceiling's high and
there's nothing to tamp down the reverberations. You might note that all
the windows are well above reach and have metal waffle grilles over them.
There's a sort of makeshift stage at one end and I see a couple of Easter
bunnies hopping around (no kidding: pink bunnies with long floppy ears,
hopping), and not only bunnies, there's half a dozen animated eggs with
painted bands around their middles. Crazy, I know, but remember, I said
it was Easter, and let's not forget where we are, Jellybean City.

There she is. There's "Anna." With all the racket I hadn't noticed
her way over there in the corner. She doesn't see me, or anyway pretends
not to—with Anna you usually can't tell. The person I'm looking at as
I approach is a stranger to me, this woman called Anna Thorwald. There
was a time when I thought I knew her pretty well, when she and I were
young and the world was that terrific pearly oyster we all want it to be.
We were good friends, Anna and I; Frankie and I were friends, she and
Jenny were friends, she and I took acting lessons together; it was a kind
of mutual admiration society from which we both profited. We held each
other's hands and gassed on the phone and went to Barney's Beanery for
chili and admired each other's new cars and applauded each other's progress and were caught up in all the starry Hollywood bullshit. And that was
all right because we were all right, our heads weren't stuck in the sand,
we weren't ostriches, we knew which way was up. We had college educa-
tions, good ones, we knew our way around, spoke the King's English,
wore two-tone spectators, and had what lots of other people envied. If we
got sucked in by the All-American Dream, well, whose fault was that? It
still takes two to tango.

Now *that* lady is *this* lady, and there she is, a wan, dough-faced
woman in a drab skirt and a shapeless sweater, with iron-gray hair and
sallow skin, who, as I cross the rugless floor of this large bleak gymnasium
of a place, sits so awkwardly, crimping the knitted bottom of her sweater
between gnarled, nervous fingers. Believe me, this person I do not know
well. In the faulty light I peer closer, distrustful of my eyes, of her, of the
life she lived that has brought her here to this place. There are things in
life that just aren't fair; this is one.

Her smile is perfunctory, tentative, mere nod to that same shared
long-ago.

I go into my act. Here in the Community Room, where the bunnies
are bouncing around and the colored eggs are talking falsetto and a briskly
determined lady in harlequin glasses waves her palms in tempo, I stick on
my smiling cheery face, I tender my Easter greeting and proffer up my

little treats with too much false enthusiasm, too little real feeling. Here's the box of chocolate-covered filberts, a paperback *(Birds of America)*, a fluffy pink box containing three bars of the soap she likes, set in little nests of orchid-tinted excelsior, three pairs of L'eggs pantyhose, a Ronnie/ Nancy paper-doll book, and so on. (She had asked for a pair of scissors last time, but scissors are *verboten*. I hope she doesn't mention them.)

First words out of her mouth: "Where are my scissors I asked for? I distinctly said a pair of scissors, remember?" Sheepishly I say I must have forgotten, but she pouts anyway. "I think you're really hateful," she says ignoring the bounty from the shopping bag. I apologize. She frowns making her face *so* unattractive. That face—Helen's face—yes, *the* Helen the one that launched those thousand ships and tumbled the topless towers of Ilium; that Helen—United Artists' Helen in that sweet summer of Italian madness, the well-remembered Summer of the Purple Grape. Yes that glorious, smiling, suntanned, all-American face. Has it really turned into this lump of dough?

I look at the doll she has clutched in one hand, the saddest, most forlorn creature in all dolldom. She calls it "Clarabelle," and she sleeps with it, too. The doctor tells me it's the maternal instinct being gratified She says Clarabelle's father is "Frankie," which is more or less self-explanatory, I guess.

One thing I do notice today: there's a tiny glimmer in those dead eyes. Just a glimmer, but I'm grasping at straws. She's had an Easter card from Vi. "Thanks, Vi," I think, "you're the nuts." No—I'll tell you what's nuts. This is: just the other day Anna's "roomie," Ida, stuck a plastic bag over her head and smothered herself to death. On the mirror she wrote "By-by all—write when you get work." Poor bitch couldn't even spell "bye-bye." Where'd she get the bag, anyway? People in this place shouldn't have access to things like that; they're as lethal as any scissors —more.

Of course, it was Anna who had to find the dead roomie. In the morning, when she woke up, there Ida was, mouth agape, breathless Anna had this crazy notion that she'd been wrapped for Christmas—off by about eight months. She complains of the fact that around there people often say or print the word "Xmas."

"Why is that, I wonder?" she says.

I explain that certain people substitute the "X" for "Christ."

"Jews, probably," she reflects somberly. My God, I think, has she become anti-Semitic, too? I open the window and comment on the fine weather we're enjoying. "We're having a wet spring. See how green the grass is? It's emerald. Like Ireland."

Emeralds or Ireland, she's not interested. She asks about Jenny, and I have to remind her again that Jenny and I aren't married anymore. Then I suggest our seeing how things may be outside, a breath of fresh air? By now the room is really getting noisy. Someone's banging on the piano and two eggs are dueting "Let Me Entertain You." Seriously. Anna thinks over my suggestion and finally she guesses we can go out. We do.

Mrs. Kraft catches sight of us in the hall and waves, then comes toward us. Mrs. Kraft is "done up" Easterwise, a bunny corsage on her sweater lapel and a fresh hairdo. Don't get me wrong, I'm not knocking Mrs. Kraft; the place couldn't get along without Corallee Kraft. She is interested in being shown the various items in Anna's shopping bag, and exclaims over Ronnie and Nancy in paper-doll form. She volunteers to send blunt-end scissors, the kind we had in kindergarten, with no points. Later.

Outside, Anna and I walk along the cement walk, then cut across the lawn and sit on a rusty glider under the pepper tree where a frayed hammock swings tiredly between it and its fellow. I smile at her, she stares at me. The bright sun brings out all her pallor, her hopelessness, the feeble struggle to go on. Her bitten nails look especially unattractive, her hair is limp and unkempt. But it's good for her, being outdoors. I can see that right away.

Her brittle, coarse voice has softened a little, she appears less nervous, almost docile, always a good sign. A meek Anna's easier to cope with than a belligerent one. I'm relieved, and pretty soon I start my Scheherazade act, telling endless stories to occupy her mind, maybe snare a flicker of interest. Because of the Easter card, I mention that I've been to see Vi a day or so ago; dropped by her house in Beverly Hills. Vi's indestructible, always a good role model; Anna shows a gleam.

"How old can she be anyway, Vi?" she asks seriously.

I hazard a guess: eighty if she's a day, maybe eighty-five? Sam's younger by a good ten years, but retired to Cathedral Wells. This oblique reference causes Anna to ask about Angie; have I seen her? No, I lie, not a glimpse. These days Angie's far sicker than Anna; in Desert Springs Hospital and not expected to live. Big C. But Angie's one of the ones Anna enjoys remembering. Sometimes Frank, though Frank's actually sort of a phantom, this dark, mysterious phantom, like Rochester or Heathcliff. And Bud's taboo, absolutely. Belinda's name pops up sometimes—and Claire's, ha ha. With Anna, Claire's always a joke; Anna claims Claire will bury us all. I find it tricky negotiating these conversational reefs and shoals, where some people—many people—are dangerous to mention.

I confide what I hope is an edifying item. Mrs. Kraft has told me they'll show *Brighter Promise* sometime in the Community Room, if Anna likes. Unfortunately Anna doesn't like, not a bit. I explain that the audience will probably ask questions afterward; she still doesn't like. She doesn't even remember the movie, which comes as no big surprise to me.

Showing the movie turns out to be the doctor's suggestion. Dr. Kern has been on this case since he was a young man. He doesn't seem discouraged, either, and you have to envy such zealousness. As if tomorrow Anna would somehow suddenly spring back to life and say, "Hey! I remember! I remember it all!" I don't know, though—if I were Anna, would *I* want to remember what *she* has to remember? As far as she's concerned, her whole life's been one great big Freudian slip.

Dr. Kern's a Jungian, though. At least *he* claims he is; you couldn't prove it by me. Frankly, I don't see what difference it makes; she's mad as a hatter any way you cut it. There's no way she's ever going to get out of here. I know it, the doc knows it—so, I assume, does Anna. This is the last stop on the line, where the pavement ends, grass growing out of the cement and all that. You don't go home from here. Here *is* home.

After a while it's time for lunch, and we adjourn to the cafeteria, more institution green with homey little touches—violet Easter bunnies scissored out of construction paper adorning the walls, multicolored egg cut-outs pasted on the windowpanes, little yellow chicks, and so on. The echoing clatter of mass food consumption, the chink and clink of heavy chinaware, the blat of many voices, raucous, high-pitched, agitated, sometimes unrestrained.

Even though it's Easter, the luncheon menu holds little attraction. I have my choice of Virginia ham with raisin sauce or the cold plate. I take the salad on my pressed-pockets plastic tray. Plastic knife, fork, spoon—what did lunatic asylums do before the age of plastic? Those around us take no more notice of Anna than anyone else. If they "know," there's hardly any sign of it. I once heard her referred to as "Virginia." Someone pointed at her and screamed, "Virginia's on the rug!" They could only have been referring to Olivia de Havilland in *The Snake Pit*. Interesting, how they had a rug on the floor in that movie but no one was ever allowed to walk on it, and here there's not a rug in sight; only miles of industrial linoleum, enough to cover the tarmac at a jetport.

The good Dr. Kern stops by the table, sits with folded hands, pencil tops and pens picketed along his pocket edge. Serious glasses, white coat, white buckskin shoes, nylon socks, professional demeanor. I forgive him; what else can he do? There are over five hundred patients incarcerated here and he's responsible for a lot of them.

"Well, how are things today, Anna?" he asks in his Leo Genn–ish voice, edged with wry humor. Thank God he never says "How are *we?*" the way one of the nurses, Miss Pope, does. Despite the gluey manner, he's really trying his damnedest. Nothing's easy at Libertad, present company not excepted. The doctor has only so much time; he consults the wall clock and then with regrets pushes on to another table.

"You can go, too, if you like," Miss Pope comes and tells me flatly. She's "Popey" around here. I ask Anna if she wants me to leave. "I don't care." I know she means it; she doesn't care.

"I'd like to stay," I say and ask her how she might like to pass the afternoon. She thinks, shrugs, sighs.

"Ohhh . . . I don't know. . . ."

Carefully, with malice aforethought, I drop a name—a name not unknown in Hollywood annals—just to observe what her reaction is today. "What do you hear from April?" I ask blandly.

She gives me a blank stare. "Who?"

"You know—April—your friend April Rains?"

"I don't know any April Rains."

Alas.

That's the way it is on Easter Sunday of 1982. April Rains is strictly out to lunch. The only thing Anna is likely to remember about April is that she had a pretty name, a camel-hair polo coat with a belt in the back, and is dead. Asked if she remembers April's husband, she signifies no in a decisive manner. "Why does everyone keep asking me about her?" she demands. "What business is it of theirs, anyway? Why is she so important? You'd think I murdered her or something."

"Did you?"

"I never murdered anyone, much less someone I scarcely knew."

"How well *did* you know her?"

"I don't know. Stop asking me. I—you—stop—"

I can see she's getting upset again. No more along these lines or they'll be putting her back in the rubber room.

The doctors have for years been pursuing the all-important relation between Anna Thorwald and April Rains. She can't get beyond the obvious fact that both names begin with an "A." Show her a movie still or a snapshot; she may or may not recognize the pretty blonde actress, a movie queen of the early sixties. Sometimes I think, "*I* can't remember what happened *yesterday*, how's *she* supposed to remember twenty *years* ago?"

One thing's for sure: she's dead, April. Everyone agrees on that— those who know the whole story, those who don't but may suspect. But those who know best are all gone now, except me. As for Anna, she'll be dead, later if not sooner, and she'll take the story with her when she goes. Like the cast of *Gone With the Wind;* after over forty years, who's left? Butterfly McQueen, Olivia de Havilland, and some ex-gaffer named Rudy Hatch who lives in Panorama City and won a cup playing miniature golf. One who does know the story is Irene Fender. Irene's another of the looneytunes, but whenever she chances across Anna the mere sight of her presses every one of Irene's buttons. She salivates like Pavlov's dog and begins to twitch and her voice skids up an octave and a half.

"I know you!" she'll scream, pointing. "I know you! Look, everybody, it's April! April Rains! I ain't kiddin', girls! I seen her in the movies! She was fuckin' Frankie Adonis!"

God help you, Irene Fender, you've got a rotten mouth. I know you have your problems, you're a classic pathologue, but, God, I wish you'd put a sock in it. Anna doesn't need that kind of stuff, though most days Anna doesn't really know what Irene means, because she simply *isn't* April. I mean, honest to God, she *isn't*. April Rains is as remote to her as the surface of the moon.

Unlike Peg Entwhistle, April didn't come to Hollywood *from* anywhere. She was born right here, raised here, went to school here, a native Californian—one of those local girls who made good. And she was a real hot Frank Adonis discovery. You've probably forgotten it by now, but you first saw the face of April Rains on the June 1959 cover of *Look* magazine. The caption read: "America's Loveliest Coeds." Frank said actually it was Vi Ueberroth who spotted "that puss" in the Turf Club at Santa Anita. A copy of the magazine was lying on a cocktail table when Vi sat down in the lounge, and for once she found something of greater interest than the next race. That appealing face with its freckles and suntan, the sunstreaked hair done in a Ginger Rogers pageboy roll, the exuberant, all-American-girl smile with its perfect teeth—a natural, is what Vi thought, and set out to prove herself right. She showed the cover to Frank, who was quick to agree.

She *was* a natural, April. You can see it in that first film she made, the same sweet, healthy winsomeness that Esther Williams had, that gorgeous, well-constructed American chassis that made guys sit up and take notice, all kinds of guys; the kind of healthy outdoors girl that only the state of California seems able to breed so well. Only Esther, smart girl, never made the mistake of falling in love with Frankie Adonis, married guy. And if you just drove up and asked Esther whether it had all been fun, she'd probably say, Yeah, sure it was fun, I had a ball. Not so April. You could never say it was fun for her. She never had a ball. In fact she hated it. "Just *like* some people," I remember hearing one Hollywood cutie say. "Give some people the world on a silver platter and they don't want it. Imagine not wanting to be a star!"

But April didn't. Never wanted it, never liked it, never enjoyed it. She used to break out in rashes before starting a new picture. Had to stop a take to go and throw up before she could continue. Couldn't wait to get off the soundstage, out of the sight of people, all those eyes watching, the grips trudging around with boxes and cables, men she was too shy to talk to or become friendly with. Claire Regrett knew the names of every crew member on any of her pictures, their wives and kids, too, she made it part of her business; but April was plain scared and they called her stuck-up, snotty, above-it-all. It wasn't that way at all. She just wasn't cut out for the game.

April was Frank's own creation. She was a lovely piece of marble that he shaped, cut, and chiseled into something beautiful to look at, that he breathed life into and that he had the failed wit to fall in love with, his Galatea. With Babe, Claire, others, it was business with a little love tossed in; with April Rains it was the real thing. There ought to be a law about married men and little girls who don't know enough to come in out of the rain.

If she'd been something else, a secretary, a commercial artist, or if she'd remained a scholar, which is what she wanted to be—English literature, classical history—she might have been all right; it was the combination of living at the back end of Back Street and being a highly visible personality—a star—that did her in. Hollywood is like the beast in nature that eats its young; it has little sympathy for the weak or frail, certainly none for those who refuse to play the game the Hollywood way, and the seeds of disaster were sown right from the beginning. Even if there hadn't been a Frances in the picture, even if Frank could have simply swept April up and made her the little missus, it would have been stormy weather. As it was, they all lost, Frank, April, even Frances.

People today say, "Oh, *I* remember *her!*" like they'd forgotten her totally, but suddenly it all comes back again—Frances Deering, of course! "The Wife." Frank's wife, the one who made all the stink, caused all the trouble; sure, you remember. Frances, "The Other Woman." Since when was the wife ever the other woman? The *other* woman is always the other woman.

Let's go back:

Frank had married Frances Deering in October of 1942, to much Hollywood fanfare and panoply. It certainly was *not* a marriage made in heaven, but it was nonetheless the legal union of man and woman, sanctified by Holy Mother Church (Frances was also a Catholic and a staunch one), and whom God hath joined together let no man—or woman —put asunder. By 1960, the year Frank began to feel the stirrings of love for April, his marriage was badly foundering. More than once Frances had consulted her lawyer (Greg Bautzer, then everyone's fashionable attorney-about-town, ex-swain of Joan Crawford and other filmdom beauties). Though if anyone thought that a little college coed from Westwood was going to pop out of the shrubbery and snatch Frank Adonis away from his Frances, she had another thing coming; Frances never gave up anything without a struggle, least of all a husband. But by then Frank was primed to go and it was to be a struggle to the death.

Everyone makes mistakes, we know that—some large, others small, but we all make them. In his lifetime Frank Adonis obviously made his share, mistakes like Claire Regrett, like the little carhop at Dolores Drive-In, or the cowgirl at the Buckaroo Bar-bee-cue in Cathedral Wells, but those were relatively minor didos, quickly forgotten in the face of Frank's magnetic persona, which demanded leeway for little lapses of taste or judgment. No, without question, the biggest mistake of his life was marrying Frances in the first place. Some people simply aren't good mates, aren't "meant for each other," and in the opinion of many, me included, Frank and Frances were oil and water, east and west, day and night, black and white. They were as mismatched a couple as you could hope to see, while Frank and April fit hand and glove, ham and eggs, like that. Frank, a product of the slums, a tough New York kid whose family had come steerage from Naples and Salerno, whose father never learned to speak English and whose mother still said, *Mamma mia!*" The careful polish Frank had so assiduously acquired, the quiet, gentlemanly manners, the air of swank about his dress, the high-class and high-power circles he moved in, his appreciation of the finer things in life, much of this veneer stemmed from his attachment to Frances Deering, who, recognizing a diamond in the rough, took the trouble to polish and make it sparkle.

Frances herself had all the polish in the world. The Deerings, a lumber family out of the Great Northwest, were socially prominent, Frances had made her debut at the Gold Circle Ball in Seattle, and while in London had been presented at Court and been taken up by the elegant Cliveden Set. Frances was one of those super-cool, patrician beauties, to the manner born, wallowing in the wherewithal, and she was long used to getting what she wanted. She wanted Frank and, like Barkis, Frank was willing.

Frances had a way with her that people found charming, a refinement combined with a natural ease and good humor that Frank recognized as a highly desirable and marketable property. On the other hand, his own smoldering good looks, his racy background, the *frisson* of gangsterism at a safe distance, his reputation as a boudoir Romeo (by this time a reputation well sampled by Frances), and his charming demeanor all combined to make him Frances's idea of a good catch. There was a jumbo wedding on the typical Hollywood scale, a honeymoon in Waikiki, the well-publicized return, lei'd to their ears, suntanned and smiling, to settle down in domestic bliss in a fake-Tudor house on Bristol Avenue in Brentwood.

The wise among us appreciate that it's always well to take life on its own terms, to make use of what it offers and not try to bend it to one's will; this Frank knew, and this is why he was probably so free of unhappiness for so many years. Except for April Rains I think he may have got nearly everything he ever wanted, and certainly everything he deserved. I think it fair to say he married Frances in good faith and with the best of intentions. I won't say he was crazy in love with her, but he always had a finely honed appreciation of his womenfolk and I'm sure this stretched to his own chosen mate and helpmeet. Frances was class, and class was the name of the game so far as Frank went.

The trouble was, Frances played the game according to some weird set of rules she alone seemed to comprehend. She married the man, but she didn't really want *that* man, our Frankie, the guy she got; she wanted to get him and then make him over into her private vision of what she thought he *ought* to be. She regarded him as an attachment to herself, possibly even something she had bought and paid for, an expensive toy. It couldn't possibly have worked.

But Frances was Catholic, remember, and it was for better or for worse. Her own younger sister had taken vows and been ordained as Sister Mary Rose. Frances also maintained a particularly close relationship with Father Mallory, who later became Monsignor Mallory, and who made sure Frances was on good terms with the Bishop and that His Grace could be counted on to honor her table three or four times a year. It was within this snugly carpentered framework that she became known for her charitable works and generous contributions to the sundry charities of the diocese.

And because of this, divorce was always out of the question. The only time in their more than twenty years together she apparently ever considered such a thing (in this instance it was annulment) was in 1947, after Frank's casual connection with Bugsy Siegel was made public. In time, Frances even got the Pope involved, but nothing ever came of that, because in the end she wouldn't give Frankie up. No more than she would give him up years later when April came along, although in that case it was more than her strict convent upbringing at work: she had no intention of presenting her gossiping friends with the chance to laugh and say Frank had dumped her for someone younger. No, Frances was determined to hang on until the last gong rang, the last whistle blew, and when the going got really bumpy and Frank simply "refused to see the light," she showed her truest colors.

Frances certainly said and did all the "right" things, dressed the part right down to the little white gloves and hats the matronry of Brentwood and Bel Air copied from San Francisco ladies hot out of the Garden Court at the Palace. Her speaking voice, low, dulcet, just a tad Junior League, was always one of her charms. More than one Hollywood stud fell victim to it, to say nothing of the great Frankie himself.

But you could draw a black line right down through Frank's years with Frances and mark them B.A. and A.A.—Before April and After. Because when April came along, she changed him, changed his life and changed the way he acted and thought about things, and after she was gone he was never the same. Not ever. After seeing that picture of her on the cover of *Look* he tracked down the photographer, who told him the girl's name was Anna Thorwald, and that since graduating from UCLA in June she'd been working as a model at I. Magnin's. Frank checked it out, found the girl in a Norell, purchased the dress, then slipped her his card. She'd never heard of the Adonis Agency. "Would you like to be in the movies?" and like that ensued, and No, came back the answer, the young woman wasn't interested. Now, this was an odd thing, for if there's one ineluctable law of nature at work in the universe, it is that every girl under the age of thirty wants to be in the movies. Not April. She only did it for Frank. Frank was persuasion walking.

Like Babe, like Claire, like Belinda and Angie and Julie Figueroa and all the rest of that elite sorority, April was susceptible to the male of her species. Certainly she was susceptible to the charms of a Frank Adonis. He was then past fifty, temples silvering, but looking foxy, and he'd lost none of his charm or skill with the ladies, still the kind of dynamite-looking dude who gets under a woman's skin right away and starts her juices trickling. Those sooty-soft Italian eyes never made any secret of his amorous feelings; they told a woman that for that one single moment she was the most important and exciting thing in his life, the most beautiful, the sexiest, the most desirable and intelligent and worthwhile he'd ever come across. And so it was with Anna Thorwald, soon to become April Rains. She and Frank were—as we all later came to believe—destined to meet. And when they did, everything sat right there in the well-known lap of the gods.

No sooner had Frank secured his newest client a contract at Metro and changed her name than he proceeded to fall in love with her. Maybe it would have been better if he had taken her to Zanuck over at Fox, or even Harry Cohn at Columbia. Unhappily, she fell under the tutorial eye of the Great Mogul himself, Samuel B. Ueberroth, who, having heard about her through Vi, deigned to interest himself in her budding career. The name alone enchanted him. And with her golden hair and fresh-scrubbed look, April Rains was perfect MGM fodder, and he blithely confided to Frank that the girl's stardom was practically guaranteed. He himself would see to it.

But Sam had troubles in more ways than one. I can hear him scream-ing, "Whaddya mean she doesn't *wanna* be in the movies? Fa Chrise sakes, is she out of her mind?"

No, she wasn't; not then. But Sam's question was valid. When Frank had first started giving her the "You ought to be in pictures" routine, she'd only laughed at him; it seemed so farfetched, such an unlikely career for her to pursue. "Who, me? Don't be crazy." At the beginning, whenever anything came up about movies, she always disclaimed any real connec-tion. "Oh, I'm not *really* an actress, I'm just playing around for fun."

But Frank was Frank and that meant never taking no for an answer. He saw that Thing in her; she had it, too, the Star Quality they always talk about. And the more she said no, the more determined he was to prove he could do it. And fell in love at the same time.

That wasn't very bright of him. There were plenty of other girls around if he wanted to get laid, and there were plenty of other blondes to make into screen tootsies if *that* was what he wanted. But April Rains had that extra spark that demands full attention, that catches the eye or the mind, that goes beyond tootsie-ism, that gets a girl's face in *Photoplay* and keeps it up there on the silver screen.

Would he have insisted, had he known just how it was all going to turn out? I don't think so, he wasn't that kind. He really believed in his Italian heart of hearts that he was showing her the way to a good life, the grand life, that which he himself had craved. The trouble was that she just wasn't ambitious; what *she* wanted was marriage, motherhood, two cars in the garage. But before she knew it, there she went, through that old sausage grinder, and out came Metro product, Metro glossed and coiffed, Metro pretty.

She had a boyfriend or two, actually "beaux," as Donna enjoyed calling them (Donna was April's mother). So April didn't sit home Satur-day nights watching Lawrence Welk. She went out—sat in the balcony and ate popcorn while Elvis abused his guitar and sang "Hound Dog."

A good sound crack at a Ph.D. might have done her a world of good, whereas getting a scene from *Barefoot in the Park* to heart seemed a waste of time. But she did it, and others beside, Julie from *Jezebel*, Regina from *Little Foxes.*

She was then studying acting with Feldy Eskenazy, the celebrated European actress who'd won two Academy Awards yet been dropped by Metro. Feldy was earning a living by giving acting lessons and doing special coaching at the Stage Society Workshop in a rundown building on La Cienega, and, as it chanced, I too was studying with her. In fact, I was working on Essex to April's Queen Elizabeth. One evening we "performed," and Frank and Sam both came, along with Vi, and April was a complete wreck. She flubbed her lines and dropped her prop mirror and generally made a mess of things. We'd also worked on a scene from *The Glass Menagerie,* and after we'd bombed as Elizabeth and Essex I told them we were going to do the other one, with April playing Laura to my Gentleman Caller, and that went much better. April even got a laugh, which delighted her. Sam went out chortling, and wanted to drive her home. Vi said no. Vi knew her brother; his antennae were already buzzing, and while he was that Hollywood oddity, "a happily married man," Sam's eye swiveled for a pretty girl, and Vi didn't want him playing pattycakes with the newest discovery.

At this point in his long career Sam was one of the last mainstays of the studio system. He had started as a two-bit shill, barking for a downtown theatre in Los Angeles. Sam eventually found himself a studio flack at the old AyanBee Studio, where his sister, Viola, a then-secretary, had procured him a job, and in time he became a moneymaking, and therefore powerful, producer. Later he moved to Metro, where, following the death of Irving Thalberg and the departure of David Selznick for *Gone With the Wind* and greener pastures, he held down the number-one producing spot. In those days a film with the credit

A Sam'l B. Ueberroth Production

meant lines around the block and money in the bank, and many is the blonde tootsie who put in her lap time, sitting cozily with Sam while he told her the story of his next script and checked out the glands.

Then to the cast of the brewing melodrama was added that up-and-coming young thespian Floyd "Bud" Ayres, rechristened Kit Carson, the lad who really took it on the chin. Bud was a beauty, and not only in the physical sense. It's true, when the girls got an eyeful of that Nordic face, that beach-tanned body, that cornsilk hair, and the green eyes, they creamed their undies. But Bud was not merely that famous Hollywood commodity, the Boy Next Door; he was made of rarer stuff, the guy everybody thought would become the next hot rave after Van Johnson and Monty Clift. For a kid from El Segundo, son of a plant worker at Hughes Tool and Die, whom Jenny and I first saw parking cars, Bud did okay for himself.

It was our wedding anniversary and Jen and I decided to celebrate at La Rue, our then-favorite restaurant. As we pulled up to the entrance, a young man appeared in a red jacket and took the car away. On our way in Jenny squeezed my arm, remarked on how gorgeous he was, then, to my annoyance, mentioned him again during dinner. Later, when he returned our car to us, I decided to give him the once-over. Jen was right, he was impressive—tall, wide shoulders, blonde hair bleached to white from sun and surfing, a whalebone smile, and kind of funny eyes; by funny I mean with something intrinsically interesting in them, something hidden, a bit inscrutable, a definite oddity in a Santa Monica beach type.

Certainly he was a good bet for pictures, and when I next saw Frank I casually made mention of the fact to him, then promptly forgot about it until another evening, when we returned to La Rue and a different attendant took our car. When I commented on the change, Jenny said in her blithe way, "Oh, Bud's not here anymore; Frank has him working at the office." I soon learned that Frank had also signed his newest find to an actor's-representative contract, and it wasn't long before he had located cheap digs for him in our own neighborhood, a few turns down the hill, in the guest apartment above a friend's garage.

Even with Jenny's enthusiasm, which was enough for both of us, I had to admit that this new beach jock of Frank's had it over most Hollywood hopefuls that I'd come across; "star quality" it's called, and almost against my will I found myself liking him. He was twenty-two that year, which gave him a good ten years on me, and we made him part of the household, along with the dog and the cat and the cleaning lady.

In those early years Bud was like an apple ripening on the bough. He dressed like a beach bum and drove around in an old Ford woodie with a rack on top for skis or his surfboard, and if he stooped to wearing shoes it was a pair of battered sneakers, and in a time of short hair, his was always in need of a trim. He was nature's boy, an unsophisticate with a degree in engineering from the Colorado School of Mines. But he was the raw material that movie stars are often fashioned from, one who if there was justice in the world should have become a big, big star. He did, too—for a while, until life intervened. That oft-repeated agents' and producers' cliché "You don't have to act in the movies" is just so much agent-producer canned crap. Someone who looks like Bud Ayres may not *have* to act but it damn well helps—and, oddly, he could, a little.

And no sooner had Frank taken on this diamond-in-the-rough and changed his name to Kit Carson than he turned him over to Feldy Eskenazy, who took him under her wing and began the process of "polishing" him until he was ready to be sprung on a world hungry for blonde, six-foot, green-eyed heroes, just like in the comic strips. It was at Feldy's studio that Kit, like Frank before him, would take one look at April and go the same head-over-heels route. And by the time the whole thing was over, it would be this "Kit Carson" who would pay the ultimate price, the loss of his career and worse—and for what? For having faithfully loved the girl of his dreams and lost her? And, by the way, not to Frank, not altogether to him, but more to screaming headlines and bad press, and to being in the wrong spot at the wrong time.

Meanwhile, it wasn't too long before the newly christened Kit Carson started turning up stag at Frances's coveted Sunday-night soirées, wearing his tux borrowed from me, and you could see the Las Floristas Ball ladies checking out the basket, eager to have him light their cigarettes (once, at Frank's house, the stinko wife of a prominent director got into the john, whose lock Bud had neglected to turn; attacking him while he was peeing, she created a scene of some vividness, and when Bud emerged from the encounter, he stood resolved in the firm belief that his shining career was over before he'd ever put a foot in front of a camera).

Actually, his career was about to begin. The minute Feldy Eskenazy slipped Frank the word that Kit was ready, Frank took him out to Culver City and turned him over to Sam Ueberroth to be tested. As it happened, I was shooting a film on the old Selznick backlot (then Desilu, I believe; this was in '59). I had got into the habit of brown-bagging my lunch, not bothering with the studio commissary. One morning whom do I spot among the day players but Kit Carson got up as a Nazi—his first movie part. He had four lines, all in heavy Kraut, which I, who spoke none, thought he ripped through with professional aplomb.

We'd been so busy lately that neither Jenny nor I had seen Bud in quite a while, and at lunchtime I took him along to my "private dining room," which happened to be the front porch of Scarlett O'Hara's Tara. In those days the old *Gone With the Wind* set was still standing, regrettably much the worse for wear after nearly twenty years of neglect, and in the approximate spot where Scarlett had sat with the red-headed Tarleton twins on the eve of the Civil War, I shared my deviled eggs and tuna sandwich with Kit, all got up in a Nazi uniform about two sizes too large.

We sat around talking acting, directors, his future, the whole movie bit, and I was as impressed as ever by his guileless charm, still so evident despite the recent changes in his life. He spoke admiringly of Frank, giving all due credit and taking none for his own obvious physical assets, and when I complimented him on his morning's work, he brushed it aside as small potatoes.

There was an important part coming up in a picture at Metro that he hoped to be considered for. When he mentioned the title, I started: I knew all about that one, a big, all-out western, and *I* wanted that part. Frank had already promised me a crack at it. I said nothing, however, and after a while Bud dug out a football from his carryall and we tossed passes on what remained of Scarlett's front lawn. From time to time I'd glance up at a window and imagine I was hearing Hattie McDaniel bawling "Miss Scawlitt, you ain't got no mo' mannahs than a field han'."

Next day I lunched again on Scarlett's porch, reading *Vengeance Is Mine*, the super-western Bud had mentioned. As things turned out, Frank didn't have Kit pegged for the same part at all; this was an epic with roles for the entire Players Directory. Kit was up for Cheeter Slade, a young ranch hand who gets chewed up in the bindery, while I was to try out for a one-armed bandit. In the wonderful way of Hollywood, it was Kit who won his chance; I lost mine. Thus endeth the reading for that day. And for many days to come. I sat around through the rainy season, staring at my bleak, leaf-strewn swimming pool, biting my nails and cursing the acting business, while Kit, who'd finished his epic at Metro, went back to school for further burnishing from Feldy.

To my mind, Kit Carson, a.k.a. Bud Ayres, stands as proof positive of the deadly destructive properties of Hollywood. Here was this simple, likable guy, uncomplicated but not gullible, not a shnook, and not to be taken advantage of. He wanted to excel at his newly chosen profession and take advantage of his natural assets—God knows it was formidable equipment, and for the time he was an actor he used it well. In his brief film career he stirred audiences the way the good actor, the wise actor, the valuable actor, always hopes to stir his audience. He had the real thing, in spades. The moment he appeared onscreen he had them eating out of his hand. Women went crazy for him; older men envied him, while the younger ones idolized, trying to imitate his leggy lope, his cheerful, earnest manner, his solemn quiet. He walked in the footsteps of the Duke of Wayne; like Gary Cooper, he was kissed by golden lips.

In a relatively short period he made a solid mark. From car jockey to movie star was a giant leap, but he took it in his stride. Not that others before him hadn't managed it, but those others had not undergone his meteoric rise. You could probably light the whole of Minneapolis by the candlepower of that kid from El Segundo, Bud Ayres. But El Segundo has never bothered claiming him as its own. "Here was born . . ." "Here lies . . ." "This plaque erected to the loving memory of . . ." Thus pass the glories of this world.

Feldy Eskenazy was probably in love with him. I thought so, others, too. A good twenty years older than Bud, she went to jelly from the very first, and it lasted forevermore—when he died she was ready to commit suttee. Josephine Dillon, Gable's drama coach, was twenty-five years older than Clark—and she married the guy. She never could have, though, had there been a Lombard around at the time. Feldy never stood a chance with Bud. Nothing against her except that, besides being years older, she simply wasn't his type. And anyway he hadn't been working too long with Feldy when April appeared on the scene.

I always imagine that particular epiphany to have occurred something like this: it's early evening, soft, warm, inviting. Somewhere, from a distance, heart-tugging music plays, invoking mood. The sky is violet-blue, softly velveteen. Then above some foothills or low-lying mountains there appears the evening star, Venus, lambently gleaming—Tannhäuser's star. It does not move to its place in the sky, it simply appears as if by magic, and hangs there "like a tear upon the soft cheek of night," gently glimmering. Bud, who has labored hard all day, raises his weary eyes, which come to rest on that same star. He experiences feelings of rare delight and peace and a deep, hitherto unknown stirring in his manly breast. He is fettered, bound on the instant, enslaved for life, and he pledges himself to see that such a beautiful light shall never be extinguished, shall burn forever. It is the love that surpasseth all, the faith that moves mountains. April Rains has just walked through the door.

Appropriately enough, it's been raining outside, April looks a sorry sight, dripping on the paint-spattered linoleum. She speaks Feldy's name, querying her whereabouts. Feldy's in the can, though Bud has difficulty articulating this intelligence, so banal and vulgar does it seem. He takes the visitor's wet coat, gets her a chair, brings her hot coffee, makes her at home, puts forth his name, asks hers, offers friendly confidences regarding Frank, makes small talk but no pitch, is dazzled by her, and, generally speaking, is bowled over. A star-crossed meeting if ever there was one. The rain-spattered, dewy-eyed creature is almost like a gift, a Frankie-sent gift for Bud, his own, his very own.

The fact helps that Feldy is *not* in the can, but gone to pick up her dry-cleaning before closing, where she discovers that her ribbon-woven blouse of coral pink that she bought herself last Eastertime has been lost. She is gone a good quarter of an hour, and she is not missed. Bud safely employs that entire quarter of an hour to fall in love. Yes, it was that old familiar "love at first sight"—at least on Bud's part. From that moment when she appeared dripping in the doorway of that rundown dump of an actors' studio, April had a devoted slave, one who, as he was one day to prove, would do anything for her. "Anything" making a whole world, but it was the world he offered her—himself, body and soul, his future, his money (when that came, *if* that came), everything he had was hers for the asking.

And so there developed yet another hopeless triangle, which eventually became some kind of weird five-sided figure, for in time there was Frances who loved Frank who loved April who was also loved by Sam and now by Kit, and everyone was totally miserable. One day Frank comes on the lot, heading for Stage Ten, where a Debbie Reynolds picture of Sam's is rehearsing. Sam spies Frank, takes off after him, catches up and starts the famous altercation. He calls Frank a *shnook!* Frank grabs Sam's nose and gives it a tweak plus a hop in the butt. Sam has a spasm, falls backwards into the privet hedge, where Frank abandons him. Shouting threats and imprecations, Sam lapses into a fit that may or may not be real. Despite the published depositions of one Myron Radowitch III, prominent Beverly Hills attorney, authenticating this so-called fit, Frank accuses Sam of faking injury. Fake or not, Sam ends up in Cedars of Lebanon, and Radowitch institutes legal proceedings, which make all the editions. Recommending that cooler heads prevail, Viola visits her brother in the hospital and begs him to reconsider.

vi: "Sammy, darling, didn't Mama ever tell you?"

sam: "Tell me what, Vi?"

vi: "Never go to law, Sammy, never *never* go to law if it can be avoided."

When Sam and Frank next met, Sam enjoined Dore Schary to take a unilateral stand. "Damn it, Dore, I want that dago bum barred from this lot! I don't want to see him on this side of Motor Avenue!"

"But Sammy, Sammy," Dore said, "only think—how can we bar Frank from MGM? He handles four of our biggest stars."

"What you mean is he *hondles* four of our biggest stars! It's an ultimatum here, Dore, friend. Either him or me goes!"

Frank was forthwith barred from the Culver City lot. No problem. He set up temporary quarters in the bar on Culver Boulevard across from the Thalberg Building, where he would meet with his clients in the red

Naugahyde-upholstered corner booth. It fell to Sam's wonder-working sister, Vi, to attempt to bring about peace. Since Vi and Frank always had great affection for each other, she was able to persuade him to meet her irate brother more than halfway. She invited Frank over for her regular Friday-night poker session, having already suggested that her brother stop by. When she heard Sam come in through the kitchen door, Vi asked Frank to get some more ice, her drink was warm. The two archenemies met at the sinkboard.

Sam was not pleased to find Frank in his sister's house and said as much. Frank offered to leave. Viola hurried in and began pouring oil on the troubled waters. Sam agreed to patch it up, tossing an arm around Frank and saying he was just like a son to him. Everything was fine until April's name came up again; then Sammy burst into tears and pulled out a gun, a German Luger he'd picked up in the war. Frank laughed at him, daring him to pull the trigger. Sam's aim was sufficiently faulty for him to miss the heart by two and a half feet, the bullet striking Frank in the crotch. Half an hour later he lay in a bed at Cedars of Lebanon. No charges were pressed, and an abject Sam appeared at the invalid's bedside with apologies. The incident was hushed up, and other than some wounded pride the only loss was that where, like most males, Frank had once had two of something, he now had only one.

Now what happens? By now Kit, or Bud, is head over heels for April, but it's not reciprocal. Why? Because April has already fallen for Frank. Bud's all ready to have Turkish towels monogrammed, while out on Tennessee Avenue, before going to sleep, April's kissing nighty-night a picture of Frank she cut out of *Photoplay* (the wastebasket got the other half: Frances in a two-piece sharkskin cocktail ensemble).

Frances had paid scant attention when Frank casually dropped the news that he'd signed some new piece of talent and was peddling her over at Metro. She didn't even pay much attention when Mike Connolly remarked in *The Reporter* that MGM had signed a pretty blonde cover girl, the latest filly in the glamorous stable of the Adonis Agency. Frances did, however, prick up her ears when it reached them that while her husband was supposedly attending one of Vi Ueberroth's Friday-night poker games, he was actually having dinner at Jack's-at-the-Beach, a seaside hideaway notorious for harboring clandestine meetings. Needless to say, Frances took exception, and it wasn't long before she was taking exception all over the place.

Truthfully, to know Frances was not necessarily to love her, but at least you knew where you stood with her. She liked me, I think, or anyway she did at that time—certainly she was always interested in my

meeting "the right people," and (at Frank's suggestion) had occasionally
included me as a stag free-lancer at the Sunday-night supper gatherings
she and Frank were famous for. *(Life* did one of their *"Life* Goes to a
Party" layouts; it was like a Hollywood *Who's Who.)*

It came as something of a surprise, however, to find myself attending
a Sunday-evening soirée, not stag this time, but with April Rains as my
date. This pairing came about because Jenny had flown home to Boston
for her sister's wedding, and when I came back from the airport I found
a message from the agency. Frank's secretary, Minnie, said that he wondered if I wouldn't mind bringing along my acting partner for "bits and
pieces" on Sunday at the Bristol Avenue house. Black tie *compris.*

So there I am in not completely unfamiliar surroundings. I'd been
lucky enough to be invited to a number of these fabled Sunday nights of
Frank's, where you could suddenly find yourself side by side on a piano
bench talking with Judy Garland, or off in a corner listening to David
Selznick recount his problems in trying to mount a new production for
Jennifer. (Imagine if *Gone With the Wind* had been made three years later;
goodbye, Vivien Leigh!)

I remember noting as we entered that there were at least a dozen
ranking film stars in the room, and every one of those heads swiveled in
our direction as we crossed the threshold—it wasn't me but April. Frank
was at our side on the instant, welcoming us. He was making small talk
when we saw Frances bearing down on us and I wondered what all this
boded. Nothing, apparently; it was a smooth entry into space; the two
women shook hands and bussed cheeks and were conventionally polite.
Then, as Frank spirited April off to meet Clark Gable and Bill Holden,
I was left facing Frances. Frances in her simple gown of ice-blue crepe,
Frances with her pale gold hair turned in a French twist, her pale blue eyes
made no bluer by the handsome circlet of turquoises around her neck,
Frances at her hostess-best. Her look told me she knew exactly what was
going on, and she offered her little joke about what would my wife say
when she learned I was out with a Hollywood beauty, and I made the
rejoinder that April and I were joined at the hip since we were working
on *An Enemy of the People* in class, and her bright, blank, yet telling
expression as she listened said that Frances considered me a party to the
crime, as well as a traitor to her personally. We successfully avoided each
other the rest of the evening.

Later I was talking with Kay Gable, no slouch herself when it came
to beauty, and she said, "Charlie, I'd bet money that girl's going to be the
next big star in this town. Frank is going to do magic with her."

"Frank *is* doing magic with her, darling, *lots* of magic," sang a passing voice: Claire Regrett went wafting by in a red satin dress with a bustle and a new short haircut, and her naughty laughter trailed her out onto the patio.

Later I was confronted by Vi Ueberroth, who insisted I was in collusion with Frank and a deliberate party to a conspiracy equal to the Guy Fawkes Gunpowder Plot. "What on earth does he want with her here of all places?" she demanded when she caught me at the bar and pinned me against the wall. "Is he trying to let the whole world in on what's happening?"

I played dumb as only one who is in the soup can play dumb. I said I supposed Frank wanted April to get a taste of the Beverly Hills social scene. And I must say, that evening at Frank's house she looked as if she belonged, April. It was ironic that the home of Frances Deering Adano was the perfect setting, but April was pearls on velvet that night. The most interesting thing to me was that those same people, all movie pros from the word "go," already recognized what April had, they all could recognize star quality on the hoof, and they accepted her as a peer, not just some dumb starlet someone was pushing into the studio sausage grinder. Before we left, Kay Gable slipped me the word that already Clark wanted her for his next. Frank knew he had a new Grace Kelly, but what he didn't know was that neither he nor she would be living out a fairy tale.

Frank in love was something to see. Like others truly in love, he couldn't hide it, couldn't hope to. It was there in his eyes, the open book for all to read. There was a drugstore downstairs from his office and one day I heard the girl behind the register say to a friend, "Frankie Adonis has got it real bad, kid. He better not let the little woman find out; she'll have him sent up for thirty years."

That's the way it was. I mean, it wasn't any secret; the butcher, the baker, the candlestick maker, everybody knew—though everyone was pretending he didn't. Certainly *Frances* knew. But, being Frances, she kept her mouth shut, bided her time, and waited for her chance to give April the shiv. You could definitely see what was coming, though no one thought it could go to the lengths it did.

The one who was really concerned was April's mother, Donna, a really nice woman, one of those typical independent widows who keep things going. Having buried two husbands—April's father, and after him April's stepfather, A. J. Curry, who'd left her an annuity—she was comfortably off. Still, she was in charge of the "Knitting Corner" at Magnin's and stayed in the everyday world, wearing smart clothes, having her hair done every Friday, a smiling, happy woman with lots of friends. Everyone liked Donna Curry. The thing that most deeply interested her was her daughter's own happiness, and if a married man was going to make April happy, who was her mother to object?

Yet she worried. "Will she divorce him, do you think?" she asked me one time when I was picking up April (her Ford was in the shop). I answered as diplomatically as I could—it was no secret that Frank and Frances were running on a one-way street, and in Hollywood who could tell who would stay married and who wouldn't? I didn't drop a hint of my own true thoughts in the matter, but already I was convinced that things weren't going to end up well; I just never believed April and Frank would make it to the altar. And secretly I wondered how Donna, a Methodist, and Frank's mother, Maxine Fargo, devout Catholic, would get on together.

Born and raised in Hollywood, Donna was on to its various cat-claw ways, and when the question of April's going into the movies first came up, she raised no objections, though that firm, quiet character of hers harbored a-many. The plain fact was, she never cottoned to the idea of her daughter's becoming a movie actress—worse, a star. Donna's keen intelligence was sufficient to appreciate the sacrifices that would have to be made, and if April was going to be placed in the harsh limelight glare, nothing good could ever come from an affair with her married agent. His being unhappily married had nothing to do with it, and though Donna was always pleasant to Frank Adonis, she was wary. She wanted to like him, marriage would have been fine if he'd been single or if a divorce were in the offing, but Back Street was no place for her little girl. Ten other girls could be up there on the silver screen, but somehow she never thought it was right for "April"—a name she could never quite accept as natural; she found it just a little contrived, which of course it was.

"I'd really rather she just went on and got another degree and married some nice fellow," she said to me one evening (the Ford was still in the shop and I'd dropped April home). While she made coffee, Donna and I were talking about the screen test Frank had arranged for April in the Sam Ueberroth picture she was up for. "It won't wash, you know," she said.

What wouldn't wash, I asked.

"Anna, being in the movies. Oh, it'll be all right on the surface, I guess, but she really isn't made for all that—" She said "nonsense" but meant "bullshit." She was savvy enough not to express her misgivings either to April or to Frank, but she was hoping that, given the practicality she accorded both Jenny and me, we'd be able to talk some sense into

April's head. Since I was going to do the test with her, we were often together; I'd promised Frank I'd help as much as I could.

We shot the test, Sam gave her the part (by then Sam was head over heels in love with her himself, and truthfully no other actress even came close to playing it *but* April). As director Sam hired the great Mamoulian, who easily exploited every bit of beauty and talent placed in his hands; neither Frank nor April could have hoped for more. And I give her credit, she really tried. (Remember, she was a total beginner; she'd done a "personality" test, sitting on a stool and talking to someone off camera, but this was a job of acting.)

At some point along in here Frank had faced the astonishing realization that his happiness now depended on her happiness, depended on it utterly and without argument. April had become the keystone to his existence, the one that held up the arch. Here was a guy used to having almost every woman he set his sights on, who never wasted much time getting a lady into bed, and now he found himself in a hot froth but couldn't, or wouldn't, do anything about it. Though he was determined to possess her, he revered her, and it was touching to see him acting for a change like a high-school kid on a date, as if he were courting her in the old-fashioned way, with Benny Goodman records and white gardenia corsages and necking dates in the balcony Friday nights.

Maybe his was a calculated approach, maybe he knew exactly what he was doing—but I don't think so. At fifty-odd he'd fallen into the grip of something primitive, something so powerful and overwhelming that he simply couldn't stop himself. Fault? Is there fault in these things, the eternal triangles? I know this: it was a beautiful thing to see; beautiful to watch, even to be a part of. It's what they wrote the book of love for.

April was like nothing he'd ever known before; her freshness and honesty made their convincing appeal, especially after glitzy dames like Babe and Claire, with their heavy doses of sex and glamour, their crepe gowns and slubbed satin sheaths and needle-heel sling pumps and combed upsweeps. April was like a spring freshet, a sweet, cooling rain in the face.

And April was that true Hollywood oddity, a virgin. She'd never been made love to by a man and wasn't especially anxious to do so. (Remember, we'd just come through the fifties.) Bud's eager advances she easily repelled, even though his ideas of conquest were perfectly plain. Frank, on the other hand, was a surprise, since he hadn't made the least overture. A connoisseur of woman-flesh, he had found the all-time prize and he wasn't going to rush it.

If it had been up to Donna, she'd a thousand, ten thousand, times, have picked Bud Ayres over Frank Adonis. An unscrupulous mother might well have jumped at the chance to see her daughter mistress to such an important movie figure; not Mrs. Curry. She had her feet on the ground and, as I said, she didn't want her little girl mixed up in the movie business in the first place. Yet week by week she watched April slip more desperately, more eagerly, in love with the dark figure regarded by many as notorious, by some even as dangerous.

By this time Sam's picture *The Scarlet Roan* was being previewed in San Bernardino, and, having learned of the sneak, Maxine Fargo had tucked herself away in the movie-house balcony, her eyes straining as she watched this all-important performance by the girl her son loved. "Well, she's got it, she's got it," she said to herself on the way home, and the evidence was indisputable; what Maxine had seen was soon to be seen by the whole town, the country, and the world: "She had it." However hard it was for April to stand the gaff, she had stood it. Under the lights, in front of the lens, she had blossomed, her little touches of awkwardness and nervous giveaways had been skillfully disguised by the director, and she had emerged just as Frank had decided she would, not quite a star, but the next-best thing to; another picture would put her over the top. She was on her way.

With only ten days off she went from *Scarlet Roan* into her next picture. By now there seemed little doubt about her future. Hedda by this time knew how the wind was slanting, and that anything to do with April Rains was a hot item, especially where it concerned Frankie—Hedda and Frances Adano were let's-have-lunch-and-wear-hats buddies—and she was sniffing around, trying any way she could to dig up enough dirt to plant some bulbs.

Meanwhile, April was thinking that maybe it wasn't so bad, maybe she *could* be a star. Acting comes harder to some than to others, and to yet others, like April, it comes even harder. But once she got in front of the camera, under those lights, she was okay. What she really didn't like was all the claptrap, the heavy glitz, the tinsel glamour. She hated the klieg lights, the parties and premieres, the personal appearances, the interviews, that whole fox-fur-and-rhinestones part of the act. It's a job, like any other job, but there are ways and ways of performing it. Hepburn did it one way —her way—but her way would not have been possible for many, since you have to be a rugged individualist and utterly true to some inner force or posture: Certainly that way was not for April. She couldn't tell an autograph seeker to go screw or simply not go into public restaurants. Claire Regrett had her own way, too, which was to take the tiger by the tail and shake the son-of-a-bitch until he yelped, but Claire's long gone from the movie scene, while Hepburn's still hard at it, whatever that may prove.

The thing was, everybody liked April. You couldn't help liking her. She had no pretensions, she was just toe-to-toe with whoever you happened to be. She never put on much of an act; they had to make up things for her to say to Hedda and Louella, things to say in interviews; otherwise she came over a little flat, and God forbid any starlet should ever come over a little flat. Better she should screw her way from bed to bed, from producer to producer, than be a shrinking violet.

"You've got to get out and sell yourself, honey," the studio publicity gang used to tell her. "And don't be so brainy. Forget the music, show your tits a little. Give 'em the ole Marilyn wiggle."

In three years she played parts in nine major films, supporting parts, then starring parts. When her name went up in lights she cried. They opened her second picture at the Bruin in Westwood; local girl makes good was the theme, a sell-out, but despite everything it came as a surprise to me that she was a star. I still tended to think of her as the girl who'd come in out of the rain, the greenhorn Feldy had struggled to turn into a screen actress. Because April herself always joked about her inability to act, it constantly surprised me to see that she could. She wasn't Eleonora Duse, but she had this natural quality that came over well on the screen.

They put her in light stuff mostly—*The Scarlet Roan, Skies of the West, Pretty Peppy*—nothing to tax her abilities. It wasn't until she played the lunchstand waitress in *Thirty-six Hours* and got terrific reviews that they really began to take notice. In Hollywood, when a star is born, I mean, it's BORN! They really let you know about it; you couldn't pick up a magazine or a paper and not read about or see a picture of April Rains.

Frank wasn't merely happy; he was ecstatic. This was his new superstar, the girl whose footprints would go down in Sid Grauman's cement. One girl like this was worth the grief and misery of all the rest, God rest their boobs. Louella wept tears of joy in welcoming her to the pantheon, the greatest potential star since Audrey Hepburn, since Marilyn, since— gee, Lolly couldn't think of another. Sidney Skolsky, who was reputed to do his news column from a booth at Schwab's Drugstore, became April's knight in shining armor; hardly a day went by when he didn't byline one or more items about the rising star.

She did make a pretty light, you know. She was gracious and friendly, always trying to smile, waving at the camera; she seemed to be there for you, for everybody. When she attended premieres she often went with Donna, because there was no main squeeze for her; Bud came in for his share of squiring, but it was the old "just friends" routine. And that was true; just friends. Not so with Frank, however; a little more than friends, I'm afraid, though everybody was running around trying to stifle that item, asking Sidney not to print it, muzzling Hedda, putting a sock in Louella.

Because I'd been her acting partner, because I knew her so well by the time she began getting better known, because she was so likable, so lovable, I took a strong interest in her rising career. Though Jenny was by nature a jealous sort, where April was concerned she only dittoed my encouragement and support; April wasn't just my friend but Jenny's as well. I remembered how the four of us—we two, April with Bud—went one night to see *Green Hills of Kentucky* at the old Picwood movie house over on Pico Boulevard, where you could sit in those big soft rocking-chair seats and smoke your heads off; we heard the comments of others around us, whispering about how beautiful she was, how terrific, and believe me, they wasn't talkin' about the horse!

There was a new star up there in the Hollywood sky, and as I say, it made a lovely light. And the light had turned green, it was GO all the way. She won the Photoplay Award, then the Look Award; *Life* did a cover story backing up the original cover shot; she was made guest of honor at a Foreign Press Association Christmas luncheon (she came and left with Hedda); she'd been on three cross-country publicity tours, two of them with Bud (well chaperoned, of course). She went on working with Feldy at the Stage Society, and was taking her work very seriously. Then the head of studio publicity took her to lunch at the Derby "for a little private talk." He talked about careers and how hard they were to build and how much stood at risk by unsavory personal associations, and why didn't she give some thought to tying the knot with Bud, who adored her anyway. And the fans would eat it up. The studio would foot all the bills, including two weeks at a first-class hotel of their choice.

Over her Cobb salad, April explained that she wasn't interested. Dore Schary, then top dog at MGM, had a talk with her: Stop seeing Frank on a private level. Remember, he was a married man, his wife was a prominent figure in her own right and had the Bishop in her pocket. April accepted Dore's warning with thanks but chose to ignore it.

By this time there was no stopping either the career or the affair. Each was going its own way, soaring up among the stars, where when you fell you fell a long way. Until the release of *Brighter Promise* the affair hadn't in the strict sense been consummated. But sooner or later there comes a time for everything, especially lovemaking, and the point at last arrived when they mutually agreed that the time had come. Jack's-at-the-Beach was okay for quiet talks and furtive hand holding, but the moment had arrived to put away childish things and act grown up about it all. The place they decided on for this consummation was Frankie's beach house. They drove out to Malibu. Since Frances had decided she really didn't care for the beach, Frank had the place to himself, and it was here that the big romance really took fire. The beach house was romantic and invested with a sort of trembling aura of magic. The weather report was lousy, but if you thought about it, it really didn't matter. He was with her, she was with him, they were together. They had the whole weekend. Only fifteen miles from town, but no one would know where they were.

Since noon the Coast Guard had been posting storm warnings all up and down the line from San Diego to Point Mugu, and it looked as if Malibu was in for a heavy blow. Inside the house all was cozy and warm. Frank built a fire and carried in a good supply of wood to keep it going. He put on his old beat-up weekend clothes, his Black Watch shirt and turtleneck, his belted corduroy jacket, and later they went for a walk on the beach, where the surf was thundering onto the sand, sending up geysers of white foam.

The gathering storm exhilarated her, roused feelings that choked her with their intensity. People went by, and she felt odd, nervous. Everyone was out walking, it seemed, the world was out walking. She slipped her hand in his jacket pocket and they made it all the way up to Paradise Cove without saying much. A dog, a golden retriever, joined them and they threw a stick for him to chase. The wool of Frank's turtleneck scratched her when she nuzzled him or they kissed, and the waves drew the sand in pockets from beneath their bare feet. "It's like the end of the world," she murmured, gazing out to where the overcast rolled forward across the surf, and the salt blow pricked her eyes. Everything looked gray and pewtery and the gulls flew as if on kite strings against the wind.

It was dark by the time they got back to the house, and they'd forgotten to turn on the lights. Suddenly she felt intimidated, afraid to go in. It wasn't her house, she was an interloper. Another woman's house, another woman's husband—nothing was hers. Even someone else's dog. "Shoo! Shoo!" she told it, trembling. "Go home!"

Inside, Frank blew up a fire with an antique leather bellows studded with brass nail heads, a present from Frances, then put steaks on to broil; corn was steaming in a pot. She went around turning down the lights— she had the feeling people could see in, and this bothered her.

She was positive she wouldn't be hungry, but she was. They had all of tonight and all the rest of tomorrow, then all of Sunday, too, till seven, when she'd promised Donna she'd be back. She wanted to talk—there were important things to talk about—but somehow they only joked, all of it casual. Afterward, when they had got rid of the dishes and were curled up by the fire, there was a bang on the door; they jumped up. Frank's neighbor: the surf was getting high. Coast Guard lights flashing up and down the beach. A power boat was having trouble making it down to the marina. Just letting him know. When Frank followed him outside she sat huddled in the window seat under a red-and-black buffalo-plaid blanket. It made her think of horses, and that made her think of *The Scarlet Roan*, the film about the stallion in which she'd made such an impression, and *that* made her think of careers, and *that* made her think of all kinds of problems. Suddenly, faces appeared at the window to frighten her. Blessedly, one of them was Frank's, but by the time the three men trooped in, she was hiding in the bathroom.

They didn't stay long, and when they left Frank coaxed her out.

"Sweetheart, don't—it's all right. They're friends, they won't say anything."

Outside, the rising wind screamed itself into a tearing tumult and the heavy waves kept crashing underneath the house. It will wash us away, she thought, as she heard the tide rattle the stones and pebbles. This was all there was, this fire, this room, and the two of them. They were "Outward Bound," passengers on a fog-shrouded ship carrying them—whither? How sweet, how blessed it was. She was ready; tonight she would give everything. She loved him, and something told her she would never love another man. It was this one; this one or none at all. They were in love. Nothing like this, ever. All beings should love like this, this was what it was meant to be, what the gods intended from the beginning. This, only this. She'd give anything—anything to have it, keep it, guard it.

That night he carried her to bed and it was everything they'd hoped for, more, and they knew now it had to be, somehow had to be. Gone were thoughts of Frances. This was their bed, their sheets, their pillows. Hungry bodies ate and tasted, ate again, and still not enough. More, I want more; the dark lay all around and they reached and touched so close they could wrap themselves in each other's skins. He had her hair across his lips, he could taste it; drew the strand away, spoke in her ear, his voice rumbling deep in his throat.

The angry sea roared and rushed about the under-porch pilings, jolting the house; the wind tore at the shingles. There was something ultra-theatrical about it, as if the storm had been engineered just for them. They slept a little, woke up, made love again in the gray early morning, slept some more. The oystery eye of dawn opened in the east; she could hear early-Saturday-morning traffic out on the road; the sky lightened bit by bit. She felt prescient. Something boded.

He slept late. She tidied up, bathed, dressed, was reading an old *National Geographic* about the Eskimos in Baffin Island when she happened to glance up and was startled to see a man standing outside on the porch, peering in at her. He wore boots and a slicker and a sou'wester, and he watched her intently. Then he clumped across the deck and out of sight. Fisherman? Irate neighbor? What business had he around there? The same bedraggled retriever came back, scratched to get in. She ignored the animal, then tossed it the T-bone from last night. He trotted off with it between sandy jaws. Once he stopped, looked back, went on. The sea had quieted now.

Frank woke up; she cooked breakfast. They had curried eggs and popovers and Bloody Bulls with celery stalks to swizzle. He told her her coffee was the best. She told him about the man on the porch; he wasn't overly concerned—maybe the guy was checking for damage. They lazed around all morning; then when she started lunch he said he wanted to go next door.

She thought of Frances as she looked through the kitchen drawers, saw her as a tallish, darkish, forbidding statue, bronzy and cold to the touch, intractable, implacable, remorseless. "He's mine," she heard her say, "I found him first, you can't have him." She looked at all the photographs on the hall chest, autographed to Frank and Frances. Belinda, Babe, Maude and Crispin Antrim—how much a "couple" they seemed, how well suited to each other, how they "shared" the space in the picture. She felt as if she were prying among secret things, fingers poking into private little corners. A life, but another's. Hers was on Tennessee Avenue with Donna, not in Malibu.

Frank wasn't gone long. There was a lot of damage along the beachfront, he reported; several houses had flooded, one had washed away. He was lucky; his house was well built. The storm had washed a sea beast onto the strand, a small whale. Weak, dying, nothing to be done for it; the Park Service was making arrangements to tow it away. April didn't go out to view it, didn't even go onto the deck. She felt time pressing at her, heard its hoofs thundering amid the crash of the waves.

He explained that the neighbors wanted them to come over later for cocktails. The thought frightened her, but she said all right and when the time came she put on slacks, a cashmere sweater, and a jacket and they went. It was the local beach crowd, eight of them. All perfectly cool, no one thought—no, no one *said*—a thing. No Frances. Frances didn't exist here.

Actually she liked them, the beach crowd. Warm, friendly, interested, admiring of Frank. "Isn't he the best guy!" exclaimed the one called

Barb. "Some girls have all the luck, no kidding." April had the grace to blush. She heard the others talking in the kitchen about divorce and Frances's name was being bandied. But they were nice to her; they made it clear that all they wanted was Frank's happiness.

The two of them were sent home with a pitcher of martinis and plastic throwaway cups. Carrying these, they climbed out onto Seal Rocks, where the sea, calmer now, lay before them, pitted with brazen gold and throwing glittering flecks of light onto their faces. They sipped their drinks and gazed out to sea, saying little, nothing, volumes.

The waves had greedily eaten away at the beach, cutting away a four-foot shelf that the neighbors' kids were gleefully leaping from into the foam as it rolled onto the strand. The air was filled with spindrift, which settled on their faces; the whole world seemed painted in sunset hues all the way up to Point Dume, whose jutting headland cut off the further view. "Look, how pretty they are," April said, pointing up the beach. Slowly approaching them were two riders on horseback; at the angle they resembled centaurs.

"Come again?"

"Centaurs," she repeated.

He laughed. "I thought you said 'senators.' I know—centaurs. Who were they?"

"A mythological race of man-horse creatures who lived in Thessaly."

"Sicily? Cecily? Sassily?"

"Thessaly. They were killed by the Lapithae and driven out of Greece forever."

"Poor senators. Impeached. Where did they end up?"

"There." She pointed down the beach. "They came to Sunny California."

"With the rest of the cast-me-offs and nutburgers."

The horses had stopped, their riders side by side gazing outward to the horizon, figures unreal and merely imagined, mythic beasts in the coppery sea. She stirred in his arms and he heard her voice in his ear.

> *"One by one in the moonlight there*
> *Neighing far off on the haunted air*
> *The unicorns come down to the sea."*

She trailed off.

"Pretty. Whose?" he asked.

"Conrad Aiken."

"My Aiken back? I know him well."

"Joker. Fool. Madman. Aiken's poem. Called 'Evening Song.' "

"Nice. Pretty pretty." He crooned in her ear, nuzzled her cheek. Gin and love were at work together; love instead of dry vermouth. Ah, sweet sweetness. He wished for no more than this. This was happiness, only this. The hell with 430 North Rodeo. The hell with movies and studios and Sam Ueberroth. This was heaven in the here and now. His arm circling her back, her blowing hair tickling his nose, her smell, touch, sound—her all. From his heart came the longing shout for freedom—*Let me go, damn it! Slip my bonds, crack my fetters, release me*—and the pale face of Frances, his wedded wife, swam to him from out of the gathering fog, spoiling the moment. Frances the lumberman's daughter. Marry in haste, repent at leisure. God. April made a tiny murmur and stirred in his arms.

He apologized, hadn't realized he was squeezing so hard. "Some more, please," he said in a husky voice. "More lines."

She thought a moment, then recited,

> *"It is evening, Senlin says, and in the evening,*
> *By a silent shore, by a far distant sea,*
> *White unicorns come gravely down to the water.*
> *In the lilac dusk they come, they are white and stately,*
> *. . . One by one they come and drink their fill;*
> *And daisies burn like stars on the darkened hill."*

He liked it; pretty images. "What's it called?"

"Senlin," she told him.

"Senlin who?"

"Just 'Senlin.' "

He got up, brushed his trousers, and held out his hand. "Let's go back, want to? Play doctor?"

She laughed that laugh and sat up, touched his cheek, murmured something he failed to catch, words lost to the wind. It was no longer Malibu but the Cornish coast. He was Tristan; she, Isolde; Francis King, Mark; and their love was the love of the ages. At twenty-five, April Rains was legendary. He kissed her. They clung together, lost out on the Cornish rocks in the rolling fog. Horses and riders had gone. Darkness was theirs. No one to see, no one to care. "I love you. Darling, I love you. Love me. Please love me."

"Yes. Yes, darling, I love you, too."

Words, merely, but a comfort to say them. How long since he'd said them to any woman? Common everyday movie words, but so great a comfort. The most important words.

They went in, lovers, not married, into Frances's house, his and *hers*, not his and hers. Inside the still room the fire was there and the shadows, safe, enveloping, blessed dark, and where they lay and how, that was love's old story. People should be happy? Yes, happy, men and women making babies by the firelight.

At the thought she pulled suddenly away.

"What?" he asked, drowsy with the gin.

"Nothing . . ." Her Mona Lisa smile in the firelight.

To have his baby! Terrifying, wondrous thought—to bear her young for him, fruit of his loins. What Fran could never do, give him babies, little *bambini* in diapers, rompers. Toddlers all over the place. How pleased and happy Maxine would be.

Then, finally, disaster. They were asleep and a hot coal must have jumped onto the flokati rug. The neighbors saw billowing smoke, called the fire department; strangers came dashing into the house from everywhere, "to the rescue," and the lovers were caught—not even "doing anything," but *in flagrante* was *in flagrante*, even in the Malibu Colony. The dead whale was one story; a better one was the fire.

"Conflagration . . . house of Frank Adonis . . . present on the scene was Frankie . . . with a business associate." Hedda was on the phone posthaste, going racka-racka-racka. The power of the press, the printed word. It went from the Hat to the Fat One and pretty soon everybody was playing guessing games. Who was the lady at the house of Frances Deering Adano when it caught fire and burned on the Sunday of the Big Storm?

The real reason Frank had been able to spend a whole weekend alone with April was that Frances had gone to Seattle to visit her father in the hospital. A mild stroke had him bedded and she wanted to be at his side in the emergency. Also she wanted to discuss her current domestic situation with her mother, a conversation that may be easily imagined.

But Frances's absence was not prolonged, and it was some time before Frank was able to spend another such interval in April's company. It happened the following spring; by then Frances was occupying the Bristol house alone and Frank was temporarily in rooms at his club. It being Maxine's birthday, he ran down to San Bernardino to surprise her, and with him came April, whom he introduced to his mother as his client, adding nothing more. But Maxine Fargo was smarter than that. She wanted to hear all about April, knowing perfectly well that there were things her son wasn't telling her. It made her sad to think that her Franco was doing things he shouldn't, and with a girl not yet half his age, beautiful though she was. In her own Maxi-way she went straight to the heart of things. She took April to see her garden, and while they walked among the rows of butter lettuce and tomato plants she interrogated her, in a kind, pleasant way, but her intentions were clear. She wanted to know if this willowy college blonde was a home-wrecker, someone who was bad for her Franco, someone who would bring him pain and misery. But by the time they got to the Swiss chard, Maxine was convinced that April was an angel from on high. Her mother's heart told her that this was the one who could erase that look from her Frankie's eyes, that empty look that frightened her and made her ill.

As things fell out, Maxine saw April only once again. This was on the eve of April's departure for Italy that summer, during which time, by a perfectly natural arrangement, she would see Maxine's son, also summering on the Boot.

This European venture came about as follows:

One afternoon as Frank came in from the track, he bumped into Kit Carson in the agency parking lot and invited him up to the office where he'd once been an office boy. As they stepped into the elevator another passenger entered behind them. This was Tonio Gatti, the assistant to a large-scale Italian producer, the famous Alessandro Cannis (*Cave* Cannis, as he was known along the Via Veneto). Top dog among the producer's underlings, Gatti, a good-looking, amiable Latin with an atrocious accent, was in Los Angeles scouting American talent to fill several roles in the gargantuan epic now in pre-production in Rome, *The Trojan Horse*.

"Thees ees-a quite amusing, *amico mio*," Tonio greeted Frank, "but I was just-a now on my way to see you. And, tell me, who 'ave we 'ere? An actor, no doubt." He took in Kit's six-foot-three frame, ending with the blonde hair and green eyes. Frank introduced the two and the upshot was that within days Kit was signed to play Hector in the Trojan epic and was packing to fly off to Rome.

Soon after, Frank arranged for Tonio to meet another of his young, attractive clients, April Rains, who instantly captivated the Italian. Though married, Tonio was something of a Lothario, and almost before she knew it, April likewise found herself preparing for an extended junket to sunny Italy. Cannis was borrowing her from Metro, at three times her normal salary.

April and Kit flew together to New York, where they performed the usual studio publicity chores, and when they were done they went on to

Rome. Then, after a discreet lapse, Frank himself followed, ostensibly to Britain, to pave the way for yet another client, Babe Austrian, soon to make her debut at a London nitery. Naturally he would drop down to Rome to check on the progress of the *Horse*. A trip with pleasant prospects all around, inasmuch as he was to travel unhampered by Frances, who was in the throes of redecorating the Bristol house (yet again); besides which, her father hadn't fully recovered from his stroke.

That year, Rome was a beehive, and it seemed as if everyone was in town, including Jenny and me. I'd wrapped my picture in North Africa a few weeks earlier, and Frank wanted me in Rome to see if he could squeeze me into *The Trojan Horse* as well. In any case, he'd already had a firm offer for me to start another picture in Europe, so one way or the other I was career-carefree and on hand for the duration.

This was the great time of Italian picturemaking. Rome was Hollywood-on-the-Tiber, and every last foot of production space was leased to filmmakers, foreign and otherwise. These were the glorious days falling on the heels of Fox's *Cleopatra*, the days of the Burton-Taylor-Fisher debacle and the field day the press had enjoyed, ringing their chimes on that triangle. Now *la prezza di Roma* was hungrily searching for another tasty pudding to dish up. On the Via Veneto the faces sitting in the cafés drinking espressos were just like all the faces at Pupi's on the Sunset Strip drinking café espressos. You saw everyone you'd left at home, stars as well as nobodies. Many had come trying to wangle a job; they were all beating a path to Tonio Gatti's door; Tonio, it seemed, had invented the better mousetrap.

By now Kit and April were deep into the film, currently on location at Ostia, where the embarkation of the Greek army was being shot. *The Trojan Horse* is one of those Hollywood extravaganzas of twenty-odd years ago that you never hear anything about these days. Mercifully, it seldom turns up on the *Late Show*, and isn't the sort of picture you're likely to come across in the revival houses. It featured the usual cast of thousands, an unending number of battle sequences, plus some equally stunning love scenes between Paris and Helen, but that's about it for the *Horse*. By now it's long since joined that boneyard of unmourned Hollywood turkeys like *Solomon and Sheba*, Tyrone Power's swansong, like *Samson and Delilah*, like *Pandora and the Flying Dutchman*, like *King Richard and the Crusaders* and the late, unlamented second version of *The Charge of the Light Brigade*.

There came a time when the company moved farther down the Boot, to where the city of Troy had been raised in rubber and plaster along the Pontine Marshes. With the switch in scheduling, April wasn't being carried on the callsheet, and no sooner had she been given her temporary release than she disappeared and no one but Tonio Gatti knew anything of her whereabouts.

In the meantime Jenny and I had come up from Sicily to Naples and had hopped the *motoscafo* over to Capri, where we put up at the Quissisana Hotel to indulge ourselves in a bit of well-earned *dolce vita*. Shortly after our arrival we were discreetly joined by a friend who signed the register as "Anna Thorwald," and she occupied the room on our left. Shortly after that a gentleman signed in as one "Orlando Gatti" and he took the room to our right. Since all the rooms connected, the balconies as well, we were a merry troupe, indeed we were.

And thus commenced the famous Summer of the Purple Grape, the name we later gave to those weeks, those happy, sun-filled weeks of Italian summer, a little less than paradise—but only a little. And in those weeks we watched a beautiful flower come slowly, gorgeously, into full blossom. The flower's name was April, and I thought this must be what watching a night-blooming cereus was like. I was no gardening buff, but I knew horticulture when I saw it.

Seeing lovers together wasn't anything so new, I'd observed my share, but this was a rare piece of drama we were witnessing, Jenny and I. Romance was in the air, night and day. They were like two young lovers, yes, yet at times they looked like the oldest married couple we knew, two old shoes, so comfortable and relaxed they were, at ease with each other and with us and with the world. There's that tired old cliché you still hear a lot, "meant for each other," but we had the feeling that in this case it really applied. Somehow you knew it, they were God's couple, but what made it really poignant to me was knowing how close to zilch were their chances of making a go of it. Even if April gave up her career, which I knew wouldn't have bothered her much, even if she left the public eye, what were the chances of Frances's ever bending enough to give Frankie the divorce he so desperately wanted? And while April was radiantly happy in the role of young lover, she was not the type to last as Official Mistress to a married man.

Realizing this, Frank told us he was resolved that upon returning to California he would absolutely force Frances to divorce him. Jenny and I thought this a fairly unrealistic approach on his part. That he did not perceive, or simply chose to ignore, the truth wasn't much to his credit, but he was a man deeply enamored, and what could anybody do about that?

But during this interval of enchantment—it's true, they were both enchanted—they acted as if a divorce were the likeliest event in the world it was only a question of time before things worked out and they'd be man and wife. To look at them no one would have guessed there was anything amiss, they seemed so happy, so natural together. As I say, meant for each other.

I see them still, hand in hand as they stroll along the narrow cobbled streets of Capri, in shorts and shirts and straw hats, dark glasses, sandals, touches of gold jewelry, he dark as mahogany, she a glorious tawny gold with just that touch of pink lipstick, white teeth flashing, blonde hair—she twenty-four, he—fifty-three! Almost thirty years older, yet you could see how little it really mattered. How could it? She might be a widow before most girls her age, but who could think about that now? Who could think about anything except that they belonged together, they were already married to each other even though no papers had been signed, no ceremony had been performed.

I watch them walking by the seaside and try to distinguish them from teen-agers, two sweethearts poised on the threshold of life, poor but honest, as they say; see how they duck their heads and smile or lean toward the other's cheek. See them pick up a shell, examine it, carry it to the ear, listen for the wave that lies within, forever sounding. The Mediterranean laps their tanned ankles, blue water under bluer sky, a movie's blue lagoon —it could be Long Island Sound but for the drying nets festooning the stone walls of the breakwater, the pink and blue houses. They go hither, thither, buy a bangle, buy a bead, buy a watch. She spends all of a thousand lire for a watch; he has only the one Frances had given him, she'd rather he went timeless than see it. This one has "Mikee Maus" using yellow gloves to tell the time.

See the *signorine* in the windows above them, nodding, laughing— pretty girls with flowers in their hair, they know *amor* when they spot it. *Ah, il americano, com'è bello, com'è sexy. Ciào, bello! Buon giorno, bella signorina!* They laugh and chatter and comb their hair and put in ribbons. Where will they find such a *bello* for themselves? *Ma, è italiano, non è verro, questo ragazzo? Ma cinquante? Non è possibile! Ciào, bello! Ciào, Franco!* No man looks like that at fifty!

Who can imagine how happy they are, how they are blessed? These are golden hours, stolen from the great world. But for how long? Not very . . .

At this point the whole Boot of Italy was swarming with a clamoring horde of international press. Had anyone divined the arrangements that were operational on Capri, there would have been hell to pay, and April was not the kind of girl to deal with that kind of hell. That her career might be in jeopardy wouldn't have worried her—it might actually have been a relief. But the thought of all the pressure, the scandal, the publicity —it didn't merely worry her, it terrified her.

One evening Jenny pleaded fatigue and went to bed early. I had been doing a little writing and stuck my nose in some pages while Frank and April took the funicular up to Anacapri. Later I went out and sat on the balcony, enjoying the view. I heard April's door and presently their voices. Someone had recognized April in the chapel up above; now she was upset and Frank was trying to calm her down. Then she began to weep, and I realized how badly she was troubled by her situation. She was telling him she would rather end it now, here at Capri, clean and cold, than go on hoping he was ever going to marry her while they went on sneaking around, always afraid some photographer would pop out and take their picture together and it would come out in the papers.

"But what does it matter?" I heard Frank say. "The only important thing is that we love each other, isn't it? A picture in the paper isn't going to hurt us, is it?"

He cajoled her until her tears subsided; then I heard her laugh, that pretty sound that was so much hers. Leave it to Frank to get her smiling again, and so quickly. Still, I knew this little episode was only the precursor to others, the foreshadowing of further tears to be shed.

The low murmur of Frank's voice went on; I didn't catch the words but I could imagine them.

"Darling, we belong together, that's all that's important. The hell with the rest of them. Frances is only playing a waiting game, but in the end she'll come round. She'll try to make us miserable as she can for a while, but in the end she'll give in, you'll see."

And April's bright response: "Yes, of course, you're right, you're always right. I'm just being foolish. Let's forget the whole thing."

And of course it was forgotten; at least no one spoke of it, though I doubt anything was *really* forgotten. You didn't just forget about Frances, even though she was ten thousand miles away . . . except, damn it all, she wasn't ten thousand miles away, but a lot closer, as events were shortly to prove.

Though Frank had brushed off the incident, nonetheless their having been recognized at Anacapri had its effect. Somehow the word got out, the *paparazzi* arrived in swarms, and the lovers decamped while Jenny and I laid a general smoke screen. They went into hiding again. What little dignity remained to them was spent in fleeing by car up the Autostrada del Sol, heading for a safe haven and the high walls of a villa belonging to Frank's kind friend, the celebrated and newsworthy Contessa Dodi Ingrisi.

Dodi was a rich American heiress who owned a luxurious antique villa at Civitavecchia, built on the ruins of one of the Emperor Tiberius's play spots. Sixty-five and more, Dodi was gay and charming, wore lots of Puccis—screeching pinks and parrot greens and lavenders—and ran about her estate in a pink-painted golf cart. She was a doyenne of the Rome social scene, but was as the veritable tomb when it came to keeping a secret.

It was here at the ochre-tinted Villa Pinati that the lovers managed to catch their breath. Here no one bothered them; few even knew they were in residence. Dodi was happy to share their company if they were so inclined; otherwise she gave them the widest kind of berth. And for eleven days they remained sequestered, safe from prying eyes and the probing lenses of the *paparazzi*. They strolled in the cool gardens that were filled with blank-eyed tufa statues and tall palms, played games of *bocci* on the lawn that looked like a billiard table, rode horseback along the ragged Mediterranean shore, climbed among the rocks looking for crabs, or went out in the little pink-hulled ketch that Dodi had supplied them with.

This pink ketch was their undoing. Christened the *Dodo Bird* by its owner (who never boarded the vessel; Dodi hated being on the water), it was for Frank the answer to a prayer. Once at her helm he could put himself entirely at ease, cutting himself off from everything except the sun, sky, and salt water he loved. And by dint of lashing her tiller and setting her a straight course, he could contrive to enjoy his inamorata in the cozy cabin below decks, where there were two narrow bunks, one of which they appropriated for their own uses.

One afternoon while they were love-wrapt in the cabin, a squall sprang up out of nowhere and came rushing across the bay to fling itself upon the little boat. Taken unawares, Frank staggered above deck to find his craft about to capsize. While he jumped to unlash the rudder, April gamely hauled down the flapping mainsail, and together they tried to muscle out the driving squall that seemed bent on destroying both the boat and themselves. The sky had gone an eerie black, the waves were dangerously high, and there wasn't another vessel in sight. And while they were in full view of the beach, a quarter mile distant, there were no people in sight.

Frank was a good sailor and he put up a brave fight, but though he kept his bow headed close into the wind, the waves were choppy and the gale sprang now from one quarter, now another. They began shipping water, bailing became a hopeless necessity, and soon the boat started to go down.

They abandoned the sinking craft and struck out for the shore. The waves were strong, and when April tired, Frank put his arm around her and hugged her close, certain the wind would carry them to the shore. April couldn't speak, but Frank kept muttering in her ear, "I love you, baby," over and over. "I love you, baby, love you, baby."

This misadventure ended happily when they washed up on the sand, where they were helped by locals whom an anxious Dodi had dispatched in search of them. The ketch was gone forever, beneath the Civitavecchian waves, not so far from the spot where the poet Shelley had suffered a more fatal mishap 150 years before.

This dramatic business of the shipwreck led to notable results. First, it served to strengthen the ever-deepening love between Frank and April. Having faced the peril of the storm in each other's arms, they were more than ever resolved to cleave together, whatever this might entail. Nobody could prevent their being together, and if Frances wouldn't give him the divorce he demanded, so be it. He'd find another way; he had to.

Second, and worse luck, the mishap again set the bloodhounds on their tails. Not unnaturally, such an incident was bound to attract the attention of the press, and upon learning that the lost vessel had belonged to the Contessa Ingrisi, reporters gathered to investigate. Since April was still presumed to be with Jenny and me at Capri, and Frank in London, no connection was yet made between them and the pair on the boat, whom Dodi passed off merely as relations of her former husband. The reporters bought it, all but one droll type who, with considerable resourcefulness, made a friend of the cook's scullery boy and learned from him that an "American couple" was being sheltered under *la Contessa*'s roof—no names, but the boy thought maybe *il cinema*, maybe, they talked *molto molto* about the movies—and in no time the wind was up. Accompanied by his photographer, the reporter camped out in a van in a nearby pine grove until Dodi called up the local *carabinieri* and had them dislodged.

Still their identities went undetected, and after a day or two they relaxed vigilance. They were idling on the villa's *terrazzo;* April was trimming Frank's hair. Out in the bay a yacht was lying calm in the water; Frank recognized it as the *Calliope* but paid no attention as his black curls fell about his chair seat, an antique bronze lion on which she'd perched him. Too late he saw that the yacht had been slipping closer inshore. He could make out figures along the rail, and he realized that binoculars were trained their way; maybe even cameras? The barber and her customer hightailed it inside, but the damage was done: pictures of this intimate domestic scene appeared in Thursday's *Oggi* with suitable comments.

Now the jig was up for sure and they fled in earnest and nocturnally, this time in the Contessa's Karman-Ghia. With Dodi herself chauffeuring them, they crouched ignominiously on the floor, covered by blankets and some valises, arriving in Rome during the early hours, before the heavy traffic had begun its din. At a convenient corner Frank was let out to get back to his hotel by taxi, while April was driven straight to the Stazione Termine, where she boarded the *rapido* for Naples. By lunchtime she was again with us on the terrace of the Quissisana.

Meanwhile, when Frank came strolling into his hotel he found a worried Tonio Gatti in the lobby. He'd been there for nearly two whole days, waiting to warn him. The word was out all over town, and, worse, Frances was upstairs. "And, Franco, I'm-a sorry to tell you this, but you must know. She 'ave brought *un 'amica*. Ees 'Edda 'Opper."

Grounds for suicide.

It was true, with Frances had come the GrassHopper, Hedda herself, all ready to twang her legs and bare her pancaked breast to the world. The whole thing stank of trouble, the serious kind that makes headlines and ruins careers—and lives. Hedda would doubtless sharpen up her pen and pillory Frank and April the same way she had Ingrid Bergman years before. Frank would be made the villain of the piece, the philandering playboy-agent husband, while April would be painted up in shades of scarlet, the conniving home-wrecker, leaving Frances to continue in her adopted role as the long-suffering wife, come to extricate her poor blind spouse from the clutches of this collegiate femme fatale.

As a background for drama, Rome now became a potential setting for public exposure, denouncement, and shame. How we hated to let Frank face it alone, but he was determined to protect April however he could.

The plan was, we would stay on Capri until the coast was clear; then, when the Dread Hopper had been disarmed or otherwise knocked out of commission—Frances, also—we would return to Rome, where we would be met by Kit Carson, at which point we would then all four reappear along the Via Veneto, a happy young American quartet returning after a private holiday. Let Hopper write what she wanted, no one could really be sure what had happened. We thought it was very clever.

Frank's call was long in coming, and though he treated serious matters with his usual bantering style, I knew he was being made to run the gantlet. When he glibly reported that he had Hedda eating from the palm of his hand, I had a good idea what that must have cost. It had cost plenty. In exchange for the columnist's solemn agreement not to break the story of Frank's errant holiday, he had promised not to see April again. Rather, he must reestablish himself with Frances as her spouse—in all senses of that word—and when his current business was finished in Rome, he was to depart without having made an attempt to get in touch with April by *any means* whatsoever.

There was no help for it; Frank had already heavily impressed this fact on me. He would keep his end of the bargain at all costs, as he knew Hedda would keep hers. Bitchy though she could be when it came to handing out public reprimands and scourgings, bigoted and contentious in her opinions and political beliefs, Hedda had a good side as well as a bad; she could be both a good friend and a dangerous enemy, but at least you pretty much knew where you stood with her. And she had always had a warm spot for the Swanky Wop.

The hot wind cooled, the whole storm blew over—for the moment. April's career, along with Frank's marriage, was saved, and only the parties involved were privy to what had actually taken place. When the three of us sneaked into Rome, tails between legs and still scared to hell that something would leak out, we learned that Frank and Frances had already departed, but the lady scribe was still in town. We took rooms at the Hotel de la Ville, next door to the Hassler atop the Trinita de Monte.

The day after our arrival, April announced that she was going shopping. Not with Jenny, who occasionally accompanied her on such forays, but with Tonio and his wife, Djiberta, who called promptly at ten and off they went to the Via Condotti. Jenny was rinsing out some things in the washbowl and I was sitting out on the balcony when who knocked at our door but the GrassHopper herself! She looked like a Helen Hokinson club lady in her dotted shirtwaist dress, with a giant garden hat tied under her chin and a large bag of dyed raffia clutched in her hand. Grim as iron, she marched to the center of the room, where she stood in that bandy-legged stance so inimitably hers.

"All right, don't play games with me," she began, looking around the room. "Where is she?"

"If you mean Jenny, she's Luxing out her undies, the way Irene Dunne used to do."

My attempt at humor fell flat. "Don't fool around with me, Charlie. You know who I mean."

I explained that April had gone shopping and wasn't expected back. "Not till late, anyway," I added.

"Jenny! Come in here," Hedda commanded.

Jenny dutifully appeared, drying her hands and facing the music. "Now, look, you two," Hedda began, "I'm going to say something to you both and you'd better get it straight because I won't say it again. I want this thing stopped. Got it? No, don't stand there making sheep's eyes at me, you know darn well what I'm talking about. You all think you're mighty clever, running all over Italy, playing the Innocents Abroad. Well, you're abroad all right, but you're not innocent."

When I tried to protest this high-handedness, I was warned not to interfere, and I made no attempt to test her powers of destruction.

"Now, I'm leaving for London this afternoon," she went on, "and I just stopped by to tell your friend that if she dares to see Frankie Adonis even once, I'll blast her and her career along with her! Understand? You just tell her she's to keep away from him—"

Jenny interrupted. "I don't see how she's to do that, when he's her agent."

"Agents have been known to work out of their offices, or in the commissary or on the set. I've no quarrel with that. I'm talking late-night tête-à-têtes and snuggling down at Dodi Ingrisi's. My God, Charlie, *you* should know better if these other ninnies don't."

"Why should Charlie know better?" demanded Jenny.

"Because he's been around, that's why! And if you haven't got the sense God gave a chicken, someone should. Frank's gone to London. With Frances. They've made it up; they did it in front of me, so I know. But you can tell little Miss Betty Coed that if I hear of any more cute pranks on her part, I'll hand MGM an earful that'll get Frank barred from the lot for the rest of his natural-born days. Get it? Good!"

There was more in this vein, and then, just as Hedda snatched up her bag and turned to go, the door opened and Tonio and Djiberta Gatti appeared on the threshold with April between them.

"Were your ears burning, dear?" Hedda called out sweetly as they trooped in. Tonio's helpless expression said nothing yet spoke volumes, while April seemed dazed as she stared at her persecutor. Hedda walked to the door, gave it a good slam, then marched back to April and began another harangue of the sort we'd just been treated to, shaking her finger under the speechless girl's nose.

"Don't do that," April said, drawing back nervously.

"Never mind, my girl, you just sit down smartly and listen to what I've got to say." She pushed April into a chair and stood over her, then repeated the threats she had just made to me and Jenny.

"You'll be washed up, April Rains, by the time I'm finished with you! You'll never work another day in front of the camera—do you hear me?"

Hedda's racka-racka had April staring glassy-eyed, an agonized expression freezing her face while tears streamed down her cheeks.

"Can't you see you're frightening her?" Djiberta said, unafraid to stand up to Hedda.

Tonio spoke up. "Yes, please, Mees'ees 'Opper, be gentle, be nice—thees-a young lady, she don't feel so good."

"She'll feel a lot worse by the time I'm finished. What's wrong with her?"

"I think she ate something bad, she's-a need lie down."

"Food poisoning? Well, don't just stand there, someone call a doctor!"

"No!" April leaped from her chair and stood tottering as if she would fall. Jenny moved to her and put an arm around her waist. "I'm not sick!" April declared. "I just want to lie down."

Crusty Hedda jerked her chin at her. "Then do it. But I warn you, my girl, and this is my last word. If you get up to any more of these tricks with a certain married guy, I'll have your scalp nailed up at Ciro's, I promise! Ask Ingrid, she knows."

April took a gulp of air and her eyes blazed. "Oh, shut up! Can't you just be quiet? What business is it of yours, anyway? You're nothing but a miserable gossip-monger, all you want to do is hurt people. It's none of your business, or anyone's! I love him! Don't you understand? I love him —he loves me—we want to be together, we *have* to be together!"

"You do, do you? You've apparently forgotten that the gentleman just *happens* to have a wife, a home, marital responsibility."

"But he doesn't love her!"

"So he tells you, but I know better. It's been a sound marriage, no matter what anyone says. If you'd only stay away from him!"

"Wait a minute, Hedda," I said, stepping between her and April. "Give her a break; she's not alone in this. Besides, can't you see she's upset?"

"She'll be a darn sight more upset when I'm done. Face it, you're in hot water, my girl."

Hedda's censorious finger came into play once more, but instead of quieting April, it galvanized her; she leaned forward and her teeth clamped down.

"She's biting me!" Hedda cried and tried to rescue her finger, but those teeth held fast. "Stop—you're hurting!"

Again I was forced to intervene, this time physically. April's eyes rolled with hysteria, she was making strange, guttural sounds in her throat, and her head was turned at an odd angle, trying to keep her hold on Hedda's finger. But before I could effect a release, Hedda's other hand flashed out, striking April's cheek. April released her hold, and sank to the floor like a felled ox.

"*Dio mio,* be careful, *il bambino!*" I heard Tonio exclaim. The fateful words sprang out unchecked; then we heard him draw breath through his teeth and saw him dart a fiercely apologetic look in my direction. "*Madre di Dio,* I'm-a so sorry—"

Without pause I scooped April up and, followed by Jenny, I rushed her into the bedroom and laid her on the bed. Leaving Jenny in attendance, I hurried back into the other room, where Hedda was nursing a sore finger and ferociously interrogating the crestfallen Tonio.

As he tried once again to apologize, I told him to forget it and turned to Hedda. "Well, there's a cat out of the bag for you," I said. "What are you going to do?"

It was Hedda's moment of triumph, the moment she'd come to Rome for. "I'll tell you what I'm going to do, Charlie-boy. Your old Aunt Elda's going to spread this tidbit across the front page of every one of my newspapers, *that's* what I'm going to do!" She crossed thin arms over her withered bosom and dared me to contradict her. I hung dog.

Her threat was appalling, the thought of April's ruin brought about in Hopper's ninety-eight newspapers.

"You can't!"

"You're darn tootin' I can. Unless . . . ."

"Unless what? What do you want?"

"The truth! I want the whole story from April herself! Start to finish. The works. Then I want her to promise to leave Frank Adonis alone. When I've got that promise, it'll remain our little secret. Just between us."

I tended to doubt she would go so far as to expose Frank and humiliate Frances this way, but even so I decided to play along with her. "You mean you won't print it?"

"Not if she does what I ask."

Again it was a question of ethics—Hedda's. And we had no choice. We had to believe her or see the career of April Rains disappear down the tubes. Hedda plunked herself down and ordered tea while I explained the situation to Jenny and April in the bedroom. April washed her face, put on lipstick, and came out to beard the lioness in her parlor.

"What do you want?" she asked dully.

"You know what I want, and you'd better give it to me. Once I have it you can forget all about it—I won't write a word. Not unless this gets to Lolly and *she* prints it. After that it'll be no holds barred. Now, sit down and have some tea, you'll feel better. Surely you're not going to go through with it—this baby?"

"Yes."

Hedda was aghast. "But how can you? It won't have a father!"

"Frank is its father. The baby will be Frank Junior."

"I think Mrs. Adano may have something to say about that."

"No she won't. She's going to divorce him."

"You're either out of your mind or the most foolish creature I've ever seen. For your information, yesterday, before they left, the Adanos, man and wife, had an audience with His Holiness. A *private* audience, mind, in which their marital differences were discussed and ironed out. *Ironed*, my dear—and it was the Pope who did the pressing. When you see tomorrow's paper you'll get the whole picture, and in the meantime I'd advise you to collect yourself. I'm told you have two weeks left on this Trojan opus. If I were you, I'd get them polished off and then skedaddle for Sunny Cal. The Adanos are at present in London, staying at the Savoy, and if I hear one word about you crossing the English Channel to get to Frank, I'll do worse than nail your scalp up at Ciro's, I'll skin you in print so you won't ever be able to go home. Do you get the picture?"

Dry-eyed but white-faced, April nodded acquiescence; but I for one didn't believe her.

"Good. Now that we understand things, dear," Hedda said smoothly, "I can tell you, the talk is that you're coming over very well in the picture. In fact I heard in the bar last night that Agyar wants you for a film. Take my advice, dear, be a star, not a husband stealer; there's more in it for you. And when we get home, I'll call you and you'll come over to Tropical Drive and we'll have lunch and laugh about the narrow squeak we had in Rome."

See? That was Hedda, a wire-wheeled bitch one instant and your sainted Aunt Elda the next. Racka-racka . . .

Photographs of the papal audience at Castel Gondolfo duly appeared in the Rome press. We were shocked to see Frank in his best bib and tucker, side by side with the black-clad Frances wearing an embroidered Spanish veil and looking stern and gaunt. Too gaunt by far, and I called up Hedda to ask about it.

"For me to know, you to find out, Skeezix," she said, and flew off on her broom.

And that was the end of that; except it wasn't, of course. Not even close to the end. But it was at this point that it struck me hard—Jen and I often talked about it—that, whatever voyage April may have thought she'd embarked on, it was a trip to nowhere. A secretary in Sioux City may fall in love with her married boss and get her nose nicked a bit, but for a growing luminary in the Hollywood firmament to put all her eggs in the basket of one of the town's best-known citizens, one with a spouse determined to have and to hold him, well, this was plain folly. Jenny sometimes took it upon herself to talk to April about it, and it was just at this point that there seemed to surface the first cracks in the plate, auguring broken pieces to come. Just now April was nearly as much a curiosity as a "star"; people were interested in her not merely in the way they might be interested in an Esther Williams or a Doris Day; they were interested because of her direct relation to one person: Frank Adonis. If she'd chosen to break things off at this juncture, she and Frank going their own ways, she might have continued indefinitely, attaining the stardom he'd wanted for her. But there was to be no finding out because they didn't part, even though she was reeling badly from the pressures of stardom, the bear-trap jaws of fame, the required decorum in such touchy situations; nor had the fact that Hopper had sided so violently against her helped matters. It was a no-win situation.

I telephoned Frank in London to check out his current state of mind. He was Happy Frank again; you'd never know he had a problem in the world. "Look after baby, will you," he said before hanging up. No problem, I told him. Besides, Kit Carson was back on the scene, and I knew Bud would perform yeoman service in the cheering-up department.

It doesn't take much imagination to appreciate April's fragile state of mind when *The Trojan Horse* wrapped and she arrived in Paris. Her agent and lover being one and the same individual, she could hardly look to him for aid or comfort in her extremity; in fact, Hedda had been exact and explicit in the matter: no congress of any sort whatever was to pass between them. Yet one of the first things April did upon arriving was to go into Charvet and buy a pair of cuff links, the famous Charvet silk knot, but in 24-carat gold, and a polka-dotted silk bowtie, requesting they be sent to Frank at his London hotel in time for his birthday. The tie cost only thirty-five dollars; the cuff links were expensive. It was the sort of impulsive gesture she loved making, but in the circumstances it was imprudent.

The fact that with April's arrival in the City of Light she was separated from her lover by no more than the width of the English Channel meant only that it was that much harder for her to be away from him. So near and yet so far. Given the opportunity, she would have camped out at Calais with a spyglass, pondering invasion of what was left of the British Empire, longing to cross the water and once again find herself wrapped in those arms she loved. As luck would have it, though, she was not obliged to bridge the gulf, for before too long Frank appeared at her side, for what he believed to be one final scene.

But before that there were other arrivals. First arrived Kit Carson, also liberated from *The Trojan Horse*. April was elated by Bud's appearance; she got him a room at her hotel and together they set out to see the sights. Flushed with the success of his latest venture and with *molto lire* burning a hole in his pocket, Bud proposed marriage twice, once on the Eiffel Tower, once in a *bateau mouche*. He'd even bought her a ring from Buccellati. She declined both times and refused the ring.

This was pretty well the set-up when Frank turned up. Jenny and I had been with him in London and getting lots of attitude from Frances, who regarded us two as traitors to her cause and was icy to freezing, depending on the time of day. There were problems everywhere, and Frank had trumped up this business about having to go check things out at the Trocadéro for Babe Austrian's opening, still months away. And so he did the forbidden thing and crossed the Channel, while we stayed on in London and awaited reports from the front.

He arrived on a Friday, and after lunching at the Tour d'Argent with a party of business acquaintances, he had his hired chauffeur drive him to an address on the Ile St.-Louis, to an apartment belonging to Tonio Gatti. It was here that Frank and April kept their last rendezvous. The apartment was costly and expensively furnished in French and Italian antiques, and had an impressive view of the city from the tenth floor. Many well-known people, including several international film stars as well as an English duchess, occupied the premises. Frank and April found their rendezvous a bittersweet one, but each regarded it as necessary; the threat of Hedda notwithstanding, there were important matters to be discussed. They talked for several hours, each entertaining the foolish notion that all they were doing was "straightening out a few things," and that they weren't there to make love at all.

They conversed quietly on the terrace until sundown, when the Parisian evening drew on in all its soft violet splendor, painting the old buildings that remarkable shade that lends its name to "*l'heure bleu,*" the blue hour of cocktail time and romance *à la Parisienne*. Under the circumstances, the hour was well named. It *was* romantic; certainly it was blue; it would get bluer.

Frank never said much afterward about this particular evening, but I know it was an anguishing episode for him. It was Jenny who heard all about it from April, later, when we three were in Yugoslavia together. She and Frank had talked at length until, as the evening chill came on, they moved inside, where they had a fire, sweet reminder of Malibu nights. There was a polar-bear rug in front of the hearth, and when they found they couldn't deny themselves any longer, they took off their clothes and made love.

It was a scene of much passion and infinite tenderness, played as if each knew that it was to be the last time they would be together like this. Painful, aching, hindered by their mutual feelings of unfulfillment, they lay together on the white bearskin, while the firelight danced on their faces. In that stranger's room, unfamiliar to both of them but serving admirably their present purpose, high above the crooked streets of the ancient island in the Seine and the traditional sounds of taxis crossing the Pont Marie, they yearned in each other's arms. It always surprised her how, large as he was, he never hurt her, he was so gentle, and even in their climb up the mountain he was never hurting, and when they fell off the mountain together and went floating out over purple Paris, it was ecstasy of the highest order. Could Bud give her this? Could any other man?

There was only this moment, this bit of time stolen from the outside world and those who made it painful for them, and they wanted to make the night something always to be remembered and cherished. If they were to part—and it seemed they were; no matter what had been said, each knew perfectly well that in the end Frances would prevail—they would strive to make it a memorable parting. Locked in embrace, they whispered the ancient litanies of passion, devotion, and love everlasting, knowing that before the night was out they would no longer be one, but two, two who through no fault of theirs would then be forced apart. However tightly they might cling together in the Paris night, sipping French champagne and breathing French air, in their hearts they knew they were bound to lose.

When at last their bodies parted, Frank poured them more champagne and they sat gazing out the window onto the Paris rooftops. A scene from *La Bohème*, only he was no starving tenor, he had all the money in the world; his walls were hung with Manet and Monet, Braque and Utrillo; a Rodin bronze crouched in the garden and guests rid their ashes in the Baccarat. He had sixteen wheels on four foreign cars plus spares and would never have to worry about his old age; everything he desired except the one thing he desired most in the world. A bitter pill, and he choked on it. He thought of that long list of women he had couched, women to whom he'd been friend or lover or both, but never lover like this, no, not like this.

The champagne was dry and tangy on his palate and he'd had sufficient to feel the least bit pissed, just a little smashed, and he held her more tightly. They were in robes now and she sat on his lap in the chair by the window—the way she'd refused to sit on Sam's lap, "talking movie stardom." She was trembling and she wound her arms more tightly about his neck. "What is it?" he whispered, lifting her hair away from her ear.

She'd begun to weep, something she rarely did. "I'm afraid," she said, shivering.

"No, no, you don't want to say that. You're not afraid, because there's nothing to be afraid of. This isn't the end for us, we're going to go on seeing each other, you know that."

"Do I?"

"Sure you do. It's going to work out. You'll see. She can't hold out forever. I know her. She's acting this way because it's part of her nature. She doesn't want me, but right now she doesn't want anyone else to have me, either."

"She must hate me."

"It doesn't matter. She'd hate anyone who—look, she isn't going to stick around over here much longer. She's itching to get home, I can tell. She doesn't like to be away from the house for this long—you know how she is about that goddamn house. And after she goes, you can come to London, or I'll be coming here with Babe. And anyway, there's your new part. I'm going to fix up that deal with Agyar."

That was Frank, always "fixing deals," with Agyar or someone else. His gold ring flashed in the candlelight, the ring Frances had given him at the altar, and on another finger another ring, another gift from her, rings to which she'd attached heavy chains. Murder was in his heart that night in Paris.

Then it was time to go. They'd already lingered on the Ile St.-Louis long past the hour when he should have been at his hotel: Frances would be calling. Then, as only bad luck would have it, they were noticed coming out of the elevator: friends he couldn't slough off. Foolishness to have left together, but he couldn't bear leaving her and wanted to drive her back to her hotel.

That unfortunate encounter didn't get into the papers until after April's trouble began, and by then it hardly mattered. But what happened next was far worse. By a piece of ill luck, before going back to London Frank had spoken with the notorious Ilya Agyar, the Hungarian producer who had arrived in Paris to set up a co-production deal with a French-Italian company. He'd heard all about this movie-actress friend of Frank's, and he was showing a panting enthusiasm. Thinking this might be the best answer to her current problems, Frank asked Agyar to invite her to his office for an interview, with an eye to giving her the lead in his production.

What occurred made headlines, further adding to the shabby legend of Ilya Agyar, but doing nothing at all for April's already tattered reputation. He invited her to take tea with him at the Ritz, and afterward the innocent April unwisely accepted his invitation to dinner at his apartment, where, presumably, Madame Agyar was to be on hand. April arrived suitably dressed (she thought) for such an occasion, hoping that she would leave with what she had come for, the plum part in a big movie. The ensuing scene proved the most banal in the world, the cliché of clichés. She and Agyar sat in the best room, champagne and a sturgeon pâté were offered, and the talk centered on the person of Frank Adonis, thus providing April with a lively and interesting raconteur as well as a sympathetic shoulder to cry on. But as time passed, it became more and more evident that there was no Madame Agyar poised to make her entrance (Ilya had this wife, an ex–opera diva, but one seldom if ever saw her anymore).

What next took place became a matter of major conjecture. April's apprehension turned to fear as Agyar made his pass, gross as his own gross character; her screams were sufficiently loud to bring other tenants to the apartment, plus the concierge, pounding on the Third Empire doors, threatening the Hungarian with the constabulary, but when the door was opened and his guest escaped with her virtue intact and a torn dress, such was her peculiar behavior that the gendarmes were indeed summoned.

There emerged a tale difficult to judge for truth, for while the guest claimed she had been forcibly attacked, the host confided to the police that the young mademoiselle was a bit off her head and ought to be placed under observation. She—*he* claimed—had forced her way into his apartment in the hope of gaining the lead role in a production of his (he made sure to mention its name several times over), and, having been told by him that she wasn't right for the part, she had begun to tear off her clothes and had attempted to lure him by exposing various parts of her anatomy, along with making suggestions that they investigate the bed, a generous offer, *bien sûr*, but one which Monsieur had declined, since everyone in the world knew that he was the happiest of married men, also *bien sûr*.

This horrible business was bound to have its effect on April. Not only did the story find its way into the Paris papers, but it made its way in turn to Rome, to London, and certainly to Hollywood, where both Hedda and Louella pounced on it. Frank was still in London, and because he was engaged in the tricky business of presenting Babe Austrian to the British upper crust, there wasn't much he could do other than see that April had the necessary attention. Since it was attention not to her physical state but to her frayed mental condition that was needed, it fell to one Dr. Rand to see to her welfare. And since Dr. Rand, an eminent specialist in mental disorders, ran a fashionable clinic in the *banlieues* of Paris, at Passy, it was there that April was put to bed under the care of round-the-clock nurses, the doctor being instructed to report daily to Frank in London.

At Passy, in comfortable quarters overlooking a private garden, April Rains, née Anna Thorwald of Westwood Village in Los Angeles, sat reading old *Reader's Digest*'s in their original English, interesting herself in the How to Improve Your Vocabulary and The Most Interesting Character I Ever Met departments.

Meanwhile, Bud took up residence at a country inn some two kilometers away from the Rand Clinique de Très Bonne Santé, as the place was designated. Every day he would ride a rented bicycle there, and spend hours hoping to be allowed to visit with her. Meanwhile, he sat among the birch trunks studying French from a paperback Hugo's grammar he'd picked up at the Gare du Nord. He learned reflexive verbs and the list of sixteen adjectives that preceded the noun, while the leaves fell faster around his little chair. His French improved; April did not.

It was a real dyed-in-the-wool mess; you couldn't have found a worse one. Jenny and I bled for her, for him, for both of them. By then Babe had closed at the Café de Paris in London and crossed the Channel. We came, too, Frank's guests. The Adanos took a suite at the Crillon, Jen and I stayed with friends, and Frank got us a car and driver; we drove out to Passy and tried to reassure April, Bud too, and carried somewhat edited versions of her present state back to Frank.

She was determined he wasn't to know about the baby, and of course we bowed to her wishes; we would have agreed to anything short of murder to bring her some measure of peace. Anyway, the doctor recommended that she be indulged, and it wasn't difficult to do so, we felt so damned sorry for her. Anyone would have. They were keeping her well iced, like a Friday mackerel.

By now Frank was no longer in Paris, for Babe Austrian had suffered her fall and was recuperating at a Swiss clinic where Frank had gone to shore her up. Finally he was able to come. "Have I done this?" he asked himself when he saw her. "Is this what our love has brought her to?" On a scale of ten, Passy was about a two; worse was to come. For now they chose to enact, each of them, a role: "I'm all right, you're all right, we're all right." This thing here, this business of Passy, was merely a little hitch, a rest, if you liked, a chance to catch the breath. The Summer of the Purple Grape had got a bit out of hand, but now all was calm again, or soon would be. The doctor said she was coming along just fine, she could go home any time; what they both needed was to get back to Sunny Cal, and pick up the thread of things at home. They played the old saws: Frances was bound to come round, later if not sooner, Frank was sure of it. Next year —surely by next year—everything would be straightened out. He'd have his freedom, they'd announce their wedding plans, they'd even go back to Italy, to Civitavecchia; Dodi Ingrisi would give them a wedding—a wedding of weddings!

But she didn't want to hear it, none of it. And she said she didn't want to go home, though not *why* she didn't want to go home. It was the baby again. If she was going to have it, it must be here in Europe, some out-of-the-way place, no prying eyes. The doctor would see to it; she'd already talked to him.

Frank didn't understand. How could he? It was eating at him, everything, tearing him apart. Big strong Frankie wasn't feeling so big and strong these days. She began to weep; he put his arms around her and held her. Crushed her against his chest, saying over and over, "Love me love me love me," with that desperation in his voice he couldn't overcome.

Later they walked in the little park with the white birches, the gravel crunching underfoot, walking not like lovers now, but more like father/daughter—should she drop out of Bennington in her sixth semester to go live on the Left Bank and paint landscapes of Notre Dame?—or brother/sister—Look, Mother needs this operation; how are you fixed for cash? They formed a melancholy picture in their dark clothes, seated knees together on the little iron chairs—he'd spread his handkerchief for her—among the peeling trunks of white birch and their gold leaves that fell around them like money, eight kilometers south of Paris, where you got squab for dinner even if you *were* mentally disturbed.

They still talked of love, but such a different kind of love from that of the Summer of the Purple Grape. Now love was heartbreak and anguish, but not—not yet—regret. Regret was to come, in the Winter of the Discontent. Now was the Autumn of the Gold, and what they learned together in their explorations of their present situation was that Passy was a dead end.

The truth was, as he later confessed to me, Frank was feeling the worst fear of his life, the deepest terror. This was when he related to me the agony of indecision and despair he was in, though he fought to keep her from seeing the widening chinks in his armor. The thought that he'd hurt her, the last person in the world he would ever hurt, made him tremble with self-loathing and fury.

What have I done, what have I done? Over and over, *mea culpa, mea culpa*. And its corollary, What shall I do now? Their talk was awkward and fumbling, they were the halt and the blind, groping amid the white birches, lending helping hands that were little help.

Another parting tore at them; the pain was excruciating—she masking it with a mustered dignity and no more tears, for she knew how it upset him, her crying, he making rash promises. In the end he left, back to Paris on a wet road, a near-accident as his Peugeot skidded onto the narrow, leaf-strewn shoulder, and the violet-blue air seemed haunted in a world of steamy damp and fog and leafless trees. He thought of the white unicorns that came down to the sea at Malibu, "neighing far off on the haunted air. . . ."

For Frank it was Chicken Little time, the sky was definitely falling. He had to get back to his office in Los Angeles, it couldn't be avoided. Meanwhile, help was on the way: Donna Curry was coming. Jenny and I stayed as close to April as we could until my picture got its shooting date and I was off for the steppes of Yugoslavia. April seemed in reasonably stable condition and Dr. Rand had high hopes of a complete recovery if she would just steer clear of Frank, who was now being labeled in her medical reports a "deleterious influence." And since by now he was some seven thousand miles away, the horizon seemed clear.

Then, surprise: at the beginning of the month who should turn up at Zagreb but April and her mother, and I could tell that Donna was deeply worried about April. Shocked to find out her daughter had been in the clinic, she let me know how disappointed she was in me for not having said anything.

"I guess we should have told you," I apologized, "but April made me absolutely promise we wouldn't. She didn't want you to know."

"Oh, Charlie—Charlie," she said in such a sad way my heart went out to her, "how have things come to this? And is it going to happen again?"

Downplaying things as best I could, I repeated what Rand had said —April would be all right if she stayed away from Frank.

Donna rejected it all. "Does anyone actually think she'll keep away from Frank? It's a mess, and, much as I hate to say it—well, let's just say I don't think it can end happily for either of them. Charlie, I wish they'd never met. I wish he'd never put her in pictures."

She paused while the waiter brought tea. When he left, Donna resumed. "I went to that pretty church on the square, the one with all the flowers in front, and I prayed. Do you know what I prayed? That they can part without wounds, that they can just quietly get it over with now and go their separate ways. Is that too much to ask? I don't want to see her hurt anymore."

"What about the baby?" I asked.

She shrugged helplessly. "She insists she's going to go ahead and have it."

"She mustn't. It'll ruin her. Hedda—"

It wasn't to be thought of. When April reappeared, Donna discreetly withdrew, leaving me to talk turkey with her daughter. Yet, though I spoke as persuasively as I knew how, I could tell I wasn't getting anywhere.

"Hedda doesn't scare me, and Frank wants a child. Frances can't give him one. I can. I'm going to. I don't care what happens, I'm going to do it. For him. A son and heir."

Greater love hath no woman than that she should give up a blooming movie career for her lover whom she can never have, but to whom she can present an illegitimate son. But what was to happen to the kid? This wasn't the eighties, when women could have out-of-wedlock children and so what? This was still the early sixties, when such things were mightily frowned upon.

I was forced to tell Donna I'd struck out. And soon we began seeing another, less serene April. The sweetness seemed to evaporate; she became nettlesome and crabby. I began feeling nervous around her. Jenny said it was because of the baby; I didn't think so. One day she cut her hair off at a whack, dyed it brown, gave up makeup, began wearing weird clothes, talking to herself. It was scrambled-eggs time again. In truth, there are certain people you meet up with who have an aura of doom. It has nothing to do with a dark or perverse nature, nothing malign, but you sense that they're just not going to make it, that sooner or later things are going to go sour and there's a bad end waiting for them. It was beginning to seem that that's how it was with April.

We loved her, we cared about her, we feared for her. She was falling apart before our eyes and we couldn't help her. I called Dr. Rand once, twice, three times, burning up the wires to Paris until he hung up on me, then wouldn't take my calls. April kept saying that things were closing in on her, and I assumed it was because of the Frank situation. But it was so much more. Because for someone in her position, everything was doubled, trebled, quadrupled. By now she was living in that rarefied atmosphere of the star, she was even getting a star complex, but at the same time detesting all the circumstances that made this possible. "It's strangling me," I remember her once saying. "I can't breathe. I can't catch my breath. I hate it. Oh, Charlie—I really hate it!"

She did, too; she hated it but was trapped by it—just one more specimen in the Hollywood zoo, the Metro menagerie. Ava Gardner was living in Rome at the time and she and April had met, become friendly. Ava was a girl who'd sorted things out for herself, however painfully, and she had good advice for the younger girl—Get out, baby—but April was oddly passive even as she was being swept up into the maelstrom, round and round and round, then sucked down and down, out of sight, to the place where the only written word is *finis*.

Time passed. Lots of time. We even lost track of her, and though we waited for cocktail-party seepage concerning the scheduled birth, none was forthcoming. By now Jen and I were having a few problems of our own, domestic variety, and after the picture wrapped she decided to stay on in London for a while, and I returned home alone over the Pole. When I got to Hollywood, the rumor factory was grinding out talk pertaining to Frances: it was being bruited that she was in a hospital "for observation." The word was first made public in Lenny Lyons's column, then it came out in Hedda, who until now had been insisting that Frances had entered St. John's Hospital in Santa Monica for an "exploratory operation," and Frank confirmed it all when I saw him.

Frank was often distracted, stumbling for the first time in his life that I knew of, and trying desperately to put together a new deal under his Adonis Productions banner. Having spent prodigally to buy the rights to a current Broadway stage hit, starring a prominent actress, he vowed to have the success of his career (incidentally, earmarking the role of the daughter as April's).

"What can Frankie Adonis be thinking of?" carped Hedda in her morning pillar. "Going around town telling all his friends that none other than April Rains will play Cassandra in his new movie. A fatal move if ever I heard one. Between you and me and the gatepost, April is rumored not much up to playing much of anything, since she is presently horse de combat [sic] in a Connecticut rest home." Racka-racka.

Hedda was right about one thing: April was definitely a patient at the Hartford Retreat, a mental hospital where various notables from sundry branches of show business have gone at one time or other; the place was on a par with Menninger's. Judy Garland had been in and out several times during her periods of depression, other celebrities as well.

On my next trip east I hired a car and drove up to Hartford to see my family, then went to visit April. It proved to be the unhappiest visit of all. "Hello, Charlie," she said as I came into her bungalow.

"Hello yourself. How're you doing?"

"All right, I guess. They don't complain about me. I may be getting out of here soon. Maybe."

"Good news, baby." I kissed her. She didn't look so hot. "Not off your feed, are you?"

"A little." She pulled a droll face. "How's Jenny?"

It was my turn to make a face. I explained that Jenny was still in London and for the time being we'd agreed to disagree. I said I'd been in touch with Donna, but just now April seemed more interested in my vicissitudes than in my correspondence with her mother. I dealt with my boring story briefly, then maneuvered the conversation around to her again. "Well, beauty, how's it going? And remember, this is your old pal Chazz. Don't try to kid me."

"I guess you know—I lost the son and heir, woe is me." Woe is her was right. When I touched her hand, it started to tremble and her face began working; I slipped quickly to her side and put my arms tight around her.

"Don't, hey, don't, please." I might have said, "Hey, it won't help," but maybe it would have; whose arms had she cried in lately? Who was there for her to turn to except guys with Easter Island faces and shrink degrees from Vienna? She had every right to shed tears. What worse calamity for a woman than to lose the baby of her body? April was a staunch and stalwart girl; but I knew that she'd suffered profoundly the loss of this child—Frank's child, which she'd endured so much to bring into the world, only to find out eleven days later that the baby had died in its crib, what the doctors call S.I.D.—Sudden Infant Death—fine one minute, not breathing the next. It had been a bitter, bitter blow, one she never fully recovered from. Her guilt had been overwhelming. Did people think she'd suffocated it on purpose? Did Frank think she'd been negligent? *Had* she been? Lots of nutty ideas like that.

In time her body healed, but her mind was something else again; that was unstitched, too, and soon began to unravel.

"Sorry, honey, I'm so sorry. I know how much you wanted it." She had me weeping against her cheek; this scene really undid me. I mean, what do you say? Frank's kid.

"He wanted it so much," she said, pulling some Kleenex from a box on the table, some for her, some for me. We blotted up each other's faces. "I guess it just wasn't in the cards." She sniffed and balled her tissue, then backboarded it into the wastebasket. "Bad genes, maybe. I read this article that says everything's in the genes. I wanted him to be a present to Frank. He wanted it so much. Damn. I screwed up his kid. And now there won't be any more, doctor says."

I told her she wasn't the first one all this had happened to. "It's how things happen sometimes." In my heart I pitied her, a thing I knew she'd hate me for, and I masked it as best I could, saying that since it was such a lovely day outside, why not enjoy it?

Outside, nature seemed to spread itself generously on all sides as if purely for our benefit—green, green everywhere, with patches of flowers and attractive glimpses of water. I could see that she was receiving good treatment, and what was better, she seemed to be responding. But she was having problems, lots of problems. By now it was pretty clear to her that the movie career was in jeopardy, but she didn't care about that. Surprisingly, she also failed to show much interest in ever getting it together with Frank again. It was a case of a bit too much water over the dam, I thought, too much blood under the bridge.

"Frank . . ." I began, then stopped, wondering how to go on with what I had to tell her.

She smiled. "Yes? Frank what?" She spoke quickly, as if to dispense with the matter in a businesslike fashion. "What about him?"

"I talked to him the other day. I told him—in fact I promised him I'd come and see you."

"How is Frank?" she asked. I didn't like the way that question sounded; flat, impersonal, uncaring.

Fine, I replied, Frank was fine.

"He always is, isn't he?" I glanced quickly at her, searching for something behind the words, but I could tell from her blank expression there was nothing hidden intended; it was only a commonplace. "What's he up to these days?"

Those last words answered my unspoken question; she hadn't heard from him, was probably ignorant of the recent changes in his life. I mentioned one or two matters involving him that I thought might arouse her interest, but she showed little. Then I said, "I'm supposed to tell you —he wants you to know: Frances is in the hospital."

April was genuinely upset. "Nothing serious, I hope."

"I'm afraid so."

"Oh." She lowered her lids as though to obscure her thought. "Poor, poor Frank. As if he didn't have enough problems. What is it? Not cancer?" I nodded. "Can they do anything?"

I shook my head. "It seems to be that old question of time."

"Oh."

I paused fractionally, then: "April?"

"Yes?"

"Do you understand what that means? If Frances dies, I mean?"

"Oh God." She shut her eyes again and sat down abruptly on a bench, as if her knees had given out all at once. "Don't say it. Please, Charlie, I don't want to hear it."

"Hear what?"

"What you're getting up the nerve to say. Whatever you've come here to tell me. If it's about Frank—I don't want to hear it."

"You don't mean that."

"I do. Charlie—this is it. I'm not going to see him anymore. I'm sorry his wife's dying, but I don't want to see him. I'm cutting off. I'm getting out. Before—before—"

"Before you hurt him more, you mean."

"*No!* Before I go—g-go down the tubes."

"You're not going down the tubes—don't say that."

"I am, I am, I feel it, every day it gets worse. They can't really help me here, I tell you it's not *going to work!*"

"What makes you think that?"

Her sad smile as she shook her head; I'll never forget it. She was turning in her number; they'd retire it, of course, but the game was over. And what then?

"April, honey, listen to me, you're upset. The baby, Frank—don't—don't tell him this, not now—not yet."

"No, Charlie. I want *you* to tell him. I want you to go to him and tell him I've stopped loving him, that no matter what happens I can't marry him, that he can't marry me. It isn't possible anymore. It's too late. The boat sailed. The good ship *Lollipop.*" She gave a hopeless shrug, then laughed. "It's like *Rebecca*, isn't it? The first wife, reaching back from the grave to twist the lives of those who come after; the second wife, who's so mousy she doesn't even have a name—except *Rebecca* had a happy ending, didn't it? I don't think there's a happy ending for me and Frank." She shook her head sadly. "No, I don't think so. . . ."

She trailed off into some vague distance. I had to say something, just to break the silence. "He'd come and see you if you'd let him. Let him, honey, please let him."

"No, I don't think so. Paris was—well, Paris, but I don't want to see him anymore. Besides, it's bound to get into the papers—Hedda would have a field day. So let's skip it, hm?" Her voice was hollow and she spoke with utter finality. "Do you need any more explanation?" she added.

No, I said, not really; she didn't owe anyone any explanations. Except maybe Frank.

"You'll do that for me, won't you, please? Put it the best way you know how, tell him—" She broke off, got up, walked in a circle with her hands over her face. After a little while she took them away and I saw her defeated look. She tried to brighten it a bit, saying, "I'm really sorry about Frances, though. It's an awful thing, cancer. I dread the thought."

I, too, was dreading the thought—the thought that, for no reason I could comprehend, she was turning thumbs down on any possible future with Frank. Worse, I had this feeling about her—this really bad feeling. Screws were being loosened, the back door was coming off its hinges.

When I asked about her future plans, she grew cloudy, the light dimmed. "Will you be coming back to Hollywood?" I asked. "I saw in *Variety* how they're holding the Wilder picture open for you."

"It's a lovely part, but I don't think—I'm sure I won't be doing it. I don't think I'd be up to it."

"Well, Frank mentioned he was looking for something for you, his own production, good part . . . lotsa bucks?"

She shook her head. "Frank's just being frivolous again. I don't think —well, I just think he'd be unwise. Anyway, I couldn't make another picture, I can't act anymore. I'd be too afraid."

I hated it all, but I had to take it as the gospel according to April. She volunteered the information that her mother was coming to stay with her, and I thought that was a good idea. Certainly someone should be with her; the doctor said she was disinclined to make friends among the patients. Then she rose abruptly and faced me.

"You're sweet, Chazz," she said, "and I appreciate your coming to see me. But—" She shaded her eyes. "Here comes Miss Menzies. It's time for my routine. Miss Menzies is really a clockwork nurse."

I felt devastated. More, I was angry. Here I'd thought I was bringing her tidings that could alter her entire life, and she'd just steamrolled the whole thing. Down, down, she was on the down escalator. I couldn't get her off it.

I left her in the garden and drove despondently back to New York. The car radio wasn't playing but I kept hearing music in my ears, sad, bitter music. I was being forced to acknowledge something I didn't want to believe: no matter what help she was getting at the Retreat, it wasn't going to be enough. Nothing was ever going to be enough now; there wasn't any cure for what ailed her.

Donna did come on; she stayed in the Hartford area for over a month, doing her best, but her best wasn't good enough. She had a job and was obliged to return. It was through Donna that I learned that Bud Ayres had taken over the watch, was in fact staying at a nearby hotel to be close to April. This news naturally made its way into print, and soon reporters began descending on the place from New York and Boston. By this time Bud was adept at dealing with the press, and, using his considerable charm, he fended off the reporters as well as anyone could. You had to hand it to them, though; the guys were sympathetic to his plight, for he made it plain that he loved April and wanted to marry her as soon as she was well enough. The old saw rang true, "All the world loves a lover," and April and Bud had everyone rooting for them. People wanted them to win out, to get together and be a married couple; they wanted them to have the success and happiness that were supposed to accrue to them by virtue of their being movie stars. It went with the package: there *was* a pot of gold at the end of the rainbow.

As for the other leading couple in the drama, the matter of divorce between Frances and Frank, of course, hung fire as she faced her illness and eventual end. And if Frank had any idea of what was going on in Hartford, he certainly wasn't saying—not to me, not to anybody. With time Frances's condition had become stabilized and she was reported to be in remission. He spent hours, days, at the hospital, where there was little he could do to help. But he was there.

Then he had a bad blow, a terrible one. Maxine Fargo died unexpectedly. He'd gone down the week before and taken her out to dinner; afterward they'd stopped by the Buckaroo to have drinks with Angie, then started for San Bernardino and home. He noticed that Maxine looked tired, but she kept insisting she was all right. Three days later Chui Alvarez, the Mexican on the place, telephoned to say that she was real bad and Frank should hurry. He'd promised Frances to come to the hospital, and this delayed him, so that by the time he got to San Bernardino, Maxine was gone. Chui took him out to the garden to show him where she'd had her attack.

"There, Señor Frank, in the tomato patch." He pointed to the flattened plants where she'd been stricken. Frank sank down on an overturned peach basket and wept. *"Mamma mia, Mamma mia."* He was not to be comforted, and Chui had to drive him back to town. For weeks after, he remained profoundly shaken, trying to encompass his loss. It was as though Maxine dead meant that everyone in the world was fallible, everyone's time must come, including his own.

Desperate to do something, he declared that his mother was going to have the biggest and best funeral anyone ever had, though his mother had expressly asked for a quiet end. He argued with the priest for hours, but finally gave in. The obsequies were limited and circumspectly handled. He wanted her buried at Forest Lawn, but Father Mendoza said that her desire was to rest in the desert, the closer to her garden the better.

Among the host of condolences he received was one he showed me. It was a typical Hallmark type card with suitable sentiments inside, signed not with a name but simply as "a friend." He asked me to look at the handwriting; was it April's? I examined the words, but truthfully I couldn't tell. I even compared it with the signature on a birthday card she'd once sent me, but still I couldn't tell.

One day Feldy Eskenazy telephoned, asking if she could come and see me; she had something to tell. Yes, I said, come up soonest.

Feldy was much more a part of our lives in this period than I've probably indicated. Far more than just my acting coach, she'd become a friend. There was no nonsense to her, and she told me straight out what she'd come to say. Yesterday afternoon April and Kit Carson had married in Connecticut and were honeymooning in Nassau. Our first thought was naturally of Frank: had he heard, and how would he take it? Feldy thought it better for me to break the news—that was what April had wanted. I stopped by his office that evening and relayed the details. He took it philosophically, but I could see how badly it hurt him to hear it. Despite everything that had happened, he had hoped against hope that things would somehow iron themselves out, but now she'd turned to Bud, and that was that.

Later he went to Orgell's and sent them a classy Georgian wine cooler as a wedding gift.

We stood by, along with all his other friends, helpless to do much more than stay close. He handled everything with strength and sureness. A stranger couldn't have told from his calm demeanor that he was being torn to pieces inside. At the office it was business as usual, and he had a new girl he'd discovered and was going to bring along. He did things— went to dinners, or down to the Springs overnight to play some tennis with Angie, see his friends, have a few laughs with Alice Faye and Phil Harris at the Racquet Club, then hop back to town and take up his chair at the hospital again.

And he was always interested to hear news of April and Bud. By now Bud was doing a picture in the East (this was *Red Coat Hunt*, being shot in the Tidewater and fox-hunting country of Virginia) and his co-star was none other than his bride. It was April's wedding present to him, her promise to do the film, since she'd already said she wouldn't make any more pictures. It proved to be a lucky gamble. Bud had talked her into it as a therapeutic device, the doctors had approved, and the result was the most popular picture either of them ever made—as well as the last.

Frank never said anything about it to me, but I learned through his office that, although he'd found the story and originally set Bud up in the deal, before shooting began Bud had written asking for his agency release and April's as well. I thought then that it was a lousy thing for him to have done, but later I saw that he was probably right, that they both should have representation elsewhere. Things were much too close with Frank, and they needed a less personal professional environment. Frank took it all with good grace. Then, when the picture was finished, Bud and April stayed on in the East, having fallen in love with the state of Virginia; soon afterward, they bought a farm there and took up being horse folk.

Almost at once the Carsons were in solid with the hunting set, and would make another picture only if they really liked the script. Meanwhile, they were enjoying country life and starting a herd of Herefords. The apple trees blossomed pink and white in May at High Farm, the purple clover came in and the alfalfa, and the two-year-olds threw their foals, and Squire Carson and wife were out in rough-out boots, chopping kindling and digging postholes for a new paddock. There was never talk anywhere of any baby; there was no nursery room at High Farm. Remembering Passy, I already had the answer there: no little Kits or Kats would be running about the pastures of High Farm in Virginia.

Then Frances died in California. By now Jenny and I had made up our differences and she'd returned from London. We'd taken a jaunt down to an isolated little spot in Mexico we were fond of, and one afternoon a boat carried over a message from Frank. We caught the next plane out of Puerto Vallarta and arrived home in time to catch him on the eleven o'clock local news. He looked haggard, and a host of reporters and cameramen were shoving microphones at his face.

With Frances's death, he was bound to assume the burden of guilt. He'd experienced a lot of anguish, bad health had dogged him through the preceding four or five years, and he was feeling the strain. He'd set himself a Spartan vigil to see Frances through to the end, knowing it was what she wanted, to go out as though nothing had ever come between them, nothing had happened in their married life to cause the least rift, the slightest pain. With her, appearances were everything, even the passage through Death's Door. She had herself well buttressed with the Church, the Bishop, the Archbishop, the old family priest, Father Mallory, the nuns, and of course her own blood sister, Sister Mary Rose, all gathered around, joining hands as though to ward off the evils attendant on her for having been for over twenty-five years the devoted wife of the well-publicized and controversial Hollywood figure, the loving, patient, and understanding wife of Frank Adano.

Frances was laid to rest in the family vault at her aunt's house in Pasadena. I was there, and when I saw those bronze doors swing shut on the sepulcher I thought of that poor, unhappy woman and all the misery she'd caused in one lifetime. Afterward, Frank asked me to ride back in his car and I sat beside him amid the gray velvet upholstery, watching the freeway traffic hustle by on both sides. Most limousine drivers are such careful drivers, pokey, even, wouldn't speed if their lives depended on it. We crept and thought, and he swigged some from the flask he'd brought along. I'd brought a flask. He didn't talk, neither did I. But I thought we must be thinking the same thing: Frances was dead, Frank was free. But where was April? Fox-hunting in Virginia.

Back at the Bristol house, Frank invited me in and told the driver to wait. I followed him into the front hall, where he stood looking around into those rooms that were perfect marvels of beauty, utility, and convenience. The hand of Frances Deering Adano lay everywhere. Suddenly he turned to me with a fierce expression. "I'll sell it, you know," he muttered as we went on to the bar. He cursed and flung off his coat. "God, how I hate this place. It's like a Ross Hunter set." He raised his glass. "To the Short Happy Life of Frances Adano," he said in his low, dark voice. "*Pax vobiscum* and R.I.P." He lifted it again to the Alexander Brooks portrait of Frances above the mantel, then made a pistol of his thumb and finger and shot at it.

"Do you hate her?" I asked.

He looked out the window and gulped some of his Scotch, hiked his shoulders, then wearily let them fall. "No. It might be easier, but I can't. And at the last she was sorry. She really was. She'd come to dislike herself. But . . ." He ran his fingertip along one side of his mustache. "I knew what I was getting into, right from the start. I'm no rose, you know. She used me, I used her, that's how it was. She had the class, the money, she was upper-crust; I had the glamour, I was Hollywood. But oil and water, never the twain. Hell, looking back, I think I must have been out of my mind. I'd have been better off with Claire. Or—" He jammed his fists in his pocket. "What the hell," he said, "we all make our own beds, don't we?"

People who saw Bud and April together after they were married said they'd never seen two more contented people; they were a modern Adam and Eve, happily playing in their Eden, ignoring both apple and serpent. And their loyal fans admired Bud as the All-American Man, while loving April for being a survivor, for having weathered her tragedies and having found love at last.

In the spring of their second year of marriage, while they were still living in the East, basking in the success of *Red Coat Hunt*, they were invited to go on a promotional junket to Hawaii, Bud to be photographed by *Sports Illustrated* for a six-page color layout called "Sports Hawaii." They would be guests on the famous Parker Ranch on the Big Island. There, amid parties and publicity chores, April learned to eat Rocky Mountain oysters, knowing full well they were bull's balls; she went into the rain forest, rode a horse along the surf, and played water polo on horseback with the paniolos, the island equivalent of Texas cowboys. She even caught a marlin leaping in the blue waters off the roads.

Along on the junket were the magazine photographer, a studio-unit publicist, a wardrobe man, and a sports equipment specialist. Bud was a hotshot with bow and arrow, and the idea was to get him knocking down some of the wild boar that were to be found in the hillside bush. He'd already done one archery layout with bull's-eyes in the butts, but this was to be one of action, showing his skill with the ancient weapon.

They started just after early breakfast, fortified with coffee and oatmeal, thirteen people on the trail that wound itself upwards along the slopes of Mauna Kea. The accident happened on the last foray of the day, while the paniolos were readying the camp for the trek downhill again. Mickey, the sturdy Portuguese-Hawaiian whose task it was to look out for April at all times, had performed his assignment admirably, but just at that one moment he was occupied, digging a stone out of the hock of her horse. April was seated on a stump in the middle of the clearing when the dogs began a scuffle in the underbrush. Suddenly and with shocking speed, like some short-legged hairy hound of hell, an alarming shape came rushing out of the brake, head down, grunting, snorting, rushing forth into the waning light. Four ambitious hounds harried the boar, two on a side, leaping in to sink their jaws into the pig's tough hide, nimbly escaping those angry tusks as it continued its mad charge, heading straight for the figure on the stump. Bud saw it, shouted, April leaped up, jumped onto the stump, while the boar rushed toward her.

In a flash Bud had sent three feathered arrows into its back and neck, yet still it came on, screaming with pain and fury, the arrows sticking out like the *banderillas* from a bull's neck at a *corrida*. Bud ran headlong into the clearing like a matador into the arena, to do battle, waving his jacket to distract the boar's attention from April, shouting, until, just shy of the stump, the beast swerved, then pulled up short, uncertain, its wet nostrils quivering as it scented another prey. Then, backing one or two steps, making its ugly snuffling sounds, it leaped forward at Bud, and as they closed, with both hands Bud enclosed the snorting head with his jacket, then threw his weight on the boar's back and wrestled it to the ground.

Muffled in the coat of heavy corduroy, the boar pulled away, freed itself, then, as Bud rolled free in the opposite direction and struggled to his knees, it sprang at him, landing full-force on his back and bearing him to the ground, where with cries of fury it gored him with its tusks. In another second two shots rang out and the boar crumpled on top of Bud, where both lay still.

Mickey came running, he and April, and together they dragged the boar from Bud's back. He was alive, but he couldn't move. April cradled his bloodied head while Mickey ran for help. The sun was already going by the time they'd got a stretcher made up and were able to begin the difficult descent; it was full dark by the time they reached base camp.

The boar had done wicked damage before it died. Raking Bud's back with its tusks, it had torn the flesh and bone and severed important nerves, so that he had lost the use of his body from the waist down. Time would tell if the damage was reparable. In any case, it was already a tragedy. April stayed by Bud's side, refusing to leave him for an instant while the doctors worked over him, patching him up.

One of those soonest apprised of the accident was Frank, who flew out aboard Howard Hughes's Monitor Six, loaned for the occasion. And what were Frank's thoughts during that mournful flight across the Pacific? With the surprise marriage of April and Bud, he'd seen the end of his own dream of happiness; now there was an end to hers, too.

Being Frank, upon arriving he assumed full charge of the tragedy, as if it were his own. And in a way it was, Bud being almost like a son. Though the studio had sent out its own representatives, and though an invisible wall was set up so the media couldn't trample the story into the ground, the thing was headline news and had to be treated as such. Restrained bulletins were given out, but no photographers were permitted. The governor of the state, a friend of Frank's, himself stepped in when the press became antsy over the paucity of details, both threatening and cosseting them. All too soon the truth came out in big black headlines: Kit Carson would not walk again.

The success of the Hollywood star system is built mainly on publicity, but publicity of this sort is publicity nobody needs or wants. For four days the eyes and ears of the world were glued on the drama as it unfolded on the Big Island of Hawaii, which hadn't had so much attention since the volcano erupted. And since both participants in the drama were liked by both press and public, the matter was regarded as a double tragedy. So young to be so stricken; never to walk again, never to make another movie appearance.

I happened to be in Arizona at the time, with a unit filming outside Phoenix in the Superstition Mountains. I heard the news from the wardrobe man who handed me the afternoon edition of the *Arizona Republic*. I managed to track Frank down through Viola, and reached him by phone at the Mauna Kea Hotel. We talked for over half an hour, and next day, the local press having been alerted that I was on the horn to Hawaii, I was besieged by the media people. Soon our outdoor location was being overrun with reporters from as far away as Kansas City, until Jenny and I fled our hotel and took refuge in Scottsdale.

We'd flown back to Hollywood by the time Frank returned with Bud, and of course April. The plane set down on the private Santa Monica airstrip near Hughes Tool and Die, where reporters had been staking out the place for days. It was a mob scene that not even hardened veterans of such shoddy circuses were prepared for, and Howard himself showed his face in an effort to assist Frank. April's own exit from the plane was screened as much as possible, but so slowly executed that the wolf pack descended with slathering jaws. Worse came when Bud was brought off the plane on a stretcher. Though every precaution was taken—the reporters and photographers had been cleared from the tarmac by Hughes uniformed guards as well as Santa Monica police—the victim was pounced upon by two newsmen pretending to be security officers as he was being transferred into the waiting ambulance. That was when April started to scream. And then no sooner had the arriving party left the airport than the press began howling at the doors of the hospital, whose entrances were now shut to all visitors without special passes.

Nothing of what had happened was easy on Frank. He was enormously fond of Bud, and, unhappily, he was still wildly in love with Bud's wife. A man doesn't get over something like that just because the woman in question goes off with some other guy. Though Frank tried to hide it, you could see the suffering in his eyes. By then he'd sold the place that Frances had redecorated a total of four times, and was living at Regency House on Doheny Drive, and I saw him frequently. He'd aged, that was plain—the flop picture that bore his name as producer, the heavy toll that Frances's and his mother's deaths had taken, and now this, all had wreaked their havoc.

But it was lovely to see the way he behaved around April, the kindness and consideration he showed, helping her along every way he could, trying to cheer her up. We were all terrified of another breakdown, but she seemed to be making it through, mostly for Bud's sake. She even stood up to a press conference, explaining in detail how the accident had happened, giving another medical report on Bud's condition, and informing one and all that they'd decided to leave Hollywood, they'd go and live in Santa Fe; Virginia could only remind them of the past, and Bud liked the great open spaces. And it was in those great open spaces that Bud Ayres got lost, and with him, April, his wife.

The great trouper throughout all this had been Donna. I believe if

it hadn't been for her there was no chance that April would have ever go
through Bud's accident and the aftermath. Like Frank before him, Bud
sang Donna's praises to the sky, and he made sure she was a frequent
visitor to New Mexico, especially at holiday times, periods when April
was often victim to a lingering depression.

After a while you didn't hear so much about the couple who were
starting a new life at Santa Fe. From time to time there might be some
mention of them in *Time* or *Newsweek*, or there'd be a shot of them in
Life, Bud in the mechanical wheelchair to which his paralysis had
confined him, both of them looking cheerful and content. Occasionally a
report would make its way into the papers, there'd be a halfhearted
interview, but these somehow fell flat; there was only so much you could
say about them now, America's Sweethearts, who were living out their
life together according to some undisclosed plan. Happy? Sure, why not?
Snug as two bugs in a rug. People were really surprised at the nimble way
Bud got around on his wheels and the way April had shrugged off the
tragedy and was forging ahead.

When movie queens abdicate, they tend to lose that movie-queen
look, that patent Hollywood gloss that was so much a part of them up on
the screen; they revert to a more ordinary state—not an unnatural thing
since they are, after all, only mortals, they'd come from a common clay
to which they'd now elected to return. This is how it was with April; she
wasn't as strikingly beautiful, the glow that made her famous had been
dimmed; she was just one more inhabitant of the town. And that, she
always said, was fine with her; she had no desire to get in front of a camera
again. She was still pointed out—"There goes April Rains . . . you know"
—but she took it all in stride.

Her hair got darker, at least in photographs, and she was showing
definite signs of strain. Bud was drinking—heavily, Donna told me; he had
put on weight, there were spats, then quarrels. Then one day everything
ended when the gun he used for skeet-shooting went off accidentally and
killed him.

So this was the end he was fated for, his destiny—carelessness with
a loaded weapon. When Donna called me, I was more shocked by this
news than I had been by Bud's accident. Yet I could understand it, we
all could: one moment's negligence and it's all over. We said goodbye to
the great guy who had been Kit Carson, Frank's Kit Carson, who had
made his marks on the Hollywood track; Bud Ayres, Hollywood nice
guy, never to be forgotten, but what a way to go.

But not even such tragedies can hog the headlines forever, and—with
time—the media hustled other stories and little by little the names of April

Rains and Kit Carson slipped from view, and for a while April had at last achieved the privacy she had craved for so long. No one was interested, and that was fine with her, just fine.

But now, with Bud gone and Frances gone, the big question became, What would happen between her and Frank? Would there be wedding bells for the unhappy couple? There was little reason to think so. On the contrary, April appeared to be going out of her way to avoid Frank. Leaving Bud buried in Tesuque, she moved back to Los Angeles, where Frank tried every way he could think of to see her, to manage a word with her. But she cut herself off completely, refusing to speak to him and returning each of the letters he sent her. Pleas from Jenny and me proved futile; she listened, but was adamant. At Hartford she'd told me she wanted nothing more to do with him, and if I hadn't been able to believe her then, I had good reason to now. As far as April was concerned, Frank Adonis was a chapter in her life that was over and done with; she had performed surgery on herself, she was cut off from him forever.

When Bud died, movie offers had come flooding in from hotshot producers trying to cash in on all the publicity, but she had turned thumbs down to everything. No more movies for April Rains. She moved back to Hollywood—it was where she came from, after all—and found a small apartment in Georgian House, off Doheny, a mile and a half away from where Donna lived and not far from where Frank had been living since selling his house. She went on rebuffing any effort on his part to reach her, however, and though I saw her from time to time, she seemed to rate me as Frank's friend and as such to be shunned. I felt sorry for her, I thought she needed friends around her, but I could see she was determined to change things as much as possible, back to the simple life she'd planned before Frank Adonis had come along. She was back in school, working toward her M.A., and there were few discernible traces of April Rains about her, though I noted she hung on to the name, and I wondered why.

I felt sorriest for Frank. He was in a pretty bad way these days. Though business had improved, he was often moody, the victim of fits of black depression, so unlike the Frank we had known for so long. It was easy enough for some people to kiss him off, but I couldn't do that; I kept in close touch and stayed as near as he'd allow. Once he got me so angry I let go with both barrels; afterward he told me I was right and we shook, but it had driven a wedge between us that left a big crack, a crack I wasn't sure was ever going to get repaired.

Then one day—Bud had been dead for well over a year—he and April ran into each other. It was at the Beverly Hills post office—the old revolving-door bit, he was going in, she was coming out. Each stared in wordless surprise at confronting the other's face, the beloved's face.

It's not so surprising that the coals of love, however heavily banked, may again leap into sudden flame if they are given a breath or two, a touch of the bellows. The two of them stopped right there on the post-office steps like old friends; then they walked a bit, as far as the little park on the other side of Big Santa Monica, where the gardening force was changing the plantings in the city flower beds, putting down the canna lilies that always look so ratty a week later.

They sat on a bench and talked some more. He said his car was parked over in the municipal lot, would she go for a little ride, maybe out to the beach?—it was such a fine day. They drove out through the Wilshire Corridor to Santa Monica, then headed south down through all the little beach communities, Venice, El Segundo, Manhattan Beach, Hermosa and Redondo, and so on.

They continued on down to Palos Verdes, where they stopped for lunch. They looked in at Marineland and saw the whale and the talking porpoises. They saw the glass cathedral, which was closed, then drove some more, past Long Beach, Newport, San Juan Capistrano, as far as La Jolla, 120 miles from Los Angeles, where he tried to convince her to go with him over to the peninsula and take a room at the Del Coronado, but she wouldn't. He found her very changed, but there was enough of the old April there to break his heart with longing.

They turned around and headed back. At Torrey Pines they pulled onto the palisade and sat there in the car, talking while the sun went down. It was anguish of the worst kind. He had her, she was here now beside him, close, but he didn't really have her at all. There was no way he could reach her. His sense of the fitness of things told him not to try to make physical love to her—it wasn't the time and she wasn't responding in the old ways—and he kept his ardor under control. To a certain degree she frightened him—she seemed like a bird trapped in a cage, desperately beating its wings against the bars in a struggle to get out. Yet he thought that, having come across her in this unexpected way, he saw a chance and he would take it if he could. And so he poured out his heart to her, told her of his unhappiness, the loneliness he had felt for so long. It had never ended for him, would never end, not while he—and she—lived. He loved her, she had captured his soul, he existed for her alone, couldn't she— wouldn't she?

She was listening, he could tell, listening intently to every word. She wept and clutched his hand and her hot tears fell on his flesh. And she told him how she'd missed him and how glad she was he'd found her again. She'd been so unhappy. She wanted to be with him, she really did, no one could know how much, if only—

She couldn't explain, somehow couldn't get the words out. She was deeply troubled, he could see it, she was groping toward him for help. And he wanted more than anything in the world to help her, but he couldn't. It wrenched at them both, shook them. They clung together in desperation, like two people on a life raft, hoping for rescue but seeing none anywhere on the horizon. These were not two children in the throes of first love, they weren't Jimmy Dean and Natalie Wood struggling through the plot twists of *Rebel Without a Cause*. These were two mature adults who had loved each other deeply, who'd suffered much, endured much because of their love, two who had lost their spouses and were alone and who needed each other. Bad timing—it had all been bad timing.

They talked and talked until the sun became a giant red ball hanging over the distant horizon line. It pulsed and glowed, some sort of burning icon. Then it began to sink, and it seemed to them both an act of finality. Planet Earth was spinning somewhere in space and the sun was doing what it always does; this evening it was setting, tomorrow morning it would be rising again, but to them, alone in the car on the high headland, it was the last sunset, the last they would ever see together. Unless—unless he could do something to change her mind. This was the moment—now —soon—it must happen right away. If not, no hope—the end.

Wordlessly they sought their way back toward each other, and it was as if they were holding on for dear life, holding on to the globe itself, they mustn't fall off. Lower and lower sank the sun into the golden sea. Now only the top half of its red rim remained, a melon slice poised above the glittering plane of water; then in moments it, too, was gone, sunk behind the wavering horizon. And what had gone with it? With every breath he took something told him he was going to lose her again. So near and yet so far. Yet he couldn't let that happen, he must never lose her.

Purple turned to blue, to black, day was night. The day was all gone, that memorable day. They drove back in darkness but in hope—some kind of hope had entered their souls today. They didn't know what they could still mean to each other, not really, but they both knew in their hearts that they needed each other desperately and that if they were going to have anything further out of life, they must fight to stay together.

"No matter what," he told her, "I love you. I loved you from the first, I will never love anyone else. Remember how I love you, April. Don't let anybody make you think different. Will you promise me that?"

She promised him. It made them both feel better. She told him how sorry she'd been when Maxine died. "I know how much you loved her.

I wanted to write but I didn't know what to say—I sent you a card, though," she added, an afterthought.

He felt a ripple of warm surprise. He remembered it, of course he did, the card signed with those two words, "a friend"—the card he'd asked me to look at. It had been hers all the time.

When they got back to Beverly Hills, it was ten o'clock. He drove her to the lot where her car was parked. The lot was locked. She let him take her home.

"Wait," he said as she started to open the car door. "Don't go. Not just yet."

"I have to."

"Oh God—there's so much I want to tell you, the time went so fast —it seems as if we've barely been together an hour."

"It's late, I really have to go in. I have an early class in the morning."

He reached for her hand and held it. "April, tell me you love me. Say it, just once, can't you? Say it so I can hear it. Can't you, for me—just once?"

She began to tremble. "I—I'm not sure, everything's going around in my head right now. I need time to think."

He asked when he could see her again; she said she didn't know, she'd call. He extracted her promise to call him. He jumped out on his side, ran around to open her door. As she stepped out he pulled her into his arms and began kissing her. "April, April, I love you so much. Just to hold you, oh God, don't let me lose you again." He was kissing her and crushing her in his arms, under the cadmium-blue streetlight with cars passing by, and she began to struggle against him.

"Let me go—please let me go. Don't touch me—I don't want you to!"

"But—April—wait, if you love me—"

"I didn't say I loved you! I *can't* say it! Don't you understand—I can't. Bud's dead and I'm alive and—I just can't! Please! You mustn't try to see me anymore!"

She tore away and ran sobbing up the walk into the vestibule. He watched her use her key and go in. He wasn't depressed, he told himself, as he got back into his car; he understood. She'd get over it. He'd seen her, talked to her, spent hours with her, and things were bound to change; he felt sure of it. He'd won a great victory that day, he'd begun to come back to life again, and he vowed to himself that whatever else happened, one day they'd be married.

She didn't call him. He waited and waited, but she never called.

Jenny and I heard all about this from him one night when he came for dinner. He was paralyzed by the whole thing—afraid to take a step for fear of screwing it up.

I took it on myself to call her. We met for coffee, and she seemed glad to see me again and anxious to talk. But I saw right off what Frank had been talking about; it wasn't the old April, the golden girl we'd known. April had become some other month, August, September. I detected some hairline fissures in that armored exterior, stridencies where there had been only calm, a hidden urgency where there had been relaxed humor, a tighter grip on things, as if she feared something was slipping from her grasp, something—I wasn't sure what—she had planned on and needed, something human and cherished. Was it Frank? Her career? Her sanity? Life? I didn't know, couldn't tell, and we'd lost that fine vein of communication we'd enjoyed ever since Feldy's studio. We talked but didn't confide, didn't absorb. Our trains were running on different tracks.

Where before she simply *was*, now I got the feeling she was working at things, trying too hard. She laughed that pretty laugh, but in its sound there were traces of brittleness. She looked thinner, more angular, she'd lost that pleasing harmony of soft curves; she had cheekbones, the kind that looked great on Angie Brown, but somehow didn't suit April. She'd done something with her hair, too; I didn't like the change. And she'd widened her lipline, darkened her shade of lipstick. Cherry Wine was now Lilac Smoke (or something like that)—and since when mascara?

Donna Curry couldn't have picked a worse time to die, but she was gone, a terrible blow to April. This was six or eight months later, during a rainy February. The maid had come in as usual on a Monday morning and found Donna still in bed, but she wasn't to be awakened, ever. Her heart had simply stopped. Her death paralyzed April, playing havoc with her already disordered mind, and making her feel guiltier than ever. A week or so after the funeral, her telephone rang. When she picked up the receiver, the party hung up. Five minutes later there was a knock at the door. She put on a robe and went to answer.

"Who is it?"

"Please let me in."

"Frank—I can't. I'm just going to bed, it's late."

He pleaded through the door that he had to see her. Five minutes only, and he'd go. She undid the latch and let him in.

"Are you all right?" he asked. "I've been calling and calling but you're never home. I was worried."

No, she said, she was fine, just exhausted and not answering.

"I'm sorry about your mother. I know how you'll miss her."

"Like you miss Maxine. I expect it'll get easier."

They sat down and talked stumblingly of one or two things, nothing terribly important; then she pointedly smoothed the folds of her robe and retied the sash. "Frank, I'm really tired, so please would you just say what you have to say and . . . I'm sorry, but I don't feel terribly well."

"Yeah, I know it's late, but—look, do we have to keep going around and around like this? Can't we—couldn't we just sit down and talk it all out?"

"Yes, maybe, only not now. This is not the time."

"It's never the time. I'm going to New York at the end of the week, then to London, I won't be around for a while. If I could just go away knowing that—well, knowing that we're all right."

She gave him a blank look and dropped her gaze.

He got down on his knees and peered up into her face. "Oh, April, things don't have to be like this, you know. We don't have to go on suffering, both of us, if you'd only—"

"If I'd what?"

"Just let go a little."

"Are you trying to say you want me to go to bed with you?"

"I'm trying to say I want you to marry me! What the hell are we doing, anyway? All the wasted time, all the lousy things that happened —now's our chance. Finally. Don't you want it anymore?"

He leaned toward her, trying to look into her eyes. She had her hands over her face. Presently she took them away and straightened in her chair.

"Yes. Yes I do. Only—"

"No. No only's. All you have to do is say yes."

He gathered her into his arms and kissed her, running his hand down the fall of hair that lay against her cheek, smelling her sweetness, excited by her closeness. He took a deep breath, feeling that at last he'd reached her. "Say you will. Tell me you love me and say, 'I'll marry you, Frank.' Go on, say it. I'm not leaving here until you do."

He was holding her tightly with both hands. She kept her head down, as she bit her lip and thought. Then she looked up abruptly and her words surprised him.

"All right, Frank—I'll marry you."

"You will? You mean it? When? When can we be married?"

"Right away, if you want. You decide—but, please, let's not make it a big wedding."

"Fine by me." He buried his face in her hair. "Oh God, baby, you're making me the happiest guy in the world. Hey—wait right here, don't move—I'll be right back—"

He ran out the door and came back with a chilled bottle of Dom Pérignon. He uncorked it in the kitchen and came in carrying the bottle and two wine glasses. "Aren't you ever going to get proper champagne glasses?" he asked, setting them down on the coffee table, where some of her glass animals were grouped. "Maybe someone'll give us some for a wedding present."

She was looking at him steadily, as if appraising him. "You must have been awfully sure."

He looked at her quizzically, then at the bottle in his hand. Then he laughed. "I wasn't sure at all. But I was praying a lot." When he filled the glasses, he got up and turned the lights down. After lighting the candles on the shelf and turning over the stack of records on the turntable, he sat on the couch and held her close. It was the moment he'd dreamed of for so long. It was all coming true; this was the beginning, only the beginning. More than anything he wanted to take her into the bedroom and make love to her. How long was it since they'd lain naked in each other's arms? But soon they'd be making love all they wanted; tonight he wouldn't press his luck.

He leaned forward to pour them more champagne. As he sat back he dribbled a little on the table, and in trying to catch it he knocked over one of the glass figurines.

"Oh Jesus, I'm sorry."

It was the unicorn; he'd broken it. She sat with her hands in her lap.

" 'Blue roses,' " she murmured, picking up the pieces and putting them in a dish.

"Hm? Blue what?"

Not *blue roses—pleurosis*, she explained. Tennessee Williams, *Glass Menagerie*, Laura and the Gentleman Caller. She had a broken unicorn, too. April began to cry, softly, turning her head away so he couldn't see her tears.

"Gosh, honey, I really am sorry. I'll get you another, we'll find one, don't cry."

"It's—not the unicorn." She emptied the glass pieces into the wastebasket, then took up a brush and began brushing her hair. She yawned. "The champagne—making me sleepy," she said. "Now you've got me, won't you go so I can get some sleep? You need it, too, you look worse than I do."

He left. There were some kisses at the door; then she slipped out of his arms, opening the door so it swung between them. Going down the walk to his car, he had a weird sense that it had all been just a dream, one that wasn't going to come true.

He saw her only once more before he left for New York, and she

seemed perfectly fine to him, promised to pick him up at the airport when
he came back—he was to let her know when. She kissed him goodbye and
he left her, wondering what might happen now, fearful of something's
going wrong while he wasn't around to take care of her. He called her
frequently from New York and they talked, calmly, sensibly, lovingly.
He'd been to Cartier's for a ring. Bought her a new fur, some diamonds.
She was breathless with excitement; she couldn't wait for him to come
home again.

"Be there," he told her.

"Don't worry," she said. "I'm not going anywhere."

Her statement had the ring of truth all right, only it wasn't true. One
day our telephone rang and it was April. She asked if Jenny was home;
I said no, it was Jen's day at the Good Will Thrift Shop where she'd been
putting in some volunteer time—could I do anything? April said she
wanted a ride to the doctor. When I asked if her car needed looking after,
she said no, but she didn't like to drive these days. Too nervous, having
some vision trouble. I said I'd come over and take her.

The doctor's office was at the UCLA Medical Center, and we
drove over Malcolm Avenue to Wilshire and cut through the campus to
the hospital. I wasn't particularly aware of anything's being wrong, but
suddenly, with no warning, April let out a shriek, and though we were
doing thirty she flung open the door and leapt out of the moving car. I
shouted, then swerved, barely missing the car in front as I tried to see
behind me. I pulled over and jumped out. April lay sprawled in the
street. A bus was bearing down on her, there was a screech of rubber,
the driver leaned hard on his horn, and I saw a figure dart from the curb
to drag her from the bus's path. I ran up and took her from the man.
"What are you doing?" I demanded, furious. "Don't you know you
could have been killed?"

I set her on her feet and she stared blankly at me. She didn't remember any of it, didn't even know who I was. Then, after I'd taken my eyes
from her for only a moment to retrieve her bag and its strewn contents,
I couldn't find her. Some bystanders pointed her out, dashing pellmell
across the campus lawn. Following a hunch, I got back in the car and
drove around trying to find the doctor's office. When I explained to the
nurse what had happened and who I was, she slipped inside, then returned
with the doctor, who brought me into his office and talked to me. April
was in another room, being sedated. She'd arrived in a hysterical state (this
wasn't news), but apparently uninjured. For a shrink the guy was pretty
open and aboveboard, none of the typical "I can't discuss the case" crap.
He queried me as to my relationship with April, and after I'd gone into

some detail, he left me alone for a moment when a nurse beckoned him away.

I noticed the manila file on his desk and read April's name upside down. I slid the folder toward me and began glancing through the pages of transcription. I hadn't got very far before another nurse came in and archly confiscated the file. But I'd seen enough to realize that April's illness was more serious than I'd suspected.

That evening she was transferred to the Medical Center, where she was kept under observation. I was permitted to visit and saw a gratifying daily response to treatment. I tracked Frank down and he flew home immediately. Rather than turn her over to another team of doctors, he suggested she be sent back to the Hartford Retreat and be put in the care of her former doctors there. He insisted on taking her himself and seeing her installed, and he stayed as long as he could. I know that before he left, the head psychiatrist confided to him that the prognosis wasn't good and told him not to hold any great hopes for a cure. As for thinking of marriage, that was really out of the question now. The next time I saw Frank, after he'd returned to Los Angeles, he looked like a ghost, and I asked myself when it was going to stop. When?

Then, to everybody's surprise and relief, she began getting well. The doctors declared themselves pleased with her new approach to reality, and they recommended her return to a normal kind of existence. Again Frank flew direct to Hartford to bring her back. Few knew she was coming, few cared. This wasn't the old days when she could hardly go anywhere without a dozen or more *paparazzi* on her trail. Now she was a has-been, which was how she wanted it. I went to meet the plane at LAX, and as I caught my first glimpse of Frank and April disembarking, I had the feeling that everything was going to be okay now. Since she no longer had a place to stay (her apartment had been emptied, her things were in storage), she went to a bungalow at the Beverly Hills Hotel, using the side entrance and keeping out of sight. The first thing she wanted was to visit Donna's grave, where she placed flowers; then she wanted to go to the County Museum to see the current exhibition of Rembrandts. She wore dark shades and a scarf; not a soul recognized her, or if they did they left her alone.

Frank persuaded her to leave the hotel and come stay with him at the beach. At first she didn't want to; then she gave in. She would be entering Frances's house again, and it was going to be *Rebecca*-time, yet she did it anyway. For his sake.

They seemed now to have come full circle, for they had come back to Malibu, the place where it all seemed to have begun. Here they resumed their life together, the life of man and wife, for though they were not yet made one in the eyes of church or state, they were one in love and purpose, and as happy as they could be. She was well again, they both lived in that belief, and with her well they could afford to plan, to look forward to the day, not so far off, when they would really be married.

He didn't want to push her. Didn't want to corner her or make her feel trapped, by him or by their circumstances. What had been had been, the bad things were all in the past now, they must look forward to the happiness that had been waiting for them. They believed it. I did, too.

And yet . . . and yet. Something wasn't quite right, I could tell. And it wasn't just the vestiges of her illness, either. She appeared perfectly well, at least to my untrained eye. She *seemed* well, put it that way. And Frank stated that she was. But mental illness is a tricky business.

I took care not to intrude on them, but they seemed eager for my company, so I'd drive out at least once a week, sometimes more. It was then—sitting outdoors in sweaters, for it was in the winter and though there weren't any storms it was chill and gray, "unicorn" weather, as April called it—it was then that she told me about the Aiken poem, and about the time she'd come to this same house with Frank and had lost her virginity. Not "lost" but voluntarily surrendered.

Frank was nervous about leaving her alone in the house, but he was buried in business deals at that point and had to be at the office every day. Sometimes I'd take my work along and spend the day with her; she'd make lunch, we'd talk, go for walks, but it was strange—the more time I spent with her, the more I realized just how much she'd changed. Subtle changes, admittedly, sometimes you couldn't put your finger on them, but changes nonetheless. Small wonder, I told myself, after what she'd been through; but now where was she heading?

They were to be married in the spring, in April, which coincidentally was her birth month, too. She was making bridal plans, picking out a dress and so on. They would be married right there in the beach house, with just a few friends present; then they were going to honeymoon in Italy. They wanted to go back to Capri, where they'd been so happy, and see Civitavecchia again. Dodi Ingrisi had died several years back, but friends had bought the villa and would make it available to the bridal couple for two weeks in June.

On a Friday, Jenny and I drove out to Malibu for the weekend—mainly at April's insistence. Frank, too, seemed happy to see us, though I thought we'd end up as fifth wheels. Things went pleasantly enough.

We got there an hour or so before sunset; Jenny and I threw on our sweatsuits and joined Frank and April for a run on the beach. When April lagged, Jenny hung back with her, while Frank and I huffed and puffed until we were winded. We returned to our blankets, where we sat wrapped in them, our bare toes dug into the damp cool sand, to watch the sunset. The sun was going down behind a silvery veil of cold mist. The light died slowly at first, then more and more quickly.

"Say, what was that poem, anyway?" Frank asked suddenly, speaking to April. "The one about the white unicorns, the guy with the sore back?"

She laughed, and Jen squeezed my hand: that was good. April remembered the Aiken, those romantic lines from the Evening Song of "Senlin."

> *"The stars hang over a sea like polished glass . . .*
> *And solemnly one by one in the darkness there*
> *Neighing far off on the haunted air*
> *White unicorns come gravely down to the water. . . ."*

April recited the lines in a hushed tone, as though afraid to put her voice to them. But they resonated in the quiet air, and though I was warm in my blanket I felt a chill. "The haunted air," that was it. Was that what Frank was asking? I didn't know. The lines floated away with the spindrift. I had never read the poem, but Frank had told me about that time —right over there on Seal Rocks—and I wondered if he was reliving it, the night they first made love.

Glancing at them side by side, I could see their two profiles in silhouette; they looked like bedouins in their blanket, she tanned but without makeup, he with his five o'clock beard that made him look so swarthy. He had her hand resting on his knee, and he kept touching it with his lips as if it were his most treasured and precious possession. He told me afterward that he was trying to believe his good fortune, that she was well again and they'd soon be married.

Jenny had a call to make, so, leaving the others, we went on inside. While she telephoned her sister I made a fire, then went outside to bring some things in from the deck. I could see the dark huddled shape Frank and April made, sitting where we'd left them, eerily frozen in that same spot as they stared out to sea. Together, finally, and I breathed my own calm contentment at the sight.

It was full dark before they came in, still blanket-covered, teeth chattering as they hopped around in front of the fire. As she passed me, April paused to give me a quick kiss on the cheek. "That's for being you," she said. I glanced over at Frank, still at the fire, watching with an intent expression, his dark eyes flashing in the firelight.

"Ain't she somethin'?" he muttered when she'd gone upstairs. He came toward me with his buccaneer's grin. "She's fine, Chazz," he said in a low voice, "she really is."

"And you? You fine, too?" I asked.

"Believe it, kiddo. I'm right as Rains."

I winced at the pun, he put up his dukes, then gave me two playful jabs, one on each cheek.

"I'm hitting the showers," he said, and disappeared upstairs two at a time.

By seven dinner was on; the girls made the salad and coffee, Frank let me cook the steaks; he was on the phone now. He came in with a joke about Sam Ueberroth, whose house was a stone's throw up the beach. "Sam wants us to come down after dinner," he said.

"I'm not budging," April said. I thought, Good god, don't tell me Sam's still chasing after all these years? Jen must have read my thought; she smiled at me and Frank caught it. His look was noncommittal. We dined right there around the fire, off pewter plates, with a deep-red burgundy that had plenty of tang and matched itself well to the rare beef. Frank and April sat as close as possible. It crossed my mind that Frank hadn't enjoyed himself like this for many moons. He kept cracking the latest office jokes and telling how Sam had made a fool of himself at the last Producers' Guild meeting, when he got up to make a speech and couldn't remember his words. Vi had to lean over and prompt him. I decided Frank looked younger, healthier, and more relaxed than I'd seen him in a long time, and I told myself this was the big turnaround, from here on in everything would be fine.

As things turned out later, Frank was thinking the same himself. The fact that we were all together again, a reliving of the Summer of the Purple Grape, that we were laughing and having fun, seemed to put things in their proper perspective. They even talked us into being in the bridal party, I best man, Jenny matron of honor.

During coffee he brought out a small box, the kind jewelry comes in; she opened it to find inside a pin in the shape of a unicorn, encrusted with diamonds, the horn a shaft of platinum.

"*That's* why you wanted to hear the poem," Jenny said. "It's a set-up."

Jenny and I carried out the dishes and cleaned up the kitchen, taking lots of time; then by prearranged agreement we came in yawning and saying it was time for bed. "Wait a minute," Frank said, grabbing the last bottle of wine, "we want to drink a toast, April and I." He filled glasses and Jen asked whom we were toasting.

"You, woman," Frank said. "And Chazz here. We want you to know how grateful we are, April and I, that while all the rats were deserting the ship, you stuck by us. We haven't forgotten it, and we won't. Just promise us you'll let us go on sharing our happiness with you."

I never heard anything so touching, especially from Frank, who wasn't the kind to vent his sentiments. But he was Italian, and he felt things, and Jen and I were both flattered to have him express them in this manner.

Before going to sleep, we lay under the down comforter, talking about that touching moment, how well they both looked and how happy, and how swell it was that things were finally coming together.

Meanwhile, downstairs, Frank and April lay stretched out in front of the embering fire, also talking. He couldn't believe that his prayers finally were being answered; he wished Maxine were there to see it.

"Don't say that," April said, laying her fingers across his lips. "We mustn't wish for too much. Let's just be happy with what we've got."

He put his nose in her hair, the way he always loved doing, and held her closer. They talked about their coming trip to Italy, waxing nostalgic about places they'd been, things they'd seen and done. It was good to laugh again, freely and without constraint, and not have to glance nervously back over their shoulders to see what monsters were traveling in their footsteps. He kissed her over and over, while she whispered love words in his ear. They laughed about the time the flokati rug caught fire and the fire department came and embarrassed them, here in this same room. What a long time ago that was. They even spoke of Frances and felt sorry for her. It was a luxury they could afford, now that she was gone.

The sound of the waves lulled them, the clattering rocks under the foundation; they didn't want to make physical love, they were just happy being together like this, in the place that had meant so much to them. Feeling as he did, with the euphoria that comes from knowing that the heart's desire has at last been won, he began talking about how he was going to find the perfect role for her, that he was going to see her make her comeback in a really big way, that if he could work things right she'd end up with an Oscar. She grew alarmed at his words, saying she didn't want an Oscar, didn't want to act again. He should have read the signs, but he was too happy, too far out on a pink cloud; all he could think of was making her happy and putting her back on top. Those were the terms he was used to thinking in; he wanted to see his filly back at the gate, wanted her to run the race and win it; he forgot that the filly was gate-shy and never wanted to run again. She wanted to be put out to pasture, not to stand in front of an audience hoping to be liked.

What happened next might have happened anyway, in some other time; the fact was, it happened that night, and, regrettably, it was Frank's fault. We heard the door slam, heard Frank's call after her; then the door opened and he ran out. We sat up, frozen with alarm, straining to hear something. Jenny shoved me out of bed and urged me to go see. I hiked on my pants, and sweatshirt and crept down the stairs. The wind was rushing through the open door, which swung on its hinges without banging. I ran out onto the deck and looked. I could make out the small figure of Frank way up the beach, but he was alone. I thought, If he goes that way, I'll go the other.

I walked north to the far end of the Colony, but there wasn't a sign of her. The houses were mostly dark; a dog barked at me and followed me a ways, then disappeared.

I was out of the house for an hour, and when I came back Frank was having coffee with Jenny, so worried he could hardly talk. I had never seen him so upset; he simply came undone at the seams. Wouldn't call the police, didn't want her name in the papers again; she'd come home, we'd just wait it out. He blamed himself, over and over; he smote his brow for a fool. Why hadn't he seen what he was doing? What could possibly have come from his foolish desire to see her a star, Oscar in her hand? What had possessed him to even bring up such a thing when he knew how much she'd hated it all?

He went out and paced the deck, then went up on the highway and stood under the streetlight, as if she might take it into her head to reappear. We knew different, Jenny and I. Frank was wasting his time; she wasn't coming home. And she never did, not to that house. She was picked up next day loitering at the magazine stand of a local supermarket. She'd been reading movie magazines for hours; the cashier got suspicious. But he had no idea who she was, just another cheapskate smudging the pages.

The Malibu cops were good guys, they knew Frank; he came and got her, drove her back to town. That evening she was back at UCLA Medical Center, and no one the wiser that she'd had another breakdown. She stayed there for maybe two months; then Frank had her transferred to a private sanitarium in Woodland Hills.

No sooner did he have her settled in than he had to leave town; he came to me, asking if Jenny and I would keep tabs. Alas, our marriage was really on the fritz, and I said I didn't think Jenny would be around much, but that I'd stay close. And I did. I went nearly every weekend to have the midday meal with April, bring her the latest magazines, keep her company. She wasn't in good shape, but nothing like she became later. I tried to establish a bridge to the doctor, and he came to trust me, as I did him. He was an April fan from way back and he was worried about her, more than he let on.

Frank kept in touch by phone; I gave my weekly reports and tried to buoy him with any good news I could drum up. When he came back he drove out to Woodland Hills directly from the airport and spent the weekend assessing for himself exactly how things were. I already knew what he was busy finding out: things weren't good. He'd been shocked to see how she looked—she'd really let herself go, her body was badly run down, her appetite bad. When he left she handed him a small parcel, asking him not to open it until he was home. He didn't wait, but opened it in the car; it held the diamond unicorn pin he'd given her that night at Malibu. The brief note the package contained asked him not to come anymore; it was too painful and his visits left her distressed.

So there it was: she wasn't going to marry him; worse, she held no hope now for the future. He wrote her a letter, saying he understood, and releasing her from any previous understanding they'd had. He loved her and would be there for her any time she needed him. But the awful truth was, she didn't need him anymore. What she needed was her sanity, and if she stood any chance of getting that back she couldn't go on seeing him.

It was a brutal blow for Frank, and he really took it on the chin. In the passing months I saw a lot of him, because I too was nursing wounds of my own. One night we had dinner, he and I, and in a booth at Frascatti's I saw him weep for a second time. He'd lost Maxine, now he'd lost April; there wasn't much else to lose, except his own life, and that, too, waited around the corner.

As a result of Bud's manager's crooked shenanigans, the till was all but bare, and Frank was picking up the tabs. He'd previously arranged to pay for April's upkeep at Woodland, relying on monies left him by Frances, but the family had successfully contested the will, leaving him in somewhat straitened circumstances. April stayed on at Woodland for nearly two years, with horrendous expenses that drained Frank's pocketbook, and then, after he was killed and her own money ran out, she made the trip to Libertad, taking the road to Simi Valley, the long road that led to nowhere. And I began my pilgrimages, the Sunday and holiday trips that have gone on for so many years. Read it and weep, as I do.

What with one thing and another, my life changed drastically in the next year and a half. Somewhere along the line I'd begun writing, and I'd started in on a small book. I felt the work suited me and I kept a typewriter in my trailer and worked during set-ups and at nights. Jenny was in Kenya, doing a safari picture, and we were pretty well out of touch. When the book was nearing publication, I found myself spending more and more time in New York, where I'd begun it all so many years before, and enjoying it. I had an apartment with a colossal view, and so sure was I that I'd be sticking to Manhattan that I had boxes of expensive stationery engraved with my new address. No sooner was I at home than who should appear on my doorstep but Jenny; we kissed and made up, swore we'd never part. She went out and bought me a purebred German shepherd we called Bones; I remember we used to walk him a lot and meet all kinds of friends along Central Park West. Jenny started to get itchy; she stayed only a month, we waltzed all around town, East Side, West Side; then she asked me to come back to Los Angeles.

By now I was hard at work on my second book and didn't want to be uprooted. The fact that I was having an unlooked-for success in my new career wasn't necessarily helping our home life. I'd fly to the Coast for a fortnight, sometimes just the weekend, but it wasn't working. We crabbed and bickered and were both exhausted from the energy spent in futile argument. I was also fed up with Los Angeles and wanted to make a clean break, so I went back to my apartment in New York, to work cheek-by-jowl with my editor. Absence failing to make our hearts grow fonder, when I returned to Los Angeles the next time, it wasn't to our Sunset Plaza Drive house but to a solitary room at the Villa Lorraine on the Strip.

Not too long after that, I made yet another quite astonishing move when, thanks to Frank, I found myself living in the hallowed precincts of Sunnyside, the Crispin Antrim showplace, where my landlady was none other than Maude Antrim herself. Stranger things have probably happened in my life, though I can't think of them right now. And it was there at Sunnyside that I got to observe firsthand the last days of Frank Adonis.

With Frank's death had gone all that remained of the old April, the girl you see up there on the screen or on the *Late Show*. Upon hearing the news that he'd been shot, she became uncontrollable and had to be placed under restraint.

Though we'd tried, there was no way to keep it from her—headlines were plastered everywhere, you couldn't turn on the TV without catching a late bulletin, and no one in Hollywood talked about anything else.

His death was big news, and naturally April was getting raked over the coals right along with him, and with Belinda, even with Maude; with just about any woman who'd ever had anything to do with him. Notoriety had dogged him all his life and he went out in the most scandalous manner possible. When the police photographs taken at the murder scene began circulating, one of the supermarket gossip-sheets published a spurious "Life of Frank Adonis," featuring a strip gallery of all his "ladies": Babe Austrian, Belinda Carroll, Angelina Brown, Norma Shearer, Hedy Lamarr, Claire Regrett, Frances; and of course April.

Frank's funeral had some distant echoes of the Valentino spectacle, including an emotional female—in this case, Claire Regrett—dramatically throwing herself on the flower-laden bier, sobbing and collapsing so she had to be carried from the place, the kind of hysterical display so dear to the tabloids. April, of course, wasn't there, but she heard about it anyway. And it didn't help—though by then nothing could have.

It was a perfectly natural thing that Frank should have had quantities of mourners, being loved and admired as he was. I doubt, however, that he'd have appreciated the vulgar circus the whole thing became. It really did look like a gangster's funeral, with tons of flowers, the bier covered in a blanket of roses from you-know-who, and in attendance seemingly every Italian in every black suit in the City of the Angels. It even rained, and the black silk umbrellas all came out on cue; you could have walked on them for a tenth of a mile, umbrella to umbrella. But I was touched to catch among the mourners a face I recognized; it was the gateman from MGM, holding his hat over his heart and crossing himself as he knelt by the casket. But, Jesus, the crowds of people, their emotions all geared up —it was like a bad movie. Myself, I was disgusted by the whole thing and couldn't wait to get away, thinking how Frank would have been disgusted as well.

And California dreamin' is becomin' a reality. . . .

Right now I'm in the same chair as before and my friend Anna Thorwald is dozing in that decrepit hammock that's ready to fall apart. She's listed fourth among the ten longest-staying residents at Libertad, brick and bars and hospital green out here, off the Ventura Freeway on Route 101. Happy Dell Acres, as I call it. Thirteen years, seven months, and twenty-three days on the funny farm. And bunny shows at Easter. I don't know, maybe it beats paying taxes.

Anyway, we're still here under the pepper tree, Anna and I. The small red berries litter the hardpacked dirt where no grass grows, as if the earth had been sown with salt. I know Anna sleeps badly at night, and a sleepless night in this place I wouldn't wish on my worst enemy. God help the ones who can't sleep. You try whiling away the wee small hours unable to snap on the *Late, Late Show* any time you like, lying among the other looneytunes and staring into the darkness, the darkness you live in and breathe in but can't sleep in, the clockless creeping dark that is a world unto itself for the nonsleeper.

She's sleeping now, though. Her face is turned aside, one arm thrown across it as if to hide her identity. How vulnerable she looks, how poorly armored for this life. It was her own idea to revert to her former name: Anna Thorwald of Tennessee Avenue in Westwood. I live in hope and at the same time I despair. The odds are so lousy. She is truly alone, there's no one. Me? I don't matter; she doesn't identify me with any of the events I've just narrated. It's true, sometimes she really believes she's Frank's wife, that they got married, even that there were children. As we know, there might have been one at least, if the cards had been stacked differently. But most of her dreams are wrapped up in a single soiled doll, Clarabelle. That's an end for you, a forty-three-year-old woman with a doll. I can see the way she holds it, lightly, even maternally, as though not to injure it. Baby—the one she had with Frank. Her Gift.

God, how I always liked her. What a great girl, what a really wonderful person. The kind of girl you'd like to have for your sweetheart or you'd want your boy to marry, the famous girl-next-door they used to talk so much about. Her laugh; of course, it's not the same anymore, but I remember the way it used to sound when we were all in Italy those many years ago. I look at her now and think, Where did she go? What happened? Why is she this person now, not the other one, so changed that even I sometimes have trouble recognizing her? People change, sure, we pass them on the street and may not recognize them for a second or two, but finally we do. But not April. I defy her neighbors on Tennessee to say, Oh sure, I know her still. Maude Antrim's close to ninety, but she hasn't changed, she's still Maude, only older. She's *there.* Not April, April flew the coop. That face, that glow, gone. All gone.

I catch Nurse Popey tiptoeing across the lawn. Coming close, she asks *sotto voce* if I wouldn't like to slip along before "Anna" wakes up. No, I say, she might be upset if I didn't say goodbye. I wait. The patient stirs, awakes, tries to sit up, not an easy maneuver in that hammock. I help her out and to the other chair, into which she sinks gratefully. "How are you feeling?" I ask. She nods agreeably, as if she didn't want me worrying about her. She certainly is game. Again I'm wondering what Frank would say if he were alive and here. How would he handle it all? I look her over for signs. Are her cheeks a little less pasty? Have they a hint of color? Does she seem the least bit more relaxed?

She throws one hand out with an alarming abruptness that makes me shy, as if I thought she meant me harm. No harm, though; she merely lays her hand on mine and pats it gently. For the first time she calls me by my name. She's recognized me.

"Charlie?"

"Yes?" My heart skips a beat; I'm "Charlie" again.

"How are *you?* Are you okay?"

"Yes, sure, fine, really fine," I hastily assure her. You may not think so, but I'm telling you this is a major breakthrough, her calling me by my name.

Hints of satisfaction, traces of a smile. "I'm glad, really glad. Frank always worried about you, you know. He always wanted to be sure everything was all right for you. He was always so proud of you."

Frank was quite a guy, I counter, leading the talk away from myself.

"Oh *yes,* he *was,*" she says with conviction. "Misunderstood. He was completely misunderstood by so many people. All the things he used to do for people. He kept them secret. I'll never forget him."

"Good girl. You loved him a lot, didn't you?"

"Yes. Yes. Yes, I really did love him. What a . . . pity . . . pity . . ." She trails off, shaking her head as though to clear it. "Strange. I guess that's how things work out sometimes, isn't it? Some things just aren't meant to be. *That* wasn't meant to be. You know? It just never could work. I kept hoping—we *both* kept hoping—but . . . I kept telling my mother he was the best thing for me. She wouldn't ever believe it. You wouldn't believe how she wouldn't believe it. The way she looked at it, he was the villain in the melodrama. You know?"

I nod. "The guy with the long twisted mustaches? 'Pay the rent!' 'I can't pay the rent!' '*I'll* pay the rent!' "

She blinks. "Who'll pay the rent?" she asks, suddenly confused.

I say I supposed that would probably be the hero: "Bud."

I say the name on purpose, to see her reaction. The doctors always tell me to get her to talk about it. I'm taking advantage of this lucid moment that could turn off at any given time. "You remember Bud," I prompted.

Oh yes, she replies blithely, she remembers Bud all right. Her husband. The guy she married.

"He loved you, too," I suggest.

"Oh yes," she agrees, he did indeed. "What a nice boy," she says with

the same conviction. "Really nice. I used to call him 'True Blue Bud.'
Why do parents call their boys 'Bud' anyway? I guess it's sort of like
'Junior,' huh?"

Now a very strange phenomenon starts to occur, and I'm made aware
that she has come to a sudden grasp of matters. For the first time in years
I feel there may yet be some hope, that even at this late date the damage
could be repaired, that she could be made well, that I could even get her
out of here. I feel now that's she's actually human and real, a living person,
not some android out of a sci-fi movie, a pod-person or a zombie. God help
us all, I pray silently, and silently urge her on.

She recalls with some accuracy how she'd come into Feldy's studio
that rainy night when Bud was sitting on the corner of the makeshift stage
he'd built at the workshop, how he'd taken her coat and made coffee and
the way they'd talked. He'd made her feel at home right away.

"He was so good-looking, wasn't he?" April said. "What a guy. A
girl'd be lucky to get a fella like that, I thought. I wondered what he'd
be like, making love with him." I marvel at her words. Candid confessions
such as this are not often to be heard from her lips. I wish I was a doctor
so I could interpret them, but I'm not, so I bumble along as best I can.

"What *was* he like?" I ask boldly.

"Oh . . ." She's a bit taken aback, shy even; but that's to be expected:
my dumb question. "He was giving. Very giving. He always wanted it
to be good for me. But I don't know, maybe I'm not any judge of that."

"Why not?" She doesn't answer. "Why not, Anna?" I persist.

She looks up quickly. "What?"

"Anna? Isn't that your name—Anna?"

She laughs out loud, splaying her fingers at her chest. "Oh. Yes, I
suppose it is, isn't it? I've got so used to 'April,' though, these past years."
She thinks, presses fingers to her lips, glances sidewise at me. "Pretty
name, April."

"I think so. How'd you get it?"

She comes right out with it. "Frank gave it to me."

"When?"

"Oh gosh—back there somewhere."

"April? What year are we in?"

"What *year?*"

"Yes, what year is it?"

"Why, it's . . . nineteen . . . nineteen . . . hm. Oh gosh—fifty-
something?"

"Fifty what?"

"Oh darn, I just don't know, Charlie, I'm sorry. . . ." She drawls the words in mock despair. Then her face shows impatience and frustration. "Let me think a sec," she mutters, making fists on her knees. She thinks hard, muttering and pushing at the tips of her fingers as though ticking off the years. "I was born in nineteen thirty-nine."

"That's right, you were," I encourage. This is really good, I'm feeling excited, it's creeping up my back. "Nineteen thirty-nine. So what year is this, then?"

She gazes at me with a pleading expression, as if to say "Please, Charlie, make it be nineteen sixty again." I quickly consider. If I tell the truth, she may be so shocked she'll vanish again and I won't be able to reach her. Her being this way is so good, so wonderful—reaching her again, seeing April, not the dead doughfaced Anna. I want to hold on, clutch her, keep her here. It's as if she'd lived for a long time in a dark cave and suddenly she appears at the cave opening, standing out in the light again, blonde and beautiful. April in tennis shorts and sunstreaked hair.

"Look," I say, "I want to see you get well, we all do. The doctors and nurses, Mrs. Kraft, everyone wants to see you get well. Try, April, *try*, won't you, for Frank's sake? Think, honey, if Frank was around he wouldn't want to see you in here, in this place."

"I know. Don't you think I know that? But where would I go, anyway? If I *were* well again, where would I *go*? Who would help me then?"

God, help me, I pray, please help me to say the right things. Don't let me botch it up, don't let me send her back into the cave. Suddenly I, too, am swept up by the release of emotion; I want so desperately to keep that glimmering light from going out again and leaving her in the dark.

I talk encouragingly—about the beach, since I know how much she loves it. "I've got a place out at Venice now, you'd like it. You could come there and stay."

"Oh, I love Venice," she says. "I was only there once. For a weekend, actually." I realize she means the other Venice, in Italy, not the beach, but anything's better than her silence. Keep her talking about Venice, about Capri. She remembers all right—about the *paparazzi*, the baying hounds —but she's not fearful. She handles the memory. Bud—Frank—Frank— Bud . . .

"The only two men I ever made love with, you know," she says.

No, I didn't know, but I'm not surprised. It's the kind of girl she was. She never slept around, everyone knew that.

"You loved them both."

"Yes. I did. No, I didn't, either. Frank, I loved Frank, that's all. I married Kit but it wasn't the same. You can understand, can't you? *Can't you, Chazz?*" She grips my hand so hard it hurts. I wince but hang on.

"Yes, sure I understand. I think I do. Only, April—why not—why don't you try to explain it to me so I'm sure I have it all right? I know you and Frank couldn't get together while he was still married to Frances, but—well, Frances died, didn't she? And Frank was free to marry again. Everyone thought you would."

"I guess everyone did."

"Why didn't you marry him, then?"

"Too late. It was too late then."

"Why? *Why* too late?"

I was having trouble getting through to her; at every word I was afraid she'd slip away and get lost again.

"Why?" she wondered along with me. "I was afraid. By then they'd just about hammered me flat. The publicity, the notoriety, being chased after all the time, all those reporters, cameras . . . I didn't want to be a part of it anymore. Always hiding, ducking in and out of places, wearing dark glasses, as if dark glasses could protect you. Like Jackie Onassis—anything to shut them out. But all dark glasses do is keep the sun out; they don't keep out the world. *Nothing* keeps out the world. And, Charlie—people are so cruel, you know? Maybe not cruel exactly, but they want what they want when they want it. They don't like being told no or 'get away.'"

"They want their pound of flesh."

"Yes, that's it, flesh, they want the flesh. 'In Person.' 'For One Week Only.' But not just that. They want your mind, too. They want—inside. They really want to get inside your head."

I see her watching me, earnestly, anxiously, with such appeal in her eyes. What she has paid, I think; the awful price. And for what? A stardom she never wanted, bestowed by Frank, who thought he saw a good bet and bet heavily—and lost.

I find myself thinking of that tootsie Peg Entwhistle and her leap off the Hollywood sign—smack into the cactus patch. April's had been a far more spectacular leap; she was a regular Flying Wallenda, and without the net. She'll stand as a prime example of what can happen to one more pretty girl who gets stung by the cinema asp, who lets herself be persuaded along the paths of filmdom.

Your name in lights is a pretty rare sight, all those light bulbs flashing on and off, blink—April—blink—Rains—blink blink blink, they lay down a red carpet from the curb to the lobby, people scream and claw and shove autograph books in your face or even matchbooks, napkins, you proffer your signature—one more among thousands—the newsreel and

TV cameras whirr, "Look this way, April," "Hey April, how's your sex life?," and the studio bosses give you the fisheye, wondering exactly how much you're worth on the hoof, the movie hoof, the butchers weighing out their pounds of flesh, checking to see how long before the tits and ass fall, checking your grosses. It's all built on grosses, of course, grosses are the bottom line. "We love ya, April," but there's that taint, like fish gone bad. It doesn't take so long to do a nosedive; no matter how far or long the fall, the end's the same: splat. Some people would be better off with a frontal lobotomy than a movie contract.

"Frankie—?" she says.

"*Charlie*, honey, I'm Charlie, remember?"

"Oh." She makes a charming grimace. More and more I see the April of old, the sweet April I used to know. But there was something I wanted to get back to. "April, honey, when you married Bud—"

"Yes? What? That's all right, go on, ask it." Bravely. She isn't afraid to face things. All the shock treatments in the world couldn't bring this moment about.

"You turned Frank down and married Bud instead. But you say you didn't love him—Bud, I mean. I'm having trouble with that."

"Oh, Bud was sweet, he really was. But I couldn't love him. I loved Frank, you see. Only Bud—he was—determined. You know? You might not realize, I don't think many people did, but when Bud really set his mind to something, a Sherman tank couldn't stop him—he just couldn't be deflected. And . . . well . . . he decided he wanted me and he made up his mind he was going to get me. He just kept on and on, it's all he ever talked about. 'Marry me marry me marry me.' And of course I wasn't the kind of girl who—who'd live with him, without the ring and license, I mean. And there was the baby, too. Frank's baby—poor thing—God, I loved that baby so, that dear little thing, eleven days it lived. Frank Junior. I just—oh, I don't know!"

She was growing highly emotional; the tears welled, she choked up, and her hands started to tremble. That baby was almost twenty years ago, and it was painful to see how much it still meant to her, how deep the cut went. Indeed, time does not heal all wounds. I gripped her hands between mine and squeezed hard; after a while she became calm again and went on.

"Well, I guess that's what motherhood's all about, huh? I wanted another one, I wanted lots and lots of them, but . . . And Bud would have been such a good father, what a shame. I paid for it. I got paid back in spades. Whatever that means—getting paid in spades."

And Bud, I ventured, how did he feel?

"Oh, Bud." She made a vague gesture. "Bud thought it was all just great. Really grand. Every day was the Fourth of July. By saying yes I'd made him the happiest guy in the world. Funny, how that kind of thing can make you so happy. Must be love. There was a time if I ever could have married Frank, *I'd* have been happy just that way. You go ga-ga over somebody and you can't get it out of your head. Love's a beautiful thing, I guess—when it works. Never worked for me, though."

She paused, as though searching for something, then shrugged and went on.

"It worked for Bud okay, though. He was on Cloud Nine the minute I said yes. Winchell said we were getting spliced. Spliced—I thought that was funny. Well, we tried, we both really tried," she said, "but it just wasn't any good. I never ought to have married him in the first place, not when I felt the way I did about Frank. But I really liked him, and so I made up my mind we'd make a go of it, that maybe one day I'd really come to feel about him the way I felt about Frank. Only it never happened.

"Then he had the accident and he was crippled, in that damnable chair, and somehow I thought it was all my fault. If I hadn't been off my horse, sitting on that damn stump. But I made up my mind I'd be the best wife for him; I tried, I really did. But I couldn't fool him, you see. He was so smart, Bud, in his big dumb way, he understood me, and he knew what was going on. He knew I didn't want to make love with him, and that whatever I'd tried to do for him, I still wanted to be with Frank."

"Did you ever tell him that?"

"Good Lord, no, I tried as hard as I could never to let on. But I could have saved myself the trouble. He knew all right. And I saw that no matter what I did or tried to do, it would never be enough for Bud, he'd always want more. After a while he became bitterly disappointed because we couldn't have children. In the end I think that was what he wanted most. I said, Let's adopt, but he had this notion that an adopted child wouldn't really be his. His father had been adopted, there were problems there, he was a drunk and once tried to kill Bud's mother, so in Bud's head all adopted children were like his father.

"Oh, what's the use? We'd talked about it so often I didn't want to hear any more. The night before the—the accident, we went outside. I said he should divorce me. He'd been drinking some, he got mad, said I was just looking for an out so I could marry Frank. That wasn't true, I know it wasn't, I wouldn't have done that to Bud. I truly wanted him to be happy, just the way I wanted Frank to be happy—but it just wasn't possible. Next day, on the skeet range—that's why—"

She stopped abruptly, looked at me steadily for a moment, then dropped her eyes.

"That's why what?" I asked. "What is it?"

"That's why what happened happened. The shooting. It wasn't an accident, you know. Bud was too good with a gun—he'd never have been careless like that."

I was grappling with it. "Do you really mean it wasn't an accident?"

"Certainly not. They bought my story, that's all."

"What story?"

"The one I told them. That when he was cleaning his gun, the butt got caught on the chair arm and when he jerked it free it went off—accidentally. But he did it on purpose. He did. It was suicide. He even left a note, but I tore it up."

I digested this in shocked silence. "Do you know why?" I asked after a moment.

"Can't you guess? It doesn't take a Sherlock Holmes to figure it out. A child could."

I listened hard, not wanting to miss a word. "What did the note say?" I asked.

She gave me a twisted smile. "It said, 'This is the only way I can fix things. At least one of us should be happy. I love you.' " Her eyes grew wet and she began to weep quietly.

I waited and when she was calmer I said, "And now you feel guilty. About Bud, I mean. Have you talked about this with the doctors?"

"Sure, what else? Only there isn't any answer in talking about it. It's still there."

"If you talk about your guilt, it'll go away."

She shook her head doggedly. "Wrong, Chazz. Not this time, this isn't ever going to go away. I don't mean I hang on to it deliberately—it's not that. I'd gladly let it go if I could. I just can't, that's all. Because I'm not me anymore. Well, only a little bit, sometimes. Like now. I guess this is me, the real me—isn't it? Isn't this really me?" Her voice cracked.

I said yes, this was the real her. My heart was breaking for her, the whole thing was so pathetic; she really was split straight down the middle. "Yes, April, this is you. This is really you." I began talking hard and fast before she wasn't "you" anymore, before she became the other one, trying to make her believe that if she'd try a little harder she could merge the two into the one, into April Rains again.

"The worst thing," she went on, "was the realization that I only pitied Bud. I felt so sorry for him and I had this mixed-up idea I could help him by being his wife. He just—*wanted* it so." She drew a breath and expelled it, her face wreathed in misery. "It was all my fault. I take the blame for everything. It couldn't ever have worked."

"What couldn't? You and Frank or you and Hollywood?"

"Both—either—I don't know. I just wanted everybody to be happy."

"And afterward—after Frances had died—you didn't go to Frank."

"I couldn't. After Bud died that way I promised myself I wouldn't see Frank anymore. And I didn't. I would never marry him, it would be too terrible—to be happy because Bud had killed himself for me. I would have kept to my vow, too—but then Mother died and I didn't know how to handle it. All I felt was this awful emptiness, a void. The tunnel was all dark. But that day at the post office, I'd met Frank again. There he was, as if someone had just picked him up and set him down in my life again, as if he was *supposed* to be there. Suddenly I didn't feel so empty, didn't feel so alone. I felt safe again. And I clung to him, clung so hard, I put everything I had into it, but all the time I guess I knew."

"Knew what, April? What did you know?"

"That something was going to happen. Only I never—I n-never— Oh God, please don't make me talk about it anymore, I don't want to— I can't." She began to sob, her shoulders shaking, and I sat with her hand in mine. I slipped my arm around her shoulder and after a while she took my handkerchief and blew her nose, then, surprisingly, gave a little snort of ironic laughter.

"Crazy, it's all crazy. I'm crazy and the world's crazy, too. The other night Ida put a bag over her head and suffocated herself. Is that what I should do, I wonder? I could probably find a bag somewhere."

"Don't talk like that, damn it!"

"Don't be mad at me, Charlie," she whispered. "Be my friend."

"I *am* your friend! Believe it. April, I am!"

She paused to think. "Were you here earlier?"

"When?"

"When I woke up in the hammock. They were putting on the play. Was that you?" I nodded. "Did you bring me chocolate filberts?" I nodded. "It was you, then. I thought it was. Were we talking? A long time?"

"Quite long, yes."

"I wanted to tell you then. Only I was afraid."

"It doesn't matter, you're telling me now."

I was about to ask her something else but they were blinking the porch lights and I knew it was time. She had to go in. No more Easter eggs, no more bunnies, no more talk. Just good night, goodbye, till the next time, like always. It never changed, not really. Even with this burst of talk, of real communication, things weren't changed so far as her getting out went.

"Want me to come in?" I asked.

"Oh, that's all right," she said. "I guess I know my way. I should by this time." She smiled wryly and touched my arm. "Thanks, Chazz. You're really a good Samaritan. I hope the gods smile on you." She leaned and kissed my ear, lightly, then slipped away from me. April. April Rains.

"I'll be seeing you," I promised. She drew herself up and jerked a nod, drawing the points of her collar together at her throat. "Don't worry, I'll still be here. I'm not going anywhere, am I, Mrs. Kraft?" She turned to address the matron, who had come out of the building, her uniform exceedingly white in the shadowy dark.

"We'll hope you're better so you can go somewhere," said Mrs. Kraft. "Anywhere you want to. Where would you like to go, April?" she asked, holding the door open.

I missed her answer, and wondered what it might have been. But I already knew the real answer. I'd been given these twenty, thirty minutes, all right, but there wasn't ever to be much more. April Rains had already gone to the place where she was going.

I gave a light beep on the horn, waved at her back as she slipped inside, Mrs. Kraft holding the door for her, April's head darting as though fearing some blow. The door shut and the porch light went out. I got into my car and headed for the gate.

"Everything all right?" asked the genial guard. I nodded matter-of-factly and passed through. As the gate closed behind me, I looked back at the building that had swallowed her up, wondering which window was hers. At that moment a light came on in a third-story window and I told myself that one was it. I pictured her getting ready for bed, pictured her alone in that room, with a chipped chair painted institution green, a fakey Indian bedspread, a framed reproduction on the wall in Maxfield Parrish blue. No, they probably don't have Maxfield Parrish blue at Libertad.

The broad bleak landscape lowered with darkness, throbbed and seethed with loneliness. The molded hills rolled away against the patch of sky where the sun had died. My mind's eye saw my friend, poor gray creature split like a hewed log, half this, half that, nothing good, nothing ahead. I thought about all the years I'd been doing this, making this solitary pilgrimage to nowhere for nothing, and I felt a tug, even a sob, regret sharp as a knife, unearthly desolation.

Was this what you got for trying? She had tried, a valiant effort. A pretty girl folks would go to see, healthy and wholesome, buttered popcorn in the mezzanine on Saturday night. Her prints went down in Sid Grauman's forecourt, she won the Look Award for Most Promising Newcomer, the Photoplay Award, all of those silly but gratifying medallions to receive which you put on your spangly dress and fox furs and they curl up your hair all to hell and gone. America's true royalty. But at what a price? Don't tell me it was because she loved a married man, don't tell me it was because she wanted to give Frankie a son and heir and failed, I won't buy it. 'Twas the beasts killed the Beauty. It was Hollywood did her in.

Anna. Anna-banana. Now she was alone. Alone, Anna; alone, April. Maybe that's the way it had to be, but I didn't want to believe it. My heart was overflowing with bitterness and resentment, and as the feeling mounted in me I found that I was driving twenty miles over the limit. I slowed as I saw lights in the rear-view mirror; no cop, though, only another motorist going faster as I brought the needle down to 55. I didn't go home the same way I had come, back through the San Fernando Valley, but instead continued west on the Ventura Freeway until I hit the Pacific Coast Highway and veered south. On my left rose the granite, heavily muscled shoulders of the ancient California headlands that angled sharply down to the sea-level flats, rain-rutted cliffs of decomposed granite, said to hold firm under stress. To my right lay the sea, a broad flat plane of darkening water that stretched into the fleeing day that raced from the horizon straight to Singapore. It was not yet suppertime, and under the purple-and-gold sky I could make out darkened forms along the beach: a man, a woman, a tall boy, younger children, a wet hairy dog, plodding member of the family; silhouettes only, formed but featureless, each with its particular and incisive gesture, silent figures in a darkening landscape, actors on a vast empty stage. Silent pictures.

I fine-tune the radio and light a cigarette (I quit, a hundred times I quit; now I smoke, and I love it!). It's as if she's here with me in the car, beside me in the other bucket, yet I know where she is really, behind the green waffled grille on the third floor, folding down her bedspread. I watch the road ahead, the lights that have come on in my rear-view mirror, I take in the long stretches of empty beach as they flash by, darkening, melancholy, unpeopled, fraught with a sense of end-of-the-world-ness, that old California earthquake syndrome, every Angeleno's fantasy, in which the whole state falls into the Pacific and drowns.

Then my peripheral glance is galvanized by a sight I had not thought to look upon, not so soon, wildly bizarre in its odd, quirky appropriateness, as if it's been planned by some superior intelligence: two of them, a pair, centaurs, those man-horses, prey of the Lapithae, banished from Thessaly lo these thousands of years since and now come to California, here beside the dark waters of Ocean Pacifica, to live among the nutburgers.

I wanted to stop but couldn't, I was traveling too fast, but still I held them in my view, man-horse, *homo-equus*, creatures of the Thessalian plain with their manes and hoofs and windswept tails, their human-animal passions, their anthropomorphic lusts, their horse-tears, man-and-maid tears, tears of salt and rue.

> *One by one in the moonlight there*
> *Neighing far off on the haunted air*
> *The unicorns come down to the sea.*

Fairy creatures from a dream zoo, whisked into fragile life out of the glassblower's wand, seen for seconds only on a beach in the blue-black dark 7.6 miles from a madhouse. The unicorns come down to the sea, those solemn, crystal-horned creatures of myth and fancy, figments of man's imagination, and in seconds the fog rolls in off the water like a gray plague, a movie-fog generated by special-effects men, obliterating sea, sand, creatures, all.

In another minute I knew I'd been seeing things. Everybody knows there are no unicorns; not in this life. Only the hope of them, and that hope blessed small.

Maude

As a boy, I used to get a thrill on Monday nights when that crisp, patrician voice of Cecil B. De Mille would come over CBS radio to proclaim

LUX . . . PRESENTS . . . *HOLLYWOOD!*

What those three ringing words meant, only those who likewise heard the Lux Radio Theatre can know. It was true: a soap manufacturer was presenting to the radio-listening nation the glamorous Hollywood everybody worshipped and adored and couldn't know enough about. In a brief fifty minutes they'd wrap up the whole sad tale of *Dark Victory* or *Stella Dallas*, tears, sobs, and all, at the end of which C.B. would come on and chat intimately with the stars, Stanwyck or Davis or whoever, and you felt sure that, while broadcasting, Stanwyck was wearing a slinky satin dress and fox furs (she wasn't) and that Davis had a block-long limousine waiting to take her out dancing (she didn't). Magical place names like "Hollywood and Vine," "Del Mar," and "Trocadero" and "Lucey's" and "Toluca Lake" and "Culver City" and "La Brea Tar Pits" sent tremors through you. You got glimpses of the real thing you'd already discovered in such movies as *A Star Is Born*, or in the MGM newsreel when they concreted Mickey Rooney's footprints at Grauman's Chinese. Out in Hollywood everything appeared to have streamlined curves—buildings and women alike; it was all chrome strips and restaurants built to look like men's derbies or club sandwiches without the mayo, and the smogfree California air was filled with the promise of orchids and diamonds: the Land of Dreams. Just follow the Yellow Brick Road with Judy, leave Kansas and Auntie Em behind and come, not to emerald Oz but to silver Hollywood, where you, too, could press your hands and feet in wet cement.

Well, don't kid yourself. It's gone now; it's all gone. I don't mean just

Grauman's, I mean Hollywood. Tinseltown. Glitter City. Ham Burg. A:
gone with the wind as, well, *Gone With the Wind.* The *place* is there, five
square miles of it, eight miles from downtown L.A. as the crow flies. Look
on the movie-star maps, you'll still find it, but don't look for Carole
Lombard's house, don't look for Dolores del Rio's or John Barrymore's
don't look for Bill Powell's. The houses may be there still, only Carole
ain't home, Bill won't answer the door, Dolores blew town years ago.
Barrymore—forget it; they all went with the wind, too. The nights no
longer twinkle and shine when the stars come out—the movie stars, that
is. The air no longer exudes that heady, sweet perfume, nor does it bear
upon its breath the sultry strains of Latin music along the Sunset Strip:
Lina Romay does not shake her fringes while Cugie caresses his pet
Chihuahua. No, no, all that is gone and will not come again, nothing will
bring back those golden days, nothing will even nearly approximate them.
Those were the days of cream and butter, these are the days of skim milk
and oleo. Somewhere along the line Hollywood got real, got grim.

Even most of the old-timers who are still with us have left—New
York, London, Paris, Palm Springs; no one in his right mind sticks around
Tinseltown unless he has to. One of the few who never left—and never
would—was Maude. She'd never have even thought of living anywhere
else than Sunnyside, and since that grand old house had been built for her
(the only house in town to have a musicians' gallery high above the grand
salon) and she was happy in it, why should she go? She wasn't really a
part of the Hollywood scene, hadn't been for thirty years or more. She
just sat up there on her hill looking down on the world, letting it all pass
by, watching the snows of yesteryear melt away. She'd become a fixture,
though she hated anyone to say so. "Sounds like I should be brass-plated
and clamped to the wall of a De Mille bathroom," she said. But it was true;
she'd lived in filmland since 1919, which was a scant thirty years after Mrs.
Horace H. Wilcox dubbed her citrus ranch "Hollywood."

By the century's turn Mrs. W's dusty acreage was already being
profitably subdivided into building lots and its population was numbered
in the five hundreds. By then there were two-story houses, telephone
poles, shady trees, and some signs of city life—though few of moviemaking. Not yet had the movie cameras rolled at Biograph, at Selig, at Bison,
at IMP. Not yet did the Hollywood Hotel sprawl at Hollywood and
Highland; not yet did young Capra, young Ford, and their cronies gather
at the downtown Alexandria Hotel; not yet was there a "Hollywood," the
dream factory; not quite yet. But everything was set and waiting, a
whistle-stop town basking in the orange- and lemon-fruited orchards,
waiting with its Irving Berlin skies, its fleecy pink clouds, its caressing

palms, its seashore where Sennett beauties would romp and bounce along the sands and the saxes would wail in the dance halls on the pier, everything just waiting for the celluloid to roll.

Oddly, at the very time that Hollywood was poised to meet its destiny, back east the sovereign state of New Jersey seemed a pretty fine moviemaking place itself, and there a blonde-haired child from Bayonne was helping to mold movie history. Maudie Fagan was the daughter of an Irish tavernkeeper and one day when she was seven years old she was approached by a man in the street who spoke to her those oft-quoted words, "How'd you like to be in pictures, little lady?" And in no time, the little lady was. It was her fate, in the person of Al Christie, an early celluloid cowpoke turned director.

Maudie Fagan would in time become Maude Antrim, one of the great silent-screen stars, and when she successfully made the transition to sound, she went on—as few others did—to even greater triumphs. Mary Pickford might fall by the wayside, and all her sisters, but Maude was like the Santa Fe Railroad, she went on and on.

Off the screen, for many of those years she reigned side by side with her husband, Crispin, acting as the chatelaine of that famous and magical Hollywood domicile called "Sunnyside," like the equally famous "Pickfair" one of the town's landmark showplaces, although Maude was the first to tell you that she was never a pillar of the Hollywood Establishment. When Crispin died, she laid to rest all the social fa-fa-ra, the big parties he'd loved, the entertaining of visiting firemen, the hoity-toity dukes and duchesses, the renowned authors in tweeds and kiltie shoes, the politicians belching behind their cigars. Bernard Shaw, Richard Halliburton, Lowell Thomas, Mary and Doug, Hearst and Marion, Mrs. Pat Campbell, even Churchill, they all dined there. Perry Antrim, Maude's son, once sat on the lap of Queen Marie of Romania—indeed, Perry's elbows were always well worn from rubbing them with the famous names of this century, for few folk of any consequence weren't invited to partake of the hospitality of Sunnyside. And, not so incidentally, it remains one of my greatest joys that during a period of personal domestic upheaval, I was permitted to know the rooftree of that house; and to come to know the lady herself.

It all came about in this manner:

Jenny's and my problems didn't go away, and when I came back from New York in 1972, to ease domestic matters I'd gone to stay at the Villa Lorraine, on Sunset, that home of New York actors-away-from-home, a place I hadn't set foot inside of for almost twenty years. I dined solo at indifferent restaurants and spent lots of time working out at my gym, pretending I didn't care; but I did, and after nearly two weeks of this miserable existence I called Jenny and said I wanted to come home. She said she needed more time "to think things out"; I agreed to give it to her. Then I found out she'd been seeing a TV producer, "dating him" on the sly two or three times a week, sometimes more. Why is it the husband is always the last to know? I saw red and told her she knew what she could do with her producer; I wasn't coming home after all.

How sorry I felt for myself may be measured by the number of nights I spent on the town, falling off the wagon regularly and drinking the nights away, boring my friends with my troubles and seeking the solace of several young ladies whose vocation was the solacing of unhappy husbands like myself. I was more melancholy than Hamlet, gloomy and depressed, while life at the Villa was deadly boring. Should I chuck it all, head for New York, or just stick my head in the oven?

Then one day came the first break in the clouds. I'd put my car on the rack at the Santa-Palm Car Wash and was idly examining the celebrity pictures along the wall, when up ahead, in the small concession area where they sell printed T-shirts and the like, I caught sight of someone I hadn't seen in some time: Frankie Adonis.

There he was, standing before me, hands outspread in welcome, smiling that 24-carat smile. "What's new, kiddo?" We walked over to the Orange Julius stand on the corner, where I had a chili dog and a Julius, my immutable car-wash fare; Frank had coffee. Since I'd changed careers and he was no longer my agent, it had really been a long time since we'd talked, and, needless to say, soon I was telling him how Jenny and I were having difficulties.

"Yeah," he said, relighting his cigar, "I heard." It could only have been from Vi—Viola Ueberroth, still the latter-day Tattler, the Paul Revere of all the Hollywoods: one if by land, two if by sea, and keep the lantern burning in the Old North Church. "Want to tell me about it?" Frank asked.

I began to spin my tale, gripe by gripe, and he listened with his usual patience and commented with his usual acumen, managing to sympathize without betraying his friendship with Jenny, then asked where I was hanging my hat these days. I told him and he whistled. "That place'll depress a married man faster than a cell at San Quentin. Wait a second, kiddo, I've got to hit the can."

He went off and I sat there thinking how in Hollywood you could go for years without seeing somebody and in a flash there you were, just the way things had always been, old wine in old kegs. He'd turned sixty-four that July, the gray had sneaked into his dark hair, he'd even put on a little weight. But some silver in a man's hair can look good, a healthy tan never hurts, and he'd quit drinking at the same time Belinda joined A.A.; he hadn't smoked much since his early forties, he didn't gallivant but went to bed early, more often than not alone. He was living at the Shoreham Towers at this time, in an apartment he'd kept on and off for years, a quiet, elegant pad furnished with good Biedermeier and French antiques and his small collection of pictures—the little Renoir nude, the Modigliani.

Pretty soon I saw his car rolling off the washrack—a maroon station wagon. A careless attendant spun the wheel as he ran it to the edge of the tarmac for wiping down.

"Hey, *patchouko!*" Frank shouted, coming out of the men's room. "Take it easy on the rubber, huh?"

"Where's Blindy?" I asked as he sat down.

"I'm a golf widower. She's on the tournament circuit. She and Gravel Gertrude (his name for his old flame, Angie Brown). I'm trying to set something up for her at Fox. A biggy."

I'd seen it in the trades that she was up for an important film, *The Light in the Window,* from the best-selling novel, and Frank was counting on Belinda landing the part. These days they were an item, had been for two years. Their burgeoning relationship was part of the new Hollywood legend, a throwback to the old days, but very *au courant* and greatly applauded. Looking at him, it was hard to believe that he was now in his sixties, or that Belinda was almost fifty, with a grown daughter.

A lapse of some fourteen years hadn't let me forget that Belinda and I had once also been an item, and as I'd cared about her then, I cared about her still. I was pleased to hear that she was finding some measure of happiness at last—and with Frank. I wished them both well, and though we didn't discuss it, I hoped they'd get married; somehow it struck me as the perfect solution. I knew that Belinda's daughter, Faun, was still a problem—what I'd personally observed could easily attest to that—and I wondered if having Frank around mightn't have some good effect on her.

"Listen, kiddo," Frank said, after filling me in on Belinda's career, "I was just thinking—maybe Belinda might be a good way out for you, y'know?"

"How so?" I asked.

"Well, for a change of scenery. I was thinking—how'd you like to be living up in Benedict Canyon in a little cottage all your own? Lovely gardens, tennis court, pool, garage, maid, private entrance, the works?"

I knew he had to be talking about the guesthouse at Sunnyside, oft talked about but seldom seen. "Yeah? For which arm and which leg?" I asked.

"No—I'm serious. I'll talk to Blindy. They'd rent it to someone nice —simpatico, know what I mean?" Frank, Agent Supreme, was hard at work.

"And what do I have to do to live in this lap of luxury?"

"Nothing. Nothing at all. Just . . . well, you know. Talk to her a little, try to build up her confidence. She's really in the best shape she's been in a long time."

"Does she ever fall off the waterwagon?"

"Nary a drop."

Suddenly I was longing to see Belinda again and yearning to drop my bags in the guesthouse at Sunnyside. Home sweet home with Maude Antrim—Maude the Great.

I accepted and Frank clapped me between the shoulder blades as we headed for our cars. "I'll catch you at the hotel tonight. Good seeing you, kiddo."

That evening my phone rang; Frank had fixed everything. It was fine with Belinda; I could have the guesthouse by tomorrow afternoon, to give them the morning to have it cleaned up; it had been empty for some time.

"When's she coming up?" I asked. "Soon, I hope."

"Afraid not. She'll be away till some time in February. I'm meeting her in Acapulco for the holidays. Then she and Angie are playing a tournament in Scottsdale in January."

"Busy little bee. What's her handicap?" When he told me I whistled.

"Well, so long, kiddo, gotta go. Don't let the bastards getcha. . . ."

"Wait a minute—what do I do, just drive out there?"

"Around two should do it. You'll be expected. Use the lower gate."

"I guess I'll have the place to myself, then."

"Guess you will. Nobody there except the servants."

"And—Maude . . . ?"

"She'll be along after New Year's. You'll see her—maybe. S'long."

He hung up before I could squeeze in further questions, and that night I dreamed about Mrs. Fingerhutt, my first landlady in New York. That harpy used to climb five flights every Friday morning and stand at my door with her hand out: five bucks and all the cold water you could use. Mrs. Fingerhutt was a character straight out of Dickens—while Maude, as I was shortly to discover, was one straight out of Hollywood; only Hollywood.

What did she look like? How would she behave? Would she invite me up for *intime* little suppers *à deux*? I knew that she owned a collection of jewels that could only be labeled "fabulous," all given her by Crispin as love tokens; she'd been married to the great actor for nearly forty years, with never a whisper of divorce, never a quarrel to hear tell of, never a breath of scandal. What skeletons there were in that family closet had come from the next generation, from their errant son, Perry, the playboy. Maude had published her autobiography years ago, during what she believed at that time to be the end of her career. I was suddenly taken with the desire to reread her book, *Girl of the Golden East*, but all my books were at home. There was also Crispin Antrim's memoir, modestly titled *An Actor's Life*, and I knew just where they were—side by side in the middle bookshelf—and I wanted them.

When I called the house, there was no answer, and I decided Jenny was probably out for dinner—with her TV producer. I had my key. I hopped into the car, buzzed along the Strip, up Sunset Plaza, and pulled into my driveway. There were a couple of lights on inside, but when I rang there was no reply. I let myself in and Bones the Wonder Dog came leaping joyfully out of the dark.

"Hey, boy—hey, boy!" Our joy was mutual and complete. I petted him while he frantically licked and crooned and otherwise behaved as if he hadn't seen me in months.

I wasn't keen on being in the house without Jen's having been warned, since we'd already had some heavy drama on the phone, so I made a quick stab at finding the two books I was after. But Bones was so crazy out of his mind at seeing me that he wouldn't stop yelping. I suddenly heard a male voice thunder, *"Bones! Shut the hell up!,"* and turned to find a total stranger standing in the doorway of the hallway off the bedroom, silhouetted by the light behind. He was naked, with a towel barely covering his loins, and looked bleary-eyed. It seemed that a romantic interlude of sorts was in progress in the bedroom.

"Who the hell are you?" I demanded.

"Who the hell are *you?*" he countered.

"I happen to live here. The lady you're in bed with happens to be my wife." The towel, I noticed, had *my* monogram on it.

"Holy shit!" he said, stumbling toward me, blinking. I backed up. He wasn't bigger but he was a lot younger, and I knew he played tennis with Chuck Heston. He shoved his paw at me. "How the hell are ya? Always wanted to meetcha." And—get this: "I've read all your books."

Sure, I thought, they're on the bedside table. Only you haven't been reading today, I'll bet.

"Randy-o, what the hell's going on out there?" This was Jenny's voice, and immediately my back went up. Randy—the TV producer, *Jen's* TV producer. She entered via the same doorway, wearing the satin teddy I'd given her. Apricot ice with ivory lace, and matching panties.

"Oh. It's you," she said. "Why don't you call first, or did you forget Don Ameche invented the telephone?"

"I called. You didn't answer. Now we know why. I came by for these." I held up the two books in my hand.

"What do you want them for?"

"That's for me to know." I started out, the dog at my heels. "I'm taking Bones with me."

"You are like hell! They don't allow dogs at the Villa."

"I know, but I'm not living at the Villa anymore," I said, feeling my pulse race with a perverse joy, about to make the announcement. "I'm living at Sunnyside."

She popped her eyes. "*Sunnyside?*" You'd have thought I'd said Buckingham Palace. "With Belinda Carroll?"

"Something wrong with that?"

"I suppose next thing you'll be telling me is that you and Belinda are going to be married."

"No, I'm not going to tell you. Because it's a secret. We don't want anyone to know. Ta ta, kiddies. You can get back to your labors now." I took a step and she put out a hand.

"Wait a minute. The Crispin Antrim book, *that* one's mine."

"Fine, keep it. My book, your book. Your towel, my towel." With a quick slick move I detoweled Randy. Now he was wearing nothing but a condom over his shriveled member. "Awww, too bad, Randy-o," I said, going out, "your turtle died."

A vase crashed near my head as I reached the door and I knew it was one of the pair of antiques her Aunt Nancy had given us. I laughed as I went through the gate, with Bones far ahead of me, bounding for joy.

Back at the Villa I sneaked him up the fire escape and in through the window, which I knew was unlocked, because the lock hadn't worked since sound came in. I told him to be quiet or we'd both be thrown out. I packed my scattered belongings, then, with Bones curled on the bed beside me, I began reading *Girl of the Golden East*, remembering the profound pleasure I'd felt reading it back in my first winter in New York, in the fall of 1949. Much of what it contained I recalled, in a general sense. Certain passages reappeared like old friends, others turned up like newly discovered ones. Maude Antrim wrote with a keen, clear, and objective eye, with wit and perception. If this was what she was like, I was going to enjoy being the star boarder at Sunnyside.

As a family of actors, the Antrims went back to the Civil War, to old Colonel Antrim—that would be the great Ned—who'd distinguished himself at the Battle of Bull Run, where he'd been a brevet colonel and had commanded troops that routed the Yankees and brought victory to the men in gray. That same fellow, Ned, had become an actor when the war was over. Having lost his first wife to pneumonia, he married a beautiful actress in his stage company, one May Forlorna, by whom late in life he had two children, Crispin and Daisy. Ned Antrim was the leading actor and star of the old Redpath Stock Company in Chicago, and his Hamlet had been applauded throughout the whole Midwest. When he married his leading lady, who was a good many years younger, they were drawn down Michigan Avenue in a flower-draped carriage, with four white horses that were taken from the traces while men seized the shafts and pulled them through the streets to the steamship landing, where they boarded a private yacht and cruised the Great Lakes on their honeymoon. Crispin Antrim was born in a Loop hotel in 1883.

In my boyhood there were two film actors of prime distinction: one, the charming and ever-British Ronald Colman, the other, Crispin Antrim. They were both figures of glamour, breeding, and style, and a boy would do well to emulate them, though he did not do well to imitate their diction and manners. From silent flickers to wide-screen sound with color, Crispin grew up, grew old, died before our eyes. From *Tom Hill of Phelps Hall*, through *Gallant Raleigh* and *Bonnie Prince Charlie*, *Alfred the Great* and *Trafalgar*, his bravely dying Major Ecuyer in *Fort Pitt*, all the valiant British heroes he had essayed with such verve and success, he had found his place in America's heart. Crispin Antrim was noble in a time when there were few noble men to be found. When he died in 1952, he left a gap no one has since filled—or stands likely to.

Even as an infant Maude seemed destined for fame. At four her smiling face was on every box of Purity Soap Flakes, every bar wrapper. Her blonde mop of curls became almost as famous as Shirley Temple's decades later. At age six, she danced, sang, told jokes, did monologues. It was to Al Christie, that movie cowboy director back in New Jersey, that Crispin owed his debt of thanks; otherwise he might never have met the love of his life. Under Al's tutelage, Maude Fagan had begun her professional career, and when Christie headed west, much against her father's wishes Maude and her mother joined the troupe. And where did Christie head? Straight for Mrs. Wilcox's Hollywood. Many people, especially the younger ones, won't believe it when told that Maude worked in *early* silents, the ones where they used to wear puttees and crank the camera with the cap turned round and shoot five scripts on one studio floor at the same time. In the Land of Eternal Sunshine little Maude acted child-ingenues in a number of hootenannies for Christie, later leaving him to join the Nestor Company, for whom she revealed a budding flair for comedy, graduating to the early Vitagraph Company where she played an engaging miss who in one flicker sat upon the plump knee of the great John Bunny.

Not only was Maude Antrim in the first movie *I* ever saw, she was also in the first movie my mother had ever seen on the silver screen. The film was a two-reel silent version of *Uncle Tom's Cabin,* and Mother saw it in a nickelodeon in Germantown, Pennsylvania. I saw that same *Uncle Tom's Cabin* not so long ago—they ran it at the L.A. County Museum— and I was fascinated to view the twelve-year-old Maude Fagan being carried up to heaven on plainly visible wires, while her wings drooped tiredly and her wire halo jerked above her head. In this fashion had Maude Fagan ascended to heaven, transporting Little Eva's soul to the Pearly Gates.

When movie work slackened in Hollywood, Momma Fagan took her child to San Francisco, where she was engaged to essay more of the winsome misses she was becoming so adept at portraying, and when the company went on tour, Maude and Momma went along, too. After a money-quarrel with the management, the irate Mrs. Fagan insisted they leave the company in Bismarck, and eventually they ended up in Chicago, where she marched her little girl around to the doors of the AyanBee Company, later to move its operation to the Coast but just then filming in a warehouse on the shores of Lake Michigan.

Crispin Antrim was obliged, however, to wait half a dozen years or so before clapping eyes on the woman who was to become his third wife. This meeting occurred aboard an overnight train out of Chicago, bound for New York. Having gone to the dining car, where he found the young woman listening to a lecture from her mother, Crispin stopped, introduced himself to Mrs. Fagan, and was permitted to sit down. Within an hour he had captivated the mother and enchanted the daughter, and for the balance of the trip he stayed close to them. By the time the train arrived at New York, he had the girl signed to a personal contract and was announcing his plan to make her a star. He gave her a diamond ring, bought her a fur coat, and called her his little golden wolf. The papers played it up big. He engaged the bridal suite at the old Waldorf-Astoria and began changing her image. He taught her to eat oysters on the halfshell, snails, and caviar; he gave her her first maid to button her shoes and engaged teachers to educate her where she was most lacking, and soon he declared himself pleased as Punch with his new little wife.

Within three years Maude Antrim was playing opposite the great star in *Sherlock Holmes,* and in another year Crispin brought his production of *Romeo* into New York, with his wife as Juliet. That year she and he had performed prodigies of salesmanship in the matter of U.S. bond sales all over the East (a tour in which the young Babe Austrian had also participated), after which they sailed for Europe to entertain the troops as they came out of the trenches. They returned only six weeks before the Armistice.

Life was gay, and no one was happier than this new acting team that America was fast taking to its heart. In the next few years the lissome Maude played a wide variety of roles that caught the fancy of the public. Back to Chicago for more "flickers" at AyanBee, then on to Hollywood, for Crispin's own Sunshine Company. Crispin Antrim had fallen under the spell of Sir Walter Scott's works, and it was his Sunshine Pictures that brought to the screen such works as *Ivanhoe, Lady of the Lake,* and *The Bride of Lammermoor,* in which his wife, Maude, distinguished herself with a mad scene that is still talked about.

When Hollywood fell into panic with the coming of sound, the Antrims were ready to face the microphone. In fact, the miracle of sound only enhanced their screen personalities, and they were to earn even greater stardom. It was at that time that many of those persons whom I was subsequently to meet, and who were bound to come together and have their effect on one another, were gathering in the movie capital to make their names. Sam Ueberroth was by now a top producer. His sister, Viola, had already discovered Fedora; Frank Adonis had hit town with Babe Austrian in tow; Claire Regrett, still Cora Sue Brodsky, was on her way west.

Maude's autobiography brought it all back in its modest, direct, light-hearted way. Others might take her seriously; she did not. I was surprised when I got to the last page. Having read my way through the book in three hours flat, I fell instantly asleep. I awoke with Bones whining to be let out. I jumped when a fist pounded on my door.

"You got a dog in there?" came the bald question, followed by more banging. Dick Tracy was working late. I heard his key in the lock as Bones and I disappeared out the window, me with my bag and duffel, down the fire escape. We slept in the car that night, Bones and I; next day I paid up and checked out. I saw the gumshoe standing by the door and hollered, "Take an animal to lunch!"

Sunnyside, here I come.

One thing I'd forgotten with the passage of the years. I had always thought the name of the house had some connection with Sunshine,

Crispin's old production company, but no. Sunnyside was named after the estate Washington Irving had built on the Hudson in New York, but owed its architectural debt to the great houses of Florida, those *palazzi* that Addison Mizner erected in Palm Beach and Miami and that inflated the Florida bubble back in the twenties—another bubble that went bust.

I drove out Sunset Boulevard to Benedict Canyon and hung a right at the Beverly Hills Hotel. I passed Tropical Drive, where Hedda had lived, went by Tower Road, at whose top David Selznick had lived with Jennifer Jones in one of Hollywood's most handsomely unpretentious houses, now razed to the ground by a rock-and-roll "artiste" with pretensions to Borgian grandeur. I kept a sharp lookout for the street, Caligula Way, since Frank had said watch carefully, it was hard to find. I turned at Cielo Drive—up there was Falcon Lair, Valentino's house, and across the way the house the French actress Michele Morgan had built when she was married to one of Ginger Rogers's husbands, a French country farmhouse where the Manson gang's bloody massacre had taken place, and over there the fabled Harold Lloyd estate, now dug up like a field of turnips.

I must have missed my sign, because I did get lost, and finally had to ask directions of a Japanese gardener. To my chagrin I was actually on Caligula, smack in front of the place, though you'd never have known it. A little farther up the hill I saw the gates I'd had pointed out to me twenty years before, the gates of Sunnyside.

Remembering Frank's injunction to use the lower gates, I left the crest of the hill and drove around the descending curve until I passed another pair of gates, one of these left ajar. I backed up, stopped, got out, pushed both gates open, and drove in. And there was the guesthouse under a tall shady tree, the door wide open, and a maid in white uniform running the vacuum around the living room.

She was Chinese-Hawaiian—called Suzi-Q—and she most generously offered to help me get settled in. Since I had brought so few things, I decided instead to have a look around the place while she finished up. The lawns to the guest cottage were spare, and to the side of the house an escarpment of some sort climbed away steeply, as though to discourage investigation of the upper grounds. When I went back inside, I asked Suzi-Q if I could drive her up to the main house, but as we approached the main gate she thanked me and slipped out, to disappear through a smaller gate to one side. Like a Dickens lad, I got out and peered through the wrought-iron portals. Secretly I had hoped for a glimpse of my new landlady, but Frank had said she'd be away until after New Year's, and according to Suzi-Q there was only a male servant and herself in the house.

I soon settled into a new sort of life. I defy anyone not to have felt at home in the "Cottage," as it was called, a low-ceilinged set of nicely proportioned rooms with heavy beams of adzed oak, a large stone fireplace with cobra-shaped firedogs whose yellow eyes gleamed in the flames, and mullioned windows and windowboxes planted in varicolored impatiens. The bed was hard, the bathroom a tiled glory in black and Nile green, with a six-nozzle shower stall and a tub large enough to wash a horse in. It was like living in a country lodge cloistered in a patch of green country forest, like a château at Fontainebleau, and I blessed whoever had kept this section of Beverly Hills from being built up. I hung my things neatly in the closet, put others away in drawers, placed my copy of *Girl of the Golden East* in the window niche. Then I set my typewriter on the heavily carved table and sat myself down in front of a casement window where I could gaze out across the canyon vista and dream up whatever might occur and try to get it down on paper.

Christmas came on in a burst of fine weather, blue skies and warm temperatures. Southern California was Sunny California and those unbelievable pink- and blue-flocked Christmas trees in the little park across from the Beverly Hills post office loomed in the Yuletide heat. I was reminded of the first time I'd ever seen Maude Antrim in person. This was also at Christmastime, nearly twenty years ago: Jenny had sent me to the post office with some packages for last minute mailing to the East, I'd pulled into the parking space outside the post office and there was a car just backing out—a Rolls-Royce. I'd cut in rather close and I saw the driver lean across and roll down the window. "Would you mind moving a bit, I can't get out." I did so, with alacrity. "Merry Christmas, Miss Antrim," I called as the car drove off. She'd nodded, that was all.

But this Christmas, not a sign of her. Enjoying my new digs, my new freedom, I found I was impatient for her to come, as if something wonderful were waiting in the wings. Frank had invited me to spend the holidays at his house in the Springs, but I declined; I liked my new house. I spent New Year's Eve there, Bones my only companion. Dumb, but that's how I wanted it.

The rains came, went, and came again. It was an excessively wet winter that year, but there I was, snug as a nickel. There were no leaks anywhere; a roof at Sunnyside wouldn't dare leak! I ordered up a full cord of wood and kindling with which to stoke my fireplace; there was a venerable system of forced heated air, even in the bathroom, whose tiles stayed dry and toasty.

Bones reveled in the place. The floors of thick varnished stone flagging were impervious to all dogdom, the click of his twenty nails on the slates was pleasant to my ear, becoming silent again as he moved from the

stone to one of the braided rag rugs that were strewn about, while in front
of the fire lay a large fur rug, the skin, paws, and head of a Kodiak bear
that Crispin had shot in the Klondike; the animal must have stood twelve
or fourteen feet tall. Here I lay on my back, my head pillowed on the skull,
staring at the ceiling, while the rain pattered briskly on the roof. Ah, the
joys of solitude. The only drawback I could come up with was that the
drive-in gates were not automated; I had to get out every time to open and
close them, a nuisance of major proportions because of the rain. I had to
go out and buy an umbrella. No one in California ever carried an umbrella
—umbrellas were for New York.

Sunnyside was a domain any monarch would be proud to rule over.
And since it was now mine, without the upkeep and the taxes (what must
those be?), it was doubly pleasurable to contemplate. From the Cottage to
get to the main house you walked up a short, woodsy trail to an abruptly
visible set of stone steps, and climbing those—there were 135, I have
laboriously counted them many times—you came out on what looked like
granite abutments, like old fortifications, built to sustain much weight and
green with lichen. Proceeding upwards, you reached an esplanade, beyond which was a wide strip of well-kept lawn, and the pool, with a brick
surround and stone statues at the corners—were they the Four Seasons?
So it appeared. Across the huge pool that Crispin Antrim had ordered
built so he could keep up his muscles, past plantings of clipped yew trees
and neat boxwood hedge, sat the house itself. There were flower beds laid
out in glorious pattern, banked by *allées* of dark green Italian cypresses,
so columnar they seemed to be holding up the sky itself. The handsome
sprawling house, built in the Quattrocento style, was imposing but not
pretentious. It was reminiscent of the grand villas that dotted the hills of
Lombardy and Tuscany, sloping hip roofs of red tile nicely worn, a few
galleries and balconies, windows, grilles set into the masonry, tall, narrow
chimneys, and vents here and there. Whoever had built the place had
known what he was doing.

Between the house and the garages was the famous "Playhouse,"
which Perry Antrim and his bride, Claire, had occupied following their
honeymoon, and which, my bed-making Suzi-Q informed me, was used
these days by Belinda's daughter whenever she happened to be in town.

The view from the hilltop was magnificent. Down one slope you
looked onto the clay tennis courts, and beyond them, across the vale, the
red-tiled roofs of the old Harold Lloyd estate, now badly eaten into by
land development, growing typical two- and three-million-dollar ersatz
châteaux put up for the nouveau riche of the Nouveau Hollywood. On
the far side you overlooked Falcon Lair, and I wondered what stories

Maude Antrim could tell of fifty years ago. Did she ever wander over to Rudy's to borrow a cup of sugar? (It was three and a quarter miles to the nearest market; I had clocked it.)

Frank had said I could use the tennis courts, and one day when Jenny was out I went home and got my racquet from the closet, and I encouraged friends to come and play. They came, but were far more interested in being inside the gates of Sunnyside than in playing tennis. Meanwhile, where oh where was the lady of the manor?

I languished, lord of this empty domain hidden behind the gates of Caligula Way. She came at last—in mid-January. The manservant, of whom I'd caught no more than a glimpse, donned his livery, brought out the Rolls, passed my gate as he went down the hill. Two hours later the car was back, and I glimpsed a figure in the back seat. She never saw me, and if I reasoned that an invitation would quickly arrive for dinner, I reasoned foolishly. My invitation must have blown off the porch.

Then the wind really blew, the leaves flew, and it was, in the words of that eminent Victorian Bulwer-Lytton, "a dark and stormy night." Had been in fact a particularly stormy day, which downed the power lines in the neighborhood, giving us our dark night. My electric typewriter died an ugly death, as well as every light, and I couldn't find a flashlight. I searched everywhere for even a candle stub but found nothing. Eventually I slipped on a poncho and a rain hat and mushed up the stairs to the big house.

It brooded, the large dark house. No lights showed. Great night for a murder, I thought, as I moved along the side doors, looking for signs of life. Then I caught the faint glimmer of a candle far off; it came nearer and I suddenly found myself staring straight into the face of Dr. Fu Manchu—or better yet, the Asp out of Orphan Annie; there were the inscrutable slant eyes, the yellow skin, the sinister Oriental mien. He must have observed me on my way up to the house and alerted his mistress, for he admitted me without a word and escorted me through a far door, then through a smaller passageway into the large front hall, where he knocked on the door of another room.

"Come in, Ling," I heard a clear, pleasant voice ring out, and when the servant opened the door I walked in. The room was lighted by at least twenty candles plus the glowing fire, and there in the tall hearthside chair, a picture out of a book, sat the lady herself.

She got up briskly and came toward me; the outstretched hand she offered was warm and firm.

"Well, hel-*lo*. You are Mr. Caine, of course. I am Maude Antrim. Do come in. I thought perhaps you'd be coming up, so I asked Ling if I mightn't speak to you. I tried the telephones but I think they're out, too. Are you in the dark down there? Yes, I was afraid so. There used to be some candles but probably they're all gone and we just forgot to order more. But we can easily let you have as many as you need. Beastly out, isn't it? Won't you sit down and have some nice hot tea?"

Tea with Maude Antrim? I leaped at the chance, saying tea would be perfect.

"Yes, that's right, that's a nice comfortable chair." I sat down beside a fluted mahogany pedestal on which rested a bronze bust of Crispin Antrim as Shylock, a fine likeness.

"Now," Maude went on, "just give that cord a tug, won't you, save me getting up. Ling will appear as if by magic, you'll see."

I pulled the cord and "rang for tea." At Maude's. It was a beginning. Ling entered on cue with the tray, making not a sound as he set it down.

When he had gone, she poured in an elegant fashion and handed me my cup. "Constant Comment?" I asked. She held her sip, put down her cup, and clapped her hands: "You're—you're on my team. Only people who know C.C. can get on my tea team."

"My initials," I said, "I should know." She nodded, smiled, showed pleasure, looked lovely, beautiful, was mine. What a coup. I remembered I was a writer and made mental notes. Though she had been all alone and obviously not expecting company, she was dressed. She sat rather tall and straight; her form was slender, even spare, her hair a soft brown and done in the easy style I remembered from so many of her modern films, shaped to the head and softly curled. She wore lipstick and perhaps just a sketch of penciling along the brows. Her suit looked like a Chanel, a becoming cherry-red shade; she'd had it for years, you could tell—one of those outfits that had become her from the minute she put it on. Her wrists were delicate, her hands prominently veined with blue, and brown-spotted, the badge of age. She wore a gold wedding band, no other rings.

But her eyes—how they danced, how they sparkled. And the smile. It was a scene from some familiar movie I couldn't quite pin down, the dramatic lighting, the play of color, the solitary figure in the high-backed chair—not Miss Havisham, certainly, but there *were* echoes of something, very English chintz, very country manor. A scene without artifice or trickery, yet the candlelight tossed its amber coinage everywhere, onto the Italian marble mantel, the fruitwood boiserie, the panels of billiard-table-green damask upholstering the walls, the different tasseled velvets and brocades on the chairs beside the bookshelves—many many books of all kinds. A little world. She called the room "the Snuggery," said it was her favorite spot in the whole house, the place she had sat with her lover-husband for so much of her married life. And here she sat now, in cherry red, while the outside world was plunged by wind and rain into turbulent darkness, and made small talk with her boarder.

Easing into matters, she spoke about the weather—all the rain, her winter garden just into glorious bloom and now more rain. Whole trees were going down outside, she was afraid of damage; one year, half the hill had washed away, cost a fortune to shore it up. The house was half a century old, the electrical wiring was bad and needed redoing, but she didn't enjoy the thought of coming to grips with things like that at her age. She laughed—oh, that laugh, I knew it so well, bright and bubbly and full of high good spirits: Maude's laugh. I recalled how someone— was it Louella?—had dubbed her the "Champagne Lady"; the name had stuck.

I had a lot of questions I wanted to ask her, but I refrained. She was amused when I said I'd stayed up late one night brushing up on her. When I said I had her book down at the Cottage, she invited me to bring it up for her signature. I took this as a special favor, since she was famous for not giving autographs.

I felt she was going out of her way to be kind, but on whose behalf? Mine? Frank's, Belinda's? Or maybe Vi's. We spoke of Viola—they were longstanding friends, going all the way back to the old AyanBee days. Those were the days I longed to hear about, and soon I had her reminiscing about "Cowflop City," which was what the old-timers called the lot, which when it began had been located in the middle of a pasture.

When I noted that both Babe Austrian and Claire Regrett had also had their starts there, she paused and her glance shifted. Had I made a faux pas? I waited through the pause; then she laughed, saying that if their three ages were totaled they'd go back beyond the Battle of Bunker Hill. "Remember, I saw McKinley shot." Golly; how many people did I know who'd seen McKinley shot? When I mentioned how much I liked the films Babe had made with Crispin, she accepted the compliment gracefully but wasn't inclined to comment. The same thing with Claire. She wasn't rude, she just didn't seem interested.

"And, tell me, do you like the movies?" she asked.

"Oh yes!" I exclaimed. "I've loved movies all my life—there's nothing like the movies, nothing in the world."

"Well, nobody could ever call you a cynic, could they? I'm glad when people get excited about something—even the movies. Maybe you'll take me some night; pick out something fun and we'll go."

A date with Maude Antrim? How much could a fellow take? It wasn't so very long before the moment came when I presumed to spring on her the lines I'd rehearsed. I straightened in my seat and said, "You wouldn't remember, I know, but we *have* met before."

She didn't bat an eye. "I remember. It was Christmas of fifty-five or -six—at the post office, just before closing, you were driving a gray Ford convertible, you pulled into the parking lot and I had trouble backing out —wasn't that it?" I stared, speechless with admiration. "You were very gallant," she pursued. "You said 'Merry Christmas, Miss Antrim,' and waved me off. I've kept up with you, you know. Frank has few secrets from me; I'm always interested in his clients."

I sat mired in astonishment; this was nearly twenty years after the fact. *I* could remember, sure, but *she?* She smiled at me as if such computerized memory were nothing remarkable.

Soon she began asking the kind of questions that seemed to indicate genuine interest in me, and as we talked she grew and enlarged in my favor. By now I'd had two cups of tea and had stayed nearly an hour; it was time to drag myself away. "Oh, please don't go," she said quickly as I set down my cup and stood up, "I hate sending you out into this mess. Why not stay a bit and we'll have a little tuck right here by the fire—get acquainted. Ling will broil us a steak, a few steamed vegetables—we can just put the potatoes in the coals. Please say you'll stay, won't you?"

I would. I did. And a joyful thing that was, one of the unforgettable evenings of my life. I'd come at six, I stayed well past ten. While the Asp slipped in and out with trays of dinner, quiet as a snake, we talked and talked, shoes, ships, sealing wax, cabbages, even kings. I had to keep pressing her to talk about herself; she couldn't imagine anyone's being interested in someone her age. "I'm just a used-to-be, Mis-*tah* Caine." She was equally reluctant to discuss her films, but was flattered I'd seen so many of them, all the way back to that one with Mr. Cooper.

"Most of the new films are so awful, aren't they? Really, why can't they make better ones? I suppose the wonder is that anyone ever manages to make any good ones at all. It's so difficult. Comes of joint effort, you know, teamwork. You have to have a good creative team, that's all. Now all they care about are *deals.* Well, I did have some darned good pictures. Crispin and I both were lucky that way. Good writers, we had some good writers. It's all the story anyway; *you* know that, I'm sure. This film Blindy's doing—not a terribly good script, I'm afraid. Well, she has a couple of good scenes. Some meat on the bones. And as long as I've brought up her name—Blindy—of course I've done it on purpose, Mis-tah Caine, because I want to thank you for what you did for her." When I started to protest she stopped me with a gesture. Imperious Maude. "No, no, I'm sure you don't want to be thanked—but *I* thank you. Blindy's very valuable to me. She's m'girl, you know. She's hoed a rough row and she's come through with flying colors, thanks to you and others. Wonderful thing, your group—friends of Bill, hm?" Her look became intimate, signifying that what we were speaking of was just between us. "And what Frank's done for her!" she added. "I swear to goodness, he's made another woman out of her. You wait till she gets here, you'll see what I mean."

"Have you spoken with her lately?" I asked.

That laugh. It pealed out and rang bells. "You wouldn't be here if I hadn't," she said. "I don't rent to just anybody, you know. It was Belinda who gave you the imprimatur."

"I'm flattered you let me come."

She waved a feathery hand, created a moment out of thin air. "No need, no need. Enjoy—enjoy!"

"Frank tells me she's in good shape these days."

"Fortunately, she *is* in good shape, after a very bumpy road, thank you. Gallant, she is. Crispin used to say a gallant horse, a gallant woman, and a halfway decent port were the stuff of life. I'd die if anything happened to Belinda. 'Nuff said on that score."

When I asked when Belinda would be arriving, I got a shrug. "You know Blindy, she'll come when she comes. One morning she'll pop up, who knows when. She has Faun with her these days. I'm sure you know about Faun."

The way in which she said "Faun" spoke loud and clear. Viola had told me one day that Belinda was experiencing her usual troubles with her daughter, who was now twenty-four years old. Old enough to know better, I thought. At any rate, I didn't pursue the topic.

Maude went on, deftly maneuvering the conversation away from herself, talking about my books—clearly she had read them with care, and I was ridiculously flattered, but who wouldn't be? And, inevitably, Frank's name came up again. She spoke of him at length, and fondly; she'd known him for so long.

"Do you know," she said emphatically as she sliced into her steak, "I met Frank Adonis the very night he arrived in Hollywood, the very first night? There was a large party—perhaps it was at the Goldwyns'— my mind isn't the trap it once was for the distant past—and Frank came in with the Colmans and some other people. Wasn't he good-looking, though! How debonair! I thought he was a gangster, black hair all slicked back and the best-cut dinner jacket you ever saw. The women positively swooned on the rug. We saw lots of Frank after that, I liked him so much."

"Did your husband? Like him, too?"

"Crispin?" She debated. "Why-y, yes, I believe he did. Cris came from a different background, you see—but I know he admired Frank for the way he'd pulled himself up by his bootstraps."

I supposed Crispin Antrim must have been a bit of a snob, and this was mere *noblesse oblige;* still, it made me like him more. And I particularly liked listening to the way Maude perceived Frank, her rich appreciation of his character in its various facets, the little wop out of Hell's Kitchen making it big in the Big Time. She loved the whole movie-style story— "Very George Rafty." And I especially liked the way she called him "Frank" instead of "Frankie." It seemed to confer extra status, as if she had a fuller, deeper purchase on him than others did.

When Ling had cleared our trays away, he returned with the coffee things.

"Do you think they're good for each other?" Maude asked me rather pointedly, handing me my cup. "Belinda and Frank, I mean?"

"Maybe not back then," I suggested. "But they do seem to be now."

Maude nodded firmly. "I agree. He's her lodestar, I think. And I don't mean that in the purely romantic sense, though there is that, too, let's face it. But he's been her mentor for a long time. He's helped her over many a bump, *many* a bump."

I tried not to watch the hands of the clock on the mantel move, the pendulum ticking away the minutes that had become so important to me. Looking back on that evening, I still find it such an extraordinary experience, for how often do the Maude Antrims of the world invite you to supper? On the other hand, there was something quite commonplace about it, almost as if we'd done it before, many times. And though there was no wine on the table, still it seemed as if we'd both been imbibing, and more than once I noticed the way the little room rang with our laughter. "Snuggery," snug, safe.

I'd realized how at the mere mention of Crispin's name she beamed, and I could tell that she enjoyed talking about him. I knew that Crispin had been dead for over twenty years—yet her lips had only to pronounce that magical name and they took on a tone, soft, affectionate, fondly caressing. I decided this was a one-man woman, a woman who'd never had another lover since she'd married him. She pointed out that the chair in which I was sitting was the chair he'd always sat in, because it faced the portrait of herself on the wall—while her chair faced his matching portrait on the opposite wall.

And as she went on speaking, the very walls of the room where we now sat grew more precious to me, for she was peopling it with the famous of another time. I eased farther back in my place, and across from me sat Valentino—Rudy, if you please. And there was Vilma Banky in the doorway in chiffon and gaudy bracelets; Rod Laroque, sleekly Latin, was at her side. Cecil De Mille sat just opposite us, knees crossed, tapping his leg with his riding crop as he told an anecdote about Maude as Dido in *The Walls of Carthage.* Crispin, he was there, too, standing just to the left of the refectory table, his adoring eyes fastened upon the figure of his wife, who threw back her head and laughed. Which was lovelier, I asked myself, the laugh or the line of the slender white throat that made it?

"Listen," said she, "I believe it's stopped raining." I got up and looked out: so it had. I took it as my cue to leave.

"Well, I shan't keep you longer," she said, getting up with me, "I'm sure you've many things to do." She moved close but didn't touch me. "How I've enjoyed this evening. I hope next time we won't be so formal. Let me call you Charles—Charlie?—and you must call me Maude."

Reluctantly I tore myself from her snug and cozy room and the magical thing it had come so quickly to represent. She led me through to the studio where she painted, slid open the big glass door, gave me the power lamp, and let me out into the wet air. It was chilly, but the magic lingered like expensive perfume. We said our final farewells; she invited me to come again, insisting I come up and swim in the pool as often as I liked, it was good for my back. "I've had the pool heater turned on. It will soon be swimmable. Any time, truly, don't be a stranger and don't be shy. I won't bother you down there because you're working. If you need anything, just ring, the number's on the kitchen jamb."

As I started away, she put her hand on my arm, the lightest touch. "If you can take time off for a bite of lunch tomorrow, come up around one. I'll have Ling put a nice salad into you. Goodness, just look—the moon. Very dramatic. Very Alfred Noyes."

She struck a theatrical pose and recited:

> *"The wind was a torrent of darkness among the gusty trees,*
> *The moon was a ghostly galleon tossed upon cloudy seas,*
> *The road was a ribbon of moonlight over the purple moor,*
> *And the highwayman came riding—*
> *Riding—riding—*
> *The highwayman came riding, up to the old inn-door. . . ."*

I applauded, enchanted. "I'll bet no one's heard you do that in a long time."

She pressed my hands with hers. "Now, off you go. Into the night. Write well. Sleep well."

She waved and was gone, into the house, where Ling waited, holding the candle to light his mistress's way to her room. Had it really happened? In the gusting wind, the tears of dripping rain, I doubted my senses. But rain was never wet in dreams, was it?

Thus I entered into a new and extravagantly pleasant phase in my existence, one that was to center around this delightful person called Maude and bind me to her for the rest of her life, and mine, too, for even after her death I have kept the memory of her warm and alive. In a matter of days I found myself completely under her winding spell; our relationship was the least complicated I'd ever had with a member of the opposite sex, and one of the most rewarding. I had struck pay dirt, and I mined and mined.

Some things in life become merely habit, boring and unappreciated through constant repetition; not so with me, not at Sunnyside. I'd been given carte blanche—to come and go as I chose, to use the tennis courts, to play the piano, to swim. The more I saw of her, the more certain I became that this was one of the most appealing women who'd ever walked the earth's face.

Daily she took her exercise in her heated pool, which was positively sybaritic to swim in, and afterward she'd walk around the perimeter a dozen times or so. Her idea of heaven was putting some Mozart on the stereo and floating in the water on an air mattress, eyes closed, listening and dreaming. I knew she wasn't asleep, but she'd "let go." A secret she'd learned years ago, it was part of what kept her so young, "letting go." She had two hobbies, gardening and painting, the latter of which she'd taken up after Crispin's death. Her work showed the same winning grace the artist herself exhibited, and since I, too, occasionally dabbled, she was quick to invite me to set up an easel in the studio she'd converted from Crispin's former billiard room, where we could go at it together, side by side, over a bunch of flowers or a bowl of fruit.

As for life in general and the considerable age she'd attained, she maintained a philosophical attitude toward both. "The future is folly, my dear," she said once. "The past is a dead cat. Only in the present do I live. I'm ready, I've been ready since Cris died. Any time they want me they can come and take me. They know where to find me."

Having been raised in the New England work ethic, I was disciplined when it came to turning out my daily quota of pages; but when it came to sharing Maude's company I gladly shirked. "I'm keeping you from your machine," she'd say, and I'd promise her she wasn't and we'd do a couple more laps. The rain had departed and the sun shone in all its golden

warmth—very warm for February. Sometimes we'd have a game of croquet on the side court, and she told me how Crispin used to keep a full
pitcher of martinis at each post, and whenever you hit the post you were
permitted to refill your glass.

Her tales of Sunnyside in the old days were tales of glory, of enter-
tainments and escapades in which the famous of the world paraded themselves past my eyes. It seemed as if the history of Hollywood itself had
been written on the stones of that old house.

"Aren't you afraid I may write about all this—tell all your secrets?"
I asked her. I saw her pale for a second, as if she really thought I might.
I assured her that I was joking and promised that I never would—without
her approval, of course. When I told her that her secrets were safe with
me, she held my look a moment longer—as if to be sure of me?—making
me wonder if she did indeed have things to hide. But how was this
possible, when her life had always been an open book?

To my questions about Belinda's return to Sunnyside she still
shrugged, saying that her daughter-in-law's movements were in God's
hands, not hers. Sometimes I'd come up in the late afternoon to find her
at her Steinway in the large living room that fronted the house. I'd slip
in quietly and sit listening while she played some Chopin, some Schubert
—some Gershwin. Believe it or not, George Gershwin had sat on that
same piano bench and played his own songs; back in the early thirties,
before he suffered the stroke that killed him. And one night when the
Mountbattens came to dine Claire Regrett had stood in the bow of the
piano and sung "Depuis le Jour" from *Louise*.

"How did she sound?" I asked.

"A *lit*-tle thin," Maude recalled. "I believe she accomplished it by
rubbing her legs together."

I was to learn that Maude's wit was often sharply and verily to the
point. She wasn't being mean about Claire, she simply saw her as she was
—as everyone who knew her saw her, myself included.

When I expressed interest in the Playhouse, she asked Suzi-Q to open
up the place and gave me a tour.

This, the famous Playhouse, had been the boyhood home of Perry
Antrim, and for Maude it was a house of memories, the oft-photographed
Christie murals turning the rooms into a child's fantasy. As Maude took
me around, pointing out various mementoes and keepsakes of Perry's, I
perceived it wasn't just a house of memories, but also a memorial to her
dead son, as if throughout these fairy-tale rooms his memory burned the
brightest. The horned and hairy bison heads still hung along the carved
beams; there was Perry's pool table and ivory cue, rows of his books, his

trophies and many photographs taken on his travels. In the second-floor bedroom stood a tall stove of shiny blue porcelain, brought by Crispin from Sweden.

Just now these cozy sleeping quarters with their mullioned windows and vividly carved and painted beams, the romantically swagged bed that had been Claire's and Perry's honeymoon bed, showed signs of having been recently lived in: there were makeup things spread out on a dressing table, a pink hair dryer, a set of brightly painted false fingernails in a dish, and on hangers in the closet some female clothes, plus a lynx fur coat. These items, I learned, belonged to Faun Potter, Belinda's errant daughter who on those occasions when she was around enjoyed occupying her father's boyhood room.

Amid these charming, nostalgic surroundings Perry Antrim had lived—on his own: Crispin's edict so the boy would learn independence. Maude hadn't liked the idea, and it was obvious that while he'd lived, she'd thought the sun rose and set on her Perry. She never dreamed that when he went out into the big bad world to seek a mate and bring home the bacon, the bacon he brought home would be Cora Sue Brodsky of Brooklyn, and—*oh*, the lengths she'd gone to to snag him.

Maude was in no way vindictive, but after fifty years she knew her man—or in this case, woman. She had never been deluded about her daughter-in-law, with whom she'd never been able to make friends, and all of whose tricks she was on to. Everyone knew Claire was a climber, from Sam Ueberroth to Frank to God knew who else. When she'd met Perry at a dance in Santa Monica, she'd got the message quick enough: to be "Claire Antrim" could hardly hurt her career.

The union of the heir to the name of Antrim and the rising Hollywood star had filled newspapers and magazines for months, and theirs had been an all-too-public affair. It was Crispin's notion that he wanted them to be as happy in their early married life as he and his Maude had been in theirs, and no one was more surprised than he when his idea backfired. The young couple had lived their life, so to speak, in a golden fishbowl. When they returned from a Polynesian wedding trip, they took up their married life in the Playhouse, ogled by everyone who came and went. Not that it was ever boring, for Claire soon found herself in fairly breezy company: Aldous Huxley came to Sunnyside and dined on broiled kidneys, and so did the Prince of Wales, just an omelet, thanks, and Leopold of the Belgians ate Belgian endive, and Marie Queen of the Romanians ate romaine, and the niece of the Russian prince Youssoupoff, who'd shot and poisoned the mad monk Rasputin and then helped to drown him in the Neva; Maude couldn't recall what the niece ate.

The fan magazines had had a field day. Louella never stopped bab-
bling about lovebirds all a-twitter in the locust trees and how Maude was
revealing to her new daughter-in-law all her baking secrets. (Maude may
have had secrets, but they had nothing to do with muffins or apple turn-
overs.) Maude had been against the whole cheek-by-jowl concept of
neighboring domiciles from the beginning; she judged it the mistake of
her life to have sided with her husband in the matter, but since it kept
Perry near, she'd given in. No, life at Sunnyside was not all bliss in those
days. Claire never managed to take hold as either a homemaker or a loving
wife, since Perry was always off gallivanting, and by the second year
people were already saying the marriage was doomed. No one ever says
a marriage is doomed and it's not, and this one, like the buffalo nickel and
a good ten-cent cigar, was doomed indeed. Claire was soon gone from
Sunnyside—gone, but not forgotten.

One morning I'd been hard at work since seven when just before noon
the phone rang.

"Good morning," came that inimitable voice, "do I disturb you?"

"Not a bit. I was about to take a break and come up, as a matter of
fact."

"For lunch, I hope. And do hurry. There's someone here dying to
see you. Two someones, in fact."

She wouldn't say who and wouldn't stay on the line. I went as I was:
shorts, T-shirt, and moccasins. As I came onto the pool esplanade I saw
two women seated under the umbrella having tea. One of them jumped
up shouting "Chazzz!" in a well-whiskied baritone, then came clacking
and teetering toward me on plastic spring-o-laters, dangling ten red nails
at me.

It was Angie, and with her, for Pete's sake—Belinda, looking as
fetching as ever! When I kissed her cheek, I heard Maude's laughter
behind me. "Leave him alone, girls, I found him, he's all mine now."

"Wait a sec—*I* saw him first," said Angie with her old-time bounci-
ness. "Anyway, you've had your turn, now it's mine."

There was a lot of good-natured joking, Maude obviously delighted
to have the two younger women there. Belinda had arrived with the best
news possible: Frank had telephoned night before last, saying the part in
The Light in the Window was hers at last; shooting would start early in the
summer. I congratulated her—it was a plum role. While she glowed at the
thought of doing it, I could see that the idea of facing the cameras again
in something this important was also frightening to her. Angie had picked

up on this and we kidded her along, telling her how great it was going to be and how it would really transform her career.

Maude listened to all this with quiet approval and I could see the pride she felt, for Belinda was not just a former daughter-in-law to her but a real daughter whom she wanted to love and protect. Then, with her usual tact, she turned to Angie, suggesting that they go inside. "Come along, darling, you said you wanted to see my new paintings. Now's your chance." And they disappeared into the glass-doored studio.

I moved closer to Belinda and gave her the once-over. "It seems that desert life agrees with you, lady. You look—wonderful."

And that was truth to tell. If Angie had gone a little to late-August meadow, not so Belinda. She was still a missionary's downfall, cool, tanned, soft-crisp, clear as a Maine lake, head back, laughing like a school-girl. A woman like Belinda wears well; crow's feet, sure, a pale network of wrinkles, her face was a definite map of well-traveled roads. But she was all there, all put together, everything in the right place. How did she do it, I asked myself; what had kept this woman whole, where did she get her glow? I was so glad to see her, glad to see how well she was taking care of herself these days. Only people who had something to live for did that. And of course I recognized Frank's hand in it all—and Angie's.

"Long time no see, Chazz," she said, smiling as she returned my kiss. I kissed her again, harder; after all, there were certain vested interests here, weren't there? Hadn't we shared bed-and-board in some earlier life?

Bloodied but unbowed, that was Blindy. "She's won," I thought. But of course she'd have had to, being a winner all the way. That she was— Echo Park's gift to the movies and all of manhood, the girl who used to sing for nickels outside the Four-Square Gospel Temple, rattling a tam-bourine like Little Nellie Kelly. "What a glorious sight—my God, my eyes are really sore."

"I'll bet you tell that to all the girls." She leaned forward and touched my hand. "You don't look so bad yourself. And, Charlie, you have no idea how I've longed to see you. And how nice to have you here as Maude's star boarder."

I thanked her for her help in arranging things, then brought her up to date on Jenny's activities. Belinda made sympathetic comments about my state of marital disarray, and when I vouchsafed doubts as to whether Jen and I would ever get back together again, she grew thoughtful. I knew she was thinking about the debris of her own marriages: one, Dick, the air-force pilot; two, Perry Antrim; three, Grant Potter. Would there be a fourth? And if so, would it be Frank Adonis?

"How's the golf game?" I asked, deliberately deflecting my thought.

"Super. Never played better. How do you like the new model?" She got up and exhibited her hard-won figure.

I nodded. Indeed, I could see how all things were working to lift her out of the morass into which she'd once sunk. Ruefully I recalled the wreck of a woman whom I'd accidentally stumbled on one rainy night in Murray Hill, singing "Big Wide Wonderful World" in a neighborhood bar, and how affected I'd been by that bedraggled sight. And now, thirteen years later . . . what a change.

We fell into easy conversation, centering, naturally enough, on Angie, Maude, Frank, and, of course, the Program. Alcoholics Anonymous was a special link between us, we were still both "friends of Bill."

Later, Belinda went to help Maude with lunch—Ling had taken the Rolls in for servicing—leaving me and Angie to do some catching up on our own.

"Belinda tells me you two've been having some time of it," I said. "She really looks terrific, doesn't she?"

Angie was all enthusiasm. "I just love that gal, she's such a peach. We had the best time at Scottsdale." The voice was the husky one I'd known from the old days. "And, Chazz, how about her and Frank? Did you ever think it would happen?"

I pondered that. Had I ever? Yes, I supposed I had, maybe—sometime. "Do I smell orange blossoms?" I inquired.

"Gosh, I don't know, nothing's been mentioned. You know me, I never like to pry. And anyway . . ."

"Yes?"

"Well, there's Faun to consider. Now that she's come back."

"Oh? Is Faun—'back'? To stay?"

Angie shrugged. "Who knows? She's mercurial. To say the least."

"I guessed as much."

Angie ran her lacquered nails through her hair and shook her head; then she sighed. "Oh God, Chazz, if you only knew. If the world only knew."

"The world does, doesn't it? Know a lot, I mean."

"I guess so, but that's not Belinda's fault. They're always snooping around her personal life. They've had it in for her for so long. And don't forget, little Faunie was always good at making the headlines on her own."

"No," I said, truthfully. "I haven't forgotten." Arson, stabbing, other felonies; no, I hadn't forgotten.

Faun Antrim was scarcely the ideal offspring. For longer than I seemed to recall, she'd been Belinda's *bête noire*, upsetting the applecart at every turn, and I could only wonder if she was planning to go on making trouble forever. I couldn't say that until recently Belinda had been the best of mothers, but now, from all reports, she was really trying. Having got her own self straightened out, she was struggling to help Faun. The trouble was, so far as I could make things out, that it was simply too late.

Not that it would have been an easy matter to pinpoint when and where Belinda had gone wrong with her daughter. Faun had been a model child through her eighth year, at which point something seemed to have snapped and her behavior changed so drastically that people found it hard believing she was the same girl. She became highly emotional, demanded her own way, was impossible to handle. Measures had been taken. First she was placed in the hands of a highly recommended doctor of psychiatry who initially declared himself pleased with the progress the child was making, then after eighteen months gave up in disgust. Next came an expensive private school specializing in boilerplate cases, where Faun created so many disturbances that the mistress of the place "reluctantly" let her go. After that, a series of private tutors and instructors was hired, each in turn coming to the house to tutor the girl in school subjects as well as sports and deportment. One of these instructors had been that hapless Bucky Eaton on whom Faun developed a serious crush, and when he repelled her advances, she took steps to punish him, burning the stables down, stabbing him, and falsely accusing him of rape.

Desperate, Belinda next sent the girl to stay with friends in Surrey, where she could indulge her lively passion for horses, and when this move turned out badly she was shipped off to Switzerland, to the most fashionable girls' school in Lausanne. Things, however, had *not* worked out on the shores of Lake Geneva.

I was about to ask Angie another question when her scarlet-lacquered nails flew to her mouth in surprise. Turning, I saw standing in the doorway a figure slightly reminding me of the young Lana Turner making her entrance in *The Postman Always Rings Twice*, a young woman who gave the impression of a blank near-prettiness, filling out a white halter and shorts, a towel wound around her head turban fashion and wearing plastic mules with spike heels. Her physical endowments were generously displayed, and the whole effect of sexiness was underscored by a healthy tan that had obviously required a good deal of time and effort to acquire. The eyes were hidden by dark glasses, so I had only the mouth to go by. Pretty, luscious, but mean, I thought. Strictly forbidden fruit.

"There you are, Faun," Angie said smoothly, "we were just wondering where you'd got to. Will you come and meet our friend?" She gave my name and I partly rose in my chair.

"Hello there, nice to see you," I said noncommittally.

I still couldn't see her eyes, but she nodded as she slouched across the tiling to throw herself into a convenient chair. "Hello," she returned with a pout. "I guess you heard all about me from God's gift to the cowboys here. Talk about a round-up—you should have seen this one in Phoenix." She stuck her tongue out at Angie—not the best impression she could have made—then reached across me to snag one of Angie's cigarettes, using her lighter to light it. Blowing out an exaggerated stream of smoke through the curled tube of her pink tongue, she gave me what might possibly pass for a smile and said: "How did we manage to get you into the menagerie? Are you the new zookeeper?"

I explained that I was the tenant of the Cottage. "Another one," she said, and blew some more smoke. "Watch out, they'll have you washing windows before you're done." She raised her glasses and directed Angie a mocking look. "He looks about your speed, Angie dear; I suppose you'll be shacking up down there like you did with the Olympic team that year."

"What a sweet thing to say," Angie replied. "You must have taken your nice pills this morning." She gave Faun's cheek a pinch, only to have her hand slapped away angrily. Faun flicked her cigarette away across the lawn and gave me another lemony slice of smile.

"I hear your wife left you for another man," she said. "Too bad. Though, did you ever stop to think maybe you unloaded her at the right time? Exactly what do you do, anyway?" She might as well have asked, "How much money do you make?" Another cloud of smoke. Angie delivered me a silent plea.

"I'm a writer," I said.

"Jeez, another one—what kind?"

"Well, several kinds," I returned, trying to keep it light.

Angie dipped her oar again. "Charlie writes movies and plays and novels—all kinds of things. Who knows, he may just put you in a book, kitten."

"Kitten," I suspected, had long sharp claws and loved to drag them across the silk upholstery. I watched as she ran her tongue along her lips, top and bottom, then formed her mouth into a little O.

"If he writes movies, why doesn't he write one for Mummy? God knows she could use a job."

"Your mother *has* a job, she doesn't need me."

Just then Belinda came out between the sliding glass studio doors. She had changed her clothes and was wearing a short tommy coat with a bathing suit underneath. "There you are, Faun. Have you two met?

Good. Chazz, be an angel—Ling's not back yet, and Maude could use a strong arm to carry out the lunch tray."

I was up and moving in an instant and I heard Faun mutter something about me as she went off toward the studio. "What a nerd," is what she said.

That was a new one on me. When I returned with the tray, the four of us gathered around the umbrella table to eat the giant salad that Ling had left for us. We didn't miss Faun at lunch—it was far easier to talk without her there.

Presently Faun reappeared in the far doorway of the studio. She'd put on a bright pink bikini that must have been dipped in Day-Glo. Aware that we were watching, she tripped over to the diving board, gave a little spring, and neatly executed a swan-dive. When I admired her form, Belinda seemed pleased.

"She's always been good in the water—takes after her grandmother." She patted Maude's hand affectionately. "I even hoped for a minute she might do something with it, but—" She stopped and dealt with her salad. As the talk rolled on, I kept mum, letting the women carry the ball. Maude demanded a full rundown on the golf tournament—she herself had played the game until her last siege of back trouble. Then, when the subject of golf was exhausted, she asked Belinda, "What news of Frank? Did he get to Scottsdale?"

Belinda nodded, and Angie chimed in. "Of *course* he did—he won't leave the girl's side these days. Frankie's in love—I mean he's *in love!*"

She glanced over at Faun, who in the interim had performed several more dives—for our benefit, I thought. As she surfaced after yet another one, I caught the expression on her face and got the impression that she didn't care much for our friend Frank. After a while she got up and dragged the blue plastic float to the far corner of the pool. I'll say one thing, it was a gorgeous figure, everything inherited from her mother. Lying supine on the inflated mattress, one knee bent, she resembled one of those suntan-lotion ads, like a giant billboard plastered up above Sunset Boulevard. It was in the genes, all right; plus the athleticism Perry had been famous for. Still, I had the feeling she was completely conscious of her effect, was in fact striving to achieve it. She'd move her arm or straighten the one leg and change the angle of the other, or do something with her hair, sometimes hum along as her little plastic radio played.

When lunch was done Maude disappeared for her customary nap and I said I should be getting back to work. Angie offered to see me home, and as we walked down the steps to the Cottage, we continued where we'd left off talking about Belinda.

"What's going to happen now?" I asked, stopping to undo the gate that helped keep Bones out of mischief.

Angie shrugged. "I don't honestly know. But I'm worried, Charlie."

I asked her in and we sat in the window seat, talking. Angie's fears were solid ones. Apparently Frank was right—Belinda was terrified of starting on the picture and had even been talking about wanting out. "But she mustn't, she's got to do it," Angie said. "Not for the money, she's okay financially, but for her self-esteem. If she backs out—I'm afraid."

"Afraid of what?"

She pantomimed chug-a-lugging a drink. I understood. It had already struck me that, fine job though Belinda had done, there was always the chance that something would hit her hard and she'd quick grab a drink or two, and that would be the beginning of the long slide—wouldn't be the first time, either. A.A. history was full of such hairy tales.

"And there's more, Charlie," Angie went on, slipping a pillow behind her back. "She's writing this goddamn book."

"Belinda's writing a book?"

"*Faun* is. I don't know what it's called, but it's all about Belinda—what a rotten mother she was, her drinking bouts, her boyfriends and love affairs. The usual tripe served up again. 'How I became Hollywood's Star Brat,' that sort of thing."

I nodded. Naturally there'd be a chapter on the Summer of the Purple Grape, when Belinda was carrying on with the "flamingo dancer." And one about the dude in Harlem that took the razor to her, the story that had made *Confidential* magazine. And a lot of stuff about her and Frank. Just a royal paint job, smut and smear.

"Has she a publisher?"

Angie lit another cigarette and blew a stream of smoke through the open window. "I don't suppose she does. But even if she doesn't, she wouldn't have too much trouble getting one, would she? I mean, these days they'll publish anything that's juicy, won't they? I don't think it's just talk, Chazz. And I hate to see Blindy go through any more, honest I do." She also touched on what such a book might do to Maude's state of mind, especially if it dragged in the subject of Perry's marriages to Claire and Belinda. "I was wondering," Angie went on, "if you couldn't talk to her, steer her onto something else; then maybe she'd forget about the book." She was clearly worried.

"Have you mentioned this to Frank?"

She nodded. "He doesn't think she'll ever go through with it. Says she's rattling sabers. But I've got news. This young woman's got a memory like an elephant and she'd do the whole town in if she could. Charlie —you don't know what she's really like."

I said I'd think about it, but I honestly didn't know what I could do.

Over the past five or so years it seemed that Faun Antrim had experienced an alarming number of emotional reversals, which her mother and grandmother had been forced to deal with. Faun had been financially well off by most standards; her father's will had provided her with a substantial sum of money, to be held in trust and released to her in part when she was eighteen, the balance when she turned twenty-one. To everyone's shock, the first amount she'd turned over in its entirety to the Maharishi, not an uncommon practice among his devotees. It wasn't long, however, before she had had a falling out with the entire cult, after which she'd shaken them and gone to live in a commune at Telluride.

It was there that her child with Dane Potter had been lost, another devastating blow to the entire family. Faun had had her boy with her in a van at a drive-in movie, where she and her male companion had gone one evening. They'd left Dane untended while they went to the refreshment stand, and during the space of those few minutes someone had made off with the child. There were witnesses who stated that the abductor had been a black woman; in any case the boy was never seen again.

In the end, it seemed to friends that it was Belinda who suffered more from the loss than the actual mother, who more or less brushed the matter aside, refusing to talk about it and destroying all pictures of the baby.

Shortly after that period she'd come home, tail between her legs, and proceeded to go through the rest of her money as well as two or three shrinks over on Bedford Drive. Having given up the search for divine wisdom, on a more worldly tack she'd next decided to go to New York in search of work as an actress. Considering her notable theatrical background, you might think she'd have found some success, but nothing much materialized except when a couple of unscrupulous producers attempted to capitalize on the name. Her reviews were not encouraging, one critic writing that he found her vapid, while another said her stage personality was sharp and abrasive. Claire Regrett had been photographed attending a performance of *The Petrified Forest* in which Faun was playing Gaby, and was quoted as saying she was a chip off the old block; but which block or which chip she didn't explain.

After her New York "phase," Faun headed for London, where she camped so extensively with the parents of a schoolfriend that she was asked to leave. After further ups and downs she'd wired for money, which Belinda sent, and she'd come home to take up residence again in the Playhouse. In an attempt to establish a better relationship with her daughter, Belinda had been keeping her close by—in Palm Springs, in Acapulco, in Phoenix—hoping she'd get interested in some attractive young man but so far the score was strictly nothing to nothing.

Angie and I were still gassing when we heard the sound of a motor, which I recognized as Maude's little golf cart; I went to investigate, Angie behind me. It wasn't Maude, however, but the subject of our conversation, the Princess Faun herself, who came tootling up to my door, switched off the ignition, and stuck tanned legs out in an attractive pose.

"Mummy's looking for you," she told Angie. "I think she needs you to help her with her hair."

"Her hair?" Angie gave me a suspicious glance. "What's wrong with her hair?"

"How should I know? Probably the roots need a touch-up. Don't they always? I'm just playing messenger."

"I'd better run up and see," Angie said to me. She bent to kiss my cheek and whisper in my ear, "Don't forget—see what you can do."

"Angie dear, you don't have to go whispering about me behind your hand, you know," Faun said sarcastically.

"Does your grandmother know you're using her cart?" I inquired, after Angie had started the climb up to the house.

"She lets me drive it. She doesn't care."

"As long as you're going back, why didn't you offer Angie a ride?"

"Because I'm not going—not just yet, that is," she said suggestively as she walked toward me. "I thought you might ask me in for a drink. And don't say you haven't got anything. I brought this." She held up a bottle of champagne—Dom Pérignon, if you please. "Ice cold, too. Aren't you going to invite me in?"

I was about to send her packing; then I thought, What the hell. "Sure, why not? But, I'm afraid you'll be drinking alone. I don't indulge."

"That's all right, it won't be the first time." She obviously thought that was a good one. I found it odd: here was a young woman of twenty-four, divorced and a mother, to all intents and purposes a grownup, yet I kept getting the impression of a much younger person, almost a teen-ager. It was in her baby voice, the way she used her face and body, her pouty expression, as if she were somehow afraid of becoming mature.

"So this is where the great writer lives and works," she said, brushing by me into the Cottage and looking around.

"This is it, kid."

Her look was sharp. "Don't call me 'kid.' "

I apologized and went to find a glass. "We're not really equipped for champagne around here," I said, going into the kitchen. When I came back again I found her poking around my bedroom. "Just what is it that you're looking for?"

"I'm looking around for all the girls you've probably got hidden away here."

"Look away, you won't find them. I'm getting cured of a separation." She picked up on this. "Are you heartbroken? I heard she treated you shitty."

"Where'd you hear that?"

"Mummy. You certainly have her sympathy, don't you? Of course, she cries at card tricks. You have to carry a sponge."

"You know—you ought to speak more generously about your mother."

"Oh, God, are you going to tell me she's this absolutely fabulous creature, a goddess? Well, you're wrong—she's just another old movie broad. No one cares about her anymore—if they ever did. She's a has-been, that's all."

"They did, believe me," I said softly. "People loved her. Still love her. And I don't see how you can say someone's a has-been when she's about to take on a plum film role."

"Oh. That. Don't you know she only got that picture because Frankie has something on one of the producers? They wouldn't have touched her otherwise. It's simple: Frankie gets her work, so she puts out for him. She goes wild for that big thing of his."

"You seem to know a lot about Frankie."

"Oh . . ."—she shot me a little sidewise glance of naked prurience— "I know lots of things. You pick them up, specially around here. My mother may be old, but she's still no better than she should be."

"And you, are you better than you should be?"

"Not unless I absolutely have to be. I'm just what you see. Me. You don't like it, that's your problem, not mine."

"Forget it. Your champagne's getting warm."

"That's all right, I like it that way. But . . . most men would pour it for a lady."

"I might have, were there a lady in the room." Sorry, Belinda, I couldn't resist.

I poured her some more and it foamed over the lip. She dug into her bag and brought out a sparkly little gadget. She slid the handle and it expanded into a little gold metallic brush—"for the bubbles," she explained. Her stepfather had sent it to her for her fourteenth birthday. I asked myself what kind of father sends his daughter a gold swizzle stick on her fourteenth birthday.

"From Tiffany's," she added. "I have breakfast there all the time. Ha ha." She used her pink tongue on the swizzle.

Before today I hadn't spoken a dozen words to this young woman, yet I felt that I knew her, and I realized that to know her wasn't necessarily to love her. Yet I wanted to like her, to make some contact—if only for Belinda's sake, and Maude's. Seeking neutral ground, I volunteered the information that we'd once met.

Her brows quickly arched above the plastic rims of her glasses. "Oh? Clue me in."

I described the occasion a dozen or so years before when Frank and I had seen her with friends at the Beverly Boulevard pony ride. She frowned, then dismissed my recollection with "You must have me mixed up with someone else." I let it go.

After she went putt-putting off in Maude's golf cart I was left thinking about Belinda. The fact that she'd birthed this maverick, this voluptuous creature with a snake's tongue, both interested and troubled me. Certainly they were nothing alike, mother and daughter. Faun was like the squalling changeling whom the wicked fairies had left in the cradle after stealing away the good child. Maybe the parents were to blame; it's a generally acknowledged fact that celebrities don't necessarily make the best mothers and fathers in the world, but you couldn't go through life shoving the blame onto them; you had to take some of the responsibility yourself. Setting fire to the house and stabbing your riding instructor weren't the best ways to get on in the world, particularly if you then falsely accused him of rape. As it happened, Bucky Eaton was a really decent sort; I'd met him once when he was riding at Madison Square Garden and I was doing some research on dressage, and over drinks he told me the real story; he'd never touched her, while she kept coming on with him, wearing tight jodhpurs and turtleneck sweaters that shoved her tits at him every time he came over a jump.

Well, I promised myself that I'd make the attempt, I'd give it the old college try, but really what chance was there? The twig was bent, the tree grown; I thought its fruit would be bitter.

As the days went by, I watched her. Sometimes she'd put on her cutesie act and be pleasant and beguiling—quite effective, except you could tell that she was after something. She was clever enough not to come right out with it, but sooner or later out it would pop—could she borrow a hundred bucks, take your car, would you drive her somewhere, take her to dinner at the beach? It was amazing how she could turn it on and off, the same way she did with the tears. It was her way, probably the only one she knew. God knows she had learned it superbly.

She didn't seem to choose her companions with much care. Her boyfriend these days was a self-styled rock musician named Bobby Spurling, the wastrel son of a Beverly Hills movie producer. A couple of years younger than Faun, scrawny, with a prominent Adam's apple and riotous red hair, Bobby quickly became *persona non grata* at Sunnyside—which, of course, made Faun all the more determined to parade him before us. She ran him, nagged him, told him off, threw him out, but always back again he'd come for more. Maude was stiffly polite, while Belinda made no pretense of hiding her feelings.

It was plain from the moment she came home that where she set her foot, disharmony and discord were sure to follow. One thing seemed clear: since learning of the current closeness between her mother and Frank Adonis, Faun had fostered an intense dislike of Frank. Behind his back she referred to him as "Al Capone" and "Legs Diamond." She called Belinda "Bonnie Parker" or "the gangster's moll," and kidded her unmercifully. "I've got to hang up now," she'd say on the phone to a friend, "Mummy's waiting for a call from her hood," or "We've got Dillinger coming for lunch today," things like that. The family ignored all this, but that didn't deter our Faun.

The rest of us were happy for Frank, happy that he and Belinda were together. After Frances died and he lost April, he had suffered in ways none of us really could understand. He never talked about it, but his close friends could tell that he'd been enduring the torments of hell. The months had become years—one year, two years, three, four, five years—while he traveled that road out to Libertad to the dreary building with the green walls. Five years of devotion to a dream that had become an unending nightmare, or, if it had an end, he was the one who had to write it. And he had. Suddenly, after the Christmas of the fifth year, he simply stopped going. He'd been beating his head against a stone wall, and he cut her out of his heart as she'd cut him out of hers when she was in the Retreat; and amen to that.

Her long suffering may have had its point; *his* was needless, there was nothing to be gained by prolonging things. Ugly as the facts were, they were nonetheless facts: those woebegone buildings weren't about to surrender their prisoner; she'd drawn a life sentence, no time off for good behavior. This, his friends agreed, was the better way. Love her but leave her; goodbye.

Lap dissolve: another two years and here we were at Sunnyside, and the sun was truly shining, that golden California sunshine the Chamber of Commerce raves about; the sweet orange juice was flowing in the streets and the world had turned and everything was nifty once again. I couldn't think of a grander pleasure at that time than to be a witness to this new love affair, to watch this ex–hotshot lover and man about town, pal of Bugsy's, wooer of Babe and Claire and the rest of the broads, shyly holding hands with the ex-tootsie and movie-blonde whose initials were imprinted like dinosaur prints in the cellar cement of my boyhood house.

So Frank came and went, a constant visitor to Sunnyside, and a welcome one—to most of us. But not to all.

Tap tap tap tap-tap-tap-tap.

George Sand is hard at work on her latest "thing," her "magnum opus." *The Life and Times of a Hollywood Brat.* Good title, no? (It's mine; I doubt she'd think of it.) Under the umbrella she sits in her atoll bikini, eyes hidden by shades, plastic bracelets rattling on her wrist, a vodka tonic beside her. *Tap tap tap.* By God, she's really doing it. Every day the pile of pages grows; that thin little stack is getting thicker day by day. *Tap tap tap.*

Our Jane Austen has been laboring at this enterprise for some weeks, really going at it as though her life depended on its getting done. Her little get-rich scheme, and why not? It wouldn't be the first time it's happened. Lillian Roth did it (Lil's the one who started this whole "celebrity confessions" number—*I'll Cry Tomorrow*—but at least she was showing herself naked, not her family). They say it's a way of ridding yourself of your doubts, fears, repressions, and so on. Put it all down on paper where you can see it, where the ink is dark and legible, and you can deal with it. Out goes paranoia, in comes the Greater Peace of Mind, while other folks' reputations fall by the wayside. *Tap tap tap.*

The radio is playing that Glière symphony, I can't remember the name, but it's the one that sometimes sounds like Respighi, sometimes like "The Poem of Ecstasy." Maude's over there in the pavilion, reading a new book. She looks quite comfy in her chaise, face shaded by that old straw hat that's become such a favorite. I'm laboring over a legal-size yellow pad on my lap this morning—not the play; I'm working out a new monthly budget.

No sign of Belinda yet; she must be sleeping late. The white-winged flickers are twittering about the branches of the trees, the gardeners are sweeping, the sun is bright and warm, you couldn't ask for a grander day. All is serene, happy, content, cozy.

Tap tap tap tap tap tap tap tap tap tap. Phew!

From time to time she glances my way; once or twice she lowers her glasses to make eye contact. I know she wants my involvement in this sublime piece of literature, if only for me to tell her she mustn't do it. She's been leaving typed pages lying about invitingly, just asking for little glances, comments, "How's it coming today?" or "Is it all working out?" I never say a word. Naughty girls who pen memoirs of their famous mothers for the public's edification and their parent's sorrow, should be squashed like the nasty bugs they are.

Maude would be the first to agree with this, and I can see how worried she is. Here is something that she has no means of governing, something threatening to those she cares for. Sometimes while the typewriter taps away our looks connect, Maude's and mine, we speak a silent language. Then her look drops to her page.

Now she has laid her head back, thinking. What to do? What to do, what to do, that's what everybody around here is thinking—what to do? I'm fantasizing that maybe an accident could happen, a small fire or a large wind—a "mysterious disappearance." Maybe the trolls could come out of the woods and slip dear Faun away, no one the wiser. Or maybe—ha ha! —she'll decide to go on her own steam. What's a twenty-four-year-old woman doing living at home with Grandma to begin with?

Sometimes I'd catch Maude observing her, absently biting her lip and reflecting, as though over the sad flaws in her granddaughter's character. Wasn't it a mean trick of fate, I thought, that the Antrims had descended to this—this one—all that was left of that great acting tribe? Why couldn't *she* act? Why would the klieg lights no longer light up the sky with that illustrious theatrical name? And why must that name now be dragged through the mud, because of some slip in the genes, the bad seed making mischief through the House of Antrim? These days "Sunnyside" was not so sunny.

Tap-tap.

April was upon us; the last of the rains came and went; the bright sun shone, opening up the world and making a beautiful spring. At Sunnyside everything burst into mad bloom, Maude's gardens were glorious, and there were times I imagined I was back east, after a winter of deep snows, seeing the welcome buds opening in green New England landscapes. May, often deceptively gray and overcast, was this year clear and bright, auguring good things. My divorce was "in work," my work was proceeding, there were no clouds on the horizon—unless we're calling Miss Faun Miss Cloud. And that wouldn't be right; nothing soft or lamb-fleecy about her.

She certainly wasn't lamblike around Frank but, rather, seemed to go out of her way to be bitchy, even insulting. Her disdainful look always seemed to be saying, "What business have you here today?" But Belinda, not her daughter, was the star attraction at Sunnyside whenever Frank turned up. As soon as Faun had glowered her way across to the Playhouse, Belinda's hand would slip into Frank's, they would move closer, share looks, smiles, half words, and only the profoundest entreaty would keep Maude and me from beating a tactful retreat so they could be alone. Useless for them to pretend otherwise, for they'd been bitten and the love poison was spreading in their veins. Those were happy times, sweet times, I thought; and I allowed myself the sin of envy, for I was still feeling the sting of marital failure. I let it get into the columns that I was currently seeing a certain young lady, a new client of Frank's who reminded us both of April Rains. Her name was Lily, but she was young—too young—and our mutual interest faded in the gloaming, leaving me Looking but Not Finding.

But Lily or no, Faun was always interested in my comings and goings. Sometimes when I came home the phone would ring and there she'd be, calling on some silly pretext or other, wanting to know where I'd been, with whom, but it was only feigned interest. She was lonely, I knew, but not good enough company for me to do something about, and while I tried to be agreeable I really didn't try too hard. Besides, she had Bobby Spurling—whom I'd come to think of as Bobby the Goon.

One Saturday morning late in June—I had a lousy cold and my ass was really dragging—I drove down to the drugstore to buy some cold medicine and when I came back and got out out of my car I heard the phone. It was Maude. Belinda was having a bad morning; could I leave work and come up to the house and talk to her?

"I'm truly sorry to interrupt you," Maude said, "but perhaps you won't mind. You said—"

"It's all right, don't worry, the world can wait another day for this piece of Euripides."

Laying a towel over my work to discourage investigation from any stray trolls, I went up to the main house and found Belinda. She'd had yet another row with Faun—over Bobby Spurling, naturally—she'd lost her temper again and told Faun to get him out of her life.

"Hey," I said, "I thought we agreed, no harsh words."

She gave me a helpless look. "I *know* what we *agreed*, only—damn it, Chazz—you don't know what it's like—she gets so wickedly nasty, just plain down-home corn-row mean, I want to hit her, I really do. They were sniffing coke, right here in this studio. What if Maude had walked in? I'd be so ashamed. And—do you know what she said, that little—?"

"No, I don't," I broke in quickly. "Why don't you tell me?"

"She said, 'Well, I guess this will all make another interesting chapter in my little opus.' And, damn it, she means it. Don't you see—it's blackmail, pure and simple. The minute I take exception to anything, she threatens to get me with whatever's in that goddamn book. She's forever holding it over my head. Charlie, I'm getting scared."

"What are you afraid of?" I asked her.

"You *know* what I'm afraid of." She sounded desperate. "I'm afraid she'll get me so riled up that I'll take a drink. Just one—but that'll be all I'll need. That was the hardest thing I ever had to do in my life—I'd never be able to do it again, never! *You* know it's true! I wouldn't . . ."

She began to sob and I took her hands in mine, pressing them hard.

"Look," I began, "in the first place nobody's going to drive you to any drink, certainly not Faun. If you *take* a drink it'll be because you *let* yourself, because you *wanted* to have it. But you're not going to take a drink. No matter *what,* you're just not going to do it, so stop thinking that way. And in the second place you're going to be able to handle this situation. You know it's just threats. You know she's only doing it to get your goat. She's never going to publish that thing, so put it out of your mind, just ignore it, or laugh at it. But whatever you do, *don't let her see you're scared.* Catch?"

"Yeah, catch," she said ruefully, and blew her nose. Then she began softly weeping and I held her close, her head against my shoulder, stroking her hair. I was digging for my handkerchief when I saw two figures pass the doors—Faun and her Goon.

"Oh Jesus, get a load of that," I heard her say to Bobby as they passed by, "not him *too?*"

She shot me a look of contempt and rage, as if I'd somehow betrayed her. Then, grabbing Bobby's arm, she dragged him along, whispering in his ear. The shrill sound of her laughter drifted to us as they disappeared down the stairs toward the tennis court. "Have fun-n-n, Mumm-*eee,*" we heard her call as they dropped out of sight.

Belinda shook her head wearily and pushed her hair back. As usual, she tried to take the blame on herself. "I know it's the sixty-four-thousand-dollar question, but I wish someone would tell me, where did I go wrong? Is it that I'm just not cut out to be a mother? Like ———?" (She named a famous Metro star who would never get the Mother of the Year award.)

I argued that the man or woman didn't live who could answer a question like that, not even the most skilled psychiatrist. Faun herself had been to see enough of them, hadn't she?

I put off my morning's work and stayed close by, talking on and on, trying somehow to get Belinda's mind off darling Faun. Maude wasn't having a good day, either; she sent Ling out with her apologies—she'd lunch in her room but hoped to speak with me later. I swam and sunned with Belinda for the rest of the forenoon, got her laughing again, and we had lunch sitting at the bar in the studio. Afterward we walked around the gardens, talking about Frank, who'd gone to New York and Europe on business and whose return was now overdue.

"I spoke to the office," Belinda confided. "Minnie said, 'Expect him definitely on Monday but don't count on it altogether but look for him absolutely on any other day but Tuesday through Saturday—maybe.' Whatever you're able to make of that—Charlie, are you listening?"

"Hm? Oh yes, sure."

I'd paused at the top of the stairs and was peering down through the trees to the Cottage, finding the scene exceedingly strange. I could see directly onto the gravel drive; my front door was ajar, the gates were flung wide—and my Mercedes was gone.

I glanced at Belinda, hoping she hadn't noticed. As usual, I'd left my keys in the ignition. Obviously this negligence had been discovered, and Faun and her boyfriend had taken the car for a joyride. Well, what the hell, I wasn't going to need it until four, when I had my A.A. meeting, and when she brought the car back I'd just have to exercise cool judgment in the way I dealt with her.

But by four, when the car still wasn't back, I had to miss my meeting. I could have borrowed Belinda's car, but I didn't want her to find out what had happened. When Faun and the Goon finally showed, it was way past ten and all my "cool judgment" went flying out the window; I was really pissed off. To make things worse, the left front fender had a dent. When I asked for an explanation, I got glazed looks and foolishness. I put my damaged car away and locked up. When I switched off the outdoor lights, they were still silly-giggling as they made their way across the gravel toward the garden steps. As they mounted in the dark, I heard a laugh float down from on high, derisive, contemptuous, inane: Bobby's.

I had the dent taken care of on my insurance (one hundred dollars deductible), and said nothing to anyone. It only encouraged her. One afternoon not long after this, when I came down from my swim Bones began growling as we approached the door: someone was in the Cottage, and it wasn't Suzi-Q. I crept up to the window and sneaked a look. At the writing table, in my chair, sat Miss Trouble herself, and in the window seat lounged the Lizard of All He Surveyed. Faun was bending over my typewriter, reading aloud from my typescript, while Bobby lay on his spine, his sneakered feet crossed on the plaster wall above him, his head lolling off the seat, his long hair hanging straight down. I banged open the door and Bones bounded in, scaring the hell out of them.

"Christ! What the hell do you think you're doing?" roared the terrified Bobby.

I called Bones to heel and said, "Maybe you'll tell me just what the hell *you're* doing in here."

"We just stopped by." As if that were totally normal.

"You just stopped by—for what? To trespass? To walk into my house uninvited? To help yourself to my bar, to read my pages? Just who the hell do you think you are, anyway?"

Bobby rolled out of the window seat and swaggered over to me. "Hey, look, man," he said, doing his Brando act. "That's no way to act. We weren't doing nothing."

"You're in my home, uninvited. And since I don't want you as a guest here, I'd appreciate it if you'd get the hell out."

Faun had been taking in this dialogue with apparent amusement. "I think your play is really kind of funny," she said. "But only in spots. It needs lots of work."

"I'm real happy you think so. Now, if you'd please get out I'd like to do some work."

"Okay okay—we weren't going to stay, anyway. Come on, Bobby." She nudged him and they moved together to the door, giving Bones a wide berth. On the threshold she whispered something; Bobby sauntered off across the gravel toward the stairs, while she turned back to me.

"Yes?"

"I was just wondering," she began. "I really need to talk to you. It's important." I gave her a hard look, then told her to wait in the arbor. I changed into a pair of cut-offs and went out to join her.

"Look, I'm sorry," I apologized, "I don't like to play Billy Goat Gruff around here, but you've got to understand you can't just go barging into people's houses. This isn't your place, you know, it's mine while I'm renting it from your grandmother. So after this let me know when you're coming, okay?"

She nodded in her most endearing way and I determined to put the incident behind me. "Now, what did you want to see me about?"

Her writing, she said.

"Yes? What about it?"

"I've really been thinking and I feel I could finish my book if I had the right kind of help on it. Some really professional help. And I was thinking, well—I was just wondering if maybe you couldn't sort of steer me right on some things."

Boy, could I ever!

"Doing an autobiography's not the easiest thing, you know," she said, affording me some amazing tidings. "It's so personal, you know? You really have to have the right way of expressing yourself. Don't you think that's true?"

"Yes," I said, "it calls for a certain style. You call this work an autobiography. Why?"

"Well, because it's about me and my life."

"I see. What makes you think people—that is, the book-buying public—are going to be interested in your twenty-four-year-old life?"

She gave me a nervous little laugh. "Well, I don't know, I mean—well, I am Faun Antrim, aren't I? I mean, I'm famous, sort of, aren't I? Why wouldn't people be interested in what I have to say?"

"Okay, let's assume they are. Let's say everybody's panting to read what you have to say—though most people wait to write their autobiographies until they've done something important in their lives. What have you done that's really notable or of interest to a reader?"

"Well—people are always asking me what it's like to be the daughter of a famous star. What it's like to live in Hollywood, have the upbringing I did. And they always want to know about that whole business—"

Here it came. "Which whole business, Faun?"

"You know. About Bucky Eaton, the fire, all that. Raping me the way he did."

"Yes, I see; yes, of course you'd want to include that, wouldn't you?"

"Well, of *course!* That's the whole point. I want to give the real slant on that."

"Yes, well, I suppose to a certain type of reader there's a definite interest in lurid events like those, but—"

"But what?"

"Well, since they're bound to be so upsetting to your mother, your grandmother as well, it seems to me that you'd do better not to rake over the coals, so to speak. Some things are better off left alone, don't you think?"

Her face took on that expression I hated so, that small-mouthed, mean look. I thought, I don't give a rat's ass how pleasant she can be sometimes, I don't like her and I never will. "What do you say we just put our cards on the table, hm? I'll tell you what I think and you tell me what you think, okay? Good. I think this book you're presumably writing—"

"What do you mean, presumably? I *am* writing!"

"Good. Okay. Fine—you're writing. But why not be honest and say you're writing it just to get back at your mother? That you're doing it as a sort of blackmail to frighten her with. She's still in the public eye, you know."

"I know, but that's not why I'm doing it."

"Why, then?"

"Well, as a sort of ca—ca—what's that word?"

"I suppose you mean 'catharsis.' "

"That's it—catharsis. You'll see. One of these days you'll all see. You think I'm just Miss Stupid fucking around with a pencil and paper. But you'll see. One day . . ."

Yes, one day her prince would come, or maybe Tuesday would be her good-news day. Faun lived for "one day" and hadn't learned yet what a mistake that was for man, woman, dog, or cat. But what was the point of explaining anything to Faun? When I reminded her that Bucky Eaton *hadn't* raped her, she fuzzed that little episode over, then declared sanctimoniously that she hoped her book would make Belinda "see the light" and force her to admit she'd been a bad mother. When I suggested it might be in bad taste to chastise publicly someone who loved her, she said it was for Mummy's own good and in the end she'd be a better person for it. Catharsis, shit. No, there was no talking to our Faun.

But in the days that followed I noticed a slight shift in her view of Frank, or maybe in her relation to Frank. Since his return she hadn't acted so obviously contemptuous and scornful. Instead of sniping at him the way she used to do, she fell into affected silences (though I also noticed that she seldom took her eyes off him).

When she was wearing her shades, I wondered what feelings hid behind those Lolita lenses, but it didn't take much imagination. Her libido was doing its little dance of the seven veils, her genes were giving battle. There was one afternoon—Maude and I had been painting side by side in the studio, and I was attempting a view of the pool as seen from inside the studio. The picture was bright, very California, David Hockney–ish: the aqua-tinted water in the pool, the scattering of pool furniture, the fountain, the tubbed petunias and geraniums, the sloping hill view beyond the wall. Frank had driven up to be with Belinda (it was a Saturday), and they lay paired side by side in two of the chaises, sipping eleven o'clocks from tall frosted glasses. They made a handsome couple, their two heads cocked toward each other, dark and light together, speaking quietly and holding hands.

Then—this was creepy—a shadow fell across them and I saw Faun appear around the three tall cypresses that formed a clump there. I say "creepy" because there was something actually sinister in the way she hovered over them, casting this shadow that fell across the chaises. They didn't know she was there, Frankie was leaning forward and touching Belinda, and I grabbed up Maude's birdwatching glasses and trained them on Faun. In close focus I could see her look of—what?—disgust, contempt, loathing, ridicule? All were there, and more. I studied this display for several moments; then, setting down the glasses, I strode from the studio and called out, "Hey, you guys—" and then, pretending to have just noticed Faun, I waved—"jump in, the water's fine."

By then Frank and Belinda had both sat up and were talking to Faun, who eyed them a second longer, then slouched to the far end of the pool, where she spread out her things and began sunning.

What was there in Faun's furtive appearance that had made me uneasy? As if she were plotting some further mischief? There was no reason, yet I had been alarmed—a little, anyway. I didn't know exactly what Maude might have seen; she said nothing, I said nothing, and the incident was soon forgotten.

Frank and Belinda went on being together every chance they got, and occasionally invited Faun to join them, once to dinner, another time for a Bowl concert—Pinchas Zuckerman was playing. "I just *ha-a-a-ate* fiddle players," she complained the next morning. "Why did you go, then?" Maude asked. "Because Mummy made me," was the reply, in which there was not a word of truth. How do you force a twenty-four-year-old to go to a concert? Besides, Mummy never made Baby *do* anything; Baby did as she wanted. That was the trouble.

She seemed to think she lived some sort of super-enchanted existence by virtue of her name. This was odd, because half the time she complained about it, saying it embarrassed her and people were always asking her about her grandfather Crispin, who'd died when she was still a young child. But whenever Maude talked about Crispin, Faun would frown and express vast indifference, even boredom. If Maude noticed, she never said anything.

I recall one evening in the Snuggery when Maude had just come down, and Faun made some remark about all the framed photographs of Crispin and why so many? Maude smiled, saying there could never be too many for her, she never tired of looking at his handsome face. "Your grandfather was the kindest, dearest man in the world. I was a lucky woman to get him."

"And he never tried getting it on with other women?"

"Good heavens, whatever made you ask a thing like that?"

Faun's look was arch, her tone insinuating. "Just wondering. He must have been quite something if he stayed faithful all that time. He made those movies with Babe Austrian, didn't he? I bet he had a tough time keeping his hands off her."

"Babe Austrian had her admirers, but she was hardly your grandfather's type. And I believe, if you were to dig into your grandfather's past, you'd discover that so far as the opposite sex are concerned, his hands are lily white."

"That's because he had *you.*" Faun got up and went to give her a kiss. I wondered what she was planning to ask for this time.

It came out at the dinner table: she had a friend in town, they were going to a party, and to impress the friend she wanted Nana to ask Ling to get out the Rolls and chauffeur them. I was pleased when Maude declined on Ling's behalf. I always liked it when people said no to Faun; I thought it was good for her character. It probably wasn't, though.

When Faun's twenty-fifth birthday came round, Maude gave a small dinner party at Perino's. Her present to her granddaughter was a bracelet, a narrow circlet of pearls and diamonds, ultra-understated—apparently a bit too understated for the recipient. The recipient's pretty mother, in a skirt and top of contrasting purples, was wearing some of the family jewels, the Antrim rubies that had become Maude's upon the death of her mother-in-law. It was clear from Faun's sulky attitude that she felt short-changed with a mere wrist's worth of pearls and diamonds.

I'd like to be able to say that when she was in residence, occupying the Playhouse that had been her father's, things were pleasant and lively around the old homestead, that she added something vivid to our humdrum lives; but not so. If you enjoyed the tooth-loosening dissonances of hardcore rock, the eternal complaints of that shrill voice a man could easily come to hate, the raucous blat of telephone gabble, the noisy comings and goings of what looked to me like a herd of escapees from the cages of the municipal zoo, the rudeness, the cheapo cracks, the embarrassing language featured for its own sake, the general disruption of the lovely calm that had existed before she showed on the scene—well, you can see how it all went down the drain. It made me angry that Belinda put up with it for a minute, but that was the way things were. Angie had spelled it out for me: having ignored Faun in her formative years, Belinda was now determined to make things up to her, come what might, believing that love and a slack leash would finally do the trick.

It was apparent to me that though Maude held her own views she was going along with it, mostly for Belinda's sake. If it had been up to her alone, she would have employed sterner measures, a little more rod, a little less spoiling, but she left any disciplining to Belinda. I thought it an unhealthy situation all the way around. The most peaceful moment could be instantly shattered by an ugly or tearful scene that seemed to erupt out of nowhere—and only to keep things stirred up.

She applied herself to two things, her "book" and her tan. The tan worked out okay, the book was something else. She talked a lot about the fad for Hollywood memoirs, talked more about the money such efforts could rake in. But as the weeks went by, I convinced myself that nothing would really come of it. *Tap-tap-tap* was all well and good if you wanted to impress the help, but, knowing a little about the business, I didn't think "See Jane run, see Dick lower his trousers" was going to do it. I was waiting for the nudge of her friendly elbow about my own publishing house and would they be interested, etc., etc., etc. (Only I noticed that she wrote "ekt ekt ekt.") She'd tap away for maybe an hour, sometimes longer; then the lure of the sun was too great and she was in her bikini and on the float. She had a cute behind and liked showing her muffins off, but she wasn't doing a cookbook and muffins weren't it if you wanted a golden book contract.

The pity, of course, was that Frank might have made her the best kind of father. Frank's domestic side was not well known. His public image was one of a carefully fostered glamour: the playboy, the gambler, the tireless lover of beautiful women, the man with "underworld connections," is hardly to be viewed as the finest parental material. That Frances had been barren, that April's baby had died, that Frank had longed for children—these were things unknown to the public. And no one knew that when he and Fran were married, he'd wanted to adopt a couple of babies, but she'd balked every time, something about "bad blood." Where kids were concerned, he had lived by a cold fire.

The idea of his becoming stepfather to a girl like Faun isn't really so farfetched as it may sound. I thought he could make her a good stepfather; with his cement and trowel he could patch up that tumbledown wall that had left her so defenseless; he could have created what she probably needed most, a home.

But that was hindsight, which always comes cheap. Right now things were just sort of cooking along, not one thing, not another. For months Belinda had been getting ready to go back to work, dieting and exercising, working with Feldy, getting psyched up for facing the camera again, and except for the occasional explosion, a hastily contrived dramatic scene when Faun felt thwarted or wanted to call notice to herself, life was pretty much on an even keel.

I suppose that many of the psychiatric and psychological fraternity would deem it natural for a daughter to be jealous of her mother—and certainly Faun was. She seemed intent on vying with Belinda in every way she could think of, as if they weren't mother and daughter at all but sorority sisters at college, after the same guys to take them to the Saturday football game. On the one hand it was ridiculous, on the other it was tragic; what a waste of time and energy, and what futility it led to.

Faun's feelings toward her mother's friend—"boyfriend," if you like —must have been of the most ambivalent kind, for it was obvious that she was disguising her attraction to Frank, that she was really eager to have him take notice of her. But she was a good bit past the age of infatuation for an older male, and in one of her chameleon moods she could change in an instant, one minute going out of her way to play up to him, the next contemptuous and sarcastic. She liked to think she could chop him off at the knees any time she wanted to, while he gallantly fended off her poisoned barbs with his usual good humor. Try as she did, she seemed unable to provoke him. Poor Faun!

The time came for Belinda to leave for the eastern location of her film *The Light in the Window;* Frank was coming to drive her to the airport. When I went up for my morning swim, I glimpsed Faun as she appeared in the Playhouse doorway, her bags packed as well. She waved, I waved back.

"Going away again?" I asked when I got closer.

"Santa Fe." She had a new boyfriend over that way, a full-blooded Indian at that.

"Terrific."

"We're going to white-water the Colorado. It'll be real fun. You ought to come along."

"Sorry, got to work."

"Oh, you."

She was away six days, then came back in love with her Hiawatha, who no doubt wore a feather in his hair and sat in the town square selling fake souvenirs to tourists. She raved about how marvelous he was and how she loved him, a deathless love that lasted about another six days. Now, question: where does all the money come from to do all this tootling around? Who *buys* all this white-watering, etc.? You know. Nana does.

She was always buttering up Maude for big bucks. "Nana dear, I got this absolutely ridiculous thing from the bank this morning. I don't know what it means."

"It means you're overdrawn."

"Really? How am I supposed to know that?"

"It's stamped, dear. Three checks. NSF. Nonsufficient funds."

"What do I do about it?"

"Put some money in, dear. That's what people do with banks—put the money in."

"But I haven't any."

"Too bad. First of the month."

"First of the month" meant that cash would be deposited to her account on an automatic basis. The first of the month was always nice for her, but sometimes the first was fifteen days away or more. Maude somehow always made up the difference. "Oh, Nana darling, I could just kiss-kiss-kiss you!" Kiss kiss kiss. Maude hated it, but she put up with it. If she withheld comment or criticism, that was her business; if she indulged her, that, too, was her business, but what, I asked myself, was the result to be?

One evening I managed to persuade Maude to let me take her down the hill for a bite and a movie. She was going out more these days, and though I wanted to make it special and go somewhere glamorous, she said she wanted a hamburg, so we went to the Hamlet in Westwood. Afterward we went to see the new Woody Allen film at the Bruin. She enjoyed it and was full of talk on the way home. As we pulled in through the upper gates and approached the house, I saw headlights and a car came speeding in our direction. I gave way and the car sailed out the gates.

"Wasn't that Frank?" asked Maude in surprise.

You bet it was Frank, going like a bat out of hell. I grew wary when I considered this hasty exit. Peering through the trees, I saw the Playhouse door flung open, and Faun came running across the lawn, crying out to us, her arms waving frantically. I pulled over and jumped out, to have her rush sobbing into my arms.

"What's happened?" I asked, trying to see her face. "What is it?"

"Did you see him? Did you just pass him?" she cried. "You saw, Nana —Frank, it was Frank—" She was trembling and her words faltered. "Thank God you got here in time!"

A concerned Maude spoke up. "Faun, what is it? Come indoors, you'll catch your death out here. Are you hurt?"

She spoke firmly and with some impatience, and I felt Faun clutch at me as if for moral as well as physical support. We got her inside, where Ling came to meet us; Maude took Faun into the Snuggery and wrapped her in a blanket, then asked for an explanation.

"He attacked me, he t-tried to—to—he—I—oh God! Oh *God!*" Faun babbled incoherently and her eyes were wild.

"What are you saying?" I asked. "Do you mean he raped you?"

"He was going to! I'm sure he would have if you hadn't come. He took my robe off me—" She sobbed some more, hid her face as if in shame, sobbing into the blanket. I reached to raise her head up and stared hard at her, saying I didn't believe her. She pulled away and sobbed some more.

Maude sat down on the sofa beside her. "Faun—are you telling us that Frank Adonis came up here and attacked you?"

Looking up with wet eyes, she talked more foolishness. I knew she had to be making the whole thing up. Remember Bucky Eaton? When we'd assured ourselves that she wasn't injured in any way, Maude had Ling turn down the bed in Belinda's room and tucked Faun into it. I went to the phone and called Frank, but there was no answer. Leaving a message on his answering machine, I waited for Maude to come down again, but Ling came with the message that Faun was resting and for me to go down to bed. Once in the Cottage, I tried Frank several times more before going to sleep.

Next morning he called before eight and I could tell he was angry. I met him on the Strip for coffee and got the whole story. It wasn't terribly complicated, but it was hair-raising all right. This is what he told me:

Around seven last evening (soon after Maude and I had gone down the hill) Faun had telephoned Frank at his office. Ordinarily Minnie would have fielded the call, but since Faun sounded upset she put her through.

"She said she had to talk to me right away," Frank said. "About her mother. When I asked what about her mother, she said she couldn't tell me on the phone, it was too personal. I said I couldn't just go running up there—you know how ———'s been kicking up the dust"—he named one of his most elevated movie clients, who was suffering studio as well as marital troubles—"I said I'd get there as soon as I could. She started crying and said please could I hurry, she didn't know who else to turn to.

"I got away by nine and drove up. She was standing out on the lawn waiting for me—in a houserobe. Get the picture? When she saw me, she threw herself into my arms, bawling like hell. I walked her inside the Playhouse. She was still crying and at first I couldn't get anything out of her at all, but bit by bit I managed to drag it out of her. I thought she was going to say she'd got knocked up by one of those yoyos she hangs out with, but no, nothing like that. It was all about Blindy."

"What about her?" I asked.

" 'Mummy's dying,' she says."

"*What?*"

"Relax—it's all bullshit. She was doing one of her bits. Blindy had

X-rays taken a month or so ago; they showed a spot on one of her lungs, just a tiny dot, nothing to worry about. But Faun had been listening in on the extension so she decided to see how big she could blow the whole thing up. I finally got her calmed down and then, when I got up to go, she started coming on with me. 'What's your hurry, big man?' she says. 'Nobody's home, Nana's gone to the flicks, let's get cozy,' and like that. And damned if she didn't have the champagne all iced—she turns on the stereo, all warm bunny-rabbit as can be. I'm being set up.

"I tell her I've got work to get back to, and she begins crying again. She wasn't kidding me, I knew it was one big act, but I think, Stay a couple of minutes, maybe we can get a few things nailed down between us. So we sit there on the couch, I'm asking her questions about what she wants to do with her life, what plans she has, and all of a sudden she comes out with 'Frank, I'm in love with you.'

"I tell her if we're going to talk, then talk sense, and she says, 'I *am* talking sense.' Then she says she'd been in love with me ever since that day you and I saw her at that pony ride. Remember?"

I was as shocked by this as Frank: she couldn't have been fourteen at the pony ride.

"Doesn't matter. She said men don't realize it but young girls are filled with all kinds of sexual cravings. 'I dream about you,' she said. 'I've talked to my doctor about it, he says it's natural.' Meanwhile, she's inching closer to me on the sofa. 'Don't you think I'm pretty?' she says. 'Don't you think I have a nice body, Frank? Come on, you can level with me, Mummy's not around.'

" 'And a good thing she isn't,' I said. 'Don't you think you ought to turn your ignition off?'

" 'What for?' she says. 'What are you afraid of? What I have in mind won't hurt you. Won't hurt me, either, I enjoy it.'

"I suggested she call up her chum Bobby.

" 'But I don't want to do it with Bobby,' she says, 'I want to do it with you.' With this, she gets up and excuses herself, she's got something she wants to show me. She steps around the corner. For some crazy reason I wait, and in seconds she's back. Now she's got her robe off and she's standing there, holding out her arms to me."

"You mean she was naked?"

"Not a stitch. I said if that's how things were going to be I was getting the hell out of there. She comes running after me, catches me at the door, and throws her arms around me. 'I'll make it good for you, Frankie,' she says. And—get this—'I'm much better than Mummy, you'll see.'

" 'You've got a disgusting mouth,' I tell her, 'and you ought to have more respect for your mother.'

"She laughed. 'Who could respect *her?*' she says. 'Everybody knows Belinda Carroll was the biggest whore in Hollywood!'

"Then I slapped her; once, but hard.

"Then she really flared. 'She is! She's a *whore,* you hear me? *Whore —whore—whore—*!'

"I grabbed her by both shoulders and began shaking her until she stopped, then manhandled her back to the sofa and pushed her down. She fell against the cushions and I waited until she was still. 'By Christ!' I said when I had her attention. 'If I ever hear you talk like that again you'll wish you hadn't, you got me?' I got her robe and threw it at her; then I went out the door and headed for my car."

It was just as he'd turned on his lights and started his engine that Maude and I had driven through the front gates. Then, when he'd gone, too angry to stop, Faun had come screaming out the door with her wild talk of rape.

I turned brick red when I heard Frank's story, but it really wasn't news to me. Even when I confronted Faun with the truth she stuck to her guns, saying she wasn't the one who was lying, but Frank, and that if he ever came near her she'd call the police. It was really pathological. Maude was so ashamed she hardly knew what to say to Frank.

Evidently she talked to Faun's psychiatrist—this was hers to do, since it was she who had picked up the tab for years, a hefty one, too —and Faun was finally persuaded to apologize, saying she'd been "a little carried away." Frank graciously agreed to scratch the whole thing and we contrived that Belinda should be told nothing of what had happened.

This unattractive incident was shortly followed by yet another, and after that I felt sure Faun's Sunnyside days were numbered. She'd casually mentioned at lunch that she was having some friends over that evening and named a well-known rock star. I saw the corners of Maude's lips involuntarily make their little quirk of exasperation; then she quickly said that it sounded like fun. Later I suggested to Faun that her friends use my gate and go up to the Playhouse via the garden stairs so as not to disturb anybody.

I went out that evening and when I came home, around eleven, to my shock I found my driveway jammed with cars, a glitzy array of expensive vehicles that threw off dollar signs all over the place. Faun's "little get-together" comprised far more than "a few friends," and since my garage was blocked, I went to have a look.

The higher I climbed, the louder grew the noise. A full blast of "Yellow Submarine" hit me like an electronic thunderbolt when I came onto the esplanade. While the main house lay in darkness, the Playhouse was lit up like a department store at Christmastime. The music, I suddenly realized, wasn't taped but live—the rock star had brought his whole group as well as their instruments, and the place was wired.

As I came closer I could smell the blatant odor of grass, and from the looks of some of the ones I passed, that wasn't the only drug going around. I moved into the house, looking for Faun. A red-haired girl in a leather dress put her body up to mine and gave me some Hiya-big-boy stuff. "Where's Faun?" I asked; she covered her teeth the way Japanese girls do when they laugh and pointed upstairs.

"She's up there. With Ragtime Cowboy Joe."

Though I hadn't heard of that gentleman, I got a load of him quick enough. He was in Faun's bedroom, in her bed. Faun was with him, looking out of things, and I figured she'd been on the golden spoon again. I had to shake her to get her to listen to me. I told the guy to get the hell out of there, if he didn't the police would see to it. This threat shook some sense into Faun; she began pulling herself together. I got Cowboy Joe out, and when Faun could walk I got her downstairs. I went to the wall and yanked out the plug to the amplifier. "I think you've all partied enough," I announced, "and someone's blocking my garage, so why don't you all just get out of here?"

Cowboy Joe grabbed me the way I hated anyone to do, but I didn't hit him. "That goes for you, too, Gene Autry," I told him.

"But we were having fun," Faun wailed in my ear. "You don't have the right anyway; this isn't your house."

"Should I remind you that it isn't yours, either? You're a guest here, so start acting like one, for Christ's sake."

"You're so smart. This whole place is going to be mine someday. You hear that, guys?" She collected everybody's attention. "My grandmother's an old lady and this is all going to be mine when she dies."

"All *right*," shouted Cowboy Joe. "Let's hope it's soon."

A cheer went up, a couple of beer bottles also, foaming their beer onto the rug. When the noise died away a voice spoke from the doorway.

"I think I can promise you it won't be long, young man."

"Nana!"

"Yes, my dear, it is indeed your nana. Boys and girls—men and women—I am the old old grandmother Faun has just been speaking of. If you will kindly stop this racket so I can get some sleep I will appreciate it."

I hurried to her side and led her out. Though I could tell she was angry, she was making every effort to control it.

"It cannot go on, my dear," she said, shaking a determined head as I escorted her back to the house. "Noo-oo, noo-oo, it cannot. There must be an accounting—and before Belinda comes home again."

While I wasn't going to apologize for the rudeness of Cowboy Joe, I tried to make light of everything. But her expression and voice were grim as she frowned at me and said, "She must go, Charlie, I want her out of here before something terrible happens, something really bad. She'd do it, too, I feel it. I'm afraid. Not for me, I don't mean that, but for herself. And for Belinda—and Frank."

"What will you do?"

"I don't know. I don't *know!*" she exclaimed, and her voice shook with emotion. "She's Perry's—Perry's daughter. She was mine for all those years—how can I banish her now?"

She was fighting to keep from crying, and when we got to the house I turned her over to Ling; by then the party was breaking up, and as I walked back to the esplanade I got whistles and jeers and "spoilsport" that followed me all the way down the stairs.

The next morning I waited beside the pool until I saw Faun coming over for breakfast. She was in pretty bad shape: her face was pallid and drawn from her night's revels. She looked fragile, as if she might crack like a plate. When I suggested she'd better show some contrition, otherwise Nana was throwing her out on her fancy little derrière, she laughed.

"Oh, come on, Charlie, lighten up," she said. "Nana's not going to do anything of the kind. Mummy wouldn't hear of it; she wants me around. Nana's just making noises, that's all."

When I pointed out that "Mummy" didn't own a stake in Sunnyside but was only a guest, while Faun herself was there under sufferance, she didn't want to hear any more about it.

"Just don't say I didn't warn you." I thought she had a lot to learn about the world, especially when it came to public relations. But she got the last laugh anyway, at least for a while. This is how that scenario went:

When she came into the breakfast room Maude was not in her accustomed chair. Ling appeared, with the solemn announcement that Missy Maw' would like to see Faun upstairs; I was requested to accompany her.

We found Maude in her sitting room, up and dressed for the day, seated at her desk writing some notes. She didn't pull any punches, but laid aside her little gold-and-lapis-lazuli pen and started in with one good hard swing of the axe, saying she was fed up with Faun's erratic and unattractive behavior and that if she intended to go on upsetting the household as she was doing she had better make other arrangements. I must say, she was magnificent. A stone would have quailed at that gentle but steely voice.

Faun sat facing her, hands in lap, but by no means exhibiting any of the humility I had suggested. Rather, as Maude's stinging words fell on her, she sat immobile and unflinching, stubbornly refusing to bow before the onslaught. When it was over and she still hadn't said anything, Maude got up and walked to the window. She peered out across the grounds, that splendid view that Crispin had chosen for their bedroom, and there was something so regal yet so tense in her attitude that it made me think of the British royal family at some moment of crisis—the Abdication, a declaration of war.

Finally she turned and, with hands clasped before her, said, "Well, my dear, are you merely going to sit there saying nothing? Aren't you going to make some excuse—or say something?"

"No, Nana," I heard Faun say meekly, and when she moved her head I saw the tears trickling down her cheeks. The change was sudden and surprising. "There's nothing *to* say. You're right, of course. You've been so kind to let me stay here this long, and I really should start acting grown up, I really should. It's just that I don't know how. I'm a little girl, I guess I'll stay a little girl always. But I can't go on causing you misery at every turn—Mummy, too. You both mean too much to me. I'll go and pack."

She got up and in a flash was out the door.

Maude stared at the doorway, then sank down on the corner of the bed. "Well! What do you think of that?" she wondered aloud. I thought carefully before replying. Frankly, I thought I'd been watching a scene from the *Late, Late Show;* it was all bad Monogram again, a Kay Francis three-handkerchief deal. But I didn't tell this to Maude, just said we ought to wait and see.

Before I could leave the room the telephone rang; it was Belinda in Maine, and I waited while Maude talked; then she put me on for a word. Everything was fine with her, shooting was going well, how were things here? I lied, told her everything was great, then handed the phone back to Maude and got out.

I went down to the Cottage and worked for the rest of the morning, forgetting I hadn't eaten breakfast. I had an apple and some cheese for lunch and was hard at work again when I heard the sirens. The firehouse was at the foot of the canyon, and I assumed there must be a fire in the neighborhood. The engines went roaring past my gates, loud as hell, and then I jumped up, for I could tell from the sirens that they were turning in at the top drive.

I tried the phone but no one answered, so I went pelting up the steps to see uniformed men streaming across the lawn with some kind of apparatus.

Faun.

There was no smoke, no fire, but she was dying. The damn fool had gone straight from Maude's room that morning to her own room, where she'd swallowed pills, written a note, then laid down and gone to sleep, never to awaken. It was to be a Sleeping Beauty exit, but fortunately she'd been discovered in time. It was Maude herself who'd found her, read the note, seen the empty bottle, and called the fire department.

She'd gone over to the Playhouse to apologize.

Maude and I rode together in the ambulance to the hospital, and for six hours she stayed there, until Faun was brought fully back to life. After the usual God-awful stomach-pump routine, I found Maude on her knees at her bedside. I waited while she finished praying; then we went into Faun's room again, where I left her. I spent the better part of two hours on the phone, first trying to track Frank down somewhere, then talking with Belinda's producers. They agreed it would be best to withhold the news from her until Faun was out of danger, and only when we had the doctor's assurance did I tell her what had happened, soft-pedaling the whole thing as a minor episode, a touch of "food poisoning." Then Maude got on the horn and did a fantastic job of acting, laying down a smoke screen and never once mentioning the dread word "suicide." Then, being Maude, she made another call, to her attorney, and Felix assured her he'd do his best to keep it out of the papers.

At nine that night we were seated at the bedside where the remorseful Faun lay, still as death. The lids flickered, eyes swam, words came, falteringly.

"Nana . . . Nana . . . you didn't want me . . . nobody wanted me . . . I thought it would be easier if I went. . . ."

Oh Jesus, I thought, even at death's door she's doing *Mourning Becomes Electra.* And as I watched the whole scene being played, I kept saying to myself, "The little bitch faked the whole thing." But this is what I was really thinking, swear to God: I wish she'd gone. I damn well wish it had really worked.

I could be a bastard, too.

Interestingly enough, it eventually appeared that she had indeed faked it. Suzi-Q had gone over to tidy things up after the firemen had left, and while she was changing the bed the telephone had rung. It was Bobby

Spurling. Told that Faun wasn't there, he'd turned nasty, saying she'd called him at noon and made him promise to call her at exactly three and if he didn't get her to call the police! So it was all staged.

None of us ever let on to Belinda how bad things were that day when her precious baby had almost kicked the bucket. It was only long after the fact, when it didn't matter anymore, that I finally spun the whole story out for her. But of course by that time Frank was dead, too, and it was all spilt milk.

You might think—*I* thought—that after this there might be some lessening of the strain, some easing of the screws Faun was putting to everyone, but I was wrong, there wasn't and she didn't. When she came out of the hospital four days later, Maude and I picked her up. There she was, all bundled up in baby-blue bunting with a brave if rueful smile. She stepped out of the wheelchair and as I helped her into the car it occurred to me that sometime, somehow, these shenanigans of hers were bound to pay off: she was living too close to the edge of the precipice.

A couple of nights later Frank and I had dinner and I told him what had happened. He listened gravely, and I knew what he was thinking: this was a major problem he was taking on. We sat trying to figure what it was that kept triggering these crazy emotional pyrotechnics, and he even went so far as to consult a friend of his on the staff at Menninger's in Kansas, hoping for some answer or illumination, but that was grasping at straws and we both knew it. Like me, he was concerned for Maude, and with good reason. She was a strong lady, equipped to tackle nearly any situation that arose, but she'd spoken the truth fully that day in her bedroom—she couldn't go on. Yet she'd taken Faun back under her roof, covering up once again to spare Belinda. But at such a cost! And what could the future hold?

I knew that when Belinda came back, Frank intended to pop the question; he'd waited long enough, and he hoped she'd marry him when her film was done. The fact that Faun presented an obstacle to this plan troubled him. Like Maude, he recognized the pathological aspects of the case. He saw that Faun harbored a deep-seated jealousy of her mother's growing happiness, and that the only thing that brought Faun really alive was to see Belinda made unhappy; that had more or less become her mission in life.

The question was, what would become of Faun when he and Belinda married? The obvious choices were that she should either go on living here at Sunnyside under Maude's wing—hardly an attractive proposition for Maude—or that she should again go off somewhere on her own, not a happy possibility, based on past experience. We couldn't help wishing

for some Prince Charming to appear and carry her off to his castle (where
I privately hoped she might be locked up like Rapunzel). But was this
really very likely? It never occurred to anyone that she might actually go
to work! Frustrated and unhappy, Frank paced the floor of the Cottage
as we further chewed on the conundrum, seeking the answer that wasn't
there.

I couldn't tell what Faun really thought of him, where reality left off
and her pathological fancies took hold. Despite the gross things she'd
perpetrated, the guilt she'd tried to hang on him, despite the vicious things
she said about him, her exaggerations and downright lies, I had the feeling
that deep down she liked him and wanted him to like her back. But since
she couldn't win his favor, she chose instead to belittle him, to torment
him, and he felt obliged to put up with it all, for Belinda's sake.

When Belinda finally arrived home from location, she was thinner
and far more tired than we'd suspected her to be, but her director, when
he came to dinner one evening, was unstinting in his praise. He'd never
had an actress work so hard and to such effect.

In the meantime, the news of her success failed to move her daughter,
except to further unattractive spells of moodiness and abrasiveness.
Belinda took it all. If Faun was her cross to bear, why, then, she would
go on bearing it, in any way that she could.

When she came home, she and Frank had a long talk. By now he'd
persuaded her that time was wasting and that their affair couldn't simply
trail vaporously along for an indefinite time, and he pressed her at least
to become formally engaged. Again she put him off, but only until Christmas, she said, at which time she promised to say yes. This news, however,
was not to be communicated to Faun, for fear of the effect it might have
on her. The sad fact was that Belinda's return hadn't led to any closer
rapport between mother and daughter, while the latter treated Frank as
shabbily as ever.

One afternoon I'd been at my easel in the studio and was washing
out my brushes at the sink tap under the bar when I heard voices outside.
Through the open window I could see Frank appear between the trees
and greet Faun, who lay on a chaise, keeping up her tan at poolside. When
he said hello in his usual friendly manner, she replied in her usual sullen
one.

"Look, Faun," I heard him say, "don't you think, now that your
mother's home again, you and I ought to try to get on a little better? What
do you say, hm? It doesn't do any good to sulk, you know."

"I'm not sulking."

"You could be a little friendlier when I'm around, couldn't you?"

"If you weren't around I wouldn't have to bother." I gritted my teeth; she was so unreasonable.

"You really don't like me, do you?" Frank said.

"No."

"Well, I guess I know where I stand, then."

"I wish the hell you did. I wish you'd keep away from us. My mother doesn't love you."

"Then she's giving a pretty good imitation of it."

"I want you to stay away from her—from all of us. We don't want you here."

"Look, young woman, if I were you I'd change my tactics. Acting like this isn't going to get you anywhere. Just make up your mind to it —I love your mother, and as long as she's around, I'm around, too."

"Don't count on it."

"On being around? Oh, I do, I do."

"You'll be sorry if you do. And so will she. . . ."

There was real menace in her tone and I froze. I waited for Frank to answer, and when he didn't I realized he'd walked away from her. I picked up the phone and checked my service, raising my voice so Faun would hear me and know I'd heard her with Frank, but when I hung up and went outside, her chaise was empty and she was gone.

An isolated incident. At the end of the week she went away again; no goodbyes, she was just—"gone." It was Belinda's birthday, too, and Faun had clearly made a point of not being there. Maude said she'd gone to Santa Fe; I supposed the Colorado was embracing her again with its white waters.

With her film chores over, Belinda could relax once more. She'd been under a heavy strain, plagued with sleeplessness and loss of appetite, and was inclined to be sharp with people. More than once her temper got the better of her, but then it was gone and she'd come and apologized. I knew what she needed was to get away, but she wouldn't do that: she didn't want to leave Frank, who was tied up at his office. He did take five days and they went down to Palm Springs, where they hid themselves away behind the walls of Frank's white villa, blazing in the desert sun. From Sunday to Friday morning they played together, swam together, rode some of Frank's new horses, slept together, and returned more in love than ever. It was another high point in their relationship, but with a snap of the fingers everything suddenly turned bad again.

The following weekend it was my turn to party. Some of Angie's rich Palm Springs friends were throwing a bash aboard their boat and had invited twenty of their nearest and dearest to spend the weekend aboard.

A Catalina weekend, not one of my favorite things to do, but I went. Left Friday afternoon, 4:00 p.m., returned Sunday at 7:00. Ordinarily I'd have used the front entrance, but because I had my hands full with my bags, I entered by the side door. Bones was nowhere to be found, and I surmised he must be up with Maude. I kicked off my shoes, made myself a sandwich, and turned on the TV. After a while I heard a bark outside and then Bones was begging to be let in. When I opened the front door, a folded note fell onto the flagging.

"Come at once. Boy does not cry wolf, no fooling. Trouble abounds." It was initialed by Maude Antrim. Leaving Bones behind, I dashed up the stairs. "Trouble abounds?" What had our favorite young woman pulled this time? Had she tried to burn down the house again or had she stabbed Ling with the fish knife? Panting, I reached the top step and raced along the pool toward the house. The place was all lit up, and I could see figures moving through the rooms inside. I ran in through the living room to the place where I was sure I'd find Maude—the Snuggery —only I was wrong, she wasn't there. I bumped into Ling in the doorway.

"Missy Maw' upstair. You come, mistah?"

"What is it, Ling? What's happened?" I panted.

"Missy Blindy ver' sick, say. She plenny bad off."

"Sick? What kind of sick?"

He lowered his eyes discreetly.

"*What is it, Ling?*"

His shrug was barely perceptible. "Missy Maw' tell you. Missy Blindy maybe have little sauce."

"Sauce? You mean she's been drinking?"

"I 'fraid so, Mistah Cholly."

I fled upstairs, running along the hall, where I encountered Maude coming out of Belinda's room. As she came toward me she faltered and I reached to support her. "No, no, let me go," she said, pulling away. "I'm quite all right."

But she wasn't; I could see it right away. I let her guide me along the hall to her room, and when she sank into a chair and her face came into the light of the floor lamp I could see how white it had gone and how taxed she was. Despite her attempts to disguise it, I noted her trembling hand.

"Have you a cigarette?" she asked, to my surprise. "That's right, you don't smoke." She gestured wearily for me to pull the bellcord in the corner; then as I sat again she eased herself against the back cushion of the chair. I said nothing, waiting for her to collect herself. When Ling appeared, she asked him, "Are there some cigarettes anywhere in the house? I would like one if there are. And please bring me one or two ounces of that good Napoleon brandy." When Ling had gone, she turned to me. "Bit done in this evening, I'm afraid," she apologized. "I'm awfully glad you're back, I've missed you. I didn't want you to go into Blindy's room until I'd had a chance to talk to you. She's all right now—you can see her in a little while."

"But what happened?" I asked.

"What a mess!" she exclaimed, and as she finally began explaining, her voice broke several times. I could see how deeply she'd been affected.

It was one more scene from a Monogram cheapie. Friday night Belinda and Faun had had yet another quarrel—over the Goon, with whom Faun claimed she'd patched things up and whom she'd dragged home while she changed clothes. "He's my closest best friend in the world; I can't not see him, can I?"

Belinda, however, forbade him ever to enter the house, which provoked Faun to threaten—again—to leave *forever!* Belinda said that would be fine with her, it would probably be best in the long run. Faun had stormed out, dragging Bobby after her, and later Belinda and Maude had had dinner on tables in front of the TV and watched one of Maude's favorite shows.

Maude was sleepy; Belinda kissed her and said good night. She seemed in perfect control, though Maude sensed she was brooding over the scene with Faun. Sometime later Maude awakened, thinking she heard voices. There was the sound of a glass breaking, then a piece of furniture being overturned. She was about to investigate when a lengthy silence suggested there was no need, so she lay back on her pillow and dropped off to sleep again. When she awoke Sunday morning, all seemed serene. Belinda wasn't down yet but there were no signs of breakage or disturbance in the studio. The minute Ling came in, she questioned him. Yes, he'd found a stool overturned, a broken glass as well.

"And, Missy Maw', some blood, too."

"Blood? A lot?"

"Little bit, Missy."

"Whose blood?"

Ling showed helpless hands. "*May* be . . . Missy Blindy?" He ventured the name with the greatest delicacy.

Maude was instantly on the alert.

"Why Miss Belinda? Why not Faun?"

"No, no, Missy Maw', Missy Fonn no come home. No home aw' night."

Maude went to knock on Belinda's door. No answer. She tried the knob. The door was locked. She spoke through the linenfold paneling. No response. After persisting for a while, she gave it up. She went to her own room, where she remained through the morning, intermittently attempting to rouse Belinda. Still no reply. At lunchtime Viola Ueberroth drove up as arranged to take her to the Bel Air Hotel for lunch, but Maude was fearful and wouldn't leave the house, so Vi came in and stayed with her.

They were sitting by the pool, talking quietly, when there was a loud crash from inside the studio and, looking in, they saw Belinda at the bar, with bottle and glass. She'd tipped over another stool. Her hair was half over her eyes and she was staggering badly. Suddenly spying the two women outside, she whooped, threw up her glass in a *skoal* gesture, and with outflung arms lurched toward the door.

"No! Belinda, wait!" Viola screamed as Belinda rushed forward, bottle and drink held high. Maude later told me she was actually running by the time she hit one of the sliding glass doors. There was a terrible shattering sound as she crashed through and the pane fell in hundreds of pieces around her.

"It was terrible," Maude said, her head trembling until she hid it in her hands. Belinda had suffered forty separate cuts and lesions, on her face, neck, shoulders, arms, breasts, thighs, and legs. Over a hundred stitches had been taken, many across her forehead.

I could see the headlines:

BELINDA CARROLL SCARRED FOR LIFE IN DRUNKEN FALL

We spoke about it as such disasters are spoken of, going through and under and around, saying the same things over and over, and the question we repeated the oftenest in the next two hours was, Where had she got the bottle from?

There hung the burning question, and now, as we sat together in her bedroom, Maude showed herself at a loss to answer. I was thinking hard, trying to assimilate it all. What had happened to pop Belinda off on a drunk? Upset her enough to push her off the wagon, then provide the wherewithal? Yes, indeed, someone had set the stage, and very cleverly, too, then shoved the unsuspecting Belinda onstage in front of the footlights to play out her scene. But who? I damn well knew who got my vote. And clearly Maude was thinking the same thing. I walked over to her, pressed her shoulder. She rose and we started downstairs.

"Maude?" I said as we went down in the elevator.

"Yes, quickly, tell me what you're thinking."

"Where's the bottle? I want to see it."

"Good! I *thought* you would. I've saved it. Come along."

She took me to the butler's pantry and there on the sideboard sat the empty bottle, which had escaped the crash and the fall onto the tiles. I stared at the label, though I'd already recognized it from a distance. It was a bottle of Zubrovka vodka, the Polish brand with the blade of buffalo grass in it, one of Belinda's old favorites. Where had it come from?

I walked to the wall where a calendar hung, with the telephone number of the liquor store the household generally used. I dialed the number and got a girl; I asked if she could tell me if anyone had purchased a bottle of Polish vodka in the past twenty-four hours. Oh yes, she said, several people! Was one a blonde woman in her fifties? Oh, she thought—no, she couldn't remember any blonde of fifty, but there had been a young dark-haired woman of twenty-five or so. Was she alone? No, the girl said, she was with a male companion, a hippie type with long red hair. . . .

"What did they say?" Maude asked when I hung up. "Was it—?"

I nodded. Who else? After her quarrel with Belinda, Faun had hopped down to the liquor store and bought the stuff. Then what? How had she worked the thing, how had she insinuated the bottle into the house so the servants wouldn't notice but Belinda would? Most important, how had Faun known her mother was ready to start drinking?

Maude, poor lady, was exhausted, and she began weeping softly. I looked at her and shook my head. "Go to bed, Maude," I told her, "we can't do anything tonight."

"I want to be up when Faun comes home."

"No you don't. Not tonight. If she does come, it's not the time for a showdown. Wait. Wait until tomorrow; bad things can always keep."

"You're right, of course. I'll go." She paused just in front of me and suddenly my arms went around her. She needed my help, and I was glad to be the one she needed. At that instant I was in love with her, Maude Antrim. There are people you'll gladly die for; she was one.

She reached up and kissed my cheek. "Thank you, my dear; I really don't know what we'd do around here without you." I wanted to cry, honest to God. I held the swinging door for her and escorted her to the stairs. Then I went and sat in the Snuggery. I heard the clock strike the half hour, but I didn't know which half, I'd lost track of the time. I turned on the TV and realized it was ten-thirty. I shut off the set, and crossed the hallway. Just then headlights flashed as a car circled the drive. I sat down in the hall and waited. Presently I heard voices, then a key in the lock, the door opened, and there was Faun, accompanied by Jojo the Dog-Faced Boy.

"*Well,*" she exclaimed indignantly, as if I had no business in her house.

"Well," I repeated, hardly an answer.

"My, don't we look glum," she said. "What's the matter, did your elephant run away?"

I took her arm. "Come in here, I want to talk to you." As I pulled her along toward the Snuggery, she yelped, then wriggled free of my hand.

"Get you, man. Who was your slave last year? I'm starving. We're going to make sandwiches."

"*You're* not going to do *anything* until we've talked," I said, "so get your ass in there and just shut up." True, I wasn't operating in a very adult way, but in my anger I'd lost track of the niceties.

"You don't have any rights over me. You're not my father."

"A blessing for which I'll be eternally grateful."

Bobby tittered and I whipped around at him. "Look, you little creep, do you think everything's funny? For two cents I'd paste you one."

"Leave him out of this," Faun said.

"I'm afraid I can't. And if you won't come in there where we can talk, we can have this thing out right here where we stand."

"What thing?"

I tried to sound offhand. "I'd just like to get your side of things before I call the police."

That did something. "The police? Whatever for?" She tried to laugh; miserable failure.

"Guess."

She pretended not to have a clue. Her heels rapped on the marble as she tottered about, glancing here and there. "What's happened? Where is everyone?" She moved to the foot of the stairs and looked up. "Where's Mummy? Has something happened to her?"

"Look, pussycat, don't start with that holy innocent crap," I said, "I'm not in any mood." I grabbed her arm again and swung her around, then gave her a shove toward the Snuggery doorway.

"Hey, man, lay off." Bobby started toward me with a menacing look. I struck out and knocked him back against the wall.

Faun cried out, and then marched on me in fury. "I'll have you charged with assault."

"Fine. You just go right ahead and do that, cutie, because in a very short while I'm having you charged with murder."

"Murder!" She paled and shrank back from me, squeezing her arm in that characteristic gesture of hers.

"You heard me," I said. "Murder. Both of you."

"Yeah?" said Bobby. "Who are we supposed to have murdered?"

Ignoring him, I looked hard at Faun. "Just your mother."

I walked into the Snuggery, sure that this ploy would finally get her in there. Leaving Bobby in the hall, she came trotting in, already sobbing.

"Who killed her? How did she die?"

"A lot you care."

"She's my mother! My mother!"

"Well, she didn't die—though she damn well could have. And you did it!"

"I *didn't!* You're wrong—I haven't even been home since yesterday and I can prove it."

"Maybe you can, but it won't matter. I have proof that you and your cone-head boyfriend out there poisoned your mother. They're going to call it attempted manslaughter. You'll each get five to ten, easy."

She ran at me, began frantically pummeling my chest. "You're crazy crazy crazy! You shouldn't say such things! I never poisoned anybody! I don't know anything about any poisons! You're crazy!"

Bobby appeared in the room, touching his lip, which was bleeding, and he seemed groggier than ever. "Hey, *man*, what're you talkin', anyways?"

"You heard me, *man!*"

His look was venomous. "I can get you charged with fuckin' slander, man, fuckin' perjury. My father's Ed Spurling, y'know that?—you ever heard of E. J. Spurling? Made *The Girl in the Polka Dot Bikini?* He's a big man in Beverly Hills, he'll step all over you." His jutting jaw made a neat target and I longed to punch it, but I restrained myself.

"Maybe. But I wonder what you'll say when I tell you I can prove beyond the shadow of a doubt that you, Mr. Bobby Spurling, and you, Little Miss Daisy Duck, yesterday morning purchased a fifth of Polish vodka at the Sunset Liquor Store and brought it into this house."

Bobby stuck his hands on his hips and hung his face out at me. "Yeah? Since when is that against the law?"

"Moreover, I can prove that you did it with the sole malicious purpose of getting your mother to drink it, and drink it at the peril of her life." I swung my look on Faun. "Your mother is an alcoholic and you know damn well that for her any alcohol is a toxic substance."

"You're crazy! We bought it for ourselves!" Bobby screamed. He was terror-stricken and had tears in his eyes.

I turned on him again. "No, you didn't. You bought that bottle and left it out on the sinkboard, right under the cabinet where Faun's mother keeps her tea things—you put it there knowing she'd be bound to find it. You left it in a champagne bucket with ice, knowing that was how she liked it, ice cold. You even took the trouble to open it. Just in case she mightn't bother."

"Liar! Liar! Liar!" Bobby was screaming. "You're trying to frame us."

"Bobby—shut the fuck *up!*" Faun was a tiger now. "What happened —are you telling me she's dead, then?"

"She's had a very serious accident. She nearly bled to death. She walked through a plate-glass window. Go look in the studio if you want to."

"Oh Jesus! Jesus!" Bobby was shouting, spitting venom, the white spittle from his lips. "You scared the shit out of me. I thought she was dead!"

With a roar he jumped me from behind and tried to bear me to the floor. I whipped my shoulders around and shrugged him off, but before I could attack, Faun had grabbed my arms and swung her body between me and Bobby. I lashed out with my foot, the only way I could get at him, and caught him smack in the nuts. As he flopped over in pain, I shoved Faun aside, then dragged Bobby across the hall and out the front door, where I dumped him on the stoop.

"All right, Funny Face, you're out of here." I went back inside and slammed the door. I locked it, turned out the front lights, and ran back to the Snuggery. Faun was collapsed in a chair, sobbing into her hands.

"All right, Miss Blue-Bitch, you can turn off the waterworks now," I told her. "I'm not interested. You're acting's every bit as lousy as it was last month, so can it. What I want to know from you, now that Jo-Jo's incapacitated, is—whose idea was it? I mean, did you think it up or did he?" She'd gone all white-faced and was biting her lip hard. "Well, damn it, *did* he?"

"Stop it! Stop saying that! I didn't try to murder her! I can buy a bottle if I want to, can't I? I'm over twenty-one. You haven't got a thing on me! Now I'm going out to Bobby."

But Bobby had apparently found the good sense to get lost; we heard the screech as his car went tearing across the gravel and through the front gates. As Faun started to dash after him, I held her forcibly by the wrist, and we tugged at each other until Ling appeared in the doorway, with Maude, white-faced, behind him. Faun began to sob and wail, then she sagged and among us, we helped her to her quarters in the Playhouse. The room was chilly, there was only the porcelain stove in one corner and neither Ling nor I could get it started, so we covered her with an extra blanket. Maude got a couple of Tuinals into her, and when she'd subsided, we tiptoed out. We went back to the Snuggery, talking quietly; than I left.

The next day I talked with the doctor, who assured Maude and me that Belinda would be all right, though she'd indeed had a narrow escape.

While by no means fatal, Belinda's accident had given us all a very bad scare, a worse one to Frank, who again let business slide in order to stay close by in time of need. Angie drove up from the desert also, to be on hand during Belinda's private recuperation—the sordid details of the accident were kept from the press, even friends (one paper reported she was in the hospital for a face lift, another claimed a full body retread). When the bandages came off and the stitches were taken out, she asked me to take her to an A.A. meeting. I'll never forget her standing up in that church activities room and saying, "I'm Belinda Carroll and I'm an alcoholic. I've been sober for nineteen days." Nineteen days, after her seven long years of hard-won, so-precious sobriety, and badly robbed of it by her vicious daughter and a dumb turd of a boyfriend.

But despite what might have been a real tragedy, despite the fall from grace, that momentary lapse with the Zubrovka, Belinda bounced back. She had enormous resiliency, she was the original survivor (Maude used to say Belinda would have walked home from the *Titanic* sinking), and her injuries quickly mended. Luckily her face had escaped irreparable damage, and between the lot of us we soon had her in good spirits again. Few but the "friends of Bill" knew about her having ingested nearly a bottle of Polish vodka (she joked about having a thing for buffalo grass), and the incident resulted in no flare-up of her addiction. She confided to me that she thought that by now she'd completely lost her taste for alcohol and we counted that a blessing.

In the meantime, Faun didn't show much remorse. She was pure brass, still denying any wrongdoing in the matter. Some people are without shame; she headed the list.

Maude had a long, serious talk with her behind closed doors, though what good such talk did I couldn't have said. Still, certain changes had come about: Bobby was permanently banished. No music blared, no lights burned late. And now there was no more talk about the "tome," about pub dates and book-and-author luncheons and best-seller lists, no more *tap tap* of the typewriter, which she put away in her closet. The new broom swept clean, and Faun quickly renovated her whole style; she began wearing clothes more suitable to her age. It was a tonier, more uptown sort of look, lots of status symbols—stack heels, rings on only two fingers, hair held back with barrettes, her good jewelry. There'd even been a speech change, not so slangy, and I'd hear her toss in bits of French or Italian. Now she came around with a whole contingent of Continentals she'd fallen in with at the same club.

Belinda improved daily, and when I was sure she was going to be all right, I temporarily shifted my operations to New York, where I went through the harrowing procedure of seeing my play put on—but not for long; it closed on the third night. Among the first-nighters I stumbled across was my ex-spouse. Jenny was in town visiting friends and had come to lend moral support. We didn't get to say much more than hello-goodbye, but I took her to Jim McMullen's for lunch next day and we talked things out. It was funny how, no longer suffering the bonds of matrimony, we could relax with each other and be friends. She was "seeing" someone she'd known since childhood, a middle-aged widower up in the bucks, now looking for a second wife. Jen wanted to sell the Sunset Plaza house, and I agreed that it had served its purpose nobly; I had no wish to return there. Put it on the market and we'd split the profits. She even invited me to the wedding the following June.

When my play had fallen on its ass, I went away to lick my wounds, eventually to sneak back into L.A., tail between my legs. No matter how philosophical you try to act, a flop hurts, and I wasn't experienced enough to know how to handle it. But Maude was there to tend my wounds. The Cottage was filled with flowers, the windows sparkled, and I gratefully took up my abode again at Sunnyside. Before I knew it I was feeling at home, as if I'd lived there all my life.

Nothing much seemed to have changed around the old place. Maude's garden was showing the last of its flowers, the chrysanthemums gave the flower borders an autumnal air, and with a nip in the weather the pool heater had been turned up. We resumed our swimming sessions, and as we talked across the water it dawned on me that I'd been living at Sunnyside a whole year. By now Belinda had fully recovered from her accident—the face was fine; looked better than ever—and she'd gone back to her golf and tennis, and Frank drove by often to take her to the Wilshire Club.

And where was Faun? Faun was long gone, which, I decided, was why everyone was so relaxed these days. She'd been gone a month, not a word, nor did we have any idea when she might return—if she returned at all. Yet of course it happened; the bad penny always turns up.

It was a Friday afternoon around four; Angie had driven her station wagon up to take away some furniture Maude was getting rid of; Maude's lawyer, Felix Pass, and his wife, Mildred, had stopped by to visit, and

Frank was due as well. We were all sitting out on the terrace, enjoying the view to the west, those empty hills that run in a ridge from beyond Mulholland Drive out past the Will Rogers Ranch, straight to the junction of Malibu and Santa Monica, out past Topanga Canyon. Then we looked suddenly to the doorway, where a group of unexpected guests appeared behind Ling.

"Hi, everybody!"

A figure darted forward and it took me a second to recognize who it was. Her hair was blonder and cut short like a boy's and she'd lost weight. Like some fairy sprite she skipped across the brickwork, arms open in greeting, and leaned down to kiss Maude. "Hi, Nana! What a perfectly gorgeous color!" she exclaimed over Maude's dress, then whirled away to kiss Belinda, all the time acting as if her sudden appearance were the most natural thing in the world.

"Oh, Mummy, isn't it unbelievable? Here I am, home again," she cried gaily. "You'll never guess the incredible things I've been doing. The fabulous places I've seen! And Mummy"—she waved to her companions, who approached diffidently—"Mummy—everybody, these are my friends. Asho, darling, come here." She imperiously directed one of the young men, who came to her side, a dark, slender youth of medium height and impeccable manners. "Ashoka, come kiss Mummy," she instructed him, and he did so, taking Belinda's hand and touching his lips to it as he bent. He was all European luxe, gloss and gold jewelry, looking (Angie later said) like one of those broomstick-shaped pseudo-counts in skinny blazers with crests on the pockets who only half-wait on you at Gucci's. This royal young gentleman—no mere count, he—was introduced as "Prince," His Highness Prince Ashoka Jasamin Ashokar, hereditary heir to some Moslem principality whose name still escapes me.

"Asho was named for a horse—an Arabian stallion," Faun explained as her young friend flashed both teeth and eyes and made his way around the guests, bending over the other ladies' hands.

"Jasamin by name," Angie muttered in my ear, "and Jasamin by nature, I should think." The prince, more weeping willow than good Arabian horseflesh, exchanged nods with me as he jerked a neat bow, and it occurred to me he might have a key in his back.

"And this," proceeded Faun, leading forward a doll-like figure of a girl who locomoted herself toward us with tiny gliding steps, showing us gigantic eyes all scribbled around with pencils of many colors and a beauty mark just *there*— "this" was the prince's "sister," whom Faun called Vashti like Jane Withers in *Giant,* and when Vashti articulated some words in our direction she spoke with a British accent, having been taught by the one-time governess of Grace Kelly's children. In her nose she wore a notable diamond and from her ears hung diamond pendants.

With these impressive personages were three or four others of commoner clay, names supplied by Faun that I failed to catch, though it seemed safe to assume they were subjects of H.R.H. There was much getting up and sitting down and the exchange of hollow pleasantries, and presently this party sprang up and trooped off behind Faun to take a gander at the tennis courts, the fountains, and the pools, while the rest of us fastened our seatbelts, for, to coin a phrase, it was going to be a bumpy night.

No; I was wrong. Other nights were to prove bumpy, but not this one, for having showed off the ancestral manse to her satisfaction, having got the princeling and princessling (well accustomed to palaces, our royals) to ooh and ah a bit, she had them all troop past us again and then they were gone. Kiss-kiss, bye-bye; the toy princess waved her bedizened fingers and rolled her kohled eyes, the prince bent over all the ladies' hands again, murmuring little Continental *tendresses*, "so happy, so much, thank you, *au'voir, arrivederci*," favored me with what must have been his most sincere handshake, and then he, too, was gone.

Luckily (as we considered matters) Faun had not come home to roost (well, she had, but we didn't know it then), only to show off her grandmother to the prince, the prince to Nana, but, of course, she couldn't stay. Friend Ashoka had engaged a large suite at the Beverly Wilshire, the very quarters occupied at times by Babs Hutton and Warren Beatty (not simultaneously). Hotelward proceeded this coterie of glittering nomads; the prince apparently lived in an unending succession of hotel suites, but was here to look at houses, having decided to take up his abode somewhere in the Hollywoods.

But though Faun was not in residence, that didn't stop her from tracking emotional mud into the house. Every day there was some difficulty, something to upset everybody, tears and high-tide emotions. The capper came when she was apprehended by a store detective at Gucci's, having shoplifted some Italian scarves from a counter. Nor had Gucci's been her only victim, for an examination of the contents of her bag revealed items purloined from other shops along Rodeo Drive.

It was the same story all over again, the Big Jolt on the six o'clock news, the press hammering at the gates, Belinda Carroll's daughter held in custody, her bail set, her release, the pictures smeared all over the place, her jaded comment, "I was only doing my Christmas shopping a little early." It required Frank's smooth manipulations to get the charges quashed, he having gone from store to store making ample restitution and pausing for a friendly word here and there with owners or managers.

Yet, with things at their worst, hope lay just over the horizon. With the holidays looming, we all were afraid that Faun would start throwing her monkey wrenches around and find further ways to upset her mother or grandmother. Our pleasure may be imagined when she made the announcement that she would not be here for either Christmas or New Year's, but instead was jetting off with the prince's party to Las Brisas in Acapulco. It sounded just like a Jane Powell movie; His Highness had engaged a number of suites for his guests and was taking his own music group with him (not Ragtime Cowboy Joe, however). She inveigled Nana into furnishing her with new outfits ("Nana, do you think he'll propose to me in *these* rags? I'll pay you back, I promise, soon as we're married. I can't even think how rich I'll be"), but the thought of Nana's being repaid for the outlay seemed unlikely.

True enough, it would be hard to estimate the prince's wealth, but Faun would prove equal to the task, I felt sure. And off she went, bags and baggage, off to see the wizard again, this time south of the border. All I could think of to say was *o-lay!*

Maude, too, was happy that Faun wouldn't be around for the holidays. I could tell she'd been badly slowed down by the stress that Faun always managed to create when she was around. Ling had told me privately that Maude was suffering from bad blood pressure and hypertension, too. I was glad when among us, Belinda, Felix Pass, and I were able to persuade her in two decidedly important matters. First, I got her to let me make an appointment with her doctor, old Harvey Travers, who'd had her health in hand for years. He gave her some pills for her blood pressure. But pills or no, she was still nervous, and I knew she was suffering from insomnia and sat up watching *Cattle Queen of Montana* or *Artists and Models Abroad* on the *Late, Late Show*.

Second, I had a private talk with Felix and Mildred Pass, whose fortieth wedding anniversary fell between Christmas and New Year's Eve, and they insisted Maude come down to the desert and help celebrate. When she talked it over with me, I said what a terrific idea, she'd have a wonderful time and certainly she should go. And I went along, too, to make sure she did.

Being the originator of the Great Palm Springs Christmas Conspiracy, I arranged my schedule so I'd be spending the same amount of time away as Maude. She would guest with the Passes, I with Frank, while Belinda would stay with Angie over in Cat Wells, a scant five miles away.

I drove down with Maude in the Rolls; we arrived in the Springs shortly before four and went directly to the Passes' house, where Felix and

Mildred were waiting. When we'd been welcomed and had a look around, I said goodbye and continued on with Ling.

Lina O'Leary, one of the clan of Mexican-Irishers who were part of Frank's extended family, admitted me to his house. I hung up my dinner clothes, jumped into swim trunks, and went out to catch the last rays of sun. While I basked, I telephoned over to Cat Wells and talked with the greatest talker of them all. Angie was revved up like an Indy race car, full of questions, wanting to know all the latest dirt regarding Faun's romance, how was it going, when was the wedding, like that.

Our conversation was interrupted by the door chimes. They rang and rang, and, deciding that Lina must be elsewhere, I excused myself to Angie and went out front to investigate. There was a car in the drive but no driver. Puzzled, I went back to Angie on the phone, and just then I spotted a figure coming around the corner of the house.

"Isn't anyone even going to answer?" I heard that familiar voice call.

"Guess who just turned up at poolside?" I whispered to Angie. I uttered the magic name and said I'd call her later.

"Don't they have anyone to answer the door?" Faun complained, coming toward me. Masking my astonishment at this unexpected appearance, I offered her a drink. "We thought you were in Mexico with—"

"Don't even say it. It's all over. I came home." She hadn't been gone more than six days. Had something happened? Yes, it had. The prince had dumped her on her little round tushy. It emerged that he'd never had any intention of marrying her. What he—and his sister, the toy princess—had hoped was that after Christmas, Maude would put them up at Sunnyside. Faun had said she didn't think so. Ergo, el prince was now a thing of the past. The romance was *pfft, fini, kaputt,* over. Not only had Ashoka asked Faun to leave; more embarrassing, even before she could get her things packed, the gallant fellow had called a press conference to announce his betrothal to, of all women, his own sister Vashti, who as it turned out wasn't his sister at all but a sufficiently distant relative to make marriage possible. Ashoka Ashokar, Faun quickly learned, was under royal edict to marry his "sister" and no other; not to have wed the little Vashti meant he would not get his money, the fabled millions that were his upon his majority, and so, of course, he must do as was ordained by fate and Allah. Too bad—our Faunie had never stood a chance of reaching the throne. I could almost have felt sorry for her. Almost.

When she began to cry, I made no attempt to stop her. By this time I'd seen floods of her tears and I thought the more she shed now, the fewer she might shed later, when her mother was around. When she confessed that she'd come here to tell me "first," I took it as a compliment—though not too great a compliment. I figured I was the only one she wouldn't have felt ashamed in front of.

Eventually, I persuaded her to go into one of the guest rooms and lie down; she seemed under heavy stress, and I thought a nap would help. Then I called Angie and laid the matter out to her and said to soft-pedal everything to Belinda. At five o'clock Frank arrived as scheduled. I heard his car pull into the drive, the tires crunching on the gravel and the whine of the garage door mechanism as he drove in. Moments later he strode into the living room, exuding health and vitality. When he asked whose car was in the drive I explained that we'd had an unexpected visitor, currently resting. I saw his expression change and I knew he was assessing the possibilities, wondering what damage she might cause. When I explained what had happened to explode Faun's romance, Frank was sympathetic, though not surprised. Nobody would be, I suppose. We left her napping.

He made himself a drink, took a good swig, then slipped something from his pocket—a square velvet jeweler's box. He snapped the lid to show me the contents: a diamond ring of exquisite design, 7 carats in a platinum setting. He planned on giving it to Belinda tonight, and he wanted to be married in seven weeks, St. Valentine's Day.

Just then the phone rang and he went behind the bar to answer it. Since it seemed to be a call of some importance, to give him privacy I signaled that I was going in to grab a quick nap myself.

I don't know how long I slept, but when my eyes opened, the light coming in from outside was dim. I could hear voices, faint yet distinct, and as I lay there, I realized I was hearing Frank and Faun talking together on the patio outside the room where she'd gone to lie down.

"So you've picked tonight to announce your engagement," I heard Faun say.

"We're not going to announce it formally," Frank replied.

"I know, don't tell me—you're going to wrap little messages around flaming arrows and shoot them at all the guests."

"That'd be one way, I suppose. Don't you at least want to wish me and your mother happiness?"

"If I wish you something, it won't be happiness."

"That's too bad. What will it be?"

"I'll think of something."

"I'm glad you're here anyway; Belinda will be, too."

"Why do people always have the idea my mother is ever happy to see me?"

Frank's voice was showing his impatience. "Look, I'm sorry you and your friend broke up, but I can't really do anything about that, can I? And to tell you the truth, I don't think the prince was your type."

"I know he wasn't. I wouldn't have married him anyway. Especially when I'm in love with someone else."

"Yes? Are you?"

"You know I am. Didn't I say it? I'm in love with you."

"Come on, Faun," he begged, "please don't start in again."

"I'm not going to start in. But I want you to know it—before you make a terrible mistake. I want to live with you. Not with Mummy and you, just you and me. Didn't anyone ever tell you three's a crowd?"

"I'm sorry, I'd hoped we could be a family, the three of us. Your mother and I were both hoping someday the right guy might come along—"

"Are you cartooning? No right guy's going to come along, nobody. If he did, I wouldn't have him on a bet. It's you or nothing."

I could hear the disconsolate tone in Frank's voice as he spoke again. "Faun, you're a grown woman, you've got to stand on your own feet, you can't go on being a child forever."

"Didn't I say it? I don't want you to marry her." Faun's voice had begun to sound frantic. "Don't you know she'll only make trouble for you? She'll make you miserable, she doesn't understand you."

"All right, maybe we'd better not say any more about it. Excuse me." His feet sounded on the flagging and there wasn't any more talk, only Faun's sobs. I threw on a robe and went out. She was sprawled on a chaise, crying her heart out. Pretending I hadn't heard any of the conversation with Frank, I suggested that, since it was getting late and her mother would be expecting her at Angie's, she'd better go. She didn't argue, but left as I suggested.

Everybody in the world knew that Millie and Felix Pass threw the greatest parties in the world, and their yearly anniversary celebration had become close to an institution in the Springs; people flew in from places as far away as Chicago, Palm Beach, and New York to attend. The press was banned; this was a strictly private affair. No expense was spared, no detail overlooked. The ladies received gold pins with crossed golf clubs for favors, the men got key rings with their astrological signs. There must have been fifty waiters in green jackets, more parking boys outside. The music seldom stopped; two dance bands alternated on the stand, Latin and standard; the ceiling of the big striped circus tent was a floating cloud of pink balloons; the buffet, bracketed by towering ice sculptures of the host and hostess, was a feast, and when I passed the bar table I saw a pile of champagne bottles three feet high in the corner.

Since she hardly ever attended large gatherings, it was a mark of Maude's esteem and affection for her friends that she would have turned up for the big night. But there she was, in full fig and fine fettle, apparently having the time of her life. Soon after we'd greeted her, she urged Angie and me to get out there and dance, have a good time. I was in a mood for partying, and so we joined the other swingers on the floor. Angie reminded me she'd once won a rhumba contest, and showed she'd lost none of her old form. After Angie, I danced with Belinda, then with Millie, then with a series of other partners. But between dances both Angie and I made sure we spent a good part of our evening with Maude, no chore, believe me. It was after ten and there she sat, holding court at the table of honor. There were many who insisted on stopping by for a word, a smile from her. "Just wanted you to know we remember you," things like that. She was patient and polite to all.

One of the best rewards of that night's festivities was watching Frank and Belinda together. Nothing will ever erase the picture of those two moving together about the tent, from group to group, and you had the feeling the party was really in *their* honor, not Felix's and Millie's. At one point I saw them out on the dance floor; she was in his arms while he glided her with tricky footwork around and among the other dancers, his arm around her back, she looking up at him, her hair falling past her eye in that style I'd always liked, she smiling at him as he talked in her ear, the pair of them laughing at his joke. She was carrying a little gold mesh bag in her hand and she tapped his shoulder with it as if to say, "Aren't you terrible?" At that moment his lips touched her temple and she shut her eyes and they melted away into the crowd, dancing in a dream, and I knew the dream was taking place not down here in a rented tent but way up there among the stars, between Clouds Nine and Twelve.

I felt Angie's squeeze on my fingers, and when I looked around, her glance said to get a load of Maude. I slid her a look and saw on her face the sweetest expression imaginable as she went on watching Frank and Belinda, now in the center of the crowd, and when she caught my eye she winked. That's all, winked, but what that wink said to us.

"Maude, Chazz is dying to dance with you," Angie said, elbowing me to my feet. I didn't have to be told twice. I got Maude up and out on the floor and took her in my arms. As we danced, I felt many eyes on us, felt a wave of approval and affection surrounding us, and when flashbulbs began popping she gave me a tiny squeeze of nervousness, then turned on her most radiant smile, as if to say it was all part of the game. Maude was yet a star.

When we sat down again, it was at Vi's table. Sure, Viola was there:

she'd had friends drive her down, she'd never miss an event like this. She patted the empty seat beside her and when I joined her she wanted to hear everything I'd heard from Faun about the business at Acapulco. As if on cue, Faun herself appeared, wearing something long that showed all the right bare places. She was acting as if nothing were wrong. "Hello, Auntie Vi," she said, then leaned to kiss my cheek. Why was she being so nice, I wondered? I thought she'd be either drunk or stoned. Giving Vi and Maude the high sign, I invited her to dance. She followed well and seemed full of life, enjoying herself like any normal young woman at a dance. I had to hand it to her: she had her mother's spunk. I knew how badly she must be feeling the sting of rejection, and frankly, I'd been wondering why she'd bothered coming at all, since she clearly wasn't in a partying mood, nor had she sought her mother's or grandmother's sympathy. Every time I caught sight of her, either alone or with others, I had the feeling that she'd riveted her eyes on Frank and Belinda, as if their being together tonight were exerting some strange force on her. Then something happened that led me to believe I wasn't imagining things.

I knew that Frank hadn't wanted any special notice taken of the fact that this was to be his and Belinda's formal engagement, no speeches or cameras, and he wasn't going to make a thing out of giving her the ring. He simply waited until no one was looking and whisked her out through the back of the tent into the garden, then took her along the pool to the pavilion at the end, where, alone with her, he put the ring on her finger.

The ring was no surprise, since she knew all about it, but when she came back in, displaying it, you could tell she was as thrilled as if she'd been twenty and Frank her first fiancé. We were all seated around our table and Belinda was going from person to person showing off the ring, and as I glanced up, I saw Faun standing alone; she couldn't have been aware that anyone was looking at her or she would never have worn so naked a look on her face. I felt a chill, it was so filled with malevolence. She went on staring until I walked over and touched her; then she started as though I'd given her an electric shock and her hand covered the spot on her arm where my fingers had rested, as if she were covering a painful burn.

"Go tell your mother you're pleased," I urged, "and Frank. It would mean so much to them."

When she turned her eyes on me, I saw that the green-eyed monster was still lurking; she couldn't rid herself of it. Just then Angie joined us. "Yes, do it!" she exclaimed, slipping a friendly arm around Faun's waist and giving her a kiss. "It *would* make them happy—"

"Why should I?" Faun snapped. "What do I care if they're happy?"

She ground out the words, bitter as could be. I was about to ask her to dance again when she whirled suddenly, then started rapidly for the entrance.

"Where are you going?" Angie called.

When Faun made no reply I hurried after her. "Faun, don't leave now, don't spoil things for your mother."

"She's spoiled things for me, I guess I can do the same for her. But this time I'm going to spoil them for good."

She spoke quietly, almost in a whisper, then walked quickly away. I glanced around for Angie, who'd gone to have a word with Felix and Millie. I wandered out onto the lawn, where the air was still warm from the day's heat. As I looked out beyond the wall I saw a car come speeding out of the parking area, lights off, and as it skewed on the gravel I heard the motor with that ticking sound: there went Faun, her scarf flying out the window behind her.

"Look," Angie said, coming up beside me and pointing at the two figures silhouetted against the section of wall directly opposite us. It was the lovers, their figures made one, washed with the turquoise light from the pool. "Oh Chazz," she said, "it really *is* never too late, is it?"

She slipped an arm around my shoulder and bussed my cheek; we were happy for them, happy for everything that had brought them together, just happy.

They looked over and waved us on; we came around the pool and joined them. When Belinda asked if we'd seen Faun, I lied outright, saying I'd just danced with her and she'd gone to the ladies' room. Angie seconded the falsehood. When Belinda suggested that she go look for her, I said let's dance instead. Frank took Angie, I Belinda, and we went back inside.

But as we danced, she began speculating about Faun again, and I made up a story about not having wanted to tell her but Faun hadn't been feeling well and had gone home. I could see Belinda's immediate concern; she said she'd wait ten minutes, then call Angie's house to check on her. No, let me do it, I said; then the orchestra broke and I led Belinda back to Maude's table.

When I called Angie's house I got no answer, but I remembered Faun's having mentioned something about another party. A moment later, Maude came up, saying she was tired and was going to slip off to bed. Then everyone was saying good night. Belinda and Angie got their bags and wraps and were ready to leave with Frank, who would drive them back to Cat Wells, while Ling was hovering in the background, waiting to take me to Frank's.

I was yawning grossly when I left the party and walked out to the waiting car. Ling left me off in Frank's driveway, and after we'd planned our time of departure in the morning, he drove away. I let myself in the side door, took a soft drink from the fridge and went back to my room, undressed, had a quick shower, put on my sleeping shirt, turned on the TV, and fell into bed. I watched the end of an old clinker—so help me, *Abbott and Costello Meet Frankenstein*—and it wasn't long before I was overcome with sleepiness. I doused the set, the reading light as well, and drifted off without the least trouble.

I should have slept straight through until daylight, but I didn't. Something woke me. It was shortly after two—I know because I looked at the digital clock on top of the television set. I was sure Frank must have come in, because I'd heard a car, then the sound of the automatic door rolling up—and it seemed there was another car, though, funnily enough, I thought that the other one had driven off; I vaguely recalled the sound of the motor as it went.

As I got up to go to the bathroom, my elbow accidentally hit my drink and knocked it on the rug. I got a towel and mopped up the wet, then opened my door and went along the passage to the kitchen to get a fresh drink.

The kitchen lights were still on. I was in error, then: Frank hadn't come home at all. He must still be over at Angie's. This struck me as a little strange, because he, too, was leaving for L.A. at cockcrow.

I got my drink from the refrigerator shelf, and as I shut the door I became aware of the sound of a running motor. I peered out the window above the sink, but the driveway was empty. The noise persisted, however. I set my drink down and stepped to the connecting door to the garage. When I opened it, a burst of smoke and poisonous fumes struck me in the face. The whole garage was filled with a deathly pall of smoke. I jumped back, slapped a wet dishtowel to my face, then reached around the doorjamb and touched the electric button to raise the garage door. As the fumes gradually began to clear, I tried to see through the haze to Frank's car, which I now could make out in its usual place, with the motor steadily operating. When the smoke cleared further, I began to make out a figure hunched over the steering wheel.

My shout was involuntary. I clapped the rag over my nose again and dashed around the rear of the car to the driver's side, where I yanked open the door and pulled Frank out. I dragged him across the concrete, out to the lawn and fresh air. Not only was he out cold, but there was a lot of blood. It was then I saw the hole in his forehead, the blood still leaking out. Dead, he was stone dead.

I ran inside and called the police, woke Lina, then telephoned to Angie to come at once. "See if you can make it here alone," I suggested, but it was no use. When she rolled in, Belinda was right beside her. I told her what had happened—there wasn't any keeping it from her. She wanted to see him, but I talked her out of that idea. I don't think she ever saw him again until we went to the funeral parlor. He wasn't a pretty sight, even with the wax plugging the bullet hole.

Needless to say, nobody went home in the morning.

Frank dead. Like everybody else, I heard the words and on hearing them told myself it wasn't true. Frank dead? Frank Adonis, shot through the head? The words were stunning, and the deep welling inside left me feeling bludgeoned. They let me look at the body "for purposes of identification," and I confess, it was the deadest looking body to be seen. I left the morgue and drove straight to the Passes' house and told Felix; together he and I told Maude. Though she took the news calmly, I could see how it jolted her. She had been enormously fond of Frank; theirs was an old and special relationship, and it was a bitter blow. Crispin, Perry, and now Frank.

But it was of Belinda we all thought; Belinda, to whom the tragedy meant more than the rest of us. Much as he meant to all of us, those who knew him best, much as we loved and admired him and would miss him, it was Belinda who suffered the worst shock, the strongest blow. Belinda, whose very life hinged on him. Belinda, whose long, crooked path of life had somehow straightened itself out because of Frank. It was wicked; it was sinful; it wasn't to be borne. But she bore, we all bore, because in these times, what else is there to do?

Frank dead.

There were questions, many questions to be asked. Since the shooting had taken place in Riverside County, the whole matter was dumped into the hands of the county seat in Riverside, twenty miles away. For four days the headlines blazed reports, rumors, and hearsay. Everybody who'd been at the Pass party was questioned by the proper authorities, with special emphasis on those who'd last seen Frank alive, Angie, Belinda, myself.

Whoever had killed Frank had either lain in wait to ambush him at his house or had followed his car from Angie's house in Cathedral Wells. Frank had driven the car into his drive, used the automatic button to open his garage door, driven in, and before he could even shut off his motor he'd been shot at close range. Executed, the papers said, for it was found to be a typical gangland slaying, and it produced another addition to the list of unsolved Hollywood Who Killed Cock Robin Murders. Who killed William Desmond Taylor? Who killed Thelma Todd? Who killed Frank Adonis?

It was tabloids and Late Editions and TV time. Somebody had iced Frank Adonis and the cops were going crazy looking for a suspect. The weird thing was, there weren't any. In that silent night of Christmas week down in the desert, Frank had been shot through the head with a Saturday-night special and the only witnesses to the dirty deed were the heavenly stars that had looked down for thousands of years, and the stars weren't talking.

Who had been the last to see Frank alive? Angie and Belinda were two, a service station attendant where he stopped for gas made three— who else? Had he gone straight home or had he stopped elsewhere along the way? He'd used his car telephone, but there was no record of the calls made. A witness claimed to have seen Frank's car tooling along Palm Canyon Drive around two. If so, where was he going, or where had he been?

What fingers there were pointed merely at "person or persons unknown," faceless phantoms in the Vegas crowd, some of whom were known to have had sundry dealings with Frank.

At the trial much testimony was offered by a variety of people, by the servants, by those who had last seen him alive, including Angelina Brown, the newly affianced Belinda Carroll, myself, even Maude Antrim. None of it proved in any way helpful. As for Maude, the press had a field day with her, since she hadn't made a public appearance in over twenty years. There she was, nicely dressed, quietly answering "to the best of my ability" each of the questions put to her, but you could see she wasn't up to it.

A hundred Maude Antrims wouldn't have made much difference, since nobody knew or had anything relevant to relate. It was a homicide, all right, but not the kind the cops like. Detectives are hired by the police department to dig up clues, find suspects, take down fingerprints, deduce things, bring in culprits, only in this case there were no culprits.

There *was* the matter of the *car*, however. Lina, the Mexican servant at Frank's house, stated that at approximately one-thirty in the morning she heard what she believed to have been a backfire in the driveway, and when she roused herself further she thought she heard a car driving away. But it was dark and she couldn't see.

Miss Carroll's testimony had been taken in the form of a legal deposition; she wasn't in any shape to take the stand in Riverside County Courthouse, but lay in a private room in a Palm Springs hospital under the care of a team of doctors who kept both press and police at bay. Only the county coroner and a court clerk were present when Miss Carroll had her say. It wasn't much. They'd become engaged that night, he'd given her a diamond ring, they'd planned to be married in February, the victim was planning to retire soon from his business practice as a well-known Hollywood talent agent and producer, that was about it.

It wasn't, of course; there was plenty of other comment, most of it garbage. The news file on Frank was dragged out; that file was then tied onto Belinda's file, as well as those covering Babe Austrian and a host of other famous women, including Claire Regrett. The morgues of the *Los Angeles Times* were ransacked for the juiciest, most lurid stories with which to attract their readership. But as for "person or persons unknown," they still roamed at liberty, whoever they were, free to go about their daily tasks, free, if so moved, to murder other innocent people.

Frank Adonis murdered? The guy everybody loved? It didn't make much sense, certainly not to the police, or to the newspapers, who, though they had a fair load of tripe to sell, had little more than tripe—and knew it. Those who knew more—and there were a few of those—kept their traps shut. The identity of the murderer, along with the identity of the owner of the car that left the house on Mondrian Drive late that night, remained a family secret, one more skeleton rattling around among several other family skeletons in the oversized Antrim closet.

Nor did the fact hurt that a close friend of the deceased was at one and the same time the chief magistrate of Cathedral Wells; having over the years garnered the friendship and admiration of many influential and important men in the area, the magistrate was quick to utilize her influence. The case was dropped, not with a thud, but quietly. And if in Vegas there were those who claimed that some hit-man in the employ of old Ears Satriano had waggled the finger, they, like us, knew there was but little truth in that theory.

Since I, too, had been present during the events leading up to Frank's death, I came in for my own share of questioning, but I had little to offer in the way of a solution. I was all three monkeys—I had heard no evil and seen no evil, and I certainly told no evil. What I *thought* I knew was something else, but nobody asked me for my suspicions in the matter. And while it was hoped by the police that one or more of us, his close friends, would be able to shed some light on the killing, they were flogging a dead horse while up a blind alley. Since I was such a dull witness, I was ordered to step down, after which I was free to come and go as I wished.

I went home, to Sunnyside, to Maude. We sat there in the Snuggery, accepting facts, swallowing cold, hard, unpalatable facts. Frank was dead,

Belinda was under sedation, Faun was—acting strange. I must say, Maude took things well, but, then, didn't Maude always? I went about the arrangements for the funeral, and with Minnie's help we got things set up —not at Forest Lawn, but at Hollywood Memorial Park Cemetery.

We delayed the services until Belinda was well enough to attend. Ling drove Maude and me down to the Springs and we brought her home with us. She seemed fine, bearing up. She picked out a dress Frank had liked, the shoes and bag to go with it, and had her hair done. Such preparations hardly mattered, since, like any self-respecting Hollywood funeral, Frank's took place on a gray rainy morning, which only added to the chill bleakness of the occasion, and there were black umbrellas galore.

The same priest who had buried Maxine Fargo was intoning the service when, as I stood with Angie, Belinda, and Faun—Maude wasn't present—she'd stayed home, taking care of the cold that had bedded her for a week—doing my best to listen, I noticed another limousine pull up in an empty space at the curb. The driver helped the passenger out onto the wet grass, holding an umbrella over her. Taking the umbrella, she headed for our group, disappearing behind the sea of other umbrellas. I nudged Angie and we were able to follow the latecomer's route as she made her way among the mourners, causing considerable agitation, forcing people to give way until she emerged at the front, nearer the grave than where we were standing. She wore a large black hat with a veil, and black gloves, and as she stood there slipping a white handkerchief up under the veil to dab at her eyes I heard Angie say, "My God, it's Claire."

Claire it was. She stood there, ramrod-straight, face hidden behind that veil that was right out of studio wardrobe, until the priest terminated his remarks. As he dropped in his three shovelfuls of the wet earth piled beside the coffin, we saw Claire break from her surroundings to throw herself sobbing on the flower-bedecked casket. At this the crowd stirred and a murmur of sympathy ran through it. I could see that Claire was about to slip in the mud and I went to help her to her feet. She staggered a little, getting her footing—she was on those spike heels of hers and the heels *would* sink into the damp sod. Finally two attendants came to my rescue and led her away to her car, where the driver waited, refusing to dirty his shoes, while she picked her way across the grass, her heels sinking three inches into the greensward and causing her to stop and pull out every half dozen feet or so.

Comical? You bet. It seemed to add just the touch of comedy Frank would have wanted, and I laughed to myself, imagining that he was looking down on the scene and saying, "Atta girl, Claire."

Humor was our only refuge. And I had to give Claire credit, she really saved the day. Even Belinda later agreed that Claire's performance had helped to dry her own tears. But when we told her about it, she laughed, too. So hats off to Claire—she'd really hit the right bizarre note, though the effect she'd made wasn't exactly what she'd had in mind.

And before leaving again for New York, Claire availed herself of the opportunity to press a call at Sunnyside, where she'd not set foot in some thirty-five years. Having kept her widow's weeds on, including the veil, she had herself driven up by Viola, and only through the latter's intercession was she admitted into Maude's presence. Explaining that she'd come to condole with the bereaved Belinda, only to be informed that Belinda had left town that morning and wouldn't be back until after the weekend, Claire then turned her attentions on Maude. No mention was even made of the fact that the woman shedding crocodile tears for Belinda had once been Maude's daughter-in-law—both women seemed eager to forget that fact—nor did either of them stop to weigh the love that was not lost between them. When Claire commented that the old place didn't appear to have changed much, Maude smiled as she replied that the whole house had been redone since Claire's time. Twice, in fact. Claire recovered by saying she sincerely believed that Maude's taste in glazed chintz was nonpareil.

Since there were others waiting to have a word with Maude about the tragedy, Claire didn't stick around very long, but she was able to display herself to advantage before the cameras stationed outside the gates, where she autographed the books of a busload of tourists who'd been waiting to glimpse her—or anyone else coming or going. Throwing back her black veil to declare herself to be "the best friend Frank Adonis ever had," she signed every last book, down to the tiniest tot's, before she would consent to get into Viola's waiting car. "Bless you, darlings," she called to them, crossing herself as they drove away, thus mystifying Viola, who knew she wasn't Catholic but Jewish.

Next chapter. No—final chapter.

I had to fly home to Connecticut; there was an illness in the family. I was gone a month and when I got back to Los Angeles in late March it had been raining for eleven straight days and the world was drenched; people were building arks and loading them up, two lions, two zebras, two giraffes, even a partridge in a pear tree. Under a sky of tin the soaked earth tried desperately to shed the moisture it could no longer absorb; houses slid into infinity while freshets of rainwater red as Tara's earth came sluicing down the narrow shoulders of the roadway as I proceeded cautiously up the winding canyon. Whole chunks of sodden embankments had broken away and lay in heaps, and here and there large trees lay uprooted, leaving their root systems exposed.

The Cottage, however, was gauged for a warm welcome when I let myself in. A fire crackled cheerily in the grate and there were fresh-cut flowers arranged in a bowl. "Welcome home," said Maude's note. "*Après nous, le déluge.* Isn't our weather beastly? Bones is fine. Call me soonest. Love, M."

Some things never change, I thought. It was good to know that there were people in this world whom you could depend on utterly. I put on my oldest, baggiest cords and the moth-eaten maroon cashmere pullover Jenny had given me about two lifetimes ago. As I was putting socks away in the drawer, my eye fell on one of the photographs on the bureau-top. A Kodachrome shot taken up at the pool—my grinning face, Angie on one side, Belinda on the other, Maude directly in front. We were all tanned and redolent of good health and high spirits. I calculated that picture had been taken only eight months ago, yet how long ago it seemed now. Now everything had changed, and nothing would ever bring back those happy times again. They were gone forever, and my eyes stung at the thought.

I'd seen Belinda only three days before. The last thing I'd done prior to leaving the East was to drive up to Easton again, to that place where she'd been staying since her breakdown. Granted, she was far from those closest to her, but it seemed the logical move since it was there that she'd been cured the first time.

Belinda was going to be fine, and thus I reported when Maude and I were sitting by the fire in the Snuggery, that well-named room; and how I'd missed it. It seemed to me that nothing, not flood or fire or the Four Apocalyptic Horsemen, could disturb its intrinsic peace and harmony, the sturdy, tradition-bound look of the place with its fine old furniture, the gleam of silver and crystal, the handsome pleated drapery at the mullioned windows, the twin portraits of Maude and Crispin facing each other on the walls, Bones spread across the oval rug close to the hearth, his eyes never leaving me. Hey, boy, good boy . . .

I feared for Maude, bless her—she was showing the strain. I'd noticed it the minute I walked in and we embraced; she was thinner, she had circles under the eyes, cheeks were drawn. We sat close to the warmth of the fire, listening to the rain rattling like pebbles in the downspouts, the wind soughing through the dripping branches of the trees. Now and then a limb would brush against one of the windows. It was a scene out of Hitchcock; she was Joan Fontaine waiting to be murdered—it was something he'd put in the milk—I was the stranger out of the storm; was there a beetle-browed Mrs. Danvers sniffing about?

I went on with my account of Belinda's present circumstances. She'd taken a nosedive, a bad one. Now her liver was involved and, as the doctors had warned, if it happened again, if she went back on the booze yet another time, it could prove fatal. When she came home again, there must be no more disturbances, no more violent upsets. She was still strong, she had hidden resources, but how often could she hope to rely on those? Resources dry up. How many times could she make the trip to the well before she found it empty? And how many more times could she make the big slip and still hope to retrieve herself? Sure, you always get a little help from your friends, but in the end you damn well do it yourself. One thing was certain: she mustn't come home if her darling daughter was going to be on hand.

"How's Faun doing in New York? Wasn't she supposed to be staying at Claire's?"

Maude moved the tea table closer and began pouring. "She *was*. However . . ." She stiffened and the tea spout clicked against the porcelain rim. Dot-dot-dot.

"Was."

"Was. But it seems the blush is now off the rose so far as Faun is concerned."

"*Persona non grata?*"

"Precisely. Don't ask what they quarreled about, I couldn't say. But Faun isn't having any more New York just now."

"What's she going to do?"

"I believe she intends having some more Sunnyside. For the nonce, at least." She used the silver tongs and carefully slipped three cubes into my cup. "Says she can't take the pace, has the jitters. I suppose the big city *can* do that to one." I saw her hand tremble as she passed the cup and saucer. She saw that I saw. "Anyway, she's—back," she finished softly.

Back. Little Orphan Annie was back home again, and Mommy Warbucks was going to be shelling out again (wasn't she?). "What's she been up to in the big city, then?" I inquired casually, glancing around as if I expected to see her pop out of a corner somewhere.

Maude's brow furrowed. "I don't really know. She . . . says she's tired. Very tired."

"Of what?"

"Who knows?"

Living, maybe, I thought. This mortal coil.

"Do you mean to let her stay?"

"If she behaves herself."

"Will she?"

She gave me a look filled with bewilderment and indignation and her lip trembled. Tears sprang into her eyes and the drops trickled down her cheeks.

"What is it?" I asked. "What's she done this time?"

"Not what she's *done*," Maude replied. "What she intends *to do.*"

I felt my gut contract. I moved closer. "What is it? You don't mean —not that damn book?"

Her head moved slowly up and down. She kept her eyes averted while she dabbed at them.

"Are you telling me she's threatening you again with this nonsense? Holding it over your head?"

"She is."

"Why, that's a lot of you-know-what."

She half-laughed. "It's all right, you can say the word."

"Bullshit. It's pure unadulterated bullshit." But I knew better even as I tried to comfort her. Good Maude, kind Maude, innocent and deluded Maude. In her wildest imaginings did she think Faun was going to "behave herself," as she'd so naively put it? I doubted it. Some things were just too much to hope for. But I wasn't there to try and disabuse her of whatever consoling notions she was currently harboring, I was there to do whatever she wanted me to do. Putting myself in her place, I could understand how hard it would be to turn someone from her door—turn *Faun* from her door, Faun, her only child's only child. Even after the terrible thing she'd done—but of course Maude had refused to acknowledge that. And maybe that was just as well.

She asked me to stay to dinner, but I had to decline; there was a business obligation I was forced to honor. She suggested I stop in later and I said I'd try.

I was back at Sunnyside as early as I could manage, and found Maude where I'd left her, in the Snuggery. Hadn't touched her meal and was being scolded by Ling. I got rid of him and the food, and had him bring in tea; she would always drink tea and maybe have a biscuit with it.

When I sat down opposite her, she looked me directly in the eye, but said nothing. When I raised my brows questioningly, she raised hers in reply.

"Yes?" I prompted.

"We—are—go—ing to have a *vis—it—torr*," she said with strict enunciation, then sat back with a so-there! attitude. She didn't have to say the name; I knew who our visitor would be. I felt tired, too tired to sit and talk with Faun, but there it was; I couldn't get up and walk out. Presently there was a rap on a pane of the terrace door and through the glass I saw her figure. I got up to let her in. She put her face up to mine and when I didn't kiss her she drew quickly away. I stepped back, taking her in as she passed me, thinking she looked considerably different, hair, makeup, clothes—even attitude. For the first time ever she looked grown up to me.

"Come in, Faun," Maude said, making like a hostess. "Will you take a cup of tea?"

"Nothing, thank you, Nana." Was her voice different, too, or did I only imagine it? She slipped into a chair in what struck me as a more mature way, sliding her hand under the back of her thigh to smooth her skirt and crossing her legs in that inimitable way some women have, smart and chic. I realized later she'd probably picked it up from Maude herself. "Nana, we have to talk," she began, and when I got up to go she said no, she preferred I stay. "I want you to hear this, too," she said, so I sat down next to Maude and waited.

"Nana, the fact is—I need some money. I know—don't say it—I always need it, but this time I *really* do."

"Didn't you get your first-of-the-month check?"

Faun acknowledged that her monthly stipend had come through on schedule.

"Very well," Maude replied, avoiding argument if it was to be avoided, "if you're feeling the pinch, I'll be happy to lend you some. What shall it be, three or four thousand dollars?"

"I'm afraid that's not nearly enough. And let's not speak of loans, either—I don't know when I'd be paying you back. But since you have a great deal and I have next to nothing—"

Maude grew terse—"See here, young lady"—but Faun's hand flashed, cutting off her words with jangling bracelets.

"Nana, please let's not start with the grandmother act tonight, okay? I'm really too grown up for that these days, don't you think?" She was taking a "reasonable" tone. "You don't spend an awful lot of money, your expenses are actually quite modest, I should imagine. And what with the money both you and Grandfather must have salted away, you can't really be wanting. And since you'll be leaving it to me one day anyway—"

"Now now, just a minute, my dear. I don't know where you got that idea, but let me disabuse you of any such notion. You're making a big mistake, a very big mistake, if you're sitting around waiting for me to die so you can get your hands on my money. You had your trust fund from

Crispin, which you saw fit to give away to your Maharishi friends—"

"What can I say? I made a mistake, I admit it."

"People who give away all their money on a whim aren't deserving of having more money—unless they earn it themselves. I've already spent a considerable amount on you over the years, and if, as you say, you're grown up now, I think you should give thought to earning a living on your own. As for your anticipating any further large bequest, I'm afraid that's out of the question. My funds are carefully allotted to the charities I desire to see supported. So if we're talking real money here, I suggest you adopt a more realistic attitude."

Faun bridled and her bracelets sang again. "Frankly, Nana, I don't think you're being terribly clever, if you'll pardon me for saying so."

"When you get to be my age you'll discover it's hard to be many things. Being clever is only one of them." She sat back and folded her arms. "Continue, please."

Little by little Faun's face had been stripped of any softness, and I could see she was out for blood. "Why don't you tell your grandmother how much money you need and what you need it for," I suggested, and she swung toward me.

"That's nobody's business but mine. Everybody needs money but— the fact is—I need a lot of money and I need it fast."

Maude laughed outright. "Oh, my dear, I'm afraid you'd have a lot of trouble finding a lot of money lying around here."

"I think if you'll just open up the till you'd manage to come up with it. And Nana—if you don't—"

I saw red. "Faun, cut this out right now. I'm not going to let you sit there making threats—who do you think you are, anyway?"

"I guess we all know who I am, darling. I want the money and I think I'm right in believing I'll get it. Otherwise I'm afraid I'll be forced to do something I know you don't want me to do."

"What is that?"

Faun took a pack of cigarettes from her bag, lit one with a gold-and-onyx lighter, blew out two pencils of smoke. I thought, "My God, she's doing Claire Regrett!"

"Did either of you ever stop to wonder why you haven't heard anything about my book lately?" she asked.

"Jesus. That again?"

"Very much *that* again. Surprising as it may be to you, I have a publisher for it."

"Terrific. So where's the difficulty? Can't you get an advance on it?"

"Possibly. Depending on what I can . . . come up with."

"What does that mean?"

"What do you think? Inside stuff. You know, the *real* lowdown, the *dirt.*" She stared at me. I knew she was daring me to get upset.

"And—what dirt would that be?" I calmly asked.

"Oh—whatever might be . . . around."

"Around what?"

"Around my family, idiot. I mean—every family has its skeletons hidden away in the closets, isn't that so? Way in the back, behind the winter coats? Don't you agree, Nana?"

"Perhaps." Maude never blinked or stirred.

"What skeletons would these be?" I next inquired. Maude's eyes were on us and I knew she was waiting for the answer.

"Well, as a matter of fact—um—some interesting information has recently come to light." She looked at her grandmother. "And if you don't —help me—I'm going to have to put it in the book. You know what I'm talking about. Grandfather and—"

Maude straightened, her eyes blazing. "Stop it! You will do nothing of the kind! I forbid you to write a single word about—about—"

"About what, Nana?"

Maude clamped her lips into a tight line and her face reddened. "Hear me, young woman. If you dare to write so much as one derogatory word concerning Crispin Antrim, you will never see me again. You will never set foot in this house, your allowance will be cut off forever, and I shall alter my will to the extent that it still benefits you. Do I make myself clear?"

Faun spoke softly, reasonably. "But, Nana, don't you see, if I publish my book, I won't need an allowance; had you thought of that? It's only right now I need the money. After that you won't ever have to give me another cent. When my book gets published, I can sell the movie rights for lots and lots of money."

"You would do this thing? You would dare to write wicked things about your grandfather, that dear man—your own flesh and blood?"

"Just give me the money, then, and that'll be the end of it. I'll go away and you'll never hear from me again. That's fair enough, isn't it? Nana? Do say something."

"I shall say nothing more. I refuse to discuss it further. Either say you'll give up this vile notion or I shan't be responsible for the consequences. Now, if you'll excuse me, I want to go to bed."

"Wait, *Nana!*" she wailed. "I *need* it. You've got to give it to me or—"

"Or what? Go on, tell me."

"It won't be my fault. I'll only be doing what you've forced me to do. I don't want to do it, Nana, really I don't, but you're *making* me do it. It'll be your fault, then."

"Is that what you think? Do you really believe that? *I* am making you do it. What a joke. And what a foolish creature you are. I am more ashamed of you than of anything in my entire life. I regret the day your father ever planted the seed of you—or that your mother ever allowed you to be born."

"That's all you ever talk about—Mother! I don't want to hear about her. I'm only here to talk about what's going to happen if you don't give me the money."

Maude's indignation turned to scorn. "Money! It's always a question of money with you, isn't it? You're money-mad. You have dollar signs for eyeballs. You speak and coins fall from between your lips!"

"I *need* it!" She beat her fists on her knees and her voice strained with urgency.

"I have no doubt you may need it. But not from me, not now and not ever." She sat back and refolded her arms, defiant, contemptuous. "And tell us, my dear—is that why you—"

"Why I what?"

"Is that why you shot poor Frank, because you needed money and he wouldn't give it to you?"

"I don't know what you're talking about."

"Don't you, though!" Maude suddenly jumped up and stood over Faun, her whole body trembling. "I've had just about enough of you and your lies. No more, Miss, no more. We know perfectly well it was you. We all know. Tell her, Charlie."

Faun turned to glare at me. I could see the fear in her eyes, fear that I'd say something she didn't want to hear.

"Don't look at me as if you don't know what your grandmother's talking about," I told her. "You know goddamn well you shot him."

"You're crazy! I never did! Nobody ever accused me."

"No one accused you because we all agreed we wouldn't let you get hurt—for your mother's sake. If we'd turned you in, you'd have gone to jail, maybe you'd have been executed. Do you think your grandmother wanted that? You're goddamn lucky we didn't tell what we knew."

"You bastard! You do hate me, you've always hated me, you'd do anything to—to—"

"I'd do anything to protect your mother, if that's what you mean. I'd do anything to stop you from causing her any more trouble than you have. You're right, I do hate you. You've done nothing but cause people misery for years and years—all the way back to Bucky Eaton. Poor Bucky—what a mess you made of *his* life."

"Bucky—what's Bucky got to do with this, for God's sake?"

"He was the first of your victims, poor fellow. God knows how many others there've been. But it stops, it all stops right here, tonight, in this room it stops, do you understand? And as for this nonsense about your book, I think you're just bluffing. You don't know diddly about Crispin Antrim, so why don't you just run along and peddle your papers."

"Oh you—!" Unable to think what to call me, she unsnapped her bag with a crisp, declarative sound and her hand brought out a packet of envelopes.

"What are those supposed to be?" I demanded sarcastically.

"What do they look like? Nana—what do *you* think they are?"

Stiff in her chair, Maude regarded the letters as if they might bite her.

"Five letters, and very interesting ones. Letters of a highly incriminating nature. Look closely, Nana, maybe you'll recognize the handwriting."

She held them up so that Maude could see the superscription, then took them quickly away as if she was afraid someone might snatch them from her.

"How did you come by those?" Maude asked.

"Quite easily, as a matter of fact. When I was in New York I saw an old friend of yours, Nana. I wonder if you can guess who that might be?"

"I wasn't aware we were playing guessing games."

"This—friend of yours—had lots of interesting gossip to tell me. But, then, Claire usually does, doesn't she? Yes, *darling* Auntie Claire. And would you care to hear what I learned from her?"

"I've no time to listen to your wicked talk. I said I was going to bed and I am."

"But, Nana, don't you want to hear what Claire had to say? Don't you want to know what's in these letters? I'm sure someone like you would find it *ver-* ree interesting. *Especially* in the light of the way Claire behaved at the funeral."

Maude was struggling to maintain her equanimity in the face of this cat-and-mouse game, and I wanted to give Faun a good crack in the chops for baiting her.

"Then perhaps Charlie wants to hear. Maybe he'll appreciate what I've got here that's worth fifteen thousand dollars." She held the letters up again and I tried to grab them but she put them quickly behind her.

"Tch tch—didn't your mother tell you it's not polite to grab? Very well, I'll explain what these letters contain."

"I'd rather you did not," Maude said.

"But, Nana, he's family, I've heard you say so. To Mummy— 'Charlie's like one of the family now.' "

She slipped some pages from the first envelope and held them up. "Wait," Maude said. She looked at me. "It's true, Charlie is one of my family, but I do not care for him to hear the contents of those letters. Charlie, be kind enough to wait outside for a moment or two while I speak with Faun. Perhaps Ling could make us some coffee."

I went into the kitchen and asked Ling to put the coffeepot on. He set up the silver tray with sugar and cream; then we sat on opposite sides of the counter, hardly speaking, watching the pot, which, as is proverbial, took long to boil. Then the Snuggery numeral clicked up in the little box and Ling poured the hot brew into the silver pot and set it on the tray.

He managed to mask his indignation when I said I'd carry it in. In the Snuggery I found Maude and Faun more or less as I'd left them, only now Maude was holding the packet of letters in her hand, while Faun lit another cigarette *à la* Claire.

"Ah, I can smell Ling's coffee from here," Maude said as I set the tray down at her elbow. "We're sorry to have kept you waiting so long, Charlie, but Faun and I had certain matters to discuss. Happily, our differences have been resolved, isn't that true, Faun?"

"As far as I'm concerned, Nana dear."

I poured coffee for Maude, then offered a cup to Faun, who shook her head and yawned at me. "Not for me, thanks; I don't want to stay awake another night." She took out a prescription bottle and spilled two capsules into her palm: good old Tuinals.

I threw another log on the fire, and as I turned, she covertly showed me a filled-in check with Maude's shaky signature and made a supercilious face meant to be amusing. I didn't find it so.

"Before I toddle off, Charlie, I'll bet you'd like to know what's in those letters that's worth all that money, wouldn't you?"

"If you'd care to tell me."

"Why don't you tell, Nana?"

Maude set down her cup and picked up the packet from her lap. "Come here, Charlie, please," she said. I went and stood by her chair. She put the letters in my hand and firmly closed my fingers around them. I looked down at her, then at the letters, saw the handwriting, and identified it as Crispin's. The letters were addressed to Claire Regrett. When I looked up, I recognized the wish in Maude's eyes and bent to set the packet on top of the flaming logs.

"Thank you." Maude picked up her cup again and took a sip of coffee.

Faun began to laugh. "Fifteen thousand dollars' worth of ashes," she said as the draft carried black scraps up the chimney and out onto the marble hearth. "What do you think of that, Charlie?"

"I think it's all over now," I said sternly, "I think you have your money and I think you'd better leave. That's what I think."

"My." She put out her lip. "Very well. To bed, to bed." She got up and glanced in the mirror, but didn't seem to like what she saw. Turning, she smiled at Maude, saying, "Good night, Nana. I knew you'd see things my way. And just in case you'd thought of stopping this check"—she waved it daintily—"you'd better think twice about that. I have Xeroxes." She folded the check, and when she put it in her bag she slipped out the corners of some white folded pages.

Maude sat taking this in; then her face crumpled and she began to weep and I jumped to take the cup from her hands. I knelt beside her, murder in my heart. Maude pushed me aside and got up unsteadily, refusing to look at Faun. I rang for Ling and when he came and saw his mistress in tears he glared at Faun and then followed Maude out into the hall.

After she had gone, I turned and stared at Faun, who'd remained in her chair, curled up like a cat, idly smoking her cigarette. "Thought you were going to bed," I hinted. I, too, longed for my pillow.

She said she was going, but made no move to do so. Said she was waiting for the pills to hit her. Suddenly the lights blinked out and the room fell into darkness. "*Oh!*" She leaped up with a startled cry. "What is it? What's happened?"

"Relax. We lost our power again; it'll come back on. Do you want me to walk you over?"

Declining my offer, she stayed huddled on the sofa, her figure picked out in the firelight. I stepped into the hallway and called to Ling, but then realized he must be upstairs with Maude. I knew from experience that there wasn't any use fiddling with the fuses: the lights would come on whenever they chose to. I went back into the Snuggery and sat across from Faun, who'd helped herself to a drink. Pills and booze? Great.

I rang the bell-pull, then sat. She didn't say anything, I didn't say anything. It was eerie, sitting there like that. She eyed me in the light from the flickering flames. I wondered what it would feel like, my hands around that white neck, choking the life from her. They say it takes time to choke a person to death.

I went on staring at her and presently my look had its desired effect:

tossing her hair back, she demanded to know what I thought I was looking at.

"Only looking," I answered blandly. "Cats and kings, you know."

"But you're thinking things. Shitty things."

I laughed shortly. "Do you really want to know what I was thinking?
I was thinking of Fay Bainter."

"Who?"

"An actress; you're too young to remember her. She was a friend of
your grandmother, though. Fay Bainter was once in a film with Bette
Davis; it was called *Jezebel.* "

"What's that have to do with me?" Faun asked, feigning boredom,
but I could see she was curious.

"Suppose I tell you, then. Jezebel was a woman in the Old Testament, and when Bette asked Fay Bainter what *she* was thinking, she
replied, 'I was thinking of someone called Jezebel—who did evil in the
sight of the Lord.' "

Faun colored and leaped up. "That's a terrible thing to say!" She
stood over my chair, favoring me with her most menacing glare. "You
son-of-a—"

"I know the rest of that one. Tell me, sweet thing, what do you
intend doing with those Xeroxes you have there?"

"They're going where no one can get their hands on them. When
Nana's check is put through, I'll send them to her."

"The hell you will!"

"What's the matter, don't you trust me?"

"No, I don't!"

"It's a rough world, Charlie; a girl like me has to think of herself, you
know. Think of the check as a first installment."

"And you'll be back for more."

"A girl gets homesick sometimes."

"*Sick is right!*" I jumped to my feet and threw myself at her. She
began to scream, kicking and flailing with her arms. The table went over
with a loud crash. With one hand I held her down while with the other
I tore the bag from her. As I yanked it open and fumbled for the papers,
she sank her teeth into my hand and I let out a yowl. I struck her hard
and she went limp. I crouched at the fireplace and fed the pages, one after
the other, into the flames, while my shadow danced on the wall behind
me. As I went on my task I looked back and saw Faun unmoving on the
couch. "I've killed her," I thought, but didn't stop until the last page had
been consumed. Then I was aware of a glow from the opposite side of the
room. Maude had hurried in with a lighted oil lamp.

"What is it? What's all the noise?" she demanded, then she saw Faun hanging over the edge of the sofa. "Good heavens, Charlie, what happened? You didn't kill her?"

"I don't think so, but it's not too late," I muttered.

Maude grunted in what I took as ironic assent. Setting down the lamp, she slipped her hand into mine and gave an anxious squeeze; her fingers were like ice. I released her hold and straightened Faun out on the sofa, then put some cushions under her head.

"Thank God," Maude said as Faun stirred. "Poor thing; poor poor thing," she murmured with genuine feeling. Then to my astonishment she stroked Faun's head and laid her cheek alongside her granddaughter's.

"She loves her," I thought, "loves her after all."

We got wet towels and revived her. Suzi and Ling appeared with more lanterns and we formed a circle around Faun as she moaned, then opened her eyes. When she realized where she was and what had happened, she didn't bother with any Camille act. She jumped up and started screaming at Maude about how I'd assaulted her.

Maude paid no attention, only asked Suzi to go up and put a lamp in the yellow room and turn down the covers; Faun would be sleeping there tonight.

"Like hell I will! Do you think I want to be murdered in my bed by this Mafia motherfucker?" I saw Maude flinch and I put my arm around her. Faun burst between us, flinging us aside as she swooped up her torn bag, and we watched her go stumbling through the terrace doors into the darkness.

"Let her go," Maude said to Ling, who had started after her. A spate of strident profanity rang in the outside air, then died away as she ran across the wet grass toward the Playhouse. Maude sank wearily into her chair, then gave me a humorous look.

"My hero."

"Hero?"

"My knight in shining armor. Again you've come to my rescue. You needn't deny it. Isn't that what white knights do—defend a lady's honor? Weren't you defending mine? And my husband's?"

Embarrassed, I demurred. She smiled wanly, and when Ling and Suzi went out, she asked me to make her a drink. "Just splash a little what-have-you on some ice."

I got up to investigate. I unearthed a half-empty bottle of bourbon tucked away in the under-bar cupboard, but there wasn't any ice.

"That's all right, I'll take it neat," she said. I thought she was suddenly—oddly—cheery, and I wondered what that meant. Maude was not being Maude. Or was she acting? I splashed the bourbon into a glass and handed it to her. She sipped and made a face, then took a good gulp. "You could take the paper off a plaster wall with that." She laid her head back wearily. "So. Little man, what now? I gather we are to have the Antrim Memoirs after all. Is that correct?"

I said not to worry about it. She grinned wryly. "Did I hear something about copies? Xeroxes? You burned them, I gather. But there are others?"

"I said don't worry. Why don't I find out who her publisher is and see if the thing can't just be quashed, on a gentlemanly basis? It's been done before. Might cost a little, but . . ."

She thanked me, but no, she didn't have any faith that such an obvious ploy would work. "In any case, this is family business and I prefer to keep it in the family." She fell silent for a time and I could see that her mind was hard at work. Her hands had made fists and she was biting her lower lip, and her fingers tapped the chair arms. Then she looked up, her eyes fastened on the bronze bust of Crispin on its mahogany pedestal. After a moment she turned to me, her eyes sparkling with tears. "He doesn't deserve it, you know," she said reproachfully. "He really doesn't."

Just then the telephone rang. "Ah," she said, sitting forward. "I guess we know who that's bound to be. Let someone else answer it." After a moment Ling slipped in to say it was Missy Fonn, complaining that her lights were out, too, and her rooms were cold.

"She can't say we didn't warn her," Maude said.

"I go fix," Ling began, shrugging on the yellow slicker he'd brought along.

"Yes, all right, Ling. I'm sorry, but it might be better if you went. I'm sure she doesn't want to see me again." She took another sip from her glass, then glanced away into the fire.

"Maybe you'd like me to come along?" I suggested to Ling. He shook his head and went out through the terrace doors. I sat again; Maude was sipping her drink and staring at the ashes scattered across the hearth: *Skeletons from our Closet.*

The clock ticked, the rain dripped, the room breathed slowly, like a slumbering dog.

"Maude?"

"Hm? Oh—yes, Charles. I know. You want to know what was in those letters that I fear so much. But I won't tell you. *Can't* tell you, I should say. I pledged myself—to him—never to tell. So you'll just have to read it for yourself in Faun's book. *Skeletons* indeed."

"Are you telling me this is something that will make a difference to anybody?"

Again her eyes went to the bust on the pedestal. "It's a question of the family honor," she replied. "At my age I find that things make very little difference. She's right, you know, I won't be around much longer. I know that. I've been prepared to go for a long time. I *want* to go. It's almost twenty-one years and I still miss him, every day I miss him. I'll be so happy to see him again. But I don't want to meet him knowing that that wicked girl over there has besmirched the name of Crispin Antrim."

Her look was fervent and her glass shook, glittering in the firelight. Her voice had begun to go hoarse. "Nothing's enough for her; there isn't enough love or understanding or compassion—or money—in the whole world to satisfy the greed that's in that girl."

"You're right," I agreed. "She's bent out of shape."

Maude looked up sharply. "Bent! What a felicitous word! She *is* bent. And—*I—simply—will—NOT—have it!*" Her face was drained of its blood and she spoke in a voice of brimstone. She was Lady Macbeth or Clytemnestra, Medea, all the great vengeful women. It was something to see. When she had polished off her drink she handed me the empty glass. " 'Please, sir, may I have some more?' " What was wrong? Was she going to get plastered tonight? And on Old Overholt?

I got up and splashed a little more into her glass and carried it back to her.

"Well," she said, holding up the glass against the flames, "here's to crime."

I glanced sharply at her but she was staring into the fire again. We heard footsteps on the terrace and Ling stood in the doorway, embarrassed because of the water he was dripping onto the floor.

"It's all right, Ling, don't worry about a little wet. Come in. Is she all right?"

Ling came into the room and shut the door. "Missy Fonn all pass out. I no can move her, she go sleep on sofa."

"Oh, the foolish creature!" Maude exclaimed impatiently. "She'll catch her death over there."

"Why don't I have a look," I said. "I can carry her up to bed."

"No, you stay here, please," Maude said abruptly. "Ling, fetch me a coat, and come along."

In seconds Ling was back with another slicker. I helped Maude into it and opened the door again, letting in another damp blast of air. The two went out together; I closed the door and sat down to wait. After a few moments I went to hot up the fire again. In a moment the clock chimed. I circled the room, peering out into the darkness; then I sat and waited some more, but recurring pangs of nervous energy and curiosity propelled me from my chair again and I went to the doors, cupping my hands as

I peered out. All I could see among the dark trunks of the trees was a glimmer of light through a downstairs window over at the Playhouse. Finally I opened the door and stepped out onto the terrace. The rain had stopped, but the gutters and eaves were dripping noisily. Again I peered across to the Playhouse, then decided to investigate. I loped across the lawn until I came under the beeches, whose wet branches sent cold drops down my neck. When I came abreast of the house, I looked in the nearest window. The room was empty. I opened the door and went in. The place was cold; there was no fire.

"Hello?" I called between the stairway's carved balusters. When there was no reply, I went up. At the top I saw the dim glow of light from the bedroom. The floor squeaked badly as I crept up to the threshold and peered in. I could see Faun lying on the bed bundled under a comforter, while on the far side of the room, by the porcelain stove, Maude and Ling were huddled, lighting matches and whispering together.

"Everything all right?" I asked.

Maude all but jumped. "Oh. It's you," she said. "What a fright you gave me. You really needn't have come." I detected a note of annoyance, as if she didn't want me there. Suddenly I was no longer her hero but an inconvenience.

"Can I help?"

"No, thank you. We have it now." She nodded to Ling and they stood. Ling adjusted the gas and went to the doorway.

"She asleep?" I asked, nodding at Faun.

"See for yourself." Maude turned down the cover and I saw Faun's pale face. "Dead to the world; you couldn't wake her with an earthquake." I thought her voice sounded more natural now. She stood beside the bed, gazing down at the sleeping form, absently smoothing the cover for a moment or two; then she glanced around at the stove. "I don't think there's anything else, Ling," she said. "We can go along now."

I turned and went out, Ling behind me. Maude had started out with him, but at the last moment she went back into the room, leaving the two of us to continue along without her.

Downstairs, Ling faced me with his usual deadpan expression. His dark eyes shone in the light from the lamp that burned on the table. We waited; after a moment he went to the stairs and called up in a stage whisper. "Missy Maw' come quick now, please?"

There was a slight sound from above, then silence; presently he moved to the door and opened it. A gust blew in, wet and chilly, lifting the corners of the rug. Above us, Maude's feet came into view on the staircase. "Come, Mistah Cholly, please, we go now." Ling actually ushered me out by my elbow, and I found myself among the dark, dripping trees. A moment later, I heard Maude's voice and saw her appear in the glow of the lamp Ling held in his hand. He led her out and shut the door from the outside.

"Wait, you forgot your lantern." I started back.

"No, no—I left it," she said quickly, "for Faun. She might wake up —be frightened."

Odd, I thought, Maude having just said an earthquake couldn't waken her. She'd taken my arm and was moving me away from the entrance. "Come along, do let's get out of this nasty wet before we drown." I could feel her hand shaking and her breath came in little pants as she urged me along. We bridged the distance between the two houses and came up to the terrace doors; then we were back inside.

Maude hurried to the fire and rubbed her palms together. "I expect the coffee's gone cold. I think I'd like a fresh cup," she said, "if you'll be so kind. Charlie, coffee? Oh, what's the matter with me, you don't drink coffee at night, do you?"

Ling went out and I bent to poke up the fire. I added a couple of smallish logs, pumped the bellows, and when we had a merry flame to warm us, I joined Maude on the sofa. She looked utterly done in. I felt her shiver and asked if she was cold and would she like Ling to bring her her coffee in bed? She thanked me no, and in a moment she glanced again at the doors, then settled back against the cushions, hunching her shoulders and clasping and unclasping her hands.

I heard Ling's step along the outside hallway, and in a second he appeared in the doorway with the coffee tray. At the instant he crossed the threshold his whole figure became illuminated by a glaring burst of light that shot in through all the windows and doors, and for a second he turned white and everything on that side of the room was bathed in an eerie violet light. This blinding flash was followed by a deafening explosion and the tray literally sprang from his hands. When I felt the impact, my first reaction was to snatch Maude to me and pull her to the floor, our bodies protected by the bulk of the sofa. She crouched in my arms, shaking and murmuring to herself. As soon as I felt reasonably sure there would be no second shock, I got up and rushed to the French doors, opened them, and ran out onto the terrace.

Through the trees I could see the Playhouse engulfed in flames, while burning pieces of debris fell back to earth, parting the branches of the trees. The explosion had made a lurid light and I remembered what had been said only minutes ago about the sleep of the dead and earthquakes waking them. I was running then, running hard, but even as I ran I realized how foolish it was to imagine anything inside that house having survived such a blast.

From the gaping hole that had been ripped from the roof clear down one wall, I could assume that the explosion had happened upstairs—in the bedroom. Helpless to do anything, I danced around the conflagration, and, finding no way inside, I ran back to the big house to call for help. But the fire department needed no alert; already I could hear the wailing siren as vehicles wound their way up the canyon road.

As I came into the Snuggery, the house lights blinked on and off several times, then stayed on. Maude stood by the open doors, staring wordlessly at the blaze. Before I could say anything she turned from the sight and dropped into her chair again. The clamor of the fire engines filled my ears as the trucks pulled into the drive and a voice began barking out orders over an amplifier. Two men came running toward us, and I opened the door, letting in a gust of smoke-filled air.

"Was anybody in there?" one man asked breathlessly. Maude looked at me before answering. "Yes," she answered finally, "my granddaughter was in bed upstairs. I don't believe she could have possibly gotten out alive."

The firemen agreed and said they were sorry. They ran away with the news, and we watched while dark figures dragging hoses dashed across the wet lawn. My eyes kept going to Maude's face as she watched impassively through the glass, as if she were witnessing some event entirely unrelated to her. What a cool customer, I thought.

"Missy Maw'," said Ling from the doorway, "I will go make coffee, lots of coffee; the men will want it."

"That's a good idea, Ling, please do."

He trotted from the room, calm and collected as ever, and at that moment it struck me that for neither Maude nor Ling had there been the slightest element of surprise concerning the explosion, and it dawned on me then that it must have been expected.

"The Swedish stove, of course," I heard Maude say, peering out, while the tautened hoses began to quell the lurid flames. Outside, all was action and furor; inside, only the crackling snapping fire and the eloquent silence that lay between us. "I've been saying for years it ought to be fixed —fixed or done away with."

"Like some other things," I thought but did not say. "Done away with if they could not be fixed." In this world there were some things that could never be fixed.

"Ought we to telephone Belinda, let her know?" I asked.

"At this hour? Gracious no," she replied with her old asperity. "It's late, and I don't want to upset her before we must. Perhaps we should go out and see what the men are doing." I reached to help her to her feet but she brushed my hand aside. "I can manage, thank you. I don't need any assistance."

Her brusque words spoke for themselves. I saw it all. I understood it all. Some things were best left to the Maudes of the world—if there *were* more Maudes, *other* Maudes, which I steadfastly believed there were not. Unique, indomitable, and, I suspected, now somehow at peace. Suddenly Sunnyside, her domain, had been made safe again. Now there was nothing to touch it or harm it, not any longer. And if Maude was safe and Sunnyside was safe, then Belinda, too, was safe; no one could hurt her anymore, either. I was seized by the urge to see her, to be with her and tell her she'd been made safe again. I wanted to reassure her that Charlie would see to everything.

I felt Maude's hand steal into mine, our fingers entwined. In our hands lay a secret, almost certainly in Ling's hands as well. Maybe I should have been ashamed of what I was feeling, but there it was: relief, pure and simple relief.

There would come a time, however, when these feelings would pass and I would be left with my thoughts, heavy thoughts of the thing that had happened that night, the accident in the Playhouse, the gas stove that had breathed the flames of the lamp that had been left for Faun in case she woke up and was frightened.

I persuaded Maude to remain inside while I went out to talk to the fire officers. Yes, they said, it certainly must have been the stove, that old Swedish porcelain job with the faulty jets. Escaping gas, the burning lantern, nature had taken its course—naturally.

To be sure—quite naturally.

I said that was how we too had guessed it had been—Mrs. Antrim and I.

"Is that her?" asked the captain. "Golly, I saw her a long long time ago—when I was just a kid. She was with Jackie Cooper—can't remember the name—"

I said he must mean *Fanny and Kiddo*. "By gosh," he said, "you're right." Sure I was. Dead right.

By now the men were rolling up their hoses, the captain was checking among the smoldering ruins for hot sparks. Others were poking around with flashlights, looking for human remains. Though they kept their voices down, I knew they were telling each other that there wouldn't be much to find in that mess.

When this process came to naught, I took the captain over to speak with Maude in the Snuggery, and after a while the police arrived to deal with the situation. An officer took out his pad and respectfully wrote down our answers to his questions. Maude looked badly torn up, as if the loss of her beloved granddaughter were a great tragedy, which I supposed it was—to Faun. Maude's display of emotion was acute and beautifully articulated.

When our guests had had their fill of questions, they all trooped out amid apologies and condolences. Maude stood gallant to the end, shaking hands and giving each a polite word of gratitude for services rendered. I closed the door behind them, threw another log on the fire while, slowly —even ceremoniously—she drew the curtains across the windows, shutting out sight and sound, and we stayed there in the Snuggery until dawn, talking, shoes and ships and sealing wax, just the way we'd begun on that other dark and stormy night; cabbages and kings.

When the sun rose behind the curtains, I drew the cord to open them. Turning, I saw that Maude had slipped from the room. I didn't see her for the rest of the day. Ling said she was resting, and we agreed that was a good idea.

Later, nosing around in the Playhouse debris, I found the charred remains of a typewriter—the machine Faun had been writing her book on. But there was not a single page to be found.

In a later time we sat together, Maude and I, near the spot where the Playhouse had stood, now demolished, the blasted area now seeded into healthy green turf where the croquet court had been moved. It was evening, the air was warm, and there was a special mood to our being together there, something quiet and solemn, as well as a profound air of finality, for we each realized it would be one of the last times it would happen. And for good reason: Sunnyside was to be sold. It had been less than a month after the explosion, when workers were still cleaning up the charred debris, that Maude surprised me by saying she was going to put the place on the market. Sunnyside—her home for fifty-four years? I couldn't believe she really meant it. How could she leave the place after so long, start life over in some apartment? But that's exactly what she'd done, turned the whole estate over to Felix Pass to get rid of.

Now we lingered there, gazing out across the waist-high wall, watching the shadows lengthen, the dusk come on, while the darkening hills fell away beneath us. Along the landscape of flattened canyon peaks and knolls the glimmering lights of the neighboring houses gleamed for us, those grand old silent-movie mausoleums, Valentino, Lloyd, Pickfair, in their lofty grandeur, and, ah, the stories their stucco-and-brick walls could tell; ah, the laundry airing on the lines, sheets taken from the beds where the late great had loved and mated, movie gods who were no more gods than you or I, but only mortal creatures with feet of clay. Maude was a goddess, yes, though she'd abdicated now. Yet admirers like myself would keep her name enthroned. As for this place, this Sunnyside that Crispin had built and made his home—it had been his creation, was still his; Maude was merely its caretaker. Behind the mullioned windows of the Snuggery the flame burned; she was the keeper of that flame, and she had protected it in the only way she could.

Soon nuns of a cloistered order would stand where we now stood, gazing down on this same view, wandering the corridors of the house, whispering their litanies, their knobby devotional hands clasped in prayer, prayer for lost souls like ourselves. We were sinners; but we would not confess, either of us. We would keep our unholy secret; it would lie between us, silent and unspoken. The Inquisition tortures of a Torquemada couldn't drag it from me, while she, she would carry it to her grave. As for a possible third party, when had Ling ever spilled a bean?

Here I stood, at the purple wall where the white clematis climbed, here with Maude Antrim, Hollywood's great lady, its dowager queen, chatelaine of Sunnyside, the closest thing to Camelot that movie folk could boast. Soon the stone halls of her house would fail to echo her light step, the coigns above the musicians' gallery would no longer reverberate with her champagne laughter. At Sunnyside the clock would stop, the Snuggery's embers would die to cold ashes, and one day the last light would go out. It wouldn't be just the end of an era, but the end of an age. In my heart I sorrowed for Maude, who had chosen to go, and also for the empty rooms, which had no choice but to stay—alas, without her.

The air drew on a hint of fog, a touch of chill, and we started in. As we walked along the gravel path, our eyes were inevitably drawn to the spot, there where the little wire wickets had been inserted into the earth. Maude paused; I beside her. The name we almost never spoke came to my lips. I said I thought she'd been a poor tormented soul.

"Perhaps." Maude shook her head. Clearly, she didn't want to discuss this subject. She gave my hand a squeeze, taking me along beside her. Ling was waiting in the doorway, behind him Suzi-Q.

"Sleep well," I said to Maude as we got to the door, and I smiled and kissed first one cheek, then the other. Maude Antrim, who'd put a roof over my head and given me happy times. I loved her then, I love her still, I will always love her. *Then,* an afterthought: "Some people don't really deserve to be born," I said.

Maude came tiptoe and, as she kissed my cheek, in return she whispered some words in my ear, words that sent a chill down my back. Her smile remained unchanged as she waved me off and let Ling close the door.

I carried her words with me as I went along the path and down the steps to the Cottage, and I remembered them long afterward, when Sunnyside was no more and Maude only a memory.

"She wasn't born, you know," Maude said. "She was hatched from an egg laid in warm sand."

And I agreed.

Claire

It was well after 2:00 a.m., I had heartburn, a headache, and an annoying ringing in both ears. I was thirty-five thousand feet over the Mississippi River on a DC-10, usually referred to as the "red-eye," heading from Los Angeles to New York, where I was about to see a second play of mine be put on the boards.

Thus far our flight was a bumpy one, seatbelts were fastened, and my stomach remained as uneasy as my mind. I got up and went to the john, and on my way back, passing the magazine rack, I pulled out the latest issues of every periodical that looked interesting, all the way down to *Business Week* and *Parents Magazine*.

Flipping through the pages of a fashion magazine, I happened across an ad—one for mink furs: "What a Legend Lives For"—and I spotted That Face. There it was, staring out at me, the too-familiar planes and angles airbrushed right down to the bone structure, swathed in gleaming mink pelts, giving the world that "old black magic" look.

Take a guess at how old she is. Hard to say, isn't it? There were only the slightest traces of crepe around the eyes—those eyes, no longer as large as they once had been, but still Those Eyes. Compelling, demanding, wondering at a world she hadn't made, with a wounded touch she couldn't fully overcome. And the wide slash of the well-lipsticked mouth with its exaggerated lipline that for years had been the delight of caricaturists—now those lips that had kissed a thousand men through ten thousand nights showed the barest whisper of wrinkles that not even expert retouching could disguise, the little arroyos that drive a beauty mad with helpless frustration and horror at the creeping, implacable Specter. Time, age, sorrow, loneliness, and unhappiness may have bowed that lily neck, those shining orbs may have wept buckets on and off the screen, murder, pillage, and rapine may have dogged the wake of those size 5 feet encased in their anklestrap shoes, but by God here she was again, popping up in this slick double-truck ad, the living legend herself. (Was it Dore Skirball who'd said you could kill Claire only by plunging a stake through the heart?)

Beauty in its realest sense is more precious than gold, precious because of its rarity. It's said that if all the gold in the world were melted together in one solid lump it would form a cube not much bigger than a four-bedroom house of the Dutch-colonial design. And if all the beautiful faces were gathered in one place, what then? How large a space would be required to hold them? Walk down any street in any city on any day and look around you for the faces. You'll walk a far piece before you come across something only faintly resembling a beauty. Look for a Garbo, a Lamarr, a Colbert—look for a Regrett. I'd hate to hang for the length of time you'd be looking.

In the New York Museum of Modern Art there stands the famous bronze bust by Jacques Lipchitz that, had she never done another thing but sit for the sculptor, would have provided Claire Regrett the fame due such a physiognomy. Hers was not the mere illusion of beauty, hers was the real, the genuine, article, a face famous not only for its individual features but also for the sum total of those parts. That face never dated; no matter what changes were intermittently rung upon it, no matter how it was altered to fit the newest, most up-to-date version of the wearer, it remained instantly recognizable for its nearly half a century in the public eye, despite what seemed a new face for each of her mates—new eyebrows, new lipline, new hairdo, new hair color, the works. She had no time for last week's news or last year's model. She made herself over regularly like the latest design hot off the Detroit assembly line. And, as has been pointed out, each make-over, each new transformation, accompanied the shedding of the last husband or lover, shaking out the bedcovers and saying, Get lost, buster. In the thirties, Frank Adonis and Perry Antrim; in the forties, Sky McCord III and more Frank; the fifties, the Frenchman, Yves de Gobelins; the sixties, Quentin "Natchez" Calhoun, while the list of in-between bed pals, the ones she didn't bother marrying, is long indeed.

As a fabled idol of the silver screen, Claire Regrett was one of the Great Originals—sixty movies, 1932 to 1971, that's about forty years—but as the subject of an, as they say, in-depth laboratory dissection she was quite another thing. You can take the lady as MGM presented her to us, that gilded, silvered, lacquered, often beguiling creature swanking about in her pet paillettes and her accordion-pleated Adrians, in her horsehair garden hats and egrets, displaying those perfect breasts, those narrow curving loins, the slender flanks that belonged on a jungle cat, and from behind revealed the nether curves of both chops under a swath of gold lamé, a creature hung with the jewels of a Midas (on loan from Fredd Skrebneffsky of Beverly Hills), her hair arrangement manifesting for America's shopgirls Madame's latest whim of curl or color. That elegant, square-shouldered, supercharged, slinking, scintillating, fur-cozzened, smoke-belching, eyelash-batting, intensely striving, grimly covetous, hungry, yearning, sex-bait mantrap, and the loving spirit of modern American girlhood, Claire Regrett, née Cora Sue Brodsky of Bensonhurst, Brooklyn's ex-chorine and movie tootsie and self-incarnated screen Duse.

Claire was one of those historical phenomena produced by the Hollywood glamour mills, a first-magnitude star, a living legend at thirty-five, the Most Photographed Woman in the World, as well known as such contemporaries as Wallis Warfield Windsor, Kate Smith, Shirley Temple, Madame Chiang Kai-shek, or the Dionne Quintuplets. Claire in her own person alone was quintuplets.

How did it come about that a skinny, scab-kneed kittycat from Bensonhurst with no taste, no education, and her hair in turd-curls could invent or at any rate reinvent the film star, that slick vamp who pulled the fans into Loew's Capitol or the Orpheum, that filled the same balconies in Brooklyn theatres where at fourteen she herself had sat with a dime box of sticky jujubes, her lips black with licorice, getting felt up by the butcher's boy while she sighed over Aileen Pringle in *Dream of Love?*

But, by God, in the end I did dissect her. No, take it back; I didn't, either. I *tried* to, I damn well did try. Two years of being joined at the hip to that lady wasn't easy. It's like the old joke: first prize, a week in Philadelphia; second prize, two weeks in Philadelphia. And if in the end I did fail, whose fault was that, I wonder? I defy anyone to come close to dissecting that specimen, I mean to the point where matters may be understood, conclusions drawn, true and honest opinions formed. As for illuminating her psyche—for God's sake, leave well enough alone!

This futile endeavor of mine had not been of my own choosing, and I agreed to it for reasons beyond my own comprehension or that of any rational being. By the merest hinge of coincidence, at the time of my L.A.-N.Y. flight I had just spent a good week or more being hounded by a mutual friend about Claire Regrett. This friend was Viola Ueberroth, and she'd been pressing me to do some kind of work on Claire's latest version of memoirs, an "as told to" job. Frankly I didn't enjoy being dragged on this little piece of business and I'd laughed in her face. I told Vi flat-out that, however many memoirs Claire might produce, none of them would hold much relation to life as we know it on this planet. Life construed as Claire construed it was life misconstrued. In other words, the truth was not in her.

Yes, it all began in the late winter of 1980 when I got this phone call and heard that familiar fruit-toned voice. "Dear? That you, dear? Vi here." Here I am, soaking in the hot tub, having just returned from a weekend of skiing at Mammoth Mountain. This is around ten, about an hour before Vi's usual time for telephoning, and I judge that it may be important. I'm right. It is. She's asking a favor of me, a big fat one. Get this: Vi actually wants me to hop on a plane, go jetting off to New York, and talk with Claire Regrett about my "helping her out" with her autobiography. I tell Vi she's crazy. A guy'd have to be out of his skull to "help out" Claire Regrett in any undertaking, let alone ghost her autobiography, which is what all this came down to. In the first place she'd already published one autobiography, *The Stardust Trail*. God deliver us from such spurious works of fiction: a portrait of Claire that was as manufactured as she was —from radiator to hub caps, nickel plate all the way. And then there's that other cutesie little opus she penned, *The Glamorous Housewife;* subtitled *Hints for a Happy Home Life.* Claire Regrett may know plenty about glamour, but she knows blessed little about a happy home life—and not so damn much about housekeeping, when you come right down to it.

But Vi feels that the world is ready for the lowdown on Claire Regrett, the real skinny, and she declares that this time the lady is 100 percent ready to tell all. I'll just bet. Like what happened to that famous blue movie that she reputedly made when she was still Cora Sue Brodsky, that hot item entitled *Maid's Night Out* that so many people have claimed to have seen but of which no one has ever come up with a snippet? Lately I've seen in a Hollywood scoundrel tome some beaver shots of her from those early days, but for all we know they could be "art studies." And what about that third husband, Yves de Gobelins, who ended up behind bars and died of a heavy steam-job in the prison laundry? Or—what *was* in those letters I'd burned that night in the Snuggery at Sunnyside, letters that Maude had gone to such lengths to suppress? The situation was rife, as they say, pregnant with all sorts of possibilities, but I didn't think for a minute the Claire we all know and love was not going to open her mouth on matters like these. On that I would bet my bottom dollar.

There are things in life one is happy to do for a friend, even eager to do, to show the depths of one's feelings, to oblige, to tighten the bonds of friendship. But not this. "This" was too much, and no matter how winningly Vi might turn her phrases or tempt me with juicy tidbits, I wasn't interested in the job. I'm too old and too rich and too respectful of my peace of mind to fall into a bear-trap like this one.

"Why don't we do *your* life, Vi?" I suggested instead. "That'd straighten some hair."

I am omitting Miss Ueberroth's reply. But she had not done with me yet. Poker player that she was, Vi had cards up her sleeve.

Let's go back to Claire's own "autobiography," composed by her with the admitted help of a *Photoplay* scribe to whom she claims in the foreword she was persuaded to open her heart. Her bosom, she declared, hid no secrets, her life was an open book to be read by each and every one of her fans, and if you believe that, you'll believe the moon's made of green marzipan.

For example, throughout the entire book, every mention of Frank Adonis stamps him as merely a "friend of the Broadway years" who "assisted her" in those early days of Manhattan madness. According to Claire's Technicolored version of the life that late she led, she and Frank had had a "tiff," and when he trekked west with Babe Austrian in tow, Claire "willingly admits" that her heart was broken and that she boarded a train for Miami in company with her sister, where she let the Florida sunshine and ripe oranges cure her emotional ills. Less than a year later, so this fairy-tale narrative goes, she followed in Frankie's footsteps to Hollywood, where Babe Austrian was already starring in her second picture. It hadn't taken long for Claire to catch up, then overtake her, to become the Celluloid Soap Queen, the lady with the tear in her eye, the sob in her throat, victim of gangsters and crooked magnates, out-of-wedlock parent, the Universal Bosom on which orphans, delinquents, and ne'er-do-wells all could lay their heads, the Poor Pitiful Pearl over whom anyone in heels or jackboots, be he cowhand, gold-rusher, Tahitian pearl diver, southern plantation owner, or African bwana-devil, could walk with impunity, and in the last reel she was guaranteed to dry her extraordinary eyes and come up smelling like an American Beauty Rose.

The day following Vi's call was the day the Academy Award nominations were announced, and Belinda Carroll's name among the nominees for best actress was cause for celebration. *The Light in the Window,* the film she'd completed just before Frank's death, had been every bit as successful as he'd predicted, but after the tragedy Belinda had again withdrawn from the movie scene, refusing all offers. Three years later, however, the irresistible role came along. Maude and I persuaded her to make *The Blue Train,* shot on the Côte d'Azur and in London, and Belinda's role as Lena, the aging, neurotic actress fleeing from life, had been a standout. There were early forecasts of what would happen in the next Oscar derby, and now her nomination had come to pass.

One reason I wanted to avoid the pitfalls of Viola's proposition was that I'd had a play in and out of my typewriter for the last two years, and this time I had high hopes. I even had a producer—make that two, Feldshoe and Paultz, who'd been running a good track record in the past six or seven years. Tackling Broadway again meant I'd need my wits about me, and I couldn't see Madame Clutch playing second fiddle to any Great White Way.

A second reason for not becoming involved was my feelings for Belinda. I could just hear what she'd have to say if I told her I was going to "assist" Claire with her memoirs, even in some sort of "editorial" capacity. They were ancient rivals, back to their MGM days, and right now Belinda was flying high, wide, and handsome, while Claire had experienced setbacks and reverses. And though Belinda may have put former feuds behind her, I wasn't too sure about Claire, who always kept her box of knives well sharpened. Belinda and I were enjoying a far closer relationship than I'd ever hoped for, and now we were to be professionally involved as well, for the leading role in my new play was earmarked for her, though this fact hadn't been announced.

As for this windfall nomination by the Academy, no one was more excited than I, and as soon as I heard the news I hopped in my car and hied myself over to the Wilshire Corridor, where Belinda was currently leasing a six-room apartment. As she let me in, I could see how overwhelmed she was. I took her in my arms and kissed her, then gave her the flowers I had hidden behind my back.

"So," I began with a yard-wide grin, "the movie stork is bringing a bundle of joy to your house. How do you like the idea of a little boy named Oscar to put on your mantel?"

She laughed, said I was out of my mind, it was wonderful to be nominated but she wouldn't kid herself by thinking they'd ever give it to her. Stranger things had happened, I said, secretly wondering if she might not be this year's dark horse. True, the competition was heavy, but this was an actress who'd been in pictures since 1936, who'd paid her dues, and who'd made a lot of friends along the way. Mightn't—just mightn't it happen? I thought so. In token of which I took her to lunch and showed her off. The world was in the Polo Lounge that noontime, and friends and strangers alike stopped by to kiss and congratulate her. In time our conversation, of course, got around to the subject of Viola's ridiculous crusade. As I had foreseen, Belinda was shocked.

"Are you crazy?" she said. "Why would you want to write her memoirs? I know—you're contemplating suicide."

I told her not to joke around, that Vi was serious. Belinda fell silent and I could tell she was mulling it over. Granted, it was a screwy idea, farcical; me, of all people, considering my relationship with Belinda. People had been drawing parallels between the two actresses for years, until the ruts were deep as the Grand Canyon. It was really apples and oranges, but writers loved comparing them, contrasting their careers, commenting on the Antrim connection, Perry married now to Claire, now to Belinda, blowing up the "feud" every chance they got. And there were certain grounds for the comparisons.

Each lady in her time had found her share of misfortune. Other women may experience similar upheavals, but seldom so prominently, not in front of the whole world with everyone peeking in the window, reading newsprint over their morning grapefruit. If Belinda's life had been more scandal-ridden, more prominently publicized, if Claire had somehow managed to keep hers more or less limited to the inner circles of the industry, I judged this to be no more than the random fall of the cards. Somewhere it has been written, "It is not enough to succeed; others must fail." Each actress in turn had watched the other fail while she herself succeeded and succeed while she herself failed. Both were artists of limited range and talent, yet each in her time had risen to the heights of the profession. One difference between them was that Belinda never made mean digs about Claire—at least not in print—but when Belinda was on her downward spiral, Claire had been quick to voice her disapproval publicly. Many people said she'd kicked Belinda while she was down.

So it was no surprise that Belinda failed to take kindly to Vi's suggestion that I involve myself with Claire; let Claire go out and find an "as told to," let the shoemaker stick to his last. Practical advice from a practical woman. Naturally, I would abide by her words.

And so, despite Vi's intermittent urgings, plus a certain curiosity of my own, I remained as resolved as ever to have nothing to do with such a foolhardy plan. Let Claire go her way, let me go mine, and everything would be hunky-dory. But I hadn't reckoned on unforeseen events. Fate or some other malign agency seemed bent on throwing us together. The plan had been for me to escort Belinda to the Academy Awards, and to the Governor's Ball afterward, but at the last moment I'd been unable to attend. I had to fly to New York to meet with my Broadway producers.

So here I was, thirty-five thousand feet over St. Louis, winging east, staring at the face in the magazine. That Face. Star of Stage, Screen, Radio, and Television. The Wicked Witch of the West. Miss Everybody's Dream. The Woman America Respects Most [sic]. The Girl We'd Most Like to Be Cast on a Desert Island With. Rosie the Riveter's Sister. And

"The Luckiest Girl in the World" as in (her quote, and often) "I simply think I am the luckiest girl, etc., etc., etc."

Well, say what you might, Claire was always good copy. By now her humble origins had been so often chronicled they were stamped in the public consciousness like the discovery of Peking Man or the Scopes Monkey Trial. Everybody knew how she'd started as a salesgirl at a hosiery counter, how she'd been one of Frankie Adonis's first dates, how he'd got her interested in show business and then left her for Babe Austrian, how as a result Cora Sue Brodsky had suffered a bad setback, but how, refusing to buckle under, she'd made up her mind to be as big a star as her rival.

It wasn't just a story, it was a whole Scandinavian saga, and, give or take a stretch or two, pretty close to the truth. There *was* a "holiday" in Florida to get her nerves settled, then the trek to California and the movies. Who is there who doesn't remember even today how after an endless train ride she'd arrived broke, supported herself washing dishes in a Chinese dig-in at night, and during her days had sought employment at the studios, where, luckier than thousands of other hopefuls, she played her first role, at AyanBee, having been taken under the wing of no less a patron than the noted producer Sam Ueberroth. A steady stream of parts brought her to the attention of a favorable public. The name Cora Sue Brodsky was dispatched to limbo and she became Claire Regrett, the name of the character she'd played in that old Warner Baxter movie I'd seen the preview of as a boy, after which she was on her way up, up the ladder of success. Thanks to a push from Viola Ueberroth, this bright-eyed newcomer wound up with a contract at MGM, where she next appeared in another Fedora film, *The Daughter of Olaf Ruen*, whose Coming Attraction I could recall having seen at Poli's Theatre as a boy.

It was no secret that Claire and I went way back—not that she'd remember it, but *I* did. It was one of those formative experiences that you don't forget; for the first time it gave me an inkling of what it was like to get up on a stage and perform, and after that taste it was the smell of the crowd and the roar of the greasepaint for me. This unexpected encounter took place back during the war, when I was a sailor in the navy. It was just before the conflict ended, after they bombed Hiroshima and Nagasaki. We'd come into San Diego and the USO was putting on a live show on the deck of one of our largest flat-tops. One of the stars was Madame herself, who was then married to Skylar McCord, and she had him in tow. First they brought her out; she acted really nervous up there in front of so many men, but we gave her lots of whistles and applause, and when she settled down she sang "My Blue Heaven" for us. Not bad.

Not good, but not bad. Then she danced, sort of. No Ruby Keeler she, but she sure knew how to milk an audience. She had a filmy dress on, and the breeze kept blowing its skirt around, showing off those great gams. Then she asked for a volunteer to come up and dance with her. Numbered checks had been handed out and I had the winning number. My buddies practically threw me up there beside her.

"Can you dance?" she asked, giving me that big red smile. "A little," I said. The band kicked off, I grabbed her, and away we went. I was a jitterbugging fool but she kept right up there with me. When we finished she looked the worse for wear, but she was game, I'll say that; she really gave her all for the servicemen. We were a hit, no doubt of it. Next came Skylar, muscles and curls and 4-F, lots of flashy white teeth and shoulder pads in his houndstooth sports jacket. They did a patter routine; the jokes were corny but he got a couple of laughs, though we wondered why a polo injury had kept him out of uniform. Later, when the show was breaking up, they told me she wanted me to be in a photograph with her. The admiral was in it, too—me, Claire, and the Sixth Fleet Commander —and they sent the picture to the hometown papers. I shook the admiral's hand, and then McCord's, and when it came to her she bussed my cheek again for the camera. "Bless you, darling," she said in that deeply meaningful way of hers. I still have the shot in a beat-up old shoebox somewhere, yellow with age.

I was to encounter her yet again, this time on a strictly professional level, and the shower of "bless you"s was once again like the rain in Spain. This was three or four years after I'd landed in Movieland. Frank had got me a lead on an important dramatic TV show, the star of which was none other than Madame herself. The trade press was full of it: Claire Regrett had signed to do TV; she'd "gone over to the philistines." Still a star after almost twenty-five years, she'd recently made the industry sit up and marvel at her willingness—nay, eagerness—to take on the world of television, and in its primitive format of half-hour black-and-white anthology stuff, a grueling rehearsal schedule. But Claire was pleased to be a pioneer (some said an apostate) and wrangle with the new medium, and her name was still of sufficient candlepower that I was more than happy to attach my wagon to it. I mean, Claire Regrett! She was a *star*.

I'd left my house with a good margin for error, but due to a blowout I was late by fifteen minutes. The director had convened the cast around the table for the first read-through, and he himself was reading my part. As I came through the door it banged loudly and everyone looked up. Claire was mighty grim.

"Ah, here is our missing actor," said the director, a quiet, amiable man I'd worked for previously. "Come and meet Claire."

"Good *morning,*" sang the star from the head of the table. It was that movie voice I knew so well, clipped, and phony as a plaster saint in Little Italy. "Let me guess—you had a flat tire."

"As a matter of fact—" I began, but got no further.

"Oh, come on-n-n," she said, with obvious disbelief, rolling those big eyes heavenward, "surely you can do better than that."

"I probably can," I replied, "but it happens to be the truth."

She raked me up and down with a look freighted with suspicion. "Really? Did you hurt yourself?" she inquired, taking in my distraught appearance. My left arm hung at my side, wrapped in a beach towel from the trunk of my borrowed machine. While I was changing the tire, the axle had slipped and the handle sprang on my wrist. It hurt like sixty and I supposed it was sprained. Ignoring her, I told the director I'd take over the reading and afterward I thought I should go to the studio infirmary.

"Oh, you really *are* hurt, then."

I quoted from Browning. "'Nay sire, I am killed'; and smiling the boy fell dead." And in front of God and Claire Regrett I fainted dead away.

They told me later that she cringed and wept while the doctor worked on my arm, and afterward she was contrite as only she could be. *Nothing* was too good for little Charlie. She had my dressing trailer brought in from the street and set up next to hers, and it was chicken-soup time all the way.

Our little TV tale was one of sex and murder, a sort of *Postman Always Rings Twice* in which a greedy wife and her younger lover intend murdering her older professor-husband and getting their hands on his insurance money. We had a mere twenty-three minutes of storytelling time and that was it, hello-goodbye. But she went at it hammer and tongs, as if she were playing Lady Macbeth, exploring her every motivation with the director, trying to scrape the barnacles of cliché from the dialogue and finding ways of making the material more interesting: She suggested that her part needed a little speech in which she could exploit her impoverished background and win sympathy for her character, essentially an unsympathetic one. Her "little" speech resulted in a two-page exposition in which she revealed that as a child she'd lived in a tenement on Skid Row, and contained deathless lines like "I never even had a doll. Every little girl wants a doll, but we were too poor." And "When I began to blossom forth I could tell from the look in my stepfather's eye that he had designs on me." When the director attempted to reason with her she became mulish, so we shot the speech anyway, even though I knew it would eventually end up on the cutting-room floor.

At noon of the first day she poked her head into my dressing trailer to ask how I was feeling. We chatted a bit, touching on this and that, until she gave me one of her puzzled looks and said, "Say, where do I know you from, anyway?" She batted those eyes at me, searching my face as though for clues. When I replied matter-of-factly that I'd once danced with her on board a navy flat-top her eyes sprang a leak. "*That* was *you?* That funny sailor with the *cowlick?* Oh, my darling, how wonderful to come across you again this way!" Grabbing my hand, she dragged me all around the set, actors, producer, director, telling the story of the jitterbugging gob. "Well, it certainly is a small world, isn't it?" she concluded.

I concurred that that was about the size of it.

I was pretty hot stuff *that* day.

Claire was a real pro. Ask anyone and they'll tell you the same thing, and if you were a pro, too, you earned her respect. She was a star but on the set she was trying hard to be an actress, to show her best. She'd established her standards of hard work and she demanded that everyone on the set live up to them. She buttered her bread at every turn, making little personal remarks to the gaffers up on the grid, blessing them, too, or saying wasn't her key light a bit too hot? There wasn't a blessed thing she didn't know about film. The same wasn't to be said, however, for her acting, which was a sort of tired retread of what she'd been doing for the last fifteen years, the Spider Woman filled with lust and murder, the crisp, honeyed tones, the Beverly Hills matron dodge, the white-walled tires, monogrammed pocketbook and Hollanderized fur stole. And she wore rocks the size of grapefruit. In the long shots she had on the famous trademark anklestrap shoes, switching to bunny slippers for the close stuff.

No, the acting was strained, standard MGM fare. I recalled Dore's once saying, "Claire's idea of good movie acting is being able to shift your scalp on cue." I was later to hear others on this subject. Though they, too, had worked together, Maude Antrim had never regarded Claire as much of an actress, only a bundle of assimilated reactions to a given stimulus, invariably the wrong one. You seldom heard Maude discuss acting in the technical sense—motivations and sense memory and nailing down your reaction. Rather, she talked of hitting your marks and finding your key light and knowing your lines and were the stocking seams straight?, of truck pauses and footlights and upstaging; those were her things—flat-out, simple, no-crap things.

Here's what she had to say about Claire's performances. She acted "in quotes," she put "the dummy" in front of her, she hid behind "a cardboard

cut-out of herself," and she committed the most heinous of acting crimes
—she "indicated," a fault in which the actor merely pretends the emotion
he doesn't feel. Maude used to call Claire a "dry well"—she cried buckets
but never produced a tear, only "indicated" that she'd cried. Poor Claire
—she *wanted* to be a good actress, but *wanting* wasn't enough, you
had to *be* it. And sniffing and snotting into a monogrammed hanky
wouldn't do.

"There was one movie part Claire could play to perfection," I remember Maude commenting. "The tart with a heart of gold—because that
was she herself and she understood the character. But when she tried
playing Tess Trueheart or Lady Jane Grey, forget it. Claire was not born
to the farthingale or the fan."

But here she was, giving us another of her Westchester matrons in
a basic black nothing by Givenchy and her "good" diamonds. There
wasn't much juice in her, she was indicating like hell, and to rev herself
up she was nipping at the hundred-proof vodka.

It was during this period that we saw the start of her heavy drinking.
She was still married to the poor man's Peter Lorre, Yves de Gobelins,
that short-legged, popeyed bogus offshoot of the French nobility (*le Comte
de Gobelins*, as he registered at hotels; some believed he actually manufactured antique tapestries) who hatched the disastrous perfume scheme that
helped Claire lose so much of her money. The scent christened "Jeunesse
Dorée" was known worldwide, but famous in a far different way than
Chanel No. 5 or Joy de Patou was famous. Rather, it was notorious, with
further shocks to come as bit by bit the story of Frenchy's handling of
Claire's monies was disclosed.

Certainly Yves came in for his share of attention; and with a wife like
Claire, why not? We used to laugh when Dore referred to them as "Madame and Yves." Gobelins's hold on her was that of an octopus, and when
he visited the studio she became agitated, even angry, then relieved when
he departed. But he was on the set at all hours; I'd see him lurking back
there out of the light, his eyes glinting, the cheeks—always gunmetal blue
from a fast-growing stubble, he couldn't get from morning to evening
without a second shave—sucked in, assessing; impeccably dressed, a sort
of forties floorwalker style, even the boutonniere but without the pearl-
gray spats—and too short for his own good. I knew she liked tall men,
she said they forced her to keep her chin up, but this guy was a real troll.
The wardrobe girl said she'd never seen a guy who gave her the creeps
like this one. We thought he was exercising some kind of sinister control
over Claire, though how such a strong-minded woman would take that
crap off some popeyed Frog dwarf was beyond us.

But Frenchy wasn't long for the world, as we all know. When he got sent to Alcatraz for invasion of the federal mails and assorted bits of graft and other felonies, he went up for a four-year stretch; but he never made it out again. The story was strictly headlines. Unpopular with his fellow inmates, Yves found life behind bars a hard scrabble deal. His duties partly entailed an occasional stint in the prison laundry, where one evening his carcass came to light at the bottom of the steam transformer, looking like a New England boiled dinner, the skin flayed off his parboiled flesh, his lobster-red head unrecognizable. *Dommage.*

Watching Claire sneak a quick shot of vodka now and then, I decided she deserved a boost, being married to a guy like that. Everybody knew about this surreptitious tippling, people had been talking about it for years; her hairdresser, her makeup man, the director, even the producer, they all knew. She kept little Dixie cups of blue label Smirnoff strategically tucked away behind things on the set, making believe they were only water, and I'd catch her hiking one back before a take.

One day they were setting up for a scene where we had a heavy clinch on a bearskin rug in front of a fireplace, and when it got around to my closeup, with the camera set behind her and over the shoulder on me, she said, "Raise your chin a little," then lifted it herself. Her peremptory air annoyed me, and I said with some sullenness, "The shot's on your back, how do you know where the camera is?"

"Baby, I can smell it," was her brusque reply. "I've been making love to the camera for a lot of years and, believe me, it treats me better than most of the men I've made love to." She reached out and touched my cheek, an affectionate gesture, but the makeup man later told me that hubby Yves had picked up on it from the shadows and had spat, with a *"merde"* for me to boot.

Later, when we were getting warmed up for a take, the all-important clinch became a problem of sorts. I got at her with a good healthy smooch and she yanked back as though I'd copped a feel or something. "What the hell do you think you're doing?" she demanded.

"Kissing," I said. "It's in the script."

She looked appalled. "You can't kiss me like that. Keep your lips closed; this program goes into family homes, you'll offend mothers and fathers." This, from Hot Lips Houlihan herself.

The next time we tried the kiss, I managed it as prescribed—the way I'd kiss a maiden aunt on her annual visit. After every take I'd shoot the director a questioning look, but he'd just cross his eyes and say nothing. Later, when I went to him, he explained that, being studio bred, Claire had been taught not to kiss with open lips since it was against the old

Hollywood Code. Yet, as everybody knew, she'd been on more beds than a Wamsutta sheet. Where did she draw the line? At the television sets along the Platte River, evidently.

We finally got a printed take, but as I got up from the bearskin I caught Yves out of the corner of my eye. He glared, then disappeared inside Claire's trailer; next day when she arrived on the set she wore a wicked shiner. I happened to be at the water cooler when she came in through the door and I got a good look at it.

"Jesus, did that son-of-a—"

She put her fingers to my lips to shut me up. "Okay, Galahad, no heroics. Get me Lou quick, will you?" She ducked into her dressing room and I went to find her makeup man. Lou couldn't completely hide the bruise, and when the director saw the damage he was furious. He had to change his entire day's set-ups.

Then, after having scored points, I was so foolish as to get Claire pissed off at me. It was the last day of shooting, and as I passed her door at lunchtime she crooked her finger at me. "Darling, I'm having just a few close friends in when we wrap. Nothing fancy, but of course you'll come. Champagne, some hors d'oeuvres? I made them myself. We can mess around till flight time. Sound like fun?"

"Gosh, Claire," I blurted, "I can't. I've got something on."

I'll never forget the glazed look that came over her face. It froze blue, like a Maine pond. Her whole body tautened, and the lips formed that famous movie mouth. "*Oh.*" Quick and sharp. "Well. I'm sorry you're so busy."

I knew right away I'd made a gaffe. My whole career now had wings on it and was flapping out the window. The director came to me. "What'd you say to her?" I told him what had happened. "Jesus, can't you do something?" he pleaded. "I've still got sixteen set-ups before we wrap."

Jenny was expecting me to pick her up at the airport, but I made a call and arranged for a friend to do it. I wrote a note of explanation for Jen, then went and rapped dutifully on Madame's door.

"Come."

"Say, Claire, I got out of my thing later, and if the invitation's still open I'd like to come."

She melted like a stick of butter on a hot griddle. The huge eyes teared; she patted my cheek gratefully. "How *nice*, darling. And how enchanting of you to change your plans just for me. I hope I haven't loused things up for you."

"No, not at all," I lied. "And I want you to know I've really enjoyed working with you."

"Oh, *bless* you, darling! And *I you!* I hope we'll do it again. My prediction is—" And I got a bouquet of flowery sentiments as to my budding screen career.

At the party her husband was conventionally cordial; we exchanged a few trite remarks and that was about it, but I knew he didn't give me much. He was even rude to Jenny when she arrived, and at the last minute he managed to get in a word. "In my contree," he said to me in an aside, "I would know what to do with a *cochon bleu* like you. Now you can say to zee world you have kissed zee wife of Yves de Gobelins."

"And you, my friend, can say you've kissed the ass of the man who kissed the wife of Yves de Gobelins." I stepped back and he lunged, tripped, and fell out the doorway, where a group quickly gathered. I made a good show of helping him to his feet and brushing him off, ministrations he was forced to submit to. "They ought to do something about that first step," I said as I went to gather up my gear, "it's a bitch."

He and Claire were flying off to Vegas in only two hours, and at that moment Claire chose to reappear in her "traveling outfit," oblivious to the altercation. She looked like Wilma in *Buck Rogers*, a stripped-down movie-star model none of us had ever had a gander at before. Except for lipstick and her long eyelashes, her face was devoid of makeup, and the healthy skin gleamed from the oil or grease she'd slathered over it. She was tricked out in a khaki jumpsuit with couturier lines, mid-calf boots, military epaulettes, and a designer aviator's helmet—with pink-tinted goggles. She had three diamond bracelets slung on one wrist, a baguette diamond the size of a plum on one finger, her waist was cinched with a gold kid belt and the jumpsuit was unzipped nearly to the waist, with a generous revelation of braless freckled boobs. "The only way to fly, gang!" she laughed, wafting a glass at us. Then we got the "Bless you, darlings" routine, and at an opportune moment she drew me aside and pressed something into my hand.

"Just a little remembrance," she said. She wasn't kidding, either: a lambda peace symbol in a little plastic box. "Peace," she said, and kissed my cheek ever so butterflyly. "It *was* fun, wasn't it?"

"Yeah, fun."

"Let's do it again sometime."

"Yeah, let's."

"Bye, Charlie. You're a *good hard* worker—I *like* that." She gave me one of her deep, meaningful looks. "Bless you, darling—and thanks for your forbearance. I'm sorry if Yves was acting like a putz." At that moment I saw something I hadn't seen before, something not fully expressed, which hinted at the more sincere modes of feeling common to the race. Then she blew it. "Bless you, bless you," she tacked on in her best Greer Garson voice.

Not four days later, I received a communication through the mail.

Charles, dear [she wrote on the famous violet stationery with a Vegas postmark, and up at the top was the Gobelins coat-of-arms Yves had paid a Paris heraldry firm to design for him], Again, I can't tell you how truly nice it was working with you last week. Imagine, my "TV lover" turning out to be that cute signalman I did the Lindy Hop with! God bless you, my Knight in Shining Armor, may you always have your heart's desire and your very own "Oscar" one day.

> Devotedly
> Claire Regrett Gobelins
> (Mme. Yves de Gobelins)

P.S. Yves has been contrite as can be over our little countertemps [sic]. Such things are best forgotten, don't you agree? Our little secret.

> B.Y.D.
> (Bless You Darling)

And for the next five Christmases I received a card from her, no longer signed as above but rather as plain Claire Regrett and lavishing me with endless B.Y.D.'s.

Sometime during that period I got a call from an indignant Viola. "Charlie, why don't you ever send Claire a Christmas card?"

I was somewhat taken aback by this unexpected assault, and explained that I'd stopped sending cards years ago. "I don't even send my mother one."

"She thinks you're being very rude. After all, she sends you one every year."

"Does she do it just so she'll get one back?"

"Well . . . think of it this way, dear; you're on her A list. Very few people make her A list."

Vi made me promise to be sure and send one, but I never did, and after a while Claire's card stopped coming. I knew I'd been dropped from her A list and stuck on her shit list.

When I got to New York, I went about settling into my apartment for the duration, however long it would take to get my play on. As it happened, Vi was in New York, too, and I called her. The first thing she did was book me for dinner on the night of the Academy Awards. She had an apartment in New York, and had invited "one or two others" to watch the show, too.

When I reached her building, I gave the name of Miss Ueberroth and was astonished when the doorman informed me that I was expected: "Miss Regrett just went up five minutes ago."

So I'd been tricked. Miss Ueberroth would pay for such betrayal. I was tempted to abandon her without even putting in an appearance, but persuaded myself that, given a chance, it might somehow end up an interesting evening after all. I was not to be proved wrong. As I was admitted to the foyer, I heard that laugh I knew so well, heh heh. Star of stage, screen, radio, and TV was in the other room. I'd been framed. Yes, someone would pay.

As I came in, my eye fell immediately on Claire, seated in a high-backed chair by the fireplace, a champagne flute in one hand, a cigarette holder in the other ("The Queen is discovered onstage in a thronelike chair, etc."), and in her lap—wonder of wonders—her own Oscar (". . . in case anyone wanted to see what they really looked like"). Viola interposed her small, rotund figure between us, giving me the chance to let her know I was displeased by this unexpected turn of events. Ignoring my signals, she put her withered cheek up to be kissed. "Charlie dear, how nice that you've come; do you know—" and she introduced me to several people, among them a noted cellist and his wife, a well-known British stage actor, and a duo of butch ladies in butt-sprung slacks and sensible shoes, producers in the current Broadway theatre. "And of course you know our darling Claire," Vi said as we ended up before Madame, ensconced upon her pickled-walnut throne. When I put out my hand, she pulled a meant-to-be-charming pout.

"What, Charles—no kiss?" I bent to administer a dutiful peck, looking down into her cleavage, which was badly raddled. A diamond brooch glittered there, radiating dollar signs, and I caught a heavy whiff of perfume. "I only dab a *touch* of perfume," I remember reading in her book; "men don't like to be smothered in heavy scent, floral or otherwise."

She made me pull up a footstool and there I was, sitting at her feet, just where she intended me to be. She started off with "I've read every one of your books. How did you *ever* manage to *write* them?" Before I could reply, she seized both my hands in hers and held them tight while she looked deeply and entreatingly into my eyes, giving her head tiny, earnest quivers of intensity, and said, "What made you want to change from acting to writing? Did you *always* know?" Before I could respond she hurried on. "I know—you don't have to tell me—you longed for another mode of expression, isn't that it?" When I opened my mouth, she laid her fingers over it. "Don't say it, I *know*, I really *do.*" Now her eyes began to coruscate in the light. "Frank was *so* damned *proud* of you! And I know—I really feel sure that we were destined to stumble across each other this way. Do you believe in destiny, Charles? Of *course* you do, you *must.* You've always been metaphysical, at least I always thought so. I can usually tell, you know. You and I are on the same wavelength, aren't we?" She leaned her bare, conspiratorial shoulder at me. "It's part destiny, part luck, but mostly just plain hard work, isn't that so?" She handed away her glass for a refill. "You and I know that, don't we? I'm a workaholic, so are you, we'll go to our graves working. I in my socks and buskins, you with ink-stained fingers. How I wish *I* could write the way *you* do! You make it seem so easy, as though it all just comes dribbling out from your fingertips, as if you didn't even have to think about it a single moment."

I regarded these words as damning with faint praise, but let them pass. A brouhaha with Madame was not what I'd come to New York for, and I sat back, silent, while the flood of encomiums engulfed me. "Look at me, everyone!" she proclaimed with a little laughing sob, bringing all other conversation to a halt. "I'm crying over one of his stories! I want you all to know this fella is one of the best goddamn writers we've got! And little Claire knew him when!"

"I'll bet," declared the more mannish of the two lady-producers.

Claire put her hand up and spoke behind it, *sotto voce.* "I wish somebody would stick a finger in that dyke."

"Come on," I protested, and she shot me an angry look.

"I can take any perversion, darling, but the picture of two diesels riding a boomerang simply starches my collar. Vi only invited them because they got a Tony. How, I'll never know. Oh, darling, did I tell you I'm a legend?" she went on, veering sharply from her former topic. I told her I'd seen the magazine ad, and I saw that she was gratified.

Meanwhile, the party was rearranging itself. The uniformed help were setting up TV tables and I clutched at the opportunity to relocate my seat. Excusing myself, I went to the bathroom, but when I came out Claire crooked a finger at me, indicating the empty chair now set close beside hers.

"This one's for you, darling, come sit."

"Maybe . . ." I glanced toward the ladies.

"Don't you dare!" she muttered, reaching to pull me into the chair and resetting the folding table as though to trap me. "Now I have you, my handsome friend, I want to tell you what *I'm* up to." Here it comes, I thought, and gave Viola a grim look. Claire launched her rocket. "Charles, *I'm* writing, *too*. What do you think of that?"

I said I thought that was fine.

"Claire's starting her memoirs," said Vi, fortuitously appearing at my side. "She's got six chapters."

"Seven, but who's counting?" Claire said with a laugh meant to amuse as well as to demean her paltry efforts. "Writing's *hard*, or maybe you hadn't heard, Vi, dear."

"Don't I know it, dear. Pity Tolstoy."

"Art's hard," I ventured, my favorite solecism.

"Ain't *that* the truth!" exclaimed Claire, clutching my arm as if she intended detaching it from my person. "Oh, to be an *artist*, not just a— a hack."

I thought that was slicing the ham pretty close to the bone and looked to Vi for help but, miserable bitch, she only encouraged Claire.

"I'm ga-ga for good art," Claire said. "I absolutely *haunt* the galleries and museums. I can't seem to get enough."

The lady-producers were heard to titter—lasciviously, it seemed to me.

"Good for you," I said, sliding a sharp look to Vi before asking, "Who are your favorites, Claire?" I saw those great eyes widen, and as she swallowed I could tell that she was thinking frantically. "Well-l—let's see —I—um—I *adore* the one with all the dots. . . ."

So much for Seurat.

Despite Viola's intimations that Claire wasn't well, I thought she looked quite well, blooming, in fact. She had always been a Rembrandt with her face brushes; tonight she looked as airbrushed as her fur advertisement. Certainly she didn't look her years—which were how many? Seventy? Seventy-three? -five? I remembered Dore once having said that the only way to find out Claire's age was to saw her in half and count the rings.

"Showtime, everyone!" Vi snatched up the remote control and hastily turned on the TV set. Demanding to have her glass refilled again, Claire received it and semi-subsided. Everyone was quickly in place, digging into twelve-inch plates heaped with food from the buffet, while out in California the show began.

This year's celebration was to be no worse than that of other years, but, alas, no better, either. Naturally the big item of the evening was whether or not Belinda would cop the Oscar, and it was easy to tell how the people seated around me felt. It was Belinda all the way. Claire had adopted a condescending attitude, declaring, "When a woman reaches Belinda's age I think she deserves to be honored. But she'll have to be satisfied with the nomination, they'll never give her the statue."

In panning the audience, the camera had caught a closeup of her in her seat. This sight threw Claire's switch and she really started in. "Wouldn't you think she'd do something different with her hair? She's been wearing it like that since World War Two."

"Back when you played her mother, you mean?" one of the lady-producers muttered.

"I heard that, just in case you think I didn't." Glaring at the woman, Claire went on to criticize Belinda's gown, which I'd already seen firsthand and knew hardly bore criticism. Finally Vi sidled up again and did her best to get Claire to put a cork in it.

The next two hours were an excruciating form of torture. It was as if nothing in God's world could keep Claire from bursting out with the most tasteless and idiotic remarks. "*Sor-ree,*" she'd say when someone shushed her, grimacing at her own forgetfulness, but then out would pop another crack. Plates were cleared during the commercials, coffee and dessert appeared, and with them after-dinner drinks. I stared as Claire put away a brandy stinger as if it were sarsaparilla.

It seemed as if three days had elapsed by the time the male presenter for the Best Actress category asked for the envelope. You could almost feel the waves of suspense and emotion as he fumbled with the flap and then took his time in announcing the name. When it came, the auditorium burst into a spontaneous, rousing cheer. Belinda had won!

This was no round of polite applause, but a heartfelt tribute to the survivor of them all. I saw her blonde head bobbing as she hurried down the aisle, and the way she lifted the skirt of her gown as she went up the stairs was regal in the realest sense. Breathless, smiling, waiting for the applause to die, she clutched the Oscar in one hand and spoke in a voice filled with emotion. When she began the traditional litany of thanks, Claire angled her head and made mock-snoring noises.

"*Claire!*"

"Oh, all right, I'll shut up. I won't say another word, not one more syllable. My lips are sealed." She pantomimed locking her lips and throwing the key away.

Belinda looked marvelous, really radiant and youthful. Hollywood loves nothing more than a tribute to a beloved star, and their tumultuous reception touched her deeply, you could see it. When she'd made a few generous remarks, she lowered her head for a moment, then looked up again.

"I especially want to thank a gentleman who unfortunately is unable to be with us tonight. Who is there here who doesn't know the name Frank Adonis?" A wave of applause greeted this, and I had a lump in my throat. "This Oscar I hold in my hand is really for Frank. He's the man to whom I owe so much—to whom so many of us owe so much." She began reeling off the names he'd brought to stardom: Babe Austrian, Kit Carson, Julie Figueroa, April Rains, all of those whose lives Frank had touched; all but Claire's name. At Viola's, a hush fell on the room, and from where I sat I could see people stealing glances at Claire, who sat with her glass frozen in mid-air, her face a mask.

Belinda started away from the podium, but at the last instant she turned and leaned to the microphone again. "I just realized I've been remiss in leaving out one name, the name of a terribly important star—another of Frank's discoveries, the greatest star of all, of course you all know who I mean—Miss Claire Regrett."

Claire's was one name no one ever expected to hear from Belinda's lips. I glanced at Claire, staring open-mouthed at the TV screen.

Belinda went on: "As you all know, Claire has left us—and Hollywood—abandoned us for the glitter of New York, where she lives high up in the sky—the way a real star should. I'm sorry to hear she's been a bit ill recently, and, Claire, if you're watching back there, everyone here wishes you good health and happiness." She ended by thanking all the "friends of Bill," then went offstage to more applause.

Astounded by the unexpected tribute, a teary Claire had to borrow my handkerchief, carefully maneuvering her head while she dabbed gingerly around her eye makeup. "What the hell does she think she's doing anyway?" she growled as she handed back my handkerchief. "Telling the whole damn world I'm sick. I'm *not* sick! Where does she get off saying something like that on network television? I'll never get another job, not if they all think I'm back here croaking."

"She ought to be grateful," I heard the butch lady-producer mutter. "It's free publicity, isn't it? Something she doesn't get too much of these days."

At the opposite end of the room, Vi lent an avid ear, but failed to catch any exchange as Claire asked, "Do you think Belinda really meant what she said?"

"I'm sure she did," I replied.

"But you know she hates my guts," she protested, blowing her nose.

"Damn it, Claire, if she did, would she have said anything?"

Her brow furrowed as she considered, and I made a move to the bathroom. When I came out, I found Vi waiting to pounce: "Wasn't it marvelous? Can you imagine? What did Claire think? I'm fascinated. Tell all, dear." I recapped the dinner hour, while Vi hung wide-eyed on every word.

When the program ended, I decided to make a hasty retreat, but Vi slipped an arm through mine to ask, if it wasn't too much trouble, would I be good enough to drop Claire off?

"*Would* you, darling?" Claire gushed at me. "How sweet that would be of you. What a *wonderful* evening it's been, hasn't it?" She claimed my arm and gave me an intimate squeeze. Then she circled the room, shaking hands with each guest, her euphoric mood stretching as far as the team of lady-producers, for each of whom she managed a friendly word and compliment. I could see that she was a bit wobbly on her feet; the evening had been a long one and she'd made free with the champagne and the after-supper stingers.

Hence I found myself with a jolly companion on our way across the park, while the taxi meter seemed to jump every half block. She was waxing sentimental all over the place, doing a big number on Manhattan and how much living there had changed her. All that art and culture. Yes, I thought, I know; the ones with the dots.

While we wound along the park drive, she fell silent, and, glancing at her, I saw her head turned away, staring out the window as the trees flashed by. We came out through the Seventy-second Street exit and pulled up at her apartment building, the San Remo, one of the noblest on Central Park West, the one with the two tall lighted towers, and no sooner had the doorman opened the door—she sort of tumbled out of the cab—than she discovered to her horror that she'd lost both her earrings.

"Were you wearing earrings?" I questioned, not recalling them.

"Good God, don't you think a woman knows if she's wearing earrings or not?"

A search failed to turn them up and I felt obliged to volunteer to cab it back and look for them at Viola's.

"Oh, *would* you, dear? What a darling you are! And call me in the morning, won't you, to let me know? I'm for beddie-byes, I'm simply done in." I walked her to the elevator and as it arrived she threw her arms around me and kissed me on the mouth. Definitely *not* an MGM kiss, but with lips full open and the tongue at work. She hung on, clutching me, as if she'd be happy to stand there for hours, smooching away like Corliss Archer. I extricated myself, saying I'd better get back to Vi's before she went to bed.

"And, Charles, dear, don't forget your promise, will you?"

"What promise is that?" I asked as she stepped back into the elevator car.

"Why, to help me with my autobiography." She kissed her fingers to me as the doors began to close. "Bless you, darling."

If Viola had retired I'd damn well wake her up.

"Earrings? What's she talking about?" Vi demanded testily at my ring from downstairs. "She wasn't wearing any earrings."

Saved by the bell.

"Vi, you'd better put the lady straight on one thing. I ain't ghosting her autobiography, no way. Where'd she get the idea I would?"

"Ohh . . . you know how she is, dear."

No, I didn't know, I countered, and would frankly rather not know, if it was all the same to her. Ten minutes later, when I let myself into my apartment, the phone was ringing. Somehow I had the idea it had been ringing for some time, and a little birdie even told me who it was.

"Hello, Claire."

"Darling, you'll never guess—I found them!"

I didn't ask where but she told me anyway.

"In the bathtub, isn't that the limit? Don't ask me how. They're insured, but I'd have hated to lose them, they belonged to the Queen of Sweden. Anyway, thanks for dumping me off. I hope it wasn't any trouble. And I adored seeing you again. Now. When can we get together?"

The first part had been all smarmy and laugh-laden; the last sentence was pure cast iron, right down to the nitty-gritty.

"Well, I'm not sure—I'll have to check my schedule," I responded warily.

"*Oh.*"

That "oh." I knew the next line in advance. "Very well. If that's the way you feel. I'll just have to get someone else, I suppose." My ear chilled; the frost was on the pumpkin again.

"It really might be best at that," I said, not believing it could be this easy, then adding, "There are plenty of writers around who specialize in that kind of thing."

"You don't have to hit me over the head, you know. I can certainly see that *you're* not interested." Her voice actually broke with her poor little Claire sob. "It's just that—I felt—since you're such a good, *good* writer, you'd have a deeper appreciation of the material—having known the milieu yourself, if you get what I mean."

Did I ever.

"My legacy—to my lifelong profession," she went on in that crystal-clear voice, all choked up to hell and gone. "For the record—tell the truth for once—the truth, the whole truth, and nothing but the truth. And I just thought you and I had a—sort of—special rapport, going as far back as we do. I guess you really don't like me after all—I always thought you did."

"Sure I do. But—"

"No, you don't, either," she pouted like a child. "You never even sent me a Christmas card, not once." Now she was really into her Poor Little Match Girl number. "Every year I'd hope to find one—I literally get thousands of cards every year, but I'd look and look and there'd never be one from you and it always made me so sad to think you'd forgotten me."

"I don't send cards, Claire. I don't even send my mother—"

"No, no, it's all right. I understand, I really do. You don't have to explain. Remember Noel Coward—'Never complain, never explain.' Just forget the whole thing. It was only an idea—Vi's idea, actually. She said it was the book you were born to write. But we won't speak of it anymore. It's best we don't. Thank you and g-good night."

That tiny catch was the capper. She really choked up big and swallowed her quavery voice so all I got was the impression of gallant farewell. I'd seen the same bit in countless of her films—her "Valiant is the word for Carrie" act. She was trying to suck me in, but I still wasn't about to be sucked. Though I really didn't know her, I really knew her so damn well. She wanted to attach me. Like a salary, a used car. She wanted me as an appendage, part of her entourage: her husband, her secretary, her agent, her manager, her maid, her hairdresser, her furrier, her liquor dealer —her biographer. I was to be her scribe, running around with a stylus and a stack of cuneiform tablets, recording the Life of Our Lady of the Anecdotes, artifacts to be placed in locked receptacles for archeologists to find some three thousand years hence, like King Tut's tomb.

Yet the sob in her voice had got to me, no doubt of it. The familiar little movie-throb that by now was a Claire-cliché. My mind played tricks on me. I pictured her alone, at the end of her life, damsel in distress—that kind of thing. And who knew? Maybe she *did* have something interesting or original to say. Maybe she did need help. Maybe—even—I was the right guy. Oh shit. I fought down the urge to call her back.

I was hard at work when the phone rang, and I grabbed it without thinking. It wasn't she, however; it was old Vi. "Dear, you've hurt her terribly," she said, getting right to it. "She thinks you hate her. You've made her feel worthless. She has no self-esteem."

"Look, Vi, honey, cut the crap, will you? Her lack of self-esteem isn't my fault. I just won't be made an accessory before the fact. If she wants to commit this heinous crime, let her do it on her own. I've got my play —I wouldn't have time, anyway, so the whole thing's purely academic. Let her fry her fish and I'll fry mine, okay?"

"Yes, dear, of course, you're perfectly right, and I know exactly how you feel. And, dear, *you* don't have to tell *me*. *I* know what she's like if anybody does." She lowered her voice. "But look, dear, there's something you don't know."

"What?"

"She'd absolutely kill me if she finds out I told, but Belinda was right on the Awards show—Claire's really not well at all."

I was trying to keep from swallowing the hook. "What's wrong?" I asked in a bored tone.

"They don't know. And of course Claire doesn't say. But she doesn't want anyone to know the truth. Or face it herself."

"That's the trouble with her, she never does," I said.

"I think it has something to do with all that Christian Science stuff she practices," Vi went on. "But really, dear, I think it's only a matter of time. She's known of it a month or so. That's why I invited her last night, I feel so sorry for the poor thing—she's really being awfully courageous about it, don't you think? Lots of people couldn't bear up that way."

"How long has she?"

"*Quien sabe*, dear?" Vi replied in a hallowed voice. "So far as she's concerned her health is a closed subject. I shouldn't think it'd be too long, though. Now, look, sweetie. It wouldn't take so much time just to read through the material, would it? Then maybe you could sit down with her and tell her—in a perfectly nice way, of course—what's wrong with it."

"Good God, Vi, are you saying you want me to sit down with Claire Regrett and criticize her work? You must be off your rocker. You know how she loathes to have anyone criticize her."

"In a *nice* way, I said. Then maybe you could just knock off a few chapters yourself, to sort of show her the kind of style it needs—in your own write, as they say."

"Vi, we're talking about the life of one of the most famous movie stars in the world and you think it can be tossed off like an Erma Bombeck column?"

"No, no, of course not, they're not in the same league. We're talking major book here, big stuff! And it means so much to her, it really does. Look, do me a favor, just this one favor. For me, sweetie, your old Aunt Vi, will you? Just take her to lunch. Take her to lunch and talk to her. An hour and a half—two hours, that's all. Let her tell you her ideas. And the pictures. Sweetie, she's got photos no one knows ever existed. Really intimate shots with the Prince of Wales, with Mahatma Gandhi, with Haile Selassie."

"Terrific! What about Hitler? Bruno Hauptmann? Judge Crater?"

"Don't joke, dear, she's moribund. Be *kind*. Show your human side. Just *see* her. Take her to lunch—I'll pay. I'll even make the reservation. You still like the Four Seasons?"

So it was that by dangling lunch at one of New York's posher and better victualed restaurants Auntie Vi got me to swallow the bait. Four Seasons it was, and it marked the beginning of the winter of my discontent.

Naturally Madame was late. At the bar I ran into an acquaintance, an actor I'd known on the Coast, and I was surprised when, looking at my watch, I realized thirty minutes had elapsed in movie chitchat. I glanced over to the reception desk, where Tom Margittai, one of the owners, grinned and shrugged. I shrugged back. Claire, who usually made a business of promptness—it seemed to fit her image—was late and I suspected it was so she could make the best possible entrance. A moment later I noticed some of the bar crowd leaning over the railing into the stairwell and in seconds there was an audible buzz. Tom gave me the high-sign: Madame had arrived.

I was at the head of the stairs, from which vantage point I could observe the royal entrance. She was in smart black, a dish-sized hat with a cunning veil, the fur stole the Black Magic Fur Company had given her for posing, and her trademark anklestraps. With those huge eyes and scarlet slash of a mouth, graciously smiling and dispensing favor, she ascended, dripping her ten fingers at me. In the grill, prominent heads were craning, some people were on their feet applauding. It was the Star of Stars. Claire Regrett had arrived.

She pulled her Little Match Girl number again, the eyes wide as Christmas morning, the mouth a little O. "For me?" her look seemed to say. "Little *me?*" She kissed my cheeks, both, bestowing her patronage, then turned to beam upon our host. "Tom, how *nice* to see you. My absolute favorite restaurant in all the world. Bless you, darling. I hope you have some lovely veal, my mouth is absolutely watering."

She was breathless and lit with some inner glow that seemed to transform her into a woman much younger, vital and alive, ready to war on the whole wide world. Directing a glance toward the grill as luncheongoers returned to their squab and sole véronique, she bent to give a wavette to a face she may have recognized; then Tom conducted us back to the Fountain Room. I had a good view of the heads as they turned upward to gawk. Her progress through the bustling room was an enviable and palpable demonstration of Star Power. And she hadn't made a picture in ten years.

Since I was behind her in this royal progress I couldn't see her face, but I knew what it looked like, the great eyes shining, the red mouth in a half smile, the chin held high, Hollywood royalty showing that *noblesse* does indeed *oblige*. She tossed her furs off her shoulder with a studied casualness, and I noticed how firmly her feet moved on those high heels. When we arrived at our table and Tom set down the drinks, she thanked him effusively for his attentions, allowing her diamond to glint in the light. She draped her stole over the back of her chair and initiated the process of removing her gloves a finger at a time, truly an artful piece of stage business.

"Isn't this the *most* fun?" she exclaimed vivaciously when she'd made herself comfortable. She'd no sooner handed me her lighter to light her cigarette than two young girls in party dresses came shyly up in their maryjanes, asking her to autograph their napkins.

"We haven't got a pen," one explained.

"That's all right, you darling little thing, I never go anywhere without a pen." At the same moment, "Did you see Walter in the other room?" she muttered to me as she signed each napkin with flourishes.

"Walter who?" I muttered back.

"Cronkite. He's usually at '21.' There you are. And bless you, darlings," she said in her most queenly manner, her smile a yard wide.

"Thank you, Miss Regrett," the children chorused and trooped off with their treasures.

"Bless you . . . bless you, darlings, *mizpaw.* "

"*Mizpaw?*" I'd drawn a blank on that.

She grew this soulful look as she explained. "It's an old Indian word. It means 'May the Lord watch between thee and me while we are absent one from the other.' I read it in this book *Ten Simple Ways to a Happier and Brighter Life,* by A. F. Loveteague. Ever read him? Divine. Lives in a cabin somewhere near Missoula, commutes with nature. I think a word like *mizpaw* has a lot of meaning in this busy world. And such enchanting little girls," she said, raising her voice so others could overhear. "Darling, you'll never know how much I mourn not having had children of my own. Alas, my womb is barren."

"But mink-lined," I said to myself, taking the overscaled menu from the waiter.

Claire had already accepted hers and put on her glasses, tortoiseshell, about the size of a pair of snorkeling goggles. Looking up from her card, she smiled and gave me the benefit of her eyes. "How very very nice you look! Don't you just love New York in the spring? I think it's the most enchanting place in the world, I simply adore getting out and walking, seeing the real down-to-earth people. My telephone's been absolutely ringing off the hook. *So* many people called to say—well, you know. Radie Harris is agog. I told her I couldn't believe my ears. Imagine Belinda saying all those nice things about *me*. She has a generous soul, I always knew it. And what a terrible life—tragedy, darling, Belinda Carroll has been simply stalked by tragedy, hasn't she? Oh, look, veal, goodie, and milk-fed, too. I'm simply ravishingly hungry. How *can* they say I'm ill, when I eat the way I do? Oh, people, people, and those malicious little tongues of theirs. But they'll get it all back, darling, I promise you, they'll get it all back, if not in this world, then the next. Do you believe in reincarnation, Charles? People coming back as baby elephants or trained fleas? I'm not actually sure I'd want to come back; what if I reincarnated as a giraffe or baboon?"

We ordered, the scallopini for her, the lobster ravioli for me, Caesar salad for two, *sans* wine. By now she was on her second martini, and as she sipped I witnessed a notable exercise in how to drink from a stem glass. "I love one or two martinis, they always seem to relax me so. And, darling, speaking of Belinda, is she still on the wagon? Still A.A.? Staunch girl. Many people need that kind of group support. I'm glad I don't, I couldn't bear going to those meetings—all those awful *people*. Right off the Bowery, aren't they? I *mean* . . ." Her expression grew solemn, then downright pained. "But, you know, I've been giving things quite a bit of thought these past few days and I'm truly sorry she and I haven't been better friends over the years, truly. I think if we'd actually tried, we could have bolstered each other at times of crisis, you know what I mean—oh, you're laughing at me again. You just love laughing at me, don't you, you miserable putz? Oh no, I didn't mean that, only joking, darling."

I assured her that I had not been laughing at her. "It's just that I was never aware that you had Belinda's interests at heart."

"Oh, but you're *so* wrong, darling, really. You're *terribly* wrong. Certainly I was angry when they took away my dressing room—the dressing room that had been mine for eighteen years, it was like home to me—and gave it to her—that lousy bastard Louis Mayer—and *then* to put salt in the wounds they had it repainted that awful blue—Be-*linda* blue, can there *be* such a thing?—anyway I hope I'm a forgiving person. I've never been one to bear a grudge, I'm sure *no* one can ever say that about me. But I was brokenhearted. I walked in the front gate and out the back. Like a subway turnstile. That's Hollywood, I guess, here today, gone tomorrow; look at Luise Rainer—two Oscars and they send her over Niagara Falls in a barrel. I'd really like to show the real honest-to-God Hollywood, let the people know what really goes on, y'know? Paint the real picture."

"Do you intend doing that? Tell 'the whole truth and nothing but'?"

"Certainly I do. What the hell do you think I am, Pollyanna or something? I'm really going to get in my licks. Look out, Hollywood, here comes Momma—steamroller all the way."

"I like that," I prompted. "Give me a for-instance."

"Well, I mean, it's no secret that Hollywood was a hotcha town, is it? A girl had to get along, didn't she? If she wanted to get somewhere. You know Sam—Sam was a pincher from way back. Not just a pincher, Sam was a terror. People will be shocked to hear what used to go on up in that big white office of his—sitting around on his knee, putting in your lap time while he went over the clauses in your contract and then gave your boobs a squeeze. Then asked you if you wanted to go to the Coconut Grove for a little rhumba session. *You* were there, *you* know nothing was sacred. I know where more bodies are buried than Vi does, don't think I don't. And Momma's going to start digging them up."

She took out a cigarette, tapped the end on her thumbnail, and handed me her lighter to do the honors. She leaned, flamed the cigarette, then tossed back her head, her nostrils streaming smoke like a Chinese dragon, scales and all.

"Another thing—I really want to pay my debt to Frank with this book. If not for Frankie Adonis I'd have never seen the inside of the Thalberg Building, I'd have been at Fox playing those Loretta Young parts with ruffles and Ty Power or—" She leaned toward me with a yearning expression. "Oh, darling, what must poor Frank think of us all? What must he think of getting killed that way—some gangster letting him have it right through the eyeballs? I hope the bastard rots in—no no no, take it back, take it back—I *mustn't* say that, I must think beautiful thoughts, we *all* must think beautiful thoughts. Darling, I think maybe I'll have just one more martooni, if I may. I've got my primal scream session this afternoon and vodka releases me." When the waiter had brought her drink and discreetly withdrawn, she laid her hand over mine, saying:

"Bless you, darling, bless you so *very* much for this lovely treat. It means so much to know you care enough to invite me out. I really don't get out much at all, you know. I can't imagine how Belinda found out, but really I haven't been too well. Our little secret. No, no, dear," she hurried on, "not to worry, not to fret, Charles, we're not going to talk about my ailments today and spoil our lovely lunch, we're just going to talk about *you*. Vi says you've written a simply divine play. How terribly exciting! I've always known how terribly *special* you were—"

She gushed on in this vein and I knew she was bent on finding out as much about the play as she could. Since the producers were announcing the details on Thursday to make the Sunday edition of the *Times*, I didn't mind at all dropping my little bomb in Claire's lap. The play was called *Peking Duck*, a comedy about a New England widow who goes on a trip to China and meets a communist widower and they fall in love, only to have the children of both try to break up the affair.

"China! But what a simply entrancing idea!" Claire exclaimed rapturously. "I've always wanted to go there. Only—don't they say Beijing or some such these days? Instead of Peking or Peiping or whatever it's supposed to be? I do wish they'd make up their minds. And—um—whom did you say your star was?"

I had a forkful of salad in my mouth and had to swallow first. "Belinda," I finally managed.

She stared at me blankly. "What?" I repeated the name. "You mean —Belinda *Carroll* is going to star in your play?" I nodded, watching as the realization sank in. "But—but—she *can't*. She's scarcely been on the stage in her life."

"I wouldn't worry about that. She'll be just fine."

"Will she really? I wonder . . ." Claire mused, "Belinda Carroll—on Broadway. Somehow it doesn't—doesn't ring true—I mean—she's so *movies*, know what I mean? So absolutely Hollywood. Much more than so many others with a theatrical background. And I can't picture her playing some middle-class woman going off on some tour to China. Who's the man?"

I mentioned the name of a popular star of the day we were trying to sign. She fanned her face with the hand that had the diamond bracelet. "Well, if you ask me, you'll certainly have your work cut out for you with Belinda. If you care about your little play, and I *assume* you *do*, you'll think twice about *that* casting. Think: opening night you'll turn round and she simply won't be there. She's *terrified* of live audiences."

"Oh, I think she's got that pretty well conquered," I said.

"Well, I suppose you know what you're doing—" She paused to sip her drink. "I only wish *I'd* known you had another play in you after that ghastly flop, poor darling. That Vi's a real stinker not to have told me."

"Why?"

"To be perfectly honest, I'd have liked a crack at it myself. I was trained for the stage, you know. As a child. I once won a 'Most Beautiful Curls' contest. The Brooklyn Theatre."

"I don't think I ever knew that," I ventured cautiously. "You *have* had a checkered career."

"There's a lot of things you don't know about me. Oh, if Frank was only alive, he'd tell you. He knew me from when. And even after all those years in Hollywood and God knows how many movies, I've never stopped hankering to return to the New York stage. And, after all, I'm not *that* much older. Little Miss Goody-Goody has lopped off a couple of years, even if you don't know it." An unattractive furrow had made its way between her brows, and the corners of her mouth pinched. Then she brightened, leaning across to press my hand. "Oh, just look at big, bad Momma, here she is talking about herself again." She swooped her eyebrows at me in a sort of Ginger Rogersy way. "Oh, darling, if you only *knew* how much I want you to work on my book along with me. To—collaborate—yes, that's the word! You and me together, side by side, typewriter and pencil—*blue* pencil, of course, because you'd just have to edit me. I know it'd be a best-seller, nothing like that last one." At least she was acknowledging the bomb her last book had been; a step in the right direction. "And then there'll be the movie, of course. Lots of that good old Hollywood cabbage. Maybe David Wolper could do a miniseries. After all, you can't possibly tell it all in two hours, not *this* life! Come on, boy, what do you say? Is it a deal?"

"Well, I'd really like to," I said, "it's a mighty tempting prospect, but, you see, we'll be going into rehearsal soon. I guess you know what that's like."

"But you could find a little time, couldn't you? For me? After all, I'm not exactly chopped liver, am I? I mean—I *have* retained a following, haven't I? And think of the fun we could have meanwhile. It can't be too terribly hard, can it, writing? At least it wouldn't be with you. All you have to do is ask questions and I'll just talk away into the tape recorder. I've already taped scads. Then, when your play's opened and you're a big success, you can just take it all away and stick it together—you could go to Minorca, Hal Prince has a house there. Do you know Hal?"

"Hal's Majorca."

"Well, same thing, practically—Costa Bravo—and you could just sort of fluff it all up and arrange it chronologically and we'd have a book in no time. I even have the title. I want to call it *The Movieland Express*. It's modern and catchy, I think, don't you? And then, underneath, 'Memoirs of a Hollywood Career by Claire Regrett,' in smaller print. Don't you like it?"

"Sounds good to me."

"And I'm prepared to be generous, darling. I'll give you a really good split." She gripped my hand. "Oh, please, please please *please* say you will.

Pretty please? I won't be any trouble, I promise. I won't be difficult and I won't make trouble and—"

"And you won't tell the truth."

She drew back from me against the banquette and gave me a reproachful look. "How can you even *think* such a thing? Didn't I *say* the whole truth and nothing but? *I'll Cry Tomorrow* will read like *Rebecca of Sunnybrook Farm* compared to me. And I know exactly who I want to play me in the movie."

I steeled myself.

"Jane Fonda."

"Oh. Yes. Jane'd be very good." I could just see Jane Fonda playing Claire as a budding actress in 1932.

"She could age well, too. She's already got wrinkles around the eyes, don't think she hasn't. Aerobics doesn't do it all, you know. I've managed to keep my figure pretty well, for a girl my age. I have to remind myself I'm seventy; I keep up my massage and my schedule of facials; my beauty regimen is one of the most important parts of my day. Did you know I still eat my bran? Every morning—"

"Well, fancy meeting you here," I heard a voice greet me. I jumped up to shake hands with one of my producers; this was Marty Feldshoe and he got fat eyes when he saw whom I was with. I made suitable introductions and Claire instantly batted her lashes at him.

"I'm *so* happy to meet you. Charles has just been telling me about the play. It sounds absolutely delicious. I was saying I thought possibly a more seasoned stage actress might bring greater dimension to the role. You know, of course, that Natchez Calhoun wrote *Three Women* for me—Joan of Arc, Mistress Mary Johnson, and Emma Goldman—"

"The anarchist?" Marty's eyes were popping. "Did she get burned at the stake, too?"

"Oh, I don't really think so," Claire said glibly. "That didn't really come into it, I mean she didn't throw a bomb or anything. I was just mentioning it, you know—my stage background."

"Oh yeah, sure, I gotcha, heh heh." Marty was doing his best to represent his usual breezy self. "We're lucky to have Belinda. She's a household word; especially after the Oscar, they'll flock to see her. Say, Miss Regrett, that reminds me, we're giving her a party, a big big party—on a boat—cruising out around the Statue of Liberty and so on; we'd sure like it if you'd come. Hey—better yet, you could play hostess—you and Belinda arm in arm—the old-friends bit? Get a lot of space—a girl can't get too much publicity, y'know."

I saw Claire's eyebrows shoot up, denoting something between disdain and contempt.

"Thank you so much, Mr. Feld-shaw, but I'm afraid I shall be out of town," she said, stiff as a bed slat.

Marty glanced at me. "Oh well. Just thought I'd ask. So long. Let me send you a pair of ducats to our opening. Bring a friend."

Claire's reply had icicles on it. "I shall still be out of town."

Marty shot me another look, then made a hasty exit.

I looked at Claire. "Why'd you want to put the freeze on Marty Feldshoe?" I asked glumly. "He's a nice guy."

"I'm sure he is. And his diamonds are real cheap."

"How do you know?"

"Because I know, *buster*. They're yellow as buttercups. And his shoes needed polishing."

"He works hard. He's just been divorced. He probably didn't have time. Don't be so critical of people."

"I have high standards, that's all." She waved an arm at the room. "Besides, don't you think they're all critical of me, every last one of those bastards? You bet your ass they are. They're all watching to see little Miss Clairey spill her soup or get plotzed and fall down or something."

"They're your fans. They love you."

"And don't you forget it, buster! They've loved me for almost fifty years. Stonecutter, carve it in stone. But I don't think you've really caught my pitch. I mean, we'll sell books, *lots* of books. I'll be in every bookstore across the goddamn country. I'll be on every talk show—Merv's mad about me. This book'll make a fortune. I really think you should reconsider. I mean, you *really* should. Otherwise . . ."

"Otherwise what?"

"Otherwise Momma spank—hard."

Momma *spank?* What did that mean? She all but twisted mustachios, like the villain in a melodrama.

"Charlie," she cooed. "What if your old friend Claire was to tell you something—something *really* interesting that you might not have considered—that might affect your decision?"

"I'm always game for interesting things. Shoot."

She glanced over her shoulder. "I don't think this is quite the place to discuss it. It's a very delicate matter."

"Okay. Call me sometime."

"No, no, I really want you to have time to think this over. It involves you as well as Belin—others. I thought you ought to know, just in case—well, let's say in case you continued to say no to my idea. You know—I don't particularly like having people say no to me. It tends to get my goat."

"Far be it from me to get your goat, wherever you keep him; perhaps you'd better tell me what you're talking about."

"Didn't I say this is not the place to go into such things? Suffice it to say that what I'm talking about involves a famous Hollywood name, *very* famous—one I should imagine you'd be at pains to protect. 'Nuff said? Maybe you can find time for me this evening, we'll talk further, hm?" She smiled, folded her napkin, and set it aside, giving it a little pat as if to thank it for the meal.

I was getting angry. "Look, I don't think I quite catch your drift, but if you're threatening me about—about anything—"

"*I?* Threaten *you?* Darling, don't be silly. I simply mean to point out an area where danger—lurks, I suppose would be the word. Some skeletons are better left in the closet, don't you agree?"

Skeletons. Closet. Where had I heard those words before? I was beginning to catch the drift. Vi's lunch idea was backfiring. I was finding myself up the creek without a paddle. Claire asked for coffee—well Irished. I wondered about her next appointment: her primal scream was likely to be a howl.

I drank my decaf, thinking over what she'd said. She leaned across to let me light another cigarette for her and I marveled at the impasto of lipstick on the filter. Expelling smoke in a cloud, she glanced around her, and her eye fell on the portly figure of Marty Feldshoe at the corner table where he was talking with our publicity man and a newspaper reporter.

Turning back to me, she fanned away the smoke as if to see me better and said, "It was a lovely luncheon, Charles, I've enjoyed it immensely. But may we get one thing straight before we break things up? Your Mr. Feldshow with his yellow diamonds—if it's really his quaint notion that I hostess a party for Belinda Carroll on board the good ship *Lollipop*, give him a message for me, huh?"

"Sure."

"Tell him Claire said to go fuck himself. And give our little talk some thought, will you? I must be off. Bless you, darling. Lovely veal." And she teetered off on her high heels.

"Claire—wait!" Heads whirled, necks craned, and what was left of the luncheon crowd ogled Claire's uncertain passage back through the room as she made a ludicrous effort to maintain her balance, managing to bump into a waiter, who only just saved the contents of his tray.

Fortunately Tom Margittai stopped her with a word at the head of the stairs, giving me a chance to catch up with her. She tossed her furs about and repeated her stage business with her gloves, having trouble with the fingers.

"Did you enjoy your lunch, Miss Regrett?" Tom asked politely.

"Bless you, darling, of course. The veal was scrumptious. See you soon." She kissed his cheek, gave her stole another hike, waved to Walter in the grill, took three steps, and her feet went out from under her. She hit the stairs with her bottom in the most awkward, splat-legged pose imaginable. Tom and I rushed to help her up, only to be scorned.

"No one touch me!" she commanded. "I can get up myself." Summoning what remained of her dignity, she managed to accomplish this with a minimum of effort, balancing unsteadily and clutching the brass railing, while a sea of faces gazed down into the stairwell from all sides. Another buzz flittered among the onlookers, and I thanked God there were no photographers on hand to record this moment of ignominy. Without a backward look she made her way gingerly down the stairs, one by one, obviously feeling the effects of her accident. Exit star, tottering.

The results of this minor debacle were several. To begin with, Claire's accident proved far more serious than anyone had thought, and the next day I learned from Vi that she'd been put in Roosevelt Hospital for a fractured coccyx. Being in any hospital did not set well with Madame since she was a devout Christian Scientist and didn't believe in medical help. Instead, she kept her Science practitioner at her side, helping her pray her way back to health, though the fact that she was encased in plaster-of-Paris from her chest to her lower back indicated that a more conventional treatment was needed as well.

Also, the accident further served to embroil me in the clutches of— Miss Clutch, who else? Feeling in some small way guilty about her accident, I loaded up on flowers and went to visit the patient in her sickroom, a veritable bower of blooms. Cards and affectionate reminders from a host of notables were everywhere displayed, she was got up in her favorite negligee, her hair freshly done and a ribbon in it, as if she were waiting for the photographers. They'd already come and gone.

When I came in, she settled back against her pillows and began putting on her Lady of the Manor act, cooing over my floral offering and making me look at each bouquet she'd received and read each card.

"Aren't people simply *wonderful?* How thoughtful, how kind they all are. And how kind you are for coming to see me after all those terrible things I said. Taking time out of your busy schedule." Now she was into "Little Me" again. She tilted her head to one side, and smiled coyly. "Charles," she went on, "I'm glad you've come, because I've been lying here wondering if you've forgotten what we were talking about just before I slipped. At the restaurant?"

I'd hardly forgotten about our conversation at the Four Seasons; rather, it had been hanging over me like the Sword of Damocles. What did she have up her sleeve, really?

"Your venom is caking," I said.

Her brows shot in surprise. "What a thing to say! I'm only attempting to get things straight between us."

"Sorry, it sounded like a threat. You know—'my knife is sharp, mind your liver and lights.' Suppose you just cut the jokes and level with me."

She maintained a consistently blithe attitude. "Frankly, I don't think your word 'threat' is appropriate. You know me better than that, darling; I don't go around making threats. At least—not *idle* ones." Her smile beamed, then turned to glass, and the bitch had the nerve to bat her eyelashes at me, all four feet of them.

"What I am referring to—and I think you already know what I'm going to say—I am referring to some letters. Letters written to me many years ago by a certain party. A rather famous party, who though now dead would attract a lot of attention wherever that name happened to be mentioned. Letters written to me by that party and stolen from me by another party—a relation. Letters that, should they come to light, would doubtless prove embarrassing to still *other* certain parties. *Now* do you catch my drift?"

"I do, but I think if you checked, you'd find that the letters you refer to no longer exist."

"Are you quite certain?"

"I should be, I burned them myself—*without reading them*, let me mention—I burned them in the fireplace of the Snuggery."

Claire positively purred. "Ahh, the Snuggery—how well I remember that cozy nook. English as all get-out. Maude in matching sweater sets, her daytime pearls, at the desk writing those gracious notes, Crispin in his high-backed chair, having his bourbon-and-branch, puffing away on his pipe, looking like Sherlock Holmes. And you—*burned* them, you say? The letters?"

"I did. So you see, if you're plotting a little blackmail in order to get me to do your book, why, then—the letters are ashes, and ashes don't read very well, do you think?"

"The actual letters are beside the point, we needn't consider them."

I tossed up my hands. "Well, there we are. That said, what next?"

"What say we put our cards on the table. Let's talk about that certain famous party, my ex-father-in-law, the master of Sunnyside."

"Crispin Antrim? By all means. I'd be interested in hearing what you have to say—since the letters were written to you."

"You noticed, did you? Well, I can't say it's no secret because it is —or was. And it's my guess that the Widow Antrim, I refer to your darling Belinda, would want to have it go on being kept secret."

"Why don't we leave Belinda out of this and you just tell me all about it. Let me be the judge?"

"All right." She licked her lips around and toothed off some lipstick, a habit of hers. "Well, let's see—Crispin. He and I go way back, but you probably didn't know that, most people didn't. He was the big cheese around AyanBee when I first came on the lot. He didn't know who I was —which was understandable, since I wasn't anybody. I'd walk by him, he never gave me a flick. I'd see him in the commissary but he never noticed me. Until—well, it was Christmas, you know? And he was alone. Nobody likes being alone on Christmas."

This surprised me. "Alone? Are you telling me that Maude wasn't with him at Christmas?"

"Her father had died, she'd gone back to New Jersey. So Crispin was high and dry on Christmas. Christmas Eve, to be exact. His show was working late, so was mine. Not a lot of work was getting done. Everybody was partying all over the lot, over in the offices, on the stages, everybody was feeling merry. Only he wasn't, because he was alone. I was alone, too. That's how it started."

"You and him, you mean?"

She nodded thoughtfully. "Me 'n' him. Just like that. He was going one way, I was going the other, we passed on the sidewalk. He looked, I looked, nobody said anything. I went to my dressing room; I was taking off my makeup when he knocked on the screen. 'May we come in?' he says, nice and polite. Crispin Antrim was the politest man I ever met. He says something like 'Since it is the Yuletide and everyone seems to be partaking of the seasonal cheer, it occurred to me that you might partake of a little cheer yourself. Or do I detain you? Perhaps you have other plans?' No, I say quick, I didn't have any plans at all. So he pulls out this bottle of shampoo, ice cold. He uncorks it, I get a couple of paper cups, and there we were toasting Christmas and drinking bubbly together. Me and Crispin Antrim! He said how Maude was back in New Jersey and he dreaded going home with her not there. He's got this book with him —*War and Peace*. Big. About the fattest book I ever picked up. He starts telling me all about this Russian family—two families, I guess it was—and how it's one of the great novels. He says he's read it four times, this is the fifth, and when I ask him why so many times if he knows how it turns out, he smiles. Nice. 'For the beauty, my dear,' he says, 'for the joy of the words. Once beauty presents itself to me I am able to enjoy it over and over. Like a beautiful piece of music, a Beethoven symphony, or a Mozart sonata.' So I'm drinking my shampoo and I'm thinking, 'Get a load of you, kid, here's Crispin Antrim talking to you about Mozart and you don't even know the guy.'

"Well, we polish off the bottle and then it's time to go, only he doesn't want to. He asks me if he can drive me home. In his chauffeured car yet. Everything's really gentlemanly; he asks me about my movie, wants to know what plans Sam has for me, just shop talk, and when I say good night he insists on walking me to my door. I was living on Hyperion Avenue then, and when we get there he says can he come in and see my apartment. I make coffee, he sits and talks some more, all about how much he loves Maude and his boy, Perry—from the way his old man talked about him I figured he must be plenty spoiled—and he was, believe me. His father's worried about how he'll turn out. Needs a nice girl, that stuff —and I think, Is he going to fix me up with his son? Uh uh. I know the guy's just looking for a shoulder to cry on, it being Christmas and everything. I figure he'll talk himself to death and then take off for home. Only—"

Only instead he'd stayed long after the coffee had been drunk, and in the end he'd stayed and made love to her. When they saw each other again at the studio, they talked about the miserable Christmases they'd each had, and he asked her out to dinner. They went to Musso & Frank's in Hollywood, then they returned to Hyperion to talk, and ended up in bed again.

He came back a third time, a fourth. One night she cooked for him, corned beef and cabbage, his favorite. Next time she did chicken fricassee with dumplings. He always came to talk but always stayed to make love. Somehow Viola got wind of these trysts and advised Claire to knock it off before there was trouble. Vi might have gone to Sam with the tale but she didn't, she kept her mouth shut. When Maude came home, Crispin was there to meet her. She was to know nothing.

"But he felt guilty," Claire said. "All the time guilty. You know how it was—they'd been married twenty years now, he had a roving eye. I was young, he loved my body. And I made him laugh. I'll tell you this, it's a lot easier getting a guy if you make him laugh than just being terrific in the sack."

"Did Frank know what was going on?"

"Sure. Frank knew, but he never said much. I think he was ashamed because of the shabby way he'd treated me in New York. He figured it wasn't any of his business anyway. Then he and Babe started having those arguments right out in public; she'd haul off and sock him—and he'd sock her back—and I knew he was getting tired of her carrying on like that. So when he dumped her I see that here's my chance to get him back. So I write Crispin this letter, breaking it off, saying I can't see him anymore or it's going to mean trouble for everybody. I say, Don't come around me at the studio, don't come to the apartment, and don't call. So he starts writing these letters, pleading with me to see him, he doesn't want to lose me. Really passionate letters, you've no idea.

"He knew it wasn't any good; just moments in his life. He was hog-tied to Maude. He told me he'd never been unfaithful to her before me, and I'll tell you something—I don't think he was unfaithful after, either. And he helped me: he made Sam give me the Fedora picture, and the other one at MGM. I never regretted a thing."

"What about later, when you and Perry were married and you lived at Sunnyside? How did he feel then, you being so near?"

Claire shrugged. "The whole thing was his own idea. He was gung-ho for our getting married, me and Perry. Crispin didn't like him running off all the time. He thought I'd make him a good wife and maybe he'd stop his gallivanting. Maude wasn't keen on our living over there in the Play-house, but Crispin really thought it was terrific, having me right there next door to him."

"Did he ever try to start up again? I mean did he ever—"

"Put the make on me? Are you kidding? He was just 'Daddy dear.' You'd never have known there was anything between us. I was his daughter now; I was supposed to produce an heir for him. But it was no dice. God knows I tried; any time Perry wanted to party, okay with me. Only —no kids in the nursery."

Further talk along these lines was cut off when the night nurse came in, all smiles, but telling me I had to go, it was long after Miss Regrett's lights-out. While the nurse plumped the pillows and buzzed the bed down flat, Claire's eyes lingered on me, as if to ask, Well, what do you think of all that? I didn't know what to think, but it gave me plenty of food for thought until I could see her again. I wasn't able to come back for two days, since I was tied up every minute with the play. Belinda was due in at the end of the week, and once she got here it would be full speed ahead. Meanwhile, we were trying to cast the lead male.

I finally got back to Room 804, this time lugging in a hothouse gardenia tree in full bloom. As I trucked in I was met by Claire's Christian Science practitioner, Mrs. Conklin, a pleasant-faced woman of sixty or so who gave me a friendly smile and a firm handshake. We chatted briefly;

then she kissed Claire and left to get some books at the library, she said. I liked it that Claire seemed so fond of this woman; Mrs. Conklin seemed one person who might do some real good in Claire's hectic and unfocused life.

I was anxious for her to go on with her story, and it didn't take much urging on my part. She proceeded now to enlighten me on the reason Faun had been so desperate to get her hands on the fifteen thousand dollars she'd told Maude she had to have. It was pure chance that had caused Claire and Faun to meet at the L.A. airport following Frank's funeral and Claire's untimely visit at Sunnyside. They'd ended up sitting next to each other on the flight, and by the time they got to New York they were on good terms. Faun was invited to stay for the weekend, and managed to stay for over two months. Not surprisingly, they didn't get along. There were several nasty scenes. Once Claire's maid caught Faun snooping in the files which no one but Claire was allowed to touch, and when Claire heard about it she read the riot act. Then things simmered down a bit until the next, the final, upset.

It seemed that the tenants in the apartment below Claire's, a Japanese doctor named Sadikichi and his American wife, were among the few couples in the building with whom Claire was on speaking terms. When Mrs. Sadikichi expressed the desire to entertain the daughter of Belinda Carroll, Claire obliged. Before the meal was served, the doctor invited Faun to help select a good Burgundy to go with the beef. He had showed off his notable collection of vintages, some of them costing as much as five hundred or even a thousand dollars a bottle, one being worth far more, a rare-vintaged Château Lafite.

When Claire named this figure, I began adding it all up. "Faun stole it?" I asked.

"Not that night. She waited until the Sadikichis had gone to their country house; then she went down and told the maid she'd left her cigarette lighter somewhere and wondered if it might have slipped in between the sofa cushions. The maid told Faun to take a look around. Faun looked, not in the sofa but in the wine cabinet, and she made off with the most expensive bottle. When I confronted her with the theft, she denied it all, but I knew she was lying. She'd gone to visit friends at Southampton and taken the bottle along as a house present. The host realized it was an expensive wine and didn't want to open it, but Faun insisted. I knew the people vaguely—they lived in Gin Lane—so I checked up and out came the whole story. Faced with this, darling Faun confessed. Then, by God, if she didn't talk me into paying Dr. Sadikichi and said she'd get the money from Maude. That's when she went to the goddamn files and stole the letters—Crispin's letters. Only I didn't find out about that until later. Then when she got killed, I thought, I'm never going to see that dough again. But I didn't reckon with Maude. I wrote and explained what had happened, and I got a check back just like that. It was Maude who told me about the letters, and when I looked in the files —sure enough, they were missing. Maude also sent me back that letter I'd written to Crispin all those years ago."

"Her way of telling you she knew?"

"I guess. Said she'd unearthed it among his things after he died. I felt bad that she found out. It hurt her. But what I have to tell you is, because Faun was threatening to use Crispin's letters in that book she was writing —yeah, I heard all about that one—I figure Maude got so angry she'd have done anything short of murder to keep it all quiet—even *not* short of murder . . . hm? What do you think, Charles?"

"She was upset, sure, why shouldn't she be? But more than that—"

"More than that you don't care to say. I don't blame you, darling; in your shoes I wouldn't, either."

"In my shoes? What does that mean?"

"It means that you're very interested in keeping this whole unsavory business a private matter. And I don't blame you. It's hardly in the Antrim image, is it?"

"I don't know what you're getting at."

She sucked in her cheeks and gave me that oh-come-on smirk of hers. "Don't play coy with me, laddie, you damn well *do* know what I'm talking about. I'm talking about the fact that there was some skulduggery at the crossroads. Maude's dead, a scandal couldn't hurt her anymore. But *if*—notice I say *if*—if word started getting around about those letters and what Faun threatened to do, people might—notice I say *might*—get the wrong impression. And you wouldn't want that to happen, would you? Charles? Especially if you care about what happens to our friend Blindy."

I still couldn't see what she was getting at, but I knew it spelled trouble. "Claire," I said soberly, "I think you ought to know that Belinda and I plan to be married after the play opens."

I was simply letting her know how things stood, but the face I saw was that of the Wicked Queen in *Snow White*. I'd struck a nerve.

Up went the brows, down went the mouth. "Married? You don't say. And you never told me, you sly puss. Well, well, love comes to Honey Brewster, huh? And at her age, too. Well, I guess there's nothing wrong with sex after sixty, unless it brings on an attack of sciatica. Congratulations, Charles. I wish you every happiness. *And*—notice I say *and*—this news leads me to believe you'd be that much more interested in keeping

Belinda's name free of any scandal, especially when your little play is about to open."

More than ever I wanted to kiss her off. "Why don't you stop screwing around and just say what's on your mind," I growled.

She smiled, radiating sweetness and light. "No need to get surly, darling. Put it this way: give me what I want and I'll give you what you want. That's fair enough, isn't it?"

"I don't know—what is it you want?"

"Just say you'll help me with my book, as I've been asking you to do, and I'll throw away the key." She did her little pantomime of locking her lips and disposing of the key.

"This key being—"

"—being a very strong suspicion that somebody had tinkered with that blue stove in the Playhouse bedroom. In fact, I think I know just who arranged that—accident."

"I see. And supposing it *wasn't* an accident, who gets your vote?"

"You, sweetie, you get my vote."

"Oh, you're wrong, sweetie, you're way out in left field somewhere pulling daisies."

"Am I? No, I am not. And if you think I didn't mean what I say—I'll just put the whole nasty business in my own book. Now, how do you like them apples?"

"They sound awfully sour to me."

"But do you agree? My silence for your pen?"

There I was, being gored on the horns of a dilemma. Jesus. I said I'd have to think it over, which, of course, told her lots: either that she was right or plenty close to it—even that I'd have to agree to her terms. I never liked her less than I did when I looked at her there, well pillowed in her four-way bed of pain.

I left the hospital and walked home through the park. I knew I wanted to talk things over with someone, but I didn't know who. Vi? I considered that to be unwise, given Vi's penchant for gossip, but it was she who eventually brought the thing up to me. She'd had all the facts, whether from Claire or some other source I hadn't a clue. "Do it, dear," she said. "Do it or she'll have you roasted for dinner with an apple in your mouth."

So ominous was this warning that I was forced to take it to heart. Finally, believing discretion much the better part of valor, I caved in to Claire. I called her and agreed to her terms, and was relieved when she didn't gloat but merely accepted it as my good business sense. Belinda Carroll opening on Broadway to a blast in the papers about Claire's affair with Crispin Antrim plus the odd circumstances surrounding the demise of Belinda's daughter hardly would stack up as the best kind of publicity.

In return, however, I got Claire's promise to hostess the party my producers were throwing aboard the cruise boat. Hordes of press would be on board, and what better way to hype the evening than for Claire Regrett to be on hand, Claire encouraging her "old friend" Belinda, who was about to embark on her Broadway stage career?

I came home from the hospital to find a message that Vi had called. "Sweetie, how absolutely wonderful!" she crowed when I rang her up. "I knew you couldn't turn the poor thing down, especially now when she's *in extremis.* You really have a very kind heart, dear. And she's going to go full-out for you on the party thing. Won't Belinda be pleased!"

This remained to be seen. Belinda arrived in New York too nervous to join me in my East Side love nest, instead taking rooms at a nearby hotel. I chose my time—we were in bed eating openface steak sandwiches —to invoke her blessing on Claire's hostessing the party. She took it all in stride, then grew suspicious when I laid on her the arrangements concerning Claire's book.

"Ghostwriter? *You? You're* mad. You're a novelist, a playwright, a screenwriter—but you don't ghostwrite! And you certainly don't ghost-write Claire Regrett!"

"That's what you think." When I explained that I *had* to do it, Belinda laughed.

"Don't tell me—she's blackmailing you." Seeing my expression, she sat up and gave me a hard look. "My gosh—you mean she *is* blackmailing you?"

I said it was a sort of semi-hemi-demi-blackmailing. Then it all came out in the wash. Lunch at the Four Seasons, the conversations at the hospital, my ultimate capitulation.

"She threatened to tell? She wouldn't dare!"

I said I thought she might.

"But I won't have you doing it—it's nonsense. Besides, you've enough to do with rewrites for me."

I said yes, I knew. "But I'm doing this for you, too. And the first thing you've got to do is pay her a visit. A sort of conciliatory thing. They want photographs—you can autograph her cast, right under Walter Cronkite."

Upsetting her coffee, Belinda dove for the bathroom and slammed the door. A minute later she bounded out, flying into my arms, crying, "Greater love hath no man. . . ."

Two days later, I met Belinda after her exercise class and we walked from Columbus Circle up to the San Remo, where we found the publicity man and several representatives of *People* magazine on hand. I knew she was entering into this meeting warily, but it quickly appeared that she had nothing to fear. Claire merely wanted to shine, and if Belinda was to shine as well, it would be a matter of reflection.

A neat-looking, calm-eyed black woman in skirt and blouse let us in. As we milled around in the foyer, I thought about the democratic principles at work here: in the old days any maid of Claire's would have been in uniform with cap and apron, looking like Louise Beavers and drippin' molasses. The sizable living room was a mix of weird antique pieces and contemporary kitsch. Yellow had been used liberally, along with white and green, and accented with black. Though the effect was crisp and bright, it was somehow tacky; the antiques seemed to abhor the flashy colors. Some decorator must have talked her into it. To cap the *outré* effect, the upholstered pieces all were covered in clear plastic vinyl! I'd heard but never really believed it. Belinda and I looked at each other, then looked away before we started to snicker.

Claire greeted us in the "library," a room that revealed a distinct absence of books. She was grandly ensconced on a chaise longue, well bolstered by pillows, a cane prominently displayed, the medical corset she wore artfully covered by her arm. On her lap was her toy poodle. The chaise, she claimed, had once belonged to the Spanish Ambassador, though no explanation was forthcoming about how it had fallen into her hands.

"Darling!" she cried, throwing her arms wide and forcing Belinda to lean to do ladies' kiss-kiss. But not before the photographer had his cameras ready, four of them dangling from his neck. Claire's hands were on Belinda's upper arms and I could see how she held her there in the awkward position, managing to stick her face full into the lens.

"But isn't this all thrilling!" she went on, releasing Belinda. "Charles dear, take the lady's coat. And, Belinda, do sit down, you must be exhausted; Viola's been telling me about your schedule. They're relentless, aren't they? Bless you, darling, for coming here like this; I'm afraid I'm still a bit shaky on my feet. But I'll be on deck on the night, never you fear. What color do you plan on wearing?"

"My gown's green," Belinda ventured, sitting up in the awkward straightback chair placed beside Claire's chaise, and I noticed Belinda trying to cover her knees against the camera.

"Green?" screeched Claire, making a terrible face which the camera caught. "I'm wearing red. We'll look like fucking Christmas."

"You always look so good in red," Belinda said, playing Melanie as only she could.

"Not cherry red, not fireman's red, but a scarlet. As a matter of fact, I had the material dyed to match the Cardinal's robes. I invited His Grace, but he has another engagement. But he said he'd be there in spirit. I want you to meet him, darling, he's the most divine man and he's seen some of your movies, one or two. I told him you weren't Catholic, but he's very open-minded; after all, neither am I."

I admired Belinda's example of studied calm as she sat smiling, listening to Claire run on in grand style. All the time she talked she gestured with one hand, petting the dog with the other or holding him up and encouraging him to lick her cheek. "Now now, Doodoo, don't you be such a ham," she cautioned, smiling radiantly. "Honestly, the minute he sees a camera he's up to his tricks. Naughty naughty, Momma 'pank."

When the photographer asked if Claire could stand for a couple of shots, she put on one of her acts, a touch of dubiety as to whether she could possibly manage, then a brief cloud of heavy thought, followed by determination, some teeth-clenching, finally the summoning of the necessary effort.

"No no, don't help me, anyone," she commanded again, "just—let —me—do—this by myself." Belinda still had the good sense to assist her, for the flashes kept going off, and when they stood side by side Claire put out her palm. "My mirror, please, someone"—and we waited while she gave the Face a critical review in the glass. She touched her hair in several places, scrutinized an angle, and handed away the mirror. "All right, now, quickly, let's get the photos done, while I can still stand."

She linked arms with her guest and the two ex-beauties smiled for the birdie. In the brief flash of light Claire's face looked old and sallow, and her drooping chin showed, while, nearly fifteen years younger, Belinda gave off a natural radiance and health that Claire could never hope to match. Claire herself must have been feeling something of the kind, because, when the photographer let go of one camera and took up another, she waved her hand and said in a tired voice, "That's enough, I think. I'm a bit tuckered." Grimacing, she lowered herself onto the chaise, making another show of gameness, then took up the dog and gave it the old kootchie-koo while *People* recorded the event for posterity. When they were satisfied, Belinda swung away from the group to have a look at Claire's art collection.

"You have a lot of pictures, don't you?" she said brightly. "Who does the cute little tykes with the big goo-goo eyes?" Claire pronounced the name of the artist. "Oh yes, of course, I've heard of her."

Claire seemed mollified. She adored these lemur-eyed monstrosities. "I may not know much about art, but I do know what I like. And I adore my little orphans, as I call them. It's the eyes that do it for me. The eyes are the windows of the soul, aren't they?" Belinda's expression told me these were awfully *big* windows. Claire sighed. "If I had a little girl I'd want her to look just like those. I could just gobble up the one in the blue hair ribbon."

She reached for her cigarettes and lit one, then offered the pack to Belinda, who thanked her but didn't smoke. Claire looked at the clock. "You'll excuse me if I don't get up again; this chaise is so cozy. It came from the Spanish Ambassador's house right over there across the park. One hundred percent down."

Our producers had gone all-out on Belinda's welcoming party, and the press turned out in Roman phalanxes. There were easily 150 of New York's most famous faces in attendance; name them, they were there. Happily, the weather proved agreeable, and we were able to be out on the decks of the romantically decorated river vessel. Claire made a show of being prompt—I was already on board—and she engineered her usual star entrance dressed in a fire-engine-red satin sheath and a clever evening hat bound to cause comment. Belinda hurried forward, they kissed air, hugged, and obligingly posed for the cameras. I caught the adroit way in which Claire disengaged herself and went to pose solo at the rail, looking off and up, giving them the Roman-coin profile.

For a while, in the heat of things, I lost track of her, but from time to time I'd glimpse her, glass in hand, the focus of one group or another. She was playing the hostess bit to the hilt, this was *her* party, and I found myself thinking: Blindy, beware. But there was no need to fear. It all went smooth as glass, bubbly like one huge Alka-Seltzer. I divided my time, eating a part of my supper with Belinda, the other half with Claire, and at no time did the one mention the other.

Claire was too busy displaying her sensitivity. "Simply enchanting," she breathed with an ecstatic tremor as I joined her at the ship's rail. "How I adore it. New York's the heart of the world, it always was." She preempted my arm and put it around her shoulder, then snuggled up against me intimately, clinging to my wrist with both hands as we walked along the deck, a little as if she were trying to wear me. "I'm *so* glad I came," she crooned huskily. "I'm just awfully glad I said I'd do it. It was worth it, every bit. And you were so kind to ask me. You really are a nice friend and I'm terribly proud to see the way you've developed over the years. I know I can depend on you. I can—can't I?" She all but threw her eyes at me.

After a while she released her hold on me, then looked up; I could see those long long Hollywood lashes, the exaggerated Max Factored mouth, and I knew that seventy-year-old ladies were capable of longing. When she shivered, I took the opportunity to suggest that she must be getting cold and we'd best join the others. (I also knew Belinda would be wondering where I was.) As I took her arm, Claire came tiptoe to press her lips to mine.

"That's for being so nice," she whispered. As we went through the doorway, I blotted my lips with my handkerchief. "Wait, let me," she said, taking over the job. "Later," she added, "when we get home, we'll talk some more." Subtlety was never Claire's long suit and I got the picture. I was to pay the pound of flesh, the blood as well.

When we docked, there must have been fifty to a hundred limousines jammed at crazy angles, waiting for their passengers. Amid the noisy pandemonium of farewells I glimpsed Claire coming off, escorted by our publicity man. He took her to her car, then came looking for me.

"She wants you to drive home with her."

"I can't. I promised to take Belinda back to her hotel."

He shrugged. The ball was in my court. I went to Belinda and explained; she was understanding and said she could get home on her own hook. Belinda was a big girl. Not so Claire, whom I found curled up in the back of her limousine, one big throbbing pout cradled in all that plush.

"Boy, have you got some nerve," she began as I got in beside her and we drove off. "And I tried so hard for you," she sniffed. "You have to admit that. Don't you? You thought I was going to get pissed, fall on my face, didn't you? I told you I wouldn't and I didn't."

"That's right, you didn't," I replied, thinking *"Gott sei danke."* I thanked her warmly and profusely for her efforts; she really had done a terrific job and I wanted her to realize it. "I know you didn't and I thank you."

She began to sob, like a little girl who's been kept from going to the circus or something. She dug out a handkerchief and wept into it, her furred shoulders quivering.

I was desperate and saw the driver looking at us in the rear-view mirror. "I'm really sorry."

"People always say they're sorry, but it doesn't help when you hurt people. Oh, what's the use—I guess I should be used to being hurt by now.

People are so thoughtless, so inconsiderate. This was a mistake, I shouldn't have attempted it; much better if I'd stayed home by myself and you got Lana Turner or someone to do it. I'm no use to anyone anymore. I should just shut myself up like a witch in a castle and not bother."

When we arrived at Central Park West, she was really a mess; her eyes were like a raccoon's from smudged liner and mascara, and her face had gone pistachio; the lipstick was all bitten off. She wouldn't get out until she'd made emergency repairs; then she wouldn't let me go, but dragged me in, insisting I must see her to her door. As we stepped off the elevator and stood in the vestibule, she handed me her keys, suggesting that I open the door like the gentleman she knew me to be. She then insisted I come in "for a little nightcap." I knew what a little nightcap with Claire was going to mean. We sat in the library, where she splashed vodka over ice and curled up in a chair while I checked my phone service. I gave her perhaps fifteen minutes, then said I had to get home, there were things I needed to take care of. When I bent over to peck her cheek and thanked her again, she pulled away.

"I didn't do it for you, damn it, and I certainly didn't do it for her. But I kept my part of the bargain. Now, my man, you can keep yours. You *do* intend *keeping* our bargain?" she added.

I hastened to assure her that I did and started on my getaway, but no. "I'll pick you up for lunch tomorrow. Around noon. There's something I want to show you, I think it will help you get a better perspective on me."

When I said I couldn't have lunch, her lips clenched. "I've got rehearsal," I explained. "I can't just not be on deck. It's the first day."

To get myself out of there I rashly agreed to lunch on Saturday. When I stepped into the elevator, she ordered me to wait, hurried inside, and reappeared with a manila envelope.

"The first ten chapters. Read them and we'll speak."

I nodded, the door closed, I sagged against the wall as the car began its descent. "Bless you, darling." I heard the charm float down to me through the elevator shaft.

"She's a real honey of a dame, isn't she?" said the beaming elevator man.

"Yes," I said, "a *real* honey of a dame."

Next morning, when I went to bring the paper in, I found Claire's material still on the hall table. I made coffee, then stepped out on the terrace and, eschewing the *Times*, I opened the manila envelope and took out what amounted to about seventy pages, cleanly typed on expensive paper. I thumbed through it, glimpsed words like "enchanting" and "divine" and "very, very" all over the place. But I tackled the job.

I read slowly to begin with, to "get the flow," then when I'd got it I read faster, then faster, then skimmed, then threw the pile of pages down in a heap. Even while I was lying there wondering what kind of ass I was to have got involved in such a thing, the phone rang: Vi.

"She says she gave you the chapters. Have you read them yet? What do you think?" I told her what I thought. "But that's exactly what I've been telling you, sweetie, she needs you to straighten her out."

"Sweetie, it's the biggest carload of bullshit I ever read. And in her own words, '*Just whom is kidding whom?*' That's not writing, that's barbarism." Viola made pigeon coos and said there never was a word put on paper that couldn't be fixed. I was inclined to disagree; nothing could fix what I'd been reading.

But I was committed, not only to the book but to a mysterious excursion. Therefore, on Saturday morning, when they rang from downstairs to say Miss Regrett's car was waiting, I slung on a jacket and went down. She was lounging in that negligent, modelly way of hers (I'll say one thing for Claire: she always knew how to sit a limousine), wearing one of her jumpsuits and her fur coat, though the day was fair and warmish. We drove east to Second Avenue and then downtown. She asked me how rehearsals were going, was interested to hear my comments about her rival's performance.

"I hear tell you're not happy with my work," she began, having lighted her prop cigarette. From the corner of my eye I could see the Fabulous Profile inviting my attention; obviously she didn't care to look straight at me. "Now, before you start in, let me say this. I *know* what you're going to say, I *know* it's not what we're after, but it's a *start,* isn't it? I knew you weren't going to like it anyway, so I'm glad we're through that. But I think I have a new approach on things. Is that fair?"

I said yes, it seemed so; but where were we going? She gave me a cryptic look, and when I saw us turn onto the approach to the Fifty-ninth Street Bridge, I became more puzzled than ever. Pretty soon we were winding through the mazes of Astoria, and eventually we found ourselves in Brooklyn. Then I got the idea: she was making a sentimental pilgrimage.

"We wouldn't be going to the ancestral homestead, would we?"

She darted me a frown. "Very clever of you. That's exactly where we're going. You are about to gaze upon one of the rare sights of the world, the birthplace of Cora Sue Brodsky."

When we'd traveled another dozen blocks into the teeming warrens of Brooklyn, giving crisp directions to her driver, she eventually ordered him to pull over and we got out.

Here we stood on a corner, staring up at a grimy windowed, tired-looking building of some six stories, every inch of which looked its century of age. We crossed the street and came up on the near corner, close to a red brick tenement building. An old woman sat on the stoop eating an apple while she addressed another woman leaning on a pillow over a windowsill.

"She could be Ma," Claire said in an emotionless voice. "Look. Up there," she said, pointing to a window. "That's the one, right there."

"That was your room?"

"Uh uh, that was the front room. Come on." She guided me to the alley that ran beside the building, separating it from its neighbor. "*That's* my room, up there. Hasn't changed a bit. Some things never do, I guess."

The solitary window at the rear was small and begrimed with soot; I wondered what light could come through those forlorn-looking panes to light the life of a five-year-old child who slept there with her sister.

"See the fire escape?" she asked. "That's where I used to keep my flowers and plants. In the summer I used to sleep out there. Or up on the roof. Some nights you could hardly find a spot to put your bedding: it was so hot the whole building would empty out. Like people sleeping in air-raid shelters."

I saw the woman on the steps giving us the eye and taking in every word. As she munched on her apple she inspected the core after every bite.

Claire stepped back to the curb, gave the doleful sight a long look, then turned on her heel and stalked off. As we passed her, the woman on the steps said to her companion at the window, "Why would she wanta come back here?"

"Just taking a walk down Memory Lane, Mrs. Beller," said Claire over her shoulder. Her car appeared and as we got in the woman pitched her apple core after us.

I knew she'd lured me to Brooklyn to demonstrate in a visual and hence dramatic manner the deprived background she'd come from and how hard she'd had to struggle to climb the ladder. To show up almost sixty years later in a mink coat and diamonds outside the door of her old tenement house was the sort of theatrical gesture she doted on.

When we were on our way again, her mood brightened. "Well, darling, now that you've looked over the family manse, you certainly ought to have a better idea of where I'm coming from. Of course, I've changed three hundred and eighty degrees since that little girl used to sit on that fire escape watering her geraniums, but there's a lot of me that's still her. You get what I mean, don't you? No matter how hard I may have tried to get rid of Bensonhurst, it's still there, it's inside, deep, deep. Now, here's what I want you to do, Charles. Take these—" She handed me a plastic cosmetics bag inside which I glimpsed half a dozen cassette tapes. "I've been talking into my machine," she went on. "I just let it come, sort of stream of consciousness, with no order at all. You know, what did I really think of so and so, that kind of thing. There's lots of stuff there about Perry, bless him, the poor lost darling—and there's good stuff about Frank —another lost darling—and I talk some about Yves, that creep, just to give you some of the real lowdown. And for sure there's Sam, dear Sammy, who gave me my start, and Vi. There's one smart cookie, Vi; I don't understand why at her age the brain hasn't warped, but she just seems to go on, doesn't she? It's us Jews, we age like old oaks."

I got out, clutching the bag of tapes, and she put her cheek up, demanding a peck. We arranged to meet again next week, and I drew a healthy breath as I went up.

The tapes, for which I held high hopes, were a total washout. It was nothing but a lot more bullshit. The first cassette dealt with her feelings of rejection after Frank Adonis had left her—"dumped me" was her phrase—and her sister, Bella, had taken her to recuperate in Florida, where they stayed with relatives in Clearwater. This was followed by a sentimental anecdote dealing with a bunch of cute Boy Scouts she'd chanced across on the train that had first taken her west, and I recalled her having divested herself of this item in her first book. Then there was the same old tripe about how Viola had found her and brought her to her brother, Sam, who'd made her a star, presumably overnight. Ho hum! The next tape dealt with her love affair with Perry Antrim, and it sounded like something out of *Ladies' Home Journal*. Then how Perry had swept her off her feet, how she'd been at loggerheads with the Antrim tribe, how she and Perry had eloped and been married by the captain of a sailing vessel. Yawn. And there were the little dinner parties she and Perry used to give (I remembered how Dore used to laugh at her setting out place cards for only four guests and calling the napkins "serviettes"). And on and on about Perry, how tender and loving he was on their first night, that he rocked her to sleep in his arms without exercising a bridegroom's privileges. And then the many vicissitudes of the doomed production of *Three Women*, to which her fourth mate, the eminent playwright Natchez Calhoun, had given of his heart's blood. Zzzzzz . . .

After a while her voice became as monotonous as a dial tone. I could tell she was half-crocked and pumping out the treacle as if she'd cut her veins; talking about her favorite recipe for grouse, which Carole (Lombard, one supposed) had given her, and saying that Skylar McCord, hubby number two, loved having her cook *Sauerbraten mit Spaetzle;* what a nifty sportsman Sky was, how he could bring down a whole bag of doves at a shot, racketing on about how she used to rub Absorbine Jr. on his polo injuries and sing him to sleep with "By a Waterfall." Yoo hoo-hoo-hoo. Then back to the "boy genius," Quentin "Natchez" Calhoun, that son of the Old South, how she had labored to make a happy home for him while he ground out one masterpiece after another, until everything had "futzed."

The longer I listened, the madder I got, until I called Vi up and laid it on her. Unless Claire was really going to loosen up and get over her case of the cutes, the whole deal was off. I was sick to death of being jerked around by her bullshit, was tired of playing court jester, was too old to be a typist or even a stenographer, and besides, I had too many other fish to fry, not the least of which was my play. And furthermore, I couldn't possibly dump this stuff on my publisher and convince him we were going to make any kind of decent book out of it.

"Yes, dear, of course, you're perfectly right. Let Auntie Vi have another little talk with her. . . ."

I left Vi prepped to leap into the breach, and later on I got a message on my machine saying Claire wanted to see me on the morrow's eve, after rehearsals would be convenient. As I made the pilgrimage across the park, I did some heavy thinking, but nothing had really changed, and I could only reach the old conclusion: it was my responsibility to keep her satisfactorily muzzled, and to see that Maude was given no reason to spin in her grave. Truth I wanted, yes, but not at the price of blackening Maude's or Belinda's name. I'd stab Claire first.

The same immaculate black woman who'd admitted me the last time did so again, taking the trouble to introduce herself. "I'm Ivarene; I expect we'll be seeing a lot of you." Claire came in, wearing fall-down clothes: black jeans and shirt, cordovan boots, a billed cap, no makeup, no jewelry; her high-tech look. As always under such conditions, her individual features appeared overscaled, exaggerated into the newspaper caricature we knew so well. It's a wonder Gutzon Borglum didn't place her among the great Mount Rushmore heads; it was always that kind of face to me. Tonight, I quickly realized, she wasn't playing star with the capital "S," she was the Little Match Girl.

I followed her into the den, which I hadn't seen that first day with Belinda and which she was eager to show off. It turned out to be the trophy room as well and, Jesus, did she have the trophies! Every award including Oscar was there, and an oversized golden banana made of satin sat in a corner. There was a shelf of Paddington bears as well, chairs upholstered in fake leopard or maybe ocelot, a neon sculpture, bad Victorian bric-à-brac, worse 1910 department-store pieces in golden oak, a not-old patchwork quilt on one wall, and on another a corny collection of reproduction soda-fountain mirrors with menus printed on them.

There were other notable items as well: an assortment of framed letters from famous folk through the decades, Noel Coward, Amelia Earhart, Lindbergh, Admiral Byrd, Lowell Thomas, J.F.K., Arturo Toscanini. Then she was leading me by the hand along the bedroom passageway, on whose walls was hung an awesome display of celebrity glossies, each one autographed to her.

"I call it my Memory Lane wall," she explained as we moved along.

Next she showed me the living room, about the size of Grand Central Station, where on the piano she displayed her "special gallery." In silver frames there were portraits of more famous folk, Alphonso of Spain, the Duke and Duchess of Windsor, Mr. and Mrs. Roosevelt, even a small portrait in oils on an easel of Claire herself, which she said had been "essayed" by darling Noel when she'd visited him in Jamaica.

It was all very fascinating but not really fodder for our work, and I was anxious to get down to the job. When I asked where we would talk, she led me back along the same passageway to the library, with a fireplace and a suite of worn velvet chairs, deep and comfortable, upholstered in a rich plum color. "I bought these out of the MGM auction," she explained. "They were made for my penthouse in *The Ladies' Hour*. Comfy, aren't they?"

I concurred, taking the nearest chair and setting out my equipment and a fresh cassette.

"Vi says you weren't pleased with the tapes," she began, assuming an attractive pose and arranging her hair in a nearby mirror. "I spill my guts out for him and he doesn't like it. He thinks it's too tame, too namsy-pamsy, too airy-fairy." She laughed as if to herself. I wasn't in on the gag.

"What's the joke?" I inquired.

She shook her head wonderingly. "You don't get it, do you? You just don't get it. People simply don't understand what it's like to be a famous person. Did you know? Adela Rogers St. Johns called me the most famous movie icon of my generation."

"Didn't she like Garbo?"

Claire bolted upright and drilled me with a tigerish look. "Garbo's different. And she hasn't worked in forty years, she's famous in another way. But when you come right down to it, I have the same trouble opening up as Greta does. Can you imagine ever being tired of who you are? That's the way I think it is with Greta, that's the way it is with me sometimes."

I nodded, thinking how for those forty years that Garbo had been a recluse, Claire had been currying favor with the public, offering herself up as a burnt offering in the incensed rites of fame and fortune.

She lit a cigarette and blew out a cloud of smoke, like Mount Saint Helens. Then she swirled the cubes in her glass, drained it, and went to the bar to fix herself another. When she returned, she picked away an imaginary fleck of tobacco from her lower lip. Raising her chin to just the right angle to take up the slack under the jaw, she contemplated the ceiling, as if thereupon she could see the scene she was about to paint for me. I clicked on my cassette recorder.

"So, you really want it, hm?" she demanded, her eyebrows arching. "The *facts*, as you call them? All the garbage? Okay, buster, you asked for it, you got it. You just check your little tape recorder there and sit back, because Momma's going to give it to you straight, without the chaser. Straight as a die. Where'll we start? Not at the beginning, that's too boring; I showed you the beautiful slum I lived in as a girl. Now let's pick it up somewhere after Frank gave me the brush-off. You heard the part about my sister and me moving to Florida 'for my health' after Frankie dumped me. Well, he did dump me, that much is true, but the rest isn't, it's all a crock. There wasn't anything wrong with my health, I just needed to turn a buck. Plenty of bucks. The old lady was in the hospital with a goiter, so Bella and I got our asses on the Miami Express. We didn't take berths, just seats in the chair car. Then, on the trip, we'd work the club car."

"Work?"

"You're getting the picture, baby. Bella and I were the make-out sisters, and, let me tell you, we made out. There'd be some butter-and-egg man with his cigar and stock-market report and we'd come in and he'd start eying us. I'd show him a little leg, he'd ask to buy us a drink, we'd get chummy, you know the bit. And believe me, little Cora Sue and her big sister did all right."

"You mean you were hooking on the train?"

She barked a laugh. "Hooking, but with style. Strictly a class operation, no duds or hicks, only guys with a jingle in their jeans. Most of those guys were rolling in dough; they were happy to meet a couple of girls with a well-turned leg and fun ideas."

"What did you do when you got to Miami?"

"Sometimes, if we hadn't done too well on the run, we'd head right back for New York and then make another trip down on the next train. Or if we'd done okay, we'd meet our gents at whatever hotel they were staying at. A couple of times we got invited over to Cuba. Havana was a wild town in those days, and we'd have a ball. There'd be hotcha parties, all the champagne you could drink, the ponies would be running at the track, and we could go to the casinos any time."

"Did you win a lot?"

"Won some, lost some, you know how it goes. Sam was one who took me to Havana. Sammy was a high roller."

"Sam who?" I asked innocently.

"Sam Ueberroth, who the hell else?" She saw the look of disbelief on my face. "I know everybody thinks we met in Hollywood, Vi included, but it really wasn't that way at all. We met on the Bluebird, in the club car, just like I met all the other guys. He was going to Florida for his health —I guess they were all going there for their health. Sam was all alone and we got together. He says to me, I'm a producer, movies, Hollywood, and I think to myself, Sure, Mr. Bigshot, go wax your mustache. But when he really lays it on, I start to think, Hey, baby, you got a live wire here. By the time we get down to Miami, Sam's telling me he wants to put me in the talkies. So I sort of moved in with him, then he takes me over to Havana on this yacht some friends have, he buys me a couple of trinkets and this really elegant dress, stockings, like that, then when he's on his way home he says I should look him up when I get back to New York.

"Hell, I wasn't about to let this big fish off my hook, so I tell him I'm coming back to town with him. Off we go, back to New York. No sooner there than Sam slips his leash and the next thing I know he's scrammay-vooed back to the Coast. I had to stick around town because of Ma, but Sam had given me about two hundred bucks, gratis, and he says he's serious about putting me in the movies. You could have bowled me over with a feather."

"So off you went? Just like that?"

"Pretty much. I caught the train out of New York and I'm in the day coach. I'm thinking, if I could just turn a couple of tricks on the way, why not try it? I mean, a train's a train. Only this trip I'm not making out at all. I'd had this lousy cold, and I lost some weight, so maybe I wasn't looking my best. You remember my telling you about the Boy Scouts on the train to the Coast?" She laughed. "Well, I made all that up. What it was, they were boys all right, and they were in uniform, too, but they weren't Boy Scouts, they were U.S. marines—five of them. They were in the day coach, too, and after a while we got real friendly. We didn't have any private compartment to fool around in, but we had the last three seats in the car and we had some blankets. The boys fixed up this sort of tent thing. You'd have never known what was going on under there unless you really looked, and, well, you can figure out that scene, I guess."

"Could you be a little more graphic, just for the record?"

Claire got as graphic as only she could be graphic. It made a vivid picture, and it all went down on the cassette. She took another drink, paused to grind out her cigarette and light another. "What'll we talk about now?"

"Tell me something about Sam and Viola," I suggested.

"Oh, Sam, Sam was such a putz in those days. But he was kind of sweet, too. You know what a hound he always was for the girls. He was just sitting waiting for little Miss Claire to pull into the station and get off the train. He sent Osky Hamburg down to meet me; there was bug-eyed Osky with his jug ears and this big bouquet of wilted flowers. He drove me to my hotel and got me all set up, and that afternoon he took me to the studio. Sam was leaning out the window with this big cigar in his mouth and this leer on his face. He chucked Osky out, then he swept me up and dumped me on the couch and started unbuttoning his fly. That old leather couch must have been a hundred years old, and he really got down to business. Kept telling me how he was going to put me in his next picture and make a big star out of me.

"Of course, he didn't mean a goddamn word of it. He'd just given me the fare out so he could keep me around to screw. What a rat. But it was through Sam that I met his sister. Vi was the charm, believe me."

I knew that Claire's career had got a boost from Viola Ueberroth, who'd also found Fedora on that trolley car out to the beach, but I was never aware of just how much she'd had to do with Claire's rise in films. Apparently Vi saw something in this raw, untrained creature that she believed could be made into a valuable property. She persuaded Sam to stick her in a picture, after which she carefully observed how Claire attracted some audience interest. Her second part was that of the waitress in *Olaf Ruen*, whence came her new name.

"Whose idea was that anyway, the name?" I asked.

Claire laughed. "Mine, baby, nobody else's. I give credit where credit is due, but believe me, that change was all my own idea. By that time I had a little apartment over on Hyperion, close to the studio. In those days the whole place was practically all orange groves and turnip fields. You could see clear to the mountains, and hardly a house in between. Sam got me the apartment; he liked having me close by so he could stop in. He also gave me a private dressing room on the lot, where he'd visit me whenever he got the urge."

"Did Vi know what was going on?"

"Hah! That's a hot one. Vi always knew everything that was going on. And she had the inside track with Frankie, so that helped. Vi might be my agent right then, but I knew that one day Frankie and I were going to be a team again.

"Anyway, because of Pauline—Sam's wife, what a pill *she* was, a real pain in the ass—he used to talk about dumping her and marrying me, but I knew he was just bullshitting me. I thought, 'Sam, never crap a crapper,' you know? Anyway, we always kept things quiet because he was married and all, and if it had got out it would have been bad for both of us. Pretty soon I was doing four or five pictures a year and climbing up. Then I met Crispin Antrim. We've—um—pretty well covered that episode, haven't we? Let's press on."

I asked her how things stood with Frank when she got there.

"Things stood zilch with Frank. Frankie didn't know little Cora Sue was alive."

"Did you try to get in touch with him?"

"Yeah, sort of. What a laugh, I thought I'd show myself and he'd come running, I'd snatch him right out from under that plump pigeon of his; but no dice. One day I ran into them at the track and he doesn't even introduce me to her. Frankie never gave me the time of day till Sam took me over to Metro; then he'd put the Babe on ice and was hot to trot again. Trouble was, he starts in with Frances, too. Now, *she* was a big hole in the road; I mean, she had blood in her veins like the bluing Ma used for the Monday wash. But she never knew what was going on with Frank and me when he'd come by my place at five for a nice ladies' hour before going home to the ball and chain. Frankie's problem was, the ball and chain were twenty-four-carat gold and he was always a sucker for the bucks and the bluebook."

"How did you feel about starting up with him again?"

"Hell—for Frankie I'd have laid my back on a bed of nails like a swami. And as for Frances, I figured if he wants that icicle in his bed, okay by me, let him."

"You really loved Frank, did you?"

"*Ohhh,* Frank. He was my *guy*! I don't care about all those lousy broads he had, he was *my* guy. Ohh, what a man. There was nobody like him. He was sure there the day they were giving it away—he got it *all*. Looks, brains, he had the best case of street smarts I ever saw. Nobody wore the duds like he did—he looked divine in white tie and tails, the swanky way they used to get got-up. Did you ever notice his eyelashes? They were the longest, thickest, curliest—all the girls envied them. I'd of married him in a second if he'd ever asked me. He never did, though. But that didn't keep me from loving him. Our affair went on for a long time —nobody knew, but we stayed hot for thirty years. He'd stop by my house late, around eleven or so, and he'd start pulling my clothes off and we'd get down to business right there on the living-room rug—God, he was hot.

"You know what was the giveaway with Frank? His eyes. Oh, those eyes! They were deadly. One look and you were a goner. They could be so maddeningly sexy—'bedroom eyes,' they used to call them back then —and they could get so little-boy, so really innocent and honest, as if they'd never seen a rotten trick in their life.

"They'll never be able to tell Frankie's story, not the whole story, the *real* story. I know plenty, but even after all those years I don't know it all. No one does, really. It makes me laugh, how he peeled off the streets right here in New York and went out there to Hollywood and made them set up and beg. Had them eating out of his palm, the whole goddamn bunch.

"Sure, he was connected, everyone knew that, he was tied into the mob, here in New York, out there, too, especially the Vegas bunch. He and Ears Satriano were chummy. And Bugsy—he and Bugsy were just like this, the two of 'em. They'd grown up together. In those days Bugs wasn't such a slicker. Big ears, big nose, a real thug. He worshipped Frankie, he'd have done anything for him." She chuckled to herself, drank, puffed, blew smoke, tossed her hair. Certain of my attention, she went on:

"You want to hear something funny? Something *really* weird? It'll show you on what little hooks our lives hang, you know? You've heard about the night they sprayed Bugsy Siegel, at his house on Angelo Drive? Well, you know that Frank had stopped by. He was sitting right on that sofa where Bugsy got hit. But Frank had this rendezvous and so he split, and less than ten minutes later they blew Bugsy away. Rat-a-tat-tat on the glazed chintz. You saw the pictures, it was like the Chicago stockyards, blood all over the place." She leaned toward me. "But listen to this, baby. Frank had left a little early 'cause he needed to make an important stop. Know where? Schwab's Drugstore. Know why? For a pack of French ticklers. He had a date, he wanted to be up for a big night. Know who the date was? You're looking at her, buster, you're looking at her.

"There we were in my bed, Frankie was catching his second wind or maybe his third. The radio was on. A bulletin came over. Christ, did he pull out and fly out of my place. Jumped into his pants and he was gone in six seconds. I mean—*he was gone!* He borrowed Howard Hughes's private plane and flew up to Frisco, then hotfooted it straight for Waikiki Beach. The manager of the Royal Hawaiian was a friend of his, he back-dated the registration card so Frank had an alibi—perfect. Then he called me and told me to get to Honolulu quick. I was there in fifteen hours; I got on the *China Clipper* and took the heat off him. Nobody believed that big-mouth maid who told the cops she'd let him into my house that evening. I really fired her ass. Frank was solid alibi'd, they couldn't touch him."

She emptied her glass, wiped the bottom on her napkin, and set it aside. "Louis B. gave us these glasses for a wedding present, Sky and me." She looked up suddenly. "Damn it, I almost forgot!" she exclaimed. "It's time for din-din. Hope you like it."

Presently she returned, wearing a frilly apron with a poodle stenciled on the pocket, and ushered me into the formal dining room, where we sat across from each other at the table, in whose center rested a ceramic head from which protruded at varying angles a dozen plastic anemones. The meal had already been set out in plastic serving dishes and Claire urged me to help myself. "I hope you're hungry. I like my men to eat. Pretend you're Jewish and I'll be your *yiddische mama.* "

Any self-respecting *yiddische mama* would have blanched to see our plates: a small casserole, a seafood dish with bread crumbs and sliced hardboiled eggs paprika'd on top. I complimented her on it, and she beamed, saying it was just an old "o-grotten" thing she'd been doing for years. Salad with cottage cheese and pineapple topped with a green mara-schino cherry, and gluten bread eked out the sumptuous menu.

As we ate, and since I didn't want to waste a minute, I led her on to other topics and she talked willingly, eagerly, toasting me with the vodka-rocks she'd brought along to the table. The liquor was having its usual effect on her. Sometimes she slurred her words, her eyes glittered. She ate with care, remembering the table manners she'd so assiduously taught herself. By now she was into her Lady of the Manor, and I mar-veled at her little touches: how she used her "serviette" and cutlery with studied elegance.

While we ate, she painted pictures for me, her brush again favoring scenes from her youth. She relished talking about her Brooklyn childhood and what life had been like in Bensonhurst.

"Saturday, after *shul,* we'd always gather in the front room—front room, hah, it was practically the *only* goddamn room we had, I slept in a closet in the back—and the rabbi would start reading from the Torah. Everybody'd be squashed in like sardines, Ma, Pa, me, Ira, Bella, the aunts and the uncles, ten or fifteen in that tiny room, and everybody'd be praying together. And that goddamn rabbi—we called him Uncle Casimir, only he was a cousin—what a creep. He was the original dirty old man. He always insisted that Ma sit me next to him and all through the boiled beef he'd have his hand stuck up my dress."

"The rabbi?" I asked in some surprise.

"You better believe it. I really had to laugh, you know—Pa was so religious, during Rosh Hashanah he'd always have someone come in and turn off the lights or start the bathwater. And there's Uncle Casimir copping a feel while he passed the potatoes. But I fixed him good."

"What did you do?"

"One day I was passing around the cabbage soup; it was hot off the stove, and I just dumped the whole bowl right in his lap. You never saw anything like it, the way he jumped out of that chair.

" 'You done dat on poipose!' he screams at me. 'Oh no, Uncle Casimir, it slipped,' I say in my most innocent voice. You'd of thought he'd finally learned his lesson with his scalded crotch, but no, he kept on snatching and grabbing at me every chance he got."

"Did you ever tell your father what was going on?"

She heaved a sigh. "What use? He'd have said I was only making it up. He said I made everything up." She giggled. "He didn't know how right he was. I made up my whole life, I kid you not." She placed her knife and fork beside her plate rim and used her "serviette" to good purpose.

"What became of Uncle Casimir?"

"He went to matzoh ball heaven, and I'll bet he's still copping feels off little girl angels. Perry used to really break up hearing me talk about Uncle Casimir. He thought it was funny. I said—'You should live so long!' "

"Let's talk about your marriage to Perry Antrim. Were you happy with him?"

"God, yes, at first it was divine, he was the handsomest man you ever saw—even better-looking than his father. One look and I was a goner. I mean, I flipped, right out of my gourd. I thought, 'Screw you, Frankie Adano with your high-society wife, look what I got now!' I'd caught the brass ring first time out. But time proved me wrong—as it has so many times since."

"Explain that for the tape."

"Listen, our marriage didn't stand a chance in that hospice on the hill. It was like Shepheard's Hotel in Cairo, sooner or later everyone in the world showed up. You try living directly under the eye of your in-laws, eating their food at their table, sleeping on their sheets and pillowcases, having their laundress iron your clothes, driving in their cars, swimming in their pool. We even had their dogs.

"I begged Perry, Let's go out and buy a house of our own, but he wouldn't hear of it. He said that when he went off on one of his adventures he wanted to know that I was protected and looked after. So he kept me plunked down right there at Sunnyside, and off he'd skip, looking for tsetse flies or lost missionaries or whatever, and there I'd be, having dinner with the Mountbattens or some potentate. Ye gods, how I hated it.

"Sure, I know I made a big stink, saying he wanted his freedom to go out and conquer the world, swim the deepest ocean, climb the highest mountain, all that crap, but we'd no sooner divorced than I turned around to find out he'd married our little Miss Carroll, and I thought that was really dirty pool. And god damn if the *next* thing I read in Hopper isn't that he's gone into the jungle looking for some goddamn doctor and he ends up missionary pie.

"First I lost Perry, then Frankie. Of course, Frankie was my great love, you know that. And . . . Charles"—here she changed gears, her voice dropped, became ultra-grave—"I know you'll understand this. *That's* why I got so terribly upset at Frank's funeral. You remember what happened. I'm so sorry it turned into such a spectacle, a farce, really, wasn't it? Come on, you can be honest with me, it really was a farce. But I didn't know what I was doing, I was *so-o* upset. Honestly, Charlie, I wasn't even going to attend—really, I thought it would really be *de trop*. I had to knock back a couple of tall ones, just to get up the nerve to go. Then we were slowed up by the rain, and when I saw that sea of umbrellas, I just plowed on through. I wanted to get to the casket, but the goddamn idiots wouldn't move, the slobs, so I just shoved them out of the way, those Hollywood phonies who didn't even give a rat's ass about him when he was alive, and now he was dead and they all wanted to weep over him and—oh, I don't know, it all just got to me. And then I saw Belinda. There she was, plunked right down in front for the world to see, all done up in black with this darling hat and a veil—I mean, she looked like Jackie Kennedy or something. And then they said I was trying to steal the limelight, but that's a goddamn lie. I mean, if anyone knows how to behave at a funeral, this little gal does."

"It must have been quite a blow, losing Frank," I ventured sympathetically.

"You can say that again." She stubbed out another cigarette, then got up, stretched, and opened the terrace door. I could see her standing at the parapet, gazing out over the city. When I joined her, without looking she handed me her glass for a refill. As I carried it to her, I glanced at the tape recorder that had been taking everything down. Should I bring it outside or give it a rest? Deciding on the latter, I rejoined her on the terrace, where she was stretched out on a chaise. Her red nails glinted as she took the glass and pointed for me to sit at her foot—that famous foot at which so many other men had sat. "Thanks," she said and put her lips to the rim of the glass, tilted her head, and drank. "That's what I thought," she said moodily, though I'd lost the thread of the talk. "Perry being a grand guy, I mean."

"You were happy with him? Or not?"

"Depends on how you look at things. I guess we were, all things considered. For a while, anyway." She chuckled, then spun round, eyes sparkling. "Well, biographer mine, are you enjoying these confessions of a movie queen? *Ex*–movie queen, I should say."

She held out her empty glass again, but I seized that as my cue to *partir*.

"Golly, it's late," I puffed, looking at my watch with consternation. "Sorry, but tomorrow's a working day."

She stood and faced me. "All right, scribe of mine, I guess that'll hold you for tonight. Tune in tomorrow night for another chapter in the continuing saga of Claire Regrett, girl-wonder. God, haven't I banged on, though?" She gave my cheek an affectionate pat. I went inside, slipped my recorder and my notes into my briefcase, and started out. Catching up, she put her arm through mine and we traversed the passageway while her little dog trotted in our footsteps, its nails clicking on the parquet squares. Before opening the front door and allowing me to escape, Claire lifted her brows to ask, "What time shall we expect you tomorrow? I'm really going to cook up a storm, my special stuffed pork chops. Sound yummy?"

I had intended to effect an orderly exit from Fortress Claire. Though this was only my first "interview," I'd known it would be tough sledding. One night, okay—two nights in a row, no. I had my excuse prepared. "I'm afraid I can't meet tomorrow. Sorry."

"Whaddya mean, you can't meet? Not at all?" came the granite voice.

I explained I had a complex series of meetings, morning, lunch, and afternoon.

"What about tomorrow night? I thought at least the nights would be mine. We've only just begun."

I had a dinner engagement with an "old friend," a fact I frankly would have preferred to conceal, but she was ahead of me there. "Don't tell me, you're having dinner with Madame Nhu. *Old* is right."

I confessed that this was true, like it or lump it.

"Damn it, I should think that a serious author would regard his work as all-important. Maybe you could come by afterward? It's Friday. At Belinda's age you don't want to keep her up too late; all her nuts will loosen and the bolts will fall out and then her ass will drop off. By the way, I heard that Her Nibs has had her face done again."

"A little nip and tuck, nothing major."

Her brassy laugh rang out. "Come on, Charlie, get real. She's had the whole road resurfaced like the Alcan Highway."

With a bad show of grace she yanked open the door and buzzed for the elevator. "It takes a year sometimes." She scowled as she inspected the mirrors, then removed the handkerchief from my jacket pocket and rubbed off some smudges her ever-keen eye had discerned. It didn't take much to see that she was pissed off.

On the way down in the car I gave my trusty tape recorder a friendly pat. Panasonic gives good Claire . . . nice stuff tonight.

The days went by and I labored like a Trojan. I was probably deceiving myself that I was searching for the key to her character. That key had been tossed away long ago. When I asked one day if she'd ever been psychoanalyzed, she blew up at me and did twenty minutes on what she thought of the profession of psychiatry, all that Freudian bunk. She didn't need to be stuck on a couch, she goddamn well knew who she was; what's more, she'd read an article in *Reader's Digest* exposing all that nutty dream stuff. The problems weren't in people's dreams but in their diets. Low cholesterol and wheat germ would do a lot more for her than remembering how the grocery boy once tried to stick his finger in her panties.

One afternoon I stopped by after a grueling rehearsal; we hadn't been long at work when the telephone rang: for me, she said, and handed me the receiver along with a look. She didn't care what it was, you were with her and she wanted every minute of your time, the whole enchilada, rag, bone, and hank of hair.

"Belinda-baby?" she said meanly when I hung up.

"As a matter of fact, no, it was my dentist, changing an appointment on Friday."

"Don't go!" she commanded, fixing me with her rigid index finger. "Go to Dr. Millsap, he's the absolute best in the city, he even does Garbo."

When I said I was perfectly happy with my own dentist, she got smartie-pants, made another grimace, then leaned forward and blew a huge cloud of smoke in my face; her little joke. "What now, scribe of mine? What shall I talk about as the evening grows later and my brain grows fuzzier?"

I made no suggestion, but let her follow her own meanderings. Pretty soon she fell into a sentimental vein; she was full of the old MGM days, all good stuff, and I didn't have to guide or steer her at all. She growled and gnawed her words, the expletives and four-letter jobs exploded on all sides, and it was all going onto tape "for posterity."

As she talked she went on sipping her vodka. The more she drank, the less discreet she became and the more slangy her talk, the less cultured her accents. I was amused, for one of the things I'd always enjoyed noticing about her was the eternal struggle against her background. Yet struggle to hide it though she might, like murder it would out, willy-nilly. "Y'know what Frank used to say?" she asked rhetorically. "You must have heard him. 'Don't let the bastards get you.' Good advice, if you ask me. They're bastards all right, they'll chop you off at the knees if they feel like it. They're all great white sharks out there; the big fish eat up the little ones; then the little ones get big and grow teeth and they eat up the next batch. You don't meet any nice ones, ones you want to remember. I've been in the business for fifty years and I tell you for a fact, I don't know how a movie ever gets made, some of the assholes they've got working on them. The minute you drive through the gate somebody's trying to jerk you around, swear to Christ."

She blatted on about Hollywood and how much she hated it until she subsided, more from weariness than contempt for the place. I saw what it was: Hollywood didn't want her anymore. She was stuck up here in her ivory tower and the movies just didn't give a rat's ass. Louis B. was dead and she knew a boy who used to empty the wastebaskets at MCA and now that pimply office boy was a hotshot producer with an Oscar to his credit. He didn't want her, they didn't want her, no one wanted her. And while I was forced to agree that much of what she said held truth, it was simply the way the Hollywood cookie crumbled. *Sic transit gloria Claire.*

I even thought I knew what was coming next; I was right: "If Frank were alive he'd show them, see if he wouldn't. He'd find me a part, he'd have me up there, he'd . . . Or, shit, maybe he wouldn't," she broke off philosophically, and you had to respect her for that.

"You've never stinted at praising him, have you?" I said.

She gave me an indignant look. "What the hell do you think I am, anyway? I believe in giving credit where credit's due. I owe Frank Adonis a lot. If he hadn't taken me to Metro, God knows how I'd have ended up at AyanBee. That joint folded so quickly. And if, after I left MGM, Frank hadn't got Sam Ueberroth to give me *Wages of Sin,* would I ever have won my Oscar? Answer: no, Claire dear, you would not have won your Oscar. You would be singing 'Abide with Me' with the goddamn Salvation Army."

"While we're on the subject," I prompted, moving the recorder closer and leaning to check the amount of tape in the cassette, "what about your getting that Oscar? Just what help was Frank in that matter?"

Instantly she became furious. "Look, *buster,* let's just can the crap, okay? Let's just can it for all time, huh? If you or any other bozos think Frankie or anybody else snapped his fingers to get me my Oscar, that's pure crap. Nobody ever got Osky for me except me! *I* got it, it was all mine, I won it fair and square, I don't care what anybody says." Obviously I had pushed a button and I decided to let her get it all out. "True, I wasn't going to finish the picture; I was sick and I just couldn't face going to the goddamn studio. If you remember, I was married to Skylar at the time and Skylar—he—he—made me terribly nervous, he used to belt me around sometimes, I wasn't sleeping and I'd lost a lot of weight, but—*I won that fucking Oscar for myself! Wages of Sin* is the best damned performance I ever gave; it was my apogee, they said in *Time* magazine, and I'm proud of every second I'm on that screen. *That's* the *real* Claire Regrett. That's what I wanted to be. An actress! A goddamn good one, too! And if they didn't think so, well, they wouldn't have voted for me, would they? So why the hell do people still say I didn't really win it, or that it should have gone to Belinda that year? Or that Sam bribed his way to win? Bullcrap, my fine man, pure bullcrap!"

She sat back with crossed arms, stubbed out her butt, and tossed me her lighter to perform service. I shied and put my hands behind me.

"No help from me," I said. We'd already been round the subject of her incessant smoking.

"Well, screw you, buster. You're not my guardian, you know. You're only my biographer. Ask me something. Anything. I'll give it to you straight arrow." She lit her own cigarette and squinted at me through the smoke. "What're you thinking, anyway? That I'm a bitch in heels? You always get that look on your puss. Like you're sniffing something out, like you're analyzing me, like you're going to take a scalpel to my hide. I gotta tough hide, baby, you better believe it. I'm a fuckin' Sherman tank!"

"Nice to meet you, Miss Sherman. Suppose you tell me one or two things about number three on your marital Hit Parade."

"Number—? Let's see. . . ." She counted on her fingers. "Perry, one; Skylar, two—why, you must mean Yves. Yves wasn't a husband, he was an aberration, the reason girls leave home. I used to call him my dwarf; I wanted him to have a hump, and a wart right here. Ugh." She touched the end of her nose and I conjured up that round, plump, blue-bearded visage of Yves de Gobelins, the phony count, would-be international financier, and general all-purpose prick. Claire groaned aloud.

"Frankly, I'll never know what I thought I saw in that gnome. I was crazy to marry him, but he was the biggest con-artist in the world. Any woman married to that one was better off dead." She eyed me through a thick cloud of cigarette smoke, then waved it away as if to see me better.

"We had a row over you after that time you lunged at him on the set. He didn't like you one bit. But don't take it personally, he was a *very* odd type, Yves. And short people can get awfully mean."

"How much did he lose you on that perfume deal?"

"Oh-h God, thousands. *Millions.* I never knew what hit me when the auditors started coming out of the woodwork. He'd skimmed off the whole company. Left me with a ton of debts. I broke my ass paying them off."

"How would you say Yves stacked up against the others? Frank, for instance?"

"Frank?" She widened her eyes and craned her head back in mock surprise. "Are you out of your gourd? Listen, baby, there's one constant in this life, and that's that there was never *anybody* better than Frankie when it came to the ladies' hour. Absolutely no one, no one ever came close, I'll go on record on that. But Yves ran him a close second. In the sack he was something else, I kid you not.

"But *he* was the one who wanted to marry *me*. He kept chasing me; you remember how it was in all the papers. He wanted to show me off and use my name to get his picture printed. Anyway, besides the sex, he sort of intrigued me. He was interesting in a way lots of American men aren't. He had this sense of mystery about him, like you could never know everything about him, so there wasn't any point of trying. He thrilled me, and I had this feeling of something dangerous around all the time."

"But who said you had to stay married to him? Why didn't you just dump him?"

She laughed that wicked, snarly laugh of hers. "Believe me, I tried to! But when I told him I was fed up with him and wanted a divorce, he just stood there and laughed at me. That popeyed little midget laughed at me! Right then I knew I was in real trouble. He started having me followed, he'd make threats, he beat me up really bad, I was scared. And I don't scare easy."

"What sort of threats?"

"He said he'd pay someone big bucks to throw acid at me and disfigure my face. Then he threatened to have my kneecaps broken with a baseball bat. He even threatened to put me in a box and have me dropped into the Pacific—alive! He got me so scared I couldn't sleep or work or do anything." I watched the flood of emotions that played across her face as she spoke. "He also threatened to blackmail me."

"What did he have to blackmail you over?"

Her mouth twisted down in a scarlet grimace. "That's for me to know and you to find out. Anyway, there was the business of all the money. My hard-earned bucks! He was bleeding me dry. He just wanted more and more of everything, and the more I gave him, the more he demanded. All for Marie-Claire Parfums Incorporated. He didn't know the first goddamn thing about operating a big company like that, so he ran it right into the ground. Any time he needed cash to gamble with, he'd just go to the bank—my bank. He had some weird system of double-entry bookkeeping that nobody but him and this weasely accountant seemed to understand."

"That's how he ended up in prison, right?"

She laughed again and I picked up the deadly irony in its sound. "Not exactly," she said shortly. "He got sent up because that was probably his destiny. Plus which, he had some unlooked-for assistance."

"Mm-hm? And what was that?" I asked carefully.

"Poor Yves, he went to the slammer because that's where he belonged. But he probably never would have done a day's time if—certain steps hadn't been taken to ensure this."

I cocked an ear. "Can you be more explicit?"

She eyed me with suspicion. "Will this go in La Book?"

"How can I tell until you tell me? Come on, Claire, don't beat around the bush, out with it. What are you talking about?"

The tip of her tongue slicked around the curves of her lips. "Well, Ma taught me never to talk ill of the dead because they can't talk back, but Yves is another story. Don't say you heard it here, but it's a fact that he was railroaded into the can. I'm not kidding. There was this certain party you and I used to know who was able to arrange such things. He set up a trap and Yves walked straight into it."

"Are you telling me he was framed?"

"Like the Mona Lisa. Did you ever hear of Frankie's friend, Al 'Vegas' da Prima?" I allowed as how the name was not unfamiliar to me. "Well, Vegas and his pal Ears Satriano arranged the whole thing. They put the finger on Monsieur Yves and he got sent up. Alcatraz, just like Humphrey Bogart. Now, if he'd been a good boy, he might have got out on parole, but he was a naughty boy."

"You're saying he got what he deserved?"

"Look, as far as that little Frog was concerned, I could be in a cement suit by now if it wasn't for Frankie and his pals. It was him or me, you could say."

This was an unexpected revelation, one I doubted I could use, however. This was not the kind of stuff that movie-star autobiographies usually were made of.

"Yves was probably the biggest mistake of my whole life," Claire went on. "Look, I'm not bitter, I'm really not, but I'm damned if I'll go on letting everybody take advantage of my good nature. All those Holly-wood putzes, those crummy bastards who think they can just shove you around and walk all over you. Nuts to the whole bunch! And double-nuts to anyone who thinks any dame who comes along is fair game, just another roundheels pushover. That's what they decided I was, just a pushover—all you had to do was push me down and there'd be a Simmons mattress under me."

Her lip curled and she actually seemed to spit; her teeth were bared like a cat about to pounce.

"Huh," she expostulated, "they say I was a cast-iron bitch, with ice water in my veins. Well, maybe I was—now and then. I had to be. To get anywhere you goddamn well have to be—out there. You have to learn to give as good as you get, and, believe me, I did. They say I had balls —nobody who'd been to bed with me would ever have said that, but what the hell—and a lot of the time I clanged when I walked, I gotta admit. But only because I *had* to. It's a man's world, right? Anyway," she concluded, "if Frank had some unsavory friends, well, who doesn't, if it comes to that? But I wasn't sorry when Bugsy got shot. I think Bugsy would have got Frank into a lot of trouble if he'd stayed alive. And by God—!"

With no warning she jumped up, grabbed my hand and dragged me across the room, flung open the door, and pulled me out onto the terrace to the parapet. We stood there, looking downtown over the park to Central Park South. She planted her feet and raised a fist and shook it at the glittering panorama of lights. "I licked you, you bastards!" she shouted. "I said I'd lick you and I goddamn well did! *Bastards! I licked you!* Now you can all go take a flying fuck at a rolling donut! Bless you, darlings—bless you all, my darlings."

Laughing, crying, throwing kisses, posturing outrageously, she was tight as a tick, partly illuminated by the light from indoors, partly by the bright moonlight overhead.

" 'O Romeo, Romeo! wherefore art thou Romeo? Deny thy father, and refuse thy name; or, if thou wilt not, be but sworn my love, and I'll no longer be a Capulet.' "

Jesus, I thought, she still remembers Juliet's lines; what a bear-trap that brain of hers was. When I remarked on her memory, she gave me that smug look and said, "Of course I remember. I'll never forget. It's the greatest failure of my life that I never was brave enough to get out on a stage and play fucking Juliet. What a little pisser *she* was!" Then she gave me her wistful smile, corrugated her marble forehead, and modestly dropped her head, the way you would to smell the roses, but there weren't any roses to smell. "Shakespeare doesn't come easily to most Americans, I guess." I knew this for a fact, having myself had a go at the Bard and tripped on his iambic pentameter.

"Listen, Charlie, let me tell you something, screw the iambic pentameter, know what I mean? Who needs it? Not me. I'm a star. You understand that word. I may not have been a lot of things, I may have come from shit, but I'm a *star!* Not too many of those around these days. I don't mean these piddling little quacks and creeps today, I mean the old-time, old-style STAR. Five-pointed and it makes a gorgeous light. That's the prettiest and the greatest four-letter word in the English language, get me?"

I decided to play with her. "What about l-o-v-e? It has four letters, it's a pretty word."

"Oh *yeah?* Let me tell you something about l-o-v-e. It's nice, but, believe me, it doesn't hold up. Maybe they should have given it more letters or something, but when you come down to it, s-t-a-r is more important and it lasts longer. They don't put your name up there in lights for being in love. I'll take the star every time."

"Why not love?"

"I couldn't make it work, you know? I was always looking for Mr. Right, only I was always Miss Wrong. Who can figure?"

"Did you think Skylar was Mr. Right?"

"Bet your ass. Or I'd never have married. And I never should have. What a b—" She closed her lips and shook her head as if shutting out the memory, but I wanted her to go on.

"I remember the pictures of the wedding," I prompted to get her started. "In Vi's garden, wasn't it? The rose arbor?"

The look she gave me was clabbered milk. "Pretty Jesus, do we have to talk about that?" She blew out smoke and took a sip of her drink. "I suppose we do. Okay, baby, crank up the Victrola and Momma will play the record. Only I warn you in advance, the record's cracked."

We "repaired" (her word) to the library, her *sanctum sanctorum,* and as she plunked down she tossed a look toward the bar and, taking my cue, I went and poured her a vodka over ice, then joined her. It was half-past twelve, well past my witching hour, but I felt I was on the trail of something here and I really pressed. In seconds I had my recorder ready for more of Madame's deathless words. She handed me the generally accepted rundown on the gent in question, Skylar J. D. McCord III. Of course I already knew the oft-told story of how they'd met at a dinner party at Merle Oberon's house, and how in the space of four hours he'd swept Claire off her feet. Skylar was the scion of a wealthy department-store family in town, and he had a long history of playboy wildness. Due to a polo injury (he'd got his skull cracked by a mallet and wore a steel plate in his head), during the war years he was 4-F and available, and any girl's bait. Besides being a super polo player, he was also a tennis ace of considerable merit, as well as a trophy-winning golfer. He could usually be seen tooling around town in a lowslung convertible with balloon tires, wide sidewalls, white leather upholstery, and a robin's-egg-blue paint job. He combed his hair with a center part the way Scott Fitzgerald used to, and had been the figurative if not the literal death of many a Los Angeles lovely. His pals referred to him as "The Cherry Picker."

He asked Claire to marry him and she said, Sure, why not? Since her wedding to Perry had been an elopement, this time she insisted on doing it up big with a full-blown ceremony and reception. Vi helped her arrange things, even to planning her wedding dress, which was designed by Edith Head herself.

There was lots more cutesy fan-mag stuff, pictures of the two sweethearts peeking through big hearts of paper carnations, cuddling under furs in a box at the Hollywood Bowl, and like that. This was one of Claire's avowed domestic periods; she was always being photographed in ruffles and dirndls and platform wedgies, or in a gingham apron, rolling out a pie crust for the magazines. They talked a lot about how many babies she and Sky were going to have, and she was keeping one of the bedrooms in reserve to make over into a nursery. You never saw candids of her anymore unless Sky was included, flashing that big Hardy Boy grin as he hugged her or sat her on his lap.

When she did a USO stint and visited the troops, there was Sky right at her side. She'd get him up onstage and he'd crack his corny jokes, but the boys ate it up. He did it that night in San Diego, on the deck of the aircraft carrier, when I'd been lucky enough to get a ticket for the show and I danced the Lindy with Claire. After that I went back to sea, and during that time I read that she'd had a miscarriage and she and Sky had separated. Shortly thereafter she put on a big hat and went to court in Santa Monica to get her divorce, and was quoted as saying, "We'll always be friends."

"Yeah, friends," Claire growled. "With friends like him, who needs enemies?" She sprang up and went to the mirror over the bar and began inspecting her face as if to be sure she had remembered to put it on. The pause stretched out, to say the least, as she began stalking about the room like a tigress. I shut off the recorder and waited. She looked over at me as though making up her mind about something, then she strode back to her chair and flung herself into the seat.

"We can talk about something else, if you want," I suggested tactfully, seeing how upset she was.

"What the hell, we may as well get the bastard out of the way. It still makes me sick every time I think of him. I grew to hate him so."

"*Not* friends?" I ventured tactfully.

"You catch on fast, baby. Definitely not friends. I despised him then and I hate him now—no, take it back, take it back—I won't let myself hate anyone. I believe some Divine Power meant him to come into my life at that time, though I'm damned if I know why. Anyway—" She drew a deep breath and held it for a couple of beats, then expelled it and recrossed her legs. "Today I guess it probably doesn't seem like much, considering all the medicine and drugs they have to cure things, but at the time, back in the forties, it was a big deal. People just didn't get things like that, not public figures like me, not movie stars anyway."

"What things?"

She widened her eyes at me, then dropped the bomb. "Things like syphilis."

I stared in astonishment. "Skylar McCord gave you syphilis?"

"You're goddamned right he did! Here was dear old Claire trying to make like the best little wife in the world, playing Betty Crocker, cooking his dinner, working my butt off to keep him happy and occupied, and he goes out and gets a big dose of boom-chick-a-boom-chick from this Mexican broad he met at the fights—at the *fights*, mind you! And he comes home and passes it on to me."

This was astonishing; I'd never had a hint of this, not from Vi, not from anyone. How had it been kept hushed up all these years?

"What did you do?" I managed.

"What would you have done—what would anybody have done? I went to my doctor; he did the test and it came out positive. It was the only time in my life I ever failed. I was thinking of ways to do myself in. I couldn't bear the shame. I kept seeing the headlines: 'Claire Regrett Dies of the Clap.' Oh, I tell you, it was all so sordid. He almost ruined me. I'm not kidding—after all my work, after I was finally getting someplace, that big collegiate fucker almost finished me off! I kicked him out that night, and next day I had all the locks changed. I wasn't going to have that diseased leper back in my house, not if he had to sleep in the streets."

"What did he say?"

"Said he was sorry, didn't know how it ever happened, he'd been faithful, never played around—maybe he'd caught it off a toilet seat! What a laugh that was. I said, 'Look, schmuck, we're not talking crabs here, we're talking major major.' He tried talking me out of it, said he'd never do it again—can you imagine him doing it *again?* He even gave me an expensive piece of jewelry—it's the only time in my life I sent back a diamond bracelet. I was doing *Wages of Sin* and couldn't leave town; otherwise I'd have got out of there quick. I began to lose weight, the director was worried, the cameraman said he couldn't shoot me, I looked so awful. Finally they shut down and gave me a couple of weeks off. Catch syphilis and they give you ten days in Borrego Springs."

She suppressed a sigh and stared somewhere into space. Her revelation explained a number of things to me—the weird behavior she'd exhibited at the time, refusing to see anyone, going into seclusion, and then turning down the next important role that had come of her winning the Oscar that year. This had been regarded as especially peculiar behavior for her, since getting better parts had been the reason behind her leaving MGM in the first place.

"But I really stuck it to Skylar," she went on. "I sicked Jerry Geisler on him. Jerry'd got Errol Flynn off on his rape charge, and he held Sky up for a million and a half bucks in the settlement. But even after I'd washed him out of my life I still felt dirty, y'know? I had the whole house painted, inside and out, and anything he'd left around I stuck in the trash."

She fell silent. I stared at her, then away, feeling a sudden wave of embarrassment. Secret Memoirs of a Screen Queen: "And then I got the syph." These were the confidences the book would thrive on, and it all ought to go in, but I really felt bad for her. She was right: syphilis in the early forties wasn't syphilis in the eighties. Those were the pre-penicillin days, and the sulfa drugs just didn't do it.

While I reflected on this and turned over the cassette, I heard her sob; then she began to shake all over. The blood drained from her face, her eyes enlarged, and her breath came in spurts. Certain she was hyperventilating, I started for the house intercom to call a doctor.

"No, damn it! No doctor! No doctor!" she hollered, struggling up from the sofa.

"But you're ill!"

"*No doctor!*" she ground out between clenched teeth. "Call ———"
She gave me a number. "Ask for Mrs. Conklin."

I dialed the number and spoke with the practitioner I'd met in the hospital. "It's all right," she said calmly, "just say I'm on my way."

I hung up and tried to make Claire comfortable until the buzzer rang and the doorman said a visitor was on her way up.

Hazel Conklin was one of those sweet, for-real candy-box grandmothers, a kind of Spring Byington type, with a bright, lively air, and you had the feeling she knew more than she let on. Her coat was already off as she greeted me and hurried to Claire's side.

"If we could just get her into the bedroom, where she and I can talk quietly," she suggested. "Can you lift her? No, Claire, don't try to walk," she said, "let him do it."

I bent and picked Claire up, blanket and all, and carried her toward the bedroom while Mrs. Conklin hurried ahead.

"Oh, put me down, damn it," Claire moaned, but her feeble protests were useless. She was weak as a baby.

"She's all yours," I said to Mrs. Conklin and got out of there pronto.

Her attack wasn't severe and she recovered quickly. Mrs. Conklin was much in evidence during those days and I sometimes saw her leaving as I came in. I liked her; she was a nice, square, practical woman and I saw how much Claire depended on her. Fortunately she lived in the neighborhood and was never far away. I felt the better for having her around. There were others available as well, should they be needed—downstairs the Japanese medico Dr. Sadikichi (whom she wouldn't let near her with a stethoscope) and his wife, and upstairs an elderly couple whose company Claire occasionally enjoyed, the Steins, who were quiet as two mice and disinclined to meddle.

But for me, a newcomer, so to speak, it was never easy. You didn't just come and go with Claire, you were "there," bound with hoops of steel. If you wanted her loyalty, you had to prove your own, and I had trouble proving a loyalty I didn't necessarily feel. She was the bottomless well, the great gaping pit of "I want, I need, I wish, I am." Gimme, gimme, she always seemed to be saying, fill me up, complete me. I am a holy vessel, meet my requirements and my lips shall smile on you. You will be my chosen one, my darling, and I will bless your name in the years to come, the words writ large upon pages of amethyst stationery engraved with curly initials. Two alabaster arms reaching out, entwining, clutching, grappling, the Spider Woman in Manhattan.

I really wish I could say I liked her more, but the honest fact was that I didn't. No matter how I tried to add it all up in her favor, it never came out that way, I couldn't *make* it come out that way. Einstein himself couldn't have pulled that one off.

I got a breather from Miss Clutch when rehearsals ended and the time came for *Peking Duck* to wend its way to Boston. We spent a month at the Colonial Theatre, playing to packed houses after surprisingly good notices, then brought it in for our Fourth of July opening on Broadway.

Suddenly there it was, curtain up, characters onstage, Belinda acting as if she'd sprung full-blown from Jove's brow. She captured New York, her name in lights made a spectacular gleam on the Great White Way, and, to make a long story short, we were a hit.

I'd invited Claire to the opening, only to have her decline; it didn't surprise me much, sure as I was that seeing Belinda triumph in my "little play," as Claire liked referring to it, was too much for her to bear. She pleaded sick, a *"soupçon* of flu" was the diagnosis, and I sent Belinda flowers with a card from Claire, it never occurring to me that, of course, she would want to thank Claire for them. She did, and to my amazement I heard Claire say, "I'm so glad you liked them. Bless you, darling, *mizpaw.* "

And here began a new, happier chapter in my life. Success never hurts, unless you let it. I wasn't letting it. My joy at having a hit show was overmatched by my knowing I'd pulled it off for Belinda, who shone in it. As soon as she got settled in for a run she gave up hotel living and moved into my place. New York lay literally at her feet, neither of us was too old or too jaded to revel in the whole thing, and as we swung into full summer all I could think was, "Ain't life strange—ain't life grand?"

But the Lord giveth and the Lord taketh away. He giveth a good solid hit that the producers agreed would run two years (Belinda had committed for one), and taketh away my peace of mind, since, my theatrical chores seen to, I was now fully at liberty to attack Claire's masterwork again.

Like a mongoose awaiting its cobra prey, Claire had bided her time. She did not call me; I called her to say I was back on the dime and her willing and obedient servant, ready to do or die. I was surprised when I heard a cheery, full-throttle voice on the phone, telling me to get my ass over there, we had work to do. Before another hour elapsed I was back on Memory Lane again, listening to Madame crack the Hollywood eggs and serve up another of her romantic omelets. By now it was tough sledding and I was feeling the strain, but, resolved to keep my end of the bargain, I resumed where I'd left off, grinding it out as well and as quickly as I could.

In the following weeks things became more or less routine: either she talked and I queried, or she allowed me to rummage around among the chock-a-block filled drawers in that famous automated filing system. If drawers could only talk! And these did; Claire Regrett had the only talking drawers in all the world. It was like cleaning the Augean stables —how much horseshit would get swept out, how much would go into the book. Still, one persevered. I'd lunched with Vi and she listened glassy-eyed while I told her some of the things that had been going on. "You mustn't give up, dear, it'll be fine, you're sure to have another best-seller —and the respect of your peers as well." I'd left Vi realizing there was bullshit and then there was *bullshit*.

Now I became confronted with a further distillation of the Myth of Madame R. The stories of her were legion and I had a good time remembering some of them, even though I was determined never to swallow them whole. Yet there were tempting moments, to wit: the minor, perhaps even apocryphal, incident concerning film and TV star Loretta Young's famous "swear-box." It seems that in her heyday the famous actress took exception to the use of profanity on her set, and any time she heard a member of her cast or crew use a four-letter word, she required him or her to drop a coin in the slot of her "swear-box," the amount determined by a sliding scale, ten cents for a "damn," say, twenty-five for a "shit," fifty for a "son-of-a-bitch," and so on. Once, hearing Claire divest herself of a four-letter word, Loretta wagged a finger and said her "goddamn" would cost her half a buck. "Really, darling?" queried Claire; "and how much will it cost me to tell you to go fuck yourself?" Loretta's reply is not known to history.

Give her this: Claire never did less than speak her mind, and her mind was a receptacle for endless bits of interesting trivia of old Hollywood. She thrived on tales of the Golden Days, and through them she kept her past close around her; it was the warm fur mantle that shielded her from life's wintry blasts.

Much of her life was now being made plain to me merely by pushing the buttons of the filing system, where she allowed me to roam at will. Needless to say, I was both awed and fascinated by that miniature Hall of Fame she had stuck away in the back room. I loved it that there were separate files tabbed "Husbands: Antrim," "Husbands: McCord," "Husbands: Gobelins," and "Husbands: Calhoun." Each of these folders was filled with sentimental savings, the bits of string and tinfoil from forty years of marital disaster, valentines, birthday cards, snapshots, pressed flowers (true), due-bills and billets-doux, folders of sundry material in divorce proceedings, bills stamped "paid" for jewelry and other presents, a pipe for one, a gold lighter or belt buckle for another, plus lists of the individual failings and flaws of each gentleman, character sketches from her own hand, fragments of languid verse, all the flotsam and jetsam gathered on the choppy seas of matrimony.

Since I knew only a little about him I was particularly interested in the folder marked "Husbands: Calhoun." Natchez Calhoun's was an especially sad tale, though it started out like all of the rest of her romances, on Cloud Nine, drinking pink champagne from a glass slipper while the dish ran away with the spoon. From the purple passion expressed in some of Our Author's love notes, it appeared that he was energetically devoted to sex with his bride and would lay aside his typewriter at any moment to throw her in the sack.

It was interesting if predictable to trace the downward spiral of this union. With Claire's having publicly declared herself just one more Holly-wood bachelor-girl after the debacle of Yves Gobelins, and her having stated via Hedda's column (where everything was always writ in stone) that she'd never wed again, it had come as something of a surprise when she married the famous southern playwright and Pulitzer Prize winner Quentin "Natchez" Calhoun in a midnight ceremony held in the haybarn at his farm in Cornwall, Connecticut. Thereafter she changed the engrav-ing on her stationery and promised fervently and worldwide that "this time it was for keeps," a quote she'd already employed to advantage several times before.

She now entered upon her pastorale period, retiring to the mountain greenery (where God paints the scenery) of Black Beauty Farm, whence she dispatched frequent bulletins to a faithful public. She was Little Bo-Peep and Old MacDonald rolled up in a great ball of calico and kitchen rick-rack. (She even wore a straw hat—by Farmer John Fredericks.) She got up with the chickens and went to bed with the cows, and as usual *Modern Screen* and *Photoplay* came round to record the wedded bliss.

Because of her association with a spate of Muses on the highest level, she got bitten by the creative bug. She attempted short stories (one was published in *Liberty*), brought out a slim book of verse (dedicated to "My Only Quentin and Eliz. Barrett Browning," why, no one could figure). As if these triumphs weren't sufficient, she began formulating an awesome plan that they, Mr. and Mrs., should become one of the great teams of the American theatre. A large, expensive studio was built, half of which was hers to paint in, the other half his to write in. It was leaked (by Claire?) that the Pulitzer winner was currently working on a play to star his actress-spouse in her initial theatrical foray. In this piece she was to essay not one but three historical characters whose trials had been unjust—Joan of Arc; Mary Johnson, a minor Puritan figure tried and hanged for witch-craft; and Emma Goldman, the notorious anarchist. It was called, simply, *Three Women*.

From its inception things boded ill. Rehearsals went on indefinitely, with the large cast invited up to Cornwall for extended stays, and as time and money wore on, Claire was bulletined as having contracted a variety of ailments. Avoiding a local tryout, the cast trekked west, where the show played four nights at a Detroit theatre and where, since they were already in bad trouble, Claire took up the pen herself and performed major rewrite surgery. Not a good idea. Josh Logan was called in to doctor it: another not-good idea. After the worst notices in the history of the city of Detroit, the play shut down. "No Regretts" was the contemptible joke, and Claire was heard to say it was the last time she'd "ever screw around with any historical broads."

From this debacle, Natchez Calhoun was bound to have emerged a sadder man, but how wiser remained to be seen. Suddenly all the flaws in his wife, heretofore well disguised, began to be made apparent and Natchez was quoted as confessing to intimates that he wondered why he'd ever married her. Certainly not for her mind, and her body was then fifty years old. This union was to be her last. Thumbing her nose at gingham and calico, Claire hied herself back to Manhattan by hired limo to oust her sublease tenants from her penthouse (for leaving the windows open while they were summering on Fire Island, thus ruining her carpets). She replaced the rugs, had the floors sanded where they'd been marred, and set about writing her memoirs, second edition.

A name unmentioned in that masterpiece—and, in fact, never spoken by her at all—was that of Dore Skirball. As far as she was concerned he'd never existed, and, ever avoiding conflict, thus far I hadn't broached the subject. But one afternoon when we were digging through some old boxes of photographs, I came upon him, camping in one of her big hats, jeans rolled to show off a pair of anklestrap shoes. As I chuckled, Claire snatched the picture from me, tore it to bits, and threw them on the floor.

"I thought I'd got rid of all of those. I can't stand the sight of that queen," she muttered.

The moment had come to do a little mining of gold; I remembered how unhappy Dore had been over the breakup of his friendship with Claire. "You used to like him, didn't you? You and he were great friends at one point."

She spun around and gave me a glare. "Dore Skirball's not anybody I want to talk about—not to you, not to anyone!"

"All right, if you don't, so be it. Scratch Dore Skirball." I drew a line through the air.

"That silly bastard, that—never mind, let's skip it for something more important."

"He was very fond of you. It hurt him that you'd fallen out with each other."

"Then he should have watched his step. I told him time and time again one day he'd go too far."

"How far did he go?"

"Well, for one thing, he wasn't loyal. I demand loyalty in my friends or we simply aren't friends, that's all. I have to *depend* on my friends, who else have I anymore?"

"How was he disloyal?"

"He bitched me behind my back. He told Vi I was worth more dead than alive."

"Why?" I asked.

"Because they could use my skin to make alligator bags." Suddenly she laughed, as if in spite of herself. "He really *was* divinely fun, you know. I felt sorry for him, I *tried* to help him. Even Frank was fond of him, but— And then he insisted on being friends with Belinda and Angelina Brown and, frankly, I didn't like that. And then he betrayed me! He betrayed me in public, he held me up to public ridicule in that act of his, and I never forgave him. Never *will* forgive him! Who the hell did he think he was, anyway? Nobody can do Claire but Claire. Anyway, I don't want to hear any more about Dore Skirball!" she blazed.

I could see she was getting upset, not good for her precarious health, but if she had a bug up her ass, so did I. And I wanted her to understand about Dore.

"I don't think you realize how much he cared about you. And he was a major talent, even if you couldn't see it."

"What *I* saw was a mediocre drag queen trading on his friendships with me and other famous people. In the end he never made it, he lived and died in obscurity, where he belonged. Truthfully, I never understood why a clever man like Frank Adonis could go around telling people Dore would be a star. I know star quality when I see it, and he was not it."

I rejoiced, thinking of the gasket she'd blow if I laid it on her about Dore's not being a star, but I wasn't going to level, not yet, not with this Claire. She sat there with such a smug look that finally I opened up.

"Claire, you know something? You're really full of shit sometimes." The words popped out of my mouth before I could help it. She leaped up and threw her glass away. It smashed on the wall and spattered one of her bug-eyed urchins.

"You really don't like me much, do you?" she demanded with narrowed, appraising eyes.

Her question caught me offguard; I knew I'd gone too far and I all but stammered my reply. "Sure. Sure I do. Why do you say that? Do I act as if I don't?"

"Come on, buster, I mean it. I want you to level with me. You *don't* like me, do you? You really don't. Don't be afraid to say it."

I actually backed away from her. "Why? Why do you want me to say it? You never like hearing negatives about yourself."

She softened a little, and I could see she was getting Sincere. By now I knew all about Claire and Sincere. "Yes I do. I really do. When they're positive negatives. I've lived long enough to be able to face up to my flaws. My errors. Isn't that a nice word? It's so gutsy. So come on, *you* be gutsy and come across with the truth. I *want* you to tell me the truth about myself. I *need* to hear it."

I watched her expression carefully, trying to decipher it, wondering whether I really should pump her full of truth slugs. "Sure, sure I like you," I told her. "You're okay, Claire, you really are. *You're* really gutsy, you know. You're a survivor and I admire that will to survive. You're your own memorial, your own testament to the long battle. And I respect that."

"Maybe, but you still don't *like* me, do you? Come on, level with me. Just say it. I won't get mad or anything, I won't hold it against you, I just want to know. I really like to know where I stand with people. Especially ones close to me."

"Oh shit," I thought, "how can I get her off this dumb kick?" I didn't want to be having this conversation, this bared-soul confessional kind of thing. I knew her and the whole cast of characters she loved parading before people—the Iron Maiden, the Poor Little Match Girl, the Ice Queen, Carrie Nation, the Duchess of Brattlebutt, Mother Earth, Nurse Edith Cavell, Mary Baker Eddy, the whole kit and caboodle. But most of all I disliked the present company, the Great Searcher After Truth. It was the phoniest in the whole pantheon, since I judged her unable to recognize the truth if she fell over it.

I felt her eyes staring at me with increasing awareness. I saw them express by turns dawning realization, apprehension, puzzlement, hurt, then fear, and, inevitably, anger.

"Why, you lousy son of a bitch!" she blazed out at me. "You really *don't* like me! Do you! God damn, you *don't!* Who the hell do you think you are, anyway? Here I've gone out of my way, bent over backwards to help you, trying to get this book just the way it should be, trying to instill an honesty in it, to make it *memorable*—here I sit pouring out my heart to you night after night, dredging up all my secrets, and you dare to sit there looking so goddamn *smug* and telling me you don't like me! Who the hell are you not to like *me! You don't even know me!*"

I stared hang-mouthed at this explosion. But before I could protest, she was at me again.

"You know, you really ought to take a good look at yourself, buster! As if *you* knew anything about what it's like to be me! As if you could feel all the things I feel, the lousy rotten dirty things they made me feel. Well, let me tell you this, I don't give a rat's ass what you think of me. Got that? It's so easy to criticize others, you know? All you have to do is open your mouth and all the shit comes spilling out. And, you know, when you come right down to it, I don't think I really like you, either. I don't know how I got you around here, anyway. It's all Vi's fault, Mrs. Buttinski as usual, always sticking her nose in things when she isn't wanted."

"Okay, that's enough," I blurted. I'd heard enough. "Why don't you knock off all this dreary crap, anyway? In the first place, going back to our original discussion, I never said I didn't like you. In the second place, *you're* not bending over to help *anyone*, you never have and you never will. And if you think I enjoy listening to you bare your soul, you're dead wrong! And while we're on the subject, I may as well tell you—no, I *don't* like you, god damn it, you're not an easy person to like. I don't even know what the hell I'm doing here, I don't know why I'm doing this stupid book of yours— Oh, God damn it, it's happening, I said it wouldn't, I promised I wouldn't let it, but it is, it's happening—"

"What are you talking about?"

"I promised myself I wouldn't get into one of these crazy scenes with you."

"Then why don't you just get the hell out? I'm fed up with you anyway!" She kicked aside an embroidered stool in her effort to get at me. "And while you're at it, maybe you'll tell me just who the hell you think you are, coming around here to my house and criticizing me. Well, I've heard all I'm going to, buster—I think you're full of absolute shit!"

"Claire—"

"Naw—don't give me that 'Claire' routine, I'm sick of it. You hear me, sick sick *sick!* I don't need you! I don't need anyone! And I don't need your goddamn flowers stuck in these goddamn vases all over the goddamn place, either." She hefted up a vase of the flowers I'd given her and sent it crashing on the hearth, the glass scattering, the water splattering across rugs and furniture. "*That's* why I have plastic covers!" she crowed and folded her arms in triumph. I eyed the transparent slips that covered everything like the Mer de Glace.

"Thank God for plastic," I muttered. "Where would she be without it?"

"You lousy bastard—I keep those covers on so that the goddamn upholstery won't mildew!"

"The goddamn upholstery wouldn't *dare* mildew." I faced her in the middle of the room. "Look, damn it, I don't need another of your scenes, so save it for someone who'll appreciate it. If you want me out of here, fine, then I'm out of here. And don't bother looking for me, because I won't be back. But remember to ask your next publisher to send me a copy of your book—when it comes out. *If* it comes out."

I grabbed up my briefcase and coat and headed for the door. I heard the heels of her mules on the parquet as she flew after me; then she grabbed my arm and yanked me around to her. "Wait a minute, buster," she snarled, actually baring her teeth, "you're not just going to get up and walk out of here—"

"I thought that was what you wanted me to do."

"You're damn right I do, but first I've got a couple of things to say to you."

I tossed aside my things and dropped into the nearest chair, crossing a foot over my knee. "Okay, shoot."

"I said don't get smartass with me. You're just like all the rest of them. I know you're only using me. All your bunch wants is your pound of true confessions, then you'll go marching out of here, making fun of me. Everybody seems to think I'm just some kind of big Hollywood joke they can go around laughing about behind my back. It's that goddamn Viola. She's the one who started this whole thing, saying I should write my memoirs, and that she could get you to do it for me. With a snap of her fingers!"

This was interesting news. "Is that what Viola said, really?"

"You're fucking well told she did! And if she was here right now I'd tear that wig off her head, I'd scratch her eyes out! Some friend she is! And you just go tell her that—I never want to see her or hear from her again."

She flung herself onto the Ambassador's chaise, burst into tears, and grew so hysterical that I became alarmed and called for the maid.

No sooner had Ivarene appeared than Claire leaped up again and dashed across the room and through the door. As she went, the heel of her mule caught on the threshold and she pitched forward into the hall-way. There was an ugly sound as she struck the floor and lay still. While Ivarene fetched water, I carried Claire to the bedroom. She was out cold; she didn't stir when I laid her on the bed and tried to revive her. Not even cold water did the trick, and when I asked Ivarene what to do she hurried onto the terrace and called down to the apartment below.

"Mrs. Sadikichi, can the doctor come quickly? Miss Regrett has had a fall."

In short order the doctor came hurrying through the front door with his little black bag. He examined Claire, then drew up a chair and waited. "Miss Regrett—Miss Regrett—can you hear me? Wake up, please. I am your friend of downstairs, Dr. Sadikichi. Wake up, please." Meanwhile, Ivarene slipped in to me and said that she'd called the practitioner; Mrs. Conklin would be on her way in fifteen minutes.

Presently Claire's lids fluttered and she revived. It was the old "Where am I? What happened?" routine. We explained that she'd had a fall, but no damage had been done. We didn't mention that her grogginess was due to the shot the doctor had given her.

Later she was remorseful in the way I'd become familiar with. She'd done no damage to herself, or, I felt, to our relationship. With the passing of time I'd become more or less accustomed to these outbursts and was learning to take them in my stride.

Not long after these all-too-forgettable events, one day in early August when we'd been hard at it for some hours, Claire suggested that we go for a walk in the park. We'd had a lot of rain that summer; the park foliage was a deep country green, the day was warm and humid. Everywhere you looked there were crowds of shirtsleeved New Yorkers doing what New Yorkers do: sitting, walking, running; dogs, children, babies in shiny blue prams with fat white rubber tires. I could see that Claire was glad to be out-of-doors. We walked beside the lake, then crossed over the Bow Bridge toward the Conservatory Basin, where youngsters were sailing their toy craft in the breeze. We sat down on a newly painted bench, and she remained quiet, watching the merry children and the flashing sails as the rented boats sprang forward across the water. I kept wondering what the passing crowds would think if they realized that this was the famous Claire Regrett strolling among them, Star of You Know What, this shrunken, wrinkled woman. I thought of the Cora Sue Brodsky she'd once been, that skinny girl in a Dutchboy bob nursing rusty cans of geraniums on a fire escape where the wash hung on the line. Great oaks from little acorns grow; great stars from little salesgirls, too. Mentally I covered that long long stretch of ground since she'd tossed up her job to "go on the stage," when she met her fate in the person of the cigar-chomping Sam Ueberroth, who'd set her feet on the path to fame and glory.

Today she was subdued in a way I couldn't recall having seen before. I knew she'd been talking a lot recently with Mrs. Conklin about Christian Science, and though she never discussed these sessions with me, holding them private above all things, I suspected that she was giving way to fits of depression. Recently she'd been neglecting her usual household schedule, and she often became bored with talking into my recorder. The cassettes had piled up on my desk, but I sometimes found myself wondering if the candle was worth the game, if there would ever be a book.

One thing I'd been noticing lately was a definite softening of attitudes; she didn't seem so quick to rush to judgment, not so free with her gibes and criticisms. Though the reasons for this weathervane swing escaped me, I believed it a good idea to make the most of it, for who knew when things might veer, the climate alter again?

For two or three minutes the silence between us continued; then she sighed and finally spoke. "You can quit, if you want," she murmured, as if such a thought had just floated into her head. "You don't have to go on. I don't care, honestly. And as far as the letters go, all that Crispin stuff —I wouldn't have done it, you know."

"Done what?" I asked.

"Blown the whistle on you, sold you out, you, Maude, Belinda. I just said that so you'd agree to work with me. You knew that."

No, I said, I hadn't known. If I had, I probably wouldn't have started. She laughed at that; it amused her to think how she'd hooked me with her threats. "I'm not that much of a bitch," she said. "So you can relax. Belinda, too. I had to laugh, seeing how uptight she was, the time she came to the apartment. As if I was going to give away the gag then and there."

I said I'd been aware of the tension, that day and later at the party, but it was all water over the dam now. "Anyway, you don't really want to quit, do you? You shouldn't, you know. We should keep on. There's a lot of good stuff there."

Ironic, my encouraging her to keep on with her book. She gave me a quick glance to see if I meant what I said; satisfied that I did, she touched my arm. "We'll see, we'll see"—the eternal mother's reply to her child.

Together we watched the sun drop behind the twin apartment towers where she lived, the only towers on the West Side that lighted up at night, like two lighthouses high above Fortress Regrett. After a while we got up and started back. I took her arm, but instead of crossing the Bow Bridge again, we continued on to the corner of Seventy-second Street, past the rustic arbor where the purple and white wisteria bloomed in the springtime.

The traffic signal was against us and we stopped close to where four or five West Side ladies sat talking on a bench, like so many sacks of potatoes. The light turned green, and as we prepared to cross one woman spoke up loudly.

"Look who it is—can you believe it? Claire—Claire Regrett. Such a sight." I felt Claire stiffen at my side; her arm began to shake; then she pulled away from me. I watched her shove her way past the people in front of her and dash headlong off the curb and into the street. I shouted a warning: there was a taxi heading straight toward her. The driver's eyes bugged as she dashed into his path. Honking his horn, he jammed on his brakes with a squeal of rubber; he spun his wheel hard, but he hit her all the same, knocking her to the ground. I shouted and elbowed my way past the onlookers at the curb, passing the hood of the taxi, which had run up on the sidewalk and collided with a trash container, pushing my way through the crowd that had already gathered around the fallen figure of Claire, who lay on her side, outstretched, her face looking up, a dazed, pained expression in her eyes.

I tried to help her up but I could see she'd been hurt. I pulled off my jacket and laid it over her, then knelt down and held her head in my lap until the ambulance came. Another woman offered her long coat and I accepted it.

"Oh gosh," she murmured, "it's Claire Regrett."

"Claire Regrett . . . Claire Regrett . . . Claire Regrett . . ." The name buzzed about the circle of curious faces gaping at the sight of a famous movie star felled in the street. "Is she drunk?" a man wondered aloud.

Claire jerked him a look of molten fury. "No, she isn't, god damn it, but she wishes she was." Hey hey. She got a little round of applause for that. A squad car arrived, two of New York's finest jumped out and stood guard over her. An ABC news team appeared with a camera set-up and began shooting. C.R. was back in the movies.

"Kin I have your autograph, Miss Regrett?" I heard a voice say, and I roared at the stupid woman to get the hell away.

The ambulance wailed up and I rode with Claire to the hospital, which happened to be Roosevelt, over on Columbus Avenue at Fifty-ninth Street. They rolled her away on a gurney and I made some phone calls, including one to Mrs. Conklin, then I commenced that tedious interval known as hospital waiting.

After a considerable time, a young intern came to report. She'd broken her hip and had multiple contusions as well.

"She's going to be all right, isn't she?" I asked when the intern seemed dubious.

"We'll do everything we can. Are you her son?"

I explained that I was a colleague. "You know who she is, don't you?"

"Nope."

I supplied the name and his eyes popped. "No kidding! She got any hospitalization? Blue Cross? Whatever, you'll have to fill out the forms." He pointed me in one direction, he took off in another, and by the time I'd finished struggling with a ton of paperwork, the word was all over the place that Claire Regrett was on 8 with a fractured hip and the nurses were gathering along the halls, looking me over, since they knew I had some connection with the new patient.

Reports of the accident were on the evening news. I stared in fascination at a full replay of the grotesque tableau: Claire laid out, head cradled in my lap, me with my mouth hanging open, looking frantic and dazed, she covered by a donated shepherd's coat of soiled goat's wool with embroidered epaulettes, the crazy woman demanding an autograph, my ferocious roar, the works. By the time Claire was settled into bed, in a plaster cast, the whole world knew of her mishap.

I'd already contacted Vi in Los Angeles, and later she called back saying the pictures had been on network news out there and her phone had been ringing off the hook. Next morning the media descended on the hospital, equipped with cameras attached to mobile units: three networks and some local stations. There were photographers and reporters clamoring for interviews, and again the question seemed to be, Was the lady drunk?

I found myself a reluctant spokesman in the affair, but I set them straight. Anyway, I could see that Claire was lapping it all up. It was what she lived for, the attention and hullabaloo, the curiosity and enthusiasm, this new wave of publicity that engulfed her, proving that her name could still sell papers.

I had to admit she performed admirably. It was strictly Oscar-time; she dragged out Valiant Carrie and Poor Pitiful Pearl and whipped them up together in a sort of soufflé; then she gave us some Mary Noble, Backstage Wife, and a couple of other soap-opera heroines, with a dash of *All My Children* tossed in. She joked with the press and explained how she'd been saying a prayer for the health of a woman she'd just passed in the street, and consequently wasn't looking where she was going.

Naturally, they'd seen that she was bedded down on the "Gold Coast," the celebrity floor where you were allowed special privileges and the staff indulged you because you were a star. The food was above par, you were allowed round-the-clock visitors, and you could even keep liquor in the room. She offered it to all comers but didn't touch a drop herself.

This was a Claire I hadn't known or even envisioned. She really rose to the occasion, displaying a brand of spunkiness I never knew she possessed. She didn't utter a word of complaint, was sweet to the nurses, tolerant of inconvenience—the cast itched and I brought her a Chinese bamboo scratcher. She was philosophical about her plight: she didn't want to be in the hospital, but she had no choice; she was determined to make the best of things. The presence of a famous star in Room 811 considerably energized the hospital's routine. The nurses thrived on all the excitement, and the parade of celebrated faces in and out of 811 added to the *frisson* of glamour and show-biz spice that floor nurses love. By the time she left to go home, her cast bore thirty-seven famous signatures.

When she was safely returned to her apartment, I initiated a fairly regular series of visits, always bringing along my tape recorder so we could resume our sessions. I'd pull up the roomy, tufted Napoleon III boudoir chair and set the apparatus on the vanity bench close to the bed and push the ON button and she'd start talking.

Though she'd been putting on her brave show, once she was in her own bed again and enjoying the privacy of her home I was dismayed to see how quickly she reverted to type. She became tetchy and irascible, inclined to petty fault-finding and occasionally behaving so impossibly that I simply packed up and left; not even intimates such as Mrs. Conklin and Ivarene escaped her wrath: the meal tray wasn't set right, flower petals had dropped on the bureau top, the flowers hadn't been watered, her meat was overcooked, there was music coming from somewhere, couldn't somebody do something to shut it up?

Hazel Conklin was in frequent attendance, sitting bedside and talking in that sweet, soft voice of hers, then slipping quietly away like a little mouse. And when Claire became agitated, forced to remain immobile because of the fracture, I could see the anxious expression creep upon her and I knew she was fretting but didn't want anyone to know. And there now arrived an added affliction, and a serious one: insomnia, which wreaked its own havoc on her, physically and mentally. By the sheerest of coincidences, I, who lived across the park in the East Seventies, could stand in my library, where I worked, and by means of my "cityscape" telescope I could see clear across Central Park to her apartment, and I'd see that light burning. She'd taken up reading as a serious hobby and sometimes, working late myself, or coming in with Belinda from an after-theatre supper, I'd see that the light was still on. Occasionally I'd call her up. "What are you reading?" She'd tell me, with no prologue and no surprise at my call. She'd chat, I'd respond, then we'd say good night. Not one of those hour-and-a-half phone calls for which she was famous, but brief and to the point.

By now I felt I knew her well enough to tackle a crucial—and delicate —issue. One afternoon I said, "Listen, Claire, there's one thing we're going to have to deal with here, and we may as well get it out of the way now, rather than letting it go until later. Are you game?"

"Game? I don't believe I know what you mean, Charles," she answered stiffly. She'd had a few drinks that day, and when she was under the influence she invariably referred to me as "Charles"; it seemed to fit her inflated sense of dignity. "I hope you're not going to press me. I'm not well, you know."

"You know what I mean," I persisted. "About the movie."

She was off wool-gathering, staring at the ceiling. "Movie? Whatever movie do you mean?" she asked in her archduchessiest voice. "I made so many."

"I'm talking about the monochrome movie. The one you're supposed to have done that was shot 'all blue.'"

"Oh. That." Her look darkened slightly. "Claire Regrett's alleged porn epic, you mean. All right, buster, now I see what you're getting at, go ahead. Go ahead and ask me. No holds barred. If you think it'll get you anywhere."

"Well—did you make one? Or more than one? And if you did, what were the circumstances?"

Now the scowl returned to crease her brows and her lip curled. "All I've got to say is, fuck you for openers. That goddamn story's been dogging me more than half my life. I've done some dumb things in my time, but I wasn't ever that dumb—or that hard up for cash. There's not a foot of film ever exposed on me that wasn't shot on a legit Hollywood set or in my own backyard on a Kodak, and that's the truth. If you don't believe me, you know what you can do."

"Sure I believe you. But you once mentioned that Yves threatened you, and yet you never told me what kind of blackmail. I thought maybe —well, was it this blue movie?"

"I told you, there *is* no movie! And if I *had* done this famous epic, do you think I'd have let my own husband look at it? Listen, buster, I've heard stories like that about myself since the Year One. It's like that ridiculous story that used to go around about Shirley Temple being Kate Smith's baby. It really makes you stop and wonder where stupid things like that ever get started. What moron makes them up? Are they just joking, and then with repetition people start believing them?" She took a handkerchief and did a thorough job of blowing her nose. "It must be this permissive age we live in," she went on. "A girl doesn't have to show tits and ass to get the point across. And a guy doesn't have to flash the family jewels in the camera's face, either. It makes me sick to see the way pictures have degenerated into filth and idiocy that no one wants to go see. Who wants to pay dollars to watch the crap these Hollywood fly-by-nights are grinding out? Those guys are robbing their own bank, believe me, and I wouldn't walk to the corner to see a one of them." And on and on she went—with no further word on the matter before the court.

I excused myself to go to the bathroom.

The time came when I had to go west again. Leaving Belinda in New York, I flew out to talk about writing a script. I had planned on a month's stay, but one became two, two three, with only quick weekend junkets to be with Belinda, and it was Christmastime before I could resume New York living.

While I was gone, I'd often thought about Claire and her offer to let me off the hook, thinking how strange it was that, after all the trouble and misery she'd caused because of her book, she was now willing to forget the whole thing. From L.A. I'd kept in touch with her by phone and the occasional hastily typed letter, but even with the best of intentions, my schedule prevented me from really keeping up with her.

Belinda and I spent Christmas in Connecticut, and as soon as I came into town I called across the park to discover Madame's current state of health, but there was no answer. No Claire, no Ivarene, no Mrs. Conklin, nobody. I pondered the problem for a moment, then dialed information and asked for the number of Hazel Conklin. When I rang her up, I received no answer. A few hours later I tried again.

"Hello?" said that pleasant voice. I gave my name. "Oh yes, of course I remember you!" she exclaimed, "I suppose you must be calling about our friend. Was there something I can do for you?"

When I said I'd been trying to raise somebody at Claire's, Mrs. Conklin explained that Claire and Ivarene had gone to the movies. "At the Regency. A double-bill of *Wages of Sin* and *The Ladies' Hour*. They should be back before long. I shouldn't worry if I were you."

I asked about the state of Claire's health and was assured that she was doing as well as might be expected. There'd been an alarming hike in her blood sugar and a diabetic situation was developing. It was her refusal to take insulin that was causing the problem. ". . . but we have that more or less under control for the moment," Mrs. Conklin ventured.

"And what is her ailment called?" I asked, trying to sound casual.

"Well, as we know, her pancreas isn't healthy; in fact, it's badly inflamed."

"How do you know, if she won't have a doctor?"

"She let Dr. Sadikichi have a look. But no hospitals, no insulin. It's the drinks, of course, all the years."

I knew that pancreatic malfunctioning could be the sequel to heavy boozing, and when I expressed surprise that Claire was still downing the vodka, Mrs. Conklin interrupted me, saying, "Goodness, that's right, you don't know. She isn't drinking anymore. She's taken the Pledge."

I couldn't believe my ears. "Don't tell me she went to A.A.?"

"Nothing of the sort," Mrs. Conklin assured me. "She simply stopped, just like that. It was like turning off a faucet. One night she said to Ivarene, 'I quit,' and that's exactly what she did."

So Claire's bar was closed for the duration. This at least was heartening news, and I went to sit in my library, watching across the park to see when Claire and Ivarene got home. Around ten I saw the lights snap off in the library, which meant they were back. I was too tired to call, but I did phone the following day. Ivarene urged me to hurry over—Mrs. Conklin had told her I was in town. I went to make my command appearance.

She was waiting for me in the library, where, in the light of day, she looked more haggard and hollow-eyed than I'd ever seen her. I felt sorrier for her than I would have imagined possible, and I wanted to say something, do something—anything to make it easier for her. Still, she was showing pluck, and I stood in silent admiration of her quiet tenacity, the gritty discipline with which she ruled herself. She was every bit as formidable as before, yet the sound of angel wings was definitely beating in my ears, just as it must have been in hers.

I was surprised at the way so much of her former glitz and glamour had gone by the board, how much bark had peeled off that old tree, enough to make an Indian canoe. Was it possible that Our Lady of the Anecdotes had mended her ways? When I commented to Mrs. Conklin on this remarkable change, she smiled and nodded. "Yes, I know, Ivarene and I often talk about it. Claire's problem is that she's recently been quite overcome by her own incipient love of humanity. She's groping with the peculiar notion that people are nice, that she herself might even be nice —and that others might even like her. What do you think of that?"

"The thing is," I said, "she can't imagine that she's in the least bit related to the rest of the human race."

Mrs. Conklin nodded sagely. "She'll come to it. Most people do when—"

"When what, Mrs. Conklin?"

"Say 'Hazel,'" said Ivarene, "she doesn't like being called Missus. She means when the Angel of Death is hovering over the house." There was a moment of silence while each of us considered the prospect that loomed before us.

Claire was at one and the same time far more independent and yet more dependent on the little "family" she'd gathered about her. That I now found myself part of such a family was surprising, yet I forwent a number of other pleasures in order to stand by. And we got back to work. By dint of keeping my seat glued to the chair, it looked as if we might actually prevail and La Book see publication at last.

"One thing I'm curious about," I remarked one day, pursuing a gap in her story that I hoped to stitch together on the literary sewing machine. Claire was curled in her fireside chair, with the dog on his cushion at her elbow. The Mendelssohn Violin Concerto was softly playing; snow was falling outside, while a flock of birds pecked hungrily at the feed Claire had had put out for them. She looked at me from behind her glasses and smiled acknowledgment.

"When," I asked, "did you get this feeling for religion? I mean, you were brought up in the Jewish faith. Then you were thinking of turning Catholic. When did you become a Christian Scientist? Or were you always one?"

"No, I wasn't always. It's only recently that I've been investigating it again, after God knows how long. Let me go back. Way back, I mean. It was on that train trip I told you about, my first one—when I met those five marines. Sure, that was all fun while it was going on, but afterward I started getting really depressed, thinking, Is this what's going to happen to me, am I just going to go around taking on servicemen? I suppose, if you really sort things out, that cross-country train trip was one of the most eventful in my whole life."

"In what way?"

"Because of this really incredible thing that happened. That's when I really got some true religion, a feeling there really was a God. Everybody kept talking about when we'd be coming over the Rockies, there was this pass—the Donner Pass, it turned out to be, where they ate all those people, cannibals—and it had begun snowing hard outside. They wouldn't let our train try the Pass until daytime, so we pulled into this jerkwater town where they took on coal and water, and they told us we could get off the train and go to the hotel if we liked.

"The guys said they wanted to treat me to a good meal, sort of a thank-you present. I really felt down in the dumps, but I went along to the hotel and we ate in the Moose Room—lots and lots of antlers. Anyway, there was this one couple, real squares, they'd got off the train, too; they looked like farmers—or what I thought farmers looked like—and they kept glancing over at our table, nosy as can be, and I really got a bug up my ass about them, because I thought they must know I'd been screwing these guys in the smoker. They kept on staring and I could tell they were dumping on me, saying all these lousy things about my morals. I couldn't eat a thing.

"Later, when I was going to the john, I passed close by their table and I decided to tell them off. 'Well, I certainly hope you lowlifes got a load of me and my friends all right,' I said. Then I went to the john and when I came out I sat in this chair made out of steer horns, and I was thumbing through some old magazines when I saw the couple standing in the doorway, staring at me again. I really got mad, so I slammed down the magazine; then they came over and sat down near me. This geezer up and says something like, 'Excuse me, I'm afraid we've been staring at you, and I'd like to tell you why.' So he explains that his wife and he both think I'm the spitting image of their daughter, who'd drowned in this accident a long time ago. The woman—their names were Pollard, she was Annie —she comes over and shows me this photograph of the daughter. Her name was Amy, and damned if she didn't look like me, kind of.

"So we start talking and I can see they're really a nice couple. And they don't know anything about me playing pattycakes with the marines, or if they do they aren't saying. So, we start getting friendly, and I ask them how they got over losing Amy—they really loved her, you could tell, and they didn't have any other children. So he explains about how their faith in God got them through it all, and he started talking about this Christian Science stuff. He wasn't anything like a preacher, but the way he talked, I was impressed, honest. I really liked listening to him.

"Anyway, they said there were seats beside them in the parlor car and suggested I ride with them. That was okay with me, I didn't want to be with the boys anymore, so Mr. Pollard—Eustace was his first name—he went and moved my luggage while I went with Mrs. Pollard, who gave me the window seat. We spent the night on the train; it was freezing, but they had a blanket and a lantern and we sat there talking all by ourselves. I don't know how long we were like that, but it was quite a ways."

"What did you talk about?"

"Oh, lots and lots of things. Mostly about getting on in the world, trying to make something good of your life, about happiness, things like that. Eustace started explaining all about Mary Baker Eddy and some of the things they believed in. I'd never heard of Mary Baker Eddy, but I was interested. And as I listened to them, I just felt this wonderful sense of peace coming over me. Like all the burdens and worries I was carrying just up and evaporated. I felt like I was clean and good, and I could really make something out of my miserable life. Like it could start all over again.

"Next day, when we woke up, it had snowed all over the place. They started shoveling the tracks and then the train started off. We climbed and climbed, slowly, up to the top of the Pass; then through the afternoon we went down. Mrs. Pollard says to me, 'If you've never been to California, you're in for a treat. By tomorrow you'll think you're in the land of milk and honey.'

"And, you know, that's just what happened. It was so cold and lonesome-feeling up in those Rocky Mountains, I wanted to cry all the time, but when we got down onto the plain of the valley, here was this whole new world. Like the Promised Land. The weather was so nice and warm, not hot but just right, and there were palm trees everywhere and the biggest fields, all planted and green. Alfalfa and artichokes. I didn't even know what an artichoke was, and Eustace borrowed a pencil off the conductor and drew me a picture of one. My first artichoke. Then we pulled into Oakland and everybody got off, end of the line, and I had to say goodbye to the Pollards, because they were going across the bay to visit San Francisco, where her sister ran this boardinghouse."

"So you split up?"

"Not right away. They invited me to come and stay for a while. And I wasn't in a hurry to get down to L.A., so I took them up on the offer. They kept me for eight days, and I was never so happy in my life. They treated me like nobody'd ever treated me before. And Mattie, Eustace's sister, said nothing but the best would do for me, and I wasn't even a paying boarder. She was Christian Science, too—she'd actually met Mary Baker Eddy, had pictures and letters—and they'd take me down to Hyde Street to where the meetings were, and I got to meet lots of people and make friends.

"But then I had to leave. I'd called Sam and he was steaming, asking where the hell I am, he's getting real horny. So I pack up and take the train. They all came to see me off, gave me flowers, a box of chocolates, I cried, they cried, it was a real sad scene. I just hated leaving them."

"Why didn't you stay?"

"*Because.* I *had* to go to *Hollywood.*"

I was finding this very interesting. "Why 'had' to?"

"Because." She stared down at her open palm. "I knew it was my destiny. I was being drawn there. Like I was following a star—like the three wise men."

"Did you keep in touch with them, the Pollards?" I pursued.

"We corresponded for years and years. Annie and I wrote each other all the time. That's where I got my violet stationery from; it was her favorite shade and she used it herself. And do you know what—after Eustace died, Annie died less than a month later. Just think of it, they'd been married forty-five years, and when he went she made up her mind she'd follow right behind him.

"But you know how it goes. Little by little I forgot all the things I'd learned from Eustace and Annie, and for years and years I never even so much as thought about it. It was only here, in New York City, that I really got into things again. That's where Hazel came in."

"How did that happen?"

"Well, I was walking down Fifth Avenue one afternoon and I passed a Christian Science Reading Room, and just for the hell of it I went in. I took some pamphlets from the desk and went to the back of the room and sat there looking through this literature. When I glanced up, I saw the woman behind the desk watching me. That didn't bother me, but when I was leaving she smiled and said she recognized me. She asked if I was Christian Science, and I said no, not really. Then I happened to mention Eustace's name. 'Oh, Eustace Pollard, of course! Please come with me,' she says and takes me to a corner of the room and there, you wouldn't believe it, hanging on the wall there's this picture of Eustace. Can you believe it? He was one of the most famous people in the movement and he'd written all these tracts and works.

"After that I used to stop in from time to time, and that's where I met Hazel Conklin. She came in one rainy afternoon, her umbrella had blown inside out, and I tried to help her fix it. I saw that sweet face, that lovely smile, and we talked. We became friends right off the bat, and then we found out we lived near each other and we both knitted. I invited her up for tea. She sat right there where you're sitting, and I realized I'd made an important friend. Hazel Conklin's a saint, I swear she is."

This much I'd already figured out. I'd never met a kinder, nicer, more thoughtful woman in my life. And she had a mission in life—to see that Claire Regrett ended hers as easily, peacefully, and happily as could be arranged. There are only ten of Hazel Conklin in the entire world; I was lucky to meet one in my lifetime.

But how long would Claire hold on? Who knew? Sometimes I expected to get the bad news at any moment; other times I thought she might just keep on rolling along like Ole Man River. Tenacious, that was Claire; she'd clawed her way to the top; now with those claws she was clinging to the side of the cliff, with the pit yawning below. I've heard people laugh, or anyway titter, at Claire's religious leanings—"pretensions," I've heard them called. But, look, who is she to be laughed at for her faith? Why shouldn't she investigate, search, hope, yearn, need? Why shouldn't she want that thing outside and beyond ourselves that every human being gropes for? Just because she was Claire Regrett, did that mean she didn't have a soul? I guess people think that if you get as much as she did out of life, you don't need a soul, but those people are full of shit. Claire dying was a far more interesting specimen than Claire living; at least that's how I saw it, and if I'd laughed at her before, I wasn't laughing anymore.

One evening, when I'd spent a couple of hours with her going over some notes and trying to pin her down on a few of the more elusive statements she'd made into the recorder, she seemed especially cranky. We'd been talking about the time she won the Oscar and, as had happened several times before, I could see that she avoided rhapsodizing over that special evening in her life, the triumph that had capped her career. Why, I wondered, did her voice drop, why was she bored, and, more particularly, what was she hiding?

"Your fans will want to know," I reminded her. She made an exasperated sound, but nothing prepared me for the storm that was in moments to erupt and pass through the San Remo tower like a Kansas cyclone.

"Oh Christ, why don't they just let me die, then?" she muttered, fretfully toying with the sash of her robe. "Why don't they just forget about me and let me go, why do they keep trying to get at me? Hate 'em, hate 'em, hate 'em."

As she muttered, she was staring hard at the gold statuette itself, her face a mask of scorn, as if the winning of a cheap titanium trophy that hundreds of others had won was a self-defeating waste of time. The look in those still-expressive eyes was one of rage mixed with bafflement, disappointment, even desperation, asking what in life was really worth anything. Somewhere along the line they'd all shortchanged her—her mother and stepfather, her sister, Sam Ueberroth, those marines on the train, Louie B., all four husbands from Perry to Natchez, and all the other guys who'd bedded her for the ladies' hour and then gone home to momma or wifie or to the club. What did it all mean, the eyes wondered, what happened to pie-in-the-sky, her piece of the cake? Where? When? How? Why?

"Frank's work, all Frank's work," she went on in a low, unhappy voice. "Forty years, and for what? As for our little twelve-dollar friend here," she went on, waving the statuette at me, "*nobody* knows the real story about this little gold-plated bastard." She paused theatrically, slowly closing the skirt of her housecoat, the eyes glittering, the mouth an ugly grimace. Then the dam burst and it all came pouring out. She brought up her arm and with a burst of violence she sent Oscar crashing against the mantel, where it struck with a metallic sound, then bounced into the air again and fell to the floor. She hurried to snatch it up, then began smashing it repeatedly against the mantel, sobbing with every blow.

I was riveted, yet I did nothing; it was better to let her get it out of her system, whatever emotions were moving her to this appalling sacrilege. At that moment it seemed as if she hated everything in the world; the Oscar had become some bizarre symbol of all her frustrations, all the years of people laughing at her, of disappointments, slights, and hurts, the symbol of Hollywood achievement that she thought she'd pinned down but never really had. I watched her loft the statuette and wing it at her portrait over the fireplace. It struck the canvas, tore a hole in it, then bounced to the floor a second time. She spun wildly around, searching for something else to vent her wrath on.

Leaving Oscar where he lay, she headed for the fireplace, where with one violent sweep she cleared the mantel of its array of bric-à-brac, then seized the fireplace tools from their brass stand and sent them clanging across the room. Next she began yanking the pictures from the wall, hurling them to the floor and stamping on them.

Sobbing, panting, she dashed out into the passageway, where she attacked the trophy wall, tearing from their hooks the collection of framed certificates, plaques, photographs, and other memorials. "Memory Lane" was soon only a bare wall. Then she flung open the office door and went to work on the filing system. Methodically she pillaged it section by section, pushing the buttons so the apparatus revolved, then yanking out the files and flinging them frantically about. There was a carton of photographs in the corner and she lugged it out to the terrace, heaved it onto the parapet, and overturned the contents into the wind.

I'd followed her and stood transfixed by the amazing sight of hundreds of faces—that fabulous face—rising and falling all about me, 8×10 glossies with the famous lipsticked smile, the arched eyebrows, those two huge eyes staring out at me, here, there, everywhere. The face seemed to mock the world: "This is where I am, this is where I got to, damn it," the expression still said. I leaned over the parapet to look down into the street, where pedestrians were peering up, reaching to capture a photograph as it fell toward their outstretched hands.

She's flipped, I thought; *she's flipped straight to Mars.*

I turned back inside to find her collapsed in a chair, no longer sobbing, but staring mutely. Her hands hung limp over the ends of the chair arms and every few seconds they'd twitch.

"Claire?" Her swollen lids fluttered. "You've cut yourself. You'd better come in the bathroom and let me have a look at that hand."

"It doesn't matter," she returned dully, then got up and wearily left the room. I went after her to find her sprawled on her bed, the blood from the cut running onto the pillow. I wet a washcloth and tried to wipe away the blood; she groaned with impatience and pushed me away.

I went to use the office phone and called Hazel Conklin, who listened patiently, then said she'd come within the half hour.

By the time I returned to the bedroom, Claire was flooded with remorse, and for the very first time I heard her admit she was wrong about something. She was abject over her behavior and seemed afraid that she might lose me as a friend. "I wouldn't blame you if you hated me," she said, adding, "I deserve it. I deserve the hate of everyone in the whole world, everyone I've ever met. What a mess, what a lousy mess I am." She lay back against the pillow, spent and exhausted, and in her eyes I saw a desperate pleading to be helped, to be understood. She turned away and stared up at the window; the lights had gone on in the building next door and the stars began to show themselves in the darkening sky.

" 'Starlight, starbright, first star I've seen tonight . . .' " she murmured and folded her hands under her chin in a particularly childlike gesture. She could have been a little girl in bed saying her prayers to her mother.

I leaned down to see which star she was looking at. She stirred under the bedclothes, unlaced her hands, and for an instant her fingers touched the back of my hand. She murmured something in amusement.

"What?" I asked.

"Do you want to know something? I've never told anybody else in my whole life, and this is strictly off the record—I don't want any Panasonic listening in."

"Okay. I'm listening."

"Of course you are—you're always listening—like one great big ear. But after I've told you, I want you to forget you ever heard it, understand? I'm going to tell you all about little Claire's dream of Hollywood—I should say, little Cora Sue's dream. You remember that fire escape I showed you, where I used to grow my geraniums and raise tomatoes? And how we used to sleep out on hot nights? When I'd be out there and I'd look up at the sky and see all those stars, I used to imagine—now, don't tell me it's crazy, I know it—I used to pretend that every one of those stars was a movie star. I believed that every time a star was born—a Hollywood star, that is—the star in the sky would dim. And that meant that the star had come down to earth, where all the movie stars lived together in this big white tent, like a circus tent. Every star had her own little canvas cubicle, and they'd all sit around in there, waiting until they were called on to come be in a movie. There were costumes hanging on the wall, and a makeup table with lots of bright lights and little brushes and pencils and paints and putty noses laid out on a towel, and wigs on a stand, and whatever anyone needed to step in front of the camera.

"After they were finished on whichever their movie was, they went back to their cubicle to wait for the next one. And while they were waiting they could all mingle together and get to know each other, they could dance and kiss and make love—there was even this big pool in the tent so they could wear their bathing suits and go swimming. It was the most glamorous thing in the world. It used to make me so happy to think of living in that white tent.

"Then, when they got old and were dying, somebody came and took them away to this place out in back of the tent and dumped them on this big trash heap that was there, and then when nobody was looking, they'd put out their hands and float away. They'd be carried back up into the heavens and there the star that had dimmed before would brighten again. And the stars would stay bright forever and all the people who were still alive on earth would look up and remember them. . . ."

She trailed off, then darted me a sheepish little smile and drew the covers over her face. Lowering them again, she asked, "Isn't that silly? I was only seven or eight, but it's funny how I always remembered it."

"You must have wanted it a lot. To be a star."

"You have to, you know. I never wanted anything so much in my life. I really couldn't believe it would happen, but I kept hearing this little voice somewhere. . . ." She was quiet for a moment and I had to prompt.

"What did it say, this voice?"

"I'm not sure, but something like 'Do it, Cora Sue, do it, you can do it, and don't worry, everything will be all right.' "

"And so you did it."

"Yes. I did it."

"Have you always heard that voice? Do you still?"

"Not always. It stopped. One day I suddenly realized I wasn't hearing it anymore. It had left me. But you know, the wonderful thing—I got them both back, my faith and my voice, too. Yes, I can hear it these days. Not very loud, but I can hear it."

"What does it say now?"

"Same thing. Everything's going to be all right."

"Good. You keep listening, it knows what it's talking about."

She smiled again; her lids drooped, closed; I tiptoed out. In the passageway I came across Mrs. Conklin taking off her coat.

"How is she?" she asked.

"She's all right. Just corked off."

She walked me to the door. "Sometime get her to tell you about the big circus tent," I said as I rang for the elevator.

"You mean where all the movie stars live? Goodness, I know all about that tent. She's told us all a hundred times. Good night, now, sweet dreams."

I buzzed for the elevator, and when it came, the operator apologetically handed me a sheaf of badly soiled glossies, speculating as to how they'd blown off the terrace. The doorman had collected them out on the street; there were others blowing all over Central Park West, and should he send the porter to gather them up? No, I said, it wasn't necessary. There were plenty more where those came from.

Leaving the building, I could see the photographs scattered everywhere, face-side up and down, caught, like pamphlets after a parade, in the street gutters and in the branches of the trees. Those smiling red lips, those big brown eyes . . . S-T-A-R.

April Fool. I ask myself again, will there ever be a book? I cry on the shoulder of Miss U, who got me into this mess to begin with. "Don't worry, dear," Vi says, "you need a rest, then you can get back on it. Sweetie, you don't know what you've missed!" (Ah, do I not? Viola reports that Claire invited her friends—Viola, the Sadikichis from downstairs, the Steins from upstairs—and read them a chapter or two—or ten or fifteen. That must have been quite an evening; happily, Belinda and I were in the country eating our curds and whey.) The thing's a "treat," Vi says. *Loved* the part about the catfight in Loper's dress salon. Only this time Claire's the winner and all-time champion, not Angie. So much for truth.

My screenplay's done, the film's in pre-production. I'm outlining another book; *not* biographical. On Saturdays and Sundays Belinda's leaving hobnail prints all over the golf course. I chop wood and get muscles—a few small ones. Spring's around the corner; the weeping willows are greening, always the first to show a leaf. The country's fine, calm and placid; too placid. I hanker for the bright lights. I miss them. Woody Allen doesn't have the only patent on The Big Apple. Sometimes I think of "Manhattan Tower," that forty-year-old chestnut concocted by Gordon Jenkins and recorded on Capitol Records, that rousing paean to big-town highlife in a Manhattan highrise:

No-ah, oh-oh No-ah,
Get out the glasses, get out the ice,
'Cause we're havin' a party
And the people are nice.

Like the guy in the song I'm lured back, always back, to my Manhattan tower, my piece of real estate that's part of the Big Apple skyline. It seems to me the lights shining from my penthouse windows are part of the whole picture. If I'm not around to turn them on, people could be missing those lights.

So much for trips abroad, trips to California, trips anywhere. I'm back.

The first familiar face I stumble across in the street is herself, Viola Ueberroth. She seems glad to see me. Why aren't you in L.A., I ask? Why aren't *you?* she counters. We abandon Bonwit's for the Four Seasons and a pow-wow. There's lots to palaver about. With Vi there always is.

Since lunch was her idea—I really haven't time for lunch today—I order well and expensively and will enjoy seeing her pick up the check. I seem to recall another lunch, right over there by the fountain, a lunch for which I am still owed. Vi is occasionally neglectful, especially in money matters.

Over my steak tartare a host of names was arrayed before me. It seems sometimes that the whole world of show business in all its ramifications grows out of Vi Ueberroth's personal and private knowledge of that world, which she seemed to have hiked onto her shoulders like a female Atlas. From the pink stucco villas of the Springs of Palm to the walnut-boiseried offices of Beverly Hills to the storied penthouses of Manhattan, Vi knew what film projects had been given their start dates, which wives were dumping their husbands and taking which Impressionists with them, which husbands were screwing their secretaries or the stars of the movies that had got their start dates, if Burt Reynolds was at present bankable, what was to become of Robert Evans, and if the holograph was going to make it as the latest entertainment wrinkle. Ah, sweet Viola, my love, while you live, Louella Parsons is not dead.

She saved the best—or worst—for last. It was over the chocolate mousse cake that there fell from her lips the fatal name of Claire Regrett.

"Yes?" I said, sitting up brightly, paying attention. "I was just about to ask."

Viola drooped her lids and wagged a solemn head at me. "Oh dear, you've no idea what I've been through with that poor creature. It's so sad, really, *terribly* sad. You'd scarcely know her, she's changed so much."

"Changed how?"

"She's *très malade,* dear. Between you and me, this must be the end."
Right away I started feeling guilty. "Is she seeing a doctor?"
"You *know* she won't have a doctor. It's against her religion."
"Do you see her?"
Vi nodded. "Much as it distresses me. It's all I can do to go up there, honestly. She's like a gothic movie. She slops around that penthouse with no one but that poor Ivarene to look out for things. And, *dear,* you can't imagine the scene I witnessed last week. Up I went, and what do you think? When I came in, I glanced through to the living room and I saw this character sitting in this wheelchair, staring out the window. He was wearing dark glasses, and hadn't the faintest idea who he was. Can you guess? Of course you can't. It was Natchez, dear. Natchez Calhoun. He had a beard and his hair had all gone stark white. He could have been Santa Claus, dear."

"What was he doing there?"

"Well, when I pressed Claire for details, she confided that he'd recently been released from a hospital down in Virginia. He was stony, he'd lost all his money and was now nearly destitute. The poor man was living over there on West End Avenue with some relative, and once every couple of weeks she invited him to the apartment and cooked dinner for him. The place positively reeked of liver and onions.

" 'Natchez is seeking his peace with God. I'm trying to help him,' she told me. 'He likes me to read from the Book of Common Prayer. He likes *Peanuts,* too. We've really become quite good friends again.' Now, *what* do you think of *that,* dear?"

I subsequently discovered that Claire wasn't merely cooking for her ex-husband but was shelling out to the relative for his upkeep, as well as paying a share of his medical expenses. This news struck me profoundly; it was so unlike Claire, that old Claire, Miss Clutch. But, then, I decided, it was quite in keeping with the new one.

I rang her up, then went to see her and was shocked by her appearance. I don't know what I'd expected, but not this, this little old lady with a dowager's hump, splotched skin, her hair piled up like a washerwoman's. She resembled nothing so much as a shrunken doll in the old drip-dry housecoat she'd put on.

The plain fact was, Vi was right—she was dying. She should have been in a doctor's care, certainly; but there wasn't a chance of that, she still wasn't seeing any doctors. She was determined to rely only on her faith and the dictates of Mary Baker Eddy. Hazel Conklin had pleaded with her to check into a Christian Science nursing home where she could have proper care, but Claire was having none of that. She intended staying in that apartment until they had to carry her out on a door.

As the springtime waxed, I was making frequent pilgrimages across the park to Claire's. My main worry was my quandary about the book. It seemed to me a lost cause, impossible to finish, though she and I both maintained the fiction that it would one day see the light of day. But each of us realized that this was an unlikelihood, that the spotty assortment of pages hardly constituted a book and could be regarded only as a by-fits-and-starts account of a life without shape or form, rhyme or reason, a life that had gone into limbo and now would never be pegged or nailed down. These days she was more reclusive than ever. She saw the Sadikichis, trading dinners, and the Steins, joining them for a "musical evening." Few others got past the doorman. She'd changed her telephone number and given the new one to only a chosen few, me among them, but I seldom made use of it. "Why don't you ever call?" she'd say. "That's why I gave you my number, so you could get me, but you never do." She knew that telephoning as a pastime was not my thing, I generally avoided the instrument like the plague, but this hardly served as an excuse where she was concerned. So to please her I'd ring up when I was having a soak in the tub or at some other reasonably convenient time. The trouble was, once you had her on the line you couldn't get her off, and I perceived that the telephonic connection between us was a kind of lifeline, that I couldn't just cut her off short or say there was somebody at the door. And so I disciplined myself to undergo these "little chats" and actually got to the point where I enjoyed them. She could be very funny sometimes, and somehow these days her tongue didn't seem to be as acid as before; in fact she made me laugh a lot. And as she talked and as I listened, the more I came to realize that something was working changes in her. At age seventy-one, Claire Regrett had mellowed out. All her sharp edges seemed to have been sanded off and nicely rounded, the hard ceramic aspects of her softened to the clay they had been fired from. Her touch was light, that sharp, garish quality evaporated, her rigidity become malleable; something innocent, even childlike showed itself in both word and action. Claire sweet? It's true, she was.

The thing that struck me the most was the sense of inner peace she'd achieved, the feeling that she had reached the end of a long and difficult journey, and that with the end in sight she could easily afford to let the world go by. Even the timbre of her voice had altered now; it was feebler, yes, but also softer, warmer, as though nothing in the world could ever persuade her again to raise it for any reason. Her spirit had become tranquil, and if she was living on borrowed time, she had no wish to go dashing around trying to make the most of every last hour left her. Rather, she had shifted her gears into LO. She treasured her solitude, listening to music that pleased her, reading books, visiting with a few close friends, talking about cooking, flower-gardening, clothes, needlework.

In my heart I felt shamed. I recalled word for word that ugly scene when she'd hectored me about my not liking her, and I'd jumped all over her. Or the time she drove me over to Brooklyn; I ought then to have seen what was real as well as what was not.

There was also the business of her will. Whatever she left would be divided equally between Mrs. Conklin and Ivarene Hawkins, the rest to go to the favored charities as specified in the will. I couldn't help thinking that if she'd died ten years earlier, all that money would have gone toward building herself a pyramid! With a good view of the river.

So a far better Claire, but still no book. "How's it coming?" my friends ask, and when I give them That Look they pat my back and say, "We know." Fuck they do. By now you'd think Claire had ground out every last morsel of information, every tidbit of gossip any book could hold; but no. It's still only a collection of assorted anecdotes. Meanwhile, I grasp at straws.

"Tell me one thing. If you can," I ask one day, seeking an end to the torture.

"I can't, don't ask," she says. She's as weary of it all as I am.

"Sure, I know, but try."

"Go on, then."

"What was it like? What was it really, really like? The essence of the whole thing. Being a Hollywood star?"

"There isn't any essence. Making movies hasn't an essence—except when they stink, then they have *lots* of essence."

"Can you boil it down for me, the total experience? Isn't there one nugget, something you really feel about it? For example, Barbara Stanwyck once said it was like living between the pages of *Modern Screen.*"

"She was putting them on. Barbara always loved putting them on, it's the Brooklyn in her. 'Every minute of every day, boys, just like *Modern Screen.* Nurse, will you please take the baby, I have a dress fitting.'"

"Come on, be serious."

"I am, darling, I am." Her look sobered and she shook her head slowly, thinking. "Nobody who hasn't been through it can possibly comprehend it. You really had to be there, you know?" She spoke the words ruefully, as though forty years of international stardom was indeed a heavy burden for a girl to carry.

"Does that mean you didn't enjoy it?"

"Sure I enjoyed it, do you think I'm a total fool? But—" She stopped suddenly, reining in on her thought.

"Go on, what were you going to say?"

"Hell, I don't know." Again the weary note crept in. "Sometimes it seems as if my whole life's been nothing but one big mistake. I used to wonder sometimes why I even bothered getting up in the morning, I was bound to go out and make fifty bad mistakes before lunch. I tried not to, I made a real effort to conduct myself rationally and properly, and I really wanted to love people and to have them love me. I've spent half my life looking for love, for that one man to come along and love me the way I thought I should be loved—only it never happened." Her smile was self-deprecating. "I don't know why, it just didn't. I got on the best way I knew how. I thought that if I worked hard and paid strict attention to my job, that would be enough to do it, but I found out it wasn't. I was loyal to the studio, I gave it my all for all those years; then when the chips were down, I found myself out on my ass in the snow. Is that all there was? I got to keep the hatboxes? People are cruel—they love to hit you when you're down. Sure I was a bitch sometimes, but we all were, we had to be—iron fists in velvet gloves. We took it on the chin so we kicked 'em in the balls. You get to the point where the limo and the best hotel suite are important and they better have the fucking fruit bowl on the table or look out, manager! You get what you can while you can before they take it all away. Dore called me Miss Clutch—you bet I clutched! I clutched like hell—I had to."

"Dore knew that."

"I guess he did. I'd really like to see Dore again, I'd like to tell him —oh, never mind. . . ."

"No, wait—what would you tell him?"

"Well, I think I might tell him how much I appreciated all the things he used to do for me, and that I'm sorry for the way I walked all over him. I really did. I used him, I really put the screws to him, then I just kicked him out. He tried to see me, to write to me, but I wouldn't, I just turned him off. He really needed me, you know. He died in obscurity, on that damned chicken ranch of his aunt's, down there—Texas or someplace? No, Arizona, wasn't it?"

"Yes. Near Yuma."

"Dore thought he could really be a big name in show business. Too bad, it just never happened. And—this is a big laugh—he used to say he wanted to be buried right next to me—at Forest Lawn. I used to think that was such a laugh—crazy Dore buried in all that Hollywood splendor.

"Of course, he *was* terribly amusing." Suddenly she broke out in a peal of laughter. "Did he ever tell you how he broke up my dinner party for Noel Coward? He got into blackface drag with a maid's cap and came in with the entrée and I never noticed a thing until he goes and drops this huge platter on the floor and when he bent over to pick it up—you can imagine. He was bare-assed—*white* bare-assed."

I gave no sign of ever having heard this story before.

"And the nun—you *must* have heard about the nun—"

Yes, I allowed as how I knew all about Dore's infamous nun.

"But he wasn't the only one I treated shittily, don't think he was. I turned my back on a lot of people who'd meant something to me, even when they were reaching out to me. I always wanted to help people, and there they were, wanting to be helped, and I didn't—I couldn't—I never even recognized the fact that they wanted my help. God, I was a wire-wheeled bitch."

"And are you still?"

"I . . . I don't know . . . do you think I am?"

"Not that I've noticed. Not lately." She took this in thoughtfully, and I was pleased to see she found no quarrel with my words. "Claire—would you like me to tell you something interesting about Dore Skirball? Something only a few people know about?"

She turned those eyes on me and nodded. "Yes, please," she said meekly.

"He didn't die the way you think," I began. "Not in obscurity, not down on the chicken ranch with Aunt Bob. Dore Skirball died one of the most famous people in the world."

"You're joking—Dore famous?"

"Yes. And do you want to know where he's buried? He's planted in back of Paramount, at Hollywood Memorial Park. In a granite tomb. A tomb marked . . ."

As I spoke the name aloud she stared, shaking her head in disbelief. It was quite a moment. For another hour I talked my way through the details of the masquerade, Dore's joke on the world, revealing how with Frank's help he had created something that was as much his own creation as Claire was Cora Sue's. At the conclusion of my tale she whooped with glee.

Yes, the Iron Maiden had mellowed for sure.

"Boy, was I wrong!" she exclaimed. "When we finish my book, you should think of writing that story."

I took it as a measure of her newfound peace of mind that she accepted the story at face value, simply acknowledging it as one more manifestation of the oddities abroad in the world—God's world, as she looked on it. It occurred to me that the old Claire might never have believed a word: Dore Skirball as Babe Austrian? Ridiculous!

The next time we were together, however, I thought she seemed restive, and as I observed her more closely, I could see how she was controlling an ill-concealed anxiety; this puzzled me, since until now she'd shown such tranquillity, as if everything worth the worry now lay behind her. I pretended not to notice; I went to have a word with Ivarene, and when I got back to the bedroom, the look was more pronounced.

"I guess I'm all set," I said offhandedly, "but I'll be back. Is there anything you wanted to say before I go?"

She'd been looking at me but now she shifted, deliberately avoiding my eyes.

I came and sat down again. "You can tell me, you know. If you want."

She looked more anxious. "Will it go in the book?"

"Not if you don't want it to."

"No, I don't. But I want you to know. It's something I've been keeping from you. From everybody, actually." Her fingers tugged at the bedclothes. Should I, shouldn't I? she was asking herself. I waited, allowing her to make up her own mind. Finally she sighed and said, "I guess I should get it off my chest. God knows there isn't much time left. Can you stay a while longer?"

I said I could, wondering what this confession would bring.

"It's about Oscar."

"What about Oscar?"

"He doesn't belong to me. He never did. Not from the night they gave it to me."

"Wait a minute—are you saying your Academy Award doesn't belong to you? Whom does it belong to, then?"

"Belinda Carroll. Don't look so surprised, it's true. It should have gone to Belinda, she earned it. I got it because someone cut a deal for me."

I scoffed. "What do you mean, 'cut a deal'? People don't cut deals for Oscars. Remember Price, Waterhouse?"

"Maybe so today, but in the old days . . . Sit back and put your feet up, and Auntie Claire will lay it on you."

I sat back, though I didn't put my feet up, and geared myself for what was to be the last of Scheherazade's tales, the denouement to a longstanding mystery, as if now, at the end or close to the end, she was sufficiently open to reveal a secret that must have been a torture to her for too many years even to think about.

"Sham, it was all sham. I never won it, not really. It was all Bugsy's doing, you see."

I was baffled. "Bugsy *Siegel*?"

"I never could stand the guy; he gave me the creeps with those ice-blue eyes, and I don't care how he charmed the ladies, he was a killer. Even back in New York he was a killer, and I knew enough about him then to send him to Sing-Sing for life. I couldn't stand being around him, not then, not later. He came to me one night at a party, in Vi's garden this was, and he told me he wanted me. I laughed in his face. I said, 'You couldn't get Cora Sue Brodsky, you sure as hell aren't going to get Claire Regrett.' He just gave me this iceberg stare and promised that he would, and he started telling me what he was going to do when he got me in bed. I told him he'd end up with a girl from Madame Barratt's before he saw that day. He said, 'One of these days you'll come begging for it, you'll say, "Gimme it, Bugsy," and it'll be okay, I'll still give it to you.' I ran inside, and when Frankie found me I was crying. He asked what was wrong, I wouldn't tell him. Next thing I knew he and Bugsy were in the garden scrapping—that fight you always read about."

"Go on, what happened then?" I asked. She dragged on her cigarette, then let the smoke curl out her open mouth.

"What happened was this. Nobody ever expected much from *Wages of Sin*, but when I got nominated and I saw there was a real chance for me to win, I went to Bugsy. He was up in Vegas, so I flew up there. I asked him to come to my room and I told him—I said—oh God, I hate this—"

"You told him you wanted the Oscar, was that it?"

She nodded. "I said if he'd fix it for me—and he was in a position to—he could have whatever he wanted from me. It was the moment he'd been waiting for, to slap me down. 'What makes you think I still want you?'

" 'I haven't changed that much, have I?' I said.

" 'Maybe *I* have,' he said. He was playing one of his games, he wanted to make me squirm and crawl. Finally he agreed—but not for the price he'd stated—not for *just* the price. There was one more stipulation. He said that I couldn't ever see Frankie again, that I had to promise to cut it off with him and make him stay away." She gulped and pushed back her hair in the mirror. "So after all those years he was getting back at me for those days in New York when I was plain Sadie Glutz and wouldn't let the bum near me."

"What did you do about it? The deal, I mean?"

"What do you think I did? I wanted that damn statue. I knew it was now or never, I wouldn't get a chance like this one again. He was one of the lousiest guys I'd ever been to bed with. The funny part was, I never had to get rid of Frankie, because when Frankie found out what I'd done, he wouldn't come near me anyway. Frank, you see, was going hell-bent for leather to swing the MGM block of votes to Belinda; he was determined that his blue-eyed little baby was going to cop it.

"But came the night . . ." She described that famous evening, that was supposed to be the greatest moment in the life of any movie actress, how she'd heard her name announced, which had catapulted her out of her seat and sent her rushing down the aisle, swept along on the applause, up the steps to the stage, where the presenter stood grinning and holding out the gold statuette, how she had taken it in her hands and clasped it to her breast and, sobbing, had bent to the microphone and said, "This is the only guy I've ever wanted to sleep with."

How the audience had gasped and waited for more, how she'd triumphantly carried Oscar to the Governor's Ball, then how, at home alone, she'd sat and cried over the statuette, knowing he didn't really belong to her but to Belinda, and how for all the years since, the knowledge had eaten away at her, body and soul.

"And the worst thing was, I lost Frank because of it. He never spoke to me again until years later. He and Bugsy made it up, but I was off his list."

I asked her why, if she felt like that, she hadn't returned the statuette to the Academy.

"How could I? They wouldn't have accepted it unless I told the truth. And if I had, the boys would have come after me with a gun. I didn't want to end up in the Tujunga Wash."

She got up and walked to the window, where she stood staring moodily out at Central Park. "Funny, isn't it, how you can want and want something so much and then when you get it it doesn't mean much at all."

Busy gathering my things together, I had my back to her, then I heard her voice: low, sultry, movie-Claire. "Hey, take a look, baby." I turned to see her leaning provocatively against the jamb, with the fold of her housecoat pulled back, showing off her leg in the classic show-biz stance. "Not bad pins for seventy-one, huh?" she growled.

"You better believe it," I replied with a show of enthusiasm. "In fact, damn good." True, those underpinnings were indestructible.

She laughed sardonically. "Before long, I won't be needing them anymore."

"Well, you can always have them bronzed and leave them to a museum."

"I may just do that," she said. I smiled and turned to go, but her next words halted me. "Wait a minute, laddie. Before you get out of here, there's something else I've decided to tell you. I wasn't going to, but what the hell, I was up all night thinking it over. I told you a lie—the same lie I've been telling the world for fifty years. Protecting the image, y'know? Playing goddess, all the time goddess."

"Are you saying the goddess has feet of clay?"

"Does she ever. Do you know what I'm talking about?" I didn't, but was all ears. "One of my movies, one of the real early ones. In fact, the earliest. And I don't mean the one with Fedora. They didn't make this movie at AyanBee, they shot it in a hotel in Brooklyn. Don't look so dumb, you know what I'm talking about."

"*Maid's Night Out?*"

"That's the one, bubbie. I thought I'd go to my grave before I admitted it, but—now you know. Do with it as you will. Claire's famous blue movie. The old story, I needed the dough. Some girls will do a lot when they need money."

"So will guys. Don't sweat it."

"At my age? Not likely. And I'll tell you something else. I did the whole damn thing on my back, you know."

I turned back and stared at her. She nodded slowly as if to acknowledge what she had said.

"What?"

"You heard me. I said I did it all on my back."

"You—did . . . ?"

"Believe it, baby. We *all* did it on our backs."

"Who did?" I asked stupidly. I wasn't catching on very quickly.

Her laugh was scornful; the chin came up defiantly. "*I* did. *They* did. We *all* did. ——— did it on her back. And ——— did it on hers and ——— and ———, I mean, we *all* did it."

Those blanks represent some celebrated names, household names if you will, ladies of the silver screen one scarcely associates with having succeeded in their chosen careers through lying down on their backs, yet she had said so; I heard her.

"I *was* a star, wasn't I?" she asked.

If I didn't need to say it, still she needed to hear it: "You were the brightest of them all."

She nodded slowly. "Belinda was the better actress, but I was a bigger star. There's a difference, you know."

"I know."

Brother, did I know. It took nothing from Belinda Carroll, but it enlarged Claire Regrett to the appropriate, larger-than-life scale. Yet now things like that seemed of so little importance. What was movie stardom in the face of one's death, the end of everything?

"What about the book?" she asked. "Will you put it in? About Oscar?"

She'd said she didn't want me to; now I wasn't so sure. Still, it helped in painting a truer picture of the old Hollywood, the golden one she'd known and been a queen of, a Hollywood now gone. This was a verity. The Hollywood she had known was as dead as Baalbek or the rose-rock temples of Petra. Claire Regrett had stood for the Hollywood that Mrs. Wilcox had named so long ago, the Hollywood that thrived before green grass grew in the streets, before glum Jack Webb took to TV and Selznick Studios became Desilu Culver, before Louis Mayer went down into his grave and the whole world changed.

There came another spring, this being the year they reseeded the Sheep Meadow in the park, and Claire liked to walk over there and marvel at its verdancy. On these occasions she was lively and interested, pointing out provocative sights—a girl doing cartwheels, a rider trotting by on horseback, a red setter chasing behind, a man cutting out paper dolls, a woman reading a book under a tree.

Across the park, in our high-ceilinged bedroom with the wide picture window where the sun flooded in and where at night we could lie and look at the stars or at the lights of the Empire State Building, Belinda and I were merry and loving and we talked about what the future might hold for us. We had given up our country hideaway and by now Belinda had left the show; eighteen months on a strict diet of *Peking Duck* were six more than she'd bargained for, and she had a good movie script in hand. So, as the sun sank slowly in the east, it was fond-farewell time to New York and hello to Hollywood. I'd be following her as soon as I'd wrapped up my affairs. The day she was to leave, flowers arrived: roses, from Claire. Her card said "Bless you, darling."

Primary among the things I had to deal with were Claire herself, as well as Claire's book. This had been a good period for her, the last she was to enjoy. Recently I'd watched her settle even more comfortably into the groove she had cut for herself. Whatever grudges she may once have held she seemed to have forgotten by now. This isn't to say that she'd pulled out her knitting and turned into old Aunt Kate rocking her way to the boneyard. But the mellowing process continued day by day, the grapes fermented in the old keg, vintage wine was being made. I saw her often now, and derived much pleasure from our visits. Yet the days, lovely as they were, had an impermanence to them; and though I knew what was happening, I tried to ignore the fact that the Grim Reaper was sharpening up his scythe.

Two years had elapsed since the morning Vi had called me in my tub and broached the idea of the book, slightly less long since I'd taken Claire to lunch and she'd fallen down the stairs at the Four Seasons. Now that the book was as complete as it would ever be, various parties at my publishers were reading the manuscript. I drew a long breath; it had not been exactly a labor of love, most of the time mere and sheer labor, but it was done. It was called *Movie Star*, and I hoped it would be out in time for the Christmas trade. Claire had read her way through the text several times and had made innumerable corrections, but the last time I'd turned up at the San Remo she at last pronounced herself satisfied—no mean accomplishment.

One early evening we were sitting in the library, she in her favorite chair, the dog curled on its cushion. The New York world outside the windows had turned blue, all the ultramarine shadows of a Monet. In the gathering dusk, amber lights pierced the blue with shades of peach and yellow.

"Pretty, isn't it?" Claire asked. Her voice sounded unusually hoarse this evening. "It's New York at its best. Not like the Bensonhurst days, huh?" She spoke lingeringly, even hauntingly, of her life as a child in Brooklyn, "the terror of the block" who used to slug it out with the boys. "Imagine, those people never in their lives get above a fifth or sixth floor, they never are up, looking down. Never in, looking out. Just always down, always out. I guess that's why they call it down and out.

"Well," she went on, "there's one thing you can do at my age. Erase it all. Just clean off the blackboard." She chuckled into the dog's fur. "That was sure some way to clean out the place, wasn't it?" She was referring to that night she'd wrecked the joint. "I should have done it a long time ago, just set fire to all the junk. What a lot of useless stuff we shlep around with us, what a lot of worries we could just as well do without. But," she took care to add, like a chastened little girl, "I was wrong to pull a tantrum like that. Tantrums are for children, not grownups."

When I assured her that, all things considered, I thought she'd learned a hell of a lot, she accepted the homage without comment. These days she was depending more and more on the presence of Hazel Conklin. Often I'd hear them speaking in low voices about matters that didn't concern me, I knew, but I assumed they had their heads together in an attempt to reach some deeper form of perception, coming to terms with things, letting Claire's spirit, whether diminished or enlarged, circulate freely in the small space that now confined her existence.

As long as she could sit up and hold a pen, the flow of violet-tinted notes had seldom ceased from the tower penthouse. Like a never-ending river of script they'd gone into the brass mail slot, down the chute, into the canvas bag in the lobby, and from there to the four corners of the world. I found it remarkable that the woman's legend was such that, with her being all but removed from the world, so many fans, most of them strangers, had things to communicate to her, each one telling her she was still someone of consequence among her fellow human beings.

To handle these and other minor matters, Claire had engaged a youngish woman who also did bits of shopping, who "kept the files up," and—a more important task—who read to her. Claire's eyes had been weak for the past few years, and so it fell to this Rosalie Spivak to sit at her bedside or with her in the library, going through newspaper gossip columns, magazine articles and stories, books, religious tracts, whatever might interest Claire.

Rosalie was a fan of the first water, had seen every available film that Claire had been in; she'd written her a letter fifteen years ago and now was resolutely serving her however she could. The author of the day happened to be Tolstoy, the book—wonder of wonders—was *War and Peace*.

"I always promised myself I'd read it," Claire said. "It's one of the things I want to accomplish before I go. Some book, huh?"

I conceded that it was indeed "some book," than asked how it was she hadn't read it before now.

"I've tried a couple of times, but I never could get past all those goddamn Russian names. And the battles and characters running around all over the place. But I know what it's all about anyway—I read a synopsis in a book of plots."

I said I thought that was as good a way as another to get a fix on such a daunting work.

"Perry gave me a boxed set of Proust one Christmas," she went on, "but I couldn't hack it, I used it for correctional posture."

I had a picture of Claire Regrett answering the door with three volumes of *Remembrance of Things Past* balanced on her head.

And as the days passed, one by one, I came to share Rosalie's fear that Claire would never reach the end of the Wars of Napoleon, or see Pierre at last win Natasha.

Still, there was no immediate hint of the end, which stole upon us suddenly. There are always "last times" for everything, and, as I'd known it must and would, there arrived an abrupt termination to this life that I'd been chronicling for so long. Again I'd come back to the city; this was about a week after Labor Day, when the place was filling up again with New Yorkers reopening their apartments after the summer's hiatus in the country or at the beach. I flew in early one evening through a sky sultry with heat, with sizzling hints of an electrical storm in the curry-purple haze across which moved huge buffalo heads of roving clouds whose undersides were turned to bright golden fleece by a sun that had retained its noonday heat.

Once in my apartment I unpacked my bags, had a cold shower, then went and sat on the terrace, from which I could see all the way across town to that other apartment. I had no notion of the present state of affairs there, yet as I studied the building through my telescope, I had an uncanny feeling that they might not be so happy. When the lens disclosed no signs of life behind the windows, on a sudden urge I carried the telephone outside and dialed. I used our signal, then hung up and dialed again; no answer. When I repeated the action, I got the same result. I hung up again, waited, then set the phone down at my side. Puzzled at the lack of a response, I shifted my gaze to the southern view of the city, which even at sundown was throwing off heat in palpable waves. Feeling it, I took the phone back inside and started up the Casablanca fan in my bedroom. I finished putting things away; then, as I picked up the phone to make a call, it rang in my lap.

"Was that you?" asked Claire's little-girl voice. I acknowledged that it was. She sounded glad to hear from me. She'd been on the potty. I asked how she was doing and she tried to bypass the question, declaring that she was perfectly well and there was no need to delve into her health. Even so, I gleaned certain facts. She said she was ambulatory, that she was capable of looking after herself, that Rosalie was reading to her, and that she'd like to see me. I was listening hard, trying to gauge things from her voice. She asked questions about my own situation, and though her voice had timbre, to my ear it sounded faulty and weak, as if the conversation were taxing her, but when I said something to end it, she insisted that we go on. "Why don't we save it until I can come visit," I said.

"They're having fireworks with the Philharmonic tomorrow evening. If you come over, we could watch." She laughed. "Unless you're the kind who doesn't like fireworks. By the way—it's my birthday, in case you've forgotten."

I hadn't forgotten, I just hadn't realized it. But I assured her of a longstanding fondness for fireworks and accepted the date. Then I rang up Hazel to double-check.

"Not good," I was told. "Not good at all." I could tell she was worried. The pancreatic inflammation had worsened, execrin was secreting into the stomach, she was weakening and could go at any time. To satisfy my anxiety, Hazel went into some detail, and when I asked if I should go over, she said no, let her rest.

That night she had a violent upset, but since Hazel had promised no hospital she sent for Dr. Sadikichi again. By then Claire had slipped into unconsciousness, and while she was comatose he gave her a couple of hefty shots of insulin. When I called next morning, she had rallied. "The party's still on," Ivarene told me. "She talked the doctor into it. But don't stay late."

I left my apartment on the stroke of seven. As I cabbed my way across Central Park, to my bland California eye the evening seemed pleasantly rife with promise; one of those rare New York evenings filled with the super-glamour and heightened air of excitement that only a large city offers, the idea of wonderful things happening or about to happen. Couples strolled along under the dark trees, came into the glow of a streetlamp, then half disappeared among the shadows, while the hum of traffic lulled around the curves of the road. Horses' hoofs clopped nimbly as a pair of hackney coaches passed by. Out on the lawn the final inning of a softball game was just breaking up, the players' white T-shirts glimmering as the dusk came on.

At the San Remo the elevator operator greeted me in a friendly way as I stepped into the waiting car and we started up. It was Ivarene who answered my buzz. "How is she?" I whispered as she ushered me in.

"Somewhat better. I thought we'd lost her there, but—" Her look was eloquent. "She doesn't know the doctor shot her up." I got the picture.

From up ahead I could hear the sounds of conversation. We came onto the terrace to find Claire ensconced on a chaise. I was shocked to see how wasted she looked, but I pretended not to notice.

"How's the birthday girl?" I asked, bending down to her.

Stretching out her arms, she gave me a hug and kissed both my cheeks. "Now the party can start." How tired she sounded, how un-Claire. The high-tech was all gone, this was lavender and old lace.

When I'd added my gift to the small arrangement on the table, I shook hands with Dr. Sadikichi and his wife, then the Steins, and finally with Hazel Conklin, who sat to one side, a light sweater over her shoulders, her glasses twinkling in the light reflected from the east. On a glass-topped table was spread an array of fruit juices and soft drinks, as well as wine and several platters of hors d'oeuvres.

Ivarene came out again, accompanied by Rosalie Spivak, who also wore a party dress and had brought a gift.

Accepting a soda pop from Ivarene, I looked down at the park. Already the broad Sheep Meadow was jam-packed, and I could make out figures on the bandstand tinkering with the sound equipment. The orchestra chairs were all arranged in a semicircle, but only a few were occupied as yet.

"Claire, why not open your presents now, while it's still light enough to see?" the doctor suggested. She smiled and shook her head; she wanted to wait until after the concert. I caught Hazel's quick glance; if she managed to stay awake until the end, she meant.

We sat talking companionably, Claire and this loosely constructed "family" she had gathered around her. There were intense currents abroad in the air; I definitely felt them—currents composed of warm spirits and bonhomie and the clink of ice in glasses, of Claire's festive appearance, as well as the fact of her birthday and the small pile of gifts.

As the sun dropped from sight and the twilight turned to full dark, the lights came on and down in the park we could see the musicians moving onto the stage. They tuned their instruments, and presently Zubin Mehta appeared in his white coat, coming center stage to bow in the spotlight. Then, addressing the podium, he raised his baton and gave the downbeat. Two seconds later the music reached our ears as he began the Beethoven *Pastorale*, a fitting selection on so beautiful an evening. We settled back in our chairs to enjoy the concert.

The orchestra was only partway through the first movement when the telephone rang.

"Don't answer it," Claire said as Ivarene moved to pick up the receiver.

"You'd better," I said apologetically. Ivarene was permitted to see who it was; then with a look to her mistress she waved the receiver at me. It was Felix Pass calling from Los Angeles about the film negotiations we were currently involved in. I ducked into the library and shut the door; Ivarene hung up outside. It was nearly closing time in Los Angeles and Felix came on the phone with a lot of legal mumbojumbo. I had to jot down notes and figures and pay close attention to every word, and all the while, through the closed terrace door I could hear the distant strains of the concert.

The phone call, while of considerable importance, irked me because I missed almost all of the last movement of the *Pastorale*. A twenty-minute intermission followed, during which Claire's guests chatted amiably, agreeing that she was looking very well for her birthday celebration. While Ivarene and Rosalie passed plates of food, Dr. Sadikichi told a bad joke and was admonished by Mrs. Sadikichi, Rosalie reported something amusing that Liz Smith had written in her column, which made us all laugh, and everyone seemed to have reached a tacit agreement to make the most of the evening; who knew when another like it might come?

When the orchestra had reassembled, Mehta again resumed the podium and after a moment his baton drew forth the initial strains of Tchaikovsky's *1812* Overture. The music rose into the air and was carried in waves across the darkness to our ears, faintly blurred by distance. Before we realized it the climax was at hand, and when the cannon sounded in the kettle drums, the first rockets were fired into the sky. It was a moment to be remembered, if not for Tchaikovsky or the Philharmonic, then for Claire Regrett, whose life it seemed to celebrate: seven decades and a hundred rites of passage.

Maybe it was merely the way we were viewing them, but tonight's display of pyrotechnics seemed, at least to my eye, the most marvelous I'd ever seen. They rose in blazing galaxies behind the dark trees, up into the sky in starry sprays of brilliant pink and blue and yellow light, showering down in fiery arcs, rockets bursting and blazing, creating an effect of extraordinary enchantment. From down in the Sheep Meadow came appreciative cheers and the sounds of distant applause.

From time to time I found myself glancing at Claire, who reclined with her head back against the pillow-rest, her eyes shining from the reflected light. The display ended, the sky fell dark again, and all applauded their gratitude, to be surprised and delighted by one final gorgeous burst of light, and then everything was over.

After a moment's pause during which she'd remained frozen in position, Claire sat up, applauding energetically. "Wonderful! Wonderful!" she exclaimed. I saw on her face the most childlike expression. For the fraction of an instant, by the merest trick of light, an old woman was magically rendered youthful again, became a young girl. In another moment the illusion had fled and she became herself as she leaned back against the chaise, hugging her drawn-up knees.

"Did you enjoy it?" asked Hazel.

Claire nodded with enthusiasm. "But now, if you don't mind, I'd like to go in, I'm rather tired."

Easier said than done; when she swung her legs to the tiling and tried to stand, she found she could not. "Let me help you," I volunteered. This time she offered no objection. I picked her up and carried her inside. Her body felt surprisingly light; she was nothing but skin and the armature of bonework underneath. The disease that was eating at her was little by little hollowing her out inside, burning up her innards, and I realized how soon she would be dust.

"Thank you," she breathed with a grateful look. "Too much birthday, I guess. Well, it's the last of those."

Everyone pretended not to have heard her as I carried her into the bedroom and deposited her carefully on the bed.

"Don't treat me so fragile, I'm not glass." She gave me a look of mock reproach, then brightened as the others came in to say good night, the Steins followed by the Sadikichis, throwing goodbye kisses as they went out again.

"Don't go," Claire whispered to me, and I nodded. Then Rosalie came in with Ivarene, who was on her way to her sister's for the night. Mrs. Conklin, who would sleepover in one of the spare rooms, went to see them out.

Claire put out her hand and wriggled her fingers at me. "Stay a little, can you? Maybe I'll feel sleepy and then you can let yourself out."

These days I was happy to oblige her in such small things—how different from when we'd begun all that time ago. When I suggested reading to her, she willingly handed me the book from the table on the opposite side of her bed. "Rosalie didn't give me my dose of Tolstoy today. I don't suppose I'll ever get through it at the rate we're going."

I sat the book on my lap and opened it to its marker, then briefly scanned the page to get my bearings. Rosalie had left off at the place in which Prince André returns home to discover that his affianced Natasha has been having a clandestine romance with the wastrel Anatole. When I wondered how Rosalie could have stopped in the middle of all this palpitating intrigue, Claire waved a negligent hand.

"I must have fallen asleep. I often do when Rosalie's reading. I really don't remember."

I put on my glasses, then, taking up the book, recapped the scene for her. Just as I started in, Hazel Conklin slipped in and took the chair in the corner. I hadn't got very far when Claire interrupted. Had Ivarene finished up in the kitchen? Was everything put away, the lights turned off? Hazel said yes to all. At her nod, I resumed. As I read, trying to maintain a detached voice, I glanced across the top of the page to the bed where Claire lay, still in her party outfit, her head propped against the extravagant pile of pillows that she always liked. She looked utterly spent and her gaze seemed especially unfocused.

My eyes jumped forward from the lines I'd been reading to a passage I recognized, one of my favorite passages in the book, and I hurried to get to it before Claire fell asleep, for her lids were drooping. I looked at her once again and she gave me a little nod and smile of encouragement, as if to say she was enjoying it, though I wasn't sure she was. I had come to the place where Pierre, also in love with Natasha, has gone to return André's love letters to Natasha, and after a painful scene in which he speaks to her of his love, he leaves in his sledge, driving through the snowy streets of Moscow.

" 'It was clear and frosty. Above the dirty ill-lit streets, above the black roofs, stretched the dark starry sky. Only as he gazed up at the heavens did Pierre cease to feel the humiliating pettiness of all earthly things compared with the heights to which his soul had just been raised. As he drove out onto Arbatsky Square his eyes were met with a vast expanse of starry black sky. Almost in the center of this sky, above the Prichistensky Boulevard, surrounded and convoyed on every side by stars but distinguished from them all by its nearness to the earth, its white light and its long uplifted tail, shone the huge, brilliant comet of the year 1812—the comet which was said to portend all manner of horrors and the end of the world. But that bright comet with its long luminous tail aroused no feeling of fear in Pierre's heart. On the contrary, with rapture and his eyes wet with tears, he contemplated the radiant star which, after travelling in its orbit with inconceivable velocity through infinite space, seemed suddenly—like an arrow piercing the earth—to remain fast in one chosen spot in the black firmament, vigorously tossing up its tail, shining and playing with its white light amid the countless other scintillating stars. It seemed to Pierre that this comet spoke in full harmony with all that filled his own softened and uplifted soul, now blossoming into a new life.' "

I paused and glanced over at Claire, who sat waiting, her eyes wide open. "Well, that's the chapter; what say we call it a night?" I suggested, leaning toward her. Whatever reply I may have expected was not forthcoming; she said nothing.

From the corner of my eye I saw Mrs. Conklin rise from her chair and approach the bed. She stood close at my side and in another moment her hand came to rest on my shoulder. She had never touched me like that before. Then she took her hand away, went around me, and leaned down to Claire, using her hands to make some minute adjustment. When she straightened again, Claire's eyes were closed.

I put the book down, neglecting to replace the mark. That was no matter, I knew; Rosalie would have no need to find her place. When Claire met up with Crispin Antrim, she'd have to confess she never finished the book, but she could always say she'd tried. *War and Peace* was no easy job of work.

"It's all right, you know," Hazel was saying in her calm, soft voice, as together we regarded the still face against the pillows. "It's just like walking through a door. Passing from one room to another, so easily. She has gone into the other room now, that's all. It will be nice."

When I started to draw the sheet up over the face, Hazel said quickly, "No, don't do that. There's nothing to be ashamed of, we don't have to shut her away under a sheet."

I looked at Hazel's kind, expressive face. "Kiss her forehead," she said in a low voice; I got up and leaned to do as she asked. "And she never opened her presents." She glanced ruefully at the tray of gifts that Ivarene had carried in from the terrace.

Together we moved away from the bedside and spoke in whispers, talking over what was to happen now. Since the necessary preparations had all been previously made, there was nothing to do but let the proper functionaries take over their allotted duties. When we finished, she sent me along; she would stay in the room until morning, when final arrangements could be made.

"Miss Regrett's up late tonight," the elevator man observed as he took me down. It wasn't my task to inform him of what had happened upstairs, but I knew he was fond of Claire so I told him that she'd just died. He crossed himself reverently and dug inside his shirt to pull out a gold medal and kissed it.

"Dead. My gosh, that's a hard thing to believe." He shook his head to prove his point. "I guess she's the last of 'em, isn't she? The really big ones—why, she was the biggest of them all, I guess."

At that moment I felt inclined to agree. Back in my apartment I tried to reach Viola in California as I'd promised, when the need arose; she was out, the maid said she wasn't expected until late. Then I called Belinda, who was home. I told her what had happened and she was as distressed as I was—more, perhaps, since she hadn't been a witness to Claire's newfound serenity.

After a while I walked out onto the terrace and stood at the corner of the parapet, gazing across town to the same spot where we'd gathered earlier. There the bottom penthouse in the south tower lay dark; no light showed. By now the mistress of that household had traveled elsewhere. Her remains would meet their assigned end, but the spirit—that plucky spirit—was gone from the premises. To go where, I wondered?

I turned my head, looking southeast, past the bridge that had taken us to Bensonhurst that day. With only a slight degree of effort I could see from the spot where she'd been born clear to the spot where she'd died. I gauged the distance at some six miles. Not far on the odometer, but light-years away.

The rippling currents of night air made the stars glimmer and glitter the more intensely, and though I was no astronomer, I could pick out a few of the more recognizable constellations—the two Dippers, Orion's

Belt, Cassiopeia. Shadowy clouds rode the Milky Way. And, gazing up at the star-strewn sky, I thought again of that sweet Brooklyn fairy tale she'd told me about the little girl with the Dutch bob and the scabbed-over knees sitting on the steps of the rusty fire escape, gazing up at the stars and believing they came down to earth to be movie stars. I'd thought about it so many times that by now it had almost become a part of my own dreaming. With no trouble at all I could picture the tent, all the "stars" in their cubicles waiting to be called upon to make a movie, the hard work followed by socializing, the music and the dancing, the langorous love-making among the stars, all having fun, drinking champagne from long-stemmed glasses, tasting the sweet nectar of life, the glittering stars of Hollywood grouped in constellation, their own spangled universe, that sweet movie-star heaven. Little Cora Sue had decidedly grown up to live in the big tent and swim in the pool and dance and drink bubbly until the clock struck one and the tired cows came home.

It was late, I, too, was tired; I yawned without covering my mouth. Who was there to see? The buildings were dark; lights were turned off all through the midtown canyon; even the silhouette of the Empire State Building loomed in the smoky darkness like a cardboard sentinel. The dark shapes of apartments with their silhouetted water towers looked dramatically cinematic, the cardboard cut-out set Busby Berkeley used in a Gold Diggers movie. "The hip-hooray and ballyhoo, the Lullaby of Broadway . . ."

Had she licked them? Sure she had. Licked the whole world, if it came to that. Success, fame, it was all hers. Tomorrow, more headlines. She'd ridden the Hollywood merry-go-round, caught the brass ring which entitled her to a couple of free rides; she'd lived to see Tinseltown hit the pavement like a dead stegosaurus, while the studio that had made her turned out bubble-gum flicks and crumbled around the edges in the Culver City sun. It was a lot to think about.

Yawning, I went inside to my room. As I sat on the edge of the bed and took off my shoes, I looked out through the big window, and my eye was again attracted upwards, where a solitary star glowed more brightly than its fellows. Had that star been there earlier or had it just appeared? I couldn't tell. I snapped off the light and lay back, keeping the star within my line of vision. It pulsed and throbbed against the dark sky, as if sending secret messages. I knew what the messages were. And as I dropped off to sleep I heard a voice, hers or mine I couldn't tell, but it was there.

"*Bless you, darling . . .*" it said.

That was the end. But even dead she made big news—her picture, circa age sixty-five, was on page one of *The New York Times*, while the *Post* gave her a whole banner line:

CLAIRE IS GONE

with many pictures and a four-column obit. In the *News*, Liz Smith reviewed the forty-year career and had nice things to say. There would be no service, only a cremation and private burial.

I went. I was surprised at how few people were there, but it was out of town and probably inconvenient. Maybe she'd wanted it that way on purpose. Far from dreams of glorious Forest Lawn, she's buried in the cemetery of a little church up in Connecticut, in the village that she'd loved when she was married to Natchez. Since then I've made a point of going through there once or twice to take another look at the gravesite. Once I found the local graffiti artists had been hard at work: emblazoned on the simple stone I read, in lipstick yet, "We loved you Clare." Not so hot in the spelling department, but the sentiment was plain. I left the words to weather out; maybe they're there still.

I felt her passing keenly, I can honestly say I did. In my mind she'd joined the others whose lives had touched me in one way or other, Babe and Dore, Frank, Frances, April, Maude, God rest her. And if Claire was where my fancy had allowed me to place her, up there in the sky, what more fitting spot?

When I went back to the Coast, Blindy was waiting. We drove up to Carmel and got married, honeymooned in San Francisco, at the St. Francis. I'd never thought about it until she mentioned the fact; we were having breakfast in bed and she turned to me to ask, "Didn't you honeymoon here once before?"

"Sure," I said without blinking an eye, "but that was down in seven-oh-eight and the room wasn't on the Square." I really had forgotten, and Belinda was much amused, only asking if I'd made a reservation for the next time.

That afternoon, when we were walking around, we went into a bookstore and a clerk asked me when the Claire Regrett book would be published. Unhappily, I had to report that it wasn't ever coming out, and I said it with regret, forgive the pun. Despite all our labors, somehow the whole thing just didn't pull together. There were a lot of Claires in there, maybe too many; they clashed and the story came over as spurious. I'd failed to find the heart of it, but as they say, "Heart's hard." I told my editor I'd do another one in its place. This is it.

You can't write intelligently about Hollywood; it's just writing about dreams, there's not much flesh there, only fantasy. It's a fantasy, even now, in this latter age of cable and MTV. But we have a VCR, you probably do, too; we put on old Claire Regrett movies and Belinda movies and Maude and Crispin movies, and Babe movies, April movies, Fedora and all the rest, their movies—we watch the screen over the tips of our toes, we seldom go out on the town. If by chance I happen to be over in Hollywood, I'll wander in to take a look at Grauman's forecourt. They're all there, in cement, and I look at the names and the footprints, then I look at the faces of the people, the tourists from Keokuk and Duluth who've come in their Hawaiian shirts and Bemberg sheers to gawk and stare at the cement iconography. I'm not putting them down, Keokuk and Duluth, or the people, either; those folk are *interested*, they care, that's the main thing.

They go back to Duluth with stories about the glittering stars in the sidewalks, the breath of romance under rustling palms, tales of an old real estate sign above a cactus patch where a movie blonde threw herself down in despair, of the star dust that fell from the sky in lieu of tears.

Pretty soon it'll be the hundredth anniversary of the name Mrs. Wilcox gave the waving barley fields and orange groves that started the whole thing, and pretty soon the earthquake will come—the *BIG* one, number ten on the Richter—and the whole of California west of the San Andreas Fault will have broken off and dropped onto the Continental Shelf, leaving a jagged edge of decomposed granite, a couple of gas stations, and an army of signs warning "Slide Area." Our Peg Enwhistle's real estate sign will have disappeared, too:

> *"My name is Hollywood, city of cities:*
> *Look on my works, ye Mighty, and despair!"*
> *Nothing beside remains . . .*

Maybe it really will be gone-with-the-wind time, when a hollow wind will whistle through the dead sound stages, when the desert tumbleweeds will bumble along the empty streets and the last foot of printed celluloid will have fallen to dust. Or maybe it was never real at all, maybe it was only a dream, the kind of tinsel and cellophane dream that slips away little by little, no matter how hard you try holding onto it—and you know in your heart of hearts it could never have been real.

It couldn't have been—could it . . . ?